*It was a war that turned boys
into men, women into widows,
and sent a ruptured nation
rushing into the great unknown.*

**James Bannon of the 4th Virginia:** Exiled in disgrace
from his father's home and sent south to VMI, he lives with
a searing memory that shattered his dreams forever. Now,
marching with the "Lexington Volunteers" and facing the
great divide known as the Mason-Dixon Line, he seeks the
one challenge that will bring redemption . . .

**Lt. Kevin Bannon of the 4th New Jersey:** His older
brother always protected him—from their father and from
the world. But now he must learn to stand alone, as a newly
commissioned First Lieutenant in the 4th New Jersey Volunteer Infantry Regiment. Kevin must find a cause worth
fighting for—and a reason to live . . .

---

**Praise for *New York Times* Bestselling Author
Harold Coyle**

"The Tom Clancy of ground warfare."
—W.E.B. Griffin

"Coyle is at his best when he's depicting soldiers
facing death. . . . He knows soldiers and he understands
the brotherhood-of-arms mystique that transcends
national boundaries."
—*The New York Times Book Review*

**Mary Beth McPherson:** A true daughter of the South, she has fallen in love with a Yankee estranged from his home: James Bannon. Although she inflames his passions and touches his soul, she knows she must find a way to heal the secret wound buried deep within him . . .

**Harriet Ann Shields:** As beautiful as she is strong-willed, the daughter of a prominent New Jersey judge and politician is prepared to defy her family and her social rank to risk her life for her two greatest loves: the Union cause and Kevin Bannon, the son of an Irishman . . .

"Coyle captures the stress, exhilaration, and terror of combat."
—*Cincinnati Post*

"In many ways Coyle is even better than Clancy. . . . What sets Coyle's work apart is his absolute authenticity."
—*Phoenix Gazette*

**Edward Bannon:** A man of wealth, power and prestige, he has always been a cruel and tyrannical father to his two sons, James and Kevin. Now he is willing to use them to further his own ambitions and protect his financial interests. For him the outbreak of war is a threat to business, and he is determined to turn the bloodshed to his advantage . . .

**Will McPherson:** James' fellow cadet at VMI, he is a young man full of joy, energy and enthusiasm. He alone has drawn James back from the brink of despair. But in the 4th Virginia, in a cruel and savage war, he will lead James to the edge of an even more terrible hell . . .

---

"Coyle is good at conveying the confusion
and freewheeling terror of modern combat."
—*Milwaukee Sentinel*

"Coyle's examination of individuals caught in the
complexities and cruelties of combat is first-rate."
—*Booklist*

## Books by Harold Coyle

Look Away
Code of Honor
The Ten Thousand
Trial by Fire
Bright Star
Sword Point
Team Yankee

# HAROLD COYLE

# LOOK AWAY

**POCKET BOOKS**

New York London Toronto Sydney Tokyo Singapore

This book is a work of fiction. Names, characters, places and incidents are products of the author's imagination or are used fictitiously. Any resemblance to actual events or locales or persons, living or dead, is entirely coincidental.

 POCKET BOOKS, a division of Simon & Schuster Inc.
1230 Avenue of the Americas, New York, NY 10020

Copyright © 1995 by Harold Coyle

All rights reserved, including the right to reproduce
this book or portions thereof in any form whatsoever.
For information address Simon & Schuster Inc.,
1230 Avenue of the Americas, New York, NY 10020

ISBN: 0-671-52819-X

First Pocket Books printing January 1996

10  9  8  7  6  5  4  3  2  1

POCKET and colophon are registered trademarks of
Simon & Schuster Inc.

Stepback art by Karen Barnes / Wood Ronsaville Harlin, Inc.

Printed in the U.S.A.

# ACKNOWLEDGMENTS

# October 17th, 1994
# Leavenworth, Kansas

Writing this book has been a great adventure for me, for it is a deviation from the sure and tested path that I have been trotting down these past nine years. Not only have I changed from a genre that has been my bread and butter, I have thrown myself into what is probably the most written about period in American history. In doing so, I realize that not only do I face the prospect of losing loyal fans of my past works, but that I also leave myself open to the close scrutiny and criticism of historians and Civil War buffs of every caliber. Only with the help of old friends, and an entire host of new ones, have I been able to bring this project to a successful conclusion.

First in my long list of people to whom I owe a great debt of gratitude is Michael Korda of Simon & Schuster. Not only has he overseen all aspects of this project, lending his sage advice at all stages, his belief in me as a writer permitted me the opportunity to do a book about the American Civil War. Without his nod this story never would have seen the light of day.

Standing there next to Michael throughout the entire process has been Paul McCarthy of Pocket Books, my primary editor. Paul has literally been in the trenches with me throughout the entire process. His dedication to his profession and drive to draw out the best in me as a writer has made this book far better than it could ever have been had I not had him at my side.

In writing this book, I had to do a great deal of research, gathering new experiences and perspectives not only on the conduct of war during the 1860s but also on the lives of the people who lived then and the society in which they lived. I owe a great deal of thanks to countless people at National Parks throughout the East, college, university, and public libraries in New Jersey and Virginia, and just plain helpful folks all over this country.

Especially critical in this process have been my experiences with the reenacting community. By donning the uniform and marching in the ranks of the 3rd Missouri Volunteer Infantry, (CSA), and the 17th Virginia Volunteers, I gained an insight into the War Between the States that no amount of study could ever equal.

I owe special thanks to Tom Dyer, Bob Burnos, Willie Evens, and Dave Schmitt of the 3rd Missouri Volunteer Infantry a unit that was, for nearly two years, my home unit.

In doing my research back East, I became associated with the men and women of the 17th Virginia Volunteer Infantry, under the capable leadership of Marty Wilson. The sights, sounds, feelings, and smells of many a fight, marching shoulder to shoulder in the ranks with Mike Snyder, Page Johnson, Cory Johnson, Karl Kramer and his son, Rich Nead, Nick Shannon, Jack Quigley, Phil Adams, and the other members of the company, have served me well time and time again during this project. Of equal importance were the women of the 17th Virginia, especially Jennifer Legates and Trish Remick, who gave me insights into the trials and tribulations of women and their society during the war.

Another Virginian who has lent me his support has been Rick Britton, commander of the 3rd Battalion, Army of Northern Virginia. Not only did he take the time to read and comment on the unfinished manuscript, he is the finest battalion commander in reenacting I have served under. His actions and conduct on and off the field provided me with a perspective on what a good regimental commander must have been like during the war.

Not to be forgotten is Jim Tapley of South Carolina. The three days I spent with him and the rest of the "Cracker" company, marching on the Red River in April of 1994, were, for me, as enjoyable and educational as they were painful and frustrating.

And of course, there are all those great masses of reenactors, North and South, men and women, who marched and fought side by side with me all over this country. On many fields I tripped over them and, in turn, was stepped upon by them. We stood toe-to-toe firing at each other, charging and chasing one another in turn, and, in general, having a hell of a good time, rain or shine, keeping the memories of our forefathers alive and trying to bring their story to masses of Americans.

In the area of research, Will Greene of the Association for the Preservation of Civil War Sites deserves special thanks for two reasons. Not only was his insight valuable to my research assistant during the 1993 Smithsonian tour of the Eastern battlefields, his efforts on behalf of all Americans to preserve the battlefields of the Civil War have made my efforts easy as well as enjoyable. In walking the many scattered sites, both preserved and abandoned, which are mentioned in this book, I was struck by how much of our heritage is being plowed under without a second thought and converted into parking lots and strip malls. The work of Will Greene and all those engaged in historical preservation is a critical and important effort that deserves the support and thanks of every American working for the preservation of our past.

At the Virginia Military Institute, Colonel Ed Dooley has been of great assistance in making the assets of that institution available to me as well as sharing with me his own research and notes on the Civil War. Also, Dr. Daniel J. Beattie of Charlottesville, Virginia, deserves my thanks and gratitude for taking the time to plow through my manuscript and make corrections.

At her request, I am prevented from mentioning the name of my chief assistant. Yet I cannot put this manuscript to rest without mentioning what her contributions have meant to me. Throughout this project, she not only plowed through piles and piles of books, manuscripts, and material, she also served as my first reader, adviser on women's issues, and a sounding board for ideas. Without her insight, much of this story would have been dull, lifeless, and shallow. Her advice, comments, and help have, in my opinion, taken this book to a level that it never could have attained without her.

As always, I have been, and continue to be, supported by my loving wife of twenty years, Pat. She is, and always will be, the spark in my life that makes all of this worthwhile.

H. W. Coyle

six of me to one thing; at each turn, changing and changing it;
an other in any, and in general, taking a hell of a good time
than anything, keeping the memories of an isolation, ship and
leaving, to bring their ideas in memory of Americans.

In the need of genuine, Will Greene, of the Association, for
that revelation of Civil War Sites, deserves special thanks; I
owe, upon . . . I of any, was the thirst available to my research
assistant during the 199-. Statements; some of the Eastern battlefields; this effort, on behalf of all, I hope are to preserve the
battlefields of the Civil War, have made my efforts stay, as well
as enjoyable. In watching the many teachers, alike, both preserved and abandoned, which are integrated in full scale, I was
struck by how much of our heritage is being slowed under
commercial . . . second thought and converted into parking lots and
strip malls. The goal of Will Greene and all those engaged in
historical preservation is a critical and important effort that
deserves the support and attention of every American working for
the preservation of our past.

At the Virginia Military Institute, Colonel Ed Dooley has
been of great assistance in making the people at that institution
available to me as well as sharing with me his own research and
notes on the Civil War. Also, The Daniel Library librarians at the
Citadel, Virginia deserves my thanks, and gratitude for taking the
time to plow through my transcripts and make corrections.

As he tapered, I am prepared from recounting the rank of
my chief assistant. Yet I cannot put this manuscript together
without mentioning what her contributions have meant to me.
Throughout the phases, she not only played through plus and
other obvious manuscript and material, she also served as
my first reader, adviser on historic issues, and a signature
friend for them. Without her several matched this story simply
have been dull. If she is any, Aullhew . . . there, as if a, empathic
and help have, in tremendous about this book to a level that it
never could have attained without her.

As always, I have been, and continue to be, supported by my
loving wife of twenty years, Pat. She is, and always will be, the
spark in my life that makes all of this worthwhile.

H. W. COYLE

*This book is dedicated to my mother and father,*
*Evelyn and Harry Coyle,*
*who gave me all they could, including*
*the best years of their lives.*

# Contents

# Contents

*It was the best of times, it was the worst of times*

Charles Dickens, *A Tale of Two Cities*

N.Y. | CONN.

PA.
Area of
Detail
N.J.
MD.
VA.
N.C.
S.C.

Atlantic
Ocean

York

PENNSYLVANIA

Chambersburg

Gettysburg
July 1-3, 1863

Westminster

Antietam
Sept. 17, 1862
Sharpsburg
Harper's
Ferry
Frederick
South Mountain
Sept. 14, 1862

Baltimore

Winchester
Kernstown
Mar. 23, 1862
Strasburg

Leesburg

MARYLAND

Annapolis

Washington

Bull Run
(1st) July 21, 1861
(2nd) Aug. 27-30, 1862

Manassas
Junction

Alexandria

Culpeper
Cedar Mt.
Rapidan R.

Chancellorsville
May 1-6, 1863

Orange

Aquia Cr.

Fredericksburg
Dec. 13, 1862

Gordonsville

Charlottesville

N. Anna R.

VIRGINIA

S. Anna R.

Bowling
Green

James R.

Gaines's Mill
June 27, 1862

Urbanna

West Point

EASTERN
CAMPAIGNS of
the CIVIL WAR
1861–1863

Richmond

Harrison's
Landing

Williamsburg

Petersburg

Yorktown

0    Miles    20

Ft.
Monroe

Chesapeake Bay

Potomac R.

Rappahannock R.

Mattapony R.

Chickahominy R.

BLUE RIDGE

Shenandoah R.

MANASSAS
GAP

©1958 A. Karl & J. Kemp

# PROLOGUE

# May, 1856
# Southeastern Kansas

PULLING BACK ON THE REINS OF THE HORSE THAT ALSO PULLED his plow when it was planting time back on his small farm near Osawatomie, Kansas, the tired young farmer came to a halt. Two other men following him, half asleep, hardly took note of his sudden stop. Instead, they lazily turned their own horses aside to avoid a collision and continued to ride on through the darkness toward home. After his companions had gone past him, the farmer, with one hand planted firmly on the rump of his horse and the other on the saddle horn, lifted himself half out of the saddle and twisted his body about until he was facing back to the southwest.

Back there, somewhere in the darkness, lay Pottawatomie Creek. Other than the fact that it was populated by pro-slavery settlers, there was no real difference between that part of Kansas and where he lived. But to their leader, who viewed slavery as evil and all slaveholders as sinners, there was a vast difference. "So long as another human being is kept in bondage," John Brown had preached, "we cannot allow ourselves any rest, any comfort." So, under no higher authority than his own, Brown had ridden out with his small band at noon the previous day, on a mission to bring vengeance on those sinners.

While the young farmer and the other members of this small expedition were of like mind on the evils of slavery and had followed Brown willingly enough, the violence that they had just visited on five of the settlers back there was beginning to bother him. He couldn't imagine why he hadn't felt this way before they had struck in the dead of night. Even while they were dragging the pro-slavers out of their log huts so that they

1

could be more easily butchered, the young farmer hadn't hesitated. Perhaps, he thought, it was Brown's rhetoric that kept him to task. Maybe it was the excitement. Or, God forbid, it could be that they, and not the victims of their vengeance, were the real demons, the true sinners in the eyes of the Lord. Only now, however, were such thoughts coming to his mind, now that the excitement in his heart was calmed by exhaustion, just as the blood on his hands was dried and caked now by the passing of time.

Thoughts of his hands and the bloody work they had performed that night sent a shiver down his spine. Slowly he turned back to the front, easing himself down into the saddle. Once settled, he brought his hands up before his face. In an effort to see them, he squinted in the darkness as he turned his rough hands this way and that, inches from his eyes. He was thus occupied and paying no attention when, from one side, he suddenly heard a sharp voice bark at him. "What is it? Have you lost something? Are you hurt?"

Startled, the young farmer dropped his hands and turned in the direction of Salmon Brown's voice as he repeated his question. "What is it?"

Like a child caught by a parent doing something that he shouldn't be doing, the young farmer shook his head and responded without thinking. "Nothin's wrong. Nothin' at all."

"Then why," demanded Salmon Brown, "did you stop?"

Shyly, the young farmer looked around before he spoke. When he did, his voice was hushed and troubled. "I was thinking, Salmon. I mean, what did those folks back there do to deserve what we did to them? I mean—"

Salmon cut the young farmer off before he could finish. "They were slavers, man! Godless trash who defame the Lord's word by holding others down on their knees in bondage. And because they refuse to mend the error of their ways, and seek instead to spread that institution, it is our duty to annihilate them and their kind."

The young farmer was unconvinced. He had heard all of this before. Their leader, the self-styled Captain John Brown himself, had used words very similar to those being spoken by Salmon. Like other men who had listened to Captain Brown, the farmer believed them. Now, in the aftermath of their raid,

2

and with images of their deeds impaled upon his tired and troubled mind, those words were beginning to pale. The young farmer shook his head again. "Salmon, those men back there, they were farmers, just like us. Not a one of them owned a slave. They were nothin' but sodbusters, just like me. What gives me the right to pull a man out of his bed in the middle of the night and hack him to death in front of his wife and children just because he don't agree with me? I mean, it may be that we, not they, are the sinners. My God, Salmon, we just committed *murder!*"

With the same flame of passion that animated his father, Salmon Brown's eyes sparkled as he pulled back and stood in his stirrups. "How dare you question our purpose! We are doing God's work. Was it not they who struck first, two days ago in Lawrence? And didn't their kind freely, and without remorse, slay five God-fearing Free-Soilers this past winter? We, and not that pro-slave trash, are the ones living in a state of sin. As my father has declared, without the shedding of blood, there can be no remission of sins."

Tired and confused, the young farmer didn't respond at first. Instead, the two men looked across the darkness at each other. Finally, the young farmer, in a most tentative manner, asked the son of his leader, "Where will all of this lead us? What are we really trying to do out here, killing each other in the night?"

Salmon smiled, a big broad toothy smile that the young farmer could see even in the darkness. "We are just the beginning. Tonight is just a small battle in a great war that will see all good, God-fearing men throughout this country rise up and throw off the yoke of the oppressor. We, and many like us, have been given a mandate by God to light the flames of passion in the good people throughout the North, and stoke those flames until they burn hot enough to destroy every Southern slaver and their damnable institution."

As if on cue, another rider rode up next to Salmon. He didn't need to speak for the young farmer to know it was Captain Brown, for now every feature of that man, like the images of the mutilated bodies they had left behind, was burned into his memory. "What is the problem? You are falling behind, and we still have a hard ride before dawn."

The young farmer was about to voice his concerns to Brown

3

himself, but didn't. Instead, he lapsed into silence. It was war, he thought, that Captain Brown was after, a terrible and bloody war. The man he saw before him, whom he had once regarded as nothing more than an outspoken leader of Free-Soilers, had taken on a new image that night. It had been quite by accident, quite unexpected, but nevertheless, real and horrifying. In the midst of their grisly work, while he held a torch, the young farmer had looked over at Brown. In the eerie red glow of the torchlight the farmer watched as Brown raised his long double-edged sword up over his head. Holding that weapon aloft, a weapon already dripping with the blood of an earlier victim, the young farmer saw on Brown's face an expression that could only be described as demonic. Brown's wild, windblown hair and gray wiry beard, speckled with specks of blood, framed an expression that was both cold and haunting. The grin he sported, not to mention the twinkle of the torchlight in Brown's eyes that the young farmer hadn't thought about then, now haunted him as did the brutal butchery he had so willingly joined.

Glancing behind him one more time, the young farmer thought for a moment. How, he asked himself, had a good, God-fearing Christian and family man allowed himself to become caught up with such a man? Then, as Brown's horse snorted, impatient to be moving again, he realized the question was no longer important. Whether he liked it or not, he had committed himself to Brown's cause, and had, by his own hand, murdered another human being for no other reason than that he lived in a different county and dared to believe in something that John Brown didn't.

Turning his head back toward Brown and his son Salmon, the young farmer was about to say something but decided not to. There was nothing more to say. Blood had been spilled. Now, nothing but more blood would quench the fire that they were fanning.

Without another word, he turned away from the pair and rode on into the darkness that hid them, for now.

4

# PART ONE

# A HOUSE DIVIDED

# PART ONE

# A HOUSE
# DIVIDED

# CHAPTER 1

# December, 1859
# Perth Amboy,
# New Jersey

FROM WHERE HE STOOD JUST SHORT OF THE BANK OF THE
Raritan River, young John O'Keeth could clearly see the body
as it bobbed up and down in the river some twenty feet out.
Behind him a growing crowd, from God only knew where, was
gathering to watch. Only those with the foresight to bring a
lantern were permitted to go forward, down to the riverbank
itself, where O'Keeth and his fellow police officer pondered
the situation.

He was called Johnny O by those on the small Perth Amboy
police force who liked him, Paddy by those who disliked working with an Irishman. While there was much that John enjoyed
about his new job, despite the harassment he received simply
because he had been born in Ireland, there was much to be
disliked. To the good, there was none of the backbreaking work
that had been his daily fare while working in the Bannon terra-
cotta works where he had labored six days a week for seventy-
five cents a day. Nor did he, as a policeman, carry home every
night dirt and clay ground into every stitch of his clothing and
clogging every pore in his body. Often, at the end of a particularly hard day, O'Keeth hadn't even had enough strength left
to make it through his evening meal. It had not been unusual
for him to pass out from exhaustion at the table and find himself, the next morning, still in his filthy work clothes from the
day before, with nothing but the grim promise of another day
of menial labor to look forward to. Yes, O'Keeth thought to
himself, there were advantages to this job, but Lord, there were
duties, like those he faced tonight, that would make a saint cry.

7

From the riverbank, the other policeman, a German by the name of Frederick Himmel, turned and called out to him. "Well, Johnny O, looks like you'll have to go in after it. There's no way to reach it from here."

"Can't we wait for the boat to arrive, Frederick?"

Himmel shook his head. "The tide is going out, lad. If whatever snagged the body lets go, we'll have a devil of a time finding it, if ever. No, you've got to go in after it now, while it's still within reach."

Lord, John thought, it's going to be freezing. The mere thought of stepping out into the dark, fast-running river sent a shiver up his spine. As bad as it would be while he was in the river, he knew that it would be worse when he got out. Already the driving wind from the open bay cut through his coat and foretold a storm coming in from sea that would soon be there. But he had to go. The people gathered behind him expected as much. He held up the lantern in his hand a little higher over his head and shielded his eyes from its glow with his right hand. The lantern's faint glow fell upon the dark body, arms outstretched, still bobbing up and down with the motion of the choppy waves.

From behind him, a voice in the crowd called out. "What's a matter, Mick? Afraid the river'll clean some of the filth off you?"

Angered by the comment and the chorus of chuckles that followed, O'Keeth turned and glared at the crowd. Though he knew that he wouldn't be able to find the offender, for anyone in the throng could have made the comment, to stand there and take the insult would have been too much for the fiery young man.

Sensing the younger man's growing anger, Himmel called to him, "Johnny, get going, will you? My feet are freezing."

Twisting his head, O'Keeth looked down to where Himmel waited impatiently. After flashing one last scowl at the crowd, John turned his back to it and sat down on the riverbank. Behind him, Himmel patted him on the shoulder. "Ignore them, lad. They're nothing but a bunch of drunken ghouls out after a little mischief. Now, let's get this over with before the cold takes us and we both join that poor soul on the other side."

Looking up at the older man, John nodded. He was right, of course. Still, his being right didn't make the taunting any easier to take. Setting down the lantern, O'Keeth stripped off his coat, throwing it down next to the lantern. He began to take off his shoes. Himmel cautioned him. "Might be a good idea if you leave those shoes of yours on, lad. There's a lot of sharp brick-bats and broken glass about, compliments of our friends behind us."

John looked up. "There's no way I'm going into that water with my new shoes on, Frederick. I paid five dollars for these two weeks ago, the first pair of custom-fit shoes I've ever had."

Raising his hands, Himmel nodded. "Fine, fine. But when you cut your feet to ribbons and have to spend a week off from work with no pay, don't look to me for sympathy."

"I might have to go into the bloody river after a corpse," John mumbled to himself, "but I damned well don't need to ruin a new pair of shoes. The bloody Department will never pay me back for 'em." O'Keeth was about to tell Himmel to watch the shoes for him, but didn't. The German was one of the few men on the force who was truly civil to him and, on occasion, kind. To ask him to do something that should be taken for granted might insult him. Instead, O'Keeth stood up, took one more long look at the body, and began to step gingerly forward into the freezing water.

The exposure of his feet to the cold, wet mud of the river-bank did nothing to prepare him for the shock of entering the river. Within seconds his feet were numb. If they were being cut up by rocks and discarded beer bottles, O'Keeth thought, he wouldn't be able to tell. After the first step or two, he was no longer able to feel the muck of dark brown river mud that his feet sank into up to his ankles when they were not slipping off of slime-covered rocks. In an effort to minimize the impact of the cold, John turned his attention to the object of his labors.

There was no doubt that whoever it was in the river was dead, beyond help. Other than the motion caused by waves, the body hadn't moved or changed position for several minutes. There was nothing that O'Keeth or Frederick could do to change that. When he was a few feet out, he turned toward the crowd and looked at them for a moment. It was a motley collection of people that continued to grow as more stumbled out of nearby homes and taverns when word had spread that someone had drowned in the river. They stood there, massing together in an effort to stay warm as they watched and waited.

Turning his head back to his front, John began to curse himself for joining the police force. There would be no glory gained here, not for recovering a dead body from a cold river. With every step he took, the glamour of being a policeman washed away more and more. This was a dirty job. Though it was different from the one he had held at the terra-cotta works, like everything else in life, it had its nasty sides. One of them, John quickly found out, was that the youngest or the smallest or the newest person always got the worst shift, or the dirtiest assignments, or the nasty little jobs. It had been that way in Ireland and, despite the wild talk back there, it was the same in America.

Shaking his head, John continued to work his way forward despite the numbing of every part of his body that touched the river. He wanted to rush forth, retrieve the body, and get back as quickly as possible. The slime of the riverbed, the current, and the numbness of his limbs, however, made progress slow, painfully slow. By the time he was up to his waist, his teeth were chattering uncontrollably. As much as he tried, and wanted to, he could go no faster. Fixing his eyes on the body, John concentrated instead on his goal in an attempt to block out the cold and his agony. In the faint and flickering light of the lantern held aloft by Himmel back on the riverbank, he could see the body lazily bobbing up and down with each passing wave. This job ain't worth the ten dollars a month the city is payin' me. Not by a long shot it ain't. At least, he thought, when I was workin' in the factory I got to spend me nights at home in a warm bed, not in the middle of a big bloody cold river.

By the time O'Keeth reached the body, the river was up to his armpits, forcing him to hold his arms high above his head lest they too be numbed by the freezing water. Now that he had reached the body, he was unsure what to do next. The thought of being next to the body was suddenly repulsive. On the boat, coming over from Ireland, the old man he had shared a bunk with had died during the night. The image of that man's vacant stare and lifeless eyes was suddenly as sharp and clear to O'Keeth as it had been that morning when he woke to discover the old man was dead.

But he was determined to go through with his task at hand,

despite the fact that he couldn't remember any time in his life when he had ever been so cold. Without further thought, John reached out and grabbed a handful of the body's clothing. He pulled it in toward him. It moved a foot or so but stopped. Shifting about, he adjusted his footing as best he could, then gave another tug. This time, all he met with was resistance. As Himmel had suspected, the body was caught on something, something underwater, and whatever was holding the body wasn't going to let go without a struggle.

As distasteful as it was, O'Keeth wrapped his arm around the body's waist. He had no difficulty doing this as the body had a very small waist. Once he had it firmly against his side, John began to run his free hand down the body in order to find out what was holding it fast. Slowly he groped in the dark, cold river in his efforts to find out what was holding the body while he struggled to keep his footing and contend with what seemed like endless yards of skirt and crinoline that the waves caused to billow out. Finally, he found that the leg of the body that was next to his was free and floating with the current. He let go of that leg and searched for the other.

As soon as he grabbed it, he knew it was the one that was stuck. It was stretched out and taut. As he had with the other, O'Keeth ran his hand down the leg, which was no easy task. His hand, numb from the cold, had little feeling. He concentrated on trying to find whatever it was that was holding the body. He did. The body's ankle was snagged in a branch or some type of debris on the riverbed. After what seemed to be an eternity of fumbling around, he grabbed the ankle and, with a jerk, forced it out of the debris that entrapped it.

Suddenly freed from its anchor, the body was swept along with the current. O'Keeth was not ready for this. He tried to hang on to the body and pull it in to him but lost his footing. The weight of the body and its wet clothes dragged him under. He panicked for a moment but did not let go of the body. John knew that he was being carried way into the bay. He also knew that he had come too far and suffered too much to lose the damned thing now. Clawing through the water with his free hand in what he thought was the direction of the riverbank, he struggled to regain his footing on the bottom. He could feel his lungs begin to ache. He had had no time to catch a proper breath before he had been swept underwater, and his lungs were now screaming for air.

O'Keeth's desperate and frantic efforts were rewarded. His foot hit upon a flat rock that stopped him and gave him some firm footing. He brought his other foot up next to it, and with all his effort, he pushed his head up out of the water. His first instinct, as soon as his face broke the surface, was to gasp for a breath of air. Then he turned his full attention to his struggle to balance himself on the rock as the current continued to threaten to sweep him away. Only when he had steadied himself did O'Keeth bother to look about. He had been swept about thirty yards downriver and a little farther out. He could see the crowd on the shoreline running down the riverbank until they were even with him. Above the roar of the crowd, muffled by water in his ears, he could hear Himmel's deep voice shouting out to them, "He's still got it! He's got it!" He turned and looked behind him. The body was still with him, held by a hand that had long since lost feeling.

By the time O'Keeth regained the riverbank, the chief of police had arrived. O'Keeth, numb and exhausted, did not take notice at first. Only when O'Keeth was a few feet away from shore did Himmel and some of the bystanders offer to relieve him of his burden. Two men waded into the river and took the body while another wrapped O'Keeth's coat around him. It was, as he had expected, worse when he got out. O'Keeth shivered and shook uncontrollably, even with his coat wrapped about him. An arm from the crowd offered him a drink from a metal flask. Without thinking, he took the flask and attempted to drink but could not because of his shaking. Someone helped him steady his hand and get a mouthful of whisky, half of which ran down his cheeks because of his shivering. Only after the second gulp was he finally able to calm down and start looking about.

It was beginning to snow. He had not noticed that before. He turned toward the two men who had taken the body from him. They had dragged the body ashore and laid it out. A boy with a lantern followed the chief of police, holding it high as the chief and Himmel knelt down to examine the body. "It's a woman," someone on the edge of the crowd called out to others behind him who could not see. "And by the looks of her clothes, a rich one."

It was Himmel who turned the face toward the light. After he had done so, there was a moment of silence before his entire body stiffened noticeably. Standing up, he looked at the chief as he stood staring down at the body. Shaking his head, the chief muttered to no one in particular, "Lord help us." The whispers of the crowd also were hushed. Only when someone asked who it was did O'Keeth understand why the chief had reacted as he did. In a subdued and troubled voice, Frederick Himmel announced to all who could hear, "It's Martha Anderson, the mayor's only daughter."

In the windswept cemetery of St. Peter's churchyard, two young men huddled behind an ancient headstone for protection against both the cutting wind and the vicious nightmare that their collective hatred had spawned. The older of the two, James Edward Bannon, held his younger brother close to him and stared out at the bay. The clouds and falling snow hid Staten Island, just a short distance across the bay, from view. James could see it though, in his mind's eye, sitting there as always. The view never changed. The leaves on the trees on the island might change color in the autumn and fall off in the winter, but they always came back. Every spring they were there, fresh, green, and alive. James knew they would be there again next spring. He wondered, however, as he held his shivering brother, if he would be there to see them.

It was natural that the two brothers would come back to this place that had always offered them sanctuary and safety. At times, when they had problems or their father turned on them and beat them in a rage, James and his brother, Kevin, would come to this haven of calm and safety. There, amongst the headstones, they would hide while they sought an answer or solution to the issue at hand. It had always seemed to work before. The tranquillity and solitude of the old cemetery worked to clear and steady the mind, allowing James to find an answer. The two brothers, born little more than a year apart, prided themselves on being able to work their way out of tight spots.

Without a mother and condemned to live with an unloving father, they had to learn to do so early. Tonight, however, James was unable to focus his thoughts. He had, in his eighteen years, never faced a problem of such magnitude. An eight-year-old boy out to prove he was tough by breaking a shopkeeper's window was one thing. Murder, even if it was accidental, was quite another.

James' mind raced like a runaway locomotive. Thoughts and images tumbled over each other in random order, preventing him from focusing on any one in particular. Ever since his return from his first semester at Princeton, his mind and life had been a muddle. James had always assumed that he would marry Martha, the mayor's daughter, a young girl of seventeen. Her pledge of fidelity to him at his departure for Princeton had, at times, been all that had sustained him during his first grueling months of college. Not even her failure to respond to his desperate love letters diminished his feelings for her. "I have," he told his roommate one night, "found something worth cherishing and loving in this world, and I swear that no one is going to come between it and me."

When he had said that, he had been referring to Martha's father, who frowned upon his daughter's association with a boy he called "Irish riff-raff," and to his own father, Edward Bannon, who had, in James' eyes, been little more than an unending source of pain and scorn. It therefore came as a shock to James when he was greeted in his own home the day he arrived there for Christmas break by his own brother, with Martha hanging on his arm. Kevin's simple announcement that he and Martha were secretly engaged left James devastated. From that moment on, there was no peace between them. Fight followed fight, each one more vicious and more heated. During one, which ended in a brawl, James threatened to kill Kevin if he ever saw him with Martha again.

As his mind tripped from one thought to another, he recalled the twisted, tangled events that had led to the confrontation that evening. While city police struggled to contain a growing mob of day laborers and protesters who filled the streets near the docks at the rumor that two of John Brown's men were enroute by steamer to be buried at the Utopian community's cemetery at Eaglewood, James had gone in search of his brother and Martha.

In the gathering darkness of the cold winter day, James found them where he had expected to, at a small secluded boat dock on the river, where the two brothers kept a small rowboat. Like the cemetery, the rowboat had often served as a refuge from their father's vicious temper. There, in the boat, drifting freely on the tides of Raritan Bay, both James and Kevin could pretend for a while that they were free from the harsh, tyrannical rule of their father. As children they would often pretend that they were sailing back to Ireland, in search of their dead mother. She had passed away within days of giving birth to Kevin, leaving neither boy any memory of her. Yet, in their minds, she was more real than all the saints that the Church could muster. Her death and absence left her, in their fantasies, pure and untarnished by the sins of a world made dark and cruel by their father.

In an eruption of raw and unrestrained emotions, logic and past loyalties were swept away by Kevin's fear of his brother's threat and James' anger at the betrayal he felt from the only two people who had ever mattered to him. When James found them, Martha was standing in the boat, waiting for Kevin to finish untying it and join her. Coming out of the darkness, James had shouted at Kevin, causing him to spin about and drop the rope as he faced his approaching brother. Though James couldn't recall his exact words, they were sufficient to cause Kevin to reach down into his coat pocket, from which he drew the revolver that he had taken from their father's desk drawer in his study. "James," Kevin shouted in fright as the hand holding the pistol shook, "you've got to let me explain, please." But James wanted no explanation. He had been hurt, hurt worse than his father had managed to hurt him. All James wanted, at that moment, was to make his brother feel the hurt that he felt in his heart. Rushing forward toward his brother without a word, James grabbed at the hand that held the pistol.

Before James was able to seize Kevin's arm, Kevin managed to cock the piece. Yet even when he was confronted, face to face, with the full wrath of his older brother, Kevin wasn't able, or willing, to bring the pistol to bear on James. That thought had never crossed his mind. James, after all, had been his shield and sole source of comfort, the only protection he had between himself and their father. Kevin had taken the pistol for no other reason than to hold James at bay while he explained as best he could how he had come to fall for a girl who had pledged herself to his older brother. He hadn't counted on James' sudden appearance from out of nowhere and his lightning response, just as he hadn't expected the discharge, the sheet of flame from the pistol he held. Pushing away from each other, the two brothers gasped in horror. In his excitement, Kevin dropped the weapon, while James exclaimed breathlessly, "Dear God in heaven, what are we doing?"

Kevin, shaken as he had never been shaken before, stuttered. "I . . . I never meant . . . sweet Jesus, James. I never meant to hurt you. But . . ." He was about to reach out with his right hand and grasp his brother's shoulder when he froze. Whipping his head to the side, he looked over to where Martha had been standing uneasily as the boat had rocked in the gentle waves. To his horror, he saw neither Martha nor the boat.

Noticing his brother's distraction, James too turned and looked over to where the boat had been. With a desperateness that made his scream sound like the howl of a wounded animal, James yelled to her in vain, "Martha! Martha!" There was, of course, no answer. Together, both brothers bounded over to the edge of the dock where the boat had been. But instead of seeing Martha in the boat, all they saw was the keel of the capsized boat, bobbing up and down on the placid waves. "Dear God, she's tipped the boat and gone in," James shouted.

Kevin, in a voice that betrayed the fear that gripped him, added, "I shot her. Mother of God, I shot her."

While still looking for any sign of Martha or her struggles in the water, James snapped at his brother. "You don't know that for sure. Maybe the discharge of the pistol frightened her. That could have made her lose her balance and fall in."

"No, James, I killed her. I know I shot her dead."

Turning to his brother, James gripped Kevin's shoulders. "You don't know that for sure. Now shut up and keep a sharp eye on the other side of the dock. She's got to come up somewhere near here."

"And when she does, James, then what?"

"Damn it, I don't know. Just look."

Though they looked, neither of them saw any sign of Martha. In desperation, James stripped off his jacket and shoes and went into the water to search under the boat in the hope that she was trapped under it. But she wasn't there. Nor was she under the dock, or washed onto the nearby shore. Like the anger that had sparked the confrontation between the two brothers, Martha had disappeared into the vast darkness that the merging of the black river and starless night sky created. In a sudden fit of panic, James and Kevin turned their backs on the lonely dock and fled into the same darkness that had so completely engulfed Martha.

The confusion of the night, prompted by the near riot caused by the decision by the Utopian community south of the river to bury two of John Brown's companions, allowed James and Kevin to make their way to St. Peter's cemetery unnoticed. James hoped in vain that something would come to him, that somehow a solution to their problem would be found. But none came. In his tired and befuddled mind, numbed by the course of events as well as the bitter cold that raked his body from head to toe, James saw no good solution, other than escape. Shaking his brother from a sleep that bordered on death itself, James informed him that they had best go home and get some rest. With a voice that betrayed his grogginess, Kevin asked if that was wise.

"We have, Brother, no other choice."

Blinking his eyes, Kevin shook his head. "But they'll suspect us. Surely they'll come and ask us what happened to Martha?"

"Yes, they'll suspect us. But if we say nothing, if we both plead ignorance, how can they prove anything?"

"I don't know, James, I just don't know."

"What," James asked, "don't you know? In the name of God, what would you have us do? March into town and turn ourselves in? For what? We don't even know that Martha's dead. For all we know, she might have fallen out of the boat into the river and swum ashore. She could be home right this moment, safe in her bed, with nothing more than a bad scare and wet clothes."

"And if she's not?"

"We'll deal with that if and when we have to. Until then, we

17

stick together, as always. If anyone asks, you keep your mouth shut, no matter what. You let me do the talking.'' Moving about so that he faced his brother, James placed his hands on Kevin's shoulders and looked into his eyes. Though they were barely a foot away, all he saw was two faint white circles, but he knew he had Kevin's attention. ''We have survived all these years by sticking together. So long as we have each other, no one, not Father, not the hypocrites who love him for his money, not even the respectable people of this town who hold us in contempt because their ancestors came to this country a generation or two before we did, can beat us. So long as you let me handle this and follow my lead, we have nothing to fear. Besides,'' James added with a hint of sorrow in his voice, ''we have no choice.''

Too tired and shaken to argue, Kevin nodded in agreement. Helping each other up, the two brothers left their sanctuary and turned to home, where they would wait in silence; for what, they did not know.

As was their custom, the business associates of Edward Bannon gathered in the parlor of his grand and gracious home on the morning after any major event in their city, state, or the nation occurred. There, amidst fine ornaments and ornate draperies painstakingly chosen by an untrained male eye for their apparent value and not their beauty, the men would discuss the event and figure out how they might contrive to profit from it or protect themselves and their growing fortunes. Edward Bannon and his confederates practiced their incestuous business relationships and arrangements in the same spirit that backwoods families, isolated from the rest of the world, marry their own kin. Of the six men sitting about in their expensive frock coats, smoking cigars or sipping coffee laced with fine brandy, not one was born to wealth or power. Like Edward himself, they had made their own fortunes by hook or—more often than not—crook. Though none of them was a criminal in the conventional sense, each and every one of them used every means available to further his own fortunes, regardless of the price he, and those who stood in his way, had to pay. At best, the established families of Perth Amboy and Middlesex County referred to these men and their families as nouveau riche. Usually they were dismissed as little more than tasteless upstarts, or worse.

Though all of these men, in particular Edward, pretended that these snubs didn't bother them, the idea that their self-proclaimed social betters would never accept them, no matter how rich or powerful they became, bothered them. It was, Edward once remarked after a particularly vicious slight, "as if they ruled this country and its society by divine right." To prove that they didn't, and couldn't, had become something of an obsession with Edward O'Bannon, an obsession that was even greater than his need to amass more money and more power. To this end he had raised his first son, James, from birth, in a manner that would permit him to enter into a society that Edward's own humble Irish birth denied him. "If I cannot do it myself," Edward often bragged to friends, "then I will breed a son who will beat them at their own game and, in time, rub their upturned noses in their own dirt."

Such thoughts, however, were, for the moment, secondary to the issues that had necessitated the gathering of Edward's business associates. While news of John Brown's raid on the Harpers Ferry Arsenal in Virginia less than two months ago threatened to tear the nation apart like a speeding, ungoverned engine, the full impact of that event hadn't been driven home to Edward and his friends until the previous day. "That the ripples of a trivial affair on the Potomac, like John Brown's raid, can shake us here, on the Raritan, speaks ill for the future of this country," Edward warned as he leaned forward in his overstuffed chair.

Waving his cigar about, an associate of Edward's who sat with him on the bank's board of directors spoke in an effort to downplay Edward's concern. "There have been slave uprisings in the South before. So long as those damned fool abolitionists are allowed to preach their own peculiar brand of self-righteousness, we and the South are going to be annoyed by wild-eyed radicals like Brown."

"Yes," another man exclaimed, jabbing his cigar at the speaker like a finger. "But this time, it's different. The Virginians and their Southern brethren are more than annoyed.

19

Many more people, reasonable people, on both sides of the Mason-Dixon, are beginning to take sides. Just look at what happened here last night. Our own workers, men who have no earthly idea where Harpers Ferry is or who John Brown was, nearly tore this city apart simply because the bodies of two of his men were going to be landed here on our own city's dock.''

"Yes," Edward stated dryly. "And fortunately for all of us, those damned fools from Eaglewood and the steamer's captain had enough sense to dock on the south side of the river. I shudder to think what would have happened if that mob had gotten hold of those coffins."

"Might I ask, sir," enjoined another man, "what difference it would have made to us if the mob had succeeded in ripping the corpses of two radicals apart?"

Edward looked at the last speaker for a moment before answering. "Surely you can see the danger that this whole John Brown affair has created? There isn't a man in this room who doesn't have daily business dealings with men from the South. Why, you know as well as I do that the South walks on Newark leather. From shoes to fire bricks, the six of us, and nearly every manufacturer in this state, depend on the South; in business and in politics, we're more a part of the South than we are of the North."

"So? How do that and the bloody abolitionists affect us?"

Doing little to hide his anger, Edward shifted in his chair. "Are you daft, man? Haven't you been watching and listening? It's not only the abolitionists that we need to worry about anymore, it's the secessionists too. Good men, reasonable men like us, are beginning to listen—I mean *really* listen—to the radicals. In the North and South radicals and the views they espouse, views that wouldn't have been given a second thought a month ago, are beginning to gain popularity. When men like Governor Wise of Virginia begin to sound like those damned fool radicals in South Carolina, it's time for men like us to sit up and take notice."

From the corner of the room, Thomas Howorth joined the conversation. "What would you have us do, Edward?"

Edward glanced over to Howorth before answering. Of the six men, Howorth was, without argument, the only one in the room who was truly odious. Even his appearance was contemptible. Fat to the point of obesity, Howorth made no effort to keep his person or clothing clean. One of his law partners once commented that Howorth maintained enough crumbs of food on his shirt and vest to feed a shipload of Irish immigrants for a week. Though Edward, like the others, didn't care for associating with the man, his skill as a lawyer and his political connections throughout New Jersey made him a man too powerful to ignore. Unfit to associate with the more genteel classes and better families of the state, Howorth had wormed his way into Edward's little group. As his price of admission, Howorth freely served as the group's legal advisor and key to the corridors of power throughout New Jersey. Still, Edward didn't like the man or his smug attitude.

Taking a deep breath, Edward pondered his response. When he was finally ready to respond to Howorth's question, Edward spoke slowly, carefully picking his words. ''The reactions of our brothers down South and our neighbors up here to the John Brown affair make it clear that this 'irrepressible conflict' isn't going to go away soon or on its own. Somehow, sometime in the future, there is going to be a crisis, a real crisis, that will shake this country. What we must do, each and every one of us, is work together to not only protect our own interests, but seize, when the time comes, any opportunity that this conflict may bring our way. While making sure that our Southern friends don't boycott our goods, we must ensure that we don't alienate ourselves from our workers and our own people here, back home.''

''In other words,'' Howorth added, ''you want us to walk the picket fence, like a cat.''

''Yes,'' Edward exclaimed. ''That, sir, is exactly what we must do. For until we know on which side safety lies, we must be careful. If we openly express our sympathies with our friends in the South, then many of our neighbors and friends here at home who view the abolitionist cause as just will sever their political and business ties with us. On the other hand, if we embrace the liberation of the Negro, our own workers, who see freed blacks as a threat to their livelihood, will riot, as they did last night.''

While the others nodded their approval of Edward's advice, Howorth pulled his watch from his pocket and looked at the time. With a grunt, he stood up, snapped the watch cover closed, and announced to the gathering, in a rather pompous manner, "Well, gentlemen, it has been a pleasure. I must, however, excuse myself. I have a client in New Brunswick, and if I am to meet my appointment on time, I must leave now."

Standing, Edward bowed stiffly at the waist. "I am sorry you must go. May I show you to the door, Thomas?"

With a sly grin, Howorth nodded. "Yes, of course, Edward."

Once out of the room, Howorth turned to Edward. "While I agree with you, do not wait too long, my friend."

Edward paused and feigned lack of understanding. "Wait for what?"

Howorth chuckled and he struggled with his heavy overcoat. "Why to jump, my dear Edward, to jump. For if you sit upon that picket fence too long, you're liable to be shot off of it." Then, with a serious note in his voice he added, "It might be a good idea to have one or both of your sons sign on with a local militia company."

Edward's expression was one of shock. "Oh? And how would that further my ventures?"

Shaking his head, Howorth held back his laughter. Strange, he thought, how after all these years in America, somehow Irishmen still equated uniforms with Crown law and oppression. "If this so-called irrepressible conflict comes to a head, our state will, like every state, be called on to contribute to whatever cause New Jersey eventually decides to support. Though I for one believe that this state will never leave the Union, no matter how much we depend on trade with the South, a son planted in the militia is sure to become involved. You see, in this country there is no better way to establish one's respectability in society than being one of the first to go marching off to war in defense of home and hearth. A degree from Princeton is good, but a wound suffered on the battlefield is, in politics, priceless. Besides, with a son in the ranks, you will have to do or say nothing to prove your own loyalty. All you'll need to do, on occasion, is smile and remind those about you of your noble son, off with the Army, suffering privation and danger in the name of liberty."

Cocking his head to one side, Edward thought about that. As

he did so, a smile began to light his face. Yes, perhaps the fat old goat was right. "I take your point," he said.

"Good, I'm glad you do." Turning, Howorth was about to leave but then stopped. Shaking his head, he looked over his shoulder to Edward. "You know, if I were lucky enough to have two fine sons like yours, I'd send one south."

Taken aback by this comment, especially after Howorth's advice that one son enlist in the militia, Edward shook his head. "I don't understand. Why, if you think that the state will stay in the Union, would you want one son to go south? That would, according to your logic, place him on the wrong side."

Howorth spun about and puffed out his chest, a broad grin on his face. "Because, my dear Edward, the South just might go their own way. If that happens, then you would have one foot planted firmly here, in the old country, and the other in the new South. In effect, you could stay on the fence while your sons make the commitment for you. While that might cause some hard feelings for a while, remember, blood is always thicker than water. Yes," Howorth concluded with a wink, "you are, sir, indeed a lucky man. Very lucky. And you could do almost anything with that luck of yours if only—"

"If only what?" Edward responded impatiently, for he hated the casual, almost coy manner in which Howorth loved to ease into important issues.

Though he sensed Edward's impatience, Howorth wouldn't be rushed. "As you know, my friend, dropping the 'O' from your surname made a big difference when we were working to get your son James into Princeton. Though it didn't change the fact that he's Irish through and through, everyone there that mattered was able to pretend that he wasn't."

Edward now became angry, making no effort to hide it this time. "It was that hefty donation that made the difference, not the name."

Howorth grinned. "My dear man, you overestimate the power of your money. These fine gentlemen we deal with on a daily basis do have pride and certain standards they wish to maintain. Your habit of flaunting your Irish lineage simply adds friction to already delicate business relationships."

"Well," Edward thundered back, "I'm as proud of my heritage as they are of theirs. When an English lord robbed me of my pride and land when I was a boy, I swore I'd never bow my head to another man."

"Edward, I am not asking you to grovel. Lord knows, I'd never ask another man to do that. But please bear in mind, if you really want your sons to succeed, you're going to have to learn to bend a little on matters of pride. Remember, you're still the outsider." With that and a tip of his hat, Howorth turned and was off. Standing in the open doorway, Edward watched him walk down the path to the sidewalk. Thinking about what Howorth had said, Edward didn't notice the chief of police stop at the gate at the end of the path. He let Howorth pass, then turned, passed through the gate and down the path, straight for Edward. Only when the police chief's first footfall hit the bottom step of the porch did Edward take any note of him. When he did, Edward shook his head, flashed as warm a smile as he could, and greeted the chief. "Patrick, good day to you. What brings you out and about so early?"

With his head bowed down, Patrick Flanahan said nothing until he was within inches of Edward. Looking over Edward's shoulder into the house, he saw the men gathered in the parlor. Bending down until his lips were within inches of Edward's ear, Flanahan mumbled, "If you don't mind, sir, I need to have word with you, in private."

Leaning back, Edward studied the policeman's face for a moment. It was grim and worried. Nodding, Edward stepped aside, whispering as Flanahan went by, "Please, in the study. I'll join you in a minute."

When the police chief had disappeared into the study, Edward made his way into the parlor. "Gentlemen, you'll have to excuse me. Something important has come up that demands my immediate attention."

One man, with a playful grin on his face, stood up and faced Edward. "Well, Edward, whatever it is, don't forget to include us if there's any chance of a profit." While the other men laughed and went about retrieving their coats from an English maid, who had appeared on cue, Edward bit back a sharp comment as he nervously glanced over at the study. "Of course I'll remember you, George. I always do." Not waiting to see them off, Edward turned, marched into the study, and closed the doors behind him.

When Edward saw Flanahan standing in the middle of the room, hat in hand, he knew that this visit was either official or that Flanahan was in search of another favor. Regardless of the reason, Edward was put off by being interrupted by a mere civil servant and let his displeasure show. With the greatest restraint, he crossed the room to his desk. Taking a seat behind the large, imposing mahogany desk, he pulled himself forward until he could rest his forearms on the clean, highly polished desktop. When he was ready, Edward looked up, motioning for the chief to take a seat. When Flanahan shook his head and continued to stand, Edward knew that there had been trouble. Unable to hold back, he simply blurted, "Well, what is it?"

Without a word, Flanahan reached into his pocket, pulling out an object wrapped in a blue-and-white checkered rag. Holding the bundle in one hand, he carefully peeled away the cloth. Even before Flanahan finished, Edward froze, his eyes growing large as he recognized the contents of the cloth. The sudden change in Edward's demeanor, accompanied by an audible drawing in of a deep breath, caught Flanahan's attention. Glancing up, he took note of Edward's wide-eyed expression, riveted on the half-covered object. That look answered Flanahan's question even before he asked. Suppressing an urge to smile, he continued to slowly unwrap the pistol. Finished, he held it up. In a rather matter-of-fact manner, Flanahan asked, "Sir, do you recognize this weapon?"

Coming to his senses, Edward leaned back into his seat, allowing his right hand to fall to his side as he did so. As carefully as he could, Edward eased the top right-hand drawer open an inch or so, while pretending to study the pistol Flanahan held. Glancing down at the partially open desk drawer, Edward confirmed his worst suspicion. The pistol Flanahan held was his. Still, Flanahan's circumspect manner hinted that perhaps, just perhaps, things weren't as serious as his runaway imagination was leading him to believe. Slowly, he brought his right hand back up onto the desktop and clasped his hands. "What concern, Chief, is this matter to me?"

Again Flanahan held back his urge to smile. The old man was hedging. It was his pistol, all right, but he wasn't going to admit to it, not to him or anyone else. Though he knew that he could prove it, Flanahan also was wise enough in the ways of

25

the world to know that Edward Bannon had more than enough influence to manipulate the truth to fit his needs. He knew Bannon would do just about anything to protect his name and the position in the community he had so carefully created for himself. This left Bannon open-minded when it came to dealing with such "inconvenient" situations. No, Flanahan reasoned as he watched Edward begin to squirm in his seat, the old man will deal with me and be happy to do so.

Sure of himself now, Flanahan puffed out his chest. "It seems, sir, that this pistol was found on a dock not too far from your terra-cotta works, just before dawn, by one of my boys."

"And what, may I ask you, were your men doing poking around my property at all hours of the night? Surely there wasn't any more trouble with those fools who were gathering to contest the burial at Eaglewood?"

"Oh, no, sir. As best I can determine, this had nothing to do with the mob last night. No, sir, they were there looking into another matter."

"Well," Edward shot out, becoming upset at Flanahan's deliberate and circumspect manner, "what matter were they concerned with?"

"I don't suppose you have heard about the mayor's daughter. No, come to think of it, you wouldn't know about the poor dear child's death. The mayor and his lovely wife . . ."

In an instant, Edward's anger transformed itself into shock that sent him reeling back in his chair. Dear God in heaven, he pleaded in his mind, please, please don't let my boys be involved in this.

"Sir," Flanahan called out coyly as he paused, "is there something wrong?"

Edward was barely able to hold the anger that came rushing forth as a result of Flanahan's smug attitude as Flanahan continued to toy with him. With a shake of his head, Edward snapped, "No! Nothing's wrong. Now, if you please, I am very busy and I would appreciate it if you got to the point, man."

Seeing that the old man was ripe for the picking, Flanahan spoke directly. "The mayor's daughter was found dead this morning, in the river. At first we thought it was a simple case of drowning. But when the women began to undress the poor dear soul's body to clean it up for the wake, they found that sweet innocent Martha had been shot in the chest. While Doctor Kempler examined the body, I had my boys search the riverbank for evidence. That's when one of them found this pistol on the dock, the small one that's just upriver from your brick works.''

''What makes you think there's a connection?''

''The ball, sir, Doctor Kempler took from poor Martha's chest is the same caliber as this pistol. One chamber of this pistol has been discharged, probably last night, since it still had the smell of fresh-burned powder and there was no rust.''

In an effort to call his bluff, Edward held his anger while he feigned curiosity. ''Why have you come to me with this?''

''Well, sir, you can appreciate that there is need for a full investigation, this involving the mayor's poor young daughter and all. And since I recall seeing a piece like this one in your possession not too long ago, well, I naturally had to come by and find out if this could possibly be yours. After all, I do need to start somewhere, and I thought it best if I could clear your name before anyone started asking embarrassing questions.''

As he cursed the pride that had caused him to show off the custom-made .36 caliber pistol, initials and all, that Flanahan now held, Edward thought fast. ''That mob last night was pretty unruly, wasn't it?''

Flanahan smiled. ''Oh, no, sir. My boys, they kept those drunks and ruffians in hand.''

''But,'' Edward pressed, ''they did get out of hand, once or twice. I've heard that from several people.''

''That may be true, but there was no shooting. None of my boys reported seeing any guns or such. In fact, the mob was—''

Having reached his limit, Edward slammed his fist down on the desk. ''Damn it, man! Isn't it possible, just possible, that one of those hotheads shot the girl? Isn't it?''

Flanahan had won. Now, for the first time, he could let the sly smile he had been holding back creep across his face as he looked over at Edward. He had Edward and both men knew it. But despite that fact, the ''rules'' of the game they were playing required that Flanahan continue in a rather circumspect manner. Despite Flanahan's having been paid by Edward on numerous occasions before to turn a blind eye to his son's indiscretions, or problems with his workers, neither man ever dropped the pretense of respectability or honesty, even in private. Rocking back on his heels and looking up at the ceiling, Flanahan thought for a moment. "Oh, I suppose that poor Martha's sad ending *could* have been the result of last night's fracas down at the city dock. Some of the meaner types in that mob were pretty drunk, it's true."

"Yes, I heard they were," Edward said. "And I'm sure that not all of them went home right after your boys broke them up, did they?"

"As a matter of fact, sir, that's true," Flanahan mused, taking up Edward's train of thought. "Officer Frederick Himmel mentioned to me that they rousted out a couple of drunks passed out here and there during our search along the riverbank. Seems they either lost their way or they went wandering about to blow off steam and cool off."

Locking eyes with Flanahan, Edward asked, "You don't suppose . . ."

For the longest time, Flanahan looked into Edward's eyes. Flanahan could clearly see that they were desperate eyes, pleading with him. Holding himself back, Flanahan decided to adopt Edward's explanation. After all, he reasoned, it would do no one any good to push a serious investigation. Though the death of the mayor's daughter was a terrible tragedy, to pass up a wonderful opportunity to look out for his own future would be a terrible sin.

Taking a step forward, Flanahan placed the pistol on the front edge of Edward's desk, draping the blue-and-white checkered cloth over it as he did so. "One of my new boys found this. Smart lad, he is. Brought it right to me. Didn't tell anyone."

For the first time, Edward breathed a sigh of relief. "Yes, Chief, he is a smart lad. You don't suppose I could have a word with him in a few days, do you?"

Flanahan smiled. "He would be happy to, sir. Seems he had been hoping to get a chance to do just that. I hear he has some relatives due in from Ireland soon. They'll be needing jobs and a place to stay."

Edward smiled. A couple of jobs and an apartment would be a small price to pay, if, in fact, the dumb little Irish policeman kept his mouth shut. Of course, Flanahan hadn't named *his* price yet, and that, Edward knew, could be expensive. And though he wanted to finish this deal here and now, Edward didn't feel like pushing the issue. Flanahan would need some time to figure out his price, and Edward, needing to tend to family matters, was not in the mood to bicker with the police chief. Standing up, he moved around the desk, throwing his arm around Flanahan's shoulder as Flanahan spun about and started to head for the door. "And you, Chief. Don't you forget to come by later on this week. I would like to hear how that new house you're building over on High Street is doing."

The less-than-subtle hint caused Flanahan to smile broadly. With a gleam in his eye, he turned when he reached the door and shook Edward's hand. "Well, yes, come to mention it, the missus and I are quite excited about finishing our new home and moving in. We've been looking at furniture, you know."

"Yes, I'm sure. And I know that when the time comes, you'll settle for nothing but the best."

"That," Flanahan stated with a nod and a broad toothy grin, "you can count on. Good day, sir."

Slamming the door shut as soon as he could do so, Edward spun about and leaned against it. That he had escaped a major embarrassment by the narrowest margin, one that could have undone years, if not decades, of hard work, left Edward shaken. Without taking the time to ponder the issues or consider matters of innocence or guilt, Edward Bannon wondered how his oldest son, James, could have done such a thing to him. How *could* he? The idea that a lovely young girl, just past her seventeenth birthday, had died didn't enter into Edward's anguished thoughts. To Edward, women, while entertaining on occasion, had little use other than to produce an heir and tend to the home. Outside of that, they were an expensive ornament that held no special charm for him. His older son and the future that he had so carefully planned and worked for were all that mattered. And to have James jeopardize it in such a frivolous manner was simply too much for Edward to deal with.

With a scream that caused the cook, at the rear of the house, to jump, Edward called for Ellen, his English maid. Rushing into the foyer of the house, Ellen stopped as soon as she saw Edward. Wide-eyed and shaking, she didn't have a chance to ask what he wanted. "Go find my worthless son and tell him I want to see him in my study, *now*."

Without needing to ask which son he wanted, for everyone in the Bannon household knew that only the older boy mattered to Edward, Ellen scurried up the circular staircase to James' room. After watching her skirts and slips disappear up the broad stairs, Edward briskly moved from the front door to his study. There, he planted himself behind his desk and waited for his son.

The frantic knock on his door, and the excited tone in Ellen's voice, told James all he needed to know. Somehow, he and Kevin had been found out, the connection between their meeting last night and the death of Martha had been made. Now, all that remained was the accounting of and atonement for his sins. James had, in the back of his mind, been expecting this. He had been, in fact, ready, fully dressed for better than an hour and sitting quietly in his room, attempting to read a book of poetry in an effort to ease his troubled mind. When Ellen knocked, James laid the book to one side, stood up, straightened the jacket of his suit, and called out that he would be downstairs in a moment. After waiting until the rustle of Ellen's skirts disappeared down the hall outside of his door, James wiped a bit of moisture that was dripping from his nose with a new white handkerchief, crossed the room, and began the long slow descent to Edward Bannon's study with a gait not unlike that of a condemned man taking his last walk.

In a ritual often played out in the past, James came to the closed doors of the study, knocked, and waited to be called in by his father. The gruff, deep-throated "Enter" barked out by his father was no different today than in the past. Even the old man's face, when James pulled the two sliding doors apart, was set in the same dark scowl he always wore when preparing to admonish his son. Taking his cue, James walked in, closed the doors behind him, and walked over to one of the chairs that faced the mahogany desk. Even before he was halfway down in the seat, Edward growled, "I didn't tell you to sit."

Had the circumstances been different, James would have chuckled and responded to the old man with nothing but a smile. Instead, he continued to settle into the chair. When he was finally ready, he locked eyes with Edward. "Yes, I know."

This defiant, unprecedented break from the established routine angered Edward, and his face showed it. Yet, he said nothing. Instead, he reached across the broad expanse of the desk, grabbed a corner of the blue-and-white checkered bundle that sat there, and gave it a jerk. With a clatter, the pistol, freed from the cloth, fell from the desk and hit the floor, spinning a half turn before coming to a stop in the dead silence of the room.

If the action was meant to surprise or shock James, it didn't. Instead, James sat there, looking at the pistol for the briefest of moments, then slowly raised his eyes again until his stare met Edward's. Angered that his son had, for a second time, defied his efforts to rattle him, Edward gave up on the preliminaries and launched right into his attack. "How could you? Damn you, how could you?"

James, faced with the moment that he had been hours preparing for, was about to answer when, without waiting for a response, Edward began to berate him. "Damn you. After all that I have done for you, after everything that I have given you, how could you throw that, and your future, away on such a mindless, trivial fit of passion?"

James was caught completely off guard. Edward's anger was not due to the death of Martha, he realized, but rather it stemmed from the loss of the bright and wonderful future that he had, single-handedly, designed and engineered for James. Awed by this display of insensitivity and misplaced rage, James started to respond, trying to point out that his love for Martha wasn't trivial. But Edward was in no mood to listen. He didn't want justice, he didn't want explanations. All he wanted to do was to lash out. "Don't you dare interrupt me, you ungrateful cur. You've spent your entire life whining and sniveling while I tried to make a man of you, and how do you repay me? HOW? By disgracing the family name and honor."

Pride and honor, two themes that Edward loved to discuss but never put into practice, always managed to become an issue whenever Edward was berating his sons. Though it angered James that his father put these two concepts over all else, he knew it would be pointless to argue, just as he knew it would be pointless to try to explain what happened and why. He had, James realized, been tried, convicted, and sentenced. He was the older of the two brothers and, as such, responsible for everything they did. It had always been that way. Now all he needed to do was endure his father's tirade and wait for him to announce his punishment.

With no need to pay close attention to what his father was saying, for he had heard it all before, James began to realize that he, as a person, had never really mattered. In fact, he wondered if anyone, other than himself, mattered to Edward Bannon. In the past, despite the harsh manner in which Edward had raised his two sons, James had always been able to make excuses. At first, he and Kevin had both pretended that their father's anger was not directed at them personally, but was rather a form of mourning due to the loss of his wife, their mother. When, as the years slipped by, Edward's behavior became so demanding that it bordered on cruelty, the brothers reasoned that he was being overworked by the many projects and business he had become involved with. "Don't worry," James would comfort Kevin. "He's not angry because Mother died giving birth to you," a fear that Kevin was never able to shake. "He's only working hard and doing his best to become a rich and powerful man in this town so that we can all live together in a nice, big house, just like all the happy families on Market Street do." Accepting this explanation, more out of desperation than out of conviction, Kevin used James as his shield and source of comfort as the two boys waited, in vain, for the happy days to come.

Over the years, as the boys matured and Edward continued to seek more wealth, power, and prestige without changing, the two brothers continued to cling to the stubborn hope that one day, everything would change, that all would be made well. But that day never came. Even when James went to college at Princeton University, there was no softening in his father. Even his final words to James on the day he had departed that August for the school were bitter and cutting. "I have worked long and hard, boy, to get you into that college," Edward told him at the station as he jammed a stiff index finger into James' chest. "Don't you dare fail me."

Now, sitting here, just as he had as a small boy, listening to his father's admonishments and criticisms, the terrible truth finally struck home with a vengeance. The old man, this poor excuse for a human being that both he and Kevin called Father, was incapable of loving anyone or anything except himself. Yet, as disturbing as this revelation was, even more shattering to James was the realization that he too was losing sight of the cause of this whole scene. Not once since he had entered the room had Martha's death been mentioned, nor, after retreating into his own thoughts, had James himself given her plight or the anguish that her family had to be feeling a second thought. Rather, he sat there, bemoaning his fate, just as his father, seated behind his desk across the room, was doing. Looking up at his father, James exclaimed, as if out of the clear blue, "My God, I'm becoming just like you!"

James' unsolicited comment brought Edward's tantrum to a sudden halt. Looking over at him, Edward thought for a moment. Finally, in a low and menacing voice, Edward replied. "No, never. You, boy, are both spineless and of no account. You don't know what hard work is. You have never known suffering or privation. You are," he continued, raising his index finger to him, "incapable of filling my shoes, or the shoes of any decent, hardworking man. In short, boy, you are a disgrace and a waste."

Like a jack-in-the-box, James jumped to his feet. His face flushed with anger and arms held tightly to his sides with both fists clenched as tight as he could, he all but exploded, spitting as he yelled in response, "Better a disgrace, sir, than a miserable, heartless bastard."

Pushing back away from his desk, in fear of physical violence as much as in genuine surprise, Edward looked at James and began to speak, but wasn't given the chance by his son, whose anger had galvanized him. "For years," James lashed out at his father with the same fury that Edward had used on him, "you have made our lives a living hell. Rather than a parent, Kevin and I were cursed with a taskmaster, more cruel and demanding than the meanest dregs you use to extract every ounce of work you can from the laborers foolish enough to work for you. Why I didn't take Kevin and flee years ago, just as you fled the tyranny of the English landlords in Ireland, I'll never know." James thrust his right index finger into the air. "I'll not live under this roof another day," he said.

For a moment, there was a stunned silence in the room as

father and son glared at each other, each taking the other's measure and wondering what to do next. During this confrontation, Thomas Howorth's words to him, spoken just minutes ago, came to Edward's mind. As if struck by a divine revelation, he suddenly saw a solution to this confusing and very messy dilemma, one that would allow him to continue to appear to be a caring and respectable father while serving his own interests.

To James' surprise and confusion, a smile, a small and wicked one, lit his father's face. Then, letting it fade as he replaced it with a stern and uncompromising expression, Edward stood up, allowing his fingertips to lightly touch the desktop. "In spite of your profane abuse of me, I am your father and, as you know, blood is thicker than water. While I must, in some manner, make you pay for what you did, both to me and the mayor's daughter, I cannot forsake one of my sons and cast him out, without means or prospects. Cast you out I will, for your miserable conduct and ingratitude, last night and this morning, leaves me little choice. But it will be to a place where you can, by the grace of God, learn a profession and lay down new roots. Now, go, and leave me here to dwell on this a little longer."

Still shaken by the events of the night before, and disarmed by the sudden and unexpected rally of his father's nerve and poise, James did not know what to do. He had, he realized, spoken out of anger, letting passion and not logic put words into his mouth. Though he was quite sincere about his resolve to leave, the sudden realization of what that meant was only now beginning to sink into his troubled mind. Unable to think clearly, James did as he always had done when faced by his father like this; he obeyed. Dropping his arms to his sides and bowing his head, as much in exhaustion as in a show of capitulation, James turned and left his father's study, returning to his room to await his fate.

# CHAPTER 2

# January, 1860
# The Virginia Military
# Institute,
# Lexington, Virginia

FINISHED WITH A WELCOME THAT COULD ONLY BE DESCRIBED
as stiff and formal, James Bannon sat outside of the superintendent's office, waiting for the cadet who would take him on
the next, and final, leg of his journey south. Like a condemned
man facing his hangman, he was anxious to be done with it,
nervously tapping the arm of the wooden chair he sat in while
he watched the door leading out into the courtyard of the barracks.

In many ways the manner in which Colonel Francis Smith,
the superintendent, explained the Institute to James was similar
to the detached and exact manner in which his own father had
spelled out James' fate. "For you to stay here would be unthinkable," his father had announced like a judge passing sentence. "You'd be an embarrassment to me and a threat to the
family, especially if that lout of an Irishman who calls himself
the chief of police ever decides he wants or needs another
favor."

Edward Bannon's ability to conveniently forget his own
roots and adopt all the snobbery and prejudice that was a trade-
mark of the Anglo-Saxon upper class of Perth Amboy always
amazed James. "He's become a fine gentleman, your father
has," an old Irish brickworker who had befriended James commented as he watched Edward Bannon strut through the brickyard during one of his infrequent tours. "A fine gentleman

indeed. And to think he came over in the same boat I did.''
Whether or not the brickworker was pulling James' leg about
coming over in the same boat didn't matter. The point that he
was making, and that James understood, was that his father
had, in all his greed, turned his back on his own kind.

There was, however, a limit, on how far a man could go,
even for Edward Bannon. "I'm of a mind to throw you out into
the snow and forget I ever had two sons," he told James in all
sincerity. "But I cannot. You are my blood, and I cannot turn
my back on that. I'm too good a Christian for that. Instead, I'm
sending you to a place where, I hope, someone can instill in
you the discipline that I have been unable to beat into you. In
deference to your dear mother's memory, I am going to provide
you with an opportunity to begin a new life, which is far more
than my drunken father, may he burn in hell, ever did for me.
All I ask, no, what I *demand*, of you, is your promise that you
will never, ever, cross this threshold again."

The temptation to tell his father what he could do with his
"generous" offer crossed James' mind, but only for a moment.
Prepared for far worse, James was thrown by this apparent
show of leniency. With no other options, and with the same
stiff-necked stoicism with which he had accepted his father's
punishments in the past, James bowed in silence to his fate and
made his promise. Now, as the minutes on the office clock
ticked away, James began to have serious thoughts again about
his decision to obey his father. While it was good to be bringing this trip to an end, he knew the true ordeal was only just
beginning. Indeed, in many ways, it had already begun.

Though he had never had the opportunity to travel much,
since his father was a busy man with little time for family
concerns, the steamboat from Perth Amboy, New Jersey, to
Philadelphia was familiar and comfortable enough. Any
thoughts he had entertained on that leg of the journey, about
switching to a westbound train in Philadelphia and striking out
on his own, were easily forgotten in the relief he felt at being
out from under the harsh rule of his father. Together with the
prospect of going to the Old South, even the murderous events
that led up to his journey and his brother's tearful farewell were
pushed aside with surprising ease as the train from Philadelphia
turned south for Baltimore. He was, he convinced himself, on

an adventure to a new place, a new beginning, much like the one that had led his father to the United States many years ago.

These dreams, however, were quickly replaced with the harsh realities of life in a nation that was eager to allow itself to be divided by sectional strife. During the railroad ride from Philadelphia to Baltimore, then to Richmond, James realized that this trip involved more than a simple change in residence. As on a journey into a foreign land, the attitudes of the people who surrounded James in the crowded railcar changed as quickly as the scenery outside the cold pane of glass that he leaned against began to change as the train sped southward.

Stranded and alone in his own thoughts, James didn't notice this change at first. Not until a man, wearing an overcoat of fine gray wool and a black silk stovepipe hat, drew James out of his own thoughts. Settled into his seat, James was waiting for the train to pull out of the station in Washington, D.C., when the gentleman came up the aisle and paused next to the bench where James sat. Clearing his throat in an effort to draw James' attention, the gentleman motioned to the vacant seat next to James when he turned to face him. "Sir," the gentleman asked with a twang in his voice that was unmistakably Southern, "would it bother you terribly if I joined you?"

Confused by the inquiry while, at the same time, fascinated by the gentleman, James hesitated as he studied the gentleman for a moment. The gentleman, for his part, was confused by James' hesitation. Bending slightly at the waist, he repeated his request, speaking with a deliberate slowness, as if to ensure that his request was understood. Realizing that he was being rude, James flashed the best smile he could and nodded toward the vacant seat. "Yes, please, by all means. Be my guest."

To James' surprise, the expression on the gentleman's face suddenly turned from confusion to anger. Standing bolt upright, he looked down at James with a disapproving frown. Turning, he marched down the aisle. Watching the gentleman's progress, James saw him stop next to the only other vacant seat in the car, one next to a very heavy man. As he had with James, the gentleman in the gray coat asked if he could join the fat man. Anxious for company the fat man smiled, responding with a sickly sweet Southern accent. "Why, of course, sir. It would be my pleasure to share this seat with you."

37

With a glance back at James, the gentleman bowed and then, with a flourish, announced in a voice that just about everyone in the car could hear, "I thank you, sir. In these times of trials and tribulations, it is comforting to find a fellow gentleman from the South such as yourself to travel with."

Noticing the attention that the gentleman had been giving James, the fat man looked over to James, then, with an inquisitive look, up at his new traveling partner. Without needing to be asked, the gentleman announced, again in a voice that was meant to be heard by everyone about, "An Irish Yankee."

Stunned, James looked into the gentleman's eyes, then into those of the fat man. Whether it was the disdain in the gentleman's voice, or the shock that he had been labeled so quickly a misfit, didn't really matter. What did count was that, from that moment on, he felt like an outcast. Even the conductor, who had not been present during the confrontation between James and the gentleman, treated James in a gruff manner that bordered on rudeness. It was, James thought, as if he wore the mark of Cain. Had this been all, James could have dealt with it. But more abuse followed. As if notified by a silent telegraphic system that he could not detect, every new passenger who came through the car to replace ones who left avoided James. Even the women showed their disdain by hoisting their skirts and petticoats away from James as they would to avoid the droppings of an animal on a busy street.

He was, James realized, in a world turned inside out, where all that he had known and all of the skills that had served him so well in the past no longer applied. The tragic series of events that had led to the death of the first woman he had ever loved, then the separation from his brother, had placed him in a world that seemed to relish being openly hostile to him simply because of his ancestry and his accent. Combined, this seemingly unending trail of tragedies left James sapped of whatever reserve of strength and fortitude he had. With no will to fight back, even if he knew who to strike out at, James abandoned himself to a fatalism that the old brickworker had once described as the hallmark and strength of the Celtic race. "There are times, lad," he told James and Kevin one day as they followed him through the tenements of Perth Amboy where the day laborers lived, "when all you can do is roll with the punch.

'Cause if ya don't, they'll break you for sure." When James asked how you knew when to fight and when to give way, the old brickworker chuckled and looked up at the sky. Then he looked down at James and winked. "You'll know, lad. Believe me, you'll know."

Now, as James allowed himself to be carried south, away from a city and a state that had been the only home he had known to the stark drabness of a snow-covered Shenandoah Valley, he realized that what the old brickworker had said was true.

Heralded by a blast of cold air that rushed into the small anteroom that served as an outer office for the superintendent when the door was open, a cadet in an overcoat with white crossed belts came striding in. The color in his frost-blushed cheeks almost matched the redness of his hair, now matted down in a tight ring where his cadet's gray kepi had been. Glancing over first to the superintendent's assistant, and then to James, the cadet smiled and nodded, giving each of them a crisp, cheery, "Good morning, sir."

James, by now used to the sullen and unfriendly attitude all had taken toward him since the incident on the train in Washington, was heartened, for a moment, by this cadet's manner. Then, as quickly as that feeling came to him, the voice of reason within James' mind shouted out a warning. Even before his face managed to crack a smile, James' guard was up and his thoughts and feelings were kept hidden behind an expressionless mask.

If the cadet noticed James' reaction, he didn't let it deter him. With quick, sure strides, he closed the distance between the door and James, reaching out with his right hand and letting his smile widen as he drew near. "Hi! I'm Cadet Private William S. McPherson. You must be the new cadet from up North, James Bannon."

Prepared for everything but a warm welcome, James came to his feet and shoved his right hand out in front of him without saying a word. There must have been a look of bewilderment or surprise on his face, for William McPherson grabbed James' hand and spoke freely while he was pumping it. "Yes, Mr. Bannon, we have been expecting you. You are, you know, the talk of the day about here."

After a shudder that William felt, James pulled back slightly. Seeing the discomfort that his comment had caused James, William quickly tried to put James' rising fears at rest. Dropping his hand to his side, William continued to smile. "Oh, I know what you're thinking. Lord save me, the cursed Virginians are lying in ambush and waiting for me." Leaning forward, William looked over at the superintendent's assistant out of the corner of his eye and whispered to James with a serious look on his face. "Truth is, they are. But then, the upperclassmen are always lying in wait for any new man who is foolish enough to enter these hallowed halls of higher education."

Pulling back, William allowed his smile to return. "And I can truly appreciate your apprehensions, Mr. Bannon. No doubt, sir, you're saying to yourself, right this minute, 'My God, they're going to tear me apart because I'm a Yankee.' Well, sir, you can take comfort in the knowledge that you're not the first."

James shook his head as if he were trying to clear his thoughts. In the short amount of time that he'd had to prepare for his trip, he had been unable to learn much about the Virginia Military Institute, other than the fact that everyone referred to it by its initials, VMI. In his depressed and troubled state of mind, he pictured VMI as a secluded and dour institution crammed full of Virginia aristocrats. The manner in which his fellow travelers had treated him during his trip had done nothing to dispel that image. And his first glimpse of the place, sitting high upon the cliffs overlooking the Maury River like a great gray Gothic fortress, did nothing to dispel this gloom. The main building of the Institute, standing four stories high and wrapping around the old brick armory like a giant horseshoe, served as both barracks and classrooms for the cadets. With a mess hall and hospital at one end, and a row of houses that provided living quarters for the superintendent and some of the faculty at the other end, adjoining the broad parade ground, the Virginia Military Institute appeared to be as cold, impersonal, and imposing as he had imagined.

Yet the cheerful young man, standing as tall as he did and

looking at him with sparkling blue eyes and a disarming smile, and speaking to him with a friendly and easy manner of speech as he tried his best to put him at ease, went against the image James had formed.

Again, James' silence and expression betrayed his thoughts, for William continued. "No, as a matter of fact, I think that honor goes to a Mr. Charles Denby of Philadelphia, class of '50. He graduated fourth in his class and lives, I believe, in Indiana. The fact is, you're not even the second. Robert F. Bell of New York City, class of '61, nabbed that title. Unfortunately, he only spent nine months here, otherwise, I'm sure he'd be here to greet you. While I'm sure, Mr. Bannon, that there are some members of the F.F.V. who aren't thrilled about having another Yankee invade their sacred soil and violate this noble institution, they look down on upstart farm boys from the sticks, like me, in much the same way."

Without hesitation now, James lifted his right hand and offered it to William. "James, please, my name is James."

With a twinkle in his eye, William reached out and clasped James' hand. "It is, James, a pleasure to meet my new roommate. Now," William said as he released James' hand and lifted his kepi to his head, "we have much to do. First, to our room to drop off your trunk. Then straight to the tailor so that we can get you out of those duds and into uniform. The sooner you blend in, the better you'll feel." Before he turned to head for the door, William lifted his right index finger and, with a feigned seriousness that was meant to be transparent, added, "I must warn you, all newcomers to this place, Virginian or not, stand out rather conspicuously until they learn the strange and peculiar ways of the Institute." With that, William turned, opened the door, and with a sweep of his free arm, announced with a flourish, "After you, Mr. Bannon of New Jersey."

From the superintendent's office, William and James went straight to their duties. For the balance of the morning James followed William as they went about drawing equipment. Everything, from a bedroll and folding cot to blankets and a chair, was heaped into James' arms, and then he shuffled off with it to their room. There, each load was deposited as quickly as possible so that William could lead James off for another issue of books, equipment, and such. All the while, William spoke incessantly, in part to put James at ease, but mostly in an effort to pass on as much information as he could as quickly as possible. "You've missed the entire first term, James, when the rest of our class learned the fine art of surviving here at VMI. I've been assigned the duty of getting you caught up by our company commander and, believe me, there is a lot."

James, thankful for having been delivered from the depths of depression and gloom by this bright and cheery redheaded son of a Winchester farmer, listened intently to every one of William's words. He also watched with intent interest how William carried himself and dealt with others. Though his short stay at Princeton had served to introduce him to the college routine, this place, VMI, was another world, with its own rules, its own language, and its own ways. Somewhere along the way that morning, as they were hastening between stops and during William's cascade of information, James made a resolution. Banished by his father and cast out of his home, he would make this place, this institution and this state, his new home. Though he knew it would be difficult, and the incidents during his trip south had, he realized, been only the beginning, Cadet William McPherson, like the late morning sun breaking through the gray overcast sky that morning, provided a few warming rays that brought comfort and hope to James. Yes, James told himself as he turned his face to that pale winter sun, I will prevail. And for the first time in weeks, James smiled.

It wasn't until after James had been issued his rifle that other cadets openly commented on him for the first time. William, on guard duty, had to stop by the guardroom to report to the commander of his relief. Feeling that James knew his way around well enough, he sent him on his way up to their room on his own. Alone in the barracks for the first time, James set off with his heavy and unwieldy three-band rifled musket, which measured almost five feet long. It was while he was coming up a flight of steps, not paying attention to where he was going, that James had his first run-in, quite literally, with an upperclassman coming down the steps in the opposite direction. Holding his rifle high across his chest, bayonet and bayonet scabbard fixed on it at the muzzle, and with loosely fitted accoutrements flopping about his hips and waist, James headed up the steps. He was trying to sort out in his head the jumble of information that William had valiantly crammed into his mind. The upperclassman, loaded down with books and preoccupied with where he was headed instead of what he was doing, came charging down and almost rammed James head-on.

In midstride, with only a single step between them, James and the upperclassman came to a sudden stop when both suddenly realized, at the same instant, that their path was blocked. Wide-eyed, they looked at each other. James, unsure of the proper response, hesitated for a moment while the upperclassman pulled back and grabbed at his books in an effort to keep them from flying out of his arms. When he had secured his load, the upperclassman looked down at James, standing on a lower step, still holding his rifle across his chest as if he were at the ready, and prepared to yell at him. James, recovering his composure, mumbled out an apology, using the same terminology that he had heard William use when addressing upperclassmen. "Sir, I am sorry. I wasn't paying attention to . . ."

The upperclassman, realizing whom he was facing, let a devilish grin light his face for a moment. Then he screwed his face into a mock expression of fear, turned, and went charging back up the stairs, yelling as loud as he could along the way, "The Yankees are invading us! The Yankees are invading us! To arms, to arms!"

From practically every doorway and in every corner of the barracks, doors flew open and heads popped out. A few cadets, taking the alarm seriously, grabbed their rifles or sabers and came charging out, hatless, and some shoeless, onto the wooden stoops that all the rooms opened onto. Among them was the officer of the guard, who turned out of the guardroom with every man he had available. This, of course, included William. Within a minute, there was total pandemonium as the startled cadets looked high and low for an armed host of blue-coated Federal soldiers or crazed abolitionists. Seeing no clear threat, the officer of the guard, his saber drawn and eyes darting about, formed his guard force in the courtyard. This body of armed cadets was joined by other cadets, spilling out of their rooms and classes, their rifles held at the ready and tipped by bayonets unsheathed and fixed in preparation to repel invaders.

Only slowly, when no imminent danger appeared, did calm begin to reassert itself. It was during this period, as the guard force scanned about in search of the threatening invaders, that William saw James standing on the staircase where he had run into the upperclassman, looking around at the chaos he had caused. James, taken aback by the entire affair, didn't know what to do. William turned and was about to shout out to the officer of the guard when a stern, high-pitched voice from the doorway of one of the classrooms brought the entire guard force, and everyone within earshot, to attention.

With the same clear and piercing voice he used to direct the cadets through their artillery drill on the parade ground, Major Thomas J. Jackson called out to the officer of the guard as he began to walk toward the reinforced guard force. "What is the meaning of this, Mr. Marshall?"

Turning to face Jackson, Cadet James Keith Marshall saluted with his saber. "Sir, an alarm was sounded. There was a riot breaking out, so I assembled the guard."

Coming up to Marshall, Jackson stopped. With his cadet kepi pulled low over his eyes, he cocked his head back as he looked about at the cadets in the courtyard and assembled on the stoops above, asking Marshall, in an incredulous voice, "What, sir, was the cause of this riot?"

Unable to supply an answer, Marshall stammered as William, still looking up at James, pondered whether it would be better to say nothing or volunteer an explanation. He had just about nerved himself up to explain when, to everyone's surprise, a nervous voice with a hint of a Northern accent echoed down into the courtyard from the stairs in one corner of the barracks. "Sir, I believe, sir, I am the source of this unfortunate confusion."

All eyes turned to the source of the voice. Seeing an armed figure, clad in civilian clothing and partially hidden from view by the railing and the supports of the stoop, Jackson looked over at Marshall, then back to the figure. "And who, sir, might you be?"

"Sir, I am James Edward Bannon of New Jersey and newly enrolled in the Institute."

In an instant, Jackson knew what had happened. There had been much talk of late concerning this cadet, accompanied by much speculation. "Why," one of his fellow instructors had asked at a social gathering, "is this boy being sent to us, from the North, in midterm. Was there some type of trouble? Is the lad guilty of some terrible transgression?" Many, faculty and cadets alike, felt this was the case and, therefore, were troubled by James' coming. Even more disturbing to Jackson was the talk, mostly overheard, by cadets who were dead against allowing a Yankee into their ranks. One day, while leaving the grounds of the Institute, he overheard a cadet walking in front of him tell another, "This is not the time to be diluting our ranks with Irish riffraff from the North. We cannot allow this intolerable situation to manifest itself."

While he had said nothing concerning the suppositions about the why of James' enrollment, he could not tolerate threats, real or idle. Without preamble, Jackson called out to the two cadets before him who were complaining about James. "And how, sir, do you as a good Christian and a distinguished son of Virginia, propose to deal with this 'intolerable situation'?"

Taken aback by Old Jack's presence and his question, the two cadets turned and looked up at him with sheepish eyes. When they said nothing in response, Jackson spoke. "While there is no doubt that these are troubled times, each of you needs to remember that he is, first and foremost, a Christian and a gentleman. You are bound by your personal honor and heritage to deal with other men as such so long as they, as individuals, conduct themselves accordingly." Though he didn't make an issue of this incident, word of Jackson's feelings on the matter spread throughout the corps of cadets and mingled with those of others concerning James.

Standing in the courtyard, knowing that he needed to preserve order and discipline, Jackson saw the humor in the current situation. Looking up at James, he thought for a moment. Then, with an expression that did not betray his playfulness, Jackson called up to James. "Do you, Mr. Bannon, propose to proceed with your single-handed assault on this position, or do you wish to capitulate?"

For the first time all day, a feeling akin to panic gripped James. Far from quietly blending in, as he had hoped to do,

James now felt like every eye in the state of Virginia was squarely on him. Through no fault of his own he had been brought, front and center, to the attention of the entire corps of cadets and, now, the faculty. Looking about, James nerved himself as he drew in a deep breath. "Sir," James shouted out with a clear and booming voice, "under the circumstances, I yield."

As cadets, both in the ranks and standing about on the stoops, broke out in laughter, Jackson turned to the officer of the guard. Maintaining his stern expression and pointing to James, he addressed Cadet Marshall in a voice that could be heard throughout the courtyard. "There, sir, stands a man who can calmly evaluate his position and make a difficult but appropriate decision. Now, I leave it to you to reestablish good order and discipline." With that, he turned and walked slowly back to his classroom, glancing up once to James as he continued on past the cadets. Shaking his head, Major Jackson let all thoughts of the incident pass from his mind, content for the first time that the Irishman from New Jersey would do well.

While some were able to dismiss James without another thought and accept him as nothing more than another new cadet, others could not find it in themselves to do so. That night, not long after the bugle call for lights out was sounded, the door of William and James' room flew open with a bang. Startled, James, William, and their two roommates sprang out of their beds and turned to face the door. There, in the shadowy moonlight that provided the only illumination in the room, James saw dark forms and figures piling into their small and already crowded room. Before he had even managed to get his feet squarely on the floor, James was surrounded by five or six faceless assailants.

Pressed in from all sides and unable to see or hear anything from William or his other two roommates, James prepared for the worst. He had been beaten up before, many times. There had been the sons of the day laborer who worked for his father and, unable to do anything about the squalor that they were forced by circumstances to live in, took out their anger on the son of the man whom they blamed for their plight. There had been the sons of the well-to-do families, boys who resented James and Kevin Bannon and any upstart who dared violate the established social order of Perth Amboy. There had been the sons of the parishioners of St. Peter's Church who had sought to demonstrate that conversion of Irish Catholics to the Episcopal Church meant nothing to them. And there had been the upperclassmen at Princeton who, in an effort to cower incoming freshmen, bludgeoned James and his fellow classmates into a hasty submission. No, James thought as he braced himself for the beatings to start, it was foolish to expect anything different. And although he and Kevin had been more than able to give better than they took most of the time, James knew that this was one of those occasions when, in the words of the old brickworker, it was best to roll with the punch.

Yet, as he held his stomach muscles taut, nothing happened. In the silence of the room, James could feel the frigid night air as it curled along the floor and swept past his bare feet. Though he stood a respectable five feet eight inches, all of the intruding cadets, fully dressed in the formal forty-four button coats, towered over him. These Southerners, he thought, were leaving nothing to chance. Still, in the back of his mind, James began to wonder why they were holding back. Whatever advantage of surprise and confusion they had had when they rushed in was now lost.

As if in answer, the two cadets standing with their chests pressed up against James' face parted to the left and right, revealing the figure of a cadet of medium build standing in the doorway. Only the very fringes of this figure's uniform were illuminated by the light coming in through the door. In a way, the pale moonlight served to outline the gray figure and obscure all other details. For a moment this cadet, attired like the rest, was content to stand in the door, legs spread slightly apart and his hands clasped behind his back. If he and his companions meant to intimidate James, they had succeeded. Now, James thought, that they knew he was overwhelmed by their show of force, they would strike.

Still, they did nothing as the cold wisps of night air lapped over James' feet like tiny waves on a seashore. Finally, with a voice held low in an effort to make it more intimidating but not disguise it, the figure in the doorway spoke. "Very few people are afforded the opportunity to make an impression on their first day here as spectacular as you did, sir. I must congratulate you. First, you manage to capture the imagination of the entire corps of cadets before you set foot in Virginia, and then you create a favorable, if somewhat comical, impression on Major Jackson and many cadets, which is no easy feat. You mustn't, however, let all of this go to your head. Major Jackson is, in many ways, rather eccentric and not held in high esteem by all."

Standing in the doorway, still as a headstone in a cemetery, the shadowy figure paused. James noted what he imagined was a slight hint of regret in the words spoken by the figure. Perhaps, James thought, this person and his nocturnal companions were upset that the major with the squeaky, almost feminine, voice had chosen not to make a big to-do about the incident this afternoon. Maybe they were here, now, to rectify that in their own way. Confused, James let his guard down. Did they mean to do this by frightening him? Or, he began to wonder, was this shadowy figure bent on talking him to death.

"A little over a month ago," the figure continued, "I stood less than one hundred feet from the scaffold on which John Brown was sent to the devil. I swore then, just as I swore the day I entered this Institute, to defend my native state and our cherished way of life against all enemies."

Emboldened by his assailant's failure to physically assault him, James began to speak. "But I'm not—"

Angered by this impudent outburst, the tall cadets about James pressed in closer but still did not strike him. "We did not come here, sir," the shadowy figure in the door shouted as he stretched out his right arm, index finger thrust at James, "to debate this or any other point. We came here to serve notice that, in the end, you will be driven from this state, back North, into the arms of your accursed fellow abolitionists. Just remember in the days ahead, Mr. Bannon, that while it was your people, and not mine, who brought on this irrepressible conflict between our native states, we Virginians will prevail. For we are honorable men, men who do not take kindly to strangers who dare trifle with our homes or our way of life."

Expecting more, James was stunned when the shadowy figure came to a position of attention, pivoted, and stepped away from the doorway. On that cue, the cadets who had been surrounding him filed out of the room in silence. For a moment James, William, and the other two boys in the room stood where they had been, not daring to move or speak. Finally, William moved across the icy floor and shut the door. Turning, he brought his cold hands up to his mouth, cupped them, and then blew a warming breath into the hollow of his hands. Shivering from the coldness of the room, James watched William as he retraced his steps and quickly slipped under the blankets of his bed without a word. His other roommates were already in their beds.

James was now as confused by William's behavior as he was by the nocturnal visitors, for William showed no real concern. "Is that it?" James called over to William. "Is that all they're going to do?"

Propping himself up on his elbow, William looked across the tables that served as their desks and separated their beds. "For tonight, yes."

"And tomorrow?"

"Well," William said as he pondered the question, "I expect they, and just about every upperclassman they can convince, will be all over you, nitpicking you to death and annoying you every chance they get in an effort to drive you out or break you." Then, as if it were an afterthought, he added, "I don't suppose it matters which comes first."

Dropping down onto his bed, James sat in the darkness and thought about that for a moment. "Huh. Is that all?"

Pushing himself up, William sat in bed and looked across at James. "What do you mean, 'is that all'? Those boys are serious."

"If they were serious, William, I'd be lying in a heap on the floor, beaten to a pulp."

"James," William countered, "this is Virginia, not New Jersey. And those were members of the F.F.V., each and every one."

"Just what," James asked, "does F.F.V. mean? You mentioned it before."

"F.F.V. stands for first families of Virginia." That explanation came from one of James' other roommates, John Tyler

Jacobs of Columbia, Missouri. "Those from the Tidewater region of this state put great stock in their family heritage and expect, in return, special treatment and privileges. Though not quite as bad as the plantation owners from the Deep South, Virginia's own special class of aristocracy can be as unbearable as anyone else's."

This, and the manner in which John spoke with a mock haughtiness, made James laugh. "And this is how they intend to rid this fine Institute of poor white trash such as me? By trying to scare me and riding me into the ground?"

Chuckling at James' feeble attempt at the Southern dialect, William shook his head. "My friend, you have much to learn." Then he turned serious. "I suppose Cadet Lieutenant Abner Wirt Couper, the gentleman who stood in the doorway and spoke, would like nothing better than for you to become so outraged at the manner in which you are being treated that you will call on him, to defend your honor."

"A *duel*? He wants me to fight a duel with him?"

"Jimmy boy, as I said, this is Virginia, and our good friend Abner is a tried and true son of the Old Dominion state. Yes, he would like nothing better."

Pondering this, James almost laughed, and would have had he not taken William's warning to heart. Yes, he thought to himself, there is much that I need to learn. But, there was much that Couper and his friends needed to understand about him. That he could never tell anyone, not even William, that there was nowhere else to go didn't bother James. That, except for Kevin, with whom James had shared so much joy and sorrow, there would be no outstretched arms, abolitionist or not, waiting to greet him if he returned North was a reality that he had already accepted. Just as he accepted that this Institute, whether they realized it or not, was all he had now and would have for the foreseeable future. All of this he understood, with the grim realism of a child raised by an abusive father and scorned by practically every child and adult about him because of who he was. For James, there was no alternative, no refuge. There was only the here and now.

Lost in his thoughts, James leaned back, lifted his legs onto his bed, and curled up under his blankets. Slowly, as the sheets and blankets about him began to warm from his body heat,

James felt sleep coming on. It was an easy, comforting sleep, the like of which he hadn't experienced in a long time. Though he knew that there would be hard days ahead, and he wasn't really free to do as he liked, a cheery thought had popped into his head. Just before he passed from consciousness, he knew he was being viewed and dealt with as a man, would be judged as a man. Half awake, he mumbled out loud to William, who was already asleep: "No, Billy, it's Mr. Couper who doesn't understand. He don't scare me, not in the least."

# CHAPTER 3

# October, 1860
# The Virginia Military
# Institute,
# Lexington, Virginia

THE MONOTONOUS DRONE OF THE INSTRUCTOR'S VOICE FILLED
the section room as he moved from one side of the chalkboard
to the other, jotting down legions of figures and mathematical
symbols. It was as if he were in a race to see if he could shake
off the last of the few diehard students who were still trying
valiantly to keep up with his logic and writing. Some, realizing
the futility of this, had already given up and allowed themselves to drift off into a fitful sleep. Glancing over to his left,
James saw that his roommate Will McPherson had already
succumbed to the incessant recital of the day's trigonometry
lesson. James sighed, for he would now have to spend the best
part of the night explaining to Will what the instructor had used
an hour going over. Not that James minded, for to him it was
a way of paying Will back for the friendship and help that Will
had freely given him from the first day.

Will, with his back-country, Christian view of the world,
didn't understand James' point of view. "I'm just doing what's
right," he told James. "Besides," he went on to explain, "at
times I feel just as much an outcast as you do. Not everyone in
the corps takes kindly to us state cadets, especially some of the
more high-minded boys from the Tidewater. Though most of
them eventually get over the shock of being stripped of their
servants, not many can forgive the state for throwing them in
with the likes of me."

With a mock haughtiness in his voice, Will presented their point of view. " 'After all,' they'll freely tell you if they were of the mind to talk to you, 'why should we have to pay a full $375 tuition a year when the state cadets get to come here for free with nothing more than a pledge to perform two years' public service for the state. Why, if there were fewer of you about, we wouldn't have to stuff five cadets in a room.' " When James' laughter died down, Will went on, in a more serious tone. "What they don't tell you is that if it weren't for us, I mean us state cadets who leave here and go out as teachers, this school wouldn't have near the reputation in Virginia, not to mention the entire South, that it does. Besides, in the beginning, almost everyone who went to VMI was a state cadet. I tell you, James," Will added with a tone of exasperation, "sometimes my own people worry me more than your people."

Of course, even to the casual observer, it was easy to see why the two boys, Will and James, were able to get on so well. Will's easy and free manner, in speech as well as carriage, was more akin to that of a Midwesterner than that of a Tidewater Virginian. The quiet and unassuming manner that James fell into after arriving in Virginia, coupled with the hard-nosed realism that guided his every action, allowed him to fit in comfortably with the cadets who hailed from the western parts of Virginia and North Carolina. Were it not for this, the difficult situation that James faced daily at VMI would have been intolerable, just as Abner Couper had hoped it would be.

Not that Couper, and his friends, didn't try. From the beginning a quiet and very circumspect war was waged by those who were offended by James' presence. They worked on James almost incessantly, using every opportunity to harass and provoke him. "They're just trying to get you so riled up," Will cautioned his friend after a particularly nasty incident, "that you'll lose your temper and start something, or simply walk away. I know what they're up to. I watched my former roommates up and leave because of the abuse. Not that I'm saying you'd run away, but to fight them would be just as bad. Lord knows, given the superintendent's views on fighting, you'd be out of here on the next stage to Staunton. No sir," Will added, "a fight is just what they want. And even if you didn't get thrown out, you'd lose the respect of those who feel that the

Tidewater boys are wrong on this account. Though they don't go about making it known, there are more than a few upperclassmen pulling for you."

James, forced to take care of himself and his younger brother for years, more often than not by sheer brute force, found it difficult to heed Will's advice. Yet, the cold hard logic of his plight demanded that he do so. He understood, without having to be told, that if he were thrown out of VMI, he would lose his last and only chance to make something of himself. So James endured in silence, buoyed up by Will and, on occasion, those classmates and upperclassmen who viewed James as nothing more than just another cadet and were appalled by what they considered cruel and unnecessary harassment by those who abused him.

When the notes of the bugle announcing the end of class drifted into the section room, James jumped up from his seat and hurriedly gathered his notes and books. Will, stirring from a sound sleep, stretched and prepared to stand up. James Winchester Breedlove of Mississippi, seated next to Will, looked over at him. "Well, seems like you're not dead after all. Guess that means I lost my bet."

James and the other cadets laughed while the instructor ignored Breedlove's comment, and Will, his mind still befuddled by sleep, looked about wondering what Breedlove was talking about.

From across the room Charles Conway Flowerre of Independence, Missouri, shouted, "Don't pay Jimmy Breedlove no mind, Will. We all enjoyed your snoring. Kept the rest of us awake." Again, there was a chorus of laughter.

Finally, the instructor, Major Stapleton Crutchfield, VMI class of '55, turned around to face the cadets. He looked about the room with the gravest expression he could manage. "I do hope, gentlemen, that your spirits will be as high after you finish your exam tomorrow."

Still stirring in his seat, Will called out, to no one in particular and with a sincere innocence in his voice, "What test?"

This caused everyone, including Crutchfield, to stop what he was doing and again roar out with laughter. When it was beginning to subside, James, already halfway out the door, shouted back, "Don't worry Will, I'll explain it to you later."

"Explain what? James, hold on, will you? Explain what?"

Gathering his books, Will rushed for the door, bobbing and weaving his way past his classmates and the desks. By the time he reached the door, James was already halfway down the stoop and headed for the staircase. "James, will you hold on and wait."

"Can't, Will. I've got guard today and you-know-who is the officer of the guard."

By the time Will began to catch up with James, he was on the second stoop and making his way for the third stoop as fast as he could. "James, listen, you've got to make it through the inspection at guard mount without any demerits. If you don't, you won't be able to join me and my family this weekend, remember?"

Without looking back or slackening his stride, James nodded. "I know, I know. That's the only thing you've talked about for the last three weeks." Then, glancing over his shoulder, James smiled and added slyly, "Other than that girl of yours."

That caused Will to smile. "Well, shucks, what do you expect. I've not seen them, any of them, since I left home fifteen months ago. You know how it is, I mean keeping a girl interested in you while you're away at school."

Will's comment about his girl struck James like a hammer blow. It had been months since he had given Martha Anderson and the events that had led to that terrible night back in December more than a moment's thought. Yet time had done nothing to soften their impact or remove any of the bitterness that James still felt.

With the weight of James' dark thoughts slowing him, Will managed to catch up. "Hey, roomie, what's gotten into you? You look almost as dour and careworn as Old Jack."

Unable to tell his best friend his problem for fear that he would lose him, James shrugged off his painful reflections as best he could and quickly did his best to turn the conversation toward a new subject. "Old Jack, is it? You're now comparing me to Major Jackson. Now isn't that a fine how-do-you-do."

Seeing his friend snap out of the unexplained gloom that had so quickly darkened his mood, Will broke out into a smile again. "Well, you know, I could have done worse. I mean, I could have compared you to . . . to . . ."

"See what I mean. You've just about hit the bottom of the barrel with that comparison."

"No, I don't see it as being that bad, James. Though I hear he's near worthless as an instructor of natural philosophy, no one can criticize his abilities as an instructor of artillery. And don't forget what he did in the Mexican War. Why I'm told his fight at Chapultepec is still used as a model of battlefield conduct at West Point."

James, in a hurry to give his uniform and brass a few finishing touches before standing guard mount, gave up arguing with Will. "Well, Old Jack's accomplishments, past, present, and future, aren't going to do me a bit of good if I don't make it through this guard mount."

"James, I don't see what the problem is. Just make sure you're in the front rank today. Couper is the officer of the guard, and they inspect the rear rank."

"Please, I've tried that before, remember?"

This made Will smile. "James, you have nothing to worry about. Tom Kinney is going to be the sergeant of the guard today. I got the feeling you're going to be in the front rank."

Reaching the doorway of their room, James paused and looked over at his roommate. The sly smile he was sporting told James that there was something amiss. Though he was curious to know what was brewing, he decided that, perhaps, it was best he didn't. After all, if something went wrong with whatever Byzantine plot was brewing, James could always honestly plead ignorance. Still, he couldn't let Will get off scot free. Shaking a finger in his face, James warned, "Will McPherson, so help me. If your little scheme earns me another demerit, it'll be your hide."

In response, Will smiled. "For heaven's sake, James, you're starting to sound like my little sister. Now relax, my friend. I've never let you down, have I?"

James cocked his head. "Well, there was the time . . ."

Shoving James before him, Will berated him as only a friend could as the two cadets tumbled into the room.

If the truth were known, James was being viewed as one of the most proficient cadets in his class when it came to such matters as drill, uniforms, and other such associated military matters. "It was," as one of the upperclassmen remarked one day after inspecting the company James was in, "as if in his efforts to catch up, he missed the mark and shot right on past the rest of his classmates." And although he never made a show of this and, in fact, tried hard to shy away from praise and recognition, James was condemned to be conspicuous no matter what he did or how hard he tried to hide in the ranks. Another officer in James' company, in discussing the situation with his roommate, dryly commented, "You'd have more luck hiding an elephant in a flock of sheep than making that boy disappear here at VMI."

Holding back in the archway leading from the barracks out onto the brick roadway where they would form up, James waited for the bugle to sound assembly for the guard mount. When the first notes were sounded, he began to make his way forward, looking to his left and right in search of his nemesis. Clearing the arch without seeing any sign of Couper, James made his way into the front rank.

He was adjusting his dress and cover when a hand reached out and began to pull him backwards by his cross belts. "Oh no you don't, Mr. Bannon. You're mine today."

There was no need to look, for Cadet Lieutenant Couper's voice was as familiar and as haunting to James as his own father's had been. When he was in line with the cadets in the rear rank, the hand let go. Squeezing in between James and the cadet next to him, Couper came around from behind and placed himself square in front of James. "Yes sir. I do believe that today you'll earn just enough demerits to win you the privilege of pounding up and down these bricks all weekend long. What do you think, Mr. Bannon?"

James, coming to attention, said nothing. He didn't even make eye contact with Couper. Instead, he stared at the back of the neck of the cadet to his front and bit down hard on the leather strap of his hat.

"Well," Couper stated with a self-satisfied smirk on his face, "I've got duties to tend to. I will see you in a moment." With that, he pushed his way through the front rank and walked out six paces in front of the small guard force, just as the last note of assembly was sounding.

Then, before Couper could manage to come to attention himself and give the order to fall in, the cadet in front of James, and all those to the left of him, took one step to the side. A hand from behind James gave him a shove, propelling him into the front rank. Behind him, James could hear all the cadets who had been to his left take one step to the right. From the corner of his eye, he saw the cadet at the far left of the front rank take one step to the rear and disappear into the rear rank. In this way, with the precision of a well-drilled unit, James was moved up to the front rank and thus he was delivered from the hands of Abner Couper, his self-appointed avenging angel.

Later, after the guard mount was over and they were in the safety of their little room, Will explained to James what had happened. "Lord," he howled, "I loved the expression on old Abner's face when he about faced and saw you standing there, bigger than life, in the front rank. He couldn't have been more surprised than if someone told him he had the French disease."

Ever anxious to see Couper get his comeuppance, even if he knew that, in the end, Couper would always be back, James savored any triumph over his oppressors. Though he knew he owed this one to the efforts of friends and sympathetic cadets, a victory, for James, was a victory. And now, as both he and Will drifted off to sleep, he could contemplate the fruits of this success. "Think of it, Will. A peaceful, quiet day far from the hallowed halls of VMI, not to mention Abner Couper and associates."

The carriage ride from Lexington south to Natural Bridge was enjoyable and inspiring. The crisp fall air was as invigorating as the scenery was breathtaking. Both near and far, the Blue Ridge Mountains were covered from horizon to horizon with trees that were alive with a wild riot of fall colors set against a bright blue sky. In awed silence, James and William sat leaning back on the plush cushions of the carriage as they drank in the beauty and enjoyed the serenity. Only once, as they passed an almost incredible vista of mountains and forest, did Will dare to speak. When he did, it was with a hushed reverence, in a tone that reminded James of praying. "Lord, James. A sight such as this makes a man willing to give his life in its defense." James, absorbed in his own thoughts, attached no dark or deep significance to Will's innocent comment. Instead, he simply nodded as he continued to soak in the majestic beauty that surrounded them.

As the carriage neared the front of the inn where the McPhersons were staying, Will's eyes lit up. "James," he shouted, like a child beholding a Christmas tree, "there's my little sister!"

Turning in the direction that Will was pointing, James scanned the long porch in search of a diminutive child. When he was unable to see anything resembling a child, James looked over to Will. "I must be blind. Where is your little sister?"

"See, I told you that all the studying you've been doing at night was hurting your eyes." Then, standing up in the rocking carriage as best he could, Will pointed. "Over there, just to the right of the front door. She's the one in the bright green dress trimmed in black."

With a marked look of skepticism on his face, James turned once more toward the inn. Closer now, and with a decent description of what he was looking for, he had no trouble at all in picking her out of the crowd. When he did, James' look of skepticism melted away. It was replaced, at first, with one of confusion, then with an expression of awe as he watched a tall young woman with auburn hair neatly tucked up under a trim black riding hat and snood wave at their approaching carriage. "That," he asked Will without taking his eyes off of the tall young woman, "is your *little* sister?"

Losing his balance, Will fell back into his seat, though he continued to grin from ear to ear and wave wildly. "Sure is. That's Mary Beth."

Having seen Will's excitement and overhearing the conversation between the two cadets, the coachman pulled the carriage up as close as he could to the steps of the porch before bringing it to a halt. Will, fired up with the excitement of seeing his family for the first time in over a year, didn't wait for the coachman to dismount and open the half door for him. Grasping the sides of the carriage, he bounded up and over the side, landing within a foot of where Mary Beth stood. Mary Beth, equally thrilled at seeing her brother, nonetheless kept her poise. While Will collected himself before her, Mary Beth placed her hands on her hips and leaned forward, twisting her face into a mock scowl. "Will McPherson, where do you get off acting like a country bumpkin at a place like this? For heaven's sakes, you're supposed to be a VMI cadet, not a circus clown.''

Stung by this reprimand, Will looked down at the space between them with a hangdog expression. ''My Lord, Mary Beth, I didn't mean to get you upset. It's just that I'm so glad to see my kid sister.''

''Oh, Lord, Will. Please don't start that kid sister stuff again. I'm all of seventeen and grown up. And if you don't start behaving yourself, I'll give you such a what-for that you'll not want to see me again for another fifteen months.''

While this brother-and-sister bantering was going on, James let himself out of the carriage, tipped the coachman, and climbed up onto the porch, never once taking his eyes off of Mary Beth. Coming up behind Will, he was content to stand there quietly as the two siblings continued their exchange.

Will, looking up first to his left, then to his right at other guests on the porch, leaned forward and whispered to Mary Beth. ''Sis, do you think you could stop treating me like a child and at least act civil?''

Unrepentant, Mary Beth brought her right hand up in front of Will's face and pointed her index finger at his nose. ''Do you, Will McPherson, think you can act like a cadet from VMI and not like a ten-year-old farm boy?''

Dropping his head, Will shuffled his feet. ''Ah, I'm sorry, Mary Beth. I guess . . . Well, I'm just so happy to see you, that's all.''

Unable to hide her true emotions any longer, Mary Beth dropped her stern expression. In its place she allowed a broad, beaming smile to light up her face. Throwing out her arms, she all but leaped forward and embraced Will. ''Oh, God, Brother, you don't know how much I've missed you.''

Opening his arms, Will caught her. Embracing, the two rocked back and forth for a moment, each silently enjoying the warmth of their heartfelt greeting. After a minute or two, Mary Beth opened her eyes. When she did, they fell upon James, who was still standing behind Will, watching the scene in silence. As if she were conscious for the first time of the spectacle that they were creating in public, Mary Beth let Will go and gently pushed away from her brother. Her embarrassment was obvious, for she looked down and busied herself in rearranging her outfit. Only when she was ready did she look up again, first at James, then back at Will. "Ah, Will, darling, aren't you going to introduce me to your friend?"

At first mystified by his sister's sudden change in attitude, the mention of his friend caused Will to smile. It was a sly smile, one which told Mary Beth that he was onto her game. With a nod and a wink, he made a partial turn toward James. "Oh, well, yes, of course. Mary Beth, I would like you to meet my best of friends and roommate, Cadet James Edward Bannon of Perth Amboy, New Jersey. James, this is my little ... I mean, this is Mary Beth, my sister."

With a coy smile, Mary Beth offered James her right hand while bowing her head slightly, though she never lost eye contact with him. James, feeling awkward and more than a little uncomfortable, reached out hesitantly with his own right hand and took Mary Beth's hand, all the while wondering what to do with it once he had it. They stood there like that for several embarrassing seconds as James studied Mary Beth's face. Everything about it spoke of natural beauty. Her china-blue eyes, sparkling like precious stones, were set in a pale oval face and separated by a graceful, sculptured nose set between two high cheeks that were ever so lightly brushed with a hint of red from the crisp autumn air.

Finally, sensing Mary Beth's embarrassment, not to mention his own, James was about to speak when a loud, booming voice broke the beauty of the moment. "Will, me boy. Lord, it's good to see you so alive and well." Recognizing her father's voice, Mary Beth pulled her hand away, taking one step back and to the side of Will. James, likewise, stepped back and fell in on the other side of his roommate, clearing the way for Will's father to rush up to his elder son and grasp him in a bear hug that caught Will off guard.

From the side, James watched Will and his father. The elder McPherson was a full three inches shorter and far stockier than his son, and crowned with a thinning crop of dark brown hair, liberally streaked with gray and white. Stepping back from Will, he held his hands firmly planted on his son's upper arms. "You're looking good, William Stuart McPherson the Third."

Will nodded. "I'm feeling good too, Father."

The elder McPherson's eyes grew wide. "Father, is it? Elizabeth, would you come out here and listen to this boy. Father he called me, just like one of those fine polished Virginia gentlemen from Richmond."

In the shadows of the inn's doorway, James saw the tall, willowy figure of a woman. Her face, oval like Mary Beth's, had a serene, almost sad expression that her thin smile could not brighten. Though James could only see a few stray strands of reddish hair under the broad bonnet that Will's mother wore, they were enough to satisfy James' curiosity as to who Will and his sister took after. He was still admiring the woman, who seemed content to hold back, when a lanky, sandy-haired boy pushed his way past Elizabeth McPherson's skirts, ducked under the elder McPherson's arms, and rushed at Will. Hit square in the midsection, Will had no time to prepare himself. He had to struggle to keep his balance as the sudden impact broke his father's embrace and knocked the wind out of him. Stumbling back, he managed to bend over the lad's back and wrap his arms about the boy's waist. With all the effort he could muster, Will jerked the boy up, lifting the boy's feet off the porch. This brought a howl of protest and screams that drew the attention of every man and woman seated on the porch.

While the boy yelled, "No fair, no fair," Will shook him from side to side. Looking over at James while he held his young captive securely in his embrace, Will nodded to his father. "James, this is my father, William McPherson. And that," he motioned with his head toward the woman in the door, "is my mother. Allow me to present James, my roommate."

James, unsure of what to do as Will continued to squeeze the boy in his arms and shake him like a rag doll, smiled as best he could and nodded. "Mr. and Mrs. McPherson, it is a pleasure to meet you." After returning their smiles and nods, James looked down at the bundle of boy Will held. "I assume that this critter is your brother, Daniel."

Flailing his arms in a vain effort to strike Will, Daniel continued to howl. "No fair. No fair. You put me down and fight like a man."

Will paid his twelve-year-old captive no mind. He just grinned as he looked over at James. "Yes, my one and only brother, praise the Lord." Then, despite the handful of boy he held at bay, Will turned, Daniel and all, to face his father. "Where's Margaret?"

Mary Beth screwed up her face and responded, making no effort to hide her sarcasm. "Where do you think? My lady is still preparing for her grand entrance."

This caused Will to groan. "Please, Sis, let's not start that again. Especially not today."

Bowing her head, she apologized in a tone that was far from repentant. Then, in an effort to extract a measure of revenge, Mary Beth glanced about as Daniel continued to struggle to break his brother's hold on him. With a wicked smile on her face and a glance over at her mother, she called out to her brother with an innocent tone in her voice, "Will, if you squeeze Daniel a little harder and make him scream some more, we can draw a larger crowd."

Taking her daughter's meaning, William's mother looked about at the other guests and visitors as they looked on with disapproving stares. Seeing that her two boys were making a spectacle of themselves and the family, she finally protested, "You let your brother go now and behave like a gentleman."

A smile lit Will's face. "Yes, Mother." With that, he released his grip and let his younger brother drop to the floor of the porch, which the lad hit with a resounding thud.

Stunned for a moment, the boy lay in a heap. Elizabeth, a look of shock and surprise on her face, rushed out to Daniel, shouting, "William McPherson, how could you?"

Looking over to James, he winked. "But you told me to let him go."

Just as angry as her mother, Mary Beth stepped forward and smacked Will on the arm. "Will McPherson, you're a bully."

Will stepped back and began to rub his arm where she had hit him. "That hurt."

With a look of satisfaction, Mary Beth jutted her face forward. "Good, I hope I broke it."

Their father, now standing in the center of this chaotic family scene, looked at the other inn guests and bowed slightly, in an effort to apologize for disturbing their afternoon. Finally, he stood up, took a deep breath, and, in a booming voice, announced, "Enough! Everyone, on your feet and inside. We came here to have a peaceful dinner with my son, *whom* I haven't seen in *fifteen months*, not to tear each other apart.''

Like magic, quiet and order were restored in an instant. Looking about, and satisfied with the results of his edict, the elder McPherson turned and walked into the inn, followed by his wife, Daniel, Mary Beth, James, and Will. Just before entering, Will tapped James' shoulder. Looking back, James saw Will standing behind him, a broad smile on his face. ''Some family, huh. It's great to be together again.''

Never having been part of anything that resembled a family, James didn't know if Will was being serious or making fun. Deciding to play it safe, he nodded and gave his friend a half smile. ''Whatever you say, roommate. Now, sir,'' he added as he stepped aside and threw his right arm out, ''after you.''

Though the fare wasn't anything special, little more than a country meal of smoked ham, seasonal greens, and yams, to James and William, it tasted like a king's feast. While Will was wolfing down portions large enough for two full-grown men, James studied the McPherson family.

The father sat regally at the head of the table, enjoying his meal and the opportunity it afforded him to function as the head of his family. Occasionally he would look up from his plate and cast his gaze across his gathered brood. With a self-satisfied smile, he would nod his head and make a pronouncement like, ''fine meal,'' or ''there's nothing like a well-prepared Virginia ham, is there?'' before taking another mouthful of food. Elizabeth sat at the far end of the table. Ever attentive to the goings on of her children and their guests, she lightly pecked at her own food as she directed her children to pass a bowl of potatoes or corn to someone who seemed to be in need of it. Outside of this, she said nothing during the meal. Never having been exposed to a mother's love or way of thinking, James could not understand the simple pleasure that she apparently derived from having her family gathered about her. Yet he could tell by the warm, thin smile on her face that she was enjoying herself.

Across the table from James sat Margaret Claire Thomas, Will's fiancée. Though James had never met a Southern belle,

Margaret fit the image of what he had imagined one would look and act like. Everything about her seemed perfect. Her physical features were as elegant and exact as those of a statue lovingly sculptured by a master artist. Her skin, milky white and unblemished by work or exposure to the elements, was flawless. When she spoke, she did so with a breathless, almost hushed voice that was sweetly seductive. Still, despite all of this, or because of it, James found her to be something less than desirable. Perhaps it was because she was too perfect. Rather than being a woman whom a man could hold and love, James saw her as a fragile porcelain figure, created as an ornament to be displayed but not handled.

What, James wondered as he looked over to Will, seated to Margaret's right, did she see in him? Though Will possessed a kind and gentle soul, was exceptionally good at drill and tactics, and was, without any doubt, James' best friend, he could never be described as anything more than average. As the son of a hardworking farmer, Will didn't possess the social graces and charms that were as much a part of Margaret as any part of her anatomy. His manners, by comparison to hers, were oafish. As if to underscore this point, Will, eating like a fiend and showing no sign of letting up, reached across the table, fork in hand and without looking, in an effort to spear the last slice of ham on the serving tray.

Seeing this, and unable to restrain herself any longer, Elizabeth McPherson spoke out for the first time. ''Don't they feed you at that school?''

''Institute, Mom. It's an institute, not a school.''

Mary Beth, seated to James' right, smirked. ''Humh. Institute. Sounds like a place where they lock up lunatics and idiots.''

His sister's comment made Daniel, on the other side of James and next to his mother, giggle. ''Yeah, it does. Well, I guess we sent Will to the right place, then.''

With a hint of anger, Elizabeth drew in a deep breath. ''Now, children, let's not start again. We're in a public inn, not the barn.''

''Yes,'' the elder McPherson added, ''quite right. Now, Will,'' he said with an air of authority as he announced the close of the meal and the beginning of the after-dinner conversation, "how do you and your fellow cadets view this upcoming election?"

Though he had heard his father, Will hesitated, casting one last long look at the slice of ham he so badly wanted. Then, with an air of resignation, Will withdrew his fork, placed it across his plate, and wiped his mouth with his napkin before answering his father. "That's easy. All one needs to do is ask a fellow cadet where he's from and you have your answer. Those from the Deep South, almost to a man, support Breckenridge."

"Even a broken-down dirt farmer like me," Will's father replied with a wave of his hand and a chuckle, "knows that. It's our fellow Virginians that I am interested in."

Will, casting a forlorn look at the lonely piece of ham that remained on the serving plate before answering his father, considered his chances of getting the slice of meat without comment from his mother. Deciding that he couldn't, especially since everyone was now looking at him as they awaited his response, Will slouched in his seat and reached for his cup of coffee. Though it wouldn't be nearly as satisfying as another slice of ham, it would have to do. "The answer, Father, is the same. Those from the eastern part of the state are, with few exceptions, all Breckenridge Democrats. Further west, above the Tidewater, it begins to get hazy, with things pretty well split up between those who support Bell and his Constitutional Union Party and those who support Breckenridge. By the time you reach the Shenandoah, you can even begin to find some Douglas Democrats. West of the Valley, things are pretty mixed up between Douglas and Bell. I even heard that there's some support for the Black Republicans out there."

"Well, William, there is no accounting for those people in the western part of our state. They can be a rather strange lot of people when they set their minds to it. That, of course, doesn't account for the behavior of the rest of our fellow Virginians, or Democrats." Will's father turned sideways in his seat as a perplexed look fell across his face. "Most of us in Winchester had hoped that when Yancy and the delegates from the Deep South walked out of the convention in Charleston they were just bluffing. Everyone expected that when the party met in Baltimore, Yancy would accept the compromise plank on the slave issue and rejoin the party ranks. But when the Virginia delegates stood up and walked out of the Baltimore convention, well, we knew it was over. Seems that no one is in the mood to compromise anymore.''

Holding his cup in his hand, Will looked down at it as he answered. ''My friends from the South, the Deep South that is, keep telling me that their states are tired of compromise. They've been compromising since the Revolution. First, they gave up the slave trade. Then came the Missouri Compromise. After that, the Kansas-Nebraska Act. As one cadet from Mississippi said, the South is going to compromise itself out of existence. There is the real fear, Father, that we here in the South stand to lose everything if folks up North, Democrat or Republican, are allowed to have their way. And to tell you the truth, I can see his point. After all, if the Federal government makes slavery illegal, we're talking about depriving the South of over two billion dollars' worth of property.''

To James' surprise, Mary Beth jumped into the conversation. ''What your good friend from Mississippi means, Will, is that he's afraid that he's going to lose his slaves.''

''That, Sis, is only part of it.''

''You bet it is, Will,'' she shot back. ''A big part of it.''

''No, it's not. You see, if we let the Federal government start taking things away from us, what comes next? I mean, I know *we* never have owned slaves and that you and Mother would never tolerate such a thing. That's our choice. That doesn't, however, give us the right to dictate how others should manage their personal affairs. For us, or anyone else, to insist that another man give up his slaves simply because we don't believe in the institution would be akin to saying that the King of England has the right to insist we give up our horses because he loves animals and doesn't feel we have the right to make animals work for us without their consent.''

''Will,'' Mary Beth chided, ''you're being silly.''

''I'm not being silly. A man's property is a man's property. That's the law and it's guaranteed in the Constitution, the same one all the states agreed upon seventy-one years ago. That body of work, and the legislation that has followed, is the law of the land.''

From the corner of his eye, James could see Mary Beth was

becoming agitated. "We are talking about people, flesh-and-blood people, just like you and me."

It was clear that Will was tiring of listening to his sister. Putting his cup down, he shook his head. "Yes, Mary Beth, they are people. No one is denying that. But they are not like you and me. They're different."

Mary Beth threw her head to one side. "Oh! Is that so, dear Brother? Please, explain to me what's so different." There was a haughtiness in her voice that told James she was ready to do battle, on equal footing.

At the end of the table, Will's mother cleared her throat. When she spoke, it was with an unmistakable sternness that put everyone on notice that the "discussion" between Mary Beth and Will had gone too far. "Now, children, we are forgetting our manners. James, our guest, is being ignored. Tell me, James, what do you hear from your folks up North? How do they feel about all this?"

The question caught James off guard. He had been raised in a household where no one ever asked another member of the family his opinion. "Only one opinion," his father had told him repeatedly, "matters in this house, and that is the opinion I hold." Dinner conversation, on the rare occasions when James and Kevin were allowed to dine with their father, was restricted to hushed requests to pass food or dictatorial pronouncements by their father, given at the end of the meal and meant to instruct his sons. The genuine freedom with which everyone in the McPherson family, including women, spoke their mind was both fascinating and intimidating to him. Though the manner in which Will's father conducted himself left no doubt that he was the head of the family and he reserved the power to decide what would be done and when, everyone seemed to be free to voice their own thoughts and opinions.

James was in the midst of this thought when Elizabeth McPherson addressed him. Shaking his head, as one does when waking up, James looked first to Mrs. McPherson, then to Will's father. Nervously, he shifted about in his seat as he glanced over to Will. Though Will didn't know the exact nature of the problem, he knew that James had had no contact with his family in New Jersey since arriving in Virginia and that he had never shown any interest in discussing it despite the fact Will suspected it bothered his friend deeply. Sensing James' discomfort, Will was about to come to his aid when Margaret spoke up. "Well, Mrs. McPherson, I'm sure all of this is very interesting to Mr. McPherson and the boys. I for one, however, am tired of all this talk of politics and states' rights and secession. If I wanted to hear that, I would have stayed at home and listened to Papa." Turning to Will, she smiled broadly as she reached out and took his hand. "I came here to see Will, not to discuss Mr. Lincoln and other such silliness."

Though he felt like chiding her for referring to Lincoln and the issues of the day as silliness, Will's father didn't say anything. What, he wondered, would be the point, being that she was a woman and all, with no real need to concern herself with such matters. Besides, she was right. They had all made the long journey from Winchester to Lexington to see Will. The talk of the elections and politics was coming dangerously close to shattering the pleasure of this joyous reunion. Standing up, he placed one hand on his stomach. "Elizabeth, I am stuffed. This fine meal has put me in the mood for a long, quiet walk. Would you and Daniel care to join me?"

Understanding the purpose behind her husband's proposal, Elizabeth McPherson stood up and nodded. "Sir, it would a pleasure. Daniel, come along."

When Daniel started to protest, insisting that he stay with Will, Elizabeth looked down at him with a look that only a mother could give. Reaching down, she grabbed her younger son's upper arm and gave it a firm squeeze that told him that she would not tolerate an argument from him. "Now, Daniel, Will and James deserve some time alone with the girls."

Determined to get in the last word, Daniel made a face as he looked over at Will. "Yeah, Will wants to be alone with Margaret so they can go out back and kiss."

With a jerk, Elizabeth pulled Daniel up from his chair and whisked him out of the room before he could make another remark. Will's father, embarrassed by his younger son's last comment, bowed at the waist and followed. As they disappeared, James could hear a slap and a yelp. This brought a smile to Will's face. "Good! The little brat deserved a pop on the bottom."

"He's only telling the truth, you know," Mary Beth quipped.

Looking over to Mary Beth, James saw the same wicked look on her face that he had seen before.

Leaning over the table, Will looked at his sister with a dead-pan expression. "You know, Sis, Mom and Dad are gone now."

"William McPherson, you are getting too old to be wrestling with your sister. Besides, what would Margaret and James think? Imagine how embarrassing it would be to be beaten up by your kid sister in public."

Standing up, Will took Margaret's hand as she also rose from the table. "Sis, I'll deal with you later." Turning to James, he winked. "James, I hope you don't mind, old man, but I'm leaving you in the capable hands of my sister. But I must warn you, she has a mean left hook."

With that, Will turned and walked away as Mary Beth stuck her tongue out at him. As if he had eyes in the back of his head, Will raised his right hand and waved it without turning around to look. "I love you too, Sis."

For a moment, there was an awkward silence. James, never having been with a family such as this one, didn't quite know what to do now. Sensing his discomfort, Mary Beth stood up. James, remembering his manners, jumped to his feet and turned to face her. Standing there, inches from Mary Beth, did nothing to put James at ease. In the quiet of the small side room where they had been dining, he could almost hear her breathe. Looking down, he studied her face and eyes for the first time, as the sweet smell of the lavender soap she used filled the space between them. Where Will could only see a sister, James saw a young woman, capable, he imagined, of inflaming any man's passions.

As if she were reading James' mind, Mary Beth blushed. Casting her eyes down, she lifted her right hand up to the brooch at the collar of her blouse as she tucked her left arm across her midsection and up close under her bosom. "Would you, ah, care to escort me for a walk through the gardens? It's a bit warm in here and . . ." Mary Beth stopped in midsentence as she thought about what she had just said. Quickly, she looked up. "I mean, it would be nice to take a long walk after such a big meal."

Knowing what she had meant, James looked off to one side.

It had been a long time, he thought, since he had been in the company of a young and attractive woman. Then, like a ghost rising from the dead, the image of Martha Anderson drifted into his consciousness. In an instant, Martha's face, cold, sad, and frightened as it had been that night on the dock, danced before James' eyes. The thought of the only girl he had ever loved and the role he had played in her death sent a shiver throughout his body. Closing his eyes in an effort to erase that image, he began to sweat as he realized that it had not been long enough. And in spite of the warmth and friendliness of the McPherson clan that he had witnessed and enjoyed all afternoon, the memories of his own past were still too fresh, too overpowering to ignore. It was as if Mary Beth had touched a wound and, in her ignorance, had reopened it.

The sudden change in James' attitude cast a dark shadow over both Mary Beth and James. Unable to fathom the cause of his sudden sullenness, Mary Beth stepped away. "If you don't mind, Mr. Bannon, I suddenly feel very tired. I think I'm just going to go up to my room."

James, still lost in his own deep, dark thoughts, mumbled something that Mary Beth barely understood. Opening his eyes, he looked at her, shook his head, and turned away to flee the room, leaving Mary Beth alone, confused, and shaken.

## CHAPTER 4

# December, 1860
# New Brunswick,
# New Jersey

LIKE SO MANY OTHER GATHERINGS AND SOCIAL EVENTS THAT Christmas season, the one held by the leading citizens of New Brunswick, New Jersey, in honor of Rutgers students from some of the more noted families, was being marred by events of the day. Throughout the room, clusters of young men stood, drinks in hand, as they spoke in rapid tones that were both too loud and quite excited. About them, at a respectful distance, young ladies, attired in their best ball gowns, languished alone or in pairs as they were roundly ignored, despite their best efforts, by the animated young men.

Near a table crowded with gaily decorated plates and platters of sweets and cakes, a group of freshmen hotly debated the issues of the day with one of their professors between bites of holiday cake. "I tell you, sir," one portly young freshman bellowed as stray crumbs tumbled from his mouth and sprinkled his cravat, "South Carolina will rue the day she decided to leave the Union."

Across from him, a tall, lanky student wearing an ill-fitting frock coat jutted his small, beardless chin. "Oh, and who, sir, will be the agent of this punishment? The Regular Army? No, sir, not them. Far too many of the officers of that tiny body of professionals are Southerners. And those who are not are, all too often, more in sympathy with their fellow West Pointers than with the politicians who are supposed to be their masters. No, sir, we cannot rely on an Army that numbers less than sixteen thousand and is commanded by gentlemen who are out of step with their times."

The haughtiness of his tall classmate was just as irritating to the short, portly student as the weight of his argument. He was glancing about the half-dozen students gathered in his clutch in search of a supporter when, out of the corner of his eye, he spied the solution to his impasse. Reaching out with a hand holding a cut crystal cup, the portly student announced, triumphantly, "There, sir, is one of the messengers that will carry the standards of the Union."

Turning about to see whom he was talking about, the freshmen were surprised when they saw that the portly student was pointing to Kevin Bannon. Half of the students immediately burst out laughing. "Good Lord, Franklin," a friend of the portly student shouted out. "Given the politics of his old man, Kevin would just as soon march on Washington as Charleston. His father is in thick with those who are advocating that New Jersey hold a convention of secession."

Offended, Franklin drew in his cup and defended his claim. "Kevin Bannon is not his father."

This brought on another chorus of laughter. "You can certainly say that again," the lanky freshman said. "Why, if there weren't shadows for dear Kevin to scurry about and hide in, we'd never see the poor lad."

Though no real friend of Kevin's, Franklin refused to give up on him, especially since his announcement had caused him some embarrassment. "Let me call him over here, Trevor, so that he can speak for himself."

This caused Trevor to smile. "You may, Franklin, call him over. But unless you also arrange for his father to join him, I doubt if he'll be able to speak for himself."

As the others laughed, Franklin left the group and headed to the archway connecting the room to where the dancing was supposed to be going on and where all the serious-minded young men stood about, chatting and eating. Kevin, leaning against the archway, arms folded across his chest and one leg crossed at the ankle of the other, was lost in thought as he watched a solitary couple move gracefully across the dance floor. Franklin, coming up behind Kevin, tapped him on the shoulder. "Kevin, would you be a good fellow and come over and join us? We are having a heated discussion on the issue of suppressing the Southern rebellion and we need a military opinion.''

Without changing his pose, Kevin turned his head and looked back at the group of students that Franklin was motioning at. There, standing out in the middle of them, was Trevor Meguire Ward, the son of a wealthy industrialist in Newark. The Wards were old New Jersey stock, tracing their history back to the time when the English took New Jersey from the Dutch. Trevor's branch of the family was in the tanning and leather trade. His father owned several shoe factories in Newark that employed hundreds of Irishmen, most of whom were fresh off the boat. This fact alone, in Trevor's eyes, made Kevin "an undesirable element" who needed to be tolerated but not encouraged. "It would be unthinkable," he told his circle of friends one day when they were discussing the matter of social acceptability and pecking order, "to allow any upstart, especially an Irishman, to even think that he can buy his way into society. No, we must maintain our vigilance in order to preserve our way of life.''

Even from across the room, Kevin could see the look in Trevor's eyes. Not having any desire to cross swords with Trevor or any member of his circle, Kevin shrugged. "Franklin, I'm only a private in the state militia. Other than drill and loading a musket in nine steps, I know nothing of military matters.''

Not to be put off, Franklin protested. "So, what matter does that make? Those buffoons over there know even less of military affairs and yet they speak freely of them as if they were schooled in military science by Jomini himself.''

Shaking his head, Kevin again demurred. "No, Franklin, I'm sorry. I came here tonight to enjoy myself, not to be drawn into a pointless debate by Trevor.''

Seeing pleading was doing no good, Franklin changed his tack. "Oh, you're here to enjoy yourself? Does standing here, long faced and alone, constitute enjoyment?''

Seeing that a simple excuse was not going to be enough to shake Franklin, Kevin thought fast. "No. But I have no intention of standing here all night. I was merely looking about for a young lady worthy of my company.''

Knowing full well that many of the young women in attendance tonight had the same opinion of the new rich, especially if they were of Irish descent, that Trevor did, Franklin challenged Kevin. "Oh? And who will this lucky girl be?"

Trapped, Kevin glanced about the room until his eyes fell upon a young woman. "That one, I think. Yes, she is the one I've been considering."

Following Kevin's casual gesture, Franklin looked over at a young woman sitting alone on one of the many chairs that surrounded the nearly empty dance floor. Dressed in a deep blue satin ball gown trimmed with white velvet, the girl sat with her white gloved hands together in her lap as she looked about with a bored expression on her face. *"Her?"* Franklin asked as if he wanted to be sure. "You are interested in *her?"*

"That's right, my friend, her. Why, is there something wrong with her?"

Unable to keep from chuckling, Franklin shook his head. "Do you know who she is?"

"No."

"Well, my Irish friend, the target of your affection is none other than the daughter of Judge Melvin R. Shields. Judge Shields' family, in case you didn't know, was here to greet Trevor's family when they came to New Jersey."

"So?"

Reaching out, Franklin took Kevin by the arm as he beamed a broad, mocking smile. "My dear, dear boy. I doubt if that picture of feminine charm would give the likes of you the time of day."

Angered by Franklin's comment, and spurred on by that anger, Kevin straightened. "My dear sir, I am afraid that you are forgetting yourself and where you are. This, sir, is America, not Europe."

Put off by Kevin's reprimand, Franklin let go of him. "It may not be Europe, but proper society knows no boundaries."

The slap at his heritage was more than he could handle. With a stiffness that was cutting, Kevin excused himself. "I have wasted far too much time in such boorish conversation. Now, sir, if you would excuse me, there is a young lady waiting to dance with me." With that, he spun about and marched across the floor.

As was often the case, Kevin hadn't even reached the midpoint in his journey across the room before he began to have second thoughts. What, he wondered, would he do if the girl rebuffed him. He was already the laughingstock of his class at Rutgers. He didn't need to look behind him to know that every eye in the group gathered about Trevor was upon him, especially since Franklin, no doubt, had told them what he was about to do. No, Kevin knew that if the girl didn't dance with him, at least once, there would be no end to the comments and cutting remarks.

Still, as he neared the young woman, Kevin's pace continued to slow. It was as if the anger that had launched him from where he had been rooted was insufficient to propel him all the way. Well, he thought, if it isn't to show *them,* then I must at least go over and ask, if for no other reason than my own pride.

That thought, far from reinvigorating Kevin, only served to slow his progress almost to a dead stop. Pride, Kevin wondered, what do I know of pride? For his entire life, he had never taken, or been allowed, an opportunity to take any pride in who he was or what he did. In an effort to escape the brutality of an unloving father, Kevin had always been content to cower in the shadow of his older brother, James. He had never really stood up for himself. Though he had, on occasion, fought at his brother's side, he did so only when he had to. For as long as he could remember, James was always there, ready and willing to fight his battles for him, at home and in the neighborhood. Even in the aftermath of the bloody incident that resulted in Martha Anderson's death, he had let brother James stand up, as he always had, and take full blame for the whole ugly business. And he had done nothing, nothing at all. Stopping, Kevin let his head drop. Perhaps, he thought, they are right. Maybe I am not worthy to be part of their society. With all his drive finally dissipated, Kevin was beginning to turn away when, a few feet away, a voice called out to him.

"Pardon me for being so bold, sir." When Kevin looked up, he saw it was she, the pretty young blonde, Judge Shields' daughter. Standing before him, with a charming smile and sparkling green eyes that reminded Kevin of jade, the girl pulled at a handkerchief as she continued to speak to him.

"I know this is highly irregular and, some would consider, unseemly, but were you about to ask me to dance?"

Unable to imagine that he had been so lucky, Kevin stood dazed as he looked at her. When he finally managed to respond, he was stuttering. "Ah, well, yes, I had hoped . . . I mean, I had intended to ask you, but . . ."

Flashing a smile, the girl curtsied before him. "Well, sir, I would enjoy accompanying you to the dance floor."

Looking about, Kevin saw the lone couple go by them, twirling round and round. "Well, it seems we're here already." When he offered her his hand, she rose, took it, and came to within inches of him. Setting her right hand lightly upon his left shoulder, she cocked her head. "Well, then, let us forget all this talk of secession and war and enjoy ourselves."

For the first time, Kevin smiled. "Yes, I agree." With that, he took the girl by the waist and began to fall in step with the music as he led her lightly about the dance floor.

Still struggling with disbelief, it wasn't until the end of the dance that Kevin thought to introduce himself. Even this simple task brought him a new surprise, for when he went to give the girl his name, she laughed. "Oh, well, I already know that. You're Kevin Bannon of Perth Amboy."

Kevin, assuming that she would turn and stalk away as soon as she knew who he was, was again taken aback by this girl who was as brash as she was lovely. Chuckling, he shook his head. "Well, you have me at a disadvantage of sorts, for I do not know your first name."

"Harriet. My name is Harriet Ann Shields."

"Well, Miss Shields, I would like to thank you for dancing with me. I was, well, beginning to have second thoughts about asking you."

"And now, are you sorry that you did? I mean, dance with me?"

"No, not in the least. In fact, you have made my night." Just then, the band began a new dance, a waltz. Looking about and seeing that a few more couples had taken heart from their example and were making their way onto the dance floor, Kevin bowed low before Harriet. "Now, if you would excuse me."

"You aren't planning on leaving now, Mr. Bannon, are you?"

"Well, I am very tired and would—"

"Please, sir. Would you at least stay for this waltz?"

Looking into Harriet's shining green eyes, Kevin found it impossible to say no to her request, just as he would find it impossible to do so for the next six dances and an invitation to tea the following afternoon. Not that Kevin felt himself trapped. On the contrary. For the first time in a long time, as long as he held Harriet in his arms, he felt rather at ease. Even more amazing, Kevin felt in control, in control of the situation he found himself in and, he fantasized, in control of his life for the first time.

Between their preparations for the Sunday afternoon tea, always a very formal affair in the Shields household, and dressing themselves, Harriet's mother badgered her daughter with a blizzard of questions about the boy she had invited to join them that afternoon. Anything and everything concerning this stranger was of interest to Harriet's mother, for she knew, when the afternoon was over, her husband, whom everyone referred to as the Judge, would want a full report on the boy. Though Judge Melvin Shields was very indulgent of his only daughter, almost to the point of being unable to say no to her on any matter, he maintained strict vigilance when it came to her social activities. This caused Harriet to nickname him "Warden Shields."

Unable to pry much from her daughter, other than a first name and the sketchiest of physical descriptions, Elma Shields contented herself with the thought that if things weren't as they should be, the Judge would handle it. That theory, much to Elma's horror, was shot to hell the minute Kevin Bannon walked in the door and gave her his full name. For while she all but reared up on her haunches when she discovered that her daughter's guest was of Irish descent, Judge Shields extended Kevin a warm welcome and a handshake. "Bannon, is it?" he said with a smile on his face as they vigorously shook hands. "You wouldn't be related to Edward Bannon of Perth Amboy, would you?"

Cautiously, for Kevin knew that certain elements of New Jersey society were incapable of viewing the Irish as equals, he nodded. "Yes, sir. That is my father."

Holding Kevin's right hand, Judge Shields cupped his left over their joined hands and began shaking them anew. "Splendid, my lad, splendid." Judge Shields looked over at his wife, who was viewing this whole spectacle with something akin to disgust. "Elma, what an unexpected pleasure. Why I've had many a business dealing with this young man's father. Just the other day he was here in town, with a group of concerned Democrats, to meet with us and discuss how the state should go on the issue of secession."

The revelation that his father had been in New Brunswick within the past week was news to Kevin. That he hadn't bothered to come over and visit him at the college, however, didn't strike him as odd. "I'm sending you to Rutgers," he had announced to Kevin that summer. "Unless I hear otherwise, and I do not expect to hear otherwise, I will assume that all is going well." With that, Kevin had been sent packing, relieving Edward Bannon, for the first time in years, of the worries of having sons underfoot, and Kevin of living in a house with the man who had torn his brother away from him. "Let the college deans worry about you for a change," Edward Bannon had said at one of their last meals together. "God knows I'm paying them enough to do so."

While Judge Shields led Kevin into the parlor where tea would be served, Elma Shields and her daughter followed at a distance. When Elma was sure that they were out of earshot, she pulled Harriet to the side. "Harriet Ann Shields, what do you mean bringing an Irishman into this house!"

Harriet, knowing that Kevin's lineage would cause a stir, smiled. "But Mother, we have always had Irish in the house. Mary, the maid, she's Irish. So is our cook, Kathleen. And the Judge's coachman, John, he's—"

"Harriet! I've not raised my daughter to bring embarrassment down on this family and sully her good reputation by running about with the likes of him. You know better."

Narrowing her eyes, Harriet stood her ground defiantly. "Mother, this is 1860, not 1680. Whom I choose to see is my business."

Hearing an outburst of masculine laughter from the parlor, Elma drew in a deep breath. "Young lady, this is no time to discuss this. I will be civil to that young man. But we will discuss this, the Judge and I, later." Without waiting for a response, Elma Shields turned away from her daughter and walked into the parlor, sporting a pinched smile as she took her seat next to the Judge.

When Harriet, following her, was seated, Elma rang a small crystal bell that served to alert the Irish maid that they were ready to be served. For the next hour, while the Judge and Kevin discussed the events of the day and how they would affect the state, Elma kept her eye on her daughter. Though she might have to suffer the indignity of having an Irishman as a guest, she was determined to keep her daughter from doing anything that violated the stringent code of etiquette that she had so painstakingly schooled her in. Far too much time and effort had been expended, Elma fumed in silence as she tried hard to be civil, in preparing Harriet for the day when she would take her proper place in society as the wife of a proper gentleman. She was not about to let her daughter throw all that away for the likes of Kevin Bannon.

Harriet, for her part, knew what was on her mother's mind and took every opportunity to push the limits of acceptable behavior. Though never doing anything that could be construed as wrong, Harriet came dangerously close on a few occasions, such as when she leaned over Kevin while pouring him tea and lightly brushed the sleeve of his coat.

By the time the tea was over, Elma was beside herself with worry and anger, for while she had remained vigilant, the Judge seemed to ignore everything his daughter was doing to irritate her. When the clock struck four, Elma placed her saucer and teacup on the tray, stood up, and announced, "Well, this has indeed been a pleasure. Now, if you would excuse me, it is getting late and I must start tending to dinner."

Kevin, knowing a dismissal when he heard one, came to his feet. Turning to face Elma, he bowed at the waist, complimenting her and professing his appreciation for such an enjoyable and relaxing afternoon. Turning next to the Judge, he thanked him for having him in his house and expressed, as sincerely as he could, the hope that they would be able to finish their discussion on the issue of states' rights at a later date. He was about to turn away and excuse himself, when, in a fit of mischief, he turned to Harriet. "Miss Shields," he began in a rather stiff, formal manner, "I always find this part of afternoon a wonderful time for a walk. If your father has no objections, would you care to join me for a stroll about the park?"

Ignoring Elma Shields, who stood behind Kevin with her face contorted in horror, Harriet jumped to her feet. "Oh, that sounds delightful." Then, looking over to her father, she asked coyly, "Of course, if it's all right with you, Father."

While Elma struggled to control her rage, Judge Shields, like everyone else, ignored her for the moment. "Of course, dear. You two run along and enjoy yourselves. Just be sure," he cautioned Kevin in a stern yet fatherly voice, "you have her back by dusk."

With a smile and a wink, Kevin promised he would. With that Kevin and Harriet left the room as quickly as possible. They were no sooner gone than Elma turned on her husband. "How could you?"

Though Judge Shields wanted to ask what she was talking about, he knew better. He had managed to ignore her peevish behavior all afternoon but knew he could no longer do so. "Elma," he started, using a tone of voice that announced that he would not tolerate a protracted debate on the issue, "your behavior this afternoon has been reprehensible. You treated your daughter's invited guest, not to mention your own daughter, as if they were lepers."

Not yielding Judge Shields an inch, Elma fired back. "Judge, you of all people should know better. The very idea of allowing our only daughter to go about, in public, with the likes of him is . . . is . . ."

"Elma, enough. That boy is the son of an important man in this county. You may not like the cut of his cloth or the sound of his name, but when it comes to politics and business, it's money and the ability to generate votes that matters. And at a time when our nation, nay, our very own state, is on the verge of tearing itself apart, we must seek help and support from every source available. When the time comes to throw that scoundrel Olden out of the statehouse, we're going to need every penny we can squeeze out of old man Bannon and his cronies."

"I suppose this means," Elma protested, "that you're willing to sacrifice your daughter for your political ambitions?"

"No, Elma. I'm just as concerned as you are about her free and wild ways. God knows we've discussed this enough and, as you already know, I regret the liberal education I insisted upon, which you so wisely fought against. That damage is done, however, and there is little I can do to undo it. But don't you see, my dear, your efforts to treat her like a child are only making matters worse. If the truth be known, odds are that the only reason she invited Kevin Bannon to this house was to spite you."

"And you think, Melvin, that I was wrong, behaving as I did?"

"Yes, Elma, you were wrong. She got to you, and now she knows it."

"What, in God's name, would you have me do? Ignore her antics?"

"Yes. For now, play along with her. Don't make an issue of such trivial matters. In time she will mature. She will outgrow her desire to rebel, and, in a few years, she will settle down and begin to seek a mate more suitable for her. Perhaps, with a little encouragement, she will even go back to Thomas Ward's oldest boy, Trevor."

The sudden image of her daughter with Trevor Ward brought a smile to Elma's face. "Oh, I suppose you're right, Judge. It's just that I can't understand this girl. I was never like her, never. When I was her age, all I could think about was finding the right man, starting a family, and taking my place in society, just as my mother had done." Then, the smile left her face. "It's all those foolish ideas that she gathered in her head at that school you sent her to."

Exasperated, Judge Shields turned, throwing up his hands. "Elma, Elma. Be patient, my dear wife. All comes to he who is patient." Then, a darkness came across his face as he turned toward the door his daughter and Kevin had walked out of. "Besides, if this secession issue does come to war—and I think it will—young men, just like that one, are the ones we will send to fight it. And war," he said with a smile as he turned back to face his wife, "is always a risky business."

The two young people walked in silence as they neared the park, each lost in their own thoughts as they struggled to keep warm. Finally, Harriet looked over at Kevin. "Why did you invite me for a walk? You certainly don't look like you're enjoying yourself."

With the hint of a grin on his face, Kevin looked over at her. "You certainly are direct for a girl, aren't you?"

"Why should my being a girl make any difference?"

Kevin was caught off guard by this second question. The grin disappeared from his face. He had meant his question to be uncomfortable to Harriet. Instead, her retort had made *him* uncomfortable. Shrugging, he searched for a plausible answer. "Well, it's just that, well, every time I've ever had any dealings with a society girl such as you, they've been, well, polite, proper, and very circumspect. I mean, take last night. If you hadn't come over just when I was about to turn away and asked me to dance, we would never have met. The way I understand it, it's just not done that way, at least not in your circles."

"Does my being forward bother you, Kevin?"

There was no need to think about his response to that question. Stopping, he cocked his head back and looked at her. "Surprisingly, no. In fact—"

Missing his sudden halt, Harriet turned and faced him. "What?"

"If you must know, Miss Shields, I rather enjoy your style. It's rather . . ."

"I like to think of it as being natural."

"Yes, well, I suppose that's one way of putting it." Resuming his slow pace, with Harriet falling in closely at his side, they walked on a little further.

"Tell me, Mr. Bannon—"

"Kevin, Miss Shields. My father is Mr. Bannon. I'm just plain old Kevin."

"And if you please, I'm Harriet. Now tell me, Kevin, why did you invite me out here, in the cold, for a walk that you're not enjoying?"

Kevin laughed, blowing great clouds of frosted breath out before him. "Hmm, why did I invite you? Well, Harriet, if the truth be known, it was a test."

"Oh? And what sort of test was it?"

83

"Your mother's disapproval of me would be obvious to a man three days dead. And your father, well, he was simply trying too hard to make me feel at home. Coupled with the manner with which you dragooned me last night, it got me to thinking. 'Kevin,' I said, 'here's a woman who's either really interested in you and doesn't care what others say or'—he paused as he turned his face to look Harriet in the eye—'a spoiled child set on upsetting her mother and father for some unknown reason.' "

A twinge of guilt crossed Harriet's face as she blushed. Turning her gaze away, she looked down at the snow-covered walk and slowed her pace. "How did your invitation for a walk figure into this?"

"If, Harriet, the latter were true, and the only reason that you're interested in me is to outrage your parents, there would have been no need for you to come on this walk. Just my showing up at your house would have served that purpose. It would have been pointless for you to leave your beautiful, warm home and venture out into this miserable cold to cause any more grief to your parents."

"I see. And my accepting your invitation? What does that prove?"

"Well, if you put stock in my logic, it proves that you at least have some interest in me as a person, and not just as a means of rebelling against your parents or your society."

They walked in silence for several more minutes before Harriet spoke again. "You figured this out, all by yourself?"

"No, not all by myself. You see, Miss Shie . . . I mean, Harriet, as a boy, I used to enjoy listening to stories of the old country. The Irish workers at my father's brickyard loved to tell my brother and me all about Ireland and the pain and sufferings they had to endure at the hands of their English landlords. Some of their favorite stories were the ones about how the young daughters of the English lords, when they wanted to get back at their parents for some transgression or another, would take up with one of the tenant farmers' sons. 'Don't mess with the fair-haired daughters of the landlord,' the old men would tell us. 'It'll only break your hearts and get ya into trouble, boys.' "

"You believed them?"

Looking over into her eyes again, Kevin canted his head down. "Should I?"

Now it was Harriet who stopped. With a shy smile and a shake of her head, she responded, "No. At least, not anymore."

He was tempted to ask her why she was willing to risk censure and condemnation from her family and peers, but didn't. For the moment, such things were unimportant. Instead, he stepped toward her, reached out, and took her hands in his. Standing there, their hands locked, they looked into each other's eyes for a moment, in the growing shadows of the late afternoon. When Kevin finally spoke, he did so with the best Irish brogue he could manage. "If that be true, me lass, then will ya be seeing me again?"

Kevin's feeble attempts at an Irish accent caused Harriet to laugh. Then, doing her best to affect an upper-class English accent, she replied, "It would please me, kind sir, if you could find it in your heart to call on me again."

With a roar, he took Harriet's hand and twirled her about like a ballerina on the slick compacted snow. When she was faced about, he offered her his arm, which she accepted. Together, the two of them began to head back to her home as the darkness of the coming night began to gather about them.

# THE COMING
# FURY

PART TWO

# THE COMING FURY

## CHAPTER 5

# April, 1861
# The Virginia Military Institute, Lexington, Virginia

THERE WAS LITTLE TO CHEER JAMES BANNON AS HE TRUDGED, stooped over, his cap in one hand and his rifle in the other, through barracks toward his room that Friday evening. He tried hard not to think anymore about the mind-numbing penalty tours. While other cadets gathered in small clutches in their rooms to discuss the latest news from Charleston, James had paraded alone, back and forth, in a vain effort to work off demerits. Like millstones about his neck, the demerits that James accumulated with such ease—courtesy of Abner Couper—never seemed to go away. Despite James' best efforts, they were always there.

Worn by long nights of study, a demanding schedule of classes, and repetitive military drill, James searched his tired mind for at least one positive thought. That his current plight wasn't totally hopeless and unbearable, James kept telling himself, was something. Abner and his friends, after all, had never physically abused him. Not that they hadn't, on occasion, come close. On more than one occasion James, pushed to the limit of his patience, had been tempted to strike Abner. Will, however, was always there when James needed him the most, holding him back or providing just the right words needed to disarm tense moments. When it was James who was on the brink, Will would remind him that Colonel Smith, the superintendent, tolerated no physical harassment or fighting within the corps.

"Don't do it, Jimmy boy," Will would shout out so that everyone concerned could hear. "Just the summer before I came to VMI several upperclassmen were thrown out for hazing the plebes." What Will didn't need to say was that most of those thrown out for physically abusing other cadets were from Cadet Lieutenant Couper's class. In private, he would tell James, "Those boys remember that, and as much as they hate having you here, getting themselves dismissed from VMI over you just isn't worth it, especially now."

The "now" of which Will, and just about everyone else in the corps of cadets, spoke alluded to two impending events. The first was the graduation of Abner Couper and his class. "If you can make it till June," Will cheered James on almost daily, "Abner will be gone and we'll have the whole summer furlough, our first, to forget about him and his friends." The second event, of course, was the crisis of the Union and the resulting threat of war that so dominated the minds and discussion of the cadets that spring. As depressing as the thought of more demerits and more penalty tours was to James, the prospect of war was even more disheartening. So far, Virginia continued its refusal to secede, though by only the narrowest of margins. While other Southern states, seven to date, had left that January and February, strong Unionist sentiment kept Virginia in check. Virginia congressional leaders, in fact, were busy in Washington, D.C., in an effort to broker some type of compromise or reconciliation between Jefferson Davis of the Confederate States, sitting in the new capital of the new South, Montgomery, Alabama, and the recently installed Republican administration under Lincoln in Washington.

Time, however, and a hardening of attitudes in both the North and South were working against such efforts, as James cynically pointed out to Will one day after returning from a visit to downtown Lexington. "Will, even the dullest plebe can see that everyone is about fed up with talking. No one wants to listen anymore. No one wants to compromise. You walk through the streets of Lexington and all you hear people talking about is the Union and how it's a shame the Southern states bolted from it like they did and how they are going to rue the day they did. Then, as soon as you walk into barracks, you'd think we were in Montgomery."

Will's response, though surprising, was in character. "Yes, I know what you mean, James. Listening to those folks in town does kind of make me feel ashamed to be a Virginian. But," he added with a smile, "I'm sure that our state legislature will soon see the error of its ways and vote for secession."

The specter of secession cast a long shadow that few cadets cared to acknowledge. Not that there weren't moments of cold reality. Most of the cadets from Southern states that had already seceded went through a momentary personal crisis as each state's cadets, in turn, woke up to the fact that, without changing a thing, they were now living in a foreign country, one that might well go to war against their new nation. Cadets from Georgia, Mississippi, Alabama, Florida, Louisiana, Texas, and South Carolina now had to wonder whether their classmates and roommates from Arkansas, North Carolina, Tennessee, Missouri, Kentucky, Maryland, and Virginia would be standing with them in line of battle or arrayed against them under a flag they themselves had once been loyal to.

Youth, however, and the magic of spring soon freed most of the cadets from such troubling thoughts and deliberations. Slogans proclaiming states' rights and sovereignty were so much easier to deal with than the reality of what a war with the industrialized North would mean to the new Southern Confederacy. If anyone, in those heady spring days, harbored any serious thoughts about what such a war would mean, they tactfully kept their own counsel. This was doubly true for James. Even Will, in all his naive enthusiasm, managed to keep at least one foot on the ground, especially when dealing with James. Only once did he ask his roommate and friend what he would do if it came to war. James, who had never told Will all of the particulars concerning his exile to the South and never let on that there was no going back home, regardless of what happened, merely shook his head and shrugged. "Will, I don't know. I simply don't know." Sensing that James was uncomfortable with the issue, Will never brought the subject up again.

Still, that didn't mean that Will refrained from joining in with every display of support the pro-secession cadets put on. It wasn't unusual for James to find himself in the midst of a discussion among Will and his friends on how they could show their support for the Confederacy without getting caught. Will and two other members of the third class were, in fact, discussing just that when James came into his room.

"I tell you, Will," Bryan Lloyd of Georgia was saying, "there's no way they can do anything to us. The upperclassman that told me about this said that they were going to doctor the flagpole tonight, sometime after lights out."

Hard as he tried not to pay attention, James' ears perked up. Hefting his rifle up into the gun rack on the wall, he went about undoing his accoutrements and uniform blouse as Joshua McMann of North Carolina added his comments without paying any attention to James. "That's right, Will. All we need to do is be there when the Unionists in town go to hoist their flag, and enjoy the fun."

Will, with an impish smile on his face, looked at each of the other cadets, and shook his head. "I don't know, boys. Those folks in town might not see the humor in all this. They're not cadets, you know. They think they're playing for real. They might really get upset with us for insulting their flag." Turning to James, Will asked, innocently enough, "James, what do you think?"

James had heard enough to know that his fellow cadets were talking about causing some type of mischief at the flag-raising ceremony scheduled in Lexington the next day. Taking off his wool blouse and draping it across the back of his chair before answering, James looked at Will, then at Bryan and then Joshua in turn. "Will's right, you know. Those people in town attending their little flag ceremony may not appreciate what we pass off as a prank. Especially if the news from Charleston about Fort Sumter is to be believed."

Joshua suddenly turned serious. "Of course it's true. Why would anyone want to lie about a momentous event such as that?"

James pulled his chair away from his desk and sat down. "Josh, the firing on a Federal installation makes this dispute between the Confederacy and the Federal government more than a simple disagreement or debate. Now we're talking about armed insurrection."

"Struggle for independence, sir. What we have here now is simply a matter of free men standing up against a foreign power.'' Joshua corrected him with an indignant tone in his voice and a harsh look on his face.

"Well," James continued, choosing his words with care now, "that's just my point. You see, those folks in town, the Unionists, and most people up North don't see it that way. They believe in their country and the Union just as reverently as you believe in the principle of states' rights. They're not going to just roll over and give up on a union that their forefathers forged, not without a fight. The flag they intend to raise tomorrow is more than a piece of cloth. It is, to them, the embodiment of their beliefs. At a time like this, when everyone's passions are inflamed, they're not going to take kindly to any insult to their beliefs or any symbols of those beliefs. If their flag comes tumbling down in public, believe me, they will respond."

"James," Joshua started slowly, "you know that I appreciate your comments and I respect your views on the issue of secession. But you and Will have to understand that for those of us from the Deep South, this is no *longer* a 'simple prank,' as you put it—never was. That flag we'll be raising opposite the United States flag is now the emblem of *our* nation. Though it might look strange to you, its symbolism is as important to us as the Stars and Stripes is to you. I *do* understand what the Stars and Stripes means to the Unionists, for I too once held that flag in reverence. But ..." Josh paused. When he spoke again, there was a solemn conviction in his voice. "Things have changed. That flag, which we once all stood under and marched behind, is now a symbol of opposition and oppression to me. It represents those who would overthrow our way of life and deny us our liberties, the liberties that my forefathers fought for. It shields the abolitionists and Unionists who defy the laws of the Federal government that has, on many occasions, passed laws and statutes guaranteeing our personal rights and property. Because of all of that, and more, it has become a hated symbol, as hateful to us in the Deep South as the British flag was to the patriots in the last war of rebellion. To the good people of Charleston, the flying of that flag is akin to waving a red cape in front of a bull. And despite what those folks in town and up North say, we have as much right, under the Constitution, to fly our national flag and be proud of it as they do.''

93

"But Josh," Will said in an effort to come to his roommate's aid, "Virginia is still in the Union, mind."

Standing up, Joshua looked down at Will. His face was serious and his voice stern. "Yes, that's right. And if I were you, I'd be ashamed of that fact. Virginia, sir, is a Southern state, a slave state, no different from South Carolina, Georgia, and the rest. So long as she, as well as North Carolina, Maryland, Tennessee, Kentucky, and Missouri persist in holding aloof, those devils up North will be encouraged to make trouble for us and ignore our independence. If Virginia and the others had stood up with the rest of us, Lincoln and his Black Republicans would have conceded defeat and let the Confederacy go in peace a long time ago. So long as the issue is in doubt, they'll make trouble for us all."

Unable to respond, Will looked over to James, who turned away. Bryan, seeing that Joshua wasn't about to relent, stood up. "Josh, we need to go get ready for supper."

Suddenly understanding that things had gone too far, Joshua looked down at the floor and blushed in embarrassment. After mumbling an apology that was barely audible, Joshua and Bryan turned to leave. Will, however, stopped them by calling out. "When are we going to go into town tomorrow?"

Joshua turned, flashing a smile. "As soon as last duty is finished. I want a front-row seat for this."

Will smiled. "So do I."

Cheered by Will's response, the two cadets left. James, still sorting out his thoughts, said nothing as he stared vacantly down at his desk before him. Finally, Will spoke. "James, you don't understand."

James stopped and looked over to his roommate with a smile on his face. "Oh, Will, but I do. And if I were in your place, I'd go too."

Will grinned. "Then why don't you?"

"Because, Will, I'm not in your place. For me to be there would be . . ."

With a sigh, Will answered for James. "I know. It would be awkward. I suppose if I were you, I wouldn't go either."

"I knew you'd understand. Now, let's get ready for dinner. I'm starved to death and don't feel much like collecting a whole passel of demerits on the way to the mess hall."

Reaching across the table, Will motioned to James as he reached for his own shoe brush and polish. "Here, give me your other shoe and I'll give you a hand."

That night, while James and Will lay in their beds after lights out, they started to talk. For them, as for many other cadets, this was a very special time of day. With all the rushing about and daily duties of the day at an end, and all of the tensions and problems of daily life facing a young man in college behind them, they could discuss personal issues and problems, among friends, in the safety of the dark confines of their room. The surviving roommate from the previous year, who had endured the trials of his first year at VMI, seldom joined in. It wasn't that he was antisocial. Rather, as he liked to remind Will and James, "I'm a busy man with a lot of responsibilities. I need all the sleep I can get." And sleep he did. According to Will, he could "sleep through an earthquake." True to his habits, he was already sound asleep when Will and James started to talk, his heavy breathing, which bordered on being a snore, providing a backdrop to their conversation.

"You realize, James," Will started, "if it does come down to a war, we're going to lose our summer furlough."

James chuckled. Even at a time like this, Will had a way of reducing even the most monumental affairs of two nations into simple, easy-to-deal-with personal terms. "Yeah, Will, I guess a war would sort of put a crimp in your summer plans."

Will thought for a moment before he responded. When he did, it was almost as if he were thinking out loud. "You know, I would have liked to have spent one more summer at home. It's beautiful up there on the farm, James. Real beautiful."

"I'm sure it is, Will." James knew that Will was worried, really worried. In the past, every time he was faced with a major crisis, such as a major examination or an important event, Will would spend hours the night before talking about his home and family. It was, James figured, his way of calming himself down, of turning his mind away from the trials and tribulations that he was about to face. And it seemed the more detailed his memories, the more troubled he was. Tonight, James knew, from his tone and the nature of the description of his family's farm, that the events of the past days, and those ahead, were bothering Will greatly.

Like a tour guide, Will verbally walked James through his house and about the grounds immediately surrounding it. At intervals he would stop to discuss the members of his family when he came to the spot in the house or on the farm he most closely associated with each of them. Inevitably, the first person he would run across in his imaginary stroll was his mother. "She's always in the kitchen, it seems. I'll tell you, James, you're going to love her bread. Nothing like the hard, dry stuff we get here. No sir, hers is nice and thick and moist. She serves it up hot and fresh, so hot you can hardly hold it in your fingers without burning them. There were times when I'd make a meal of that bread, covered with a thick layer of apple butter. One bite and you'll think you died and went to heaven."

Daniel, his brother, always seemed to be just outside in the yard, tending the chickens or hanging off a branch of an apple tree in their yard, picking apples that no one else could reach. "That one should have been a monkey," Will would say with a chuckle. "Fact is, Mary Beth is always threatening to sell him to the circus. When he was young, he thought she was serious. He was so scared when a circus did come to town one year, he hid in the barn for two days. Ma was worried sick and Mare got the beating of her life."

When he got around to describing his father, Will always saw him far away, busy working in some distant field. When he spoke of him, he spoke of his labors. Will's father, it seemed, spent his days plowing, harvesting, chopping wood, or mending the miles of rail fence that enclosed their fields and orchards. Will's words described the strength, steadiness, and security that his father gave to their lives. If Will's mother was supreme in the house, his father, in Will's eyes, was the ruler and master of the small universe called the McPherson farm.

Inevitably his sister, Mary Beth, was always the last person he came across. She, unlike the others, never seemed tied to the house or any single part of the farm itself. It was, James imagined, as if she were a free-roving spirit, moving about as her mood took her, even in Will's recollections. The terms Will used in describing her were light, almost whimsical. The most recurring memories of her were those of her mounted on one of the family's horses, riding astride like a boy. "She's a sight, James, a real sight. With her sunbonnet pushed back and her long red hair trailing behind like a raging flame, she can outride anyone I ever saw. The man who tries to hitch his wagon to her is going to have the devil of a time reining her in, don't you think, Jimmy?"

Usually, by the time Will reached this point of his ramblings, he had lost James, for James would, despite his best efforts, slip away into his own thoughts. Without fail those thoughts would be of his own home and his own family. Step by step, he would contrast Will's experience and memories with his own. And step by step, as Will's recollections buoyed his spirits and brought relief to his troubled mind, James would slip slowly into a depressing gloom as his parallel journey home opened old wounds that time and distance, no matter how great, never seemed to heal. This was especially true whenever Will spoke of his mother, for there was nothing in James' past that even slightly resembled the warm, comforting feminine touch that Will's mother graced him with. The English housemaid and the cook who had joined the household when Edward Bannon's fortune permitted it were no substitute. Rather, they served only as reminders of the tyrannical and oppressive rule Edward imposed upon his household. Like James and Kevin themselves, the hired help moved about the house as if they were barefoot and walking on glass. No one in the Bannon household dared let down their guard, day or night, for fear of being subjected to Edward Bannon's harsh and uncompromising tongue. No one dared speak unless spoken to for fear of offending the old man or exposing their own thoughts and ideas to his cynical and cutting criticisms. "Impudence," he would bellow at James whenever circumstances forced James to defend himself or his brother, "will not be tolerated. Your opinion, like your very existence, is a bothersome necessity that time will soon rid me of."

Often, with the memory of such condemnations ringing in his ears, James would lose track of what Will was saying. Only Will's persistent, "Jimmy, boy, you still awake?" would serve to wrench James away from the dark shadows of his past in New Jersey and back to the silence of their room in sleepy

Lexington, Virginia. Composing himself, James would eventually respond in a murmur that he wasn't asleep. Hearing this, and satisfied that he still had an audience, Will would work his way into another subject, usually the one that had been troubling him in the first place. Tonight was no different.

"James," he started formally, "have you given any thought to what you'll do if Virginia, I mean *when* Virginia, leaves the Union?"

James had known for a long time that eventually Will would ask him that. And for a long time, he knew the day would come when he would have to answer it. Now, with the Southern Confederacy using open and unrestrained force to defend its cause, his freedom to avoid the question was all but gone. He, like Virginia herself, would have to declare himself, once and for all. There would be, as so many of his fellow cadets had stated in the past few months, no place for neutrals in this conflict. "We must all," one instructor had stated in class one day, when the class had succeeded in turning the classroom discussion to the matter of the coming war, "do what our hearts and our convictions demand. No man can do wrong so long as he is true to himself."

After staring into the darkness for several seconds, James sighed. "God, Will, I wish I could give you an answer, one that I really believed in. I wish I could promise you that whatever you do, wherever you go, I'll be there by your side, but I can't."

Will thought about his friend's answer before he responded with a voice that was as supportive as his broken heart could manage. "I understand, James, I really do. Though you've never spoken much about your family and your home state, I realize that when the time comes, you'll stand by them like I'll stand by mine."

James propped himself up on his elbow and looked over to where Will's cot was. "It's not like that, Will. Unlike you and most of the other boys here, I have no great attachment to my native state. The city where I lived is as cold and impassive as Old Jack is, filled with strangers who want nothing to do with anyone outside of their own little neighborhood. The house I grew up in was built for people I never knew. Except for my brother, the only member of my family that I really care for, the North means nothing to me, not anymore.''

Hearing the rustle of James' sheets and blankets and the desperateness in his tone, Will threw his legs over the side of his cot and sat up to face James. "But?" he asked without finishing his question.

"While it might be true that there's next to nothing for me back in New Jersey that's worth fighting for, it is equally true that there's nothing down here that I can call my own. Though I wear the uniform of the Virginia Military Institute and march behind the flag of Virginia, I am not a Virginian."

"James, I don't know what brought you here, and to tell you the truth, I don't give a hoot. The fact is, my friend, that you are more than my friend. You're more of a brother to me than my own brother. And despite what Abner Couper says, you're just as much a Virginian as any man here that drew his first breath in the Old Dominion. Hell, Jimmy, even Couper's own family started out no better than yours or mine. The only difference between his ancestors and mine and yours is that they managed to get themselves thrown out of England sooner than ours did."

Though it wasn't meant to be funny, Will's statement caused James to laugh. Will had a way of doing that, especially when he was trying to be serious. Hearing his friend's chuckle, Will paused, then started to laugh himself when he reflected on what he had just said. After several seconds, with a tone of sincerity that needed no amplification, Will began to speak again. "James Bannon, when the time comes to stand up for Virginia, and I'm thinking it will happen soon, I would consider it an honor if you were to stand with me, at my side, Abner Couper be damned."

Will's last statement, meant to be a show of support and loyalty to a trusted friend, did nothing to ease James' troubling dilemma. Instead, it made him feel as if he were a small life-boat cast adrift on a violent and heaving sea, forced to ride out whatever was thrown at him. Stubbornly, James blindly grabbed and held on to Will's faith and friendship in the hope that, somehow, the future would bring him salvation. Where that salvation would come from, James did not know. All he knew, on that quiet spring evening as he and Will quietly lay back down in their own beds, was that all he had, at that moment, was a lifeboat called VMI and a friend who had come forth to fill the void the loss of his brother had left, just as he knew that the threat of war, a war that everyone welcomed, could sweep away this tenuous hope.

Left to decipher the complexities of a math problem concerning the volume and weight of a cord of wood, in the quiet of his room, James didn't hear the first distant cries that disturbed the afternoon quiet. It wasn't until they had grown in both intensity and desperateness that James realized that something was amiss.

Within a minute the quiet and tranquillity of the day was shattered by running feet as they pounded the wooden stairs and treadways that made up the tiered stoops of the cadet barracks. James, in part angered by this disturbance, slammed his pencil down on his desk, stood up, and turned toward the door. His trip, however, was cut short when the door flew open in his face.

"James!" Before him stood a hatless and disheveled classmate, wide-eyed and shouting out breathlessly between gulps of air. "Grab your rifle and fall in. The mayor's called out the militia."

Pushing away from the doorway, the cadet was about to continue his Paul Revere–like romp down to the next room when James grabbed his arm. "Frederick, what are you talking about? What's happening?"

Grabbing the edge of the door frame with his free hand, the cadet pulled himself back until he faced James. "The Unionists, James. The Unionists started a fight when their flag came tumbling down. They knew we did it. They knew it. And they were so angry that some of them just lit into the first cadet they could get their hands on."

"The militia, Frederick? What's this about the town militia?"

"The fight started to spread when the cadets were joined by other loyal Southerners. Before you know it, people were running all over the place, chasing cadets or anyone without a Unionist lapel pin. Some say a cadet's already been killed. The mayor of Lexington sent for the Rockbridge Rifles, who were doing their weekly drill. When we saw them, some of us decided to come back here and get the rest of the corps.''

Letting go of his classmate, James looked about. On every stoop across the way he could see cadets, in every state of dress, rushing to form up with rifle in hand. Then, facing Frederick, he asked about Will. ''James, I didn't see Will. There was no time. Everything was so confused.'' Then, seeing that ranks were beginning to form, he turned away from James. ''I gotta go get my rifle and cartridge box. You coming?''

Without even a second's pause or another comment, James pulled his head into his room. In a single bound he reached the rifle rack. With measured speed, James draped his cartridge box over his left shoulder, adjusting it so that the box rested just to the rear of his right hip. Over this, he donned the thick black belt to which a cap pouch and bayonet were attached. After buckling the belt's large, highly polished brass buckle, embossed ''VMI,'' James grabbed Will's rifle and accoutrements and slung them over his left shoulder before he took his own rifle down. Pausing only long enough to grab his cap, James rushed out the door of his room, pulling his cap down till the visor was only a couple of inches from the bridge of his nose. Once out on the stoop, he joined the throng of cadets that was still spilling down the stairways and down the hill toward town.

With the same ease they used when preparing to march to chow or chapel, the cadets formed and dressed their ranks. Even at this moment, with nervous excitement running through them like an electric current, the drill and discipline that were as much a part of their daily routine as breathing asserted themselves. No one was thinking of anything but the immediate crisis. Instead, the mindless drill and uncompromising demand for precision that so annoyed many of the young and energetic cadets, who railed against every infringement upon their individuality, were taking hold. Within minutes the quiet college campus had produced a formed body of troops, armed, ready, and under the control of the cadet officers who now hastily paraded up and down the ranks checking one last time before marching off to do battle with anyone who stood in their way.

It was during this brief lull, with the cadets in the ranks standing shoulder to shoulder, rifles held tightly at their sides, that Cadet Lieutenant Abner Couper came across James. After initially glancing over James, Abner stopped short and backed up until he was standing squarely in front of him. With a look that betrayed both annoyance and surprise, Abner looked James up and down. "What are you doing here, Mr. Bannon? This fight concerns only Virginians and true sons of the South."

Up to that moment, James hadn't paused to think. He hadn't considered what his actions meant. But now, when confronted by the very question that he had so carefully avoided answering, he didn't hesitate. Looking straight ahead, James shouted in an uncompromising tone. "Sir, my friends are in danger."

"But you are a *Yankee*, Mr. Bannon."

Cocking his head back, James peered out from the dark shadows the visor of his cap cast over his eyes. Locking his eyes with those of Abner Couper, James took on a stern, uncompromising expression. "Sir, I am a VMI cadet."

For the first time, James saw something in Abner's eyes that he had never seen there before. It wasn't confusion, or the usual contempt he showed when dealing with James. Instead, James thought in those fleeting seconds, it was a look of approval. It was, he imagined, as if this had been a test, one which he had passed.

There was, however, no time to reflect upon this thought, or any other for that matter. The moment passed as the senior cadet officer present called the cadet battalion to attention and began to issue his marching orders. In response to the quick, crisp commands of the cadet battalion commander, echoed by the four cadet company commanders, the two ranks of cadets faced to the right. Without hesitation, without even a hint of confusion, every second cadet stepped to the right and forward, transforming the two long ranks of each company into a compact column standing four abreast. Taking his place at the head of this column, Captain John McCauland, one of two members of the faculty who had joined the cadets and taken charge, gave the order: forward march. In time with the first deep rumble of the corps' massed drums, the cadets stepped off.

They had just finished facing to the right when Will McPherson, fresh from his run back from town, burst into the ranks next to James. "Jimmy, Jimmy," he shouted over and over as the cadets about James gave way for Will. "This is it. There's no turning back from this. We're at war, Jimmy."

Though he was just as happy to see Will as Will was to see him, James kept his eyes fixed on the back of the cadet before him. He said nothing to his roommate as he listened and marched, unshouldering Will's accoutrements, one at a time, and passing them over to him. When Will had finished slinging his cartridge box over his own shoulder and had his belt in place and buckled, James handed Will his rifle. After tucking the rifle up against his body at shoulder arms, Will took a deep breath. "Thanks, James. Thanks a whole lot. I knew I could count on you. I just knew it." Turning his head about, to another classmate in the ranks behind them, Will rephrased his praise into a question. "Didn't I tell you that Jimmy would stand by us when the time came?"

Like James, the other cadet didn't respond. Instead, they marched off to the foot of the hill and into the yard of an inn at the end of Lexington's Main Street. To those untrained eyes watching, the cadet battalion made a grand and glorious spectacle. Their neat uniforms and even, straight ranks and files, moving forward with a purposeful stride spoke of power. Even the grim, determined expression worn by each and every cadet added to the feeling that an irresistible force was in motion. That the thoughts of those cadets didn't match their appearance never occurred to anyone, not even to many of the cadets themselves. Rather than a hard corps of professional soldiers going forth to do battle, the two hundred plus cadets, who hailed from every corner of the South were, in truth, little more than a body of well-trained boys passing mechanically forward into a great unknown.

It was, therefore, perhaps a good thing that just as the cadets were about to leave Institute property, Colonel Francis Henry Smith, the superintendent, intervened. Shocked by the sight of his charges loading rifles, forming up in ranks, and marching off into battle with townspeople who had been his neighbors for years, Smith scrambled from his bed, where he had been recovering from pneumonia. Running down the hill as best he could after them, Smith managed to reach the head of the column just as they were forming into line of battle. After relieving Captain McCauland of his command, Smith looked over the corps and pondered what he should do. He knew that he had an explosive situation on his hands that could have serious and irreversible repercussions.

"Cadets of the Virginia Military Institute," Smith began, "I do not know what led you to deploy for battle like this. I do know, as you do, that I am your commander. And if there is going to be a fight, I am going to lead you."

From the ranks came murmurs of approval. Seeing that they were listening, Smith continued. "If I am going to lead you, I must insist on prompt obedience to my orders."

Within the corps of cadets, there was a moment of hesitation. Will whispered to James, "Why's he making such a statement, at a time like this? We know he's in charge and that we'll follow." James, tight lipped, said nothing as he wondered what Smith was up to. Neither he nor the other cadets bothered to work through the confusion created by Colonel Smith. Instead, they responded with nods or lusty shouts of approval.

"Yes! Yes!" the more excitable cadets yelled as they acknowledged Colonel Smith's authority.

Satisfied that he now had some control of them, Smith issued a quick, and surprising, string of orders. "Corps, atten-tion. Right face."

Again, there was confusion. Will turned to James. "What's he doing, James? We're facing barracks, not Lexington."

James smiled when he understood Colonel Smith's game. He was about to tell Will that Smith had no intention of leading the corps into battle that day when Smith yelled out in the best command voice his frail condition would allow, "Forward march."

Though there were clear and unmistakable signs of displeasure and a great deal of grumbling, the cadet officers echoed Smith's commands and responded. Retracing their steps, the corps of cadets moved back to the barracks, where they were herded into Major John Thomas Lewis Preston's section room, which was the largest room in barracks. There, Smith, aided to varying degrees of effectiveness by other members of the faculty, endeavored to reason with the cadets. The cadets, frustrated in their efforts to stand up to the Unionists in town who had affronted them and their cause as well as endangered their

104

fellow cadets, refused to be pacified. Neither Smith nor any other member of the faculty could calm them. The faculty would just about manage to get them quieted when the anger of the cadets would flare up anew.

In the midst of this struggle of applied reason and inflamed passions, Major Thomas J. Jackson walked into the room. As was his custom, the dour and tight-lipped professor moved over to the rostrum and took his seat. There seemed, to James, little concern or excitement in his face. "Look at him, James," Will whispered as he pointed to Jackson. "He's acting like this sort of thing happens every day."

James smiled warily. "Will, don't forget that man faced, almost single-handedly, the entire garrison of Mexico City at the Battle of Chapultepec. You don't think a room full of unruly cadets is going to get him excited, do you?"

In the back of the room, a voice called out, "Major Jackson." The first voice was joined by another, then another as the cry rose, "Old Jack! Old Jack!" Though some of the cadets called out in jest, there was little doubt that some, like James, saw a great deal more behind the bright blue eyes of Thomas J. Jackson than a drier-than-dust professor.

Seeing the reactions of the cadets, Colonel Smith turned to the professor of natural philosophy. "I have driven in the nail, sir, but it needs clinching. Speak to them."

With little more than a nod, Jackson rose. As he stretched out his tall, angular frame, the room went silent. Reaching the rostrum, he paused, looking down at it as he considered his words. When he was ready, he cast his gaze across the room, looking into the eyes of as many of the cadets as he could. When he finally spoke, his high-pitched voice took on a tone that few in that room had ever heard or even imagined was possible from a man many called Tom Fool. "Military men," he started, "when they make speeches, should say but a few words and speak them to the point."

James was taken by the quality in Jackson's voice. Looking about him, he saw his fellow cadets giving the man they had called Old Jack their complete attention. Like James, they were hanging on every word, spoken in a manner that demanded their attention.

"I admire, young gentlemen, the spirit you have shown in

rushing to the defense of your comrades, but I must commend you particularly for the readiness with which you have listened to the counsel and obeyed the orders of your superior officer.'' When he paused, no one spoke. His manner and words, spoken with an earnestness that was compelling, were having their effect.

''The time,'' he continued, raising his voice slightly, ''may be near when your state will need your services, but it has not come yet. If that time comes, then draw your swords and throw away the scabbards.''

That was it. Major T. J. Jackson had said what he felt he needed to say, and, finished, he turned away from the rostrum and took his seat. For a moment, there was a silence among the cadets. Then, in ones and twos, they left Major Preston's section room. The crisis had passed.

Later that evening, while they lay in their beds, listening to their roommate snore, Will and James discussed the day's events. ''I was sure glad to see you out there today, James. Surprised, but glad.''

James thought for a moment before responding. ''To tell you the truth, Will, I was sort of surprised to find myself out there.''

''Do you know what the hardest part of all this talk of war has been for me?''

''Yes, I do, Will. Your fear for your home and family. I know I've been thinking a great deal about my own brother these past few days.''

Sitting up in bed, Will turned to face, in the darkness, in the direction of James' bed. Curling up his legs, he grabbed his ankles and pulled his feet under him as a small child did when sitting before his mother to hear a story. ''No, James, that's not it.'' Then, as was his custom when he spoke before he thought, Will corrected himself. ''Well, yes, I am worried a little about the farm and my family. But they'll be all right. They've got each other. I can't think of a power on this earth that can break them.''

To this, James said nothing. Perhaps what Will said was true. Perhaps there was nothing to worry about. There was strength in Will's family, a strength that James had never imagined possible. Still, James knew better. He had seen a dark side of humanity that Will and many of the young cadets at VMI had never imagined. He had listened, with his brother Kevin, as the old Irishmen at their father's brickyard spoke of the devastation of the Potato Famine and the oppression of the English landlords. Together with the stories told by the old German policeman, Frederick Himmel, of the suppression of the liberal movement in Germany in 1848, James knew that a family needed more than love when faced by the depredations of men at war. Still, he said nothing. No need, he figured, to get Will more excited than he already was over something that might never come to pass. Lying there, he listened as Will continued.

"No, Jimmy, this afternoon, as I was running back to the barracks with three Unionists coming up fast behind me, all that kept running through my mind was the most horrible image I could imagine. You know what that image was?"

"No, Will, I really don't."

There was a pause, as if Will was reconsidering the wisdom of continuing. Sensing this, James prodded him. "Go ahead, Will, you can tell me. Lord knows you've always told me every other thought and secret you've ever had."

"Well, if you promise not to get angry."

"I promise I won't get angry."

"Well, James, when things started to get really scary, and I'll admit, I was pretty scared there for a while, there was this one image that kept smacking me square in the face. I couldn't push it from my mind. Not until I saw you in ranks with the rest of the corps did I breathe easy."

James, though trying to be patient, was becoming exasperated as Will danced about the subject he seemed so reluctant to mention. "Yes, Will, I'm sure you were excited. I would have been too. But what, if you please, had you so scared if it wasn't the three Unionists chasing you?"

"James, though I knew you'd never do it, I couldn't help but think . . . I mean . . ." Again, there was a hesitation. Then, as if spurred on by James' impatience, Will blurted, "Well, damn it, James Bannon! The thing I feared the most was finding you, standing out there in front of barracks, with your rifle, bayonet fixed, ready to fight me. I could deal with just about anything, even though I was scared. But I don't think I can deal with seeing you go North and fight with the Unionists. It would . . .'' He paused as he mustered up the courage he needed. Then, with a soft-spoken sincerity, Will finished his sentence: "James, if you and I wind up on different sides of this fight, it will break my heart.''

Across the room, protected by the darkness that covered them both, James began to cry. Of all the fears he had, the one that had become the most compelling, most crippling, was the fear of being wrenched away from Will and the rest of his classmates.

None of the cruelties that his father had heaped on him, no amount of despair could match the pain he felt when he had considered what he would become and where he would go when war came. And it wasn't until that afternoon, in the heated rush of events, that James had found that there wasn't, and probably never had been, a real choice to be made. Slowly, day by day, step by step, he had bound himself to this state, this school, these boys whom he had come to call brothers. Though it had been a long time in coming, James finally realized that, for better or worse, he was committed to Virginia's cause. This place, his fellow cadets, and this state were his home.

"James? You asleep?"

James wiped his face with his hands. "No, Will, I'm not. And, Will?"

"Yes?"

"Thanks.''

# CHAPTER 6

# April, 1861
# New Brunswick,
# New Jersey

IT HAD BECOME A CUSTOM FOR KEVIN BANNON AND HARRIET
Shields to stroll arm in arm along the quiet streets of New
Brunswick before returning to her parents' house for Sunday
dinner. In the beginning, it wasn't easy for Kevin. The haunting
memory of his last love affair had a habit of cropping up in his
mind at the most awkward of times, leaving Kevin shaking and
Harriet confused.

*"There is much,"* Harriet recorded in her diary one night,
*"that Kevin isn't telling me. With the same ease with which a
warm spring day can give way to the most violent thunderstorm, his personality can transform itself from one of happiness and cheer to a withdrawn sullenness that is unshakable.
All I can do for now is to ignore these fits of melancholy as best
I can and hope that someday he'll trust me enough to open up
to me the innermost secrets of his heart."*

Her mother was, for Harriet, an entirely different matter.
Despite her efforts, Elma Shields couldn't keep word from
spreading that her daughter was seeing an Irishman. Harriet, of
course, had a hand in helping the word spread. When Kevin
asked why she insisted on choosing a different route each time
for their Sunday walk, Harriet smiled. "I want people to get
used to seeing us together, Kevin. Eventually, when Mother's
circle of friends finds that their vicious gossip is having no
effect, they'll find something else to talk about and leave us
alone."

Comments like this convinced Kevin that there was more to
Harriet's desire to see him and be with him than simple rebel-

109

lion. Like the flowers coming into bloom all about the city that April, the friendship between them unfolded with each visit, becoming more beautiful. This was especially true for Kevin, for Harriet's warm affection did much to replace the hollowness he had felt when his brother had left home and erase the memory of a tragic love affair. And although he was warned by many of his classmates that Harriet was strong willed and independent of mind, Kevin ignored them, for he found those qualities to his liking. It was, he confided in a friend one day, quite comforting to have someone who could think and make decisions. "I do not much care," he told his friend, "for these girls who play coy little games and flit about like butterflies that can only be admired from afar. To have a girl who knows the King's English and has a brain every bit as sharp as my own makes being with her quite enjoyable."

What he didn't bother to tell his friend, or anyone else, including Harriet, was the real reason he enjoyed her company. She was, in many regards, becoming a substitute for his lost brother, James. Try as he might, Edward Bannon could not, overnight, undo the years of damage that Kevin's dependence on his older brother had left. Nor could he keep Kevin from searching for a person to take the place of the protector, confidant, best friend, and teacher that James had been to Kevin. "You are a man now," his father would shout out whenever he detected even the slightest hint of indecision or weakness in his second son. "As the oldest surviving son, you must learn to stand on your own two feet. You must be strong. This is a cruel world, boy, a place where any sign of weakness in a man will surely lead to his undoing." Except for the part about him being the oldest surviving son, a statement that always upset him, Kevin could remember James receiving the exact same lecture.

The difference was that James could take it. There were few occasions when James took his father's abuse and criticism without responding in kind. His brother, Kevin remembered, had no problem with standing toe to toe with the old man, glaring in his father's eye with a defiance that Kevin always admired but could never emulate. Heated conversations and violent arguments, accompanied by beatings when they were young, were as routine to the Bannon boys as Sunday church services. James' departure hadn't changed anything, other than the players involved. Now it was Kevin who found himself standing where James had been. The big difference was that while James always had Kevin to turn to for solace and comfort, Kevin had no one. That is, until Harriet Shields came along.

While Harriet would never fill the gap that James' exile left, and no one could protect him from his father's wrath, she did satisfy needs that were just as important to him. Unlike other girls he had been with, back in Perth Amboy and after starting classes at Rutgers, Harriet was easy to spend time with and made an enjoyable companion. From the beginning, Kevin took great comfort in the fact that he didn't need to make all the decisions or carry the conversation. More often than not, Harriet would greet him at the door, dressed and ready, with a smile on her face. In a sweet voice, she would inform Kevin of where they were going, and with a lively step that he sometimes had trouble keeping up with, she would whisk him away to destinations unknown. Kevin ignored his classmates when they chided him for letting Harriet lead him about as she did. Every time Harriet sent him a simple note telling him nothing more than to pick her up at a certain time, Kevin's roommate would shake his head. "I tell you, my friend, it's degrading and unmanly to allow a woman to dominate you like she does. Encouraging a woman to behave in this manner is a dangerous thing. Left unchecked, they begin to expect such behavior even after marriage. Best you put her in her place now, before she becomes totally unmanageable."

Kevin had no intention of putting Harriet in her place or anywhere else. So long as she filled the void that his brother's absence had left, Kevin was more than satisfied to let Harriet have her way.

"I do not see how we cannot respond, Kevin. They did, after all, fire on our fort."

Kevin nodded. "Yes, Harriet, a fort which just happens to be right in the center of one of their busiest harbors. Now why, you might ask yourself, was Mr. Lincoln so willing to give up all those other forts, without a fight, while making such a fuss over Sumter?"

Harriet looked down at the pavement ahead of her as she walked and thought about Kevin's question. Finally, after shaking her head, she looked back at Kevin. "I really don't see what difference that makes. I mean, whether we abandoned one fort or one hundred, that does nothing to erase the fact that the Rebels fired on our flag."

Kevin cocked his head back and laughed. "Harriet, that sounds like a woman's logic."

Without looking over, he knew that her brow had gone dark and an angry expression had fallen across her face. Whenever he wanted to change the subject or get her goat, all Kevin had to do was say, "Harriet, you're starting to sound like a schoolgirl," or "is that what your mother taught you to say?" or make some such frivolous reference to her gender. In return, Harriet would chastise him, telling him he knew better than that or that he was lucky she was a woman, otherwise she would teach him a thing or two. Kevin, when he was satisfied that he had succeeded in drawing her away from the subject he had tired of, would respond by squeezing her arm or hand. With a soft gentle smile, he would remind her that she should be glad that she was a woman, "for if you weren't, my dear, I hardly imagine us walking like this, arm in arm down the middle of the sidewalk."

Today, they had just reached that part of their conversation as they entered the foyer of Harriet's home. Their gentle laughter caught the attention of her father, who called from the study. "Harriet, Kevin, would you join me."

It was a command, not a request. Looking at each other, the two young people shrugged. After Harriet had finished removing her hat, she took a moment before the hall mirror to make sure her hair was in place. Taking her by the arm, Kevin led her to the room where Judge Shields entertained important guests. Turning the corner, they had no sooner passed through the open double doors when Kevin brought their forward progress to a screeching halt. Harriet, caught off guard, was jerked back and up against Kevin by this unexpected response. Looking up at him, she saw a look on his face she couldn't understand. For while his mouth hung open in speechless surprise, there was definitely a look of fear or panic in his eyes.

Flinging her head about, she faced her father. It was then that she noticed a stranger sitting across from him. When he saw her eyeing him, the stranger stood up. "Harriet," her father announced without leaving his seat, "I would like you to meet Edward Bannon, Kevin's father."

Edward Bannon bowed stiffly, as if the act was both unnatural and painful. "It is, young lady, a pleasure to meet you."

The words were spoken as if they, like the bow, were forced. Still, Harriet flashed a smile, nodding her head slightly in acknowledgment. Kevin, totally bewildered, said and did nothing as he stood in the doorway, and Harriet tightened her grip on his arm.

Sensing the awkwardness of the situation, Judge Shields, ever the perfect host, stood up. Straightening his frock coat, he looked down at Edward Bannon, then at Kevin. Clearing his throat before speaking, as if he were calling a court to order, Judge Shields smiled. "It would seem, Harriet, that congratulations are in store for your young man."

"Oh? And what has *our* Kevin done to deserve this?"

Ignoring her emphasis on the word "our," something she did to annoy her mother, the Judge glanced back at Edward Bannon, who nodded his assent. "Well," the Judge said as he looked at Kevin and puffed out his chest, "it seems our young hero here has been granted a commission in the state militia."

Kevin reeled backwards as if he had been shot. Sensing his shock, Harriet tightened her grip on his arm in an effort to minimize this pulling back and keep him on his feet. Seeing that he was unable to speak at that moment, Harriet jumped in. "Oh, Kevin, how wonderful! An officer, in our state militia." Then, seeing that he was about to say something that she feared might be embarrassing, Harriet turned to face Kevin. Reaching up and planting her hands on his shoulders, Harriet stood on her toes and kissed the still spellbound young man. Pulling away, she looked into his eyes, which had grown wider after the kiss, the first show of real affection she had ever shown him. "Smile," she whispered. "Smile and shake my father's hand."

Thrown off guard, first by Judge Shields' announcement,

then by Harriet's kiss, Kevin shook his head as if to clear it, while Harriet stepped aside. Mechanically, he crossed the room, reached out with his right hand, and clasped the Judge's hand when he offered it to him. "Thank you, sir," was the best Kevin could manage.

Relieved that an awkward moment had passed well, Judge Shields laid his left hand on their two joined hands and shook them again. "Oh, lad, I had nothing to do with it. It was your father who did all the work. I'm just playing messenger boy."

When he finally turned to face his father, the look in Kevin's eyes had clouded over and darkened. "Ah, Judge Shields, Harriet. Could I have a word with my father, in private?"

If he sensed the anger building up in Kevin, Judge Shields never showed it. Instead, he released Kevin's hand and walked across the room to where his daughter stood. "Of course, my lad. Harriet and I will run along and tell Mrs. Shields the good news and hurry tea along." With that, the two Shieldses passed out of the room, an Irish servant closing the double doors without a command being given.

When they were alone, Edward Bannon resumed his seat and looked his son up and down. "College, it seems, agrees with you. You've put on some weight."

"Father, before you say another word, I will not—"

Cutting him off, Edward shouted back at him. "You will not what? Accept the commission? Do your duty? Do as I tell you?" Leaning back in his seat, he flashed a wary smile. "Before you start telling me what you will and will not do, you listen to me, boy."

Edward Bannon's outburst had its desired effect. The single glimmer of resistance that Kevin's passions had managed to muster up was squelched. Satisfied and quite content with himself for so easily putting his son in his place, Edward began to talk. "As soon as the Rebels in Charleston began firing on Fort Sumter on Friday, rumors started flying that the Federal government was going to call out the state militia. Seeing an opportunity to further *your* career, I wired Governor Olden and solicited him, on your behalf, for a commission."

Kevin was confused. "But I thought you had campaigned against Olden."

A self-satisfied smile came across Edward's face. "I did,

114

boy, I did. Had to. Olden's sympathies are too closely tied to the Black Republicans for his and our own good.''

"Then why would he do you a favor?"

"Politics, boy, and a return favor. This decrepit old man that you and your former brother have spent so much time learning to hate and despise is an important man in this state, one who knows how to work both sides of the tracks. Of course, I openly supported General Pierce in the last election. He was the choice of our party. But in politics, you never, never put all your eggs in one basket. With the help of Judge Shields, I, along with several other gentlemen throughout Middlesex County, secretly funneled funds into Olden's campaign. You see, the good Judge here wants a seat on the State Supreme Court and doesn't much care whose money buys it for him or which governor appoints him.''

Staggered by his father's cynicism, not to mention his mention of Judge Shields' duplicity, Kevin stepped back and sank into a chair. After a moment or two, he looked up from the floor at which he had been staring. "And what if I don't accept this commission? Many of the students over at Rutgers have already resolved to stay out of this affair. Except for the McNeel brothers from Texas and Andrew Moseley from Alabama, no one seems to be really keen on the idea of rushing off to war.''

"What other men's sons do is not my concern," Edward barked. "You, my boy, are committed.''

"Not if I refuse that commission.''

Edward Bannon leaned forward. "Would you give up that commission if it meant losing that lovely young girl? I really doubt that Judge Shields would allow his daughter to associate with a man who was chosen by the governor himself to defend his nation's honor and then refused to do his patriotic duty. Do you?''

Stunned by his father's implied threat, Kevin's face reddened as he grasped the arm of the chair with both hands. He had seen his father manipulate his brother. He had watched him use people, including himself, for his own purposes. But the idea of toying with the relationship between a man and a woman like this was unbelievable. It was, he imagined, the meanest thing that he had ever heard of. "You wouldn't dare.''

A self-satisfied smile lit Edward Bannon's face as he eased himself back into his chair. "I wouldn't dare what, boy?"

"You wouldn't dare make me out to be a shirker."

"Son, I don't have to do anything. You, and not I, would have to explain to that lovely young creature and her father why you turned down a commission in the state militia at a time when your country needs you."

Kevin's realization that his father had shoved him into a corner with the same astuteness that he used when swindling his business partners out of their fair share of profits was like a slap in the face. To accept the commission would mean placing himself in a position of responsibility that he simply was not ready for. Yet, if he didn't, he would most certainly lose Harriet. For while Judge Shields could overlook his ancestry, cowardliness, even if it was just a perception, was an entirely different matter.

Standing up, Kevin looked down at his father. There was anger in his eyes. Anger and hate. In an instant, however, the anger was gone, almost as if a safety switch had been thrown by Kevin's inability to confront his father. With a visible slumping of his shoulders, Kevin capitulated to a situation that, in truth, had been out of his control from the beginning. Satisfied that all was in order, Edward Bannon's smile softened. "Boy, why don't you run along and inform Mrs. Shields that we are ready to join them for tea. I'm sure she'll be pleased."

Without a word, Kevin turned and marched off, in compliance with his father's wishes.

## The Virginia Military Institute, Lexington, Virginia

Impatiently the cadets waited in ranks for the order that everyone had been anticipating. Since word reached them on Thursday, April 18th, that Virginia had finally for all intents and purposes seceded from the Union, there was little doubt that the corps of cadets would be called upon to defend the state. The

1860 Virginia Militia Bill, enacted in the aftermath of John Brown's raid at Harpers Ferry, recognized the cadets and their faculty officers as part of the state's military establishment. Use of the corps during time of need, such as at John Brown's hanging, was ample proof to the cadets that when the time came, they would be standing in the front ranks of Virginia's military forces. The question about which flag those forces would muster under had been solved on April 15th when Abraham Lincoln had called on all the states, including Virginia, to raise seventy-five thousand troops "to exercise the laws of the Union; and to suppress insurrection." When Governor Letcher of Virginia responded the next day to Secretary of War Simon Cameron with a note that stated that the "militia of Virginia will not be furnished to the powers in Washington for any such use or purpose as they have in view," all doubt as to how Virginia would go was gone. Months of heated debate and anxious discussions were at an end. Now, with their prayers for action finally answered, every young heart in the corps of cadets waited for the order that would send them to war.

But on that Sunday morning, after hours of feverish preparations and a hurried noon meal that few cadets ate, one hundred and seventy-six cadets and eight faculty officers waited, fully equipped and standing to in ranks, for their commander to give that order. To their chagrin, Major Thomas J. Jackson, in charge of the movement, sat calmly on a camp stool that he had produced as if by magic, and watched the barracks clock as the cadets and their officers stood idle in the ranks and watched him.

Off to one side of that formation stood Will McPherson and James Bannon. Like many of those who would remain behind, they watched Jackson as he waited for the appointed hour to strike. All told, there were forty-seven cadets who would not be making the trip to Richmond with Major Jackson and the bulk of the corps. Rather than serving as drill instructors to the military forces of Virginia now assembling there, Will, James, and the rest of those chosen to remain behind would guard the arsenal and the military stores remaining at VMI. This, of course, did not sit well with Will. "After all this time," he had shouted when he had seen his name posted as part of the guard force, "I will not be denied. I refuse to sit down here, far away

117

from the heat of battle, while everyone is up there, with the rest of Virginia's Army, teaching those Yankees a good lesson.''

Since the flagpole incident, Will no longer made an effort to hide his feelings about the North and Yankees as he had before in deference to James. ''I don't give a damn what Abner Couper says,'' he had told James after the Saturday crisis. ''In my eyes, James, you're just as much a Virginian as any man born in this Commonwealth.''

James, as always, kept his own counsel. His actions on the 13th had been a reaction, not a deliberate act. That he had stood in ranks with the other cadets for the express purpose of helping a friend did not, to him, commit him to becoming an active participant in the defense of Virginia or the Southern cause. While it was true that he could not go back home, and had no desire to do so even if the opportunity arose, it was also true that he was less than motivated to rush off to war at the first blare of the bugle. Thus his selection to remain behind to guard the Institute suited him just fine. He could do his duty for his newly adopted state without the need to actively campaign or fight.

''Good Lord!'' Will exclaimed as he thrust his arm out toward Jackson. ''Look at the man, sitting there like a bump on a log, waiting for God knows what.''

James smiled. ''It's not one o'clock yet, Will.''

''What's that got to do with it? I mean, what's he waiting for? The corps has eaten, they're formed up. Even Dr. White's prayer and invocation have been given. They're ready! Everyone but Old Jack is ready.''

With a chuckle, James folded his arms across his chest and leaned against the barracks wall. ''Oh, Major Jackson's ready, all right. He's just waiting for the clock to strike one and he'll be off.''

''But why wait, James? It seems foolish to me and, I'm sure, to every cadet out there.''

''Major Jackson's orders were to move at one and neither heaven nor hell is going to get him to budge one minute before that. You don't think something like this little ole war is going to change his manner of doing his duty, do you?''

''Well, I think it's silly. Bullheaded and silly.''

''And I, Will McPherson, think it is rather comforting and

reassuring. It's sort of nice to see at least one person who hasn't lost his head and taken to running about like a chicken with its head cut off.''

James' comment caused Will to raise an eyebrow. ''There are times when I think you're as thickheaded as he is. First you refuse to protest your posting with the guard force. Now you defend Old Jack's peculiar behavior. Sometimes, James, I worry about you.''

Glancing over at the cadets in ranks, James smiled when he saw Abner Couper standing ramrod stiff to the rear of his company. Anyone, James thought, would be delirious over the prospect of being separated from his tormentor for the first time in over a year and a half. As soon as he had found his name on the posting, James had searched for Abner's. When he saw that Abner was going to Richmond, James had cried out with joy, a cry that Will had misunderstood. Had he not been so angry over his own assignment, Will would have been able to see the advantage that the situation offered to James. But Will could not see beyond his own disappointment. Instead, he lamented, over and over again. ''Oh, Lord, this war is going to pass me by and there's nothing I can do about it.''

With the striking of one o'clock, Major Thomas J. Jackson rose from his camp stool. For a moment, he looked up and down the ranks, studying the faces of the cadets, all of whom he knew by name. Raising his head a little, Jackson drew in a deep breath and issued his first order of the war. ''By files left, march!''

With the echoing of commands and the crashing of drums, the corps of cadets, company by company, executed Jackson's orders with precision and ease. Within minutes, they were gone from view.

When only the faint rumble of drums could be heard, Will gave his forty-four-button coat a tug at its hem. ''Well, they're gone, and we're not.''

James straightened up. ''You didn't expect them to change their mind about leaving you here, did you?''

''I had hoped they would, James. Now, I have no choice.''

''What do you mean, you have no choice?''

With an angry expression on his face and an edge in his voice, Will turned to James and barked at him. ''That's just what I said. They have left me no choice. Are you coming with me or not?'' Without waiting for a response, Will turned and began to walk away from James and downhill toward Lexington.

Having no idea what his roommate was talking about, and fearful that he was about to do something foolish or rash, James followed.

In minutes they had reached the busy center of Lexington, normally quiet to the point of being dead on a Sunday afternoon. But today was anything but an ordinary Sunday. The avalanche of recent events had created an almost carnival atmosphere in the otherwise sleepy little farm community. First came the news of Fort Sumter. This event, in faraway South Carolina, had triggered the flagpole incident of the 13th. Next came Lincoln's call for troops and Letcher's response, which inflamed pro-Southern passions and all but quelled the formerly dominant Unionist voice of Lexington. Within days of this came Virginia's secession. The announcement of secession prompted the mustering in of the town's militia company, the Rockbridge Rifles. Departing on the 18th, they joined other companies from the upper Shenandoah Valley as they headed for Harpers Ferry, on Virginia's northern border.

The Rockbridge Rifles had no sooner departed when word spread throughout the county that another company, calling themselves the Rockbridge Grays, was forming. This call to arms brought a new flock of people into town. Friends and relatives, as well as the recruits themselves, gathered to witness the mustering in of that unit on Saturday, April 20th. Many were still on hand on Sunday to witness the VMI cadets as they headed out of Lexington for Richmond. The necessity of parading through town to meet the coaches that would take them to Staunton, where they would transfer onto a train, provided another patriotic event for the entertainment of the townspeople as well as an opportunity for politicians to speak and church leaders to preach.

In the midst of all of this, and in part inspired by it, the opening of recruitment for another company began in the lobby of the only hotel in town. Charles A. Emit, a prominent town lawyer, graduate of the University of Virginia, and politician-in-waiting, had missed his chance to join the Rockbridge Grays because he had been away on business. Returning to Lexington, he quickly became fired up with enthusiasm and a burning desire to "join the fun." Taking advantage of the crowd gathered to watch the Rockbridge Grays, Emit stood up in his carriage and addressed the noisy, excited throng about him. "My fellow citizens. Now, today, is the time for all loyal sons of the great state of Virginia to come to her defense. Let us not stand here, on the sidelines, and watch our friends and neighbors march off, leaving us and our honor in the dust. Rather, let every able-bodied male of Lexington rise up and defend his home, his community, and his state. Dear brothers, follow me and make your mark on history." Greeted by a thunderous ovation and joyous cries of support, by dusk, Charles Emit had enrolled better than forty men into his self-styled Lexington Defenders company. When the rally was concluded for the night and all prospective recruits either signed up or too drunk to care, he promised to reopen recruitment on Sunday, so as to build himself a full company which he, of course, would command.

Heading straight for town at a pace that was more of a run than a walk, Will said nothing to James, who was having a time keeping up with him. With a determined look, Will plowed through the crowd gathered outside the hotel with James right behind him. Making their way into the lobby, they found themselves right in the middle of another crowd drawn there by Charles Emit's recruiting effort. Pausing, the two cadets looked about. To the left, near the bar, was a gaggle of excited men milling about three tables that had been pushed together. "That must be them, James. It has to be."

Looking at the throng at the bar, James shook his head. While some were busy talking loudly and slapping each other on the back, as if congratulating each other, others were drinking freely, despite this being a Sunday. Off to the right, in ones and twos, other men stood about with their hands in their pockets, looking on. James concluded that these were either men who had come in to see what was going on or who hadn't screwed up their nerve yet to make their mark. It was then, when he saw Will make a sharp turn to the left and head for the tables near the bar, that James realized for the first time what Will was about to do. Reaching out, he took hold of his friend's arm. "Will, are you crazy? You can't go off and join up like this. Your duty is back at VMI."

Will turned and gave James a hard look. "James, no one, especially Colonel Smith, is going to stand in the way of a Virginian who's answering the call to arms. And even if he did, I'll be damned if I'm going to sit here on my hands and miss the chance to be a part of this war."

"But you won't. You are part of it already. And you have your orders. In time, when all the military supplies at the Institute have been shipped to Richmond, I'm sure we'll go too. All you have to do is be a little patient."

"James," Will pleaded. "I can't wait. You've heard what everyone said about this war. One big battle and it will all be over. I'm afraid if I wait, I'll miss that battle. And if I miss it, I'll never be able to live with myself."

Like Will, James had listened to all the talk at VMI and read every newspaper that he could lay his hands on. He wasn't taken in by all the bold and arrogant claims made by politicians such as a North Carolinian who stated that all the newly raised Confederate Army would need to do was "just throw three or four shells among those blue-bellied Yankees, and they'll scatter like sheep." Yet, he did believe that this war, out of necessity, would be a short one. "I'm sure, Will, that once the people up North see that you, I mean we, are serious about standing up for our rights, they'll give in and let the South go in peace." Then, thinking about what he had just said, James added, "It's not that the folks up North are cowards. It's just that they have different goals in life than you and the other native-born Southerners. Everyone up North is working for a better future for themselves and their children. War, especially one with fellow Americans, doesn't make sense, and as soon as they realize this, it will all be over."

That such talk had contributed to Will's single-minded drive to join up as soon as he could didn't occur to James, either then or now. Like everyone else, the two cadets were caught up in events that both pushed and pulled at them at a breakneck speed that didn't allow time for cool, reflective thinking. "We are all," a professor had stated one day to James' class, "like tiny boats caught at sea in the eye of a terrible storm. Each man must steer a wise and prudent course, weathering the storm as best he can.'' For Will, that course led straight to the table where Charles Emit sat enrolling men for his company.

''Next,'' Emit called out after the second of two lanky farmers who were brothers finished making his mark on his enlistment papers. With James just behind him, Will stepped forward. Looking up at the cadet in his natty gray uniform, Charles Emit smiled. ''What seems to be the problem here, son? Missed the stagecoach for Staunton?''

The men gathered about Will started to laugh, causing him to turn beet red in anger. ''I'm here to enlist in your company.'' The determination in his voice, combined with a hint of anger, caused another ripple of laughter to go through the gathering of men. Clenching his fists, Will looked about the room. ''I'm as good as, if not better than, any man in this room. And if any man here wants to test me, I invite him to step outside, now.''

From all over the room a chorus of jeers and sharp comments greeted Will's threat. ''Hey, Marty,'' one of the barefooted farmers yelled to his brother, ''this here child sounds serious. The captain better sign him up 'fore he runs home and tells his mama that we were mean to him.''

The comment and more laughter added to Will's anger. Turning this way and that, he looked for someone to strike at. After nerving himself up to do this, the last thing he had expected was to be heckled. Now that he was inches away from his goal, Will had no intention of backing down. Yet his temperament would not let him take lightly the comments from the men, most of them older than James and Will. James knew this and stepped forward. Taking Will's arms from behind, he leaned forward to whisper a word of caution in his friend's ear. ''That's right, sonny,'' another voice called out in a drunken slur. ''Hang on to yer friend there fer me 'cause I'm startin' ta shake in my boots.''

Seeing that things were starting to get out of hand, Charles Emit leaned forward and cleared his throat to get Will's attention. ''Ah, son, if you're here to join up, then you and your friend will have to do so as privates. The boys who signed up yesterday elected the officers last night, and we picked all of our sergeants and corporals this morning.''

Will took one last angry glance about the room before turning to face Emit. "That, sir, will be fine by us. All my friend and I want is a chance to fight."

Emit smiled. "Well, so long as you make sure you save some of your fighting for the Yankees, the two of you are welcome." With that, he handed Will a pen and showed him where to sign his enlistment paper. With a flourish, Will signed his name.

Standing up, he cocked his head back, looked about the room. Turning to James, he handed the pen to him. "Here, James, your turn."

Flabbergasted, James looked at Will, down at Charles Emit, then around the now silent room. Every eye was on him, waiting for him to sign his enlistment paper. He hadn't come down here to do this. He hadn't even known what Will had been up to until they had stepped into the fray of men milling about the table where Emit sat. That Will had done so had been a shock. That he was now expected to do so too was incredible.

Yet there he was, at his friend's side, just as he had been the week before as the corps of cadets had formed up in preparation to do battle with the town militia. Like the chain of events that had led him south, and to this moment, each step had been taken without thought, without any clear vision of what to follow. That Will's action left him no choice, just as his father had given him no choice well over a year before, became painfully obvious as Emit, Will, and every man around him grew more impatient with each second he hesitated.

Slowly, mechanically, James stepped forward, leaned over, and signed his name just below where Charles Emit pointed. Finished, he stood up and looked down at Emit's smiling face. "Welcome to the Lexington Defenders, Private Bannon. Now, belly on up to the bar and have yourself a stiff one. It looks as if you could use it."

Ignoring the laughter of the men about him, James pushed his way through the crowd. From out of nowhere, a complete stranger handed him a shot glass of whisky. "Here you are, lad. Bottoms up for Old Virginia and the Confederate States of America."

With a nod, James took the glass to his lips, closed his eyes, and jerked his head back, taking the whisky in one clean swallow. Shaking as he felt the whisky flow down his throat, James looked back at the stranger who had given him the drink. "Yes," he said, "to whatever."

Then turning away, he walked out and went back to the barracks alone.

## CHAPTER 7

# June, 1861
# Arlington Heights,
# Virginia

THE THOUGHT THAT IT WOULD SOON BE NOON AND TIME FOR a break from the morning drill did little to cheer Kevin Bannon. Like the fourth and fifth sergeants of the company, whom he stood between, he marched behind the first platoon, waiting for the order that would swing them to the right and into line. Up ahead, in front of and centered on the first platoon, was the company commander, Captain Ambrose Milner, a thirty-two-year-old lawyer from Newark with political aspirations. Directly behind Kevin, leading the second platoon, was the company's first lieutenant, Morton J. Donovan, a divinity student who had left his studies at Princeton when, in his words, "God called me forth to be his sword arm." Kevin didn't much like either of them, and they both, together and separately, returned the feeling.

The true reason for this mutual dislike was hard to pinpoint. Kevin, always sensitive about his ancestry, suspected that it was due to his Irish background. The enlisted men of the company, on the other hand, believed their commander and his deputy didn't like Kevin because he had prior military training and they didn't. Kevin soon gave up his search for a reason. His sole interest now, as it had been since joining the 2nd Regiment, New Jersey Militia, was to do what was required, avoid both Milner and Donovan as much as possible, and, at the end of his ninety days, return to Rutgers. Kevin was greatly aided in this by Milner's habit of sending him off on every detail requiring an officer that came his way. Kevin even suspected that Milner went out of his way to find additional duties at regiment that would keep Kevin from getting underfoot.

Despite his desire to stay clear of Milner, these duties, and the regularity with which he was assigned them, bothered Kevin in the beginning. Even the company's first sergeant felt Kevin was being unduly punished for being too knowledgeable about the simple drill that his company commander still found mystifying and complex. A tall man with broad shoulders who had worked as shop foreman in a Newark shoe factory, the first sergeant had a dislike for Irishmen that came as naturally to him as the breath he drew.

Still, the necessity of a common purpose overrode this feeling. As the weeks went by, the first sergeant took a liking to Kevin, complaining to him often. "Those two gentlemen," the first sergeant often remarked to Kevin, whenever their company drill was going astray, "would do well to consult you instead of sending you on all those wild-goose chases they are so fond of." Though the first sergeant's feelings about the Irish kept him from adding the "sir" that military courtesy mandated when addressing an officer, Kevin never chose to make an issue of it. That the first sergeant addressed him with a grudging respect was good enough for Kevin.

While what the first sergeant said might have been true, Kevin found that it was to his advantage to say nothing and accept the various missions and tasks. Shortly after arriving in Washington, during a particularly bad drill period, the first sergeant turned on Kevin. Fed up with watching the company move about the drill field, stumbling out of step and bumping into other companies like drunken sailors, the first sergeant blasted Kevin. "Damn it, Lieutenant," he bellowed without any regard to who heard him, "when are you going to open your mouth and go out there and take charge of this mob?"

Rather than becoming angry at the first sergeant's outburst, Kevin looked up and gave him a faint smile. "While that might be advisable, First Sergeant, from my standpoint it would not be wise. As the company's second lieutenant, I'm expected to be military in appearance and quiet as a church mouse."

Caught off guard by Kevin's composure and response, the first sergeant stared blankly at Kevin while Kevin explained.

"From our first day at Camp Olden in Trenton, every time I offered Captain Milner advice, I found myself condemned to endless hours of wandering about on some fool's errand or another. And while I agree that it would be beneficial to have someone who at least is familiar with Scott's tactics out there training the company, I'm not going to say another word." Stepping back and crossing his arms, Kevin cocked his head. "You see, First Sergeant, I am tired of counting frying pans, inspecting tentage, searching for nonexistent equipment, and other such foolishness. All I'm interested in right now is following my orders and, when the time comes, going back to my studies at Rutgers." He wanted to say "and the Union be damned" but felt that doing so would alienate him from the first sergeant and many of the men who still believed fervently in the holy mission for which they had volunteered.

After that, while the first sergeant never again pushed for Kevin to exert himself, he never missed the chance to point out, in a voice loud enough so that Kevin could hear, his displeasure with Milner's ineptitude at drill. Rather than the crisp call of "Left, right, left," the men of Milner's company only heard the first sergeant's muted curses as the company stumbled this way and that.

Kevin's response was only partially true. As May eased into June and June passed by at a snail's pace, the little tasks and duties given to him made the time pass more quickly. He even found some of the duties enjoyable, for they provided him an opportunity to visit other units. During these visits he met officers and soldiers from other states with whom he was able to strike up friendships, which eluded him in his own regiment. His duties also allowed him to see things, both in the city of Washington itself and its surrounding countryside, that he had never seen before. All the while, as he roamed about from one camp to another or from depot to depot, he was learning about the Army and the system that made it run. In doing so, he also found that he had a talent for the administrative staff work that befuddled other officers in the 2nd New Jersey Militia as completely as Scott's manual on infantry drill and tactics.

128

As he had most of the days that preceded it, Kevin marched in his assigned spot behind the company's first platoon, thinking of everything but what he was doing. What use, he wondered as he looked at the heels of the soldiers in front of him, would his new-found knowledge be when the regiment finished its ninety days of service at the end of July? There wasn't even a rumor in camp or on the streets of Washington about when the Army would move out and fight the big battle that everyone expected would end the Southern rebellion. The only forward movement Kevin's regiment had participated in had been a short march from the city of Washington itself on May 24th over the Long Bridge into Virginia. There, near Arlington Heights, they occupied the high ground at a place called Columbia Springs. After that less than spectacular advance, which was totally unopposed by the Rebels, the 2nd Regiment, New Jersey Militia, settled into the same dull routine that had occupied it on the north side of the Potomac; drill and construction of fortifications. So the little duties and tasks that Kevin's company commander seemed to contrive and invent to keep him out of sight and mind kept Kevin busy and entertained.

With his mind roaming freely over these and other, more distant thoughts, Kevin missed Milner's command, "On the right into line, guide right." Only when the fourth sergeant, to Kevin's left, nudged him, did Kevin realize that a command had been given. Looking up, he glanced to the right and saw his company commander already moving to the right flank to a point where he would serve as the first platoon's guide. In place, Milner looked back over his left shoulder and gave the command, "March."

Awkwardly the two ranks of the first platoon began their movement to the right by files. The soldier on the extreme right in the front rank was the first sergeant. On the order of march, he pivoted to the right and slowed his pace. Jerking his head to his left, he watched as the first platoon's first two files of two men each broke off and faced to the right. Marching forward, these first two files, in two ranks and shoulder to shoulder, guided toward him. In this they were successful. When he saw that each successive pair of files was facing the new company front and roughly aligned to his left, the first sergeant stepped off and began to advance to where Milner stood.

Milner, having given the order, had faced to the front and didn't see the movement of the first platoon. Only when the first sergeant came abreast of him did he belatedly give the command, "Halt."

With a disjointed jerk, the first platoon came to a stop. Without hesitation, the first sergeant stepped out to his front, faced left, and moved down to the left flank of the first platoon, quietly ordering the soldiers of that platoon to dress and cover as he went by them. Like Kevin, the first sergeant knew that Milner would, as he usually did, stand silently rooted to the piece of ground that he had planted himself on and forget to give the order to dress right. In the rear of the first platoon, Kevin looked about. Satisfied that he was in his assigned position, he looked over his shoulder to watch Donovan maneuver the second platoon around into line to the left of the first platoon.

Unfortunately, Donovan, looking straight ahead and marching with great strides, didn't issue any orders as the second platoon marched past the left end of the first. Kevin watched as the company's second sergeant, serving as the guide for the second platoon, looked to his right, then at Donovan, and then back to the right with a worried look on his face. He, as well as the first sergeant, who was watching from his post, knew that Donovan had missed his mark for giving the orders that would be necessary to bring the second platoon up in line with the first platoon. Neither man, however, said a word. They, like Kevin, had found that Donovan, like Milner, didn't take kindly to being corrected by anyone when drilling the company. So they watched, looks of disgust creeping across their faces, as the second platoon marched briskly farther and farther away from Milner and the rest of the company.

Donovan and his errant platoon had marched a good fifty yards before it dawned on Captain Milner that something was wrong. When he finally looked to his left and saw the second platoon marching off, a worried look flashed across Milner's face. Hurriedly, he took several paces out in front of the first platoon and yelled, "Lieutenant Donovan. Bring your platoon into line." Using his sword, Milner pointed to where the first sergeant stood, face turned upward toward the sky as he mumbled a silent prayer to see him through these trials. "Bring your platoon back to here," Milner shouted to Donovan. "Quickly, sir, quickly."

Realizing his error, Donovan immediately halted his platoon. Stepping to the right, he looked back at Milner, who continued to point to where he wanted Donovan to maneuver his platoon. Like an engineer confronted by a problem, Donovan looked at Milner, over his shoulder at his platoon, then back at Milner as he pondered how best to do what Milner wanted. Seeing that his first lieutenant was completely befuddled, Milner returned his sword to its sheath and stalked off to where Donovan stood. Not wanting the soldiers of the second platoon to hear what he expected to be a heated rebuke, Donovan likewise sheathed his sword and hurried toward Milner, meeting him halfway. Knowing that this would take some time, and seeing that Milner and Donovan had left both platoons at attention and at shoulder arms, Kevin called out to the first sergeant. "Have the men in both platoons come to order arms and rest."

With a sharpness in his voice that betrayed his anger, the first sergeant complied, giving the order first to the platoon he was with and then signaling to the second sergeant to do likewise. After bringing his own rifle down to order arms, the fourth sergeant turned toward Kevin. "Well, sir, looks like another long day ahead of us."

Kevin was about to respond to the fourth sergeant's cynical remark when a drummer boy, serving as a runner for the regimental staff, came trotting up to Kevin. "Sir. The adjutant requests your presence at headquarters, immediately."

Glad to be freed from the bumbling drill period, Kevin returned the drummer boy's salute. "Thank you, boy. Please run along and inform Captain Van Reipen that I'll be along in a minute." Turning to the fourth sergeant, then the fifth sergeant, Kevin smiled. "Well, gentlemen, as much as I hate to leave you, duty calls. Please inform Captain Milner, when it's convenient, where I am."

The fifth sergeant, half in jest, shouted to Kevin as he walked away, "You wouldn't be needing any help at regiment now, would you, Lieutenant?" Without looking back, Kevin laughed. Raising his right hand, he waved good-bye to the fifth sergeant as the two widely separated platoons of the company stood in ranks with nothing better to do than to bake in the hot noonday sun as they watched Milner and Donovan sort out their errors.

Expecting to be sent far afield on another assignment, Kevin was taken aback by the sight of Harriet Shields. Halting for a moment, he watched as Harriet, seated in the tent that served as the regimental adjutant's office, chatted with Colonel Henry M. Baker, the commander of the 2nd Regiment, New Jersey Militia, and Captain Cornelius Van Reipen, the regimental adjutant. Harriet was resplendently dressed in a light green skirt with matching short vest, a white blouse with great billowy sleeves, and a trim and stylish black felt riding hat. With her hands resting in her lap, she laughed politely as the colonel and the adjutant told her amusing stories of camp life. Pausing, Kevin looked down at his own dust-covered uniform, soaked with sweat and smelling quite gamy. Embarrassed for the first time in weeks over his appearance, Kevin began a vain attempt to brush off as much of the dust as he could.

Out of the corner of her eye, Harriet caught sight of Kevin's hasty and futile effort to tidy himself up. "Ah," she commented to Baker and Van Reipen, "there's my gallant young warrior."

Her use of such terms when speaking of him caused Kevin to blush, something that both Baker and Van Reipen noticed. "You might add, Miss Shields," Colonel Baker stated, "modest."

"And," Van Reipen added, "quite an effective administrator."

Looking back at Harriet, Colonel Baker explained. "You must forgive Cornelius, here. Ever since he found that your young beau has a talent for staff work and getting things done that bewilder others, he's been at me day and night with pleas to have Kevin assigned to the regimental staff as his assistant."

Uncomfortable with such talk and eager to put an end to it, Kevin stepped forward quickly and saluted as he reported to Captain Van Reipen. "Sir, the runner said you wished to see me?"

"Not I," responded Van Reipen as he nodded toward Harriet. "Miss Shields, who has graced my humble tent with her presence, demands an audience with you."

While Harriet was amused by Van Reipen's effort at gallantry, Kevin felt uncomfortable and ill at ease. Sensing this, after little more than a glance, Harriet turned to address the colonel and Van Reipen. "As much as I would love to stay and hear more of your recent adventures, I am afraid that I do not have much time and would like to spend as much of it with Kevin as possible."

Though saddened to lose Harriet's pleasant company, Colonel Baker was quick to respond that he understood. It would not do, after all, to offend the daughter of a man as politically powerful as Judge Melvin Shields or the son of a man who commanded both wealth and considerable influence back home. After casually mentioning to Van Reipen that it was time for their noonday meal, Baker and his adjutant took their leave and left for the officers' mess.

With Baker and Van Reipen gone, Kevin entered the tent, walked past Harriet, and dropped into a chair across from her. Exhausted and drained from three hours of drill in the sun, he removed his cap and began to mop the sweat from his forehead with a dirty white handkerchief he had retrieved from the breast pocket of his jacket. Only when he was ready did he look up at Harriet with a forced smile. After staring at her for a moment, he realized that he needed to say something. "Your presence is quite a surprise," he said blandly.

Seeing that he was at a loss as to what to say and tired, Harriet decided that she needed to do most of the talking for a while. "The Judge," she began to explain, "had business to tend to with members of Congress from New Jersey, as well as the Supreme Court. Since Washington is now secure from attack by the Rebels, he decided to come down here in person rather than trust sensitive matters to the mail." Though she hadn't explained what that business entailed, Kevin had no doubt that it was more political than judicial. From the beginning, Kevin had suspected that Judge Shields' warm affection toward him was purely out of necessity rather than fondness. Keeping his dark thoughts to himself, Kevin listened as Harriet went on, nodding every now and then at what he assumed was an appropriate time.

"Well, seeing as the Judge was going to come down here," Harriet continued, "I decided to tag along. Mother, of course, was dead set against it, but I refused to be put off. Lord knows when I'll get to see you again." Kevin chuckled to himself. He knew exactly when he would see her again; the day after his ninety days with the 2nd New Jersey Militia was done and he was mustered out.

He was in the midst of this thought when Harriet abruptly changed the subject. "Kevin, I brought a picnic lunch with me in the hope that we would be able to steal away for a few hours." The thought of being able to enjoy decent food and spend time alone with Harriet brought the first genuine smile to his face since he'd set eyes on her this day. Seeing that her invitation had achieved the desired effect, Harriet stood up. "If you would be so kind as to take us somewhere far from the prying eyes of your fellow soldiers," she said as she cut a sideways glance at a group of soldiers gathering outside the tent, "I promise to treat you to a feast that will carry you through this terrible war and on to victory."

Though annoyed by the sickening sweet rhetoric about victory that Harriet used, Kevin ignored it. It seemed that women everywhere, not to mention newspaper editors, were in the habit of reciting such insane comments these days. Kevin resigned himself to suffering such talk in silence, as he did his commander's fumbling efforts at company drill. Standing up, he offered Harriet his arm. "As always, Miss Shields, it would be an honor and a privilege to accompany you." Then, with an air of gallantry, he added, "The Army will simply have to go on without me for a while."

Nestled under the cool shade of trees not far from the Arlington estate of Robert E. Lee, Harriet and Kevin enjoyed the picnic lunch that had been prepared to Harriet's demanding specifications by the kitchen staff of Willard's Hotel. When they were finished, Kevin relaxed by lying on the ground with his head resting on Harriet's lap, while she read to him from a book of poetry she held in one hand. She gently ran the fingers of her other hand through Kevin's hair. Except for an occasional muttering of orders given by officers of the 8th Regiment, New York Militia, as they drilled their men in the distance, no other sounds and no person disturbed the idyllic and serene setting that Harriet had so skillfully arranged. Stretched out on his back, with his shell jacket off, collar opened, and eyes closed, Kevin felt so comfortable and at ease that he almost fell off to sleep as he listened to Harriet's sweet voice.

When she finally tired of reading, Harriet laid the book off to one side and brought her free hand down to rest on Kevin's cheek. "Why haven't you grown a beard or mustache yet, Kevin? It seems to be all the rage with many of the officers throughout the Army."

Not thinking, Kevin murmured his response. "Vermin, my dear. I see no point in providing the vermin another home to nestle in."

For the briefest of seconds she stopped running her fingers through his hair. Realizing what he had said, and feeling her tense up, Kevin opened his eyes and smiled. "Oh, sorry. I didn't mean that I have friends right now. Far as I know, I don't. But when it comes time to march off and fight the Rebs, if we ever do, then there's a good chance, the old soldiers say, of becoming a walking home for the little critters."

"What do you mean, Kevin, if you march off? Isn't this Army going to continue its march to Richmond and put down this rebellion soon?"

"Continue? We haven't even begun the march to Richmond. Our little foray into Virginia a few weeks ago was nothing more than an effort to save our own capital. No, my dear. This Army is going to need a lot more time and a damned sight more training before it's ready to move anywhere."

Appalled that he had used a curse word so casually in her presence, Harriet was about to reprimand Kevin but hesitated. He was, she told herself, in the Army after all, and that fact alone, from what she had heard, was enough in itself to corrupt a saint. Even her father, on their way down to Washington, had warned her that she would see and hear things that she hadn't before. Letting this indiscretion go, she continued to gently prod him with questions. "When do you suppose you'll be ready?"

"Well," Kevin answered with his eyes closed and a self-satisfied smile on his face. "If I'm lucky, the day after the regiment musters out."

This time there was no hiding the surprise and bewilderment she felt. With a sharpness in her voice that warned Kevin he had misspoken again, Harriet shot back, "What do you mean, after you muster out? Kevin Patrick Bannon, do you mean to tell me that you are not interested in defending the Union?"

Sitting up quickly and turning to face her, Kevin balanced himself on his knees as he reached out and gathered her hands in his. With as sincere an expression as he could manage, he hastened to undo the damage the slip of his tongue had caused. "Oh, no, dearest. That's not what I meant. Not what I meant at all. You see, I would love to go south and teach those people down in Richmond a thing or two. It's just that we're not ready. There isn't a single professional soldier in the whole regiment. All the drill and training needed to prepare for such an invasion takes time. If we were to go off now, half cocked and un-trained, the Rebels, defending their own homes, would stand a good chance of beating us."

"Are you saying," Harriet asked half in surprise, "that the secessionists are as good as our boys are?"

Her naiveté almost made him laugh. Were it not for his desire to smooth over his momentary indiscretion and the fact that the view she was expressing was a common one with many in the North, Kevin would have laughed. But he didn't. Instead, he continued to do his best to placate her. There was, he rea-soned, no sense in getting her angry over her silly ideas about a war that would soon be over. Moving closer to her on his knees without letting her hands go, Kevin continued to work his way through his dilemma. "Harriet, we all want the same thing. We all want to crush this rebellion with one mighty blow. But like everything else in life, these things take time, and try as hard as you can, they can't be rushed."

"But I thought you were ready. I mean, the newspapers are always talking about how well the regiments drill and of the grand host Mr. Lincoln has assembled here around the nation's capital. Don't tell me that all of that is a lie?"

Looking into her eyes, Kevin tried to explain to her how things in the Army worked as if she were a raw recruit. "My dearest Harriet, the newspapers oversimplify matters. You see, first the company officers and noncommissioned officers—sergeants and corporals—must learn their duties. Then they must drill their men, day after day, until they can perform all the complex maneuvers that are required to move a company about the battlefield. Once the companies are trained, they must be brought together by the regimental commander and his staff and trained to move and act as one. I will tell you, dearest, it is no easy thing to transform a regiment of more than seven hundred men from a march column on the road into a line of battle. And even when the regiments are ready, which many are not, they, in turn, must learn to work in cooperation with other regiments that they are brigaded together with. On top of all that, there are the artillery and the cavalry, for no one branch of service can work effectively without the others. So you see, like a tiny child, we must learn to walk first before we can run.''

When he was finished with his long-winded and hastily presented lecture on the basics of military tactics, Harriet looked down at their joined hands. Squeezing them, she sheepishly apologized. "I'm sorry I doubted your resolve to do your duty, Kevin. I just didn't understand what you meant when you said . . .''

Releasing her hands, Kevin moved himself around so that he was seated next to her. Wrapping his arm about her shoulders, he pulled her close to him. "There's no need to apologize. After all, Harriet, many people, including men holding high positions in the Federal government, don't understand the complexities of a modern army.''

"But I do feel badly,'' Harriet countered, "I do. After all, here you are down here, doing your duty, and I'm condemned to stay at home, in New Jersey, with nothing better to do than pine away and wait for your return.''

Harriet's lament was music to Kevin's ears, for this was the first time that she had actually admitted having deep feelings for him. What he didn't understand, and what Harriet didn't dare mention to him or anyone else, was her desire to somehow do something more concrete, more positive to help win the war for the Union. Only in her diary did she dare admit her dream of running off and joining the Army. To fight, as Kevin was preparing to do, had become her one true and burning desire. Being denied that opportunity because of her God-given gender, and frustrated in her efforts to find a role for herself that was both acceptable and useful, she found no other alternative but to live out her dreams, however vicariously, through Kevin.

Glancing to one side, Harriet watched a company of New Yorkers in the distance drill for a moment. They were young, she thought, all of them. Looking back at Kevin, she saw the same glow of unblemished youth in his smooth-shaven face. Leaning forward, she reached out with one hand and rested it on his shoulder. Kevin, not knowing what to expect, sat motionless as she brought herself up on her knees and softly kissed his forehead. Settling back on her heels, Harriet looked into Kevin's face. Kevin, feeling free of prying eyes, returned Harriet's kiss before settling down on his back with his head resting in her lap. Thus the two of them passed the rest of the afternoon lost in thoughts that neither dared reveal to the other.

# CHAPTER 8

# July, 1861
# South of Falling
# Waters, On the Road to
# Winchester, Virginia

SLUMPED OVER, WITH HIS EYES DOWNCAST, JAMES BANNON followed along behind the man to his front without thinking. Like the rest of the Lexington Defenders, he made his way slowly south through the choking dust kicked up by other units to their front. Though they had been redesignated Company J, 4th Virginia Volunteer Infantry in early May while still at Harpers Ferry, the men of the company Charles Emit had raised persisted in using their colorful and self-styled name. They were not alone in doing so. The Liberty Hall Volunteers, comprised mostly of seminary students from Washington College in Lexington, clung stubbornly to their adopted name, as did the Rockbridge Rifles. "No colonel appointed by some dad-blame governor in Richmond," one soldier in the Rifles snorted, "is going to take our proud name away."

Slowly, however, as May turned into June and June, in turn, made way for July, most of the men grew used to their new organizations, their officers, and the strict military order and changes they brought. Within days of their new brigade commander's arrival regular drill was introduced, often lasting five hours a day. Another change was the decommissioning of all militia officers above the rank of captain and their replacement with volunteers, many of whom had, at one time or another, been associated with VMI. Some who didn't, or couldn't, handle the new order of things refused to muster into regular service and, instead, returned to their homes in a huff.

139

Most of the men in James' company would have tolerated all these changes if they had been followed by some kind of immediate action. But nothing happened. The hardships and the trials of training and camp life at Harpers Ferry, made more demanding by an epidemic of measles, simply went on and on, day after day, with no promise of the big fight that everyone knew would bring an end to the war and Southern independence. This failure to come to blows with the enemy, more than anything else, grated on the men's nerves. Martin Hazard, one of James and Will's messmates, often complained bitterly about Colonel Thomas J. Jackson, their brigade commander. ''Ya'd think he was plannin' on winin' the war by outmarchin' and outdrillin' the Yanks.'' Whenever Martin made this, or a similar complaint, Will would patiently try to explain tactics and the need for drill to both Martin and his brother Matthew. Martin, however, had no head for such things and little patience. ''You don't understand, boy,'' Martin would counter. ''We ain't like you keydets. We're here for the fightin'. I wish you, your old fool professor, and all the West Pointers and keydets would go away and leave us alone. Why,'' Martin would exclaim, his eyes ablaze and his face flushed with excitement at the thought of a good fight, ''I bet we'd have this whole mess settled in less than a week, if they'd let us be.''

Will, always persistent and cheerful, and just as anxious to get into a fight as Martin and Matthew were, never gave up. ''Boys,'' he'd respond. ''Old Jack, he knows what he's doing.''

''Well,'' Martin would usually shoot back, ''he better do it soon or Matthew and I are gonna head back home. We got a farm to tend to, and I'm plannin' on marryin' as soon as I get home.'' When asked who he was planning on marrying, Martin would smile. ''Don't know yet. But as soon as I find me a good woman, I'll tell ya and then I'll tell her.''

All thoughts of marriage, the farm, or leaving had quickly left Martin's mind that morning as word was passed down early on the second day of July to form up and prepare to move. Within moments officers hurried about the camp, forming their companies or overseeing the packing of the unit equipment and supplies. Not that there was much equipment to be packed. Another change that Jackson had imposed on what was now being called the First Virginia Brigade was the elimination of all unnecessary baggage. This was almost as hard on some of the men in the brigade as the drill and reorganization. "How does Old Jack expect," Captain Charles Emit bitterly complained to anyone who cared to listen, "a gentleman to survive with little more than a waterproof ground cloth, a blanket, and a haversack?" Determined not to knuckle under to what he called military tyranny, Emit resigned his commission and returned to Lexington.

The nervous anticipation of the early morning that had put James Bannon and his regiment on the march to battle slowly faded as the promised coming to grips with the Yankees never came to pass. After rushing north from their camps near Martinsburg in the footsteps of Colonel Kenton Harper's 27th Virginia Infantry and Captain W. N. Pendleton's battery of artillery, the 4th Virginia and the 2nd Virginia did little but turn around and join the retreat south toward Winchester after Colonel Jackson confirmed that he was faced by a superior enemy force. Even when the word eventually trickled down to the men in the ranks that their overall commander, General Joseph E. Johnston, had ordered Jackson to avoid a general engagement and withdraw if the Union's Major General Robert Patterson came on in strength, few spared any kind words for their commander. "Well, boys," a man several ranks in front of James called out, "guess we just aren't drilled enough to suit Old Jack. Maybe next year."

Lost in his own thoughts, James paid no attention to Martin and Matthew's bantering. When the two brothers weren't fighting each other, they were busy trying to provoke one another. "Hey," Matthew shouted as he jammed a bony elbow into his brother's side. "There's a pretty girl up ahead that looks like your kind."

After a slight pause, Martin responded. "Well, she is kind of easy on the eyes. And besides," Martin added with a hint of mischief in his voice, "if she does do me the honor, maybe you and her horse can strike up a conversation. That is, of course, provided the horse isn't too picky about bein' seen with the likes of you."

The two brothers were in the midst of shoving each other as a prelude to a fistfight when the girl they were speaking of called out. "Will McPherson. Has anyone seen Will McPherson?"

Though he had met her only once, and that had been some nine months before, James recognized Mary Beth McPherson's voice. Lifting his head, he looked in the direction everyone else was looking in and saw her. Mounted on a big roan horse that seemed too much horse for so slight a girl, Mary Beth towered above the passing files of soldiers, her bonnet pushed back off her head and dangling on her back. James could see the worried look she wore as she scanned up and down the ranks, calling her brother's name. She, like other civilians in the area, had heard there had been a fight and come out to see what was going on or to check on loved ones.

Shifting his gear about on his shoulders, James straightened himself up. Behind him, Martin and Matthew had stopped their fighting. "Hey, Matthew, she's looking for our own Little Willie!" Martin shouted with glee in his voice. "You think she's his girl?"

"Her?" Matthew responded with a wink at his brother and a nod toward James that James did not see. "Naw, she's dressed too plain and rides that horse of hers like a boy. No self-respecting VMI keydet would associate with the likes of her."

James ignored Matthew's comment. Instead, he simply announced, so that both brothers could hear, "That's Will's sister, Mary Beth. She must have heard the firing and come out to see if Will was all right."

"Aw," Matthew announced. "Now isn't that just precious."

"Well," Martin countered, "I think it is. Shows good character in a girl to be concerned about her kinfolk. Now, if she can only cook."

Unable to ignore Martin's comment and seeing an opportunity to take a verbal swipe at him, James looked over his shoulder. "Marty," he said with an earnest look on his face, "I'm not too sure if she'd make you a good wife. Will's told me she's been to school and is planning on going to an all-girl college in Harrisonburg."

James' barb had its desired effect. The grin that had lit Martin's face turned into a frown as he looked down and thought for a moment. Then, looking up, he nodded in agreement. "Ya know, Jimmy boy, you might be right. Book learnin' has a tendency to mess up a woman's head something fierce. Maybe I'll just keep looking.'' Then, as an afterthought, he asked, ''Does she have a younger sister that hasn't learned to read yet?''

''No,'' James responded. ''Just a kid brother.''

Before Martin could say a word, Matthew chimed in, ''Well, now. He'll do nicely, seein' as how Martin's not particular.''

In a flash, Martin turned on his brother and, despite the rifle and equipment slung over his shoulder, landed a solid punch right in the center of Matthew's chest.

Ignoring the growing fistfight he had left behind him, James called out as soon as he was close enough for Mary Beth to hear and see him. ''Mary Beth. Over here.''

Not recognizing the voice or the face, she searched the mass of dirty upturned faces for its source. Only after James waved and again called out her name did she finally recognize who he was. When she did, there was no joy in her face, for she immediately looked all about James in search of her brother. ''He's not with us, Mary Beth.''

The sudden look of horror on her face told James that he'd picked his words poorly. Before he could explain to her what he meant, Mary Beth was off her horse and pushing her way through the ranks of soldiers. Pulling her horse behind her, she mumbled to herself and shouted to James as she went, ''Dear Lord, where is he? Is he hurt? Oh please, Lord, let him be all right.''

Angry at having alarmed her for no good purpose, James began to push his way forward through the ranks toward Mary Beth. Seeing the girl and her big horse rush at him and hearing James coming up behind him, the last man who stood between them stepped aside in order to avoid being mashed. This sudden move and their momentum caused the two young people to crash together. Embarrassed, Mary Beth tried to step back, but her horse's nose thumped her in the back and pushed her into James again. Reaching over her shoulder, James pushed the horse's head to one side, allowing Mary Beth to move out from between her horse and James.

Though she was now free, James, the horse, and Mary Beth were still blocking the road. From behind them several men, including an officer, shouted. ''Clear the road up ahead. Get that damned horse out of my column and off the road," the officer yelled.

Taking the horse's reins in one hand and Mary Beth's arm in the other, James escorted the two out of harm's way, muttering apologies as he went. Some of the soldiers in the company who enjoyed making fun of James and Will and were always anxious for a break in the tedium that was so much a part of military life made fun of James as he, Mary Beth, and the horse made their way past them. "Hey, boy," one gruff soldier yelled, "you plannin' on dating both of them, or can I have the girl?" As the horse went past another soldier in the company, he reached out and patted its rump. "Hey, Marty," he shouted over to Martin Hazard, "I've found you a wife!" Just then, the horse passed wind, causing the soldier to step back, waving his hands wildly before his face. "Lordy, Marty! This new girl of yours sure has the foulest breath I ever did smell."

Freed from the press of the packed soldiers and their jokes, James slid his rifle off his shoulder. Planting the butt of the rifle firmly on the ground, he leaned on it for support as someone would with a walking stick, before looking around to see if any of the officers or sergeants were eyeing him. Only First Lieutenant Theodore I. Lynn paid any attention to him, warning him not to linger too long and lose track of the regiment. Taking this as permission to stay where he was for a few minutes, James turned to Mary Beth to explain. "Will's not with us today because he was assigned to stay with the regiment's supply and baggage train when we began our march this morning."

The relief Mary Beth felt at hearing this was immediate and obvious. Bringing her right hand up to her bosom, she looked skyward and muttered a silent prayer. Finished, she looked back at James. "And you, James, are you all right?"

Smiling, he nodded. "Yes, I'm fine. We never did manage to get into the fight, not that it was much of a fight, from what I hear."

Anxious to hear news of the war firsthand, Mary Beth blurted, "Well, what happened? Can you tell me that? Because if you don't, I'll never hear anything about it."

"I need to be going. I'm sure you'd rather hear it from Will," James responded in an effort to break off their meeting.

144

"Will? Surely you can't be serious. He never tells us anything about what he's doing."

James looked at Mary Beth quizzically. "He certainly visits home often enough. You should know everything there is to know about this unit and what we do."

Mary Beth shook her head. "Not from our Will, God bless his soul. He's so afraid that he might say something that would offend Mama or get us worried that all he ever talks about is—" She was about to say "you," but stopped short. Instead, she looked down at the ground and slowly started to kick at the dirt with the toe of her boot, reminding James of something a schoolgirl would do when trying to play coy. "Well, he just doesn't say much, that's all."

Not knowing the reason for Mary Beth's sudden shyness, James cleared his throat. "Like I said, it wasn't much of a fight. A skirmish really. Colonel Harper's 27th, Pendleton's battery, and some of Colonel Stuart's Virginia Cavalry did all the fighting."

"Did we win?"

For a moment James wondered why she would ask such a question when it was obvious that they were in the middle of a retreat. Then, when he realized that she didn't know that they were retreating, he shook his head. "No, I guess we didn't."

Confused, Mary Beth looked back up at him. "What do you mean, you guess?"

"This wasn't supposed to be a major battle, Mary Beth. We were only supposed to delay them and then fall back to Winchester if the enemy came on in strength."

"Then you *did* lose. Does that mean that you're going to give up Winchester?"

"No," James responded quickly. "We're going to stop soon. At least, that's what the word is in the ranks."

"Good." She responded to this news with obvious delight. "That means that Will can come home more often." Then, turning back to her questions on the battle, "Have you seen any of the fighting?"

"No, none at all." Suddenly, he began to chuckle to himself.

Thinking that he was laughing at her questions, Mary Beth frowned. "What's so funny?"

"Oh, while we were up there, forming up to support the 27th

Virginia, a soldier from that unit came running down the road. He had no hat, no rifle, and was running for all he was worth. One of our officers tried to stop him, but the man didn't slow down a bit. When the officer yelled at him and asked why he was running, the soldier shouted back over his shoulder, "I'm runnin' 'cause I can't fly.''

James' little story caused Mary Beth to laugh. It was a light, gentle laugh that captivated him. Yes, he thought, she is a lovely and lively girl, just as Will described her. Noticing James' stare, Mary Beth again cast her eyes downward. "Mr. Bannon—''

"James, please.''

"James, I do hope that you will accept our invitation to come to dinner with Will next time. Mother and Father would love to have you. And Will would too. He thinks so much of you. Fact is, you're all he talks about. Mother always asks about you and reminds Will to bring you along every time he visits home, but you never seem to come.''

Now it was James' turn to blush. He was at a loss for words and unsure how to proceed, when a troop of riders came up behind them. A sharp, almost squeaky drawl from one of the riders caused James to spin around and come to attention without thinking. "I do hope, Mr. Bannon, that you're not planning on leaving us?''

Looking up, he saw Colonel Jackson, mounted on a short, powerfully built horse with a large neck that seemed too big for its body. Though Jackson called the horse Fancy, some of the men in the ranks were already calling the horse Little Sorrel because of its chestnut color. To Jackson's left was Lieutenant Colonel James Ewell Brown Stuart, whose simple gray uniform of the 1st Virginia Cavalry, topped with a floppy black hat sporting an ostrich feather, stood in stark contrast to Jackson's dingy blue VMI coat and cadet kepi. "Oh, no, sir," James responded quickly. "Miss McPherson, here, Cadet William McPherson's sister, had ridden out to inquire about the health of her brother.''

"I trust he is safe and in good health, sir?" Jackson inquired.

"Yes, sir. He's with the baggage train.''

"Fine, fine. Another cadet from VMI who has turned out to be a good soldier,'' Jackson commented as he looked over to

Stuart. "Now, miss," Jackson said as he looked down at Mary Beth, "we have work to do, and Mr. Bannon needs to rejoin his command." Then, without further adieu, he tipped his hat to Mary Beth and rode on. Jackson, Stuart, and the string of staff officers following him were passing by, each man tipping his hat to Mary Beth as they did so, when, out of the corner of his eye, James caught sight of a man he had thought he was through with in April: Abner Couper.

Unfortunately, Abner Couper had come to Harpers Ferry with Jackson at the end of April. Though neither James nor Abner was pleased to see the other, Couper, being assigned to the 4th Virginia as its adjutant, was in a far better position to continue his tormenting of James than he had been at VMI. The only saving grace for James was that Couper was a staff officer and, because of the chain of command and James' lowly position, James was able to avoid any direct dealing with him. Only the fact that there was far too much for the undermanned staffs of Jackson's brigade to do kept Couper from bothering James. As it was, he had little time to think about James, let alone do anything to him. Still, his mere presence was enough to bother James.

He was still watching Couper, long after he and the rest of the mounted officers had passed, when Mary Beth spoke. "I do hope that I didn't get you in trouble."

Shaking his head, he looked over at Mary Beth and smiled. "Oh, no trouble. None at all. Colonel Jackson is a tough taskmaster but he's not impossible, despite what everyone says about him."

"Will likes him too. Colonel Jackson and what he does are about the only military matters he talks about."

James canted his head to one side. "I thought you said I was the only thing that your brother ever talked about?" Though he hadn't meant it to be embarrassing, he'd obviously hit upon something that Mary Beth had not wanted him to discover, for his statement caused her eyes to widen noticeably and her cheeks to turn bright crimson. Not sure what to say or do, James looked over at the column of troops. Noticing that his regiment was well down the road, James nodded toward it. "I have to be going now." Then, without waiting, he began to back away.

Not wanting him to escape as he had before, Mary Beth took a step forward. "James?"

Seeing that she had something more to say and was determined to say it, he stopped. "Yes?"

"I was wondering if you would consider, if you have the time, of course, writing me, I mean us, every now and then and telling us about Will and camp life. Mother is always worrying about him, and she knows that he holds so much back. And Will doesn't want us to visit the camp, even when it is so close. He says an army camp is no place for a lady."

"Well," James interrupted, "he's right. Some of the boys, as you have seen, have a tendency to get a bit crude, especially when there's a woman around."

Though Mary Beth had no doubt that James was right, she had no intention of conceding the point to him. "Well, that might be true, but after being raised in the same house as two brothers, there isn't a whole lot I haven't seen or heard already."

Unwilling to argue the point, James just sighed.

"Regardless of what you and Will think," Mary Beth continued, "it would mean a great deal to me, I mean us, if we knew what he was going through and how he was faring."

Mary Beth's reaction to his comment and her stumbling about with the words "me" and "us" were the first sure indications that James had of her interest in him. Though he'd thought that he could have been mistaken at the inn at Natural Bridge, her manner this day left little doubt that she had an interest in him. As on that day at the inn in October of the previous year, James wasn't sure how he felt about Mary Beth's attention, let alone what he should do.

And as on that day, he sought resolution to the awkwardness of the situation through escape. Hoisting his rifle up and slinging it over his shoulder, James tipped his cap to Mary Beth. "Miss McPherson, I do need to be going now," he said, then turned to walk away.

From behind him, Mary Beth called out. "You will write, won't you?"

In haste, James turned his head, looked over his shoulder and, without thinking, answered quickly, "Yes, of course."

"Promise?"

He nodded. "Yes, I promise." Then, with a wave, he looked back to the front and began to pick up his pace in an effort to escape her as much as to catch up to his company.

Watching James merge back into the tightly packed ranks of soldiers and disappear, Mary Beth wondered what it was about her that made him so nervous. Thinking back over their last meeting and this one, she found nothing that she could think of in her conduct that would cause him to behave so . . . so distant. It was, she thought as she turned to remount her horse, as if he were afraid of her. That got her to wondering if James treated all girls in the same manner.

Looking down the column to where he had disappeared, Mary Beth threw her head back. "Well, Mr. Bannon, you've escaped again, but not for long." After pulling herself up into the saddle, to the cheers and hoots of passing soldiers, she looked down the long column again. Slowly, a smile lit her face. "You, sir," she said out loud, "shall be mine." With that, she dug her heels into her horse's flanks and jerked his head to the side as she galloped off toward home.

149

# CHAPTER 9

# July, 1861
# East of Centreville,
# Virginia

"*Up!* COME ON. EVERYONE UP AND ON YOUR FEET. ROLL CALL in five minutes."

The booming voice of the first sergeant startled Kevin out of what seemed like the only ten minutes of decent sleep he had managed since leaving their camp outside of Washington. With an effort, he pushed himself up from the black waterproof that separated him from the mud of the field they were bivouacked in and threw his blanket off. It was not quite dawn yet, though he could see a slight lightening of the sky off behind some trees to his left. That, he reasoned, must be east. Looking around, he could make out scores of other prone lumps and figures, soldiers like himself, still asleep under blankets on waterproofs laid out in the irregular furrows of the field they had been shuffled into.

"First Sergeant," Kevin called out with a raspiness that distorted his voice.

Without answering, the first sergeant walked over to where Kevin sat, searching for his canteen. As he passed several forms still lying motionless on the ground, the first sergeant, with the toe of his boot, lifted their blankets and kicked them off. "Come on, time to get a move on." As if to underscore this, a drum somewhere off in the distance began to beat reveille. Within seconds it was joined by a second, then a third. The succession of drumrolls, accompanied by the calls of officers and men, had become a riot of martial music and noise by the time the first sergeant reached Kevin.

While Kevin took a quick drink from his canteen in an effort to soothe his parched throat, the first sergeant squatted next to him and surveyed the scene around him. "I suppose, Lieutenant," he said half to himself, "it's always been like this—war, I mean. Funny how you never hear about the long, hot marches through clouds of choking dust or the miserable nights, sleeping in muddy farm fields."

Kevin tried to speak again, but his dry throat, irritated by the smoke thrown off by dozens of small cook fires scattered about the field, caused him to start hacking. After a moment, he was able to clear his throat again. "Well, both you and I have already found that there's a whole lot nobody's bothered to tell us about this business of war." After taking another swig, Kevin too looked about. Here and there, standing or squatting about small fires kept alive by the sentinels, soldiers were gathering, their uniforms in disarray and hands in their pockets or carrying a small coffeepot or frying pan. As on most other days since joining their company, the soldiers were taking care of what they considered their most immediate needs and doing whatever they saw fit as they waited for someone to tell them what to do. Coughing, Kevin shook his head as if to clear it, then turned to the immediate business at hand. "Has Captain Milner caught up yet?"

In the faint light, Kevin could see a look of disgust come across the first sergeant's face at the mention of their company commander's name. "No, that gentleman hasn't managed to rejoin us, Lieutenant. Seems those fancy riding boots of his cut the calves of his legs to ribbons. The man knows less about walking shoes than he does about drill."

Kevin managed only a grunt in return. While all had gone well on July 16th, the first day of their march had taken them less than three miles. The next day was different, proving little more than a disaster. Instead of reaching Fairfax Court House by late morning, in the wake of the rest of the Army, it was well into the evening before they were able to close up. Slowed by their own stragglers and hundreds from units to their front, Kevin's regiment spent the entire day on the road, moving forward only short distances in sporadic fits and starts. Sometime during this march Ambrose Milner had joined them, complaining of the heat. That was the last anyone had seen or heard of him.

"You think those gentlemen in command of this fine Army are finally going to get it moving again, Lieutenant?" the first sergeant asked with a hint of disgust in his voice.

"To tell you the truth, I've given up trying to predict what anyone outside our little company is going to do, First Sergeant."

"But do you suppose they're going to try to cross that creek again, like they did the other day?"

"The Bull Run? Of course, First Sergeant. They have to." Kevin threw his arms out as if he were trying to embrace the gathered host of men about him and looked to his left and right. "That, after all, is why we're here. The Rebels are south of the Bull Run and we're to the north. Since the Rebel generals don't seem to be in a hurry to attack us, I suppose our generals will want to attack them, and soon."

"You mean because we're supposed to muster out in a few days?"

"That, First Sergeant, and the fact that the same people in Washington who pushed our generals to begin the march on Richmond aren't going to take too kindly to seeing their Army sitting around, doing nothing just twenty-five miles farther down the road."

With a resigned air about him, the first sergeant sighed. "Well, if it comes to a fight today, Lieutenant, you'll be leading us."

Blinking his eyes, Kevin stuttered. "What do you mean, I'll be leading the company? What about Lieutenant Donovan?"

"Who?" the first sergeant responded with a hint of mischief in his voice. "Didn't I mention to you that Lieutenant Donovan went to the surgeon last night, complaining about stomach cramps?"

"No, First Sergeant, you didn't mention anything of the kind. How is he? Will he be back?"

Standing, the first sergeant looked down at Kevin and shook his head. "I have no idea. All I know is what the sentinel on duty reported to me when I was roused from my sleep this morning. Seems Mr. Donovan doesn't care much for our steady diet of salt pork and crackers." Then, looking about and seeing that the company was up and moving, the first sergeant added, "Which reminds me, unless you have any orders for the company, I'm going to hold morning roll call and have the men tend to their morning meals.''

Befuddled by the first sergeant's news, Kevin waved him away. At least, Kevin thought, as he started to feel about in search of his boots and other clothing, they were in reserve. A lot of other units crowded around Centreville farther down the road would have to be committed long before Brigadier General Runyon's Fourth Division saw any action. Of course, he reminded himself, if the fight at Blackburn's Ford on the 18th was any indication of how things would go, he might not have long to wait.

### Southwest of Centreville, Virginia, Along the Bull Run

Not long after sunrise the sound of firing somewhere off to their front alerted James, Will, and the Lexington Defenders that the fight was on. Quickly they formed up and waited, with the rest of the 4th Virginia, to be called forward into battle. When that call didn't come right away, and the anxious minutes started to stretch into an hour, and then two hours, the men began to speculate on what was happening around them as they idly lounged about in ranks. "Ya think," Matthew Hazard asked quizzically, "the Yanks are going to try crossin' the stream again today?"

"Oh, I doubt it," Will responded with an air of authority. "After all, they tried to force their way across down here the other day and failed. I doubt if they'd try again at this end, not after the way the boys of the 1st, the 11th, and the 17th Virginia under Longstreet handled them. The fighting, they say, was so fierce that a sergeant in the Bloody 17th ran out into the middle of the stream and got into a fistfight with one of the Yankees who wouldn't retreat.''

"Then why," Martin Hazard shouted, "is there so much commotion up front there?"

**153**

"Maybe," Will ventured, "General Beauregard's planning an attack of his own. I heard some of the officers talking about just such an attack last night while James and I were on guard duty up near the general's tent."

In disgust, Martin lifted his rifle, then smacked the butt of the rifle's stock on the ground as hard as he could. "Yeah, and maybe this is just like back in the valley. Maybe our hare-brained general has no idea what he's doing and we're gonna miss another battle. Maybe the real fight will be over 'fore we get there, just like before," Martin shouted.

James, who had been lying on his back on the ground, trying to sleep after being up on guard most of the night with Will, lifted his cap from his eyes. "If I were you, boys, I wouldn't worry."

Walking over to where James lay, Martin bent down over him. There was a scowl on his face and a belligerent tone in his voice. "Oh, Mr. Keydet, is that so?"

"Listen, boys," James explained in a calm, almost casual voice as he looked up at Martin. "As I recall, there are about twenty-two million folks in the Northern states and only nine million people in the Confederacy. Now, if you consider that some three and a half million of those nine million in the South are slaves, that leaves only six, maybe six and a half million white Southerners to deal with all those Yankees."

Confused, Martin pulled back. "So?"

"So," James said with an air of confidence, "if I were you, I'd sit down and relax awhile, seeing as there's more than enough Yankees to go around."

From behind him, Matthew laughed. "*Ha!* I guess he told you a thing or two."

Leaving James in peace, Martin stalked off to where his brother stood and smacked him in the stomach for laughing at him.

Within an hour a flurry of mounted riders, followed by a rushing about of their officers, announced the receipt of orders for the regiment, ending James' futile efforts to catch up on his sleep. Little time was wasted as the men fell in and began to move north, toward the sound of the guns, which had, over the course of the hour, grown closer.

Moving along a crude wagon trail through stands of cedars

and pines and open farm fields, the 4th Virginia followed along with the rest of Jackson's entire brigade. Up ahead, the growing sounds of battle served to dampen the nervous chatter in the ranks as the faces of more and more men began to show the apprehension many felt in their hearts. This would be, for most, their first battle, an event long awaited and prepared for but one that was still, to all but a few, a great mystery that was as much dreaded as it was hoped for.

Long before they reached the firing line or ever caught sight of it, Jackson's brigade began to see their first signs of battle. They began to encounter human debris, like flotsam from a shipwreck, of the unseen battle they were marching toward. First came the skulkers, individually or in small groups. These were men who, in the heat of battle, didn't measure up to their own and others' expectations. Lacking the grit needed to stand up to the enemy and face death as a soldier was expected to, they drifted back from the firing line when their officers weren't looking or went down with minor wounds. Once freed from the pressure of their comrades or the biting rebukes of their officers, which kept many men in the ranks when their personal courage began to subside, the skulkers made their way to whatever safety they could find. As they were skedaddling, or running, they shied away from formed units and the officers of those units until such time as they could muster up the courage to return to their own companies or continue their flight home. Anxious to avoid officers or the embarrassing questions of fresh, unbloodied soldiers, who always seemed to be wiser and braver than the men of a veteran unit, the skulkers avoided Jackson's brigade, heading off deep into the forest as soon as they saw the First Virginia Brigade making its way forward toward the sounds of battle.

James and Will were only vaguely aware of the presence of the skulkers as they and others around them caught fleeting glimpses of the fleeing soldiers moving through the woods in the opposite direction. Some, too tired to continue their flight, peered fugitively at the passing column from a secure hiding place as they rested or struggled with themselves in an effort to muster up the courage needed to return to the fight. To some of the Lexington Defenders, these men were unworthy to be called soldiers. They became objects of criticism and mockery. To others, however, the appearance of the skulkers served as physical reminders of their own fears and apprehensions. Silently, they ignored their taunting messmates and fellow soldiers, praying that they would not soon become the object of similar shouts and comments from the soldiers of another unit.

Next came the walking wounded, sometimes alone, sometimes in pairs or small groups. Wounded just badly enough to provide them with a bona fide excuse for leaving the firing line and seeking the relative safety of the rear, these men were often cheerful and eager to talk. "Hot fighting up there, it is." One bearded man, holding his bloodied right hand with his good one, shouted out to James as he went walking to the rear. "There's more Yankees up there screamin' and hollerin' for our blood than you can shake a stick at." Then he said with a devilish grin, "I'll save you boys a place on the train to Richmond. See y'all soon."

Will, who had been silent for the longest time, shook James' arm. "You think he's trying to be funny, James?"

James, who had been trying his best to ignore everything and everyone around him, glanced over to his friend. "Don't pay him any mind, Will. Those fellows are just trying to have some fun with you, that's all."

Looking back over his shoulder nervously, Will swallowed hard. "Well, I don't feel bad about saying so, but I think they're doing a mighty good job of it."

Laughing, James grabbed the sling of his rifle, which was hanging on his right shoulder, with his left hand and reached over and slapped Will on the back with his right. "William McPherson, don't you worry one iota. You'll do fine. I guarantee it."

Whatever effect James' assurances had on Will was short lived, for the next group of refugees from the battle were more unnerving than the other two combined. These were the seriously wounded, men whose wounds were crippling and required immediate medical attention. As there was no established ambulance service or medical evacuation system, these men depended upon their comrades to help them back to wherever their regimental or brigade surgeons had set up shop. Of course, a unit engaged in combat couldn't spare riflemen for this task, so, often, the seriously wounded, if they were helped at all during the battle, were assisted to the rear by other, less severely wounded men or some of the more fainthearted who hadn't mustered up the gumption to strike out on their own like the earlier skulkers. Using the excuse of helping a wounded comrade to leave the firing line, many a sound fighting man took himself out of harm's way without sacrificing his personal honor.

For the most part, the officers and sergeants did their best to prevent this. Unfortunately, the experience of battle was as new to them as it was to the men in their command. Suffering the same effects that fear and confusion visited upon the men in the ranks, some of the men charged with the responsibility of being leaders simply did not measure up to that task. They, like the skulkers that James and Will had passed on their move forward, had chosen to seek safety in the rear over duty. The leaders who stayed and were able to work through their own fears and the confusion of battle were often far too busy with keeping their units in hand and fighting to stop all of this bleeding away of strength through desertion and skulking. And, as the battle dragged on, more and more of the officers and sergeants themselves were becoming casualties.

Making their way to the rear, past the 4th Virginia, few of the badly wounded and their escorts paid much attention to the troops headed into battle. Unlike the slightly wounded, none made light of their plight or tried to scare the newcomers. Of course, they didn't need to say anything. The sight of a man with a leg shredded, limping along, using his rifle as a crutch, was more than enough to get James' comrades thinking. Silently, as each step took them closer to the battle, more and more began wondering what the future held in store for them. Those who hadn't already begun to worry started to as the sounds of battle grew louder, more distinct, and the number of wounded flowing past them increased.

The final group of people that the 4th had to make its way through were formed units, pulled back or thrown back from the firing line and heading to the rear to either re-form or resupply. One of the units Jackson's brigade came across was Captain John D. Imboden's battery from General Bee's brigade. Imboden, who had been with Jackson at Harpers Ferry, needed little urging to turn around and join Jackson's own artillery.

It was shortly before noon, with the sun high in the sky and stray enemy artillery rounds streaking over their heads, that the men of Jackson's brigade came out of the pine and cedar woods they had been marching through. Quickly, Jackson and his regimental commanders deployed on the rear of a hill that rose gradually to their front. All the artillery that Jackson had with him and had picked up along the way was pushed forward and deployed to the front. By the time James and the Lexington Defenders neared the edge of the woods, those guns were in line and preparing to fire.

Ordered to lie down after deploying into line, James propped himself up and looked around in order to orient himself and see what was happening out in the open to their front. Wiggling forward in an effort to join James, Will came up on his left. "Well, Jimmy boy, we're almost there. What's going on up here?"

Because of their position on the reverse side of a hill behind the artillery gun line, neither boy could see much. On the far right, just down from the crest of the hill and to the right of the artillery gun line James could make out the 5th Virginia. To the immediate left of the guns was the 2nd, commanded by Colonel James W. Allen, VMI class of '49. Though he could not see it from where the 4th was posted, to the rear of the artillery gun line and in support of the forward regiments, he suspected that the 33rd Virginia, under Colonel A. C. Cummings, VMI class of '44, was somewhere to the left of the 2nd. The 27th Virginia, temporarily under Lieutenant John W. Echols, VMI class of '43, like the 4th, was to the rear. Because of the way they were deployed and the small area they were in, the 4th and the 27th were overlapped slightly.

When the guns commanded by Captain Stanard to their front began to fire, Will shouted with glee. "Well, now. I guess we're really into this fight, aren't we?"

James, looking up and down the line of guns, said nothing. Though neither he nor Will could see who the guns were firing at, the actions and the looks on the gunners' faces told him that the enemy was near and closing. As if to underscore this, within minutes of Jackson's oversized artillery battery firing, return fire from Union guns well to their front began to whistle over the Confederate gunners' heads and explode over or among the waiting infantry behind them.

This first taste of battle, being delivered to them blindly at a time when they could do little to protect themselves or strike back at their attackers, began to rattle some of the men in the tightly packed ranks. While few of the Lexington Defenders had any idea of what their first battle would be like, none imagined that it would entail lying flat on the ground, shoving their faces into the red Virginia dirt in an effort to avoid bombs and shells fired at them by unseen assailants. This experience, from start to finish, was unnerving. Only the appearance of Jackson, mounted on his little sorrel horse, riding back and forth to their front as if on parade, kept many of the men in check.

Easing themselves back into their place in the ranks, James and Will were greeted by a rattled and agitated Martin Hazard. "Doesn't that blamed fool up there hear all those cannonballs sailing past him?"

Will glanced to where Jackson sat on his horse, directing the fire of a gun as calmly as he had while serving as the artillery drillmaster at VMI. With a grin, he looked back at Martin. "Of course he knows what's going on. That's Old Jack, the hero of Chapultapec. Why do you think we're following him?"

Martin looked at Jackson one more time, then shook his head. "I don't know about you and your crazy professor. Standing up and gettin' shot at ain't my idea of fightin'. How long do you suppose he'll sit there on his horse like a damned fool and let us get shot up before we get going out there and doin' some of our own fightin'?"

With a self-satisfied smile, Will responded with authority. "Until he's ready. But," he added, "when he does give the order, I feel sorry for the poor Yankees."

• • •

That order didn't come for some time, almost three hours in fact. In the interim, the Lexington Defenders had little to do but suffer without any chance to respond to the deadly fire that punished them as they lay there. During that time, the passage of Alabamans and Mississippians of General Bee's brigade through their ranks, headed to the rear to rally and rest, caused a stir. "Where ya headed?" Matthew Hazard shouted to one Mississippian, covered with sweat and grime.

"Back to Jackson, I hope," he replied. "I'm all used up, boys, and don't think I can take much more."

"Well, what about the Yankees?" Martin yelled as the Mississippian kept walking away. "What kind of shape did ya leave 'em in?"

Without stopping, the Mississippian looked back and grinned. "Well, if you boys stay right where you are, they'll be by here in a minute or two and you can ask 'em how they're feelin' yourselves."

As if to underscore the worn soldier's grim warning, within minutes a flurry of firing erupted to their left. "What do you suppose, James, is going on over there?" Will asked nervously.

Rousing himself from the slumber that he had managed to lull himself into despite the shelling and shouting, James rolled over and pushed himself up off the ground. Kneeling, he looked over to the left. "They must be trying to flank us."

Unsettled by his friend's casual observation, Will looked at James, then over to the left. "Do you think we're in trouble?"

James shook his head, pointing as he did so. "No, I don't think so. There goes the 33rd."

Following James' finger, Will caught a glimpse of Cummings' 33rd Virginia, dressed in blue as many Confederate units were, just as it fired a volley. Then, advancing at the double, the entire regiment disappeared into the swirling smoke that clung close to the ground over the crest of the hill to their left. When he couldn't see them anymore, Will looked at Jackson and the officers of the 4th, who were looking, like them, over to the left. "How come we're not going with them?"

James also looked about. He watched for a moment as the artillery to their front, reinforced by additional guns, continued to deliver a steady fire to their direct front. " 'Cause, Will, I imagine that there's still a whole lot of Yankees in front of us who are just as eager to push us off this hill as we are to stay.''

This little discussion between the former roommates was suddenly interrupted by a sharp explosion overhead and the screams of Martin Hazard. "OH, LORD!" he yelled with a bloodcurdling shriek. "I'm kilt boys! I'm kilt!''

Turning their heads quickly, James and Will watched as Martin jumped up and began to dance around and scream. Suddenly he bent over, grabbed his left hip and lifted his left leg up and continued to hop about on one foot, screaming all the time. "The damned Yankees have kilt me, Matthew. They've kilt me for sure.''

Jumping up and grabbing his brother, Matthew pried Martin's hands away from the hip he was clutching. Then, with a look of disgust on his face, he stepped back, made a fist, and then punched Martin in the face. Startled by this, Martin lost his balance and fell backwards onto two other men in the company. "What in blazes did you do that for, Matthew? I'm bleedin' all over.''

Reaching down, Matthew pulled Martin's canteen out from under him. Turning it around so that all could see the wide gash cut into one side of the flat canteen, Matthew shouted back at his brother. " 'Cause you ain't bleedin', you fool. They hit your canteen. That's water, not blood, runnin' down your leg.''

Sheepishly, Martin tried to explain. "Well, it sure stung bad when it hit the canteen. Really, boys, I thought I was a goner.''

Throwing Martin's canteen down, Matthew yelled at his brother. "Martin, don't you dare go scarin' me like that again or I'll really get mad and hit you like ya never been hit before.''

"But you did, Matthew.''

Matthew ignored his brother and dropped on the ground, leaving James and Will to continue their speculation as to what was happening out there before them, just on the other side of the hill.

Unfortunately for some of the men in the 4th Virginia, not all the men hit by shrapnel and shell fragments were as lucky as Martin. All about them, in James and Will's own company and others throughout the brigade, men were being hit. Not far from where James and Will knelt watching what they could of the fight, a shell went off, wounding one man in the hip and ripping off the entire right shoulder of another. The man with the hip wound died first, crying out as he did so, "Oh, Lord, have mercy on me, a poor sinner. Boys, pray for me." The other man, though it appeared that he had the more severe wound, lasted longer, almost two hours, before he died. Others, more fortunate than these two but still unlucky enough to be hit, added their moans and groans to the growing noise of battle and further eroded the courage of some of the waiting soldiers. One man, his nerves near shattered, began to wail after every nearby explosion. "Oh, Lord," he would cry. "Have mercy upon me! Have mercy upon me!" A companion lying next to him seconded his every plea, shouting as if he were a chorus, "Me too, Lord! Me too, Lord!"

Throughout this grueling trial, Jackson and the regimental officers moved back and forth or among their prone men. With his left hand held aloft and bound with a handkerchief to stop the bleeding from a minor wound, Jackson rode calmly and slowly, encouraging his men in his high-pitched voice as he did so, "Steady, men. Steady." Though some men gave in to the temptation to drift back to the rear, their officers kept most of them from getting very far. Like their commander, the men of the First Virginia Brigade suffered their wounds, held their positions, and waited.

With nothing more to see to their left, James crawled back to his place in ranks and dropped on his back. For the next hour or so he drifted back and forth into a fitful sleep, despite the unending shelling by the enemy, the gunfire by friendly artillery to his front, and the growing scenes and sounds of horror all around him. Will, animated by nervous energy, couldn't understand how James could sleep with all the racket but didn't bother him to find out. James, after all, had always had a knack for withdrawing into himself when things were going badly. Will just figured that from James' standpoint, the battle unfolding all about them was no different from a bad day back at VMI.

## *East of Centreville, Virginia*

Just outside a small hamlet with the pretentious name of Vienna, Kevin Bannon and the soldiers of the 2nd Regiment, New Jersey Militia, were also waiting. No one was sure what exactly they were waiting for, but without any orders, that's all they could do. Throughout the morning, as the sound of artillery in the distance rumbled across the horizon like a spring thunderstorm, Kevin watched the comings and goings of people along the road running from Washington, D.C., to the east and Centreville to the west. In the morning a number of well-dressed government officials, workers, and businessmen, in the company of gaily dressed women in carriages, rolled by them.

Kevin was in the midst of wondering if Harriet, if she had been in Washington, would have joined this grand parade when the first sergeant, amused by all of it, snorted as a particularly loud group passed in a bright yellow omnibus. "No doubt some of our dedicated congressmen taking advantage of this fine Sunday weather for a bit of a picnic and a ride into the country to watch the slaughter."

Kevin, who had never thought of war as a slaughter, shrugged. "Perhaps the Rebels will do us the service of dispatching some of those gentlemen for us."

The first sergeant laughed. "Lieutenant Bannon, I do not believe we will be that lucky."

"Well, at least maybe they'll see that this war is something more than entertainment and the subject of idle parlor talk."

"Perhaps," the first sergeant grunted before turning away from Kevin.

By midafternoon the flow of traffic began to reverse itself. First came couriers, mounted riders carrying dispatches and orders from the front. The appearance of these messengers caused Kevin's heart to flutter as they drew near. Only after they had passed his regiment and disappeared down the road was he able to compose himself, for Kevin had no desire to lead his company into battle. During the interlude between the passage of couriers, Kevin stalked back and forth along the road, cursing to himself silently as he went over and over in his mind the sequence of events that had, step by step, placed him in such a vulnerable position. Each time he did so, he swore to himself that once his ninety days were up, he would go back to New Jersey and do whatever was necessary to make sure that he didn't find himself in a similar spot again.

Not long after the first of the couriers had come and gone, some wounded men began to appear. Though he knew that there were field hospitals back up the road in and around Centreville, Kevin realized that some of the men he saw were using their wounds as an excuse to place themselves as far away from the battle as possible. Few of the men he saw in the early hours seemed to be too badly hurt, reinforcing his opinion. Sympathizing with them, and having no authority over these men, Kevin did nothing to stop them. In fact, he soon began to envy them. For them, he reasoned, this day's trial was over. He, on the other hand, hadn't even begun his.

News brought by these men from the front, and freely shared with anyone willing to listen, was universally good. "We have them on the run now, boys," one soldier dressed in a gaudy Zouave uniform announced as he limped by Kevin's company. "If you don't hurry, you'll miss all the fun."

Nodding, Kevin said nothing, although he hoped that the man's optimism and prediction were true. He had, Kevin reasoned, done all that his father and Harriet had expected of him. Counting his lucky stars that his duties hadn't yet included combat, he watched, waited, and hoped that fate would allow him to keep it that way.

## Southwest of Centreville, Virginia

Near three o'clock, Will shook James. "Come on, Jimmy boy. Get up. Get up. We're going forward."

Lifting his hat from his face, James looked around, noticing that all those about him were standing up and busily handling their rifles. "Are we attacking?"

"Yes, James, we're attacking," Will exclaimed with the giddy excitement of a child. "Not more than a minute ago Old Jack himself came up in front of the regiment and told Colonel Preston to hold his fire until the enemy was within fifty yards, fire, and then give them the bayonet."

James, getting himself up, grunted. "Well, that sounds like Old Jack, all right."

"He also told Colonel Preston to have us yell like furies when we went into the charge," Will added with a broad smile on his dirty face. James could see that Will, like most of the others about him, was excited and ready to go forward, regardless of what lay on the other side of the hill. James, for his part, was in no great rush. Though as new to this as Will was, James realized that once they went forward, men were going to die. While he wasn't exactly scared, James wondered how he would behave.

These and other thoughts were cut short when Colonel Preston, six paces in front of the regimental color guard, which was posted in front of the regiment, gave the order to advance. Along with the 27th Virginia, the 4th stepped off and began to move forward, angling slightly over to the left.

Moving up over the crest of the hill and to the left of their own artillery gun line, the men of the 4th Virginia were greeted with a view of the battle that, for a moment, was breathtaking and exciting. Between swirls of white smoke that moved across the field like low-hanging clouds, James saw the Union host before him. Off to their left, where the 33rd had made their charge, stood a pair of abandoned cannons, pointed at them and surrounded by motionless clumps of blue and gray. To his immediate front, and of concern to him and every man in the ranks, stood another battery of enemy guns, supported by infantry. Beyond them, off in the distance, other groups of blue-clad figures could be seen. For a moment, James wondered if Jackson had, indeed, made a mistake, throwing them at so large a body of Union soldiers.

This thought was quickly pushed aside as their company commander, echoing the regimental commander's order, shouted, "Ready!"

As mechanically as he had done at VMI and on the drill fields around Harpers Ferry, James brought his rifle up to the

165

ready, jerking the hammer back to the full-cock position as he did so.

"Aim!"

Like everyone to his left and right, James brought his rifle up to his shoulder, resting his cheek on its stock and sighting along the long barrel. As he did so, he steadied the weapon until the image of a Union soldier with a look of utter surprise on his face seemed to rest on his front sight.

With the command "fire," James, and hundreds of men to his left, right, and rear, discharged their weapons. In an instant, the image of the Yankee soldier disappeared from James' sight. Before the smoke cleared and he was able to determine if his aim had been true, the word "CHARGE!" rippled down the ranks. Without a flicker of hesitation James lowered his rifle, let out a yell that was more of a throaty shriek than a yell, and, shoulder to shoulder with Will, rushed forward.

Coming out of the smoke of their own volley, James saw the blue line they had just fired on staggering and falling apart. Here and there freshly wounded men were stumbling about, grabbing a limb or another part of their body before toppling over onto the ground. Those who hadn't been hit were visibly shaken by the unexpected appearance of the Confederates to their front and the devastation their enemy's volley had brought. Many didn't wait for the gray mass of men to reach them, choosing instead to move back away from the rifled field pieces they had been supporting. While a few simply turned and ran for all they were worth, most of the Federals before the 4th and 27th Virginia moved backwards deliberately. While this was decidedly slower, it prevented their enemy from shooting them in the back, a sure sign of cowardliness.

Whether their opponents moved back deliberately or with haste, by the time James and Will reached the enemy artillery pieces, the blue line was gone, for the moment. Officers, anxious to keep their commands in hand, pushed their way to the front. With their swords held in both hands parallel to the ground, they began to align their men, shouting for them to reload as they did so.

Turning his head to his right, James watched Will as he attempted to load his rifle. Will was nervously glancing back and forth from his rifle, which he was trying to load, over to where the Union troops they had just routed were re-forming. Excited by their charge and trying to hurry, Will was fumbling with his cartridge, spilling more of the powder on the ground than down the barrel of his rifle. Realizing that his friend was shaken and was in the process of botching the simple reload drill, James shouted out. "Will, slow down and pay attention to what you're doing."

Looking over at James with wide eyes, Will said nothing. James saw that he needed to do something fast before his friend became totally unnerved and did something foolish or rash. "Will, listen to me and follow my lead. Come to attention."

Responding to his former roommate's orders as he had done when being drilled by him at VMI, Will complied, repeating each order James gave, only louder. "Load in nine times. Load."

With that, Will and James, moving together, each grasped the muzzle end of his rifle with his left hand and brought it opposite the middle of his body. Set, each man moved his right hand around to the cartridge box resting on his right hip.

"Handle cartridge," James shouted. Retrieving a cartridge, they brought the paper-bound round of ammunition up to their mouths and grasped the end opposite where the bullet was between their teeth.

"Tear cartridge." With a tug and a jerk of their heads, they ripped the end off of the paper cartridge.

"Charge cartridge." Bringing the open end of the cartridge around to the muzzle end of their rifles, James and Will tilted the round up and emptied the contents of the cartridge into the rifle's barrel, stuffing the paper in behind the bullet.

"Draw rammer." With quick, easy motions, the men drew out their ramrods, twirled them about over their heads, and pushed the head of the ramrod into the barrel of the rifle until it was seated on the head of the bullet.

"Ram cartridge." With a quick motion, they rammed the ball and loose powder behind it down the length of the barrel, giving one more shove to ensure that all of it was seated.

"Return rammer." Drawing the rammer out of the barrel, each man again twirled it above his head and reinserted it back into place under the barrel.

"Prime." With their left hands, they raised their pieces up

until the trigger and hammer of the rifle were just above the cap box located on their belts just to the right of the belt buckle. With thumb and forefinger, they dug into the cap box, and retrieved one of the small copper caps. They gave the cap a slight pinch to squeeze it together and keep it from falling off of the cone, before they brought it up to the rifle's hammer and lock. Pulling the hammer back to the half-cock position, each man flicked the expended cap off the cone of the lock and placed the new cap on it.

When he saw that Will was ready, James gave the final command, "Shoulder arms." With that, both men brought their rifles up and into the space between their bodies and their right arms, holding them by the trigger guard with their right hands.

Absorbed in their own drill, neither James nor Will had noticed that Martin and Matthew Hazard, as well as several other nearby men, had followed James' instructions. When all of these men were ready, their company commander came up behind them. "Independent fire, men. Independent fire."

He had no sooner moved on when Will, caught up by James' instruction, absentmindedly shouted out on his own, "Ready, aim, fire."

In unison, James, Will, the Hazards, and several other men brought their rifles up and discharged them together on Will's order. Steadied by James' efforts and excited by the results his order to fire had given, Will, grinning, repeated, out loud, the reload drill. As before, the Hazards and several other men about him followed Will's commands. A few men, farther down the ranks, leaned over and shouted for Will to speak louder so that they could hear him. Though he had no rank, no one seemed to mind, not even the sergeants and corporals in the ranks or the officers to their rear. Methodically, and with the ease brought on by hours of endless drill, the 4th Virginia continued to deliver a steady and telling fire on the enemy unit to their front.

The Union forces opposite the 4th Virginia hadn't been idle. Seeing the danger that Jackson's sudden attack on their center presented, Union commanders moved reinforcements into the breach the 4th and 27th Virginia had created in their lines. After exchanging volleys with the Confederates, a regiment from Minnesota began to push uphill toward Jackson's brigade.

Neither side gave way, at first. Instead, the two opposing lines slammed into each other, volley fire giving way to hand-to-hand combat.

James, always worried about Will, was in the process of loading his own rifle while looking over at Will when he felt a sharp, cold object slide along the left side of his stomach. Turning his head back to the front, he was startled to see a wide-eyed Yankee standing face to face with him. Glancing down to his left side, James saw that the Yankee had run his bayonet through his shell jacket. Fortunately for James, the Yankee's thrust had missed his body. Looking down himself and seeing no blood, the Yankee realized his error and began to withdraw his bayonet in preparation for another try. Having no intention of letting this happen, James finished capping his rifle, brought the muzzle end of it up into his assailant's face, and pulled the trigger. In a flash and a cloud of red-and-white haze, the Yankee disappeared, tumbling over backwards without a face and leaving his rifle, hanging by its bayonet, in James' jacket.

A quick shiver ran down James' back as he recovered from his near brush with death. He was just freeing the dead man's bayonet from his jacket when Will grabbed his shoulder. "James! We're pulling back. Come on, James, hurry."

Nodding, James began to carefully step backwards, feeling his way with his feet in an effort to avoid tripping on one of the many bodies that now lay scattered about. A wounded man, anxious to be brought back, grabbed at his leg. "Please!" he pleaded. "Help me. Help me." James, busy loading his rifle as he continued to walk backwards, neither paid any attention to the man nor slowed his pace, for the Yankees were close at hand and continuing to come on fast.

When they were halfway back from their most forward position, the 4th and the 27th Virginia, now supported by the other regiments of the brigade, stopped. Squeezing himself in between Will, on his right, and Thomas Stone, James was bringing his rifle up to shoulder arms when Will looked over at him. With a note of horror in his voice, Will cried out. "James! Your leg. What happened?"

Shaken, James bent over and looked down. Across the front of his right leg were four bloody red streaks that reminded

James of a cat's claw marks. They wrapped their way around from the front of his trouser leg to the back. Though he felt no pain, James was worried. Lifting his leg, he started to look to see where the marks ended before he remembered. With a jerk, he looked up and back in the direction from which he'd come. It had been the wounded man who had made the marks, James realized, the man whom he hadn't even bothered to look down at. Peering through the drifting haze of dirty white and gray smoke that obscured the battlefield all about them, James wondered why he hadn't done anything to help his stricken comrade. Was it the excitement of the moment? Had it been the intensity of his concentration on reloading that had kept him from doing anything? Or was he simply an unfeeling, uncaring bastard who was incapable of paying any heed to anyone else's problems or feelings but his own?

This speculation was cut short by the sight of the Yankees, re-forming their own ranks, and their company commander, Captain Benjamin R. Pugh. Making his way hastily down the front of the company's ranks, Pugh was pushing men into place. "Dress and cover," he shouted as he went by, with an occasional nervous glance over his shoulder to where Yankee company commanders were busily doing the same thing to their own units. "Dress and cover, I said." Placing his left hand on James' right shoulder, Pugh was in the process of pushing James back into line when a look of surprise flashed across Pugh's face just before he pitched forward and into James.

Dropping his rifle as he struggled to keep his balance, James rocked back, bumping into Martin Hazard behind him. Martin, with his left hand, grabbed the material of James' shell jacket and helped steady him as James reached out and caught Pugh's slumping body in his arms. Pugh's dead weight dragged James to his knees. After easing his commander the rest of the way to the ground, James pulled back and looked at him. Pugh's face was frozen in an expression of shock and surprise. With a vacant stare he looked up, past James, to a sky that he no longer could see.

"Will!" James yelled. "Tell Teddy Lynn the captain's dead."

Turning his head this way and that, Will didn't see their first lieutenant. What he did see, as he searched for someone to take command of the company, was the companies to their left and right beginning to return the raggedy fire the Yankees were pounding them with. "James, I don't see Lieutenant Lynn!"

Knowing that there was nothing more he could do for the captain, James started to retrieve his rifle, which lay on the ground pinned under Pugh's body. "Do something, Will," James yelled as he tugged on the stock of the rifle with one hand and tried to roll Pugh away with the other.

Caught up in the moment and prodded by James's order, Will yelled out as he had when running through the steps of the reload drill. "Lexington Defenders. Ready . . ."

With their hearing deadened by the discharge of massed rifle fire, the firing of their own artillery, and the explosion of artillery shot and shells all about them, the men around Will didn't pay any heed to the fact that the voice shouting the order wasn't Pugh's. They only heard their name, caught glimpses of the solid enemy line through the smoke across from them, and responded as they had been trained.

"Aim . . ."

Quickly the men searched for targets or merely pointed the muzzles of their rifles in the general direction of the enemy. "Fire!"

Though it lacked the snap and crack that massed rifles firing in unison gave, the disjointed volley had the desired effect. As James stood up, careful to avoid the barrel of Martin Hazard's gun, he looked at the other companies. "Have them fire at will, Will."

At another time that comment would have brought a chuckle from everyone around them. Now, however, engaged in what they saw as a struggle for their lives, Will and the company responded without hesitation. "Independent fire," Will yelled down the line to the right and then, facing left, repeated his command, "Independent fire!"

As First Lieutenant Theodore I. Lynn finally began to exert his authority, James, Will, and their comrades traded volleys with their enemy, giving as good as they got. Other than to Will, James paid no attention to anyone or anything about him. Busy with tending to his own rifle, he didn't notice that Thomas Stone, who had been on his left, was gone, shot through the heart by a Yankee bullet. He paid only scant attention when someone behind him was hit in the face and lunged forward just as James was preparing to fire. James' only response to this was a sharp curse at having his aim spoiled like that.

Behind the firing line, Jackson was there with his men, watching and giving orders as needed. When he judged them to be ready, he again pushed his brigade forward, back across the deadly space of ground that separated them from the Yankees. Again the 4th and the 27th, along with the other three regiments of the brigade, went forward. This time they stayed, locked in desperate hand-to-hand fighting with men from Michigan, New York, Massachusetts, and Wisconsin.

Unit cohesion as well as alignment disappeared within minutes. Fighting as best they could with whatever they had on hand, both sides hacked and clawed desperately to hang on to the abandoned Union guns as if the fate of the entire nation rested on their possession. In this fight the butt of a rifle and fists were used almost as much as the bullet and the bayonet. Martin Hazard, faced by a large farm boy from Wisconsin, saw that his opponent was going to beat him in their race to reload and fire. Not wanting to lose this contest, Martin dropped his rifle, bent down, grabbed a rock, and threw it at the Yankee. Hit square in the chest, the Yankee reeled backwards from the blow, giving Martin enough time to recover his own rifle, finish loading it, and bring it to bear on the Yankee. James and Will, staying shoulder to shoulder and sometimes back to back in the blinding chaos that swirled about them, fought on as if they were one.

When this phase of the battle had lasted nearly an hour, the toll of their exertions up to that point and the terrible confusion created by units thrown into the fight haphazardly began to tell on the Union. Confused commands, renewed Confederate attacks, and fire from fresh units on their flank caused the Union troops engaged in their desperate struggle with Jackson's brigade to fall back. Their commanders had meant them to simply pull back to the base of the hill, reorganize, and try again. But the confusion caused by regiments merged together and the weight of the prolonged effort demanded of them since two that morning were too much. The gradual withdrawal became a general retreat, then a rout.

Fleeing back down off of the hill that they had fought for since noon, Union troops defied all efforts of their own and other officers to stop them, leaving James, Will, the Lexington Defenders, and Jackson's bloodied regiments in command of the field.

## *East of Centreville, Virginia*

It was almost midnight when the first sergeant came up next to Kevin and pulled him off to one side. "Sir," he whispered in the darkness, "we've lost most of the men in the ranks already and stand a good chance to lose the rest. Standing here on this road like this, trying to stem this rout, isn't doing any good. I think we need to gather everyone we have left and pull back."

Caught in the flood of refugees fleeing the battle for Washington, Kevin and his command were waging a losing battle of their own. Ordered to establish a straggler line before their position at Vienna as night began to fall, Kevin and other units of Brigadier General Runyon's Fourth Division failed to stem the endless tide of broken units and individual stragglers. With the coming of night, the officers in charge of this straggler line soon found that their own men were slipping away out of ranks and joining the massive retreat. Some of the officers even set the example by disappearing without a word.

When Kevin didn't respond, the first sergeant again pressed his point. "Sir, if we don't do something soon, we're not going to have anyone left to do anything with."

Alone and with no other officers to consult, Kevin nodded. "All right, First Sergeant, you're right. But we're not going to just up and go back to Washington on our own. I want you to gather all the men we have left and pull them away from the road. I'm going to see if I can find the regimental commander or the color company."

Shaking his head, the first sergeant tried to protest. "What's

173

the point, Lieutenant? He's probably halfway back to Washington already.''

Kevin wasn't swayed, however. "When all else fails," he firmly stated, "you can do no wrong by rallying around the flag. If that flag is still out here, I'm going to find it and form whatever we have left of the company around it."

Though he didn't understand that Kevin's response was nothing more than his habit of doing exactly what he was told without question because he lacked the fortitude to do otherwise, the first sergeant didn't protest. Instead, he saluted, pivoted, and headed off into the darkness to carry out his orders. Kevin, alone on the road in the midst of the jumbled chaos that had once been an army, began his search for the regimental commander or the regimental colors. Though he would have liked to turn and flee along the road with the rest of the mob of faceless men, Kevin knew what was expected of him and went off to comply with those dictates.

# CALM
# BEFORE
# THE STORM

PART THREE

# CALM
# BEFORE
# THE STORM

# CHAPTER 10

# August, 1861
# Trenton, New Jersey

"WELL, KEVIN, DO YOU THINK THEY'RE REALLY DONE WITH us?"

The question caught Kevin Bannon off guard. With his head resting against the pane of glass and his eyes staring vacantly out of the railcar window, he was lost in thought, oblivious to anyone and anything around him. Kevin turned his head toward his traveling companion, the quartermaster captain from the 1st Regiment, New Jersey Militia. "Excuse me. I was just thinking. What did you say?"

If he was bothered by Kevin's lack of attentiveness, the quartermaster captain didn't show it. Rather, he simply repeated his question. "Do you think they're done with us?"

In response, Kevin grunted. Looking into the captain's eyes with a cold emotionlessness that conveyed his earnestness, Kevin said nothing at first. Unlike the majority of his regiment, Kevin had been retained beyond the ninety-day term of service.

Many tasks fell upon him in the wake of the disaster that the press was calling the Battle of Bull Run. First and foremost was the seemingly simple one of gathering up all of his men. Collapse of discipline made this more difficult than it should have been. Troops, knowing that their term of service was near an end, took their liberties, visiting nearby Washington, where they drank and whored with wild abandon. Only by the sternest measures of the provost marshal's guard and the officers who could still command respect were the men brought back into line. Even then, control was all too often short lived and tenuous.

In the midst of this problem, Kevin needed to tend to the cleaning, mending, and turn-in of Federal and state equipment.

Much of it could not be accounted for, abandoned either on the march to Vienna or during the wild flight back, when men freely jettisoned everything that impeded their progress to safety. When he finished with his own company, Kevin was kept on by the regimental staff, to help them sort out problems and difficulties other units were having mustering out. It seemed that his skills in handling such matters were deemed indispensable. Unable to mount an effective argument and anxious to be done with all of this, and the Army in general, Kevin launched into his duties with energy and drive. This, he discovered, led to the first major obstacle in his plan to put Army life behind him.

At a time when despondency and anger over their defeat at Bull Run had hamstrung just about every part of the Army, Kevin's quiet, efficient performance attracted the attention of his superiors. That it had been remnants of his company that escorted the regimental colors back to Washington after Bull Run and that he and most of his company were available for immediate use were the beginning of Kevin's undoing. Politically appointed officers, in search of some good news to send home, seized upon Kevin's rather mundane achievements and magnified them in their reports to Governor Olden of New Jersey. The manner·in which he conducted himself and the efficient way he executed his orders and duties in mustering out his men and others who were without officers only served to reinforce the belief that he was a competent and efficient officer whose services were indispensable to the state and the Army. Thus, without his knowledge, and because of his own action, the seeds of his undoing were planted, fertilized, and nurtured in ground made fertile by defeat.

Finished with his duties in Washington, Kevin began his trek back to Trenton during the first week in August in the company of the last officers of the three New Jersey ninety-day militia regiments. No one in that group had any thoughts of glory or fame, for there was none to be found in their collective performance during and after the battle. As they made their way back, the fact that they had been well to the rear in reserve, safe from any danger, only served to increase their embarrassment at what could best be called a humbling experience. Even Kevin was affected by this feeling, though he, unlike many of the others, was quite willing to put all of it behind him and carry on with his life. Blinking, he finally answered the quartermaster's question. "I think when we get home, and the truth of what we did, or didn't do, becomes known, the State will be glad to be rid of us."

Kevin's indirect reference to their lack of battle honors, made more embarrassing by the precipitous flight brought on by mere rumors of Confederate cavalry, caused the quartermaster captain to nod in agreement. "We were," he responded in a rather sheepish tone, "a sorry excuse for a command." After a moment's thought, he looked out the window at the passing scenery. "I suppose you're right. The governor and everyone back home will be anxious to shove us off to the side. Still," he mused to himself, "it would have been nice to have an opportunity to avenge ourselves."

Another captain, from the 3rd Regiment, New Jersey State Militia, who had been listening, nodded in agreement. "Yes, yes, you're right. And I intend to join one of the new regiments, provided, of course, they'll have me."

"I doubt"—Kevin continued the captain's last thought —"that the governor will offer any of us another commission."

"Then," the captain from the 3rd snapped, "I'll enlist as a private. All I want is a chance to show those gentlemen from the South that Jerseymen are every bit their equal in a fair fight."

With no desire to continue this discussion, Kevin shrugged and looked back out the window. Soon, he knew, they would be in Trenton, where he would be free to separate from his bothersome company and state service. Then, he would be able to get back to school and the wooing of Harriet.

Given the glum mood of the militia officers returning home, it came as a surprise to them, Kevin in particular, when the train they were on was greeted by a band and an official party at the station in Trenton. The governor himself was there to welcome the officers and men of his militia units back home. That this was all show, meant to boost support for a war that now promised to last well beyond anyone's wildest dreams, was not lost on Kevin. Governor Olden was in a very tight spot. In December, 1860, he had worked against many of his own party in his efforts to derail New Jersey's secession movement. When the war came, his quick and energetic support of Lincoln's call for troops and funds required more political maneuvering that had cost him. Now, in the aftermath of the failure of the Union Army, and the less than stellar performance of New Jersey's troops during that battle, Olden was in a bind. He had to raise new regiments, three-year regiments, to support the protracted war that he had so energetically supported before Bull Run.

Standing on the platform, Olden and a delegation of state officials shook each man's hand as he stepped down from the railcar. Kevin, not having been privy to the dispatches that had mentioned him so favorably, was bowled over by this sudden and unwelcome attention. Only the sight of Harriet, mashed from all sides in the throng of well-wishers and officials, cheered Kevin. Even this bit of joy, however, was short lived, for in the next moment Kevin noticed that she was flanked by her father on the right and his own on the left. It was, he thought to himself as he looked into Harriet's inviting eyes from across the platform, as if she were a lamb tied out by two hunters as bait.

With Judge Shields in the lead, the trio pushed their way toward Kevin. Enroute, the Judge managed to collar Governor Olden. "Governor," he announced as they neared Kevin, "this is the young man who so gallantly saved our state colors in the field last month."

While Kevin's eyes darted back and forth between the two men, the governor looked Kevin up and down, almost as if he were trying to decide if the person before him was worthy of his attention. Finally, a smile broke across the governor's face, as if to announce that a favorable decision had been arrived at. "Yes," he pronounced with a practiced air of authority as he reached out and grabbed Kevin's hand to shake it. "He is everything that you said he was, Judge Shields. He will make a fine addition to the 4th."

Not understanding what the governor was talking about, Kevin looked blankly into the governor's eyes. When the governor failed to respond, Kevin turned to Judge Shields. Knowing that Kevin had no idea what the governor was talking about, since Harriet had begged him to keep the news a surprise, Judge Shields explained. "At my request, Kevin, the governor has decided to grant you a commission as a first lieutenant in the newly formed 4th New Jersey Volunteer Infantry Regiment."

This shocking bit of news caused Kevin to squeeze the governor's hand until he winced. Pulling his hand away from Kevin, the governor looked at the young man as he shook out his hand. At first, there was anger in his eyes, anger that both Kevin and Judge Shields noticed. Then recovering his composure, the governor glanced first at Judge Shields and then over at Edward Bannon, who had, until now, remained a little behind Judge Shields. Forcing a smile, the governor shook out his throbbing hand. "Well, one thing is for sure. He definitely has the strength needed to whip his new unit into shape."

With the awkward moment past, everyone, except Kevin, laughed. Harriet, seeing that Kevin was still reeling from the impact of the news, pushed her way past Edward Bannon, coming up next to Kevin and wrapping her hands around his arms. With a tone that hinted at mock indignation, Harriet took over. "Gentlemen, seeing how you have conspired to find new and fiendish ways of keeping Kevin away from me, I must insist that you permit me the pleasure of his company for a few hours before you hustle him away to war again." Harriet looked up at the governor and smiled as she curtsied. "I am sure, Governor, that you, my father, and Mr. Bannon have much that you need to discuss, just as I am sure Kevin is anxious to get away, at least for a while, from all this talk of war and politics."

Seizing upon the opportunity to free himself so that he could move on to bigger and more important things, the governor tipped his hat and bowed. "By all means, Miss Shields, please take your lieutenant and enjoy yourself while you can. But don't keep him too long. We have much need of his talents."

The talents that the governor was interested in didn't matter to Harriet at the moment. After smiling sweetly at her father, and then at Edward Bannon, she quickly backed away and began to push her way along the crowded railroad platform, pulling Kevin along with her as she went.

Once they were alone in the carriage, Kevin turned away from Harriet and stared blankly out the small open window. The noise of the train station and the clatter of the horses' hooves on the pavement kept Harriet from saying anything until they were well on their way. Even then, she hesitated to say anything, not knowing for sure what sort of mood Kevin was in.

Unable to ignore her any longer, Kevin turned and looked at the girl whom he thought he was in love with. "You knew about this new commission, didn't you?"

Harriet sucked in a deep breath before answering. "Yes, I did."

Kevin looked down at his lap and shook his head slowly. "You also knew that I had no desire to continue my service with the Army after my three months were over." He looked up at her again. "I told you that when you were in Washington and I told you that in my letters."

"Kevin, listen," Harriet hastened to explain. "When it became obvious that this war was going to become bigger than anyone imagined, many of the men who had hung back in the spring came forward to join up. While I am sure that most of them did so because they really believe in the cause, there are more than a few whose only interest in doing so is to make sure that their names are included in the rolls of those who answered the call to duty by the governor."

"And the three of you, my father, your father, and you, all decided that it would be to my advantage if my name was among them," Kevin snapped.

Harriet, angry that Kevin was reacting so poorly to what she had hoped would be good news, glared at him. "Yes, Kevin Bannon, we did. It was your father who came to my father to ask for his assistance in securing a second commission for you, in a three-year regiment. He is, I am convinced, very interested in ensuring that you have all the advantages you will need to build a secure and meaningful future, advantages that he never had."

Kevin was about to laugh, but held back. She didn't know his father like he did. How could she? She hadn't been raised by him. She hadn't seen the ruthless way his father ruled him and his brother. She hadn't been there when, without a second thought, he had separated them. But then, how could she know what kind of man he was. When he wanted and needed to be, Edward Bannon could be a charming and very endearing person.

"My father," she continued, "is always looking for an opportunity to do a favor for someone who has the money to support his political ambitions. That, and his desire to keep us apart, made him more than receptive to your father's request."

"And you, Harriet?" Kevin asked sharply. "What is in all this for you?"

There was much that she wanted to say to Kevin that she simply could not find a way to express. Her own burning desire to, herself, rush off to war and serve, frustrated by her gender, would sound laughable to him. Even Harriet found it impossible to picture herself in uniform, carrying a rifle and living in a tent, without seeing it as nothing more than the fanciful dream that it was. Instead, she tried to explain it in a manner that Kevin could accept. "We spoke of this before, and I know you understand it. Even though my father feigns approval and acceptance of our relationship, in his heart he agrees with my mother's view that you are an unfit suitor for me. By continuing to serve, and serve with distinction, as you have been doing, you will earn your place in society and leave them no choice but to accept you when it comes time for us to become engaged."

Kevin looked at her for a long moment. At first, he was appalled at how much she was a prisoner of her parents' desires and the dictates of the society she lived in. He was about to discount this lack of self-determination to her gender but paused when he suddenly realized that he too had spent his entire life doing little more than following the orders of either his older brother or his father. When he had thought about this in the past, he had never viewed it as weakness. "We do," his brother James had told him before he left for Virginia, "what we have to in order to survive." While he had accepted this explanation, and used it many times to justify his meek acceptance of his father's orders, Kevin knew that there had to be more to life than just accepting what was. There had to be a time, he thought, when people had to stand up and do what was right for them, regardless of the consequences. The question he pondered, as he watched the people hustling about on the sidewalks outside the carriage, was when to do so.

"Besides," Harriet added almost as an afterthought, while Kevin's thoughts wandered, "Trevor Ward has also been given a commission."

Kevin snapped his head back toward Harriet. So, he thought, that's the game. Trevor Ward, not Kevin, was the man whom both Judge Shields and his wife wanted Harriet to marry. If Trevor went to war and came back a hero, while Kevin stayed at home, he'd have no chance at all of winning Harriet's hand in marriage. Harriet knew this and was, Kevin thought, willing to gamble his life on it.

Seeing that he was becoming angry, Harriet now gave Kevin no chance to respond. "I've managed to arrange a small dinner tonight at a friend's house. Her father, Dan Worthington, is a state senator. It will give us, you, me, my father and yours, an opportunity to be together in the home of an important member of the state legislature. I'm hoping that by doing so everyone who matters will get used to seeing us together. And if Senator Worthington does what I expect him to do, and makes a big thing of your service with the militia at Bull Run, I'm hoping my father will begin to see you as an acceptable suitor."

"And," Kevin responded dryly, "if your father doesn't?"

"Oh," Harriet stated with confidence, "he will. Unlike my mother, my father's a hard-nosed realist. When he sees that he has no choice but to accept you, he'll make the best of it and be happy."

Unwilling to carry on with a conversation that he didn't much care for, Kevin shrugged and turned to look back out his window. How lucky, Kevin thought, James is. His brother, taken from him almost two years before because of an unfortunate incident brought on by Kevin's own unchecked passions, was free of all this. To Kevin's troubled mind, his brother was a truly free man, able to make his own decisions without worrying about someone's ambitious schemes or an antiquated society's stringent rules and oppressive prejudices. Yes, Kevin told himself over and over, James is the lucky one. But then, he

reasoned, he had always been lucky. He had always been able
to figure out what to do and then stand on his own two feet and
do it, regardless of the cost. Even James' acceptance of his
exile to Virginia, Kevin convinced himself, had been an act of
determination and independence. "Oh God," Kevin whispered
to himself as he considered the hopelessness of his current
plight, "how I wish you were here, dear brother."

Harriet, seeing that he wasn't going to respond, and unable
to hear his whispered prayer over the noise of the street and
clattering hooves, also looked away. In many ways, she
thought, her father was right. The Irish were a moody people.
Though Kevin was intelligent, and even seemed to have the
heart of a poet at times, his sullenness and readiness to accept
the decisions of others sometimes made Harriet wonder if he
would make a good husband. Then she smiled as she realized
that it was probably those traits, both the good ones and the
questionable ones, that drew her to him. With no chance to
make her way in the world on her own because of her gender,
Harriet would need a husband who could be easily influenced.
Trevor Ward, from an old-money family, was too self-centered,
obnoxious, and arrogant. Kevin, on the other hand, was mal-
leable. With her determination, Edward Bannon's money, and
her father's political connections, she told herself, there wasn't
anything that Kevin wouldn't be able to achieve.

The private affair that Harriet had planned on began to unravel
even before the Bannons and Shieldses left their carriage before Senator Worthington's Trenton home. What should have
been a quiet, almost vacant residential street was alive with
carriages bearing distinguished couples. Without exception, the
men were older men, well turned out and escorting well-
appointed women, many of whom appeared to be their wives.
Anxiously, Harriet looked about to see where all of these people were headed. To her horror, the carriages, without exception, halted in front of Worthington's front door. Turning to
face her father, Harriet managed to calm herself before she
spoke. "Father, I thought this was going to be a private affair."

The casual and innocent tone of his daughter's voice didn't

deceive Judge Shields. Used to her mother's habits and traits, he had suspected that his daughter was up to something from the beginning. Though he didn't quite know who was being manipulated and for what reason, he knew something was afoot. Her appearance and dress, too grand for the "casual" and private dinner, herself more radiant then he had ever seen her before, confirmed his suspicion. With a sly smile, the Judge looked over at Harriet. "Well, yes, that's true. But," he added after a slight chuckle, "when Dan Worthington heard who was coming to dinner, he insisted that he be allowed to make this a homecoming worthy of young Kevin, here." Harriet's shocked expression and furtive glances over at Kevin were all Judge Shields needed to convince him that in this little war of manipulation and staging, he had outflanked a master. Though he knew the battle had just been joined, he had both the advantage and more surprises in store.

In all of this, Kevin Bannon gave the appearance of being utterly uninterested. He wasn't, of course. The less than subtle manipulations and maneuvers being staged about him would have been obvious to a man three days dead. From his father's warm politeness to Harriet's stunning attire, everything, Kevin realized, was being played out for his benefit and, he feared, his detriment. It was, he imagined, as if he were the prize goose being fattened up and prepared for the kill.

This thought triggered a series of images, burned into his mind as few had ever been before. The memories of the wounded streaming past his company's position on the road to Washington began to fill his troubled mind. They came in droves, many little more than pitiful remnants of the strong, brave lads they had been just hours before. While the sight of stumps left by limbs freshly amputated or severed by shell fire held their own horror, it was the look on many of the faces of the wounded that struck Kevin the hardest. Ashen- or white-faced men, all wearing a look of shock, surprise, or bewilderment, marched before Kevin's eyes as Harriet and her father bantered back and forth. How terrible it must have been, Kevin thought, for those men, so young and so alive, suddenly to be faced with their own mortality in such a brutal and inhumane manner. Here and there in the crowd he recalled seeing a man go by him with a vacant look that told Kevin death was only a few moments away. What thoughts, Kevin wondered, must have passed through those men's minds? Whatever they were, he knew they died with their owner. Looking about the carriage, Kevin stared at each face in the crowd surrounding him and repeated the same question to himself in disgust, "What thoughts are those faces hiding?"

When the carriage stopped, Harriet was out and on the ground in a flash. Anxious to get inside her friend's house and see what other surprises her father had in store for her, she chafed at the delay while she waited for the others to step down from the carriage. She was tapping her toe on the brick sidewalk, waiting, when a familiar voice called out her name from behind her. "Well, Miss Shields, this is quite an unexpected pleasure."

Whirling about she found herself face to face with Trevor Meguire Ward, the young man that her mother so dearly wanted Harriet to marry. This confrontation completely unnerved Harriet. Stunned into speechlessness, Harriet stood in front of Trevor, trying to decide whether to be angry at her father for all of his fine machinations or at herself for being too clever for her own good.

With the hint of a smile, Trevor reached out and took Harriet's hand, as if it were a foregone conclusion that she was going to be with him the rest of the evening. "I had feared," he said with a smirk, "that this was going to be another one of those dreadful evenings of standing around listening to politicians puffing themselves up while they stuff their faces. Now, with you here, well, this could be an interesting and enjoyable evening."

While this little tête-à-tête between Harriet and Trevor was going on, Kevin emerged from the carriage behind his father. If he was surprised to see Trevor, holding Harriet's hand, he did not show it. Instead, his mind still awash with images of a lost battle, he dutifully followed his father, who was wearing a broad smile as he eyed the notables entering Senator Worthington's front door. There would be much to be gained tonight, he thought, just as Judge Shields had promised.

The Judge, last out of the carriage, saw Trevor and smiled. "Ah, there you are, lad. I see you have already found Harriet." Stepping down, he motioned toward Kevin with a simple wave of the hand. "You already know Kevin." Then with a flourish, he brought his hand to rest on Edward Bannon's shoulder, blocking any view of Kevin in the process. "And this distinguished gentleman is Mr. Edward Bannon, owner of the terracotta works in Perth Amboy, president of the board of that town's most prestigious bank, and part owner and board member of the new railroad line being built along the Jersey coast."

Showing the deference and respect appropriate to a man of such accomplishments and stature, Trevor let Harriet's hand go to shake Edward Bannon's. Harriet, freed from Trevor and regaining her composure, withdrew a few steps and came up next to Kevin. Leaning on him, and stretching her neck until her lips were within an inch of his ear, Harriet whispered to him, "I had nothing to do with *him* being here." Then she added, in a pleading tone, "Kevin, what do you intend to do?"

Pulled back from his own dark thoughts by Harriet's question, Kevin looked around at the faces staring at him. Though he had no idea what it was that she expected him to do, he knew exactly what he was going to do. Looking down at her with a rather bemused smile, he announced in a voice that both Edward Bannon and Judge Shields heard, "I, my sweet little arranger, intend to go into the senator's house, head straight for his liquor cabinet, and spend the balance of this evening doing my best to empty it."

Without another word, Kevin pivoted, marched up the stairs of Senator Worthington's house, and disappeared inside, leaving Harriet shocked, Edward Bannon embarrassed, Judge Shields satisfied, and Trevor smiling from ear to ear.

True to his word, Kevin could be found next to the table where the punch and wines were being served. As people came by, either to meet him or fill their own glasses, Kevin was friendly and gracious to the point of being obnoxious and a nuisance. Harriet, for her part, attempted to pry him away from there. Kevin, however, ignored her prodding and pleas, holding his position tenaciously. Frustrated, Harriet resorted to diverting her attentions to Trevor. Like Kevin, she put a great deal of effort into being seen. Unlike Kevin, she was failing to achieve her objective, for Kevin merely nodded and raised his cup in a mock toast to her every time she glanced over at him.

At first Edward Bannon attempted to ignore his son's boorish behavior. As the evening progressed and Kevin's forced conversations and laughter became louder, Edward decided that he needed to take action. Catching Kevin alone for a moment, Edward eased up next to his son. "You are acting like a damned fool. I demand that you get hold of yourself, boy, and stop embarrassing me like this."

With his tongue loosened by liquor, Kevin surprised both of them by snapping back at his father. "Dear me, Father, I am sorry. How would you prefer me to embarrass you?"

Edward's face contorted with anger. "How dare you speak to me like that."

Kevin laughed. "I don't see why you're so upset, Father. You always seemed to encourage James to talk to you like that. Of course," Kevin said with a grin, "dear brother James never seemed to need much encouragement when he was in your presence."

"DON'T you mention *that* name in front of me again or I'll . . ."

Kevin slammed his glass down on the table. Towering over his father, he looked down at Edward, noticing for the first time how small the old man really was. "Or you'll what, dear Father?"

From across the room, Judge Shields, who had been watching this confrontation out of the corner of his eye, decided that the time was right for his next move. Picking up a knife, he gently tapped the edge of his punch cup. "May I have your attention, please." A hush fell across the room except for a rustle of crinolines as people from other rooms drifted in to hear what the Judge had to say.

"Ladies and gentlemen, as you all know, the gallant young men from this state and all across our great nation have met the enemy for the first time in battle. Though I wish I could say that the results were favorable . . ."

From across the room, Kevin hoisted his glass and shouted, "Here, here."

Ignoring the rude interruption as if it had never occurred, the Judge continued. ". . . our troops were not without success.

Troops from the New Jersey Brigade were called upon to cover the retreat of our beaten but unbroken Army from the field of honor.''

Kevin snorted. "Field of honor, very good.''

Again Judge Shields let the comment pass without comment or notice. With great relish, as if to accentuate the hollowness of his words, he continued. "We are *honored*, tonight, to have one of the *heroes* of that sad day with us. Lieutenant Kevin Bannon of the 2nd Regiment of Militia held his command, virtually alone, throughout the night in the face of great and terrible odds, to cover the retreat of General McDowell's Army of Northeastern Virginia. Only when there was no need of his unit's services did he quit the field. Even then, they did so as a unit, bringing the regimental colors back with them, held high and unsullied.''

A polite round of applause drowned out another snort by Kevin.

"In recognition for his achievements,'' the Judge announced, "the governor has offered Kevin a commission as a first lieutenant in the 4th Regiment of Volunteers, where his skills and experience are so needed.''

Again, there was a round of applause. Nodding in acknowledgment, Kevin judged this to be an excellent time to state that he had no intention of accepting the offered commission. Judge Shields, however, in his haste to spring his last surprise on his languishing daughter, beat Kevin to the punch. "I might also add,'' he said with a flourish, "that we have here tonight a young man who hails from a fine and honorable family that has, from the earliest days of this great state, provided brave and capable leaders in both war and peace. Tonight, Captain Trevor Meguire Ward comes to us from Camp Olden, where his company is now in training, with the news that Kevin Bannon will be joining Captain Ward's command as his first lieutenant.''

A slap in the face could not have rattled Kevin as much as the Judge's announcement did. Both he and Harriet gasped at this announcement, looking first at the Judge, and then at each other. From start to finish, everything that she had worked so hard to arrange had been undone by either her own father's maneuvers or Kevin's outrageous behavior. Now Trevor, with

190

a name that everyone in the room was comfortable with, became the center of attention, a center that included, much to her displeasure, Harriet Shields herself. For the moment, she simply stood there, her arm locked in Trevor's as the people about them smiled, congratulated Trevor and wished him luck. With one eye cast in Kevin's direction, Trevor accepted this adoration. Kevin, alone now and unnoticed, was uncertain what, if anything, he should do about the insult that Judge Shields had so astutely engineered. That plus the sudden realization for the first time that he could actually *lose* Harriet left him totally befuddled. When Kevin finally turned to leave, after taking one more long drink from his glass, Trevor's smile broadened considerably. He gave Harriet's arm a squeeze and, like everyone else, paid no more attention to Kevin Bannon.

With morning came both sobriety and realization of what had happened the day before. Neither of these was pleasant or easy for Kevin to deal with. Still, deal with them he must. In the quiet of his room, he pondered all of his alternatives. There were few that he found to be realistic, and none of these came close to what he had wanted.

In these deliberations, he also became keenly aware of how alone he was. His elder brother, James, who had shared his troubles and provided him with counsel and support in his times of need, had been taken away from him some two years ago. That he had been the architect of the events leading up to James' exile to the South was never far from Kevin's mind. At times like this, that memory all but dominated his thinking. Harriet, a person whom Kevin had found to fill the void left by James, was also gone. Again, his own action had caused this. The best she could manage after witnessing Kevin's performance the night before was a polite note, delivered that morning by a servant, explaining that she needed to leave early for New Brunswick and that family affairs would dominate her time for the next few weeks. Though he knew Judge Shields had been instrumental in setting the stage, it had been his own actions, his drinking and rude comments, that had undone him. There was, of course, always his father. But Kevin would have preferred to face a volley of canister fired at point-blank range by a Confederate battery than go to his father that morning. So he was, as he had been that night of the battle, left on his own to make decisions that he didn't feel equipped to make.

As certainly as the sun rose in the east and set in the west, Kevin followed his natural course and did what was expected of him. Dressing in his uniform, now showing signs of wear but brushed off by the hotel valet and freshly pressed, Kevin reported to the State Adjutant General's office. There he mustered out of the 2nd Regiment, New Jersey State Militia, and accepted both his commission as a first lieutenant and his assignment to the 4th Regiment of New Jersey Volunteers. ''Your orders here, sir,'' a clerk stated with an air of unjustified authority, ''state that you're to report to Company J, Captain Ward commanding, at Camp Olden.'' Kevin, while finding the clerk's attitude annoying, was in no mood to make an issue of it. Instead, he took his orders and left the statehouse quietly, as had been his custom for so long.

The short ride out to Camp Olden was familiar. Even the camp itself was familiar. But there had been changes since he had left there just over three months before. The bright greenery of late spring was dried and turning brown after a long, hot summer. And that which the sun had not killed off had been trampled to death by the marching and drilling of soldiers who had followed the first militia regiments. Even the smell of Camp Olden had changed. While all military camps reeked of wood fires, wet wool uniforms, sweat from both man and beast, and latrines poorly tended to, old encampments tended to have a more pungent odor. The nearness of the stagnant Raritan and Delaware Canal, not to mention the state prison just opposite the camp, added their particular smells to the camp's stench. It reminded Kevin of rotting meat. That, Kevin always thought, was a good analogy, for many of the men gathered in such camps would, in time, be nothing more than that.

At regimental headquarters, Kevin was greeted with a face that was vaguely familiar. ''O'Keeth, sir. Johnny O'Keeth from Perth Amboy.''

There was a moment of thought, then Kevin's face lit up as he recognized both the name and face. ''Oh, yes. You worked in my father's brickyard and then joined the police force.''

A smile lit O'Keeth's face. "That's right, sir. I did. You'll be pleased to know, I'm sure, there are several other lads from Perth Amboy, including old Frederick Himmel. And wouldn't you know, they made him the first sergeant. He's become a right and proper Prussian drillmaster, he has."

The sight of a bright and friendly face had the effect of bringing Kevin out of the funk that he had wandered about in all morning, for O'Keeth's cheerfulness was contagious. "How many of the lads," Kevin inquired, "are there from the Amboys?"

"Oh, about twelve, if you count the ones who come up from South Amboy. There would have been more, you know, but . . ." For a moment, O'Keeth's face darkened. It was as if he had misspoken and suddenly realized it.

Kevin's curiosity was piqued by this, and he pressed the man. With a fatherly reassurance, he urged O'Keeth to continue.

"Well, if the truth be known, sir, it's the officers. Your father held a mass recruiting meeting with the idea of raising a company from the Amboys. Lots of lads from the terra-cotta works, the docks, and the railroad gangs attended. And all was going well until someone announced that the officers were all going to be from Newark. And you know what sir?" O'Keeth stopped. Fired up by his own conversation, he looked into Kevin's eyes. "Not a one of the men your father picked to lead his company was a Catholic or an Irishman."

"And that," Kevin enjoined, "made a difference?"

"Yeees, sir. I'm here to tell you it did. Some of the older fellas, you know, those from the old country, stood up and shouted that they weren't going to be the cannon fodder for some rich gentleman's son, like they had been in Ireland. Those who hadn't signed their names up and walked out. Oh, sir, it was a mess."

"But you couldn't, I guess, because you'd already signed."

His tone softened somewhat as O'Keeth, in a sheepish tone and with a shuffling of feet, admitted that he signed up after that fuss. "I was tired of being made fun of by the other lads on the police force. When Frederick Himmel, the only man who treated me decently, signed on, I decided to give it a try."

Kevin shook his head. "But nothing's changed. You're still

a private, not much different than you were as a policeman.''

"Oh, but, sir, it is different. Here I'm just as good as the next man. And I'm fighting for something that's important, something that means a great deal to me.''

"And what would that be?''

"A free country. A country that lets me do what I see fit and make my own decisions. I'm beholden to no man, for no man can tell me not to do that or not to do this. Unlike my father, who was tied to the ground that they buried him in by some lord who never knew him, I am a free man.''

This unexpected and profound statement by O'Keeth rocked Kevin back on his heels for a moment. Here was a simple man, barely able to read and write and with next to no means, with a conviction and dedication that Kevin himself had never known. Glancing down for a moment, Kevin chuckled, then looked up at O'Keeth. "Private O'Keeth, I thank you for sharing that with me. I really appreciate it.''

The momentary fear that O'Keeth had felt passed with Kevin's announcement. The broad grin lit up his face again. Before turning to lead Kevin to the company area, he commented, more to himself, "I knew I was right. I knew that once we had one of our own with us, everything would be right with the world.''

That O'Keeth considered him "one of our own'' and was glad to have him there pleased Kevin. Perhaps, Kevin thought, he had made the right choice. That, of course, was yet to be determined.

The meeting between Trevor Ward and Kevin Bannon was strained. The smugness that Trevor had displayed so well yesterday was gone. In its place, there were signs of uneasiness and concern. "I will not lie to you, Mr. Bannon,'' he announced during their meeting. "I am glad at least to have someone with military experience, other than that crazy old Prussian, to rely on.''

The manner in which Trevor referred to Himmel bothered Kevin. He did not, however, show his displeasure. Instead, he queried Trevor. "What, exactly, is it that you expect of me, *Captain* Ward?''

"I need you to do two things. First, and most important, I need your help in preparing this company for battle. I have, as

I'm sure you know, no military background. I, like you, owe my commission to my father.''

Kevin was about to remind Trevor that he, Kevin, had been a member of the militia well before the war, but said nothing. Trevor knew that and there was no need to add any more problems between them than already existed. ''And the second item you need my help with, sir?''

Trevor hesitated and looked away from Kevin as he spoke. He couldn't look into Kevin's eyes. Whether this was because of shame or disdain, Kevin could not tell. It didn't really matter, for the gist of his comments inflamed Kevin regardless of Trevor's meaning. ''I need your help in dealing with those people,'' Trevor said, gesturing vaguely out of the tent toward the company street.

''By *'those'* people, I assume you mean the Irish.''

Trevor turned his back on Kevin. ''Yes, that's exactly what I mean. Most of this company was recruited from the Horseshoe in Newark. They don't seem to be taking well to military discipline. I was hoping . . . I mean the colonel was hoping that having an Irish officer in the company would . . .''

''Pacify the men?'' Kevin finished.

Trevor looked over his shoulder. ''Yes, something like that. Do you think you can do that for us and the regiment?''

Barely managing to hide the disgust he felt, Kevin snapped back with a crisp, military response that was accented with the best Irish brogue that he could manage. ''Well, *sir*, you can be sure of that. Now don't you worry a moment. We humble Paddies will get along just fine, Captain.''

Trevor turned and faced Kevin. There was anger in his eyes. Kevin, however, didn't care. His short conversation with O'Keeth had been both enlightening and encouraging. Given time, Kevin realized that he would be able to master both situations and show, for all to see, that he, and not Trevor Ward, was the better man. Though these weren't exactly the best reasons for going to war, at the moment, they were enough for Kevin.

## CHAPTER 11

# January, 1862
# On the Romney-
# Winchester Road

WITH A START, JAMES WOKE UP. IT WASN'T THE SHIVERING that stirred him. The bitter cold they'd been dealing with for the past week left everyone shivering. Even when standing over blazing campfires, James found himself shivering. So it wasn't the shivering that brought him out of the first sound sleep he'd managed in days.

Though he felt Will's back against his, James neither felt movement nor heard any sounds from his friend. Though this caused James to panic, he was careful as he reached around with his hand to feel Will's chest since he didn't want to knock off the blanket which the two men shared for warmth. After a second, he felt Will's chest heave up as if he were laboring to catch a breath. At least, James thought, he's alive. Though still worried, James could relax a bit. Pulling his hand away quickly to cover his mouth as he began to cough uncontrollably, James decided that it was best that he leave Will alone for a while. Now that he was awake and hacking again, James knew there would be no going back to sleep. Slowly, so as not to disturb Will, James eased away from his friend and out from under their shared blanket.

Though the thin gray wool blanket, issued by the brigade quartermaster from stores captured from a Union cavalry regiment, offered scant protection from the bitter cold they had been facing since beginning their march for Romney, it was better than nothing. And nothing, he thought as he slowly pushed himself up off the ground, was what he felt he had on as the bitterly cold wind knifed through the thinning wool of his shell jacket. Automatically, his hand shot up to pull his collar closed. The hand collided with his chin as he tucked it down in an effort to trap whatever body warmth he could.

Shuffling over to a small fire several feet away and surrounded by seated and standing men, James elbowed his way into the circle without a word or an apology. There was no need to speak, for everyone standing about the fire was in the same predicament as James, cold near the point of freezing and seeking whatever available relief, however short or minor, could be had from the little heat the fire was throwing off. For the longest time no one spoke. Only the crackle of the fire, a chattering of teeth, and an occasional stomping of feet broke the silence. All of the men, like James, though exhausted, were unable to go back to sleep due to the cold. So they gathered together, like a herd of forlorn elk, in an effort to stay warm while they waited for the pale winter sun to rise and another day's march to begin.

"We'll be in Winchester by tonight for sure, boys," Andrew Caddall offered to no one in particular. "Sure as I'll bet my life, we'll be back in tonight."

A bearded man, rubbing a leg that was bruised, shook his head. "Not if them roads don't get any better." A few men, seeing the dark-haired man rubbing his thigh, nodded in agreement. The frozen roads were worn smooth as glass by the passage of wagons and artillery limbers, making them slick and treacherous for man and beast alike.

Matthew Hazard, crouched low and only inches from the fire, grunted. "Andy, if'en we don't make it back soon, I think you and a whole lot of us boys will have to pay up on that bet." Then, in a soft, mournful tone, Matthew added, "I only pray to God that Marty hasn't already done so."

Realizing that his comment had caused Matthew grief, Caddall tried to ease Matthew's fears. "I'm sure, Matty, that your brother's doing fine. They took him back better than a week ago. Why, I bet he's sitting back there in Winchester now, tucked away in some nice warm bed in a hospital, being tended to by one of those pretty young things that come around to help the surgeons."

If Caddall's words made Matthew feel any better, he didn't show it. Instead, Matthew just sat there motionless as he stared into the fire. After thinking about what Caddall had said for several seconds Matthew took in a deep breath. "I sure hope you're right, Andy. I don't know what I'd say to Ma. She's always worried 'bout us, seeing's as we never bothered to take care of ourselves proper like. She said we never did have the sense to come in out of the rain. She . . ." With tears streaking down his cheeks and his voice choking up, Matthew stopped, letting the quiet lap back over the miserable gathering of soldiers. No one offered Matthew a reassuring word or took any notice of his tears. They all felt as he did, to some degree or another, and spurred on by his recollections of his mother, were lost in their own thoughts of home.

For James, moments like this were hard, for he carried no fond memories of home like the others. The images of home that he conjured up were cold, hard, and all too often brutal and painful. Home, to James, had never been a refuge. Rather, it had always been a place to be avoided by both him and his brother, Kevin. The docks, the streets, and even the bars were far more inviting and pleasant than even his own bedroom. Were it not for the sense of responsibility that protecting his younger brother from his father had nurtured, and his love for that brother, James would have left home at an early age.

Now Kevin, like his home, were distant memories of another life that haunted him but were no longer his. But his sense of responsibility, transferred over to Will McPherson, was still very much alive. Glancing behind him, he looked over toward the dark mass of blanket he and Will shared. Seeing his concern, Andrew Caddall spoke as James looked. "Is Will doing any better, Jimmy?" There was real concern in his voice.

After looking at the blanket for another moment or two and seeing it quiver as Will coughed, James turned back to the fire, shaking his head. "He's worse. Burning up with fever now. He's got pneumonia for sure."

"Well, he's young and strong, Jimmy boy. He'll pull through all right."

James shook his head. "He's young, but he's not strong. Not anymore. He used every ounce of strength he had left to pull through that bout with diarrhea last month. I told him he needed to stay back. I told him he needed to ask the colonel to be left with the rear detachment. But he wouldn't listen. No, he said,

I'm a corporal now and I can't be hanging back in the rear like a slacker. Now, he's barely able to walk. Lord," James moaned as tears began to well up in his eyes, "I don't know if *I've* got enough strength left to help him if he can't walk today."

After a brief silence, Matthew Hazard stood up next to James. Reaching around his shoulder, Matthew gave James a light pat on the back. "Don't worry, I'll help you, Jimmy." Then looking about the fire, he nodded. "We'll all help you."

Except for an occasional crack or sputter from the logs burning in the fireplace, there were no sounds in the room where the McPhersons were gathered. The elder McPherson was asleep in his rocker, near the fireplace, as he usually was by this time of night. "The cold," he complained to his wife every day, "just takes it right out of me." His wife sat quietly in her rocker next to him. She was busy mending a pair of trousers that were too small for her younger son, Daniel. A shortage of material, and just about everything else except bad news, made it imperative that they last another year. Daniel, for his part, was lying between them on the floor. He was supposed to be doing an assignment for school but was, instead, busily drawing sketches of cannons, flags, and charging horse soldiers.

Mary Beth, seated across the room, divided her time between her efforts to read *Gulliver's Travels* and looking out the window she was seated next to. To her, the quiet seemed tedious, strained. It had been that way every night since the beginning of the new year, or more correctly, the 1st of January when Major General Thomas J. Jackson's division, accompanied by General William Loring's division, marched out of Winchester. Though the weather had been tolerably good when they had left, within a week the temperature had dropped to zero. With the snow came a deep concern for her brother Will and his friend James. Her every moment these days was filled with thoughts and fears for their safety, though no one spoke of them, except on one occasion, after dinner one night, when Elizabeth McPherson, out of the clear blue, looked up and whispered in prayer, "Lord, if only we could have reliable word that our Will was safe, I could rest."

Though no one heard her, Mary Beth added in hushed tones, "And James. Please don't forget James."

There was, however, no reliable word these days. While it was known Jackson's force had reached and taken Romney, the only thing Mary Beth heard were muted rumors carried back by the wounded and ill soldiers who were steadily filling every field hospital and many homes in and around Winchester. "Pneumonia is carrying away more of the dear boys," a family friend from town lamented, "than Yankee bullets." Anxious for news of Will and James, Mary Beth made a habit, despite her mother's warnings not to, of visiting the hospitals in search of information. While every now and then someone admitted knowing "the Cadets," as Will and James were still being collectively called, no one had any exact knowledge as to their well-being. "Oh," one soldier recovering from the loss of three fingers due to frostbite told Mary Beth, "I imagine they're out there right now, stomping their feet like everyone else so's they don't freeze to the ground." While the soldier found his remark funny, Mary Beth saw no humor in it and left. She didn't, however, give up, for Mary Beth was persistent to the point of being headstrong. "A mule," Will called her. "A mule in a skirt, that's what you are."

She was lost in the midst of that thought when a thumping at the door, like that of an animal trying to force its way in, broke the stillness. More curious than alarmed, Mary Beth's mother turned her face toward the front hall. After listening for a moment, she looked down at her son. "Daniel, if that's your dog, I'm going to give him a whipping like he's never had before."

"He's cold, Ma. He just wants to get in and be with us, at the fire."

"Well, young man, so long as I'm alive, no fleabag dog is going to share this house with me. Now go out there and quiet him down before he brings down the door."

Though complaining, Daniel got up and walked out of the room, headed to the door. Mary Beth, who loved the long blond-haired mongrel as much as her brother did, was about to tell her mother that she was being unreasonable when Daniel yelled from the front hall. "Come quick. It's Will!"

The boy's voice, betraying more shock and concern than joy,

caused both women to leap to their feet. Just before they rushed for the door, they glanced over at each other. Mary Beth could see that there was a blend of concern and dread in her mother's eyes. "We best go out there and see if they need help," she said in a matter-of-fact manner that barely hid her concern. Ignoring her husband, who was just now stirring and asking, in a stupor, what all the racket was about, Will's mother started for the front hall.

She stopped short, however, as a tall, lanky man, holding up another figure slumped down with feet dragging, came barging through the door into the room where the family had been gathered. Seeing that the stranger was looking for someplace to set his care down, Elizabeth McPherson rushed over to her vacant chair at the fireplace and turned it toward them. "Here, young man, bring him over here."

Thomas McPherson, now wide awake, leaped to his feet and bounded across the room to the two struggling men. Taking the free arm of the limp figure over his shoulder, he helped the stranger drag his charge to where Elizabeth was waiting. With a groan, the two men eased Will McPherson's ragged and haggard figure into the chair. Heaving a sigh of relief, the stranger stood up and shook himself out as he looked about the room. "I hope you be the McPhersons."

"That we are, stranger," Thomas McPherson responded, as Elizabeth began to pull off the filthy blanket wrapped about Will's shoulders. "And you?"

Rather than respond immediately, the stranger inched his way toward the fire, closing his eyes and canting his dirty, bearded face up toward the ceiling. A smile began to spread across his face as the numbness left his arms and feet and he felt true warmth for the first time. "Hazard," he said without opening his eyes as he savored the warmth of the room. "Matthew Hazard. Will and me and my brother Marty and James Bannon are all messmates."

The mention of James' name caused Mary Beth, standing off to one side, to shudder. "James Bannon. How's James Bannon? Where is he?"

From behind them, a weak voice responded. "Right here, Miss McPherson. I . . ."

Twirling around, Mary Beth saw another man, leaning

against the doorjamb of the room. James' appearance caused her to gasp. Like Will and Matthew Hazard, James was attired in ragged clothes that were both wet and filthy. His face, beet red from the cold, was just as dirty as his clothes and covered with a scraggly, tangled beard. Composing herself, Mary Beth took several quick steps up to him and tried to smile. When she looked into his feverish eyes, however, her feeble smile disappeared. Reaching out, she went to grasp James' arm in order to lead him to the fire just as his legs buckled under him. James' eyes rolled up into the back of his head as, without so much as a grunt, he collapsed on the floor in a heap.

At first, James thought that he was floating. Light-headed and groggy, he couldn't feel his arms and legs. Though, at first, this thought was pleasing, in an instant that idea was wiped away. With a start, James sat bolt upright in the bed and screamed. Mary Beth, standing across the room and folding some linen, jumped a good foot off the floor when James screamed. Dropping the tablecloth she held, she rushed over to the side of the bed, where she stood for a moment, staring at James.

With eyes wild with fear, James pushed the fluffy comforter off of him and began to frantically run his hands all over his body. Finding no wound there, he ran his hands down his legs until he reached his toes. Only then, when he was satisfied that he was all right, did his breathing slow down. Closing his eyes, he mumbled something that sounded like a prayer and then flopped backwards onto the bed.

Not understanding any of this, Mary Beth, still shaking from the fright he had given her, reached down and pulled the covers back up over James. Patiently, she stood there, waiting for James to open his eyes and greet her. When he didn't, falling backwards instead and showing no inclination to speak, Mary Beth decided to speak to him. "Are you awake, James?"

Though he heard her question, he didn't answer it, asking his own instead. "Where am I?" Then, before Mary Beth could answer, James opened his eyes and turned his head toward her. "Mary Beth, is Will . . . How is he?"

Seeing that he was now fully conscious, Mary Beth put on a

bright, brave smile. "Will's doing fine, James. In fact, he's doing better than you. He was up this morning with the sun. Made it down to the breakfast table too."

For a moment, there was a look of disbelief in James' eyes. Mary Beth reached out and felt James' forehead. Realizing that he had no idea how long they had been there, she said, "You've been here now for three days, Mr. Bannon."

"Here? In this bed?"

"Here, Mr. Bannon, in this bed, sweating out a fever."

"Three days?"

Lifting her right hand, Mary Beth held up three fingers. "Yes, three whole days."

James thought about that for a moment. Then, lifting the cover, he looked down at his body. He was wearing a clean white cotton nightshirt. His feet and the part of his legs that he could see looked clean. Easing the covers down, he looked sheepishly up at Mary Beth. "I don't suppose that you had a hand in . . ."

Mary Beth's face brightened with a broad smile. "Why, Mr. Bannon, modest, are we?"

This made James blush. "Well, I just was wondering if, I mean . . ."

"I have two brothers, one younger and one older, not to mention a father. There's not much a girl living in a family like this on a farm hasn't seen by the time she's become a woman."

Looking down for a moment, James smiled and looked back. "No, I guess not." Then, anxious to change the subject, for he was beginning to notice just how much of a woman Mary Beth was, James asked about Matthew Hazard. "Oh, he stayed the night. In the morning, Mother made him bathe; she washed his uniform, mended it as best she could, and then fed him. Lordy," Mary Beth exclaimed, "that man can eat."

The mention of food brought James' stomach to life. "We've been on short rations for days. Fact was, everything was short out there in Romney, except for the Yankees and the cold. Had plenty of them."

Mary Beth sighed. "Yes, Matty told us all about it. And he told us all about you and Will. You two apparently make quite a pair when the fighting starts."

Again, James blushed. "We just do like everyone else. Nothing more."

"Not according to Matty. He said that you should have been made a corporal, but because of a captain on the staff, another VMI man who doesn't like you, Will got the stripes."

James' face darkened at the mention of Abner Couper. After the Battle of Manassas, when a vacancy for corporal became open, Will had been nominated to fill it. Will, knowing that James, and not he, deserved the stripes, had gone to Colonel Preston and told him the story of the fight that day. The colonel, according to Will, was about to change his mind when Couper, listening to the conversation, intervened and convinced the colonel that Will was the all-round better soldier. Though the stripes really didn't mean that much to James, the idea that Abner Couper was still hovering out there, watching and waiting for any chance to get at him, bothered James.

Seeing how angry her mention of the incident made James, Mary Beth quickly changed the subject. "Mr. Hazard went back to camp the next day, taking the note from the surgeon who turned you away from the hospital."

For a moment, James had to think about what she was talking about. Slowly, he began to piece together the events of that night. Upon reaching Winchester, Matty and he had dragged Will to the nearest hospital only to find out that it was already overcrowded. The chief surgeon there, finding out that Will was a local boy, wrote out a note saying that Will was too ill to return to camp but could not be kept at the hospital. The surgeon, therefore, issued Will a medical furlough to go to his home. Though James didn't know if the surgeon had the authority to do so, he was in no shape to argue.

Sitting up suddenly, James looked about the room. "My uniform. Where's my uniform?"

"I wanted to burn it. But Mother, knowing that there's a shortage, insisted on washing and mending it. I think she's finished. Why?"

"I've got to get back to camp. The note the surgeon gave us was only for Will. They probably have me listed as absent without leave."

Mary Beth laughed. "Oh, is that all you're worried about?"

"Is that all? Mary Beth, they shoot deserters."

"Oh, don't worry. Matthew went back with a note from Mother explaining that you were also ill. An officer came by yesterday and checked on the two of you. Nice gentleman, a Lieutenant Lynn, I think. He stayed for dinner and then rushed back to his company. Before he left, he told Ma to keep you two until you were both fit and ready for service. So," Mary Beth said with a triumphant smile, "my mother is in charge of you two, and what she says is law."

Satisfied that his absence from the company was sanctioned, and quite comfortable where he was, James lay back down. "Do you think," he asked timidly, "I could have a bite to eat? It's been three days, after all."

"Well, after spending so much time in Winchester and never bothering to come home with Will for dinner, I am glad to finally have you here."

Though Mary Beth's words were not meant as a scolding, James felt a pang of embarrassment. He started to explain, but Mary Beth put her hand up to shush him as she would a child. "Mr. Bannon, I am sure you had your reasons for not coming in the past. That doesn't matter anymore. What is important now is that you're here and that you're our guest. So please, relax, rest, and I'll tend to your meal." With that, Mary Beth turned, purposely giving her skirt a slight flick so that it fluttered about her handsome form, and marched out the door of the room. As he watched her go, James realized that there was more to what she had just said than she let on. As to what, exactly, she had on her mind, he didn't have a clue. Not that it mattered for now. All that was important to James at that moment was Will. Just as important was that they were both in a dry, warm place, where food was plentiful. It was, to James, a gift from heaven that could not be ignored. It was a soldier's dream come true, and as hard as it was for him, James relaxed and tried to enjoy it.

# CHAPTER 12

# March, 1862
# Near Alexandria,
# Virginia

"LIEUTENANT BANNON, SIR, THE COMPANY'S FORMED AND ready."

"First Sergeant, your timing is incredible. Could you come in here and give me a hand with this accursed sash?"

Pushing the tent flap up, First Sergeant Frederick Himmel ducked, careful not to knock his hat off, and entered the tent shared by First Lieutenant Kevin Bannon and the company's second lieutenant, Henry Meyers from Newark, New Jersey. A lad of nineteen, Meyers had left his studies at Princeton and rushed home, where his father, like many other fathers with political connections, managed to secure him a commission in the 4th New Jersey Volunteer Regiment.

Himmel found Kevin dressed, except for the red officer's sash, belt, and sword. He was standing in the center of his tent, between the cots, holding both ends of the sash and looking at it as if it were a bothersome snake that he was having trouble controlling. Looking up at Himmel, Kevin gave a grimace of disgust. "Sorry about this, First Sergeant. Young Mr. Meyers was supposed to give me a hand, but as soon as he was dressed, he was out of here before I knew it."

"He is," Himmel replied with a fatherly chuckle, "an anxious and energetic lad. He's already out there with the company, pacing back and forth, waiting for you like a pup waiting for his boy." Then, realizing that he might have insulted Kevin, Himmel stopped to apologize. "Oh, I am sorry, sir. I didn't mean to say that you were a boy. I was just . . ."

Kevin laughed. "No need to apologize. I know what you

meant. Now, let's get on with this and see if the two of us can't tame this damnable bit of cloth.''

Leaning his rifle against Kevin's cot, the first sergeant took one end of the sash and slowly walked away from Kevin. Kevin, with the other end, found a good starting point and held the sash there, flat against his body, about two and a half feet from his end. Looking down to ensure that the red tassel on his end reached his right knee, he called out to Himmel, "Okay, here we go." Slowly, keeping one hand on the sash at his waist, Kevin began to turn, wrapping himself into the sash. The first sergeant, keeping the other end tight, but not too tight, slowly began to walk toward Kevin as more and more of the scarlet sash was wound about Kevin's body.

"Will the captain be joining us for today's grand review, sir?"

Though the first sergeant's tone was innocent enough, Kevin chose not to answer the question. He knew that neither the first sergeant, nor anyone else in the company, cared for their company commander.

Trevor Meguire Ward was everything that Kevin was not, and he took every opportunity to remind him of that. "Perhaps, Kevin," he would remind him on many occasions, with a barely concealed sneer, "when your family has spent as many generations in this country as mine has, you will appreciate why things are the way they are." Kevin, though angered by Trevor's presumptuousness and pompous attitude, always managed to hold himself back.

Often, Kevin dreamed of smashing Trevor square in his smug, pasty white face. But he didn't. To do so, after all, would simply prove Trevor's point. So instead, Kevin behaved as Trevor hoped he wouldn't. He obeyed his orders promptly and carried out his military duties smartly and efficiently. Frustrated by Kevin's response, Trevor used every opportunity to provoke Kevin into doing something rash that would prove to his peers that Kevin Bannon was nothing more than the offspring of a presumptuous and rather odious Irish immigrant of no account.

In drilling his company, Kevin found a sense of self-worth and pride that he hadn't felt before. That he began to regard Company J as his own was natural. Trevor was seldom there. With no military background at all and unable to make sense of the complex commands and maneuvering prescribed by Scott's manual on infantry tactics, he avoided drilling the company. Instead, he spent most of his time with the regimental, brigade, and division staff officers. There, in the company of other ambitious young men of means such as himself, Trevor assumed great airs. Like the others, he often spoke of grand military strategy while damning the wretched civilian politicians who interfered with the conduct of military affairs. And like so many of his peers, he was awed by the fame and power of men such as Phil Kearny, their one-armed brigade commander, and General George C. McClellan, the commander of the Army of the Potomac. In the shadow of such men, Trevor left the mundane daily concerns of training and administering his company to Kevin and First Sergeant Himmel.

In this task, Kevin excelled. Though he was, at first, unsure of himself due to his experience in the wake of the Bull Run disaster, Kevin pitched in to his duties. In part this drive was motivated by his desire to put behind him the regrettable incident that had resulted in Harriet Shields breaking off all correspondence and contact. Kevin had offered no note of apology, and Harriet made no effort to renew their courtship. The company was full of eager young men, many of them still boys, who wanted to be soldiers. They demanded Kevin's full attention, and he gave it to them. Together with Frederick Himmel, Kevin did his best to train them and care for them, earning in the process, their respect and admiration. From this unspoken affection drawn from the men charged to his responsibility, Kevin found the self-worth that his father's bitter words had so cruelly tried to deny him and his older brother's overprotection had kept him from achieving on his own. Though Trevor hadn't planned on things turning out as they did, his snubbing of Kevin diminished his and not Kevin's value in the eyes of the soldiers in the ranks.

● ● ●

Only First Sergeant Himmel's clearing his throat brought Kevin back from his tangled thoughts of Trevor and Harriet. Looking up, Kevin noticed that he had reached the end of the sash, and Himmel was waiting patiently for Kevin to relieve him of the end he had been holding. When Kevin did, Himmel asked again, in a rather nonchalant manner, if Captain Ward would be commanding the company that day.

Remembering that he had not answered the first sergeant's question, Kevin shook his head as if to clear it, then took the end of the sash from the first sergeant and began to pin and tuck the sash together. "Oh, sorry. My mind was wandering."

Used to the peculiar ways of officers, Himmel chuckled. "Oh, no problem, sir. I know you have much on your mind, what with the rumors of a march into Virginia and all."

Mention of a march into Virginia made Kevin laugh. "If I took every rumor about *this* Army moving in the near future seriously, I'd be bald from worry by now."

"It is a rather slow-moving Army, isn't it."

"Slow!" Kevin exclaimed as he finished and then turned to face Himmel. "A person has to move first before he can be slow. If it weren't for all these division and corps reviews, this army would have taken root right here where it sits."

Nodding in agreement, Himmel reflected on Kevin's comment. "Yes, yes. This is true. In the Prussian Army, even in peacetime training we marched and maneuvered a great deal. Do you suppose," he asked, "that war and what happened to General McDowell last July has made our General McClellan cautious?"

Kevin thought about Bull Run. "Yes, I suppose it did. Battle has a way of doing that, I guess." Then, he looked at the first sergeant. "And to answer your question, the company commander will not march with us today. He has been selected to serve as an escort officer for the visiting dignitaries coming down from New Jersey for this review."

Absentmindedly, as if talking to himself, Himmel lamented, "I should have figured."

Though Kevin should have reprimanded Himmel for making

a remark that was an obvious slight on a superior officer, Kevin ignored it, as he did all such remarks. If he took the time to respond every time an NCO or private made a comment like that, he'd have no time to tend to the administrative duties and training that Trevor was so ready to leave to him. Like the first sergeant, the men in the company had come to accept that Kevin, not Trevor, was the only officer who was reliable and genuinely cared for them and their welfare.

Henry Meyers, the company's second lieutenant, was caught in a dilemma. He truly admired the manner in which Kevin tended to the military chores necessary to run and maintain a company and the skills he demonstrated in maneuvering the company about the drill field. And while he would have liked to spend more time with Kevin in order to learn everything that Kevin knew about the Army and training soldiers, Henry Meyers knew it would be social and political suicide to side with "The Immigrant's Boy," as Trevor called Kevin when in the company of other officers. For Meyers, like everyone else in the regiment, sensed the tension between Kevin and Trevor. So, while Trevor was off with the regimental or brigade staffs and Henry Meyers was busy keeping out of the line of fire, Kevin was left with nothing to do except run the company and prepare it for a battle that never seemed to come.

Finished pinning his sash in place, Kevin looked down at it. "This sash, First Sergeant, isn't going to leave this tent if and when we ever march off to fight the secess."

Coming up behind Kevin with his sword belt open and ready for Kevin to put on, Himmel smiled. "Perhaps, Lieutenant Bannon, I can leave mine with yours."

With a mock look of horror on his face, Kevin protested. "Heavens no, First Sergeant. The two might mate with each other and produce more of the accursed things."

"Right you are, sir. Now, if you'll excuse me, I'll go tend to the lads."

Picking his sword up from his cot and hooking it onto his belt, Kevin nodded. "Yes, of course. I'll be right along and then we can all have a good look at our special guests. It will be interesting to see who traveled all the way from New Jersey just to see General Franklin and his band of twelve thousand."

• • •

With a precision that his old company in the 2nd Regiment of Militia never mastered, Kevin wheeled his company to the left and began the final advance toward the reviewing party. Despite the cold and dampness of early March, there was quite a large group of well turned out civilian gentlemen and ladies watching the grand review. The ladies, for their part, remained in their carriages in order to get a better view as well as to avoid the mud that made the ground slippery and tended to soil the hems of their ornately trimmed skirts and crinolines. None of the gathered spectators and guests took into account that the same mud would leave the twelve thousand soldiers of General Franklin's corps a massive cleaning chore, amounting to some twenty-four thousand shoes and twelve thousand pairs of trousers, not to mention rifles and other equipment. Soldiers, after all, were expected to do this sort of thing and enjoy it. While many a soldier did find being part of such a massive body of armed men thrilling, most tolerated it as simply another part of a soldier's lot. A few cynics, like Kevin, saw it as a waste, nothing more than another excuse for a general to impress politicians and men of wealth who someday would be expected to remember this little kindness and repay the general with a favor of their own.

Such thoughts were suddenly shoved aside as his company neared the first marker on the side of the field, which told him he was nearing the reviewing party. Watching it out of the corner of his eye, Kevin waited until he was parallel with the marker. Then, turning his head back over his left shoulder, he issued his orders in a booming voice. He had to, for he was competing with the steady roll of the company drums beating out a cadence for the soldiers as well as a full band that stood opposite the reviewing party, playing loud and fast-paced martial music. In a single motion, Kevin brought the hilt of his sword up until it was inches from where his face would be if it were turned to the front and let out his preparatory command. ''EYEEEES . . .''

Hearing his voice and the first part of the command, the soldiers of Company J braced themselves to execute the com-

211

mand that was about to follow. After a pause of a second or two, Kevin completed the command with a crisp, sharp, "RIGHT." With that, he brought his sword down with a quick, almost exaggerated motion till his right arm was angled down and out to the right. Holding his arm stiff, he snapped his head to the right and fixed his eyes on the party of generals and civilian dignitaries serving that day as the reviewing party. Except for the two soldiers in the far right-hand file, every man in Company J snapped his head to the right.

Though they were supposed to look at the man's head to their immediate right, many couldn't resist the temptation to look at the reviewing party and see who was there. From behind him, Kevin could hear the remarks of some of the men, mostly from the second rank, as the company marched past the reviewing stand. "It's only our dear senator and Little Mac," one man commented dryly. "To think," another responded, "I voted for that pompous ass. He'll not get my vote again, I can tell you." A third threw in his opinion. "Well, at least General McClellan is here." "And is that," a fourth voice with a heavy Irish accent intoned, "supposed to make us feel better about this whole big ta-do?"

Though Kevin wanted to shout back and quiet the men, he had no need to, for above the din of drums and the full brass band, the next voice he heard was that of First Sergeant Himmel. With his sharp, curt parade-ground tone made more compelling by his German accent, Himmel snapped, "Quiet! Quiet, all of you or I'll have the lot of you drilling till you drop." Though this stopped the talking, one man couldn't resist having the final say in the matter. The next sound Kevin heard, just as he marched past General McClellan, affectionately called Little Mac by his troops, was one of his men making a rude noise that sounded like a person passing wind. Even Kevin was half tempted to laugh at this, barely managing to keep a stern and serious expression on his face. Behind him he knew Himmel's face was turning beet red as his eyes darted about the soldiers to his front in an effort to discover who the offender was.

Kevin was still thinking of this when, out of the corner of his eye, he caught sight of something white flapping in the breeze. Looking away from the reviewing party without moving his head, Kevin saw a woman standing upright in a carriage, waving a handkerchief wildly at him. Though he could tell that she was indeed facing him, her bonnet and the distance hid the features of her face. Curious, Kevin watched the woman intently as he drew nearer. This almost caused him to miss the next guide marker. At the last minute, however, he caught sight of the marker, only because it was in line with the woman he was watching. Realizing his error, Kevin rushed his commands. "EYES, FRONT." This hurried command caused a disjointed ripple effect as some soldiers, quick on the uptake, turned before others, expecting the customary pause, did so. Fortunately, all eyes that mattered were already staring intently at Company K, coming up fast behind Kevin's company.

Without another thought about the woman, Kevin brought the tip of his sword up with a snap to the front of his right shoulder. With that, he turned his attention back to what he was doing, thankful that he had managed to catch himself before it was too late.

Only a request by the brigade commander, Brigadier General Phil Kearny, brought Kevin to the reception and dance held in honor of the visitors from New Jersey. Had anyone else made the request, Kevin would have declined without a second thought. To General Kearny, a man schooled in the art of war on European battlefields, a request by a superior officer was no different from an order. So Kevin, like all the other officers in the brigade, scraped the mud off his shoes, brushed the dirt from his trousers, and donned his accursed bright red sash for a second time that day. Together with his one true friend in the regiment, First Lieutenant Samuel M. Gaul of Company G, Kevin headed into Washington.

When he showed up promptly at seven o'clock, Kevin's intention was to spend as little time there as possible. He planned to share a drink or two with Samuel Gaul, let General Kearny see him, and then, slip away. Walking into the main dining room of Senator Edmund Brent's home, Kevin and Samuel stopped and took in the room. Gaul, sharing Kevin's disdain of social affairs such as this, snorted when he saw how few people were there. "I told you we should have waited some before coming. Now we'll have to wait until the room fills before we can gracefully leave."

Kevin shook his head. "No, no, no, my dear Samuel. You're wrong, my dear sir."

"Oh? And how does your Gaelic logic come up with that?"

Gaul was one of the few officers who could make fun of Kevin's Irish heritage without offending him. Kevin smirked. "The fewer people in the room, the more visible we are. Later, as others come in and incur the wrath of our esteemed brigadier, our absence shan't be noticed."

"A crafty race, you Irish. Crafty indeed."

"And thirsty," Kevin added as he poked his elbow into Gaul's ribs. "Don't forget to mention that we are a thirsty race."

"Yes, well, I thought that went without saying." Then, with an exaggerated bow, Gaul bent over and threw his hand out, motioning for Kevin to precede him into the spacious dining room, which had been cleared for the reception and dance. "After you, dear sir."

Stepping out into the center of the room, the two young officers were halfway to the table where the punch bowl sat, when a familiar voice called out. "Lieutenant Bannon?"

With a noticeable wince, Kevin came to a sudden halt and turned to face Harriet Shields as she walked out of a side room, headed straight for Kevin and Gaul. Noticing his friend's reaction and expression, Gaul leaned over and whispered in Kevin's ear. "Is she . . ."

Kevin nodded. "Umhuh. Mademoiselle Shields herself."

Dressed in a jade-green satin ball gown that didn't quite reach her shoulders and swept the floor in a smooth, gentle motion, Harriet approached Kevin and Gaul. "I was hoping to talk to you," she started as she was still approaching, "before—"

"Before Captain Ward arrived?"

Kevin's mention of Trevor's name and the sharpness of his voice brought Harriet to a dead halt before she had reached the two officers. The look of shock on her face pleased Kevin. Gaul, though he knew of the affair gone bad, was also taken aback by the rudeness of Kevin's remark. Wanting to leave before the two came to verbal blows, Gaul began to excuse himself and back away, but Kevin stopped him by grabbing his arm. "No, no, my dear fellow. I would like to introduce you to my commanding officer's fiancée, Miss Harriet Ann Shields, the daughter of the esteemed Judge Shields of New Brunswick."

Angry now, and not caring who saw it, Harriet closed up on Kevin, stopping square in front of him. *"Mister* Bannon," she said with forced politeness, "I would like to speak with you, alone."

Samuel Gaul was the only one of the three who noticed that they had become the center of attention. Nervously, he glanced about the room until his eyes hit upon a familiar face. With a slight exaggeration, he cleared his throat. "Ah, Kevin. The regimental adjutant just came in. If you don't mind, I have to discuss a discrepancy over the company rolls with him. Ah, if you don't mind, I'd like to go over and catch him now, while I can, and tend to that, ah, matter."

Noticing his friend's nervousness, Kevin looked away from Harriet's determined stare. After glancing quickly about the room he noticed the stares of others who, like them, had come early. Smiling, and nodding politely to where General Kearny and Senator Brent stood watching them, Kevin took Harriet's arm and slowly began to back away in search of a quiet corner. Gaul, seeing his opportunity, fled to seek his own refuge.

Once safely alone in a small side room, Kevin let go of Harriet and turned away from her for a moment as he collected his thoughts. When he was ready, he turned to face her.

With a mock smile on his face, Kevin leaned back and threw his hands out. "Is this suitable, dear lady, for holding our little chitchat?" Looking around, he added bitterly, "After all, I understand that it wouldn't do to have a person of your social standing seen conversing with Irish riffraff, especially by your fiancé."

Putting her hands on her hips, Harriet leaned forward and thrust her chin out. "I am not Trevor's anything. I have no more intention of marrying that bore than I do of ... of ..."

"Of what?" Kevin inquired mockingly.

In anger, she sputtered, "Than of giving up on you, you dunderhead!"

Now it was Kevin's turn to be rocked back. With a shake of

his head, he blinked twice, then looked down at the resolute face inches from his. "But I . . . you . . ."

"I what, Mr. Bannon?"

"Well, you never wrote. After that reception last August and no word from you, I assumed . . ."

"That I didn't love you? That I was going to run off and marry Trevor? You fool. You poor misguided fool. How could I?"

"Your father, my father, and you. The three of you went to so much trouble, so much effort, to make sure that I didn't spend one more minute in New Jersey than I needed to. The commission, the reception, all of it, was so well laid out that I assumed . . ."

Harriet turned away from him and walked over to one side of the room. Clasping both hands up to her bosom, she looked down at the floor for a moment. Then, slowly, she turned her head to one side. "I thought I was being clever. I thought that I could arrange things in such a manner that . . ."

"That what?" demanded Kevin, fearful that Harriet was playacting again in an effort to disarm his anger.

Harriet turned, stiffly seating herself in a chair. As she did so, the skirt of her ball gown spread out before her, like a fan opening. In the center of the fan, she rested her hands on her lap. She didn't look up at Kevin. Instead, she stared vacantly down at her hands, nervously clutching a handkerchief as she continued. "I was trying to be clever. I was trying to make Father love you as I love you."

With a snort, Kevin folded his arms across his chest and looked down at Harriet. "How? By making me look like a fool? By having me assigned to Trevor's company as his subordinate? Please, dear Harriet, do explain, for I am nothing but a dense immigrant who just fell off the boat."

Harriet's posture and demeanor didn't change. Nor did the sorrowful tone of her voice. When she spoke, again it reminded Kevin of someone giving a confession in church. "I had thought myself to be so clever, so smart. I had planned and arranged everything in the hope that somehow, someday, both Father and Mother would see you in the same way that I do. I hadn't planned on Father intervening as he did. I should have known. I should have seen it." Slowly, her tone began to change as the anger began to build up in her and spill out. "How could I be so foolish? How could I have expected my father to change his mind about you or give up his big plans without a fight?" Looking up, with tears in her eyes, Harriet pleaded with Kevin. "Can you ever forgive me for what I did?"

Suspicious, Kevin held his ground. "I suppose that I am to believe, now, that all of this is sincere? And I suppose you expect me to apologize for what happened last August when . . ."

Though his bitter words cut at her, she ignored them. Instead, she stood up and rushed across the room before he finished. When she reached him, she ducked low so that she could look up at Kevin's down-turned face. "No, Kevin. It is I who should be apologizing to you. I've been the fool." Lightly hanging on Kevin's crossed arms, Harriet looked down in shame. As she did so, she reached for Kevin's hands and gathered them up in her own. "I tried so hard to be so clever, so smart. Last June, when you told me that you wanted to leave the Army as soon as you could, I was afraid that I would lose you."

Confused, Kevin looked down at her in puzzlement. "Lose me? I don't understand."

Harriet drew in a deep breath. "By serving in the Army, I had hoped that you would eventually make Father see you as an acceptable suitor for me. Unfortunately, I've come to realize that he's as determined as my mother is to see me married off to someone who is, well . . ."

"Of your own class," Kevin added.

Rubbing the back of Kevin's arm with the tips of her thumbs, Harriet nodded.

"I know, Harriet. I guess I knew it all along."

Looking up, her eyes met his. "That sort of thing doesn't matter to me. Not anymore. In the beginning, it did. Though I tried hard to be different from my father and mother, to look beyond the cut of a man's clothes or who his parents were, I couldn't. Like my parents, I wanted to make you into something that you weren't, something that I didn't want in the first place. You see, Kevin, the reason I love you . . ."

For a second, there was a shocked look in Kevin's eyes.

Shaking his head, he managed to suppress it, and he continued to listen to Harriet's hurried explanation.

"The reason I am *attracted* to you is because of who, and what, you are . . . You're different, you're alive. Your father came to this country from Ireland with nothing. And though Father won't admit it, your father's made his way in the world based on his own abilities, his own skills—not just because his name is Ward, or Shields."

The mention of his father caused Kevin's brow to furrow and his eyes to darken. "What does my father have to do with this?"

Harriet looked down and smiled. "My father always says that the acorn doesn't fall far from the tree. Look at me. I can be just as manipulative and sly as my father. But I can change." She looked up again, reaching her arms around Kevin's as she did so. "I am not my father, but I am his child and can never escape that. Just as you are not your father but will always be your father's son. I've seen your father. I've heard what he says and I've heard what my father has said about him. While I know there is much in him that is less than admirable, I also know that he possesses great drive, willpower, and ambition. I see the same drive, the same ambition in your eyes—together with your gentle soul and kind manner. You are the sort of man whom I not only admire but have all my life dreamed of meeting and marrying."

Harriet's comments thoroughly rattled Kevin. What ambitions, he wondered, did she imagine she saw? And other than pouncing from one crisis to the next to avoid a confrontation with his father, he had no drive to speak of. What, he wondered, did she see in him that he didn't? Confused, he dropped his arms to his sides. Wishing to change the subject, he looked up into her eyes. "If you love me, then why haven't you written? Why have you waited so long to tell me this? And why tell me now?"

Looking down again, Harriet shrugged. "Because, Kevin, I was foolish. I was manipulative and foolish."

For the longest time, they stood there, in silence, as Kevin thought about what she had said. He also thought about his own feelings, feelings that he had managed, until now, to push aside. It had been easy to do so. With a company to train and

**218**

run, it had been easy to ignore Trevor's gloating and Harriet's absence. But now, with her standing before him, he could no longer bury his feelings for her. Pulling one hand free from hers, Kevin reached up, touched her chin, and gently raised her head until their eyes met again. "Harriet, I love you too. I've loved you from the first moment I saw you. And do you know what?"

With tears forming in her eyes, Harriet shook her head.

"Harriet Shields, I am going to marry you, your mother and my fool Irish father be damned."

Harriet's smile, followed by a long, loving kiss, ended all discussion. The soft sound of music from the other room drifted in, heightening the two lovers' passions and drowning out the discussion of the war that would soon engulf everyone gathered there that night, in one way or another.

# IN DEADLY EARNEST

PART FOUR

IN DEADLY
EARNEST

# CHAPTER 13

# March 23rd, 1862
# West of Kernstown,
# Virginia

THE MASS OF UNION SOLDIERS, LITTLE MORE THAN ONE HUN-
dred yards away, was not budging, despite the heavy fire that
the 4th Virginia was pouring into it. This fact was becoming
painfully obvious to James. Just as disturbing was the realization that the Yankees were more than matching their fire with
a telling return fire.

Pausing, James leaned against the tree he was using for
cover and looked about. The sun quickly nearing the western
horizon was announcing that the day was fast coming to a
close. Off to James' right, less than a foot away, were the two
Hazard brothers. As James had been moments before, they
were busy firing away at the line of unyielding Yankees. On his
left, taking shelter behind a stone wall, were men he didn't
even recognize, though he assumed they were from one of the
other Virginia regiments. Will was off somewhere over there,
tending to Lieutenant Lynn's wound and hunting up ammunition.

Besides the Hazard brothers, James could see only four other
members of the Lexington Defenders in the little group that
surrounded him. Of those four, one man, Andy Caddall, was
dying. A minié ball had struck him in the side of the head. It
must have started to tumble when it hit his jaw, for it carried
away the side of his face and a piece of his skull. The only way
that James could tell Caddall was still alive was by an occasional groan accompanied by the sound of gurgling blood that
spewed over his shattered jaw. A second man, Dale Wint, was
shot through both legs but still fighting. There hadn't been

much bleeding at all, a fact that everyone commented on. Wint, after lamenting his fate for a while, pulled himself together when he noticed no one was paying any attention to him. With the help of James and Will, who propped him up against a tree, Wint settled down to calmly loading his rifle and firing. Though quite exposed and unable to run if the Yankees decided to rush their badly sagging line again, Wint was quite content to sit where he was, popping away with everyone else. "Better," he said as he reloaded his rifle, "to be here with friends and doin' something useful than back there in the hands of those butchers this Army calls surgeons."

A third man, Lewis Jacob, was so new that he was more of a hindrance than a help. As Matthew Hazard pointed out, "I don't feel at all comfortable callin' Lewis a man. I mean, it's sort like callin' a calf a bull, if ya know what I mean." Just having turned sixteen and weighing 125 pounds soaking wet, Private Jacob, uniform, rifle, and all, was anything but impressive in appearance.

Unfortunately for James, Lewis' appearance was far better than his performance. The 4th Virginia, as well as the rest of the First Brigade, had started their march before dawn that morning outside of Strasburg, over twenty miles to the south. Not used to the blistering rate of march that General Jackson demanded of his soldiers, Lewis Jacob was struggling to keep up before the second hour had finished. By noon, Marty Hazard had taken pity on Jacob and begun to carry some of his gear, including his rifle. "Marty," Matthew protested, "what in tarnation are you doin' that for? He's a soldier. He's got to learn to carry his own blamed rifle, or suffer. Ain't nobody ever offered to carry my rifle for me."

Will McPherson, promoted to second sergeant after sickness and disease during the winter carried off some of the more senior sergeants in the company, agreed with Matthew. "He's got to learn, Marty. If he can't hack it, then he doesn't belong here." Yet when Matthew suggested that Will order Marty to at least give Jacob his rifle back, Will hesitated. "What Marty does is his business. He'll tire soon of carrying two rifles."

Defiantly, Marty shouted back with glee. "Yah, Matthew, that's right. What I do is my business and no one else's." This response provided the Hazards with just enough provocation for their daily fight, one that they were able to drag on well into the afternoon.

Keeping his own counsel on the matter, James was of two minds. While he agreed with Will on every count, he also understood why Marty had done what he had. After nearly a year of service and several hard, frustrating campaigns, those of the Lexington Defenders who were still with the colors, and that was now less than half the original number, were a hard-looking lot. With few exceptions, they sported beards and mustaches. While some did it in an effort to hide their youth, most simply didn't bother to take the time to shave.

For some, the results were rather comical. James' beard grew in patchily. Frustrated by the weak performance of his hair and tired of being razzed by both Marty and Matthew over his inability to grow "a manly beard," James shaved it off and kept himself clean shaven. "There, now," Marty complimented James after he had disposed of the offending hair, "ya startin' to look like the spry young cadet we've all growed so fond of." Will, on the other hand, grew a nice neat mustache and beard, which he kept trimmed short in the French style that had become so popular.

Marty and Matthew, on the other hand, let their beards grow wild and unkempt, which gave them a fierce look that complemented their rough-hewn features. "It's a good thing," James quipped often to the Hazards, "you boys don't use mirrors. If you did you'd scare yourselves to death for sure." While both of them pretended to resent James' insults and let him know it in no uncertain terms, James and Will caught them, on more than one occasion, slipping Will's pocket mirror out of his haversack. Sneaking off into the bushes, the two brothers would practice making the most ferocious faces they could manage. Though neither James nor Will said much about it, Marty defended his actions. "We was just prefectin' our war faces. Since those Yankees outnumber us, I figure we should scare half of 'em to death and pretty well even up the odds."

Attempts by Lewis Jacob to grow anything even resembling a beard were doomed from the start by his youth. "Don't let any milk dribble down your chin," Matthew admonished Jacob. "Otherwise a cat'll come by and lick that beard of yours right off your face." Jacob's smooth, unweathered, and hairless face looked out of place next to the hard, weatherworn faces of the veterans of Company J. Even Will couldn't help but comment on this, though he did it in private, to James. "Jimmy, I just can't help but think of my kid sister every time I look at Lewis. All I want to do is give him a good scolding and send him home to his mama, just like I used to do to Mary Beth." Though James didn't share Will's opinion that Mary Beth was nothing but a child who belonged with her mother, he understood what Will meant. In his own way, he tried hard to help Jacob every chance he could. In time, with a little patience, James was convinced that he could at least get Private Lewis Jacob to the point where he wasn't a danger to himself. If nothing else, he hoped to make the lad self-sufficient enough to survive the rigors of campaigning under Major General Thomas Jackson, who was now being called Stonewall.

There was, however, a limit to what James could do for Jacob, or for anyone else, for that matter. The regiment had just finished a hard march down from Strasburg, the second hard march in two days, and moved off the Valley Turnpike into the fields south of Kernstown, where the worn soldiers of Jackson's division expected to spend the night. Most, however, hadn't even had enough time to drop their gear when orders swept through the ranks for them to re-form into line of battle. This was done quickly, and ominously, to the accompaniment of shelling from Union artillery located on a hill just to the northwest of Kernstown. "Oh, Lordy," Andy Caddall had lamented as they formed up. "How can such a God-fearing man as General Jackson make us fight on the Sabbath?"

"Old Stonewall," Will responded when he heard Caddall's plea, "is probably the most ardent Christian I know. But when he gets his fighting blood up, boys, hell's hounds can't hold him back." So it was that day, a day when Jackson's low opinion of their brigade commander, General Dick Garnett, led Jackson to interfere with Garnett's running of the brigade and eventually brought Garnett to grief.

Following the path taken by the 33rd Virginia, which General Garnett himself had led forward, the 2nd, 4th, and 27th Virginia crossed a field, heading for the right flank. Along the way, they became exposed to enemy shell fire. That it was deadly was attested to by a smattering of dead and wounded, both man and beast, strewn along the route. Lewis Jacob found it difficult to keep up with the company. Whether it was due to his exhaustion after two long days of heavy marching, the fear that every man feels when approaching his first battlefield, or his lack of training, didn't matter. Both Will and James, in turn, pushed, pulled, and prodded Jacob in an effort to keep him up with the rest of the company.

James, feeling the effects of their marches himself, not to mention the random explosions of artillery near misses and his own excitement brought on by battle, was in no mood to listen to Jacob's complaints. Every time the young recruit began to lag behind, whining that he couldn't keep up, James reached behind him, grabbed the boy by a handful of cloth or the first cross belt that his hand lit upon, and jerked him forward. "Shut up, boy, and keep moving. Keep up." Though only a few years older than Jacob, James' eleven months in the 4th Virginia, well seasoned by hardships and privations, created a gap between the two that was immeasurable. It also created a mental attitude that Jacob did not understand.

Once they were up the hill on the far right of Jackson's line and into the woods they had been headed for, the 4th ran into a solid line of Union infantry. Coming to a halt, they were deployed by their officers and then began a lively exchange of fire with their enemies. Responsible for serving as the left-hand guide for the company, Will had no time to watch Jacob. Marty and Matthew, anxious to get into the fight, forgot all about the new private. Andy Caddall, who barely was able to overcome his own nervousness whenever the firing started, was of little help to Jacob in the beginning and none at all after he was shot. Dale Wint, who didn't pay any attention to Jacob in camp, did nothing for him here either. That left James alone to keep an eye on the new man as well as do his own fighting.

After getting off a few quick rounds and settling into a more steady pace, from behind a tree that offered some cover, James began to look over to young Lewis Jacob between taking shots. What he saw dismayed him. Through the smoke that was starting to drift, James watched as Jacob took his rifle, stuffed a cartridge down the muzzle, and rammed it home. Though slow, and with his shaking causing some of the powder to slip down the outside of the barrel, he was doing fine up to that point.

After that, however, he either became totally confused or simply forgot the drill, for Jacob never primed his rifle. Instead of putting a cap on the cone that the hammer struck, Lewis Jacob simply hoisted his rifle to his shoulder, cocked the hammer full back, and pulled the trigger. Though the trigger slammed down on the cone, there was no cap on it and, therefore, no discharge. Jacob, however, didn't realize this. Instead, he brought his rifle down, reached into his cartridge box, and began to reload his rifle again.

"LEWIS!" James yelled in an effort to be heard over the din of battle. Though he was less than three feet from where James stood, Lewis didn't hear him. Looking to his left and right, James took a breath and bounded over to Jacob, stepping over Andy Caddall, now lying on the ground, and bumping into Marty Hazard just as he took a shot. Though Marty said nothing, he gave James a dirty look, then got to the business of reloading his rifle.

Reaching Jacob just as he was about to pour the powder of another cartridge into the muzzle of his rifle, James grabbed Jacob's hand and pulled it away with a jerk. "What do you think you're doing?"

Already totally befuddled by his first taste of battle, Jacob was shocked by James' actions. Looking up into James' face didn't help. There was fire in James' eyes. That, together with smudges of black around his mouth from biting off the ends of cartridges and the skin darkened by exposure to sun and weather, gave James a fierce, almost frightening look. Jacob's mouth gaped as he tried to utter a response. James, in a hurry, didn't give him a chance. "You forgot to prime your piece, you fool. How many charges have you rammed home without firing?"

Jacob didn't respond. Instead he stood there looking at James with an expression that told James that the green recruit had no idea what he was talking about. Knowing that there was at least one charge in the barrel that hadn't been fired, and suspecting that there were more, James grabbed Jacob's rifle away from him. Bracing himself against the tree that Jacob had been using for cover, James brought the butt of the rifle down between his feet and withdrew the ramrod. In the process of doing this, he managed to ignore most of the Yankee bullets that went whizzing by them. It was, however, impossible to ignore all of them. Though it was a definite miss, smacking the tree inches from James' ear with a resounding thud, one bullet sent bark and splinters flying. This caused James to stop what he was doing as he jerked his head to the side. Jacob, who had been watching James intently, and paying no attention to anything else, was caught completely off guard. He fell flat to the ground, covering his ears with both hands. James looked down at him, shook his head, and continued to go about checking Jacob's rifle.

Bringing the ramrod up, he twirled it over his head, smoothly brought the rammer end down, and inserted it into the muzzle. He began to ram it home, but even before it was halfway down the barrel, the rammer stopped dead. James gave the ramrod one more shove but gave up when he felt it crunching against an untold number of unfired cartridges. To cap the rifle now and fire it, with God knew how many charges in it, would be more dangerous to the firer than to the enemy.

Tossing it to the side, James turned about and headed back to where Caddall lay, going by Marty, the more outspoken of the brothers, who was loading his rifle. Giving James an odd look, he shouted. "What in the hell are you doin', boy? Have you gone mad?"

Reaching down, James grabbed Caddall's rifle and wrestled it out of the dying man's hands. Then, standing up, he faced Marty for a moment. "Jacob's been loading the rifle but hasn't primed it since we got here."

Marty shot a look of disgust over at the quivering young soldier, now standing unarmed behind a tree. "To hell with him, Jimmy. If he ain't got it sorted out by now, he deserves to get his blamed fool head shot off."

A near miss went whizzing by, snapping several branches just above their heads and causing both men to duck. When he came back up, James gave Marty a pat on the shoulder. "I have to *try* to help him, at least."

Though James didn't wait for a response, Marty yelled to him as he moved back to Jacob. "Then you're as big a fool as he is."

James didn't reply. Getting back behind the tree Jacob had been leaning against, James reached into his cap box, pulled out a cap, and cocked the hammer. After putting the cap on the cone of Caddall's rifle, he hoisted the rifle up to his shoulder. Taking aim at the blue mass through the clouds of smoke that hung in the dead space between the lines, James pulled the trigger. The hammer struck the cone and set off the cap, but there was no discharge. Caddall hadn't reloaded before he had been hit. Satisfied that the rifle was clear and functional, James turned to Jacob, who had been watching without understanding what was going on. "Here," James shouted as he shoved the gun into Jacob's chest. "It works. Now take your time and remember to prime your piece before you try to fire." James turned away from Jacob as soon as the boy took Caddall's rifle. Reaching back for his own rifle, James took his place in the line between the Hazards and Dale Wint, being careful where he stepped in order to avoid Andy Caddall's twitching body, and went back to loading and firing.

Settling back into his position, James joined in the steady firing that continued without any sign of letup. Between shots, as he mechanically reloaded his rifle, he looked about, noticing that there were more people from other units mixed in with his company. How they got to be there, he had no idea. Leaning back, as if in an effort to see under the billows of grayish-white smoke that enveloped both friend and foe, James looked down toward where Will McPherson should have been. "Will McPherson, you over there?"

Listening closely, James barely heard Will's voice over the steady rifle fire that was punctuated, rather randomly, by shell fire. "Yeah, James. I'm here. You okay?"

"Yes, yes, I am. You?"

"Could be better."

Just then, Lieutenant Theodore Lynn, his bloody left arm hanging limply at his side, came by. Since reaching the woods on the hill, he had been moving back and forth behind the line, watching his own men as much as the enemy. He now stopped in the lee of a tree that offered him some shelter from Yankee gunfire. Though they were only a few feet away, Lieutenant Lynn had to shout over to James. "You need to keep your mind on what you're up to, James. I'll keep an eye on Will for you."

James looked over at Lieutenant Lynn and saw him grinning, despite his exhaustion and concern for their predicament.

James returned the smile. "You know, Lieutenant, that could prove to be quite a task."

"Well," Lynn said as he glanced nervously over to his right, "I'll do my best. In the meantime, I'd be obliged if you'd keep up the fire."

Without another word, James went back to firing as Lieutenant Lynn went on keeping the company at its task, while listening for any new orders from the regimental commander. During this interlude, James hadn't bothered to check on Jacob. Marty Hazard caught his attention: "Hey, Jimmy boy."

When James, after finishing the shot he was making, looked over, Marty Hazard grinned and nodded toward Lewis Jacob. Jacob, his back against the tree where he had been since James left him, was trying to shove his ramrod down the muzzle of his rifle but having no luck. Only three-quarters of the ramrod protruded from the rifle's muzzle. With an exasperated look on his face, James glanced back to Marty, who was turning away to continue firing. Deciding that there was nothing more that he could do for Jacob, James shook his head and tended to his own rifle. He looked over at Jacob one more time that day. When he did, Jacob was sitting on the ground, his back against the tree with his face buried in his hands. James couldn't tell if he was hit or just crying. Not that it made a difference. Matthew Hazard, James decided, had been right. It probably would have been far more charitable if Marty had let him fall out of the march that morning. Now there was the good chance that Jacob would get himself shot by a Yankee, without anything to show for his efforts.

As the day neared an end, time seemed to slow down, then stop completely. Not only was there no letup in the fighting, but from where James stood he couldn't see that there had been any changes in either army's position. It was as if both sides, through mutual consent, had agreed to stand their ground and exchange a steady fire that nibbled away, like a mouse eating cheese, at the men in the ranks. If there was a plan or a supreme guiding hand in this battle, it was not evident to James. What was evident though was that ammunition, daylight, and physical strength were all just about used up.

Even the company was being used up. Slowly, as men fell from the ranks or dropped behind the line to work on fouled rifles and the ranks closed up, James and Will found the distance between them becoming less and less. Finally, they were almost shoulder to shoulder, just like in the old days. Pausing, Will leaned over and yelled into James' ear. "This doesn't make sense to me, James." Digging into his cartridge box for his last package of rounds, James took note that Will's voice betrayed the same frustration that he felt. "Somebody has to be pushing forward on our left or right. I mean, what was the sense of starting this fight if all we were going to do was just sit here and blaze away at each other?"

Will was getting nervous. James could tell from the manner in which he kept looking about. The reason for Will's concern was easy to figure out. Earlier that afternoon, when it seemed as if they were going to halt south of Kernstown for the night, all Will talked about was his family. "Lord, Jim. If there weren't any Yankees just up the road, I could be home in less than an hour." Pacing back and forth nervously, despite the fact that they had just finished a punishing march, Will kept looking up the Valley Pike toward Winchester. Occasionally, he'd glance back at the officers of the regiment or the brigade, gathered in little knots, and shake his head before he continued his pacing. When orders finally did come to form up into line of battle and advance, Will was animated and impatient with anyone who was slow to do so. Though he rarely used strong language, his impatience to push north overrode both his exhaustion and his usual inhibitions. "Move it, damn you! Move it," he yelled to one of the men who was normally slow. "You're poking along like a damned old mule. Move it!"

When they reached their current position and began to pitch into the Yankees, Will finally managed to settle down. Now, however, with things going against them, Will was nervous again. Even the officers behind them, both on foot and mounted, had worried looks. The kindly, almost fatherly expression that their brigade commander usually wore and that had helped endear him to the men of Jackson's old brigade was gone. Instead, his face showed no emotions, no expression. It was,

James thought, like looking at a man playing poker who knew he didn't have a winning hand but had thrown too much into the pot to back out.

"James," Will McPherson went on. "I'm going a little ways down the line, over there to the right, to see if I can scare up some ammo for us."

James nodded. "Might want to check and see what's going on over there while you're at it."

Will gave James an almost guilty look, as if he had to be given permission to do something he had already decided to do. "I think I'll do that." Without another word, he was gone.

"Where's Will goin'?" Marty shouted over to James as he stepped back into the firing line.

"Oh, he's after ammo."

As if to remind him to check, Marty gave his own cartridge box a shake. "Hope he don't dally none. I'm about used up. How 'bout you?"

James, about to load one of his last ten rounds, shook his head. "Not good, Marty. Working on my last pack."

Finished loading, Marty looked over to where Lieutenant Lynn was talking to the regimental commander. "Well, whatever they be plannin' on doin', they'd best be decidin' on it and get it done 'fore we run outta bullets and daylight." With that, Marty hoisted his rifle and tucked it into his shoulder. Before firing, he gave a shout that could be heard above the din of the battle. "BILLY YANKEE! HERE COMES ANOTHER."

Will returned just as James finished firing his last round. Not only was he without ammo, for everyone on the firing line had cartridges boxes that were nearly empty, he was also angry. "We're pulling back!" James, though he understood Will's frustration, was glad. He didn't relish the idea of greeting a Union bayonet charge with an empty rifle any more than he did making such a charge himself. Since these were the only options that seemed open to them if they stayed there, retreat seemed like the only option that made sense.

Kneeling and carefully handling his rifle to keep from burning his hands any more than he already had on the hot barrel, James took a deep breath and looked about before looking into Will's eyes. Seeing that they betrayed both Will's anger and dismay, James put his right hand on Will's shoulder. "They'll be all right, Will. I know it. Despite what the newspapers say, Yankees are humans, just like us. They're not going to bring any harm to your family."

Will looked down for a moment, thought about what James had said, then looked up. The sickly smile told James that Will remained unconvinced. But he didn't say so. At least, he didn't have time to. For Lieutenant Lynn, his lifeless left arm flapping at his side, came running up behind the line. "Up, everyone up. We're pulling back. Re-form on me." Though he and the other surviving officers of the company did their best to organize the retreat, the men didn't respond. While some were simply too exhausted from two days of hard marching that had been capped off with a hard fight, others were too anxious to get away from the menacing Union lines that continued, unabated, to hurl death at them despite their best efforts. Even before it really started, the retreat fell apart.

Sensing that things were going badly, James turned and grabbed Marty by the arm. "Help me with Dale. He can't walk."

Marty looked over at Dale Wint, still sitting by his tree. Dale, with a mournful expression on his face, glanced at James, and then at Marty. Without a word, Marty slung his rifle over his shoulder and reached over to grab the arm Dale threw up at him. James did likewise. Ignoring everyone and everything about them, James and Marty began to pull Dale. At first Dale moaned and complained. "Oh, boys, slow down. Ya killing me."

Marty, never known for sensitivity, shouted back. "Oh, hush, you old fool. Would ya rather have us kill ya or the Yanks?" Seeing that he wasn't getting anywhere with Marty, Dale looked up at James. "Jimmy, boy. Have some pity on my poor broken body, would ya?"

James, in no mood for talking, said nothing. Like Marty, he simply kept dragging Dale away to where they thought the regiment would be re-forming, as quickly as possible, despite Dale's impassioned pleas and protests.

Some distance back, in a field where many men were milling about in the gathering darkness, James and Marty stopped and eased Dale down. "Oh, thank you, boys. Thank you. Though I wished ya'd been a mite more gentle, thank you all the same."

Marty, freed from his charge for the moment, looked about. "Matthew Hazard. Where in the blazes are you?"

"Right here," Matthew announced with a shout and a slap on Marty's arm. "And don't," he added in a stern tone, "let me hear ya usin' cuss words like that again. Why if Ma heard ya, she'd give you a beatin' and then one to me for not lookin' out after ya like I'm supposed to."

Despite the desperateness of their current plight, James suddenly realized why he so liked the Hazard brothers. Though in no way, shape, or form did they resemble him and his own younger brother, Kevin, the relationship between them was the same, exactly. Matthew was always looking out for Marty's welfare and Marty was always managing to get himself into trouble. And though the two boys fought each other with great ferocity every chance they got, Lord help any outsider who tried to pick on one or the other. Lost in this thought for a moment, James began to wonder where and how his brother, Kevin, was. He was pondering this when suddenly he realized that he didn't see young Lewis Jacob. "Lew Jacob," he shouted, as an expression of concern began to darken his face. "Anyone see young Jacob?"

Matthew, now that he had caught his breath, responded while he looked over the lock and cone of his rifle. "Oh, no need to worry 'bout him no more."

"He's dead?" James asked in surprise.

Without the slightest hint of concern in his voice or manner, Matthew answered, "Nah. Least not when we pulled back."

"Well, where is he?"

Matthew looked up from his rifle and over to the positions they had just left. "Well, I suppose he's gettin' ready to greet his Maker or the Yankees, I reckon." Then, with an evil grin on his face, he looked over to James. "Maybe he's fixin' to do both."

"You left him?" James asked incredulously.

"Sure! He was nothin' but a nuisance anyhow. 'Bout the only good he was to me durin' the fight was a place to get cartridges from."

Still upset, James stepped closer to Matthew. "You took his cartridges, then left him there?"

More bothered than threatened by James' manner and questions, Matthew put his rifle down and leaned on it. When he spoke, he glared at James. "Look, Mr. Keydet, that boy back there was nothin' but trouble, another worthless mouth to feed. We're better lettin' the Yanks take him and feed him than drag that sorry excuse for a man all over the place. He ain't no soldier, never was and never will be, no matter what you and Will and Marty do for him."

James looked down. He knew Matthew was right. He knew that some people, like Jacob, just weren't cut out for this sort of thing. But, still . . .

"Hey, boys," Marty interrupted. "Everyone's still goin' back. Come on, let's get Dale and keep up 'fore we lose the regiment."

Over Dale's protests, Marty and James each grabbed an arm, picked him up, and started back. Matthew, hovering protectively behind them, kept one eye over his shoulder, back toward the position they had just left. The Yankees had closed up and were firing at them, though with little effect. More threatening than the Yankees at that moment, however, were their own officers. James and his little knot of followers hadn't gone very far from their temporary rest stop when General Jackson, his face alive with rage, came riding through the throng of soldiers streaming back to where they thought to find the rear and safety. Halting a drummer boy, Jackson ordered him to beat the rally. No one, however, responded to that. Nor did they respond to his demand that they "go back and give them the bayonet."

While such pronouncements could on occasion make a difference, Jackson's orders fell on ears that were deaf, at least for the moment, to heroic words. With few exceptions, the men of Garnett's brigade were not only exhausted, they were broken, in spirit and in body. Though he too tried to end the retreat that was turning into a rout, Garnett had lost control of his brigade. There were no serious efforts to pursue the broken Army of the Shenandoah, but the damage had been done. General Thomas J. Jackson had been handed his first defeat.

236

## *Winchester, Virginia*

It was well past sundown and Mary Beth McPherson was still on her own, waiting for her mother, her father, her younger brother, anyone, to return home. While she was anxious for news of how the battle south of town had turned out, her concerns were more focused on the safety and well-being of those she loved and cared for. As the cold gray winter turned to spring, those concerns had begun to include James Bannon.

Since the 12th of the month, when Jackson had pulled his command out of Winchester in the middle of the night, the loyal citizens of that town had been confronted with one shock after another as they learned to deal with people who had once been fellow Americans but were now a foreign army bent on punishing them, their enemies. The hope that this occupation would be a temporary one had resulted in endless days of mounting tension as the seemingly imminent withdrawal of the accursed Yankees from Winchester never developed. That afternoon, as the sounds of gunfire announced the approach of Jackson's command, the tension had given way to fear and apprehension the likes of which Mary Beth had never before experienced.

Like the thunder of an approaching spring storm, the sounds of artillery fire, followed by an ever-increasing rattling of musket fire, brought the McPhersons' normal Sunday afternoon activities to an end. "I fought tooth and nail to keep those folks in Richmond from getting our horses and livestock," Thomas exclaimed loudly to his wife and anyone who cared to listen during this chaos. "I'll be darned if some fleeing Yankee scavengers are going to get them." So, like the other families in the area, the McPhersons did their best to hide their most valuable possessions. While Thomas McPherson gathered the horses and prepared to head into the woods, Daniel herded the chickens and pigs into the cellar, and Mary Beth hastily dug holes in the yard to bury silverware and the other valuables that her mother was gathering. No one thought of questioning Thomas' departure, for they knew that without their horses, it would be impossible to plow their fields. No plowing in the spring meant no crop, which, in turn, would mean starvation and death.

The only one who raised a protest was Daniel. His insistence that he be permitted to go with his father was met with an equal determination by Thomas that his young son stay at home and out of harm's way. "Look, boy," he finally announced. "One of us men has to stay here and look after the farm and the women. With your brother, Will, away with the Army and me off with the horses, that leaves you." Though he didn't much like doing so, Daniel gave up his uneven struggle.

Not long after the sounds of the battle reached the McPhersons' farm, a young boy named Lyle Morrison came running down the lane that led to the McPhersons' home. Lyle, who lived in town, was Elizabeth's nephew. Red faced and excited, the boy started yelling long before he reached the house. "Aunt Lizy! Aunt Lizy! Ya gotta come quick! Ma's havin' the baby and she says it won't wait."

Except for Lyle, Elizabeth's sister was all alone. Her husband had died of typhoid the previous fall while serving under General Robert E. Lee during the ill-fated Kanawha Valley Campaign in western Virginia. Her oldest son, Jason, had been sent to the safety of Lexington, Virginia, where he became part of the newly resurrected corps of cadets at VMI. That left her alone to deal, as best she could, with Lyle and with another child on the way. There was, therefore, no question on Elizabeth's part about whether to go or stay. Leaving Mary Beth in charge, Elizabeth gathered up a few things and ran out the door, following Lyle, who was far too excited by the growing sounds of battle to the south and the idea of having another brother to play with. It was during this mayhem that Daniel, unable to stand it any longer, made good his escape.

As soon as she discovered Daniel's absence, Mary Beth became angry. Though the idea of being disobeyed in such a manner accounted for some of her anger, a large measure of it was due to the idea that everyone had left her at a time of crisis. Though she could understand why her father, and then her mother, had left, Daniel's desertion had nothing to justify it other than foolish curiosity and stubbornness. Even Will's absence came under scrutiny and brought additional bitterness to Mary Beth's outlook. Despite her best efforts to keep herself distracted, she could hear the sounds of battle that rolled across the countryside, penetrating a house that had been for so long

238

a sanctuary of peace and security. Finding no refuge from her thoughts or the ominous rumble of a battle on whose outcome she imagined the fate of her family hung, Mary Beth gave up all efforts to do anything constructive and began to pace through the house, pausing only when she passed a window.

Soon, her anger melted away as her concern for the safety of those she loved began to hammer at her with the same ferocity that the distant cannons pounded at each other. The ebbing of the sounds of battle, receding with the setting sun, brought no comfort. As much as she dreaded the approach of battle, the sounds of battle moving farther and farther away were just as ominous, for they told of defeat. All thoughts, at least all coherent thoughts, came to an end with darkness and this realization.

It was nearly three hours after darkness had closed around the McPherson home when Mary Beth heard the front door open. Standing in the kitchen, washing a dish that she had already washed three times in the last hour, Mary Beth froze. Holding her breath, she listened to every sound, debating whether she should flee and hide or run into the hall to see who was there. She hadn't quite decided what to do when Daniel's small, quivering voice called out plaintively. "Ma? Dad? Mary Beth?" A pause after each summons resulted in the next name being called out with greater desperation.

Dropping the dish she had been scrubbing absentmindedly for many minutes, Mary Beth moved rapidly from the kitchen into the small hall that led to the front door. At the other end of the hall, just inside the front door, her brother stood, alone and forlorn. Even before she could utter a word, Daniel caught sight of her, turned, and rushed to her. Though the tall lanky youth was now taller than she was, Daniel seemed no more than a small child as he wrapped his arms around her waist and buried his face in her shoulder. For Mary Beth, the simple joy of having one of her beloved family in her arms was so overwhelming that for the longest time the two did nothing more than stand there in the silence of their home. From the living room, the steady ticking of the mantel clock, so familiar, so regular, acted as a reminder that all was well, that all would be right again.

Slowly, reluctantly, Daniel pulled away from Mary Beth.

His eyes were downcast, still swimming in tears that he struggled to hold back. Slowly, with halting words, he began to apologize. "I didn't listen. I . . . I wanted so bad . . . to see the battle for myself." He looked up at her, wiping away a tear with the sleeve of his dirty shirt. "I didn't mean to upset you . . . to get you all concerned and all. I . . ."

Reaching out, Mary Beth began to take his hands. It was then that she noticed that one was wrapped in a dirty white cloth. Any anger she had harbored because of his running off to see the battle was washed away by her concern. Taking his injured hand in hers, she looked at it, then up at Daniel's dirty face, streaked where tears had run down his cheeks. "Your hand? Is it hurt bad? Come into the kitchen, where I can see it in the light."

Obediently, Daniel followed her as he always had when he was a child and she had been left in charge. There were no objections, no false sense of pride being wounded by her actions. This was, after all, the natural order of things, and Daniel felt as comfortable following his sister as she did tending to her hurt younger brother.

In the kitchen, while Daniel sat at the table drinking the last of that day's milk and Mary Beth bustled about the room gathering everything she would need to tend to his injury, Daniel began to relax and tell her of his adventures. "It was a shell fragment, a big piece from an artillery shell that had just exploded. Well, I thought it would be a good souvenir, so I raced Dale Morton . . ."

"Dale Morton was with you? He was supposed to be minding Mrs. Beckner's cows, to make sure that none of the Yankees got any ideas about taking them when they went North."

Realizing that his unintentional slip had put his friend in jeopardy, Daniel looked around at Mary Beth. "You won't tell anyone, will you, Sis?"

Putting her hands on her hips as her mother often did when she was peeved with them, Mary Beth shook her head. "I should, you know. I really should. But . . ."

"Thanks, Sis."

Mary Beth pointed her finger at him. "When are you boys going to get over all those silly notions about war being romantic and fun and start to take this seriously?"

Her admonishment struck Daniel like a slap. But rather than being angry at her, Daniel became quiet. He looked down at the table, then back at her. She could see that his expression was changed. It was as if, she thought, a ghost that only he could see had just entered the room. Slowly, he began to speak in solemn, almost mournful tones. "We came up over a hill, just to the west of Kernstown. There were Yankee cannons all along the crest of the hill, not far from where we were, firing for all they were worth. From somewhere to the south, a battery of our cannons was firing back."

Slowly, Daniel lifted his hand and turned it before his eyes as if he were studying it. "I didn't think that a silly little piece of iron could hurt so bad." He put his hand down on the table and looked at it. "The shell exploded, almost over our heads. It looked so beautiful, so . . ." He paused, then shook his head like a person who remembered something foolish he had done. "When Dale and I both saw this big chunk of the shell land near us, well, naturally we raced over to where it landed." He paused, then continued sheepishly. "I never figured that the shell fragment would be so blamed hot. I was just so anxious to get it before Dale did that I just reached down and scooped it up in my hand."

Then he looked up at Mary Beth, who had been standing across the table from him, listening to his story. "It was like the hurt woke me up. After that, things weren't the same. I started to notice other people were hurt. There, on the hillside, a pair of artillery horses, their stomachs torn open, lay where they had been killed. Out front, down the hill and across the fields, Dale and I could see the backs of the Union soldiers as they stood there, firing steadily to their front at a hill with woods on it. From that hill we could see the flashes from the rifles of our boys returning the Yankee fire. We couldn't tell who was gettin' the worst of it, not at first. But that didn't seem to matter. Here and there, blue clumps lay in the fields behind the line. Every now and then, another man would fall backwards, as if he had been punched. It took me a little while, after seeing that a few times, to figure out that the blue clumps already on the ground were men who had been shot earlier."

Again, there was a silence. Mary Beth wanted to go over to him, to hold him and comfort him, but she didn't. Like a captive, she stood there, riveted by Daniel's tale told in a steady monotone. "Not all the Yankees who were hit were dead. Dale and I, while we were making our way around to the right, ran into a wounded sergeant. He was a big man, shot in the leg. When he saw us, he yelled over to us to give him a hand. Dale wanted to run. So did I, but I was afraid that something might happen to us if we didn't do as he said. So we helped him, Dale on one side and me on the other. We took him to a place where there were doctors working on wounded soldiers."

Daniel looked up at Mary Beth and shook his head, his pleading eyes tearing up. "It was awful, Sis. Awful. Some of those fellows laying about there I think were already dead, left to one side in their own blood. Others, waiting their turn, hollered like stuck pigs or cried and whimpered. And the doctors, God, Mary Beth, the doctors stood at a table, dragged from a house, and sawed off arms and legs like Pa does when he butchers a cow."

Looking away, Daniel took a deep breath, then a slow, reflective sip from his glass of milk. For a moment, he held the glass before him and studied it. "They were thirsty, real thirsty. Another big sergeant, who seemed to be in charge there, saw Dale and me standing there. He came over, grabbed us by our arms, and shook us once. He told us to go and find some water for the wounded Yankees and bring it back. He had such a mean and angry look on his face that both Dale and me figured we'd better do as he said." He looked up at Mary Beth. "That's where we were all this time, hauling water from a nearby farm to that awful place for wounded Yankees."

Though she didn't want to hear any more, Mary Beth was anxious to find out if her brother had seen or heard anyone who had news of James and Will. "Were there any of our boys there? Did you get to speak to them?"

As if he had to consider her question, Daniel looked away. Cocking his head to one side, he pondered his sister's question as if he were mentally flipping through an album of images. Finally, Daniel shook his head, then turned toward her. "No, I don't recall seeing any Confederates. I don't think either side moved the other much, or that our side made any charges. Least not that Dale and I could see. Both sides just stood in line and blazed away at each other. We saw plenty of wounded Yankees coming back to where we were, but that's all.'' Daniel's brow furrowed as if a strange thought had entered his head. "I guess killing Yankees is progress, isn't it?"

Her brother's question shook Mary Beth out of her trance. Moving around the table, she seated herself catercorner from him and began to tend to his hand. "I don't know about such things and don't think I care to. Now, let's see that hand."

Slowly, Daniel turned his hand over and offered it up to Mary Beth. As she took it and began to carefully unwrap it, Daniel looked up at her. "Sis?"

Mary Beth didn't respond at first, then, sensing her brother's mood, she paused in her work and looked at him. "Yes?"

"Thanks."

Though she didn't know what exactly he was thanking her for, Mary Beth gave her little brother a smile, then went back to tending his wound as best she could.

# CHAPTER 14

# June 27, 1862
# North of the
# Chickahominy River,
# near Richmond,
# Virginia

THE SMELL OF BACON COOKING OVER A SMOKY WOOD FIRE AND the sound of dozens of muted voices holding hushed conversations greeted James as he passed from a sound sleep to consciousness. Wiggling slightly, he was reminded that his bed of hastily gathered grass and leaves offered no protection from the tangle of vines and branches that he had failed to clear away before he had thrown down his blanket and wrapped himself in it barely six hours before. Taking in a deep breath, James began to cough.

"Well, Little Brother," Matthew Hazard quipped, "looks like our dear messmate is finally stirrin'."

"Ah, leave him alone, Matty," Martin Hazard pleaded. "You're just sore 'cause he got first crack at picket duty last night."

"I ain't sore at no one," Matthew countered in a loud voice, " 'specially him."

"Oh yeah? Well, what was it you were saying about Will a few minutes ago? As I recall, you said . . ."

Like many of the men who marched with the Hazard brothers, James had learned a long time ago to tune out their incessant bickering. "Like living with magpies," Will complained, "nothing but a pair of magpies." Lying there, James listened to the other sounds about him. The noise of a regiment in the field didn't seem to change. The crackling of cook fires, the sizzling of freshly issued bacon being prepared for the day's meal, and the comings and goings of men were all about him. It seemed, James thought, that it had always been this way. To imagine living any other way now was as foreign a thought as this manner of life had been to him a scant fourteen months ago, when men spoke confidently of one big battle and a short war.

Throwing the blanket off his face, James sat up, pulling his knees up to his chest as he did so. Scratching the stubble of a sparse beard that covered his dirty face, James looked about. Well, he thought, they had had their one big battle. But rather than solving anything, the fight at Manassas had only served to thin the ranks of the 4th Virginia, just as each and every battle and campaign had done since. Struck by diseases that carried away soldiers as quickly as bullets, the 4th Virginia had shrunk from nearly one thousand strong to a little more than three hundred effective. And even within that small number there were few who had been with the colors from the first day the regiment had been mustered into the Confederate Army. That got James to thinking. Without any preamble, and while the Hazard brothers were still bickering, James called out to them. "You boys ever wonder why the four of us, Will, the two of you, and me, are all still alive when there's so few of the old regiment left?"

James' strange question caught the Hazards off guard. Of the four, James had always been the quiet one, the one who soldiered on with little comment and few complaints. Marty chuckled nervously as he glanced over at his brother stirring the bacon in the fry pan with a stick. "Well, you can bet it's not 'cause of my brother's cookin'."

"You don't like my cookin'," Matthew complained, "do your own."

Anxious for an answer of some kind, James tried to head off the fight he saw brewing. "No, I mean, think of it. The four of us have been messmates now for over a year and we're all still here. There isn't another group of men from the old Lexington Defenders that can make that claim."

"Well," Marty responded, "it's not that the Yanks haven't been tryin'. There was the sickness that dang near took you and

Will and me this past winter. And Matt over there took a ball in his leg at Winchester.''

At the mention of his name, Matthew whistled. "Lordy, that thing burnt bad. Felt like the feller who shot me stuck a hot poker right through my calf muscle.''

"And even Will," Marty continued, ignoring his brother's comment, "still hasn't gotten over the gash he got from the shell fragment at Port Republic. He still can't carry anything on his back.''

"But," James countered, "we're all still alive. Will's gone from being a private to acting company commander because of all the losses.''

Sidetracked by the thought, Marty cut James off. "You think they're gonna make Will an officer?''

"Sure," Matthew answered. "He's one of those keydets that Old Jack is so fond of. When someone finally gets 'round to figurin' out that Lieutenant Lynn isn't comin' back, they'll make Will the company commander.''

Turning from his brother, Marty looked over to James. "How come you're not a sergeant yet? Will's always sayin' you're the smart one. Don't those fellas know how good you are, I mean being from VMI and doin' so well in all of our fights and all?''

For a moment, James stared at Marty, who stared back in patient expectation. James knew why but didn't answer. Matthew, however, seeing the pained expression on James' face, did. "You know damned well, you fool. Captain Couper don't like Jimmy, here. Doesn't seem to think that a former Yankee should command Virginians.''

"Well, our brigade commander," Marty shot back, "old Winder's no Virginian. He's from Maryland, a state that didn't even bother to secede, and he's in charge of five regiments of Virginians.''

"He's in command 'cause Old Jack likes him and wants to undo all the harm he thinks Dick Garnett did to us when he was in charge. And besides," Matthew added, "Couper has a personal dislike for Jimmy and all Irishmen. You know how those Tidewater folks get about those things. So long as Couper is the adjutant of this regiment, Jimmy isn't going to get promoted.''

Seeing that the subject that he had so wanted to discuss had been replaced by one that made him uncomfortable, James changed it again. "Where's Will?"

Marty was about to answer when Will McPherson came ambling up to the fire from out of the predawn darkness. "Right here, sleepyhead. While you boys have been lollygagging about, I've been over with the regimental commander with the other company commanders."

"*Well,*" Matthew exclaimed. "*Excuse* me, Sergeant McPherson."

"Oh, Matt, don't start on me like that," Will protested. "I didn't mean it to come out the way it did."

Unwilling to let go of the mood now that he knew he was getting to Will, Matthew persisted. "Well, Mr. Sergeant, sir, would you care to tell us where we're going today?"

Will chuckled. "You know Old Jack doesn't tell anyone anything about his plans. I'll bet General Winder doesn't even know what we're going to be doing today."

"Well," Marty volunteered, "you can bet wherever we go, there's going to be fighting to be done. I don't think we'll miss the fight like we did yesterday."

"No," James sighed. "I don't think we'll be that lucky." Then, as an afterthought, he was about to add that he hoped their collective luck held, but didn't. In the back of his mind, he realized that discussing things such as that, particularly before a battle, was not very smart. There was, he reasoned, no need to challenge or question whatever luck had been protecting them. Best, he figured, to let those things go unsaid.

Roused from their defensive positions facing the mighty Confederate host that was believed to be poised in Richmond, the New Jersey Brigade had been rushed north across the still black waters of the Chickahominy to join the beleaguered Fifth Corps. For a while, they were held back in reserve, away from the furious fight that raged in the low ground that surrounded the Fifth Corps's hilltop bastion like a great moat. Then, with little warning, they had been committed.

Making his way through the woods and undergrowth, Kevin Bannon found there was no need to urge his company on. In their eagerness to join the fight that was boiling up out of the woods that sprang up all about the high ground, the men of the 4th New Jersey didn't complain about the double-quick pace that the French officer from McClellan's staff insisted upon.

From his post on the flank of the company, Kevin looked all about him at the scenes of wreckage that an army in battle generates to its rear. Sometimes whole regiments came back from the firing line, such as Duryea's regiment of Zouaves, which had come to rest not far from where the 4th was deployed. With heads bowed low and their rifles carried as it suited each man, these units had the look of a railroad work gang returning from a hard day's labor. Officers, when present, walked absentmindedly alongside their men, swords and scabbards held over their shoulders the way a farmer would carry a shovel or pitchfork. Few words passed between the men in the ranks, men who were as physically and mentally exhausted as their cartridge boxes, with their unsnapped flaps flopping open, were empty. Orders were given in a hushed, almost breathless manner. When, finally, a unit found the spot where it was to halt, many of the soldiers threw themselves onto the ground, too tired even to take a drink from their canteens, if they were lucky enough to still have water in them.

Besides the units, there was a great deal of traffic that crisscrossed the high ground. There were, of course, the wounded, staggering back alone or in pairs. While watching one party of men coming back, Kevin noticed that two perfectly healthy soldiers, showing little sign of fatigue or battle, were helping one man back who seemed to have little more than a scrape on the side of his head. When one of the helpers noticed Kevin staring at him, he quickly averted his eyes and began to push the "wounded" man and the other helper away from Kevin's prying gaze. No doubt, Kevin thought as he turned away from them, the only thing the wounded man's helpers were interested in was their own welfare, and not their comrade's.

Then there were the guns of the artillery. Deployed in battery, the guns occupied much ground as they busied themselves firing at targets Kevin couldn't see. While the guns themselves didn't take up much space, the limbers, caissons, and teams of horses did. Here and there Kevin spied a limber or caisson team with an empty trace. To one side, a horse, sometimes in the throes of death, lay in a massive brown or gray heap. While Kevin wished that someone from the battery would put those poor wretched beasts that were still alive out of their misery, he could see that the drivers and gunners had their hands full serving their guns or keeping the horses to the rear of the guns steady and calm. Strange, he thought as he passed one team that was giving its handlers a great deal of trouble. He had always considered horses to be dumb animals, incapable of logic or thought. Yet, here they were, in the midst of danger, doing all they could to escape while he, a creature reputed to have intelligence, was marching of his own free will into that very same danger.

The other people who populated this crowded and confused world behind the ranks were the staff officers and couriers. These officers rode about the field, often in great haste, or stood well behind the lines, with great concern etched on their faces. The young French dandy with a pretentious name who had ridden up to their brigade commander with orders to release one regiment to him was a fine example. Wearing the rank badges of a captain, the staff officer rode up to General Taylor and began to spew a jumble of French that Taylor didn't understand. At first Kevin watched in amusement as General Taylor, with an exasperated look on his face, turned to Lieutenant Baquet of his staff and asked, "Who the devil is this, and what's he talking about?" Baquet, like all good staff officers do, responded to Taylor's demand by informing him that the young captain was the Comte de Paris, a member of General McClellan's staff. He was under orders, Baquet explained, from General Porter, to take one of General Taylor's regiments to fill a gap in the line.

At first Taylor was unsure. He looked at the French captain, then back at Baquet. "Do you know him?" There was concern and suspicion in Taylor's voice. It was, Kevin imagined, as if General Taylor was looking for a reason for not letting one of his regiments go. Baquet, however, responded with all the confidence that staff officers are noted for. "Yes, sir, I do."

After looking at Baquet for a moment, then at the staff officer from Porter, Taylor finally relented. "Very well, then," he said with a note of resignation in his voice, "give him the

4th Regiment.'' Then, he added sharply, ''And go see where he puts it and come back and report.''

While Kevin was, at first, as concerned as General Taylor had been, he quickly discounted those fears. The foreign officers who were in evidence in many of the headquarters of the Army of the Potomac were all professional soldiers, Kevin reminded himself. Even Major Hatch, their regimental adjutant, had served in the Russian Army, as a captain of cavalry. These officers, Kevin knew, were schooled and practiced in the art of war by European masters, men who knew war. And the French, well, their military prowess was historical fact, Kevin told himself. Their former brigade commander, Phil Kearny, who had lost an arm in French service, could attest to that. That Kearny was only given a division and not a corps when he left the brigade just before the start of this campaign was a surprise to many and, Kevin had no doubt, a personal insult to Kearny himself.

As the 4th New Jersey hurried in the wake of the Comte de Paris and Lieutenant Baquet, some of the men still found enough breath to speculate about their new orders. John O'Keeth, still carrying the nickname Johnny O, thanks to First Sergeant Himmel, chattered like a schoolgirl going on a picnic. ''Do ya really think we'll get a chance ta do some real fightin' this time?''

Klemm Davis, one of O'Keeth's messmates, shared O'Keeth's eagerness for battle. ''Lord, Johnny, I hope so. It would be a sin, a mortal sin to come all this way and lose all those poor boys to fever and sickness without havin' a chance to even up the score.'' A dark-haired boy who had worked in the tanneries of Newark since he was thirteen, Davis was called Jeff by everyóne in the company, including Kevin. After gulping down another breath, he added, ''I'm sure we didn't come all this way to this miserable place just to march around and pull caissons out of the mud.''

This comment brought a weak whistle from another man behind O'Keeth. ''Woo-wee. I ain't never seen mud the likes of what they got down here. Them farmers back home always talked big about bottomless roads. Heavens, I thought they was funnin' me.''

Marching in the front of the company, First Sergeant Himmel had to cock his head over his shoulder to shout. "Save your breath, lads. It'll do us all some good if you stop moving your mouths and move those legs of yours instead."

Though Kevin didn't mind the chatter, he said nothing. Himmel, his German accent becoming more pronounced as the promise of battle drew near, was another one of those soldiers trained in Europe that some of the senior ranking officers in the Army respected so much. Assuming that Himmel, like the others, knew what war was about, Kevin kept quiet. Looking over his own shoulder, he saw Henry Meyers coming up. Meyers' father owned the factory where Klemm Davis had worked. That, however, was the only connection between the two. Even their approach to battle was different. While Davis all but shoved and pushed the men in front of him in an effort to speed them up, Meyers lagged behind. With his eyes wide open, and sweat pouring profusely down his flushed face, Meyers reminded Kevin of a man on the edge, someone who could go either way when the firing really started.

From the head of the regiment, a flurry of orders began to ripple down the line. The breathless commands needed to transform the six hundred men of the 4th New Jersey from a column of four abreast to a two-rank line of battle were given rapidly and obeyed promptly. When all was set, and before the men in the ranks had completely recovered from their rapid march in the sweltering heat, the order to move forward was given.

Though the woods they entered not far from the Watt House were not that thick, the swirling clouds of choking grayish-white smoke and undergrowth made visibility past twenty to thirty yards spotty and movement for a formed unit difficult. From his post behind the company, Kevin could see as they entered the woods a line of men emerging out of the smoke to their front. Everyone who saw this, including Kevin, felt his blood rise, for the woods and smoke made identifying them difficult. Taken by the sudden sight, O'Keeth let out an excited yell. "This is it, boys. This is it!"

As Kevin strained his eyes, now watering from the acrid smoke drifting out of the woods, another officer shouted to his company. "Steady lads. Steady. They could be ours."

About that time, Kevin caught sight of their colors. "They're Union," Kevin yelled with a note of relief in his voice. "Hold your positions, men, and let them pass.'' The regiment, the one that Kevin assumed they were there to relieve, passed to the flanks of the 4th. In contrast to the even, dressed ranks of their regiment, Kevin noted that the regiment coming up from the woods came at them in staggered lines with gaps here and there. Those who could were dragging their wounded while others walked backwards, careful not to turn their backs on the enemy until they needed to. From the ranks, O'Keeth yelled out, ''What regiment?''

A grizzled old sergeant, his lips and beard stained black from biting off the ends of cartridges, shouted back without looking. ''Third Pennsylvania Reserves, Meade's brigade.''

''Who's in front of us?'' O'Keeth queried.

The Pennsylvania sergeant stopped, looked about him to make sure all the men he was responsible for were still up with him, then looked out into the smoke that hung in the woods. ''Mississippians, Alabamans, and Texans, I think. To tell you the truth, I didn't bother to ask. Not that it matters where they're from, mind you. All you boys need to worry 'bout is that there's a whole lot of 'em and more coming.'' Turning to follow his men up the hill, the Pennsylvanian added, in a fatherly tone, to soldiers his trained eye told him were new to a stand-up fight, what little comfort he could offer. ''Don't worry, boys. We'll be up over there somewhere. If you need us, we'll be back to finish the job.''

With the passing of the 3rd Pennsylvania, the 4th New Jersey prepared to go forward. Kevin was still looking to his front when he felt a tapping on his shoulder. Turning, he was surprised to see Trevor Ward standing next to him. As the company commander, Trevor should have been out in front of the company, ready to lead it forward. When he tried to speak, Trevor's words were croaked out in a dry and raspy voice from a throat unused to issuing loud commands or enduring the pungent smoke and orders of the battlefield. ''Lieutenant Bannon, I . . . my voice. I can't command the company right now. Take charge.''

To Kevin's surprise, Trevor pivoted and marched off, alone, to where the regimental adjutant was posted. Dumbfounded, Kevin stood there watching Trevor go. That Trevor would walk away from his command just as it was about to enter its first serious battle had never occurred to Kevin. Only the order to advance, repeated down the line from the regimental commander by each successive company commander, shook Kevin from his confusion and disbelief. Instinctively, Kevin repeated the preparatory order, "FORWARD!" Then, without another look back in the direction in which Trevor had gone, he began pushing his way through the tight ranks in an effort to reach Trevor's post. He was little more than a step in front of the first rank when Colonel Simpson, the regimental commander, barked the command "MARCH!"

There was no time to think about what had just happened. No time to ponder what Trevor's action would mean for him. His only thoughts at that moment were to get forward to his post and do what was expected of him. Drawing his saber as he ran, Kevin looked to his left, then to his right as he tried to gauge his alignment with the other company commanders as they began to step off with their commands. Somehow, without missing a beat, he managed to hop over the body of a Union soldier that he saw at the last moment with his peripheral vision. He couldn't tell during the brief second in which he saw the dark- and sky-blue clump whether the man was dead or wounded. All that mattered to Kevin was that he not trip over the poor soul, whoever he was.

In his haste to get to his post, Kevin hadn't had time to consider the danger he was exposing himself to. Up till now, except for the smoke and woods, the regiment's maneuvering was just like the numerous drill sessions they had been subjected to in camp outside of Washington all fall and winter. Only when the regimental commander gave the order to halt did Kevin bother to look to his front. The sight before him sent a cold shiver down his spine. While there had been doubt before, when they first saw the 3rd Pennsylvania, about who the people to their front were, there could be no doubt this time. Like shadowy apparitions stepping out of an evening fog, the ranks of the gray-clad enemy advanced slowly toward them like blind men groping about.

Again, it was only the orders of the regimental commander, reacting to the same threat that mesmerized Kevin, that galvanized Kevin into action. "FIRE BY COMPANY!" Giving his head a shake, as if to clear it, Kevin looked down to his right. His company was on the extreme left, the tenth company in the regimental line, an even-number company. He would have to wait until the commander of the eighth company gave the order to fire before he could do so. Quickly, he and his fellow company commanders ran at the double from the front of their formations to the right flank of their respective companies, taking the position the first sergeant had been holding open. Nervously, he watched and waited. One second, he was glancing down the long front ranks of the regiment to the unit his would follow in the firing sequence. The next, he was peering out to his front, keeping track of the progress of the advancing enemy, who didn't appear to be all that anxious to close up on them. Finally, after what seemed to be an eternity, Kevin heard Colonel Simpson's command to commence firing. Without hesitation, Captain Charles Meyers, of the first company in the regiment, gave his orders. With a flash and a thunderous roar, Meyers' Company fired, enveloping itself in the smoke of the discharge from their own rifles. Next, the third company fired. Then the fifth, the seventh, and finally, the men belonging to the ninth company in line, to the immediate right of Kevin, brought their rifles up, took aim as best they could, and fired on command.

By now, Kevin's nervousness was beginning to take its toll. His eyes cut from the right to the front as he waited for the even-numbered companies, starting with the second company, to start firing. Unconsciously, he began to flick the end of his saber's hilt with his right thumb. Only slowly did he notice that he was doing so. When he did, he began to think of how worthless his saber was. He had never really practiced enough with it to be confident in his ability to use it as a weapon. And even if he had, for him to use it, the enemy would literally have to be right there in his face, little more than an arm's length away from him. He didn't want that. He didn't even want the enemy where they were. For a moment he considered sheathing his saber and drawing his pistol. But he decided, after looking down the ranks and not seeing other company commanders with pistols, to hang on to his saber after all. Still . . .

As he waited, his thumb fast becoming sore from his absentminded twitching, Kevin took note of one Confederate soldier who seemed to be advancing straight for him. Kevin imagined that the Rebel, with his rifle held at the ready, had fixed his gaze upon him and no one else. Slowly, the scrawny figure drew closer, marching forward with measured cadence and deadly determination. Though Kevin wanted to look away, and he knew he needed to in order to gauge how far up the line the regimental volley had progressed, he found that he couldn't take his eyes off the man. Though in reality the smoke, the distance, and the woods prevented him from doing so, Kevin began to imagine that he could distinguish facial features. He could see, he thought, the anger and hatred in the Confederate's eyes, a hatred that knew no bounds.

Finally, Kevin heard Captain John Reynolds, commander of the eighth company in line, give his men the order to fire. Stiffening, Kevin prepared to shout out his commands, all the while keeping his eyes fixed on the lone Confederate soldier that he had singled out as his personal enemy. After forcing a swallow, he screamed his commands. "COMPANY!"

Kevin could feel the men to his left stiffen from the tension of anticipation as he had.

"READY!" With a snap, over fifty men brought their rifles up and held them across their chests, cocking the hammers of their rifles full to the rear with a snap that reverberated off the trees about them. Men in the rear rank did likewise, all the while moving their right foot back and placing it at right angles behind their left.

"AIM!" While men in the front rank were shouldering their weapons, those in the rear took one step forward and to the right, planting their right foot between the feet of the men in the front rank. At the same time, they brought their rifles up and trained them on the advancing enemy, all but resting their weapons on the shoulders of the men in front.

"FIRE!" A single, sharp explosion was followed instantly by a white choking cloud that wiped away all view of Kevin's ominous foe. His command to reload was drowned out by the discharge of his company's rifles, as were any further efforts of the regimental commander to fire organized volleys. From where Kevin stood, it was difficult to tell if their efforts had actually hit anyone. But even his personal nemesis, who had so dominated his attention, seemed to be gone, swept away by the blaze of his company's volley.

Then there was a zing, a snapping of branches, a sudden flurry of overhead leaves. These were new sounds to Kevin and his men. As was the peculiar thud, like a man hitting his chest with the flat of his hand.

But it wasn't a hand that had hit someone's chest. As if pulled down by an unseen hand, a soldier in the front rank of Kevin's company dropped to his knees. Kevin took one step to the front to see what was wrong. As if surprised by the whole thing, the soldier knelt there for a moment, eyes wide with disbelief. Without any of the others about him bothering to interrupt the reloading of their rifles, the stricken soldier began to weave a bit, as a drunk does just before he passes out. Then he jerked his head up, looking for a sky hidden by trees and smoke. After a single, soulful moan, the man flopped to the ground, face first, and twitched for a second before dying.

Again, it was the commands of his regimental commander, or someone down the line, now veiled by the smoke and haze of battle, that galvanized Kevin to action. "Independent fire! Independent fire, fire at will."

Still standing a step in front of his own company, Kevin looked down the line and echoed the command. "Independent fire! Independent fire!" repeating it, though he had no need to do so. Several men, their sense of hearing already deadened by the discharge of their own rifles or the rifle of a man in the rear rank who had fired too near another man's ear, were already firing. Within the space of a couple of minutes, all traces of the precision that had been drilled into the 4th New Jersey was lost as men up and down the regimental line began to wage their own little battles, at their own pace, against their own private enemies, real and imagined.

Seeing no need to remain where he was, Kevin stepped back away from his exposed position. With the idea that his old foe might suddenly reappear and rush at him, Kevin hurried along to where he knew that he would be needed now, behind the company. There he would be better able to keep an eye on his own men, ensuring that order was maintained, that fire was kept up, and that his timid and less-motivated charges didn't melt away into the confused and jumbled mass of men, units, and staff officers on the hill that the regiment had so recently traversed.

Sheathing his sword, Kevin started to walk back and forth along the rear of his line. Every now and then he would pause to look over the shoulder of a man who was busy loading his rifle. Out there, to the company's front, he could see images, shadowy figures, partially obscured by smoke and trees, busily loading their rifles and returning the 4th New Jersey's fire. Once, when he paused behind Johnny O'Keeth, O'Keeth stopped what he was doing and looked back at Kevin. With a scowl on his face, O'Keeth thrust his hand out toward the enemy, just missing the head of the man to his front. "Why ain't we charging? What's all this shooting for? Can't we just up and go after them?"

Though younger than O'Keeth by nearly two years, Kevin gave him a patient, fatherly smile as he put his right hand on O'Keeth's shoulder. "When the time is right, everything is set, and the regiment gets the order to do so, I'm sure we'll go out and finish them. Till then, Johnny, keep up the fire."

Stepping back, Kevin looked up and down his line. To his right, he saw a soldier, Private Thomas Green, stagger backwards. After taking one or two faltering steps, Green dropped his rifle, then reached up and clasped his head with both hands. A file closer, Third Sergeant Paul Skinner of Newark rushed over to Green. Bending over, Skinner looked up at Green's head, using his free hand to pry away one of Green's hands. In spite of Green's resistance, Skinner managed to get a good look at his wound. Though Kevin couldn't hear the words they exchanged, he figured Skinner had told Green to head back to the rear; then Skinner turned away from him and resumed his post.

Kevin watched Green as he wandered away, without his rifle, to join the chaos back up on the hill. For a moment, Kevin regarded Green with a mix of sorrow and jealousy. Kevin was genuinely sorry that Green had been injured and was being cast off, without help, to seek succor on his own. At the same time, Kevin wished, with all his heart, that it was he, and not Green, walking up that hill and away from the hellish scene the men in his command were helping to create.

He was still watching Green, oblivious to the lively exchange of fire his company was engaged in, when First Sergeant Himmel came up behind him. "He'll be all right,

Lieutenant. Ball took a clump of hair, a chunk of skin, and some bone off the side of his head, that's all.''

Kevin turned and looked at Himmel. He wanted to say, ''That's all?'' but didn't when he saw a heap of blue splattered with red lying just behind where Himmel stood.

Seeing Kevin staring at something past him, Himmel cranked his head about to see what he was looking at. With a shrug, he turned back to Kevin. ''Private Lenz. Poor lad took a bloody big ball right in the neck. Splattered blood all over dear Lieutenant Meyers.''

The mention of Meyers' name caused Kevin to look around for him. Not finding him, Kevin asked Himmel if Meyers was all right. ''Oh, he'll live, at least for a while longer. He's over there, behind a tree. Once he finishes emptying his stomach, he'll be right as rain.'' By the look on Kevin's face, Himmel could see that he hadn't gotten his meaning. ''You know how it is, sir, the first time you see a body all ripped apart and messed about.''

Kevin suddenly felt a terrible chill, as if he had been touched by the invisible hand of a ghost. He didn't know whether it was the look in Himmel's eyes, or the manner in which Himmel made his statement, that caused him to feel that way. Nor could he tell, for sure, if Himmel had baited him intentionally, for Kevin knew that Himmel had been involved in the investigation of Martha Anderson's death in 1859. Regardless of why Himmel had done it, if in fact he had done it intentionally, Kevin found himself again reeling under the memories of that terrible December night.

Closing his eyes, Kevin saw falling snow. He saw Martha. The image of her body, arms thrown out to the sides, falling backwards off the small dock, was as clear now as it had been that night. As was her face, frozen in an expression of utter dismay. He was never sure if he actually saw Martha's body fall off the dock or if his guilt-ridden conscience had created the image on its own. That of course didn't matter. Not really, for the image was there and as real to Kevin as Private Lenz's corpse was.

Kevin felt a hand on his shoulder, and opening his eyes, he saw Himmel staring at him. ''Are you all right, Lieutenant? You suddenly went pale.''

Kevin took in a deep breath, shook his head, and raised his hand. "Fine. I'm doing fine. It's just the heat."

Letting go of Kevin's shoulder, Himmel took his cap off, wiping his own forehead with his sleeve. "Yes, yes. It is devilishly hot in these woods. No breeze."

Kevin looked about him in an effort to collect his thoughts and reorient himself. When he was ready, he pointed down the line to where his company and Company I met. "I'm going to go over there and make sure we're maintaining contact to the right. Do keep an eye on the end of the line and, when you have the chance, on Lieutenant Meyers."

Himmel nodded. "That, sir, I'll do." Without another word, Himmel hoisted his rifle, brought it to shoulder arms, and began to move down the line to the left. As he did so, he looked to his right, watching the men in ranks and pausing, every now and then, to make a correction or comment. Kevin, still not free from the lingering memory of Martha Anderson's death, went to the right, doing the same.

With a yell that echoed through the dark pines that surrounded the Union-held hill, the 4th Virginia went forward. After standing for better than an hour under steady but ineffective Federal artillery fire, the men greeted General Winder's order to advance with great relief. "*Now* we'll get to do some fightin'," Matthew Hazard shouted.

Matthew's enthusiasm, however, soon was replaced by angry cries of frustration as the regiment stumbled and staggered forward in small groups through swamps and thick stands of pine trees and vines. "Why in the hell are we fightin' for this blasted swamp!" he murmured as he made his way forward. "Let the damned Yankees have it, and Richmond too. They deserve it."

From the right of the company line, Will McPherson shouted down to Matthew. "Shut your yapper, Hazard, and keep moving."

"I'm tryin'," Matthew protested, "but these blamed vines are . . ." Matthew disappeared for a second as he stumbled and fell, breaking his fall with one hand while struggling to keep his rifle out of the water. "Damn! Damn this place."

"Matty," Will repeated above the din of the battle they were closing on, "shut up." Then he shouted to James, whom he had posted on the far left of the company. "James, do you see the 2nd?"

James, struggling to keep from stumbling while maintaining his alignment with the men to his right, glanced over to the left. The drifting smoke of battle together with the gathering darkness of early evening hid any movement from him. "Can't see anyone, Will. I think they're lost." The zing of a pair of bullets passing near his head caused James to bob to one side. Looking back to his front in a desperate effort to see if he could locate his assailants, James blinked in an effort to relieve the stinging in his eyes caused by the lingering smoke. "Don't worry about the 2nd, Will. Just hang on to I Company. The Yanks are just up front, I think."

There was no response from Will, who was already doing what James had been thinking of doing even before James reminded him. Nervously, Will looked over to his right and caught sight of the second sergeant of Company I. Then, lowering his head as if he were walking into a gust of wind, Will shouted down the struggling line of men to his left. "Come on, keep up. Keep your alignment and for God's sake, keep together."

During the course of the fight, Kevin never took the time to pull out his pocket watch and check the time. He simply had too many other concerns. The stifling heat, lingering smoke generated by a steady discharge of rifles, mounting casualties, and lateness of the day, together with their efforts on the firing line, all conspired to drain away more than the strength of the 4th New Jersey. Slowly, almost imperceptibly, the resolve of the individual soldiers to stand up and execute their duties also began to ebb. The death or maiming of others about them, as well as the sickening thought that they might be next, was more than some could stand.

Like the pair of soldiers helping a slightly wounded comrade

Kevin had seen during their approach march, perfectly fit members of his own company began to ease back from the firing line, looking this way and that in an effort to find an excuse. Some, on the verge of breaking and needing no excuse, watched the officers and sergeants to the rear of the company, who served as file closers. These men looked and waited for an opportunity to step back and away from the company, the regiment, and the mortal danger that hung thick in the woods about them like the dirty white smoke of battle. Some did succeed in absenting themselves for no other reason than to escape the very real danger that randomly took an ever-increasing number of their comrades.

For any number of reasons, ranging from true conviction to simple peer pressure, most of the men in Company J, however, stayed at it. Kevin, First Sergeant Himmel, and all the mystical forces that drive men to fight were at work. Yet those same forces were also at work for their opponent. As tenacious as the men of the 4th New Jersey were about holding their ground, the Confederates all about them were just as tenacious in their efforts to drive Kevin's men from that ground. And in the end, it was a shortage of ammunition and physical endurance, and not moral courage, that led Kevin's regimental commander to yield ground.

Up and down the firing line word came that the 4th New Jersey would be pulling back. A regimental staff officer told Kevin and the other company commanders that the 11th Pennsylvania Reserve, a fresh regiment, would be relieving them. Some soldiers, such as Johnny O'Keeth, greeted this news with scorn. Most of the 4th New Jersey, however, was more than willing to count their blessings, happy that they were still alive and able to pull back for a bit of rest. One man, turning to Himmel as he was preparing to talk to Kevin, interrupted those two with his short, disjointed comments. "Not much more of this, I can tell you. Mind you, I'm no coward. But not much more of this can these tired old bones of mine take."

Understanding the sentiment, and not at all angry at being interrupted, Kevin placed his hand on the man's shoulder and gave him a slight smile. "If it's any comfort to you, these young bones of mine are hankering for a bit of a rest themselves."

"Well then," the soldier said in all sincerity, "quit the jab-
bering and get to it. Day's finished, and so are we. Time we got
back to where we're goin' and got some rest."

The withdrawal was carried out in relatively good order.
First Sergeant Himmel stood back, a little out of the line,
keeping an eye on men who might give them trouble or bolt
now that they could see safety within their grasp. Kevin, standing in what had been the rear of the company but was now the
front, kept his eyes peeled toward the center of the regiment.
Through the smoke and trees of the woods they had defended
at a cost of one man in five, he ensured that the tattered ranks
of his company maintained connection and alignment with the
other companies.

It wasn't until they were just coming out of the woods behind the 11th that Kevin noticed a line of battle drawn up to
their front, in the open. Darkness and drifting smoke prevented
him from making out their uniforms or those of another column
hastily deploying to the right of this line. Kevin, however, had
little doubt that these units were part of the support for them
and the 11th Pennsylvania. It took Lieutenant Josh Shaw of
Company B going forward on his own to see who these people
were, before the terrible truth was known.

Several shots, one of which took Shaw's sword belt, were all
Colonel Simpson needed to convince him that they were in
trouble. Quickly he issued orders to move to the right at the
double, past the enemy's flank. He was, however, going against
the inevitable, for the Confederate units were formed up sufficiently to resist that effort. With the same commands that he
himself had been issued and had, in turn, issued, he heard the
Confederate officers prepare their men to deliver volley fire.

"Down!" came the command from Colonel Simpson. "Lie
down." Few men had to be told twice and none needed encouragement. With their own cartridge boxes empty, and exhausted from their efforts on the firing line, none could see any
sense in standing up dumbly and taking an enemy volley without the means to reply in kind.

Yet the Confederate volley, fired seconds after the 4th New
Jersey went to ground, was not wasted. For while the bullets
that had been intended for the Jerseymen passed harmlessly
over them, they riddled the ranks of the 11th Pennsylvania.

This sudden fire from the rear was as much a shock to the Pennsylvanians as the appearance of the Confederates had been for the 4th. The impact was even more devastating than anyone on the other side could have hoped, for the 11th was just about to receive a charge delivered to their front. Rocked off balance, the 11th fell back to where the 4th New Jersey was still lying on the ground. Sometime during the ensuing confusion, during which Kevin tried hard to keep his men in place without unduly exposing himself, and a captain of the 11th tried to pull his men together on the same spot of ground where Kevin's company was, Colonel Simpson decided that the fight was lost.

Now the real confusion began, for while Kevin had been able to drill his company in every possible battlefield contingency that Scott's book on infantry tactics covered, he was totally unprepared for carrying out Colonel Simpson's orders to surrender. Befuddled, Kevin stood up and looked around. All about him, the men of his company and those of the 11th Pennsylvania milled about, looking at each other or at those officers who were still with them. The officers, in turn, were looking at the approaching enemy, now rushing at them in ones and twos. Apparently, Kevin thought, the sudden surrender had caught the enemy as unprepared as it had the 4th New Jersey.

All further efforts on Kevin's part to influence what was going on ended as the Confederate soldiers, dirty, raggedy scarecrows with wide-eyed grins on their faces, began to merge with the tangled blue mass of men. "Up, ya vermin. On ya feet and drop them rifles," one loud Confederate sergeant yelled as he waved his long rifle tipped with a sleek eighteen-inch bayonet in the faces of men he felt were moving too slowly. Seeing Kevin standing there, looking nervously about in bewilderment and in an effort to figure out what to do next, the loud sergeant pointed at him and yelled, "Henry, you and Gus get that Yank officer 'fore he gets away."

In an instant, two men were upon Kevin, poking their bayonets in Kevin's face. "Don't move, Yank," the shorter of the two shouted. "Don't you dare move."

Despite the warning, and the obvious threat to his life, Kevin couldn't help but step back in an effort to put some distance between himself and the menacing bayonets that were being waved inches from his face. The short Confederate shouted out in excitement. "He's tryin' to escape! He's gonna run. Shoot 'im, Gus. Kill the son of a bitch."

Without a word, the tall man raised his rifle to his shoulder, cocked the hammer back, and sighted down the long steel barrel right at Kevin's face.

"Hold it, damn you. Hold it." With his eyes firmly fixed on the muzzle of the rifle aimed at him, Kevin didn't see, at first, where the raspy, dry voice came from. It wasn't until Gus lowered his weapon to the ready position and Kevin began to regain his composure that a Confederate officer, as dirty as his men, stepped up into Kevin's view. He was young, as young as or younger than Kevin. Yet the haggard expression he wore made him look older. "I," he announced, "am Lieutenant Clarence J. Thomas of the 4th Texas." Then, with a note of anger in his voice, he added, "And *you*, sir, are *my* prisoner."

Kevin, still not recovered from his brush with certain death, stood before the Confederate officer, wide-eyed, shaking, and dumbfounded. The Confederate, not sure if Kevin had heard him and already angered at the loss of his control over his own men, shouted at Kevin, who he believed was ignoring him. "*Sir*, you are my prisoner. Surrender or I'll have my men shoot you down where you stand!"

Kevin blinked, then dropped his head till his chin almost touched his chest. "I . . ." Then he looked up. There were tears in his eyes, brought on by embarrassment and frustration. He sucked in a deep breath before looking up at the treetops. For a moment, Kevin watched the smoke of battle as it drifted away through the trees. The trees, now shaded in amber and red as the setting sun threw its long rays on the shattered landscape before him, looked out of place here. They were alive, beautiful and alive. In the distance, the sounds of battle were slowly fading as if reluctant to give this land back to the quiet peace that was to Kevin more appropriate for it.

Still, the random smattering of musket fire, punctuated by the occasional report of a cannon, reminded Kevin that the day's work wasn't yet quite finished. Having regained his composure, Kevin looked back at the impatient Confederate officer, whom he knew had no intention of shooting him. Finally, Kevin sighed. "I've never done this. What, sir, do you expect of me?"

Just as relieved by Kevin's response as Kevin was that the battle was over, the Confederate lieutenant smiled. "Your sword, sir. If you please."

Suddenly, in the midst of all the despair and destruction that surrounded him, a strange thought crossed Kevin's mind. Too bad he hadn't brought his red sash with him. Had he done so, he could have gotten rid of that bothersome piece of cloth along with his worthless saber.

Night brought neither peace nor quiet to the alien landscape that the 4th Virginia had found once it reached the hilltop that had been fought over for so long. Unable to seize an artillery battery that had been its immediate objective, the entire brigade, finally reunited in the dying moments of their attack, pulled back. Without the comfort of blankets, hastily dropped on the road before beginning their attack, the men of the 4th settled into a position, as best they could, from which they expected to continue the attack in the morning. To provide warning of a Union attack, Will McPherson was ordered to establish a line of picket posts along the regiment's front. James, who had been on the far left, found himself paired off with Marty Hazard at the far end of the picket line.

Carefully the two men felt their way forward through the pitch-black tangle of trees, vines, and wreckage. Some of that wreckage was human, though James couldn't tell whether it was Federal or Confederate. When he judged they had gone out far enough, James whispered to Marty to lie down and take up a position behind a snarled heap of dead trees. True to his nature, Marty promptly fell asleep without a word as soon as he had settled into a nice comfortable position with his head against one of the trees. James didn't much care. He was used to the Hazard brothers, as was everyone else. At times their constant bickering and eagerness to fight, even if it was with each other, became quite bothersome. This personal shortfall, which at times could be amusing, was far overshadowed by the friendship and loyalty that both brothers had extended to James and Will. In a fight, they were unequaled. While neither of the Hazard brothers had the school-taught knowledge of military matters that James and Will had, their skills as riflemen were unequaled in the company. Only Will surpassed them in their eagerness to close with the enemy. And for pure dogged determination, both brothers matched James. So if Marty or Matthew didn't always measure up to the immediate task at hand, neither Will nor James complained.

Left to himself by Marty's slumber, James settled down for a long and uncomfortable night. Had there been no battle there that afternoon, the woods they were in would have been unpleasant enough. The coming of night brought no relief from the heat and humidity of the Peninsula that all of the men of Jackson's Valley Division found intolerable. Bugs, from the omnipresent lice that populated every stitch of clothing the men wore, to the large, lumbering flies that buzzed about them continuously with impunity, added to every soldier's grief.

Then there was the human flotsam of a freshly ended battle to contend with. All about James the woods were alive with noise. They had settled in a position that had been the front line during the day and could hear the wounded, Northern and Southern, who had been left by their comrades call out for help or moan in agony. James, hardened by now to the sounds of the battlefield, listened to them for a while. Those who called out with loud or angry voices, he figured, weren't hit all that bad. They would surely make it to dawn, when someone would come along and recover them. Who would do that, James had no idea, for the rumor was that the Union corps they had fought that day had pulled south across the river that lay just out to James' front. Jackson, James knew, would surely pursue the beaten enemy and finish the task of destroying them that the setting sun had cut short. However, that was still to come. For now, all James could do was watch and wait.

From a spot not far from where James lay resting against a fallen tree, he heard the soft, almost breathless moan of a wounded man. He made no cry, uttered no words. Only an occasional, laborious, and irregular groan told James that there was someone out there, nearby, in great distress. James listened for several minutes. Gut shot, he thought. He'll be dead by dawn for sure.

Still, though he knew that there would be nothing that he could do even if he did find the man out there in the shattered landscape, James found it impossible to ignore the man's suffering. For the longest time James wondered what he could do to relieve the man's agony. As the tortured night slowly dragged on, James conjured up one plan after another in his tired brain, only to reject it summarily. Finally, around midnight, after striking upon a plan that he was sure would work, James paused in his deliberations to listen closely to the man's moans in an effort to get an idea of where, exactly, the wounded man was. It was only then that he noticed he could no longer hear the man's moans. Slowly, James raised his head above the fallen tree he was behind and pricked up his ears. Still he heard nothing. Heaving a great sigh, James eased back down and tried to push all further thoughts about the wounded man out of his head.

But he couldn't. For suddenly, the image of his brother's face, streaked with worry and fear, popped into his head. The image was as strong and as clear that moment as it had been on that terrible night in December, 1859, when Martha Anderson had died. With a muttered curse, James corrected himself. Martha Anderson had been murdered, murdered by the two of them.

The image of his brother and the memory of Martha now caused James to shake his head. How strange, James thought, the world was. Strange and fickle. Kevin, he had no doubt, had been pushed into the Army, somewhere, by their scheming father. That Kevin should be encouraged to do what James had been accused of doing by the same man struck James as twisted. Though the circumstances, James knew, surrounding Martha's death and the killing of a soldier in war were different, the end results were the same. Someone was dead, a life had been taken. The moaning soldier was now as dead as Martha was, and right or wrong, no one would be able to change that.

"Jimmy, where in thunder are you?"

Will's plea jerked James back to reality. "Over here, Will."

The slow shuffling of feet through dead leaves and an occasional cracking of a twig told James that Will was approaching. When he was a few feet away, James called out again. "Here, behind the pile of tree trunks."

Feeling his way about in the pitch black that hid friend from foe, Will eased to where James was. "God, I hate this place.

Can't say I much care for this Tidewater country," Will grumbled. "Can't see what those snotty Virginia gentlemen are so blamed proud of. I haven't seen anything but swamps, scrub oaks, and bugs since we left Ashland."

"Well, at least there're no mountains to go up and down," countered James. "I'd damned sure rather be here, bugs and all, then back in those mountains 'round Romney. Lord, I was never so cold."

Easing down until he was sitting next to James with his back against the log James had propped up his rifle on, Will rested for a moment. As the two men waited there, James reflected on how much Will had changed. It had been a gradual change, hardly noticeable. But now, in the light of this day's action, and many others like it, James realized that his good friend had matured.

That change, as James thought about it now in the darkness that was as oppressive as the heat and humidity of the Virginia Tidewater, was quite startling. The image of Will McPherson as a mature, capable leader captured James' thoughts. Will had not wanted the rank of corporal when he had been offered the stripes shortly after their first serious fight at Manassas. "You're the one who should be wearing these stripes," Will had protested loudly to James. "Not me." But he took them, in part because of James' prodding and in part because there was, in truth, no one else in the company, other than James, who deserved them more.

The transformation from a wide-eyed youth, eager to go out and conquer the world, into a battlewise noncommissioned officer wasn't easy and it didn't happen overnight. On many occasions Will told James that if the truth were to be known, he would rather have been back in the ranks, next to him. In the quiet hours, when it was just the two of them around the campfire, just before they would wrap themselves in their blankets, Will would often rub his stripes. "I'd give anything, Jimmy," he would say with a wistful tone in his voice, "to have nothing more to worry about in battle than tending to my rifle and watching out for my own hide."

Though James knew his friend was speaking the truth, he always found something to say by way of encouragement. Most of the time, he tried to be lighthearted, even funny, in his response. He could be, too, for in battle there was no hesitation, no reluctance on Will's part to do what was expected of him. Whether it was pushing men forward during a charge or keeping the ranks closed up on the regimental colors during a stand-up fight, Will was right there, doing his duty. Yes, James thought, as he remembered Will dogging a man from another company who had fallen out to discard the remains of what had once been a pair of boots, Will had come a long way.

"James," Will began slowly. "What do you think of my little sister?"

The unexpected mention of Mary Beth and the manner in which Will asked his question caught James unprepared. Unable to respond right away, James grunted. "Humph. Your sister. Well," James shot back hesitantly, "what exactly do you mean."

"What I said, Jimmy, was what do you think of Mary Beth?"

Though he had always pictured himself as a mature, responsible individual, it wasn't until he came face to face with Mary Beth McPherson that James realized that he had a lot of growing up to do. Dealing with his father and brother in New Jersey, and later, learning to survive in a strange and often hostile land had done little to prepare him for the kind of attention that Mary Beth had shown him. In the beginning, he had tried to avoid her. In part, James feared another relationship with a female. That the one girl he had loved had left him for another was, to this day, still too bitter to think about. That it had been his own brother who had taken the girl from him, and had cost that girl her life and led to James' being sent to Virginia, only added to the devastation that James felt every time the image of Martha Anderson stole its way into his troubled mind. Though he had never made a conscious vow to avoid any romantic entanglements in the future, James had made sure that his actions and the situations he permitted himself to drift into didn't allow for that possibility. Yet how to tell this to Will, at that moment, was beyond him.

The need to answer Will's question was canceled by the cracking of branches and the shuffling of feet not far from where James and Will sat. Turning around while James eased up to where his rifle sat at the ready, Will looked over the log barrier that the men were behind. Without thinking, he shouted out, "What regiment are you?"

Will's question brought the tromping of the unknown and unseen visitors to a cold, dead stop. After a second or two, a voice called out from the darkness. "Well, what regiment are you?"

Before James could stop Will from responding, Will shouted out, "4th Virginia, Winder's brigade."

When he heard the click of hammers being locked back to the full-cocked position, James grabbed Will by the scruff of the neck and pulled him down with him. The crash of a ragged volley fired by a dozen rifles whizzed wildly overhead, waking Marty Hazard. "What in hell . . ."

James reached over with his free hand to where Marty sat and covered his mouth. Marty, wide awake now, didn't struggle or complain as the three of them, breathing heavily, sat where they were and listened to the sounds of tromping feet as they faded away in the woods. When James let go of Marty's mouth, the youth spat out dirt that James' filthy hand had left on his tongue, while Will, shaken by the foolishness that could have cost him his life, tried to compose himself. Finally Marty, in fine style, spoke up. "You suppose those fellas were Yankees?"

With the tension broken by Marty's question, James laughed. "Well, it's either that or the Irishmen from the 27th Virginia out looking for a fight." As Marty wondered if James was serious, James turned around and sat shoulder to shoulder next to Will. "Well," he quipped to Will, "what do you think, Second Sergeant McPherson?"

Still shaken by the unexpected brush with death, Will fumbled about with his canteen as he looked over to Marty, and then James. "Go to hell, both of you."

Marty gave a loud, deep laugh. "Huh! Too late, Sergeant Will. We be there for sure."

With the abandon of men who had just cheated death, the three comrades burst out laughing. To the left and right the other pickets, also recovering from the scare the stray Union soldiers had caused, didn't think anything of the strange incongruity that James', Will's, and Marty's laughter made when mixed with the ever-present moans and cries of the wounded scattered about. For they knew that this was war, a terrible and strange place where emotions and passions ran deep and where a split second often was the only margin between death and laughter.

# CHAPTER 15

# July, 1862
# New Brunswick,
# New Jersey

IN ACCORDANCE WITH THE ROUTINE THAT THEY HAD SETTLED into, Elma Shields and her daughter spent the early afternoon in the parlor knitting socks for the Soldiers' Christian Relief Agency. Far from being the time of tranquil thoughts and quiet chatter between mother and daughter that Elma had hoped for, these afternoon sessions became just another opportunity for Harriet to bemoan her fate. "Why is it," she started as soon as she had walked into the room, "that the men are expected to suffer so, while the best we can do for this war is sit about, eating chocolates, gossiping about this one and that, and sewing?"

At first, Elma tried to explain to her daughter that in war it was a woman's duty to patiently tend to the home and family. "God has given us each a special place in this world," Elma lectured, "and being good Christians, we have no choice but to follow the teachings of the Bible." Inevitably, their discussions would degenerate into arguments. When the subject of nursing came up, Harriet would mention Dorothea Dix and her appointment by Lincoln as the Superintendent of Nurses. Elma responded by wrinkling her nose. "*Miss* Dix and her nurses are abominations. No proper lady would demean herself by engaging in pursuits such as nursing. All you have to do is read the requirements that Miss Dix uses in selecting her nurses and you can tell that an Army hospital is no place for a lovely young lady with a promising future."

"A future that promises what?" Harriet demanded. "Marriage to a man I don't love? Giving birth to children until a suitable heir has been produced to carry on my husband's name or my health is wrecked?''

Though she didn't mean to hurt, Harriet's indirect allusion to Elma's inability to give the Judge a male heir always struck at the very soul of her mother. ''Your father never left my side,'' Elma retorted with a rage held in check only by years of inbred restraint. ''When a lesser man would have walked out or taken a mistress, your father stood by me and prayed for me through miscarriage after miscarriage. And he forgave me. The least I can do is honor your father's love by doing what our faith and society demand of me.''

Though Harriet knew her mother really didn't place much faith in the Judge's loyalty to her, Harriet knew when she had gone too far. Besides, in many respects, her mother was right. There simply were not any opportunities as far as she could see for her to do anything of real value for the Army. *''It is a cruel fate,''* Harriet wrote in her diary, *''that has cast me in a place which offers me no real prospects for useful employment in support of our armies. I only pray that God will soon give me the wisdom to endure my fate with the same serenity that has seen Mother through all the terrible trials and tribulations that the Lord and our gender have presented her.''*

Work with the local soldiers' relief organization offered little relief to Harriet. In fact, it only served to further trivialize her role in the community. Organized by a local minister named Binford and the wife of a city alderman, the Soldiers' Christian Relief Agency of New Brunswick worked to provide soldiers from the state with items to augment the bare necessities of life that the Federal government provided to the men in the ranks. Whether it was knitting new wool socks and sewing fresh shirts or gathering Bibles and other suitable reading material, the women of the relief agency tried to do their part. Elma Shields, selected to head the sewing circle, took great pride in her position. ''I will endeavor,'' she told the gathered women in the church's parish hall, ''to measure up to the trust, confidence, and responsibility that Reverend Binford and the executive committee have bestowed upon me by giving me this office. It is my sincere hope that our efforts in the coming months will do justice to the great sacrifices that our noble husbands and brave sons face while fighting for freedom against the Southern oppressors.''

Chafing at her inability to be an active participant in the war, Harriet felt that the sentiments her mother expressed in public were a bit melodramatic. *"While I'm sure,"* Harriet wrote to Kevin, *"that we do provide some good for the soldiers, I fear that our contributions pale in comparison to the sacrifices that you are being called upon to make. Though I am as ignorant on the subject of war as the other ladies in Mother's little gaggle of friends are, I at least realize that it will take more than a fresh pair of socks and prayers to win this war. Oh, that I could be down there with you instead of here, spending more time drinking tea and gossiping than knitting. If nothing else, were you near at hand, I would be able to comfort you with a warm embrace and pleasant conversation when time and your duties permitted. But, my love, I fear that is not meant to be."*

Every day, just after lunch, Elma would call her daughter to the parlor. Moving to their seats at opposite ends of the room, each woman would take up her work where she had left it the day before. In silence, they would knit away for two hours. "As the chairman of the sewing circle," Elma announced to the Judge one evening at dinner, "I must set the example. It wouldn't do to have someone knit more socks than either I or my own daughter." While Harriet didn't mind doing the extra work every day, she felt nothing but contempt that her mother's motivation was for no other reason than to maintain appearances. But as with her disappointment at being given so small a role in so important an undertaking, Harriet kept her thoughts to herself. *"I have, these past few days, come to realize that it is pointless,"* she wrote in her diary one night, *"to aggravate my parents over such trivial concerns or pettiness. Instead, by playing the obedient daughter and holding my tongue, I hope to prove that I am both responsible and reasonable. Perhaps, when it comes time for Kevin and I to announce our intentions, they will respond in kind."* Yet that was little more than a hope, and a thin one at that. And Harriet knew it.

On this day, the two women were more solemn than normal. After so much expectation and a steady parade of cheery pronouncements that Richmond was within the grasp of the Army of the Potomac, the news from Virginia had turned, like milk left standing in the sun. First there was the panic that Stonewall Jackson's triumphs in the Shenandoah Valley had created. Then the certain victory that seemed to belong to the Army of the Potomac suddenly evaporated under heavy enemy blows. Following each of these blows came reports of casualties that made those suffered at Bull Run seem trivial. "It is," Judge Shields lamented one night after reading the daily newspaper, "as if all we have done to date has gone for nothing."

On the heels of these frustrations, nameless until now, came a real disaster that put a face on the drama being played out in Virginia. This, of course, was the news that the entire 4th New Jersey had been captured to a man. People throughout the state, even those who had no one in those units, felt shock, and indignation in that *their* regiment had somehow failed them. Judge Shields viewed the disaster in those terms. "Imagine, having those *men* fail us like that after all we have done for them. How dare they?" Only her father's concentration on how this tragedy would impact on the political future of his confederates kept him from noticing the grief and anxiety that Harriet tried so hard to hide. When Elma mentioned it to the Judge, he dismissed her concerns. "Of course she's upset, woman. That's Trevor Ward's regiment."

That Kevin Bannon, and not Trevor Ward, was the subject of their daughter's grief did not occur to either the Judge or Elma. Harriet had been very careful to ensure that her parents didn't learn of the reconciliation that had taken place between her and Kevin in March. Harriet was quite content to leave both of them assuming that nothing had changed since the previous August when Kevin had made a fool of himself at Senator Worthington's home in Trenton. Whenever Elma or the Judge mentioned anything about the rather protracted and quite formal courtship with Trevor Ward, Harriet would coyly respond that she didn't want to rush into anything while everyone was so busy with the war. Though she knew that, at best, she was deceiving her parents, she was able to rationalize to herself that at least she wasn't lying to them.

The thin veneer of the little plot that she had been hiding behind, however, was shattered when word reached New Brunswick that the 4th New Jersey had been captured whole at what was being called the Battle of Gaines's Mill. At first, there was little news other than word that the terrible event had occurred. That left Harriet in a difficult and lonely position. She could not speak to anyone or ask for specifics about Kevin Bannon without giving up her game. Nor could she do so under the guise of asking after Trevor, for any mention of concern over Trevor would be an active deception, an outright lie that could not be denied later, when the truth finally became known. So, as she had in August, Harriet found herself in an awkward position of her own design from which she saw no good escape.

When they were well into their second hour of sewing, Harriet was shaken from the almost trancelike state she had allowed herself to fall into by her mother's stirring. Looking up from the knitting that she had been toying with absentmindedly, Harriet looked about the room to see what was upsetting her mother. "Harriet," she demanded, "go see what all the commotion is out in the hall."

Laying aside the half-finished sock she had been working on, Harriet rose and began to cross the room, when the doors of the parlor were flung open by Judge Shields, startling both his wife and daughter. Harriet took a step back while Elma all but jumped from her seat. Not noticing the effect that his sudden entrance had on the two women, the Judge stormed forward into the room and began talking. "He's alive, Elma," he shouted, waving a crinkled telegraph message in his hands. "By God, he's safe and alive. Wasn't captured after all."

Still reeling from the excitement that her father's entrance and announcement had created, Harriet spoke without thinking. "Kevin? You've heard from Kevin Bannon?"

While Elma, also not quite recovered from the sudden appearance of her husband, missed the significance of Harriet's comment, the Judge did not. Like a man who had been brought to a sudden halt by a quick jab to the stomach, Judge Shields stopped in midstride and turned to face his daughter. Harriet, standing a few feet from him, saw the change in his expression and realized, for the first time, that she had made a serious mistake. Stepping backwards several feet, she brought her hand up to her mouth, then looked down at the floor.

Though Harriet's actions were an innocent reaction, they all but confirmed what the Judge suspected. "Of what interest," he demanded of her in a voice that told her he was already growing angry, "is that young man's welfare to you?"

Dropping her hand from her mouth, she brought her hands together at her waist, squeezing them until the tips of the fingers began to turn white. The Judge, his eye well trained in detecting guilt, raised his voice as he repeated his question. "Why are you concerned with Kevin Bannon?"

"Well," Harriet began feebly with her eyes still downcast to the floor, "Mr. Bannon is Trevor's first lieutenant. Seeing how Trevor was all right, I was naturally curious as to what had become of his other officers, both Lieutenants Bannon and Meyers."

Judge Shields didn't believe his daughter for a moment. He knew her too well. He started to open his mouth to say something, but didn't. Instead, he took a deep breath, looking over to his wife. The expression on her face told him that she didn't have the faintest idea of what was going on between him and their daughter. Judge Shields regarded his wife for a moment. Elma was a good woman, a fine wife who enjoyed her role within their society, and a worthy consort who would never dream of doing anything to endanger his standing in the community or his future. A man in his position, in fact, couldn't have asked for better.

Harriet, however, was an entirely different matter. Watching her as she turned away from him and resumed her seat, her eyes still downcast in an effort to avoid his, Judge Shields felt anger begin to well up in him. Strong willed and independent, Harriet was learning all too quickly how to use her charm, wit, and beauty to get what she wanted. Unfortunately, the Judge realized, her goals were not always compatible with what he thought was best for her, let alone his career. At a reception in Trenton sponsored by a member of the State Supreme Court just before Christmas, a member of that court approached Judge Shields after watching Harriet from afar. "She's a fine and spirited girl," the Supreme Court judge stated, nodding toward Harriet. Then, looking down at the cigar he was slowly rolling between his fingertips, he heaved a great sigh. "Such girls can be quite enjoyable, under the proper circumstances, you know." Then, after taking a puff from the cigar, he added as he poked his finger into Judge Shields' midsection, "but they can be a great burden to a man who aspires to greatness. A *real* millstone, if you catch my meaning.''

Judge Shields, ever sensitive to such comments, had caught the man's meaning. He remembered how he felt at the other judge's innuendo and how difficult it was for him to maintain his composure. But he did, for he understood the warning he was being given. Of course, after the affair last August, Judge Shields had assumed that the budding romance between the Irish boy from Perth Amboy and his daughter was over. Harriet's reaction to his news, however, left little doubt that somehow that relationship had been rekindled. How or when didn't matter. What mattered, Judge Shields realized, was that it be squelched as soon as possible.

Yet the direct approach, he knew, wouldn't work. Standing there, in the middle of the room, Judge Shields stared at Harriet and considered his options. When it came to dealing with people and situations, the girl took after him. An open challenge would be met with defiance. Though he knew he could manage her for a while, Harriet would eventually find a way to strike back at him. With his name now being actively considered for elevation to the State Supreme Court, he could ill afford any hint of domestic trouble or public embarrassment. No, he thought. Better to handle this in the same way that she has been dealing with us.

''Harriet?'' he called out in a calm, almost pleasant voice. ''Would you be so kind as to go and fetch me some fresh coffee from the kitchen?''

Knowing what was afoot, Harriet looked up at her father with a forced smile. ''I'll have Bridgette tend to that right away.''

''No,'' the Judge replied with a feigned smile. ''I'd prefer that you do so, if you don't mind. You always prepare my coffee just the way I like it. Just the right amount of sugar and cream.''

Realizing that he wanted her out of the room and that he would not be denied, Harriet rose, laying her knitting to one side. ''Well, if you insist, Father.''

His silence and steady stare left no doubt that he was, indeed, insisting. Once she was gone from the room, the Judge's expression turned from one of calm to one of great concern. "She's been in touch with Bannon's son, hasn't she?"

Elma, still recovering from her husband's clamorous entrance and the sudden, inexplicable change in his demeanor, stood before her seat and looked at him, puzzled. "Melvin," she demanded, "whatever are you talking about?"

"Don't be daft, woman. I'm talking about your daughter and Kevin Bannon. Somehow, he's managed to draw Harriet away from Trevor."

Still confused, Elma brought her hands up to her bosom and began to wring them. "Oh, dear." Then, after thinking about what he had said, she looked at the Judge. "Well, how do you know she's interested? I mean, I haven't noticed anything . . ."

"I know," he stormed, "because she's *my* daughter." Then, angry with himself for lashing out at Elma, Judge Shields lowered his voice. "That doesn't matter, my dear. What matters is what we are going to do to end this matter, once and for all."

Satisfied that her husband wasn't angry with her, Elma moved to his side. "Well, shouldn't we talk to her? I'm sure she'll listen to reason."

"No," the Judge said, shaking his head. "Better that we don't make an issue of this. I'd rather we try to wean her away from Mr. Bannon slowly."

"But how, dear?"

Tiring of his wife's lack of imagination, the Judge sighed. "Well, dear, to begin with, you need to make sure that she doesn't collect the mail anymore. Make sure that either you or Bridgette are on hand every morning to greet the postman in person."

"And?"

"And, my dear," he continued, "take every letter from Virginia that is not addressed by Trevor and save it for me. Next, make sure that you keep her busy with this relief agency work you two have been doing."

"Well, we already spend two hours a day working . . ."

"Double it, woman. If need be, triple it," he bellowed as his patience began to wear. "Whatever you do, make sure that Harriet is too busy to cause any mischief. I'll write Trevor and see what he can do to keep the Bannon boy busy. Maybe, just maybe, between the two of us . . ."

Just then, the door opened as Harriet, carrying a tray with clanking cups of tea and coffee on it, entered the room. "Knowing how busy you are, Father, I hurried as fast as I could."

Changing his expression, Judge Shields smiled. "As always, you are looking out for my welfare."

Knowing a cynical remark when she heard one, Harriet smiled slyly. "Why, of course, Father. Isn't that what a loving daughter should do?"

Judge Shields said nothing. The game was on, a game he was determined to win.

## Winchester, Virginia

Alone in the shade of a tree off in one corner of the field, Mary Beth McPherson sat reading a book written by Herman Melville. Though she didn't much like stories about the sea, there wasn't anything that she liked that she hadn't already read at least twice. Once, after noticing that the Yankee soldiers who made up the garrison of occupation in Winchester were always getting new books from friends and relatives in the North, Mary Beth considered asking one of them if she could borrow the books when they were finished. That idea, however, was impractical. It would have meant striking up a conversation, and perhaps even a friendship, with one of them. And that, Mary Beth knew, was something that no self-respecting Southern woman would do. "I'd rather starve and die a decent Christian woman," her aunt had told her one day, "than ask a Yankee varmint for anything."

The bellowing of one of the cows she was tending caused Mary Beth to look up and quickly scan about in search of danger. Since the issuance of Union General Pope's General Order Number 7, nothing was safe from foraging parties that scoured the countryside like a plague of locusts. "If we don't look out for ourselves," her father warned, "we'll be destitute before winter." So, like most of the farmers in the occupied portions of the valley, the McPhersons did what they could to hide livestock and harvested food from Union soldiers. Such action, however, put the McPhersons in danger, for shortly after issuing General Order Number 7, Pope issued another order, governing the treatment of anyone in occupied areas suspected of being in sympathy with the rebellion. In what was known as General Order Number 11, Pope directed the soldiers of his Army of Virginia, which included the garrison at Winchester, "to take up all active sympathizers, and either hold them as prisoners or put them beyond our lines. Handle that class without gloves, and take their property for public use."

Union soldiers, already annoyed at being taken away from their homes and having to put up with Army life, used both of these orders to strike back at the people of Winchester for the hostility against their occupiers that few bothered to hide. At a family meeting one night, made solemn by the knowledge that his older son was now fighting before the gates of Richmond in what Northern papers sent to the Winchester garrison called a most desperate struggle, Mary Beth's father explained what they would do. "We can," he laid before them, "submit quietly under the yoke of the Northern oppressors, do their bidding, and face certain starvation, or," he added after a slight pause, "defy them by hiding as much of our crop and livestock as we can." There was, of course, no debate on the subject. The McPhersons, like all of the people living in and around Winchester, were a proud people. The same spirit that had caused so many of their sons to leave in the spring of 1861 to defend their rights as Americans drove the families they left behind to go against the oppressive general orders meant to cripple the Southern cause, consequences be damned.

Like Daniel, her brother, Mary Beth took turns tending the family livestock in a secluded little field that was tucked away between two hills not far from their farm. Rumored to have once belonged to a German who had settled in Winchester after the Revolutionary War, its existence was known by few. "I hope," Mary Beth's father confided in her after they had driven their cows into the hastily erected enclosures one night, "that those lazy Yankee cavalrymen don't get too nosy. But," he warned her, "if they do and you're here when they find our critters, don't fight 'em. After all, these cows can be replaced, sweetheart. You and your brother, well . . ." He didn't finish his comment. But he hadn't needed to, as only the love they had for each other exceeded their pride.

Tending the cows out there, alone, for Mary Beth had its advantages. With no one bothering her and no chores to speak of, she found plenty of time to do what she so loved, read. Her younger brother, who had no love for schoolwork, picked at her constantly because of her studious ways. "What fella in his right mind," he'd start, "would take a girl to be his wife who's more interested in what's between the covers of a book than the covers of her bed?"

Though appalled by the vulgarity that her little brother was learning from the soldiers, Mary Beth more often than not chose to ignore him. When she did respond, she did so by casually dismissing his argument. "No soldier," she told him one day when her mother wasn't listening, "whose sole interest is a romp with me will ever rest his slippers under my bed." That she was deadly serious about this was obvious. When the Valley Army had been wintering in Winchester, Mary Beth refused invitation after invitation to attend dances and socials sponsored by various women in town for the soldiers of Jackson's command.

Though her mother wondered why she would pass up such marvelous opportunities and her father worried that he might go through life with a spinster on his hands, neither made much of the matter. It was only after Will and his friend James Bannon spent two weeks in their home that winter, recovering from the effects of Jackson's ill-fated Romney Campaign, that her parents understood Mary Beth's true motivation. Approaching Mary Beth one day while she was mending James' threadbare trousers, Elizabeth McPherson sat down across from her daughter. "Do you think he loves you as much as you do him?"

Though they had never talked about love before, especially not in connection with James Bannon, Mary Beth was not alarmed or worried by her mother's blunt question. Laying her work aside, Mary Beth had blushed a little as she looked up over her mother's shoulder and into the distance. "I think he does, Ma. I mean, when he looks at me now, the look in his eyes is so gentle, so, so sweet."

Further diverted from her book by thoughts about James, Mary Beth let the book drop into her lap, not caring that she lost her place. Her eyes, not focusing on any one thing, danced about the trees that lined the little valley their hidden field was in, as she wondered when the course of this all consuming war would let her see James again. Only slowly did she realize that someone was calling her name. Looking about, she listened intently for a moment. It was her brother Daniel. Though he was not yet in sight, his hoarse yells told her that there was trouble. After placing her book in the small basket she used to carry her sewing and lunch in, Mary Beth stood up and headed for the trail that led to their farm.

Bursting into the open, running as if he were being pursued by demons, Daniel started yelling as soon as he saw his sister. "Beth! Beth! You've got to come quick. The Yankees are gonna hang Pa!"

Despite the heat, a chill ran down Mary Beth's spine. Though she doubted that anyone, even the Yankees, would just up and hang a man without a trial, these were desperate and hard times. Mary Beth had heard far too many stories of deprivations and cruelty against loyal Southerners by invading armies for her to dismiss Daniel's claim out of hand. "Who's going to hang Pa, Daniel? Who said they were? And why?"

Stopping as soon as he saw his sister approaching him, Daniel started yelling before he had even caught his breath. "The Yankees, Beth. They came to the house and started rummaging through the barn and storage bins and everywhere. When Pa tried to stop them—this big sergeant, he put Pa under arrest. Said he was gonna take everything we had . . . And then he and his men were gonna string Pa up right there, in front of Ma and me."

For a moment Mary Beth thought about riding Bucky, their horse, back. She looked at him and started toward the animal, but stopped. If the Yankees were really serious about stripping them of everything, they'd take Bucky too. Turning her back on the horse, Mary Beth started down the path for home, followed by Daniel as soon as she reached him.

The scene that greeted Mary Beth was as bad as she had imagined. Even while she was a good distance from the rail fence that surrounded the farmhouse, she could see half a dozen

Union soldiers scurrying about between the front of their house and the barn. Next to the road sat a pile of belongings that the soldiers kept running to, dropping whatever they held in their arms. That there were more soldiers present and inside the house and barn was obvious, for every now and then an object came flying out a door or window. "Oh, Lordy," Mary Beth exclaimed as she picked up her pace. "They mean to ruin us."

When she was close to a pair of soldiers manhandling her mother's cedar chest toward the pile, Mary Beth yelled, "STOP THAT. You brigands put that back where you found it and get out of here, NOW."

Startled by her screeching, one of the soldiers, a skinny blond boy, let go of his end, allowing the chest to fall to the ground with a crash. Though it was a sturdy chest, brought over from Scotland by the first McPhersons to immigrate to America, the chest hit the ground at a bad angle, causing one side and the front to split open and spill its contents all over the front yard. This only served to further anger Mary Beth, who ran up to the two soldiers, now standing empty-handed with the shattered chest between them. With a shove, she pushed the skinny blond boy out of the way. "You animals. You despicable scum. Go away." While Daniel, still on the road, looked on, Mary Beth dropped to her knees and frantically began to gather up the fine linen and quilts that her mother kept stored in the chest.

From out of the house, a sharp voice barked at the two soldiers who had dropped the chest. "What in the blazes is going on out there, Lawrence?"

The other soldier, not much older or bigger than the skinny blond boy Mary Beth had shoved, looked to the house. "A girl, First Sergeant. There's this girl out here attackin' us."

Muttering curses that Mary Beth could barely understand, a big, barrel-chested soldier with first sergeant's stripes emerged from the house. Stopping on the porch, the barrel-chested sergeant made a quick survey of the situation. When he saw Mary Beth's small frame hunched over on the ground as she continued to gather up her mother's possessions, the first sergeant laughed. Then, after letting a scowl fall over his face, he yelled at the two soldiers. "You two are the sorriest no-accounts that I ever did lay eyes on. You mean to tell me that a little puny wretch of a sesh girl stopped you?"

The skinny blond looked sheepishly over at the first sergeant. "She came outta nowhere and caught us by surprise."

"Well," the barrel-chested first sergeant shouted at the top of his lungs, "get hold of her and send her back to wherever she came from, then get back to work."

The skinny blond partner, not wanting to incur his first sergeant's wrath, bent over to take Mary Beth by the arm. She was quicker than he was, however, and managed to spring up off the ground, lay a slap across the soldier's face, and jump back several feet. "You lay a hand on me and I'll . . ."

"You'll what?" the barrel-chested man demanded from his post on the porch.

The first sergeant's response suddenly made Mary Beth aware of her precarious position. Looking about, she noticed that all of the soldiers in the yard, and those near the windows in the house, had stopped what they were doing and were watching her. The amused smirks worn by the barrel-chested first sergeant and most of his men angered her. "You men," she shouted as soon as she got her nerve up, "are destroying private property."

"Little girl," the first sergeant responded with an air of confidence as he folded his arms across his massive chest, "we are only following orders. Me and my boys are confiscating Rebel property for public use." The soldiers, to a man, burst out laughing.

Already angry, Mary Beth grew red in the face as she all but screamed at her tormentors. "I'll have you all arrested, by your own provost guard, and see that you're brought to justice."

Rather than alarm the Union soldiers, Mary Beth's threat caused them to start howling. "Lady," the big man shouted between laughs, "we *are* the provost guard."

Frustrated and angry, Mary Beth continued to yell. "This is my house. You're destroying everything. Stop it. Stop it now!"

"If this is your house, little girl," the barrel-chested man stated as he motioned to someone standing behind him in the doorway, "then this must be your dear daddy." Stepping aside, the first sergeant made room for a corporal and two soldiers with rifles in hand. Between the armed soldiers was Mary Beth's father, with a bloody head and staggering as he went.

"If you love your daddy, little girl, you'll go away and let my men finish our work."

Somehow Mary Beth could tell that the Yankee sergeant was serious. Though no civilians had been shot as best as she knew, Mary Beth realized that all of that could change in the twinkling of an eye. Stepping out of the yard and onto the road, Mary Beth kept watching the men who held her father. In her anguish, she neither noticed the sudden change that came over the Yankees nor the sound of hooves coming up behind her. Nor did she notice the spindle-legged chair lying sideways on the ground behind her, at least, not until she tripped over it. Before she realized what was happening, she was falling over backwards. Both her bottom and the back of her head hit the hard-packed dirt road with a resounding thud, sending Mary Beth sprawling in a tangle of hair, skirt, arms, and legs.

It was while she was there, on her back with the wind knocked out of her, that she first noticed the horse and rider. They, apparently, were just as surprised by Mary Beth's sudden appearance and fall as she was to see them, for the rider had to rein in his mount sharply in order to keep it from trampling Mary Beth.

Confused, hurt, and out of breath, Mary Beth found it all but impossible to focus on what was going on about her. Looking up from where she was lying, struggling to catch her breath, Mary Beth wondered where the horse had come from. With the brightly lit pale blue sky in her eyes, all she could see was the dark form of a horse's head, jerking from one side to the other as the rider struggled for control. For a moment she thought that Bucky had followed her from the hidden pasture. But she knew that couldn't be, for she always made sure that her favorite animal was securely tied to its grazing tether.

Her head was still reeling when she felt someone's hand lift her head up off the road. "My God, are you all right? Are you hurt bad?"

Blinking, Mary Beth tried to focus on the person who was now kneeling next to her, asking her all those silly questions. But the bright sky and her rattled brain kept her eyes from forming a sensible image out of all that was around her. The best that she could manage, due to her confusion and lack of breath, was a blink of her eyes and a faint gesture with her hand, as if she were trying to shoo her savior away. Ignoring her, the person at Mary Beth's side turned his head away from her and shouted toward the house. "First Sergeant Flemming, get over here with some water and some men to help me carry this girl into the house, now."

There was authority in the man's voice, Mary Beth thought dreamily. His tone showed both anger and real concern. Who was he? Then, a thought as wild as the one she had entertained when she first saw the horse over her popped into her head. It was James. He had come back to save her and their farm. Mustering up the best smile that she could manage, Mary Beth looked up at the savior and spoke with soft, faltering words. "Oh, thank God, James, you're here."

Then all went dark.

Were it not for the throbbing pain that woke her, Mary Beth would have passed off her experience of that afternoon as nothing but a bad dream. A quick scan of the room from her bed, however, confirmed her worst nightmare. Though it was evident that someone had made an effort to undo the mess created by the rampaging Union soldiers, the broken mirror over her dresser, a knotted bundle of clothing in a corner, and the absence of every little knickknack that Mary Beth had so carefully set about her room left no doubt that it had been true. All that Mary Beth needed to do was figure out how she had gotten to her bed and what had become of the Yankees.

That would not be easy, though. As she sat up quickly, the dull pain in her head suddenly turned very sharp, causing Mary Beth to all but black out again. Falling backwards onto her pillow, she lay there for a moment, breathing rapidly until the sharp pain passed. Once she had managed to regain her composure, she called out for her mother as loud as the ache in her head permitted.

In what seemed like seconds, her mother appeared. "Oh, thank the Lord," she called out as she crossed the room. "We were so worried about you, child."

Not wanting to risk a repeat of the agonizing pain that she had experienced when she had tried to sit up before, Mary Beth simply turned her head and followed her mother about the room. "What happened? Where's Papa? Did the Yankees take him? Have the Yankees gone yet?"

Elizabeth McPherson ignored her daughter's questions for a moment while she pulled the curtains closed to shut out the low early evening sunset. Finished with that, she went over to her daughter's bed and carefully sat down next to her and took Mary Beth's hand. She gave it a squeeze and a reassuring pat before she spoke. "Now don't you worry, dear. Everything will be all right now. You just rest."

Unable to rest until she at least had some answers, Mary Beth pressed her mother. "What happened? And where's James?"

For a moment, Elizabeth looked confused. Then she remembered. "Oh, no, my dear. That wasn't James. Major Sutton said something about you calling him by his first name, which surprised him since he had never met you before. I had to explain to him that James was your, I mean, a friend of the family."

"Who's Major Sutton?"

"He's the nice young man," Elizabeth McPherson explained matter-of-factly, "on the horse who rushed to your aid and stopped those soldiers from pillaging our home. He felt so bad about you being hurt and all that he personally supervised those ruffians as they carried everything back into the house. And he promised me that he would make a full report to their commanding officer on the whole affair."

Mary Beth was slow to catch on to the implications of her mother's comments. When she did, her eyes opened wide. *"He's a Yankee?"*

Elizabeth smiled. "But of course, dear. What did you think?"

"Well I . . ."

"You thought that James Bannon had come all the way back from Richmond to save you, didn't you?"

Mary Beth sighed, looking down at the hand her mother still held. "Well, yes, I did. I guess the bump on my head sort of scrambled my thinking some."

"Major Sutton said that's to be expected when a person hits their head like you did. He even asked if he could stay until you woke up."

"Is he," Mary Beth queried in panic, "still here?"

"Yes, yes, he is. He's downstairs talking to your father

about the war. When you called, he asked if he could speak to you for a moment if you were feeling up to it.''

Her first thought was to say no. It had been a matter of pride among the women of Winchester that no women would speak to one of the invaders unless it was absolutely necessary. Unsure, she looked away from her mother. ''Do I . . . have to see him?''

For the first time Elizabeth's voice became firm. ''Yes, you do. As much as we hate having them here, the Yankees are an unpleasant fact of life we need to learn to live with. Though I will never be able to forgive those brutes who nearly destroyed our house this afternoon, Major Sutton saved us and, what's more, he's given your father his personal promise that it will never happen again.''

Though Mary Beth wondered how this major would be able to do that, she didn't press the point. Her mother seemed satisfied for the moment and that, all things being considered, was all that mattered. ''Well, if I must,'' she finally replied, with no effort to hide the resignation she felt, ''I will see this Yankee.''

Leaning forward, Elizabeth patted her daughter's cheek. ''Oh, don't be so sour. Major Sutton is a very nice young man. He's from New York, where he was going to college to be an engineer. I'll go down and fetch him.''

After her mother left, Mary Beth pondered what she would say and how she would act. It was obvious that her mother was quite taken by the Yankee major, since she felt no qualms about having him in her house. Still, that was her mother. Mary Beth was sure that she wasn't obliged to follow her mother's lead. Still . . .

A soft knock on the door caught Mary Beth in the midst of her debate. ''May I come in?''

After a momentary fit of panic, during which she wondered if her hair was all a muss, Mary Beth responded with a soft, hesitant ''Yes.''

When he entered the room, Mary Beth understood immediately what her mother had meant. Major Sutton was a tall man with an average frame. As he approached the edge of her bed, she could see that his dark blue frock coat, tailored to fit him like a glove and freshly brushed, gave him a noble and commanding presence. Yet his movements were easy, almost graceful, speaking of quiet confidence. His tanned face, high-lighted by strong, yet well-sculptured features, was framed by sandy blond hair, combed back neatly behind his ears. And his eyes . . .

"I am Major James Sutton, 39th New York."

For a moment, all Mary Beth could do was to stare at his light-green eyes, eyes that seemed to smile as he spoke. Then, blinking as if to wake herself from a trance, she asked, "I thought the 39th was made up of Italian mercenaries."

This caused the Union major to smile. "Well, Miss McPherson, not exactly. While there are some sons of Italy with us, there are also companies made up of recent German and Hungarian immigrants. And we're not mercenaries, miss. I assure you that each and every man in the 39th is a good and loyal American."

His comment about loyal Americans was lost on Mary Beth, for she was too captivated by those eyes and the pleasing voice that filled the room. Finally noticing that she was staring at him, Major Sutton became a little nervous. "I came up here to apologize, in person, for what those soldiers did here today. While they were under orders to search the homes in this area for illegal weapons and foodstuffs that could be confiscated, they had no right whatsoever to do any harm to your family or damage your personal property."

Major Sutton's apology snapped Mary Beth out of her stupor. The image of her bloody-headed father being held at gun-point and the merriment that the rampaging soldiers derived from trampling their belongings underfoot brought back her anger. "Is it really Northern policy to wage war against defenseless civilians?"

Thrown off by Mary Beth's sudden change, Major Sutton shifted his weight from one foot to the other. Then, looking down at the floor, he shook his head. "No. At least, not the way I see it." Then he looked up at her again. The hurt expression and the shame were both obvious and sincere. "You must believe me, Miss McPherson, I don't want any part of this, the war and all. I'm just doing the best I can in a very, very bad situation."

"And those men. Was that the best they can do?"

"They are good men, Miss McPherson. God-fearing men,

each and every one, with families just like yours. But this is war, a civil war. Those men no more want to be here, in Virginia, than you want us to be here.''

"Then why in God's name," Mary Beth demanded, "do they behave like that? Is this what you would like our soldiers to do in your home?''

"They are angry, Miss McPherson." There was strength in Major Sutton's voice now, unrepentant strength. "Angry that they have been taken away from their homes and angry that this war is dragging on and on. They are angry about the manner in which the women of this town ignore them and even spit on them. Even I find myself enraged when I try to talk to a pretty woman like you but find nothing but hatred and scorn behind eyes that are as beautiful as any I've ever seen.''

The mixing of his explanation and adoration for her beauty totally disarmed Mary Beth. As she had when she first saw him, Mary Beth found herself becoming lost in his eyes. Though she tried, she found herself unable to rally any anger against this handsome young man towering over her. Finally, she heaved a great sigh. "I suppose that you are right, Major Sutton.''

After a moment of silence, he finally responded. "Is there any way, Miss McPherson, that I can make some amends to you, personally?''

There was no need to think long on that matter. "Yes," she said with a smile on her face. "I have been told that it is possible to pass letters through the lines to people in the South. Is that true?''

Shuffling his feet uneasily, Major Sutton nodded his head. "It is a practice that is discouraged, and it could present some problems for the one who is doing it, but yes, it is possible.''

"Do you think that you could possibly arrange for a letter to be passed through the lines to a friend of mine?''

Major Sutton looked down at the floor, crestfallen. "To your fiancé, serving with Jackson?''

"My father told you?''

Sutton looked up into her eyes. "Your mother. I asked her how you came to know my first name, and she explained that it's your beau's first name also.''

Though she didn't know why she was doing so, Mary Beth hastened to correct the Yankee major. "Well, he's not exactly my fiancé. The fact is, I'm not sure if he really loves me at all.''

This last comment brought a smile to Sutton's face that he quickly wiped away. "In response to your request, Miss McPherson, ordinarily, I would say no. But . . ."

"I will be much in your debt if you do," Mary Beth blurted out.

"Then it shall be done," he replied with a firmness that left no doubt that it would.

"How should I get this letter to you, Major?"

"Well, I could ride out here tomorrow, if that would give you enough time to prepare it?"

"That would be lovely."

Major Sutton straightened up as if he were presenting himself to a superior ranking officer. "Then, until tomorrow, Miss McPherson."

As he was turning to leave, Mary Beth called after him. "Oh, Major?"

Pausing at the door, he looked back at her.

"If you would like, Major, you could come by early in the morning, say at about eight, and join us for breakfast. We have a rather modest fare in the morning, but . . ."

With a smile that wrinkled his cheeks, Major Sutton bowed. "It would be my pleasure, Miss McPherson."

# CHAPTER 16

# August, 1862
# Manassas Junction,
# Virginia

WITH GREAT CARE, JAMES BANNON PICKED HIS WAY THROUGH the piles of delicacies that had once belonged to Pope's Union Army of Virginia. All about him members of the 4th Virginia were less picky, pulling crates and boxes off the top of stacks and opening them through the simple expedient of dropping them on the ground. While this method worked fairly well when the contents of the boxes were in cans or were dry goods, many of the fine foods that had been intended to grace the tables in the Union officers' mess were in jars. The result, of course, was disastrous. Not only were the contents lost, but the shattered glass made walking about hazardous for those Southern soldiers who had no shoes. Those, however, seemed to be the only regrets, for the mountains of supplies that General Pope had amassed at Manassas Junction seemed limitless to soldiers long used to doing without.

Finding a box that struck his fancy, James Bannon pulled it off the shoulder-high stack and set it on the ground. With his bayonet, he pried the wooden lid off and pulled away the waxed paper that covered the tins of sardines. After stuffing three cans of them in his haversack, James sat on the ground with his back against the stack of boxes and began to open a fourth can. After giving his filthy hands a cursory wipe on his shredded trouser leg, he began to pick the tiny fish out of the tin and eat them carefully. Unable to remember when he last had been able to enjoy such a treat, James had little doubt that it would be a long time before he would be able to do so again.

He was midway through his snack when Albert Flint, another private in Company J, came up to him, holding a jar. "Say Jimmy, is this what I think it is?"

James, dropping the sardine he had in his hand into his open mouth, wiped his hands across the front of his shell jacket before he took the jar from Flint. Like several other men in the company, Albert Flint couldn't read. Albert was a nice fellow, a good soldier, a devout Christian, and a hard worker. He had just never had the opportunity to learn to read. And like other men in the company who couldn't read, Albert came to James whenever he received a letter from home—written by his local parson for Albert's wife—or wanted to send one back. When they got newspapers, James also read these out loud for those in the company who were slow readers or, like Albert, were illiterate. Looking at the label as he chewed, James nodded his head in approval. "It's mustard," James finally said with his mouth still full. "Good stuff too."

"Well," Flint asked with a smile on his face, "is it as tasty as some folks say it is?"

James finished swallowing. Holding the jar raised in one hand, James pointed at it with the other. "This stuff is the best, made in Europe. In fact," James added after licking the oil off the finger he had been pointing with, "this stuff is so good, it would make the mule meat they issue us eatable."

"Thanks, Jimmy," Albert responded as he took the jar back from him and carefully set it in his bulging haversack.

"How many jars of that do you have?" James asked out of curiosity.

Albert held his haversack open and looked down into it as if he were counting the jars. "Oh, a whole bunch. You want one so you can put it on them little fishes you're eatin'?"

"No, no thanks. I don't think mustard and sardines will mix. I was just wondering what you're going to use all of that mustard on."

"Well, Jimmy, it's not for me. I mean, I ain't intendin' to eat this stuff."

Confused, James cocked his head to one side. "Then why in the dickens are you taking so much of it? I mean, isn't there something else you'd rather have?"

Albert tapped his index finger on the side of his head. "The way I figure it, these jars will be a whole lot easier to carry than cans of food. In a couple of days, I'll be able to trade this mustard for other food that some of these fellas are stockin' up on.''

James grinned. ''Sounds like a good plan to me.''

Albert stood up, beaming at being complimented like that. ''I figured so.''

From around the corner, Marty Hazard stuck his head. ''There you are, Jimmy. Will says he wants you to gather up the boys and bring them over to where he is.''

Finishing his last sardine, James tossed the can away and stood up. ''We moving out?''

Marty shook his head. ''Not that I know. Will found somethin' and wants us all there. I'll take you over.''

''Okay, Marty. Give a shout, would you, and let's get a move on. We'll fall in over there. Albert, you help him out, would you?''

Though all three men were privates, neither Marty nor Albert minded taking orders from James. Fact was, the high casualty rate among the officers and noncommissioned officers left Will the senior ranking man in the company. With no time to appoint new officers, sergeants, and corporals due to the continuous campaigning, the men in ranks more or less chose their own leaders. James was picked in this manner, more for his steadfastness and loyalty to the unit than his education at VMI. ''That book learnin','' Matthew Hazard told him one night, ''don't impress me at all. But you're a good man to be with in a fight, and that's all that matters to me.''

The handful of men that made up Company J, 4th Virginia, found Will McPherson standing in front of an open warehouse in the middle of a heap of sky-blue trousers, sorting them out into different sizes. When he saw James, he shouted over. ''Start having the men try on these pants. Pants for those with long legs are over there, short-legged men go there, and everyone needs to look in this pile here.''

Turning to face the company gathering behind him, James repeated Will's instructions. David Sayers, a lean farmer from Natural Bridge, Virginia, made leaner by hard marching and scant rations, protested. ''You took us from all that good food just to try on pants?''

James pointed at the long, unmended rip that went from the

cuff of Sayers' mud-caked trousers almost to the crotch. "Come winter, you'll be mighty happy to have a new pair of pants. Now quit your griping and get to it. The sooner you find some pants that fit and real socks with no holes, the sooner you can get back to the food."

"What about shoes, Jimmy?" another man called out. "Think Will can find us some shoes?"

James threw his arms out as he looked about the vast piles of supplies that surrounded them on all sides. "I'm sure somewhere hereabouts there's a pair of shoes that will fit you. But first you'd best tend to finding pants that fit." Scattering, the soldiers went to the piles James had pointed out and began to rummage through the wool trousers, holding them up to their legs and waist to check for a decent fit. When each man found a pair that seemed right, he would lay down his equipment, strip off the torn and tattered pants he wore, and slip on the new pair. Will, already sporting his new pants, handed James a pair. "These should fit. They're the same size as mine." The two former VMI cadets, thrown together by nothing more than the fact that they were the same height and VMI cadet companies were organized according to height, had often shared clothing in the past.

James took the pants, shook them out, and held them at arm's length. "They look good to me, Will. They'll do." Then remembering the sardines, James draped his new pants over his arm and reached into his haversack. "Here, I brought you something that I thought you'd enjoy."

Taking the thin tin from his friend, Will turned it over as he inspected it. "Can't say that I've ever had these before."

"You'll like 'em," James reassured him.

Moving off to one side, James and Will sat down in the shade of the warehouse. While Will watched the men in his charge go about rooting through the heaps of pants, he ate the sardines. Will held one by its tail out at arm's length and studied it for a moment. "They look like minnows but taste great." When James didn't answer, he looked over to see him rereading the letter he had received from Mary Beth. "She really likes you, James."

Not paying attention to Will, James looked over at him when he heard his name. "What was that?"

"I said, she really likes you."

A thoughtful expression crossed James' face. "Oh, well, I guess she does, a little."

"A *little*," Will countered. "Ma told me in the letter that she sent along with Mary Beth's that she thought that the Yankee officer who stopped the looting of the house was you. She never made any mention of me, Ma said. All Mary Beth kept asking for after she had been knocked silly in the head was you."

Embarrassed, James shrugged. "I think she's just being kind to me."

Will shook his head. "You don't know my sister like I do. She . . . I think she's in love."

Though James had wondered about that, Will's mentioning of the subject caused him to turn his face away from his friend to hide the fact that he was blushing.

"James?" Will asked hesitantly.

"Yeah?"

"Do you love her?"

James took in a deep breath as he looked up at the sky. Then, slowly, he shook his head. "I don't know Will." Then, turning to face Will, he repeated his statement, only with more conviction this time. "I just don't know."

"It's okay James, if you do. In fact, I'd be mighty proud to call you brother. Hell, after all we've been through, we're closer—"

"It's not that," James suddenly stated. He hesitated before he proceeded, looking down at his feet as he searched for the right words. When he was ready, he looked into his friend's eyes. "Will, there isn't anything I'd like more than to be part of a family like yours. Believe me when I tell you, I've dreamed of that. It's just that . . ."

"You afraid of asking her?" Will ventured impatiently. " 'Cause if you are, I'll intercede on your behalf when it comes time. Folks in our part of the country do that sort of thing all the time, you know."

"That's not it either. Will, I don't want to hurt her. Until I'm sure about my own feelings, and I'm sure that this war has been settled, I don't want . . . I can't make any kind of commitment to anyone."

Will thought about it for a moment, then nodded in agreement. "I appreciate your concern for Sis, James. I really do." Then he looked up into James' eyes. "And I understand. Just remember, I'll always be there, by your side, whatever happens, whatever you decide."

James was about to thank Will, when a stern voice called out, "Who's in charge here?"

Looking out to where his company stood, Will saw a mounted colonel facing them. Marty Hazard pointed over to where James and Will were seated. Turning his mount's head with his reins, the colonel moved over toward them. After carefully laying his open can of sardines down, Will got to his feet and saluted. "Sergeant Will McPherson, sir."

Though the colonel wasn't much older than James and Will, the long beard and fatherly tone gave the impression of great age and wisdom. "What regiment, lad?"

"Company J, 4th Virginia Volunteers, Winder's brigade."

The colonel smiled. "Ah, some of Jackson's old command."

"Yes sir, and proud of it."

The colonel pointed over at Will's men standing about, half wearing new sky-blue trousers while the others stood watching, naked from the waist down except for tattered undergarments. "Then your officers should know that it's dangerous to let your men use Yankee uniforms. I've seen some of our own units fire on another Southern unit in the heat of battle just because some of the boys in the ranks were clad in blue trousers."

James looked over to Will, then reached down and tugged at his own ragged pants. "It's going to be winter before you know it, Colonel. Unless you can assure us that the government in Richmond is going to provide us with trousers made from the right color cloth, we need to take what we can when we can."

The colonel studied James for a moment, thinking about what he had just said. Then he looked back at Will. "You are right to look out for your men like this." Then, lifting his right hand to the brim of his hat, he bowed his head. " My compliments to your commander. Carry on, Sergeant."

"Sir?" Will called out as the colonel began to leave.

Stopping, the colonel looked back. "Yes, son?"

"How long do you think Old Jack will let us root through this depot?"

Looking about him as if the question made him nervous, the colonel shook his head. "No doubt there's hordes of Yankees pouring out of the woodwork, headed for us as we speak." He smiled when he turned back to Will and James. "Can't keep something like this a secret, you know. And they won't take kindly to us feasting on their vittles. Tonight—by morning at the latest—we'll have to be on the move. If and when they do catch us, there'll be hell to pay for sure."

"The only way those varmints will catch us," Will stated with the unwavering confidence he always seemed to have plenty of, "is if Old Jack wants them to. And when that happens, well, sir, I feel sorry for the Yanks."

This brought a smile to the colonel's face. "I wouldn't expect anything less from the Stonewall Brigade. Now, sir, I must be going. Good day and good luck."

After watching the colonel ride away for a moment, Will finally spoke. "Well, I guess I'd better go poking around and see if I can find some shoes. James, you stay here with the boys while I tend to that." Bending down to retrieve his sardines, Will smiled. "Oh, and thanks for the treat. They still look an awful lot like minnows, though."

## *North of Bull Run Creek, near Manassas Junction*

From his seat, Kevin Bannon could hear Trevor Ward as he talked incessantly about this general and that. Seated next to the regiment's lieutenant colonel, Trevor was filling the colonel's head with his wild bombast and claims. "I tried, Lord, I tried," he had exclaimed again and again, "to rejoin the regiment, but it was too late. The company, I am sure, acquitted itself well." Kevin, unable to forgive his commander for the manner in which he had passed command of the company over to him, had said nothing at Harrison's Landing, where the regiment had been exchanged by the Confederates. He didn't even bother to provide Trevor with the status of the unit, leaving that to the first sergeant. Best, Kevin thought, to avoid the man than say something that he would regret.

There was, of course, much to regret as it was. In the first place, despite the fact that they had fought well, losing almost a quarter of their strength in killed or wounded, and that the terrible position they had found themselves in was due to the precipitous flight of other units, the 4th New Jersey was a unit in disgrace. When it came time to rearm the regiment, rather than receiving first-rate .58 caliber Springfield rifles as they had had before, the 4th was issued ancient .69 caliber smoothbore muskets. Nor were they allowed a new set of colors. "No need to give the 4th another set of colors," one of the officers in another regiment in the brigade commented loudly to a friend so that he could be overheard by Kevin. "We'll just send them straight through the lines to the Rebs to hang with the other flags they collected from the Fleeing 4th." Unable to muster up the will to put on a good show, Kevin allowed himself to slump into a sullen depression as black as that shared by the men in his company.

That he'd had no word from Harriet since the terrible incident didn't help. "I don't know what I've done," he confided in his friend Sam Gaul. "I can't believe that she would let our surrender at Gaines's Mill keep her from writing." Kevin, of course, wasn't really sure about that. She had, after all, been instrumental in pushing him into the Army and keeping him there. Perhaps, he thought, he had misjudged her. Perhaps she was as bad as her mother and father when it came to the issue of appearances and social status. Of course, until he heard from her again, he was willing to give her the benefit of the doubt. Still . . .

The screeching of the train's brakes and a sudden lurch forward snapped Kevin out of his gloomy thoughts. From the car ahead of them, a brigade staff officer came in. "Rails cut up ahead. We'll have to dismount here and cover the rest of the way to Manassas Junction on foot."

"How far," a captain near the front asked, "are we from Manassas?"

"Oh, five, maybe six miles."

Amid grumbles and muttered curses, the officers began to gather up their personal belongings and prepare to dismount.

Sam Gaul turned to Kevin. "Do you really think all we'll find at Manassas is cavalry?"

Kevin grunted. "Well, I hope so. I just wish we'd waited for those two Ohio regiments."

"Well," Gaul responded, "Colonel Haupt of the railroad branch seemed to be in a hurry to get us out to Manassas."

From behind Kevin, Trevor's voice chimed in. "Well, with Jeb Stuart and Stonewall Jackson running Pope ragged, someone who knows what they're doing needs to get a handle on things. While I was at General McClellan's headquarters, waiting for the regiment to be exchanged," Trevor boasted as he held up the unloading of the railcar, "General McClellan himself told me that it would take his army to save Pope. Of course, had those people in Washington done as the general had requested, we'd be in Richmond right now instead of scrambling in an effort to save our own capital." Kevin, irked by Trevor's pompous manner, said nothing. Sam Gaul, who was facing Trevor, was careful to hide his disgust. Though Kevin had never said anything about Trevor's actions at Gaines's Mill, the word had gotten round.

Slapping his hand on Kevin's shoulder, Trevor issued him his instructions. "Form up the company, Lieutenant. I'll be along in a minute."

Turning his head, Kevin nodded his acknowledgment as he muttered a cursory "Yes, sir," before following Gaul down the aisle of the railcar.

Once outside and on the ground, he headed to the rear of the train, where First Sergeant Himmel already had the company forming in two ranks. Walking down the line, Kevin glanced up at the faces of the men in the ranks. There was, on most of their faces, an expressionless, almost placid look. Yet in their eyes, he could see signs of anger and rage. They had been humbled by the Confederates, then mocked by their fellow soldiers in camp. Kevin understood the look, for he too was anxious to avenge their humiliation.

As Kevin approached First Sergeant Himmel, who stood out in front of the company, Himmel came to attention, then called the company to attention. The men responded to this command slowly, almost sluggishly. Coming to a stop before Himmel, Kevin gave him a salute that was almost as slothful as the men's response to Himmel's order. "Thank you, First Sergeant. Take your post." Himmel, one of the few men in the entire company who seemed to have taken their temporary captivity in stride, gave Kevin a crisp salute before marching off at a brisk pace to the right of the company.

Turning around, Kevin faced the company, then looked down to his left. Seeing that the company in front of his was preparing to march off, he gave the command, "order arms," then "right face." He didn't even bother to look about for his company commander before moving the company off behind the rest of the regiment. Trevor, no doubt, was somewhere near the brigade commander.

In silence the soldiers of the 4th marched around the bend of the rail line and past the shattered wreck of two trains that the Confederates had managed to surprise the day before. After that, they came to the bridge over the Bull Run, where the 4th halted. While Kevin could see that the other regiments of the brigade were moving on, the companies ahead of him weren't moving. Giving the order for the men in the ranks to stand at ease, he started to go forward but was stopped by Trevor after going only a few feet. "Lieutenant Bannon, over here."

Looking to his left, he saw Trevor. Pivoting, he walked over to where his company commander stood waiting for him. When Kevin was within a few paces of him, Trevor started to issue him orders in his usual pompous style. "The regiment has been ordered to hold here at the bridge and guard it. My company has been given the task of deploying skirmishers to the right of the bridge, over there on the high ground overlooking the creek." Kevin nodded obediently as he followed the sweeping motions of Trevor's arms. Finished, Trevor turned to face Kevin, who was still studying the area where the company would go. "Once I Company has completed their deployment, you will take the company over to the right of the bridge and deploy it."

With a final nod of his head, Kevin turned to leave. "Lieutenant."

Kevin halted and looked back at Trevor.

"It is customary," Trevor barked, "for a junior ranking officer to salute his superior after receiving orders and wait until he has been dismissed by that officer before leaving."

Though Kevin's slight against Trevor hadn't been intentional and such conduct wasn't new, he wondered why Trevor was making an issue of it at this moment. Still, this was neither the time nor place to discuss the matter. Coming to a rigid position of attention, Kevin saluted.

Trevor, however, didn't return the salute. Instead, he took a step closer to Kevin and gave him a complete once-over. "Where is your sword, Lieutenant?"

Though he had been given the opportunity to draw a new one when the regiment was being rearmed after its exchange, Kevin had taken only a pistol. Looking at Trevor, Kevin decided not to bother explaining why he hadn't done so but, instead, he gave Trevor the first response that came to mind. "Well, sir, I imagine that it's still with Lieutenant Thomas of the 4th Texas."

Though his response had been dry and matter of fact, not at all meant to be funny, Trevor became angry. "You, Mr. Bannon, are an officer in the Union Army. As such, you will conduct yourself accordingly or I will make sure that you are drummed out of the regiment in disgrace. Do you understand?"

Though he really didn't, Kevin swallowed hard and gave Trevor a hard "Yes, *sir.*"

"And furthermore, mister, you had better remember whose company this is. In the future, you will wait until I return before you move *my* command."

Again, Kevin responded with a curt "Yes, *sir,*" rather than argue. Whatever it was that Trevor was after, Kevin decided that arguing would solve nothing. If anything, he reasoned, it just might make things worse. Or, he realized, that might be what Trevor wanted. Either way, Kevin stood there, holding his salute, while he waited for Trevor to dismiss him.

After another moment or two of hesitation, Trevor did so. "All right. Go along and deploy the company. I'll be along in a minute."

When he had the company deployed and was satisfied that the men were as well situated as they could get, Kevin told First Sergeant Himmel that he was going to cross the run and walk to the top of the rise to their front. "I should be able to see the movement of the rest of the brigade for some time from there."

"Will the captain be joining us?" Himmel asked with a wink.

Kevin gave him a half smile. "I would imagine our commanding officer will join us in ample time if the situation dictates it."

"Oh, yes," Himmel replied. "I am sure he will."

With that, Kevin made his way down to the train trestle, crossed the run, and moved up to the crest of the rise, glancing back every so often to make sure he could still see his company. To his front the ground gave way to a sharp decline and then, gradually, back up to another ridge across the way. The railroad line, running from the bridge to Kevin's right rear, ran down through this little depression and up the far ridge. Manassas Junction was just on the other side of that ridge. The brigade was already deployed in line of battle and moving up the next rise, with the 1st New Jersey on the right and the 2nd New Jersey on the left. The 3rd New Jersey was centered on the 1st and 2nd and about two hundred yards behind, still in column. From where he stood, the brigade looked grand. The gleam of sunlight on the barrels of highly polished rifles was in sharp contrast to the solid straight ranks of dark blue. With national and regimental colors fluttering to their front, they were impressive.

The report from a single cannon, followed quickly by another, then another, shattered the tranquil scene before Kevin. Looking up from where the brigade was, he noticed, for the first time, movement on the far ridge. "Rebels," he muttered as he cupped his hands above his eyes to block the bright sun. After watching and waiting several seconds, Kevin could only make out three or four gun positions. Since it seemed likely that those guns belonged to a rearguard action, the brigade continued to move forward.

The hail of shell fire, exploding overhead and plowing through the dense ranks, did little, at first, to deter the brigade's march. That it was having an effect was obvious to Kevin, for even from this distance, he could see the brigade leaving small traces of blue in its wake. Yet, except for a few officers scurrying here and there, the three New Jersey regiments maintained their alignment and pressed forward.

Then, like a thunderclap, a hidden battery cut loose with a hail of canister into the brigade's flank. Kevin watched as the brigade recoiled away from the attacks of the hidden battery like an animal that has just been kicked in the side. That, however, did no good, for no sooner had those guns finished firing than other batteries, on the flanks and along the ridge before the brigade, began to fire. This booming of artillery fire was joined by volleys of rifle fire. From where he stood, it was obvious that the enemy they faced was more than a simple raiding party. The twelve hundred men of the 1st, 2nd, and 3rd New Jersey were faced with a growing ring of fire.

Still the brigade moved forward, fixing bayonets and pressing on in the face of the grueling rifle and artillery fire. For more than ten minutes this continued until, finally realizing that they were in a trap that no amount of courage could overcome, the brigade began to withdraw. In the beginning, Kevin watched as the brigade made an effort to withdraw in an orderly manner. The 1st and 2nd withdrew through the 3rd, now fully deployed, and headed back for the bridge. With the two forward regiments well on their way, the 3rd followed, giving ground grudgingly and paying for it every step of the way.

While he was watching, Kevin realized that he would soon be in combat again. Perhaps, he thought, this would be the day when they would be able to avenge their humiliation. Turning, he looked across the run to where the company was deployed. "First Sergeant Himmel," he shouted.

Stepping out into view, Himmel waved.

"The brigade's coming back! Pass word to Captain Ward to expect an attack soon."

Himmel cupped his hands over his mouth and shouted. "Where is Captain Ward?"

Kevin chuckled to himself. So, he thought, Trevor really is a coward. "Never mind that. Just pass the word to the colonel and have the men stand to."

Himmel saluted, turned, and disappeared from view.

Looking back, Kevin was appalled at the sight that greeted him. On the left, he saw enemy cavalry threatening the brigade. The brigade, coming to the ravine at the base of the rise Kevin was on, was losing its cohesiveness. The steep slopes of the hill and the flat, smooth leather of the men's shoes made climbing up out of the ravine difficult. Pursued by artillery fire, enemy infantry, and threatened in the flank by cavalry, the brigade was breaking up. Now, rather than a disciplined withdrawal, Kevin was faced with a fleeing rabble.

Strangely, he was not panicked. Rather, he thought, as he stood there watching, how ironic it was. Many of the same men in the 1st, 2nd, and 3rd New Jersey regiments now fleeing toward him had been part of McDowell's army in July of 1861 when the Confederates had defeated it. Those regiments, though, like Kevin's militia unit, had been far to the rear, in reserve. They had missed that rout. But now, here they were, on the same stream, facing the same enemy, fleeing for their lives just as their comrades had done thirteen months previously. It was as if the gods were playing some kind of cruel joke on them, sending those regiments that had missed the rout in July of '61 back to the same place on their own special train so they too could experience the humiliation of defeat.

Such strange thoughts ended as the first of the survivors of the massive ambush reached Kevin. Giving up his position on the rise, he made his way back across the bridge to his company, pushing and shoving his way through the refugees of the other three regiments. Quickly he found both Himmel and 2nd Lieutenant Henry Meyers, standing off to the side of the bridge. "Where's the captain?"

Meyers just looked at Kevin blankly, as if he were afraid to say anything bad about his company commander. Himmel, however, had no problem with that. "I imagine he's where he usually is, sir; everywhere else but with the company."

Any other time Kevin would have appreciated the first sergeant's humor, but not now. "All right, First Sergeant," Kevin shouted out without hesitation. "You post yourself over on the right as usual. Keep an eye open to the right, and if the Confederates come around there, bend the skirmish line back and pass the word on to me. Henry, you post yourself in the center rear. Keep an eye on First Sergeant Himmel and the men. Don't let the line bend or give in the center. Keep the men at their posts until either I or the first sergeant gives the order. When we do pull back, we'll do it by ranks. First Sergeant Himmel, you'll take the first rank back. I'll follow with the second rank. Henry, you stay in the center with the file closers and keep the men from skedaddling back to the rear on their own. Now, get to it.''

Though Kevin knew that Henry Meyers would be miffed that he had been placed under the first sergeant's orders, Kevin didn't care. He knew Himmel could be relied on and, at that moment, that was all that mattered. Turning to his own part of the line, Kevin looked at the men nearest at hand. From the expressions the men wore on their faces, Kevin knew there was a crazy-quilt mixture of emotions running through their minds. Those closest to the bridge could see and hear the panicked remnants of the other three regiments as they fled past them. Kevin had expected that this part of the line would be most likely to give way first because of this. ''Steady, boys,'' he called out as loud as he could so that he could be heard by as many of his men as possible above the growing roar of battle and the cries of fleeing men. ''We'll hold here till the brigade is across, then fall back, by platoon, to where the rest of the regiment is. Listen up for the orders. When we fire, mark your targets well and keep up the fire.'' Then as an afterthought, he added, ''We can do this. If we stand together, we can do this.''

With nothing more to say, Kevin stepped back and leaned against a tree. The last of those who would make it over were on the bridge now. Across the way and to the left, Kevin could see soldiers from the brigade being gathered up by Confederate cavalry and infantry. The enemy force to their front seemed to be as disorganized and exhausted by their pursuit as their prisoners. Unlike the men in blue, however, the Rebels weren't giving up. After a brief hesitation on the rise across the Bull Run where Kevin had stood moments before, Confederate officers began leading their men down toward the run on both sides of the bridge. Though he doubted if there was anyone over to his left to hold or delay the Confederate cavalry, Kevin didn't give that matter a second thought. ''FIRST RANK! Ready,'' he bellowed.

Kevin could see the musket barrels of his men, waiting in their positions behind logs or trees, come up, accompanied by the click of hammers being pulled back to the full-cock position. God, he thought as he realized how thin his company's skirmish line was, I hope we can hold. Then, forcing doubt from his mind, Kevin continued his order. "Aim, FIRE!"

Though less impressive than a full-company volley when the men were compressed, the fire of the men normally in the first rank was enough to momentarily check the approaching enemy. Fired up by the enthusiasm of their easy victory, few of the enemy were prepared for the resistance that they were now encountering. From the far end of the line, Kevin heard First Sergeant Himmel's stern voice crying out his orders to the men of the second rank. This volley succeeded in sending some of the more timid Confederates back away from the creek. They would re-form, Kevin knew. And when their officers were ready, they would come at his thin line again, this time in force.

Glancing nervously to his left, Kevin could hear the sound of gunfire. It was difficult to tell if it was on their side of the run or not. Turning back to his own front, he judged the Confederates to be beyond the range of the ancient muskets his men were armed with. Without any contact with the regiment to his rear and determining that there was little more to be gained by maintaining his position, Kevin decided it was time to go. "First Sergeant," he called.

At the far end of the line, Kevin could see First Sergeant Himmel step out from behind the tree he had been using for cover. Cupping his hand behind his ear, Himmel stretched his neck out to indicate he was listening. "Take your rank back now. We'll alternate our move back, going twenty yards at a time." Himmel made an exaggerated nod, then bellowed out his commands. "Second rank, to the rear, march."

The movement of J Company began to draw fire, but it seemed to be ineffective. When Kevin judged that Himmel had been gone long enough, he gave the order for the second rank to move to the rear. Like Himmel's second rank, the first rank rose from behind whatever cover the men had managed to find and began to move backwards, keeping a wary eye, their musket barrels, and their fronts to the enemy. Though walking backwards was difficult and caused more than a few men to stumble, the men thought that it was preferable to turning their backs on the enemy. "Least if you're shot," Private Johnny O'Keeth explained, "you'll be shot in the front and no one can call you a coward." Even Kevin, who normally didn't worry about doing things for mere appearances' sake, found himself walking backwards as he left the bank of the Bull Run.

He was still doing so when he heard the tramping of many feet coming up behind him. Turning, he expected to see the rest of the 4th New Jersey coming up. To his surprise, however, he saw a group of strangers, all of them pushing and shoving his men out of the way, rushing up to the run. A captain, not far from Kevin, was shouting to his men, "Get moving, keep going. Push the rabble out of your way."

Realizing that it was one of the Ohio regiments that was supposed to have joined them, Kevin smiled and shouted to the captain. "The enemy is re-forming on the far side of the run. They don't seem to be . . ."

The captain, seeing Kevin, gave him an angry scowl. "Get those cowards of yours out of our way, you son of a bitch. Get them out of our way."

Not realizing that the rest of his own regiment had already up and fled in panic when the remnants of the 1st, 2nd, and 3rd New Jersey had swept by them, Kevin responded with righteous indignation. "My men are *not* cowards and I'm *no* son of a bitch."

No one in the Ohio regiment took note of Kevin's protestations, however. Instead, they continued forward, pushing and shoving him about as they did so. After their ranks had passed him, Kevin, his hat knocked off during the jostling, turned and watched them go. Seething with a blind fury that he had never felt before, Kevin stood his ground, stomping his feet and pounding his clenched right fist on his thigh, yelling at the top of his lungs, "WE ARE NOT COWARDS, DAMN YOU! WE . . . ARE . . . NOT COWARDS!"

But the renewal of the battle that he had pulled his men away from drowned out his cries. After standing there for several moments, shaking with anger, Kevin realized that there was nothing to be gained from any further protests. Turning his back on the Ohioans, he slowly began to make his way back, head hanging low between his shoulders, to where First Sergeant Himmel was rallying the company.

# CHAPTER 17

# August, 1862
# Near Groveton,
# Virginia

JAMES WATCHED WILL MCPHERSON AS HE APPROACHED THE
tree that served as James' post on the regimental picket line.
Will was moving slowly, casting a wary eye toward the crest of
a ridge on his right. James, lying in the grass on his stomach,
watched that crest too. For while the rest of the Second Corps
of the Army of Northern Virginia rested behind the ridge, their
former professor of natural philosophy and first brigade commander, T. J. Jackson, was up there, riding the little sorrel that
he so favored back and forth. When Will reached the shade of
James' tree, he sank down onto his knees. Taking his hat off,
Will wiped his sweaty brow with the sleeve of his wool shell
jacket. "Jimmy," he said without taking his eyes off of Jackson, "you have any water left? My canteen is bone dry, like my
throat."

"Sure thing, Will." James rolled over to one side as he took
his own canteen off. Uncorking it, he handed it to Will, who
reached behind him without looking.

"What do you suppose he's doing up there, Jimmy?"

"Oh, I guess what he usually does, looking for ways to get
us into a fight."

Will looked behind him at the sun, now dropping down in
the west. "You suppose he'll start a fight this late in the day?"

"Will, you've been with that man long enough to know that
if he thinks there's a chance of taking a chunk out of a Yank
army, he'll do it, weather, time of day, and terrain be damned."

"Well," Will mused after taking a sip from James' canteen, "I suppose you're right. I just wish he'd get on with it, whatever it is he's going to do."

"Will, what difference does it make when it happens? Wouldn't tomorrow be just as good as today?"

Turning his head as he recorked the canteen, Will regarded James. "Have you realized how cynical you've become, James?"

"I would prefer to think of myself as being realistic. I mean, look at what's happened in just the past six months. Last year when we were here, not more than a mile from this very spot, there were nearly a thousand men in the regiment. When we marched out of Winchester this past March, we numbered over eight hundred men. As of this morning, there is a grand total of one hundred and eighty men still with the colors. One hundred and eighty! And where, may I ask, has thirteen months of campaigning, suffering, and fighting gotten us? Right back to where we were exactly thirteen months ago."

Will turned his whole body around to face James. "I suppose you could look at it that way, Jimmy. And I guess what you say is true. But think of it. We're still free. The Yankees have hit us with their best and Southern Independence is still a reality. I'm as impatient as you are to end this whole thing but I keep remembering what we're doing this for. You know I've never said much about you not being a native Southerner, but I should remind you that me and my family have a lot at stake here. This country the Yankees are tromping through is my home. Though I have no kinfolk in these parts, my heart breaks every time I see a gutted farmhouse and a deserted homestead, because they belonged to fellow Virginians, people no better or meaner than my own family. I'd like to put an end to their suffering, the sooner the better. But not if it means surrendering those rights that Washington, Jefferson, Thomas Paine, and Patrick Henry stood for in the First War of Independence. Those Virginians, and thousands of their contemporaries from both North and South, fought for seven long years to secure those rights for us. I imagine that I can be a little patient and trust Old Jack and Bobby Lee awhile longer."

The passion of Will's words was reflected in his face. How different he was, James thought, after a year of war. How different, he reminded himself, they all were. Deciding that he had let both of their moods grow too somber, James smiled. "My, my. They haven't even confirmed your commission yet and you're already sounding like an officer."

Caught off guard by the sudden change of subjects, Will shook his head and looked at James with a confused expression. "Damn you, James Bannon. You always do this to me. You get me cranked up and then—"

A flurry of shouted orders, starting in the distance but growing louder as they were relayed down the line, caught Will's attention. Cocking his head slightly, he perked up and listened. Then, he stood up. "Come on, Jimmy. The regiment's reassembling. Looks like Old Jack finally figured out what he wants to do."

With the help of his rifle, James pushed himself up off the ground. Looking about, he could see that everyone was in motion. The fight would come today, after all. "Well," he said as he started to follow Will, who was already headed to the right, "if we're going to finish the fight today, we'd best get a move on."

Will said nothing as he motioned to the other fifteen men who made up the company once known as the Lexington Defenders.

Coming up and over the ridge, where an unfinished railroad cut ran the length of the ridge, the soldiers of the 4th Virginia were greeted by the sight of Federal units deployed to their front. The Federal line was already under an ever-increasing artillery fire from both the right and left. Guiding on a farm orchard to their front, James could see that the 4th Virginia, serving as the extreme right hand unit of the brigade, would overlap the left of the Federal line. If nothing changed in the next few minutes, he reasoned, they would be able to wrap around the enemy flank, take them enfilade, and make short work of the Yankees.

"Guide on the center," came the command from Lieutenant Colonel Robert D. Gardner, commanding the regiment that day. Since James was holding the position normally held by the company second sergeant, he instinctively glanced to his left to see where the 2nd Virginia was. They, as well as the other regiments of the brigade, were advancing in line. Turning his head sharply to his right, he checked the alignment of the soldiers in the front rank who were between him and Will McPherson, still their acting company commander. Will was doing likewise, checking his alignment with the next company to his right. Each company to the left of the center, or color, company did likewise, just as the companies to the right of the color company looked to their left to align with it. Lieutenant Colonel Gardner, followed by the regimental color sergeant and color guards, led his regiment forward, all the while keeping a wary eye to his left to ensure that the 4th Virginia maintained its alignment with the other regiments.

Suddenly, to their front, a flurry of activity caught James' attention. Looking back down the slope where they were headed, he caught sight of Union skirmishers rising up from behind their cover and starting to run back to their own lines. On order, the entire brigade halted as it prepared to deliver a volley. The orders, given crisply in the clear evening air, were heard by the fleeing Union skirmishers, allowing them to dive into the tall grass just before the Stonewall Brigade delivered its volley. When they judged that the Confederates had finished, the skirmishers were up and sprinting again.

"Can you believe that!" Matthew Hazard bellowed. "We wasted a volley on thin air. I'll bet we didn't hit a thing."

From the right, Will McPherson shouted, "Quit your griping, Matt, and reload. Those fellows they're headed for don't look like they're about to run." Looking down to where Will was pointing, James could see that the solid mass of Union soldiers, a good four to five hundred men, were holding steady, eyeing the 4th Virginia as Colonel Gardner gave the order to continue the advance. Finished loading, James brought his rifle up to the ready. Behind them the men of the second rank kept theirs at right shoulder shift. All watched to their front. Somewhere in the ranks, above the cannonading, James heard someone muttering. At first, he didn't recognize what the man was saying. It was only when a second man picked up the mumbled refrain that the words became clear. "Yea, though I walk through the valley of the shadow of death, I will fear no evil: for thou art with me . . ."

It was the Twenty-third Psalm. James thought about that as they advanced, each step taking them closer and closer to the line of grim-faced men who stood their ground. It had been a long time since he had prayed, a long time. Even during chapel services at VMI, James had done as he had as a child, going through the motions of rituals and services he didn't understand. Now however, with the ringing of their first volley still in his ears, the sight of the enemy waiting grimly for their order to fire, and the words of the psalm rising up over the steady beat of drums and artillery fire, James understood. And like several other men, he too found himself picking up the refrain, without embarrassment, without restraint. "Yea, though I walk through the valley of the shadow of death," he said as his feet carried him onward, "I will fear no evil . . ." Feeling no contact to his right, he angled over until his shoulder began to rub that of Marty Hazard. "For thou art with me."

To their front, as clear as anything he had ever witnessed, James watched as the officers of the Union regiment issued their commands. "READY!" Up came hundreds of rifles; the cocking of their hammers to the rear echoed in the still evening air.

"Thy rod and thy staff they comfort me," James and Marty muttered in unison.

"AIM!"

"Thou preparest a table before me in the presence of mine enemies."

"FIRE!"

Like a sickle cutting its way through ripe wheat, the Union volley ripped through the Stonewall Brigade's ranks. To his left and right, James could hear the dreadful thud that .58 caliber minié balls made when they hit a man. Yet they went on, forward, ignoring the yelps, screams, and groans. Like men possessed, they went on, closing up the now diminished ranks and mumbling their prophetic prayer. "Thou anointest my head with oil; my cup runneth over."

Only when they came upon a thin rail fence less than eighty yards away from their tormentors did Colonel Gardner order the 4th Virginia to halt. With this as a cue, the color sergeant, accompanied by the color guard, made their way back through the ranks.

"Surely goodness and mercy shall follow me all the days of my life." More men in Company J had joined the solemn prayer as they obeyed Colonel Gardner's order to bring their rifles up to the ready.

"And I will dwell in the house of the Lord forever."

"AIM."

"For ever."

"FIRE!"

With a yell that echoed across the valley, the men of the 4th delivered a volley as terrible and as effective as that which they had just received.

Even before James had finished reloading his own rifle, their opponents, a Wisconsin regiment wearing the old-style black felt Jeff hats, delivered a volley as devastating as their first had been. But no one wavered, not to James' left, and not to his right. Instead, they continued with the grim task of reloading and firing. With no more emotion than that of a threshing machine, the two lines began to hack away at each other, each as determined as the other to stand its ground. Only an occasional shout of "Close it up!" by some company officer or another brought any change to the methodical loading and firing sequence that absorbed each and every man in the ranks. Like most of the other men about him, whatever fears James had carried into this fight with him were gone, as he was submerged in the strange numbness that robs otherwise sane men of all reason and logic in battle.

For some minutes the Wisconsin unit, seemingly unaware of the punishment it was taking, stood fast. In the growing darkness, James watched between shots as its members went through the same steps of loading, firing, and reloading that he and his companions were performing with a terrible deliberateness that no danger could seem to hurry. Even as a new unit came up on the flank of the Wisconsin regiment and began to add its fire to the steady roar of the fearful contest, the only motion the 4th Virginia made was when an officer cried out from somewhere in the rear, "Close it up! For Godsakes, close it up!"

Late afternoon passed into early evening, then, in turn, early evening faded into night. Still the firing continued with neither side advancing, neither side yielding, and neither side dimin-

ishing its fire. Even this failed to bring an end to the fight as
both sides, unable to see the foe, took aim at the muzzle flashes
of the opposing line. James had no idea how long they had been
at this terrible business when he felt a tug at his trouser leg. At
first, he ignored it. When the tug was renewed a moment later,
he instinctively shook his leg, like a man would do in an effort
to kick away a dog pulling at his cuff. Only when a hand all but
wrapped itself about his ankle did James turn to see who was
annoying him so.

Keeping his rifle aimed to the front, James twisted his body
a half turn and looked down at the ground behind him. The
flash of a ragged volley partially lit the upturned face of a man
in distress. Though he had not gotten a good look at who it was,
a terrible feeling of dread crept over James, forcing him to bend
over, closer to the face of the man pulling at his leg. When
another volley cast its eerie light upon the man's face, James
gasped. Taking his right hand away from the stock of his rifle
but keeping it balanced with his left despite the searing heat of
the barrel, James reached over and grabbed a handful of Marty
Hazard's sleeve. Tugging at Marty just as he fired, James tried
to pull his friend over to him. Though Marty missed the shot he
had been taking, James gave him no chance to protest as he
yelled above the din, "Marty, for Godsakes, your brother."

Looking first to where James stood, then down at where he
was looking, Marty saw the prostrate figure of his brother on
the ground behind them. When friendly fire again illuminated
Matthew's face, the man's pain and distress were obvious. In a
flash, Marty dropped his rifle and sank to his knees next to his
wounded brother. James did so too, although he held onto his
rifle, still ignoring the barrel burning his calloused fingers.

"Dear God," Marty shouted. "Oh, dear God, where are you
shot?"

Though he tried, opening his mouth wide, Matthew could
not speak. His labored efforts resulted in little more than a rush
of air. "Grab his arm and get him away from here," James
commanded. Reaching under Matthew's left arm with his left
arm, James stood up, pulling Matthew up with him. Marty,
doing the same to Matthew's right, got his brother up off the
ground. Despite a pitiful shriek from Matthew, they dragged
him back several feet, over the body of another man whom

neither James nor Marty bothered to identify. Though they were far from being safe, at least they were away from the jostling firing line.

After easing Matthew down, Marty dropped to the ground and pulled Matthew's head onto his lap with James' help. With one arm cradling his brother's head and the other wrapped about his limp figure, Marty began to rock his stricken brother like a mother trying to comfort her child. "It's all right, Matthew, I'm here. It will be all right." Easing back away from the two brothers, James watched for a moment in silence. At irregular intervals the light of rifle or cannon fire illuminated Marty's face, glistening brightly off the streams of tears that ran down Marty's dirty cheeks and disappeared in his scraggly beard. "Hush, Matthew, hush," he repeated as he kept rocking Matthew. "It will be all right. I'm here with you. I'm not going to leave you. It will be all right."

Whether Marty's comforting words had any effect was hard to tell, for the same flashing light that showed his anguish also fell upon the still features of Matthew's upturned face. James watched for a moment until his own vision began to be blurred with tears that fought to be free. Though the crash of battle continued unabated, and the screams of other wounded cut through the night all about them, neither Marty nor James paid them any heed as Marty finally came to realize that his brother was gone.

From behind, a hand grabbed at James' jacket. "Back to the line, damn you, get back there, you two."

Angered by the insensitivity of the familiar voice, James leaped to his feet and turned to face Abner Couper. The rage James felt at that moment must have been reflected in his face, for Couper took a step back when James stood up in front of him. For a moment, James glared at his old tormentor, unable to speak. Couper, unsure what James was about to do, clutched the sword in his right hand as he stood facing him. Then, after his initial hesitancy passed, Couper repeated his command, though not as sharply and forcefully as before. "You and him, you need to get back up to—"

Through teeth that were clenched as tight as his fists, James hissed at Couper. "Damn you, man! That's his brother."

After staring into James' eyes for a moment, Couper looked past him and down at Marty, now holding his dead brother's head up to his bosom as he rocked back and forth, weeping without restraint. James, keyed up and ready to smash Couper in the face as soon as he uttered another word, was caught off guard when Couper suddenly sank down to his knees across from Marty. Stepping aside and turning to face the two men, James watched in amazement as Couper reached out with his free hand and ran his fingers through Matthew's matted hair. Marty paused his wailing for a moment as he looked at Couper who, in turn, looked up into Marty's eyes. Then, with a gentleness that James never imagined Couper to be capable of, Couper carefully closed Matthew's eyes, leaned forward, and kissed the dead brother on the forehead.

As he stood there, watching this, a wave of shame suddenly swept over James. In his own hatred for another, bred by years of abuse and anguish, he had imagined that everyone was as mean and as spiteful as he himself could be. That Couper was human, endowed with the compassion that he had seen so little of in his life, was both a revelation to James and source of embarrassment. For it was he, and not Couper, who had been ready to strike without thinking, without regard. Hanging his head down, James started to cry, as much for himself as he did for Matthew.

Standing up, Couper looked down at Marty and Matthew one more time, then turned away from them. Stepping closer to James, he placed his hand on James' shoulder. Leaning forward, Couper whispered in his ear. "There's nothing we can do for them now. Please, come back to the ranks."

James, his head still bowed low, nodded, then turned. Together, the two former VMI cadets walked back to the vicious firefight that raged on unabated.

The following day brought no relief to the sufferings of the diminished ranks of the 4th Virginia, for the fight that was to be known as the Battle of Groveton served as a lightning rod for the scattered elements of Pope's Union Army of Virginia.

Massing in fields that were still littered with the previous night's dead and wounded, Pope's fifty thousand began a long day's fight as he tried to destroy Jackson's eighteen thousand. From their post on the right, the men of the 4th Virginia, painfully aware that the previous night's battle had cost them almost half their number, waited in silence for their turn to renew the fight.

When Will McPherson had called out the company roll that morning, only nine men responded. Marty Hazard, who had been one of them, stood next to James throughout the morning and into the afternoon. As he waited, Marty twisted and turned his hands, still dirty from digging a shallow grave for his brother, about the barrel of his rifle. Though he said nothing, the glare in his eyes and his faraway gaze told James that he was lost to a tormented world of emotions where grief and anger twisted and turned a man's feelings until they all but choked any thread of sane reasoning. There was, James realized, no soap strong enough and not enough water to wash away Matthew's dried blood from Marty's hands. Only fresh blood, that of his enemies, would cleanse the anguish Marty felt that day.

Yet, despite the ferocity of the battle to their left and the maneuvering of Union forces to the front of the railroad cut where the 4th was posted, there was no opportunity that day for Marty Hazard to wreak his vengeance upon the enemy. Only the 2nd Virginia, holding an advanced position, was involved in any serious exchange with the enemy. And even that was a brief engagement as they checked the advance of a single enemy regiment late in the afternoon.

That did not mean that the 4th Virginia was in no danger. As the Union battle line ebbed and flowed across the fields to their front and off to the left, everyone in the Stonewall Brigade became aware of just how precarious a spot they were in. At one point in the afternoon, the center of the line was pierced, necessitating the commitment of the brigade just to the left of the Stonewall Brigade. Not long after that, a New Jersey brigade came boldly up to the railroad cut but gave ground quickly. And of course, there was the far left, where General A. P. Hill's division was located and engaged through the entire day. It was therefore not surprising that both officers and the men in the ranks grew apprehensive when clouds of dust appeared to the rear of the brigade.

"It's Longstreet," Will stated. "It's got to be Longstreet, coming through the Thoroughfare Gap."

James shook his head. "You don't sound very confident about that."

Will looked over to his friend. "To tell you the truth, I'm not."

Innocently, Private John Pitt, with the unit for less than a week, spoke up. "Well, Sergeant McPherson, what happens if it ain't General Longstreet?"

Will looked over to Pitt, studying the boy's face for a moment. "Well, I guess they have us." Will pointed over to their front left. "We can't go north toward Centreville and then back to the valley, the enemy's definitely in force." Then Will pointed to their front, where Union forces were clearly visible. "Nor can we go back that way, to Manassas Junction." Pointing over his shoulder with his thumb, in the general direction of the dust clouds, which were growing nearer, Will concluded, "So, that's either Longstreet or the people who'll march us off to captivity."

Marty Hazard spit on the ground. "The hell you say." Lifting his rifle, Marty shook it at Will. "The Yankee that takes me prisoner ain't been born."

Will looked over to Marty, nodded his head, and then looked back at dust clouds.

Finally, when the colonel was unable to wait any longer, an officer from the brigade staff was sent out to discover what units were closing up on them. Only after he came galloping back through the woods where the brigade waited apprehensively, whooping and yelling that it was, indeed, Longstreet, did anyone relax. And even then, the men throughout the brigade let go a loud and sustained yell, as if they were an overstressed steam engine letting off steam.

The appearance of General James Longstreet's troops, however, did not mean an end to the battle. Instead, as on the night before, the fighting continued well into the evening. From where James stood, he could see little had changed from that morning other than the addition of more wounded to those already left on the field from the Groveton fight.

Like a fitful child fighting the very sleep it needed, the fighting refused to die away when darkness came. Off to their left, the men of the 4th Virginia could hear brief spasms of rifle fire announce the chance meeting between nervous pickets and exhausted men moving about in the dark. To the right, a substantial little fight began at twilight as Longstreet's men came into contact with the Union left. Despite the coming of darkness, this short but vicious little action continued into the evening before it too died away and yielded the night to the shrilled cries of two days' worth of wounded men abandoned between the lines. Unable to start fires to cook their rations for fear of drawing enemy fire, the soldiers along the abandoned railroad cut, who had beaten back every effort by Pope's army, settled down and slept as best they could.

Not long after the day's fighting gave way to an uneasy calm, word was passed through the ranks of the 4th Virginia that Colonel Baylor, their brigade commander, was holding a prayer service at his tent. James, at first, dismissed the idea of attending. His religious training had been presented by a minister whom the Bannon brothers enjoyed annoying when they got bored, which was often. Later, as he grew older and tried to apply what he had learned in Sunday school, James became confused, for the people who populated his life in New Jersey bore no resemblance to the ones the church spoke of. Within his own home he watched his father, a man who professed to be a devout Christian, lie, cheat, and swindle to obtain the fortune and power that he coveted above all else. When James finally was sent to Virginia, he had no use for the church he had been raised in and attended chapel services only because it was required by regulation.

Still, as he lay there on his blanket, unable to shut out the terrible images that denied him his sleep, James felt himself being drawn to the gathering at Colonel Baylor's tent. Slowly, he lifted his weary body off the ground, leaving his rifle on the thin blanket he had been resting on. With hat in hand, he made his way, as most of the men of the brigade had already, to the circle already listening to Chaplain Abner Hopkins of the 2nd Virginia.

At first, James was quite content to stand on the outside of the circle, listening to the chaplain's words. But soon, as other latecomers came up behind him, James was slowly nudged forward. In time, he found himself in the front row, standing in the flickering light of the campfire that served as the focal point for the gathering. Will, who stood next to Captain Hugh White, commander of Company H of the 4th, was surprised to see James. With a slight nod, Will acknowledged James' presence before bowing his head again. Not far from Will was Abner Couper, a man that James had once regarded in the same manner that he did his own father but now . . .

Looking up, James stared into the night sky. The stars, valiantly trying to shine through the drifting smoke caused by fires that burned away dry grass and unattended crops, seemed to dwarf James, just like the events of the past year and a half. How small, he suddenly realized, he was. How pitifully small and insignificant. When compared to the stars that filled the sky above him, there was nothing special about him, nothing of real significance. James thought hard about his life for a moment, trying to come up with some event, a worthy achievement that made his life different or important. But he couldn't.

Lowering his head, he looked at the men to his left and right, then back over at Abner Couper. He had hated Couper, just as he had hated his father. Hate and the harsh memories of his past, he realized, had been so much a part of his life, so powerful a driving force in everything that he did, that when Mary Beth McPherson had tried to express her love for him, he had recoiled like a man being offered poison. Did that, James wondered, make him unworthy of love? Were the punishments that he had been subjected to over the years just retribution or, he wondered, had they been self-inflicted? And why, he wondered, did God choose to strike down a man like Matthew Hazard, a God-fearing man and loved by his brother, and not him? Why?

As the gathering began to sing a hymn, James slowly looked about the circle. There was, he realized at that moment, no difference between them. There were no officers, no privates, no wealthy Virginians, and no poor white trash. There were only long-suffering men absorbed by an ancient hymn handed down to them by their fathers. They sang this song softly, with passion and thoughtfulness as if they were drawing strength from it. Perhaps, James realized, that was what they *were* doing, for that was what he was doing at that moment. Like his companions, he was there not to find salvation or redemption but to find the strength he needed, not to kill, for that was simply a mechanical process, but to go on living. As they sought this strength from a shared belief, James sought it from the company of his comrades. They were, James knew, like him, little more than simple human beings, mere specks in a vast universe awash in a turbulent sea of turmoil and violence with no end, no safe haven.

As these thoughts passed through his mind, James' eyes set upon Marty Hazard. Like the other men, Marty was singing. James had heard Marty sing before, both on the march and about the campfire. There was a look, however, on Marty's face that he had never seen before. All signs of the vengeful scowl of hatred that had contorted his face earlier in the day were gone. Instead, there was a serenity that at another time James would have found strange. But he understood what was behind that expression. He understood what Marty was thinking as he watched Marty's lips carefully form the words of the hymn. This was a strange place, James thought, to discover what love was. But perhaps, he reasoned, it was fitting. And as he thought about it, a tear came to his eye as he began to miss his brother as he had never missed him before.

The new dawn, the third day of battle for Jackson's command, brought the promise of another hot day and more fighting. Jackson, though, didn't expect that they would fight and said so to Colonel Baylor as he watched the Federal troops deploy before the unfinished railroad cut. "Well," he said calmly to Baylor after several minutes, "it looks as if there will be no fight today." Then, no sooner having said that, he added, "but keep your men in line and ready."

Will McPherson, who had been craning his neck to hear

what Jackson was telling Baylor, suddenly turned to James. "James, I want you to promise me something."

James had been paying no attention to Will, Jackson, or Baylor. He was lost in his own thoughts, troubled thoughts that had plagued him, like the screaming and wailing of the abandoned wounded between the lines, throughout the night. Between the screams and an occasional stray shot or brief smattering of musketry, James had been able to find no escape in sleep. For the images and thoughts of his past that tumbled through his exhausted mind in a random and senseless manner were as uncomfortable as the dry ground he lay on.

Shaking his friend's arm, Will repeated his request. "James, I want you to promise me something."

With a slow, awkward shake of his head, James blinked twice as if to erase an image from his eyes, then turned to Will. Having been lost in his own thoughts, James paid no attention to the vacant look on Will's face. "Sure, Will, anything."

Taking a deep breath, as if he were fighting back a flood of emotions, Will hesitated for a moment. When he spoke, his voice was calm, almost distant. "James Bannon, promise me that whatever happens, no matter how long it takes, you'll see to it that I'm buried on my family's farm in Winchester."

James recoiled as if he had been slapped. Cocking his head to one side, he stared at Will with a troubled and wary look.

Seeing that his friend had been taken aback by the strange request, Will sported a slight smile as he reached out and gave James' arm a reassuring squeeze. "Look, Jimmy, seeing Matthew Hazard go down like he did and last night's prayer meeting got me to thinking. I haven't got much in this world that really matters. Fact is, except for you and my family, I don't give a hoot about anything. And when this is over, I'm sure that you'll find your place in this world. Me, my place is with my family. While we may not fight today, we're sure to fight again soon, somewhere else. Old Jack's got his fighting blood up, I saw it in his eyes. It'll make things a whole lot easier on me, James, if I know that when . . ."

Though he tried to finish his thought, the emotions choked off Will's last words. James, glancing down at the ground between them, pondered his response. He wanted so badly to reassure Will that they would both make it through the war, that everything would be all right. But he couldn't. He was simply too tired to lie like that. James looked up into Will's eyes and nodded slowly. "It will be done. I promise."

At two-thirty a sharp fight broke out between the skirmishers deployed before the section of the line where Baylor's brigade waited in support and advancing Union sharpshooters. To the right, the massed cannons of Colonel S. D. Lee's battalion of artillery opened up on the advancing Union sharpshooters. Following these preliminaries, the soldiers of the 4th Virginia, from the wood line where they were posted to the rear of the unfinished railroad cut, watched in both awe and nervous anticipation an attack their commander had doubted would come. After three rousing cheers that reverberated above the din of the fight between skirmishers, dense ranks of Union troops began to pour from the woods on a hill across from the railroad cut and begin their slow, measured advance toward Jackson's right, where the 4th Virginia stood waiting.

Like everyone else, James could feel his body tense up as he prepared for battle. Like many of the other tried and true veterans of the 4th Virginia, he pulled his cartridge box around to the front, unsnapping it and his cap box as he did so. All the while, he watched in silence as the advancing blue line drew closer. Colonel S. D. Lee's artillery had now rolled forward their smoothbore cannons, held back in reserve until now, and added the weight of their shot to the growing storm of fire that was beginning to rain down on the Union line.

Freed by the onset of combat from the disturbing images that had plagued him, James watched the Union advance with a cold, trained eye. The pageantry created by the appearance of ten thousand soldiers, arrayed in assault columns, with officers and brightly colored standards, was shattered as soon as Confederate rifle and artillery fire began to rip through the densely packed ranks. The cohesiveness of those formations began to unravel some, as some units recoiled under the impact and others surged forward as if the bloodletting were a stimulant.

Tired of taking punishment without responding, individual Union regiments began to return fire. At first, this did little other than prolong their agony, for the volleys fired did little damage while the time consumed in delivering them served only to expose the attackers to more Confederate fire. James knew, however, that the first Union volleys were little more than a means of releasing tension and frustration. The most difficult duty the Union officers had at this point of the attack, he knew, was to keep the men advancing in the face of murderous enemy fire. An occasional pause, during which their own men could return fire, was often necessary to keep an attack going.

The problem with that, however, was that sometimes the officers couldn't get their men moving again. Sometimes the men, collectively, would decide that they had done all they could or had gone as far as they dared. Even such a massive attack as the one now being unleashed against them could, piece by piece, fall apart just at the point when the attacker was about to come to grips with the defender. Average units, in this case, could be expected to stand their ground and trade shots with the defenders until their ammunition or nerve gave out. Those units with men less well motivated or lacking internal cohesion would quickly melt away.

There were, of course, the exceptional units, those units that were well led or created with a bond that brought out the best in every man who served in it. Both James and Will liked to think that the old Lexington Defenders, and indeed the 4th Virginia, were among these units. Fact was, everyone in the Stonewall Brigade felt that way. "What we lack in cold steel," Lieutenant Theodore Lynn had told the old Lexington Defenders during the Valley Campaign, when they were being pursued by forces with superior numbers, "we more than make up with raw courage."

Looking out across the unfinished railroad cut, James saw that Confederate units did not hold a monopoly on such sentiments. To the left, James watched as the 1st Virginia Battalion, known as the Irish Battalion, and the 21st Virginia of Bradley Johnson's Brigade stepped off to reinforce their sister units along the railroad cut two hundred yards to their front. Union forces, already forcing their way into the railroad cut near a wood lot, greeted these newcomers to a fight that devastated the ranks of the Irish Battalion and the 21st. With little more to do than wait their turn, James watched as those units moved forward in the face of growing Union rifle fire and growing clouds of white smoke generated by thousands of rifles being fired as fast as they could be loaded. When they finally did make it to their assigned spot on the firing line, their route of advance was marked with their dead and wounded every inch of the way.

With his attention still riveted to the commitment and decimation of the units to his left and the ceaseless roar of battle, James almost didn't hear the order to advance. David Sayers, standing next to him, poked James with his elbow. "Charge bayonets, James. The colonel gave the order to charge bayonets."

With a jerk, James turned his head to the right and saw that along the entire brigade line the front rank held their rifles at the ready, while the rear rank held their pieces at right shoulder shift. Bringing his own weapon up to the ready, James looked out across the field they would have to cross, glancing every now and then to his left, as he waited, at the debris left by the units that had just made a similar effort.

"FORWARD!" Colonel Baylor's voice bellowed out above the din of battle. Up and down the line, five hundred men stepped off in unison into the open. As soon as he lifted his left foot, James stopped thinking. There no longer was a need to. From now on, this was all mechanical, all automatic. He, Will McPherson, and those in the ranks to his right had all done this time and time again. That men like Will McPherson were starting to become pessimistic was not surprising. What was surprising to James was that it had taken so long.

As with most advances, the men of the 4th Virginia were rewarded for their courage and obedience by a devastating fire from Union troops that had captured a section of the railroad cut. James paid no heed to what was happening to his left and right until, suddenly, he could no longer feel David Sayers' sleeve rubbing against his. Glancing to his right quickly, and then to his left, he realized that he was alone. While keeping his rifle at the position of ready and facing the enemy, James twisted his body about at the waist and looked to the rear. The rest of the brigade, still reeling from the impact of the Union fire, was halted. While some men made ready to fire and others shuffled nervously in place with an occasional backwards glance as they sought a safe place to flee to, another Union volley tore into their ranks, sending more dead and wounded to the ground. Without hesitation, James backed up until he was aligned with the front rank of his regiment.

All along the line, this hesitation and confused shuffling gave a strange, quivering effect to the brigade's battle line. Even the brigade commander, Colonel Baylor, was at a momentary loss as to how to get the brigade started forward again. Then, seeing the flag bearer of the 33rd Virginia go down, Baylor knew what he had to do. Rushing to where the stricken man lay, Baylor seized the regimental colors, held them aloft, and yelled back to his command for all he was worth, "Boys, follow me!" His efforts were rewarded, for the men of the Stonewall Brigade again stepped off toward the enemy.

But there was a price to pay for this achievement and such courage. And Colonel Baylor paid it. The next Union volley sent Baylor down, riddled by several bullets and wrapped in the 33rd's colors. Again, the brigade faltered, this time easing back toward the wood line they had left but a few moments before. And again, an officer responded to the crisis by running forward and seizing the colors of the 33rd. This time it was the 4th's own Captain Hugh A. White. Pausing only long enough to wave the flag wildly, White, a theological student at Washington College before the war and cohost of the previous evening's prayer meeting with Colonel Baylor, called for the men of the brigade to follow him. Then, oblivious to the flagging morale of the brigade, White turned and ran forward into the rolling clouds of smoke that were now dominating the battlefield and obscuring everything. Before he and his followers disappeared, James noticed, to his horror, that Will was one of them.

Dumbfounded, confused, and now, for the first time that day, genuinely scared, James hesitated. Fortunately, Colonel Andrew Jackson Grigsby of the 27th Virginia didn't. Stepping forward, as both Baylor and White had, Grigsby was able to get the brigade moving forward again. This time the brigade held together. This time they continued their advance despite the vicious fire that the Union troops continued to pour into the 4th

Virginia's shredded ranks. And this time they made it, though at a heavy cost.

Gaining the railroad cut, however, didn't put an end to the 4th Virginia's suffering. Though the Union troops who had held there and punished the Stonewall Brigade without mercy readily gave way, supporting units moved forward in an effort to throw the Stonewall Brigade back. Three times they came. And three times the Stonewall Brigade threw them back.

The price the brigade paid was steep. James, with Will nowhere to be seen, rallied the handful of men who had once been known as the Lexington Defenders. With all unit alignment lost and many of the officers down, the fight became a soldiers' fight, where the individual's courage, bolstered by the proximity of a few good and trusted friends sharing his labors, made the difference between victory and defeat. With Adam Page on one side and Marty Hazard on the other, James fought on. He ignored the searing heat of his rifle barrel as it burned his callused hands. He ignored the screams and cries for help as more and more men went down, adding gray and butternut to the blue of the Union dead and wounded at their feet. The only thing he could not ignore was Will's absence. Over and over again, Will's plea to be buried on his family's farm ran through James' head. Between shots, as he loaded with an urgency spurred on by the need to release his anger as much as by the desperateness of the situation, James looked around, hoping and praying to catch a glimpse through the dense and choking smoke of his friend's face. When his efforts weren't rewarded by the time he finished loading, James would clench his teeth, hoist his rifle to his shoulder, scream a profanity, and fire at the nearest Yankee.

Together, James and Marty Hazard at his side quickly ran through their own ammunition. While James paused to scramble about on his hands and knees, looking for ammunition in the cartridge boxes of the dead and wounded, Marty couldn't be bothered. Throwing down his rifle, he bent over, grabbed the biggest rock he could find, and hoisted it over his head with both hands. Waiting until a Yankee came within striking distance, Marty let out a terrible yell and threw it. Though he missed, Marty was not dissuaded from doing this again and again.

When he had enough cartridges in his pockets, James stood up, looked around for Will, and then went back to firing. He was absorbed in this when he felt a hand on his shoulder. Instinctively, he froze, for he knew that someone behind him was coming over between him and Marty Hazard to take a shot. Out of the corner of his eye, he saw the braided sleeve of an officer's arm holding a pistol come down. After a slight pause to aim, the officer fired, then withdrew his arm. Turning, James looked into the face of Abner Couper. Couper, his dirty face streaked with sweat and creased by tension, looked into James' eyes. With a slight smile and a nod, Couper was about to turn when James grabbed his arm. "Will McPherson? Have you seen Will McPherson?"

Couper shook his head. "Not since he went forward with Hugh White."

"Well, where did they go?"

"Hugh's dead, back there in the meadow. I saw his body. He still had the 33rd's colors."

"And Will?"

"I'm sorry, James. I didn't—"

A look of horror fell across Couper's face as he looked over James' shoulder. Before James could turn to look, Couper's arm holding his pistol shot up and fired two hasty rounds. By the time James did manage to face to his front, all he saw was a Union soldier, less than six feet away, staggering backwards as he dropped his bayonet-tipped rifle at James' feet. Realizing what had happened, James turned back to thank Couper, but Couper was gone. With more Yankees coming on fast, James let the matter go for now. Turning his full attention back to the fight at hand, he paused only long enough to take another futile look about for Will before taking his next shot.

# CHAPTER 18

# September, 1862
# West of Frederick,
# Maryland,
# Near Burkittsville

THE MARCH OF THE 4TH NEW JERSEY FROM FREDERICK, MARY-
land, west to the looming South Mountains was made in silence. Not even the moderating weather or the joyous welcome
offered by the recently liberated residents of western Maryland
cut through the pall that the men in Kevin Bannon's company
carried with them.

From his post off to the right of the company, Kevin watched
as Trevor Ward kept pace with the regimental adjutant, talking
as they went despite the adjutant's efforts to shake him off.
Though Kevin tried hard to forget the manner in which Trevor
had handled the company after the disaster at the Bull Run
Bridge, he couldn't. The mere sight of the man was now enough
to anger Kevin. Trevor's words to the company after the brigade's rout at the Bull Run Bridge still rang in his ears as
clearly as if they had just been spoken.

"You're a disgrace," he had bellowed at the soldiers of
Company J as they reassembled around the curve formed by
the railroad line they had been sent to defend. "You're despicable cowards and a disgrace to your uniform and your state."
The men, already disoriented and confused by the manner in
which the relieving Ohioans had taunted and jeered them as
they went forward, became totally disheartened when Trevor lit
into them. Turning to Kevin, many of the men waited for him
to stand up for them, to tell Trevor that they had checked the

pursuit of the Rebels and had fallen back only when ordered. Kevin, however, had said nothing. Rather than exerting himself as he knew he should have, he stood there mute, taking Trevor's abuse in the same manner as he had always taken his father's.

The anger Kevin felt was not directed solely against Trevor. He thought that he had found himself growing to hate his father with a passion that he had never imagined possible. Though there had never been anything resembling love between the two of them, Kevin had never really hated Edward Bannon until recently. In a letter to a girl he knew in his heart would never read it, Kevin tried hard to express his feelings and fears. *"I've come to understand what hatred means. It is, for me, like a sickness that twists my mind and keeps me from dealing with those about me. It distorts every thought, every action, and leaves a mark on everything I touch. It has even warped the memory of my brother, for at times I have found myself blaming him for my current predicament. After all, I say to myself, if he were still here, he, and not I, would be passing through this living nightmare that I am stranded in. I now know what the old fellows meant when they said that each man creates his own hell."* Though all that he wrote was true, it was not the complete truth.

For in his effort to come to grips with the feelings and emotions that tormented him, Kevin was hamstrung by the fact that the greatest loathing and contempt he harbored was reserved for himself. *"I am,"* he wrote, *"like a man standing on a railroad bed who sees a train coming straight at him but is too frightened to do anything. In all my years, I have never had to stand up and fight my own battles, to exert myself in the manner that grown men are expected to. When I had James, he protected me, standing between me and my father's harsh tongue and heavy hand. When he was gone, I sought escape by fleeing to college. And when the war came, I had you and my letters to you to comfort and protect me."* Then, as often happened, Kevin wandered from the subject that he had been writing about and regressed to the recurring loneliness he felt. *"I miss you, Harriet. I do not blame you for your rejection of me. Though I have finally come to the realization that I am unworthy of your affections, I still pine at the thought that my weakness of mind and spirit have cost me my first true and unblemished love.''* After finishing a letter such as this, Kevin would take it and, with the fatalism that is a hallmark of the Gaelic race, he would seal it in an envelope, add it to a bundle of other unmailed letters, and carefully pack it away at the bottom of his knapsack.

From behind him, a voice snapped Kevin out of his sad and troubled thoughts. ''Do you think he knows where we're going?''

Turning, Kevin shook his head as First Sergeant Himmel came up next to him. Looking back at Trevor, Kevin grunted. ''I have no doubt that he thinks he knows where we're going, but I'll not give him the pleasure of asking him.''

''And you, Lieutenant, where do you think we're going? Some of the boys think Harpers Ferry. Me, if I had my choice, would prefer to go up the Shenandoah Valley. I've been told by some of the fellows hereabouts that there are a lot of families living about Winchester that have ancestors that hailed from Germany. I'd like to go and see if that's true.''

''Are you looking to become a vagabond, First Sergeant?''

Himmel smiled. ''The idea has occurred to me. You see, the village near Königsberg where I came from was the same village that all my ancestors came from. I can remember when a person couldn't move from the village or his farm without the local lord's permission. Junkers, we called them. In fact, everything we did was regulated, if not by the Junker himself, then by a local magistrate. When I came of age, off to the Army I went. When I finished my time with the colors, back to my village I was sent.'' Himmel paused for a moment as he looked about. ''Yes, Lieutenant, I do like the idea of being a vagabond. Just as I like the idea of being allowed to fight for the right to be one.'' Then, like a flash, the whimsical smile that had lit his face disappeared as he looked ahead to where Trevor Ward was marching, now at the side of a brigade staff officer. ''Of course, there are some things that never change. Like Johnny O's landlord and my Junker, every country has someone who would like to keep men in bonds.'' Then glancing over at Kevin, Himmel added in a whisper, ''And they're not all wearing gray.''

This caused Kevin to smile. ''You know, First Sergeant, if

my dear father had his way, I'd be just like Captain Ward, one of the ruling class.''

"But," Himmel countered, "you are not like him. That is why I look forward to the day you will command this company."

Kevin chuckled. "It will be a long time before that happens."

"Oh, I think not."

Troubled by the tone of Himmel's response, Kevin cocked his head to one side and looked at the first sergeant inquisitively. "What do you mean by that?"

Himmel gave Kevin a hard look. "You must know by now, Herr Lieutenant, that our captain is a marked man. I have heard rumors that more than one man in the company has sworn that the next battle will be his last."

Though he had heard about unpopular officers being shot by their own men in the midst of a battle, Kevin had always attributed those stories to sensationalism and fiction. "Do you know what you're saying? Whether he deserves it or not, what you're talking about is murder."

Realizing that he had misjudged Kevin, Himmel tried to disarm the alarm he had created. Boasting a broad smile, Himmel let out a loud guffaw. "Oh, you have no need to worry, Lieutenant Bannon. I am sure that it was just a bunch of angry men letting off steam. No one, I'm sure, would think about doing such a thing for real. Besides," he added, "if our dear captain's performance in the past is any measure, he'll not have to worry about being shot by anyone, unless it's done with a very long range cannon."

Though Himmel's reference to Trevor's failure to lead his own company in battle was as disturbing to Kevin as the threat to his life Himmel had alluded to, Kevin let it drop. As much as he knew that he, as an officer, should punish such disrespect, Kevin didn't have it in him to do so. He was, he thought with a sigh, doing what came naturally to him—shirking his duty. Making his apologies, First Sergeant Himmel parted from Kevin, leaving him free to lapse back into his own dark and troubled thoughts.

The 4th New Jersey, like the other units of Major General Henry W. Slocum's division of the Sixth Corps, continued west at a good pace. There was, Kevin thought as he trudged along, a real purpose behind this move, for he hadn't seen the Army move so quickly since he had joined it. As if to underscore his suspicions, around noon the silence of the late summer morning was broken by the muffled sounds of rifle and artillery fire to their front. As was customary, the first sign of battle sent a flurry of mounted staff officers and messengers riding up and down the columns. This spasm of activity had no sooner dissipated when general officers, with their aides and staffs trailing off behind them, went rushing by the 4th on their way to the front.

From the ranks, Johnny O'Keeth called out to Kevin. "Hey, Lieutenant Bannon. We gonna fight today?"

While still marching, Kevin twisted his head about and looked for O'Keeth. There, amongst the faces of other men who wondered the same thing but hadn't the nerve to ask, was O'Keeth's smiling face. The sight of this man's beaming cheerful face had always been enough to cause Kevin to smile himself. Today, despite his depressed state of mind, was no exception. Returning the grin, Kevin nodded. "Looks that way, Johnny. There's certainly enough daylight left, provided someone upstairs doesn't squander the day away."

O'Keeth thought about Kevin's comment before he nodded. In an army noted for taking its time and throwing away opportunities, nothing was a sure bet. And if anyone in the Army of the Potomac knew this, it was the hard-luck 4th New Jersey. "To date," Sam Gaul had lamented one night to a gathering of lieutenants after the disaster at the Bull Run Bridge, "our luck has been consistent. Consistently bad, that is."

Kevin, convinced that all their failures to date had been mere luck and not the fault of the men he marched with, agreed. "We will have our day," he responded with thoughtful determination as he stared into the campfire the young officers were gathered about. While all the other officers present readily agreed with him, only a few understood, like Kevin, that when that day came, the price of redemption would be blood.

Slowly, too slowly for Kevin, the Sixth Corps went through the gyrations necessary to transform an army corps of over twelve thousand men from a marching column four men abreast into a line of battle that could measure up to a mile and a half wide. Though they did this under sporadic enemy artillery fire, directed at them from the towering heights of the Blue Ridge Mountains to their front, the maneuvers were carried out promptly and efficiently. Commitment into battle, however, was not so prompt.

Sent to the right of the road they had been traveling along after passing through a small town, the 4th New Jersey found itself deployed in support, along with the 3rd New Jersey on the left, about one hundred and fifty paces behind the 1st and 2nd New Jersey. To the front of those two regiments, across plowed fields and pastures of dark green clover, was a stone wall that ran along a tree line at the base of the mountain itself. Behind it were Confederate infantry, battle flags unfurled and fluttering gently in the breeze. From where Kevin stood, the Rebels were distinguishable as individuals only when they fired. Though it was difficult to judge their number, there was no hiding the four hundred yards of open fields that any attacker would have to cover if and when the order to advance came.

That order was, as usual, slow in coming. As the hours ticked away, the 1st and 2nd New Jersey, using a rail fence as best they could for cover, exchanged fire with the enemy. During this time Trevor paced back and forth in front of the company, hunched over with his hands behind his back. Every so often he would pause to look over at the heavily wooded mountain that rose steeply up from the valley floor. Kevin too looked at the mountain and decided, like most of the officers in the regiment, that no one along this part of the line was going to be going forward, especially not against an enemy entrenched in so strong and uninviting a position.

He had pretty much resigned himself to spending another long day doing nothing but being shot at when word came down the line that the 4th was going to charge. The thought of action created a moment of tension in the ranks as men who, like Kevin, had been lulled into a state of sullen resignation now suddenly had to prepare themselves mentally for battle. From his post behind the second rank, Kevin watched Trevor as he froze, hands still behind his back, and glanced about quickly. His actions and the expression on his face reminded Kevin of a nervous cat looking for a way out of a tight spot.

When he realized that the entire company was staring at him, like Kevin, Trevor straightened up, threw out his chest, and tried hard to sport a stern expression. After a long and uncomfortable moment, Trevor cleared his throat and began to speak. "Men, we are going forward." He paused, shifting his weight nervously from one foot to the other. "When we do go forward, I don't want you to disgrace me or our noble state as you have in the past."

From the ranks, there rose a murmur. Kevin, not quite sure that he had heard right, cocked his head to one side and leaned forward until his own head was up even with those of the two men he stood behind.

"We have much to atone for," Trevor continued as his own words began to embolden him. "If you cherish your manhood, if there is a single measure of pride left in your hearts, you will go forward, nobly and unflinchingly."

The murmur in the ranks grew as men shifted about, jostling each other and turning to speak to the man next to them. Kevin, unable to believe what he was hearing from Trevor, struggled to hold his tongue. Now, leaning forward on the shoulders of the two men in the second rank in front of him, Kevin glared at Trevor. How could he say such things, Kevin wondered. How could such a loathsome creature, a man who had yet to stand up in battle with his own command, denigrate those who had? It was, Kevin realized, like listening to his father. Even here, on the verge of going into battle, it seemed as if his father's cruelty and harshness were reaching out to break his spirit.

Ignoring the growing dissension in the ranks, Trevor droned on. "I am sure that you are all man enough to stand up and do what is expected of you—"

Like a twig bent too far, Kevin snapped. With a single heave, he pushed the two men he stood behind and plowed through the next two men in the front rank, bursting out in front of the company only a few feet from Trevor. Shocked by the sudden appearance of his first lieutenant, Trevor instinctively stepped back as if in fear. Kevin's stance, shoulders back and jaw jutting out, fists tightly clenched at his sides and feet spread apart, left Trevor little doubt that he was in trouble. And had there been any doubt, the fiery expression on Kevin's face would have dispelled it.

Kevin, catapulted into action by his anger, found himself in an awkward position. Though he wanted to strike Trevor, and he probably would have had he not had to fight his way through the ranks, he suddenly realized that doing so would achieve nothing. Whatever pleasure he would have personally derived from the act would have been buried under mounds of regret that would come later.

Still, the idea of doing nothing, of meekly stepping back behind others, as he had done for so long, was just as distasteful. After taking one more long hard look at Trevor, Kevin spun around. Looking up and down the ranks with the scowl he had shown Trevor still creasing his face, Kevin lunged forward at the nearest man and grabbed his musket. Moving back so that all could see him, Kevin waved the musket over his head. "You men are not cowards," he bellowed. "You have nothing to be ashamed of. I was with you at Gaines's Mill. And I was with you at Bull Run. You did splendidly, each and every one of you, and our roster has vacant spaces left by those who fell fighting like men to prove it. When we go forward, we will go all the way."

Taking a few quick steps back to the man from whom he had taken the musket, Kevin reached over, seizing the man's bayonet and yanking it from its scabbard. Affixing it to the end of the musket as he resumed his position in front of the company, Kevin again hoisted the rifle above his head. "When we come eye to eye with the enemy, give him the bayonet, all the way to the muzzle. I know you men. We can do it. We *will* do it!" Then, raising his voice as loud as he could, shaking the musket over his head violently, he repeated, over and over again, "To the muzzle!"

Fired up by Kevin's emotional outburst, the men of Company J lifted their muskets up as high as they could, shaking them and taking up Kevin's refrain, "To the muzzle. To the muzzle."

Other officers and men up and down the line of the 3rd and 4th New Jersey looked down to see what the commotion was all about. Only the order to move forward brought Kevin's wild screaming to an end. Kevin looked quickly down to his left where the regimental commander, Colonel William B. Hatch, was holding his saber aloft as he gave the command, "Forward." Kevin, composing himself, went over to the man he had borrowed the musket from and returned it. Then, forgetting that Trevor was there, he took the company commander's post to the right of the company. Drawing his pistol, Kevin held it up as the other company commanders held their swords, echoing Hatch's order to advance and ignoring Trevor's dumbfounded stare as the company stepped off smartly.

If any of the men in Kevin's company felt fear or trepidation, they didn't show it. Passing through the prone soldiers of the 2nd New Jersey and over the rail fence the 2nd had been fighting behind, the 4th New Jersey paused only long enough to re-dress their lines. With nothing between them and the Confederates behind the stone wall except four hundred yards of plowed farm fields and patches of clover, the enemy fire began to take effect.

Kevin, paying no heed to the sharp zing of bullets as they whizzed by, stood before his company, arms outstretched, and bodily forced those men who had gone too far forward back into the ranks. "Dress it up. Come on, men, dress it up and be quick about it." Though there was a sense of urgency in his voice, Kevin's demeanor served to calm the men. When he was finished and saw that the rest of the regiment was about to step off again toward the stone wall, Kevin hastened back to his post, shouting out to the men in the ranks as he waved his pistol over his head, "Remember, to the muzzle."

When they went forward again, the entire regiment did so with a deadly earnestness that no amount of fire from the Confederates behind the wall could squelch. Not even the Rebel artillery, firing from their commanding positions on the mountain above, seemed to have an effect on the 4th. When it became obvious to the defenders of the stone wall that their best efforts were going to be for naught, they broke.

Kevin, now only yards from the stone wall, saw the enemy break. Pointing with his pistol, he pulled the hat off his head with his left hand, waved it over his head two or three times, and broke into a dead run, yelling over his shoulder as he went, "After them, boys! We've got them. We've got them."

With a deep shout, the neat lines that Kevin had dressed so

carefully collapsed as the men followed him. By the time he reached the wall, Kevin was able to leap up on it with a single bound. Pausing for a moment on the wall itself, fully exposed and vulnerable to enemy fire, Kevin again waved his hat over his head, pointing at the Rebels, now fleeing up the heavily wooded mountainside. "Up, men. Up and after them. We're going all the way to the top."

Unlike Kevin, the men of Company J didn't pause on the wall. They bounded over it with ease and started to make the arduous climb. When he was satisfied that his exhortations had had their desired effect, Kevin began to follow, pausing only long enough to direct Henry Meyers to the left of the company. "Henry, get over to the left and keep the men going. Don't let a gap develop. Keep them closed up and moving."

Meyers, thrilled at being given such an important post, smiled as he saluted with the barrel of his pistol. "Yes, sir." Then, holding his saber close to his side to keep from tripping over it, Meyers turned and made off at an angle to the men on the company's left, who already were disappearing into the woods. Taking a deep breath himself, Kevin leaped off the wall and made his way up and to the front of the company, pushing men who stood in his way aside, yelling encouragement as he went by. "Keep going, men. We've got them."

Up the 4th went. To their left, the 3rd New Jersey strove to keep up with them. Behind the 4th, the 2nd was following as fast as the rugged terrain and their feet would allow. Though neither the 2nd nor 3rd had the stigma of Gaines's Mill to overcome, their rout at the Bull Run Bridge was more than enough to fire them up with the same burning vengeance that drove Kevin, his men, and the rest of the 4th to the top. Though some of the fleeing Confederates paused to fire a shot or two, their efforts were futile.

Within minutes Kevin found himself on near level ground in the gap. Coming across a road, Colonel Hatch tried to gain some control over his now scattered command. Kevin, hearing his exhortations, turned to face his men. As before, he held his arms out straight to his sides, yelling between gulps of breath, "J Company, re-form. Re-form on me." As they came up even with Kevin, some of the men took shots at the fleeing enemy. While keeping his arms up, his hat still in his left hand and his pistol in his right, Kevin looked over his shoulder. Across a small open patch of ground, he could see the enemy troops they had been so wildly chasing mingling with a fresh batch of Confederates who were as surprised to see the Yankees in the gap as they were to see their own comrades running past them and through their ranks.

Looking quickly to his left and right, Kevin could see the rest of the brigade deploying. ''Hold your fire, men. Reload and prepare for volley fire.''

Obediently, those who had fired reloaded their muskets as fast as they could. Those who hadn't discharged their pieces yet brought them to shoulder arms and waited for Kevin's order. Taking his post to the right of the company, in front of First Sergeant Himmel, Kevin took one more quick glance down the ranks of his company before giving his orders, ignoring the blast of canister being discharged by a pair of heretofore unseen Rebel cannons across from them.

Ready, he raised his pistol. ''Company! Ready.'' When the clicking of hammers being locked back to the full cocked position stopped, he continued. ''Aim!'' He paused, dropped his pistol until he held it at arm's length, pointed toward the enemy, took one last look at the terrified expressions of the milling enemy to his front, and gave the order to fire.

In a flash, the scene before him disappeared in a cloud of smoke as his company fired as one. Not waiting for the smoke to clear, he ordered his company to reload, though some of the men, still fired up by their charge up the mountainside, hadn't waited for this last order. Turning sideways, Kevin took one step out to the front. Looking down the ranks, he watched as the men finished reloading and signified their readiness to fire again by bringing their pieces to shoulder arms. When all but one or two of the slowest men were ready, Kevin stepped back into the ranks and looked out to his front.

By now the smoke from his company's volley and the fire from other units was clearing enough to see the enemy, or what was left of them. Those Confederates who judged themselves too close to the Union ranks to make good an escape raised their rifles, butt-end upright, to signify their desire to surrender. Those who had been hit and knew that they could never crawl away to join their comrades, now fleeing down the other side of the mountain, lifted a hand and waved it. "Enough," a few yelled with a real sense of desperation that Kevin understood. Looking to the left and right, Kevin made sure that none of the units to his flanks was going to fire. Satisfied that they too were checking their fire, Kevin yelled down the ranks to Henry Meyers, instructing him to take half the company forward and gather up the prisoners. With a shout, Meyers and his men went forward, grabbing the first-rate rifles that their humbled foes offered so willingly.

Watching this for a moment, First Sergeant Himmel leaned forward and tapped Kevin on his shoulder. "It seems that it would be a waste to leave all these good Confederate rifles lying about. I imagine there's enough to rearm our unit, probably more."

Kevin, looking around as he wiped his brow with the sleeve of the arm still holding his pistol, nodded. "You're right, First Sergeant. Take the rest of the company and see to it."

As he was turning to leave, Kevin called out to Himmel. "First Sergeant, do you know where Captain Ward is?"

"Why, yes sir, I do."

When Himmel didn't say anything else, Kevin shook his head. "Well, where is he?"

"The last I saw of him was back at the rail fence, sir, where the 2nd was."

"Is he wounded?"

Himmel smiled a big toothy smile. "Well, no sir, not that I saw. But if you'd like, I can see to that."

With his mind still reeling from the rush of events and the exhaustion that fell upon him now that he was no longer in immediate danger, Kevin didn't quite understand what Himmel was saying to him. When he did, rather than being upset, Kevin threw his head back and gave out a loud guffaw. Dropping his head, he shook it from side to side. "No, that won't be necessary, First Sergeant. I think that our commander has done enough damage to himself." Then, looking about, he added, "Now get on with collecting the rifles before someone else gets the good ones. And tell the men to remember to take the cartridge boxes. Our .69 caliber buck and ball won't be of much use in those Confederate Springfields."

With a nod, Himmel turned and went about his task, leaving

Kevin, for a moment, alone. Standing there, in the midst of the turmoil created by their advance and the brief fight in the gap, Kevin let his arms fall to his sides, still holding his hat in his left hand and his pistol in his right. Looking up, he squinted at the bright sun, barely visible through the dense trees and the lingering smoke of battle. Whatever doubts anyone had had about his regiment would now be put to rest. His men had, he knew, acquitted themselves as he knew they would. But even more important, Kevin realized as he stood there, admiring the strange beauty that this late summer day showered upon the spot where he stood, he had come into his own. For the first time in his life, Kevin thought, he had stepped out of the shadows that he had been so content to stand in all his life and taken his place as a man amongst men.

Not knowing who to thank for this, Kevin was simply content to stand there for several minutes, with the sun shining in his face, until his regimental commander called for all company commanders. With the spell broken, Kevin sighed as he looked about him. Taking one last deep breath, he filled his lungs with air still pungent with burnt powder, put his hat on, and turned to get on with the business at hand.

## CHAPTER 19

# September, 1862
# North of Sharpsburg,
# Maryland, on the
# Hagerstown Pike

THOUGH THE PALE MORNING SUN RISING IN THE EAST HAD YET to burn away the morning mist and fog that still lay over the low ground and hollows, the battle unfolding before James Bannon was well progressed. From his post behind a thin rail fence, he watched the battle unfold as if he were watching a play. Exhausted by incessant marching and fighting since March, James, in his mind, viewed the scene before him as nothing more than a Greek tragedy being played out by two armies, each of which was unable to completely overthrow the other.

The Federals, to the accompaniment of a chorus of artillery, entered the stage to James' front from a cluster of woods to the north. Center stage for these Union troops was a field of tall corn that lay across the Hagerstown Pike from the 4th Virginia's position. A cluster of woods to the east, on the far side of the cornfield, and another behind the 4th Virginia, in the west, served as curtains in the wings of the stage. It had still been quite dark when the first of many determined attacks aimed at General Richard Ewell's division south of the cornfield was delivered. In silence, the men of the 4th Virginia, numbering less than one hundred, watched from their concealed position as the men of Ewell's division, commanded by Brigadier General Alexander R. Lawton today, met the lead enemy forces with devastating fire. Looking to the north, where an occasional

344

smattering of rifle fire told James that the skirmishers up that
way were engaged, he could see line after line of Union soldiers, astride the Hagerstown Road, heading their way. Though
taking heavy and effective fire from Confederate artillery
posted to the south, the Federals came on.

"Well, Marty," James commented dryly while he kept
watching the enemy's advance, "we'll be in the thick of it in
a few minutes."

Martin Hazard, lying next to James, wasn't paying any attention to him or the Yankees who were fast closing on them.
Instead, he was messing with the sergeant's stripes on his left
sleeve, which were on the verge of falling off. James looked
over and watched as Marty carefully took hold of a loose
thread. Gently, he tugged at it in the hope of tightening up the
tenuous hold it had on his tattered uniform. Oblivious to everything, even the screech and detonation of shells being traded
back and forth from all sides of the cornfield, Marty kept drawing the thread tighter until he was satisfied the stripes would
hold. Done, he smoothed the stripes down, then looked up at
James. This caused him to blush slightly. He averted his eyes
back to the stripes for a second before looking into James'
eyes. "I still think you should have gotten them and not me."

James, touched by the sorrowful tone in Marty's voice,
shook his head. "I told you at Harpers Ferry, Marty, it doesn't
matter to me. Really!"

"Well," Marty countered, "it does to me. I don't understand why the adjutant keeps comin' down on you every time
promotions are being handed out."

James looked away, back to the north. Abner Couper had
come to him while he was on picket duty the night Marty had
been promoted. "James," Couper stated apologetically, "I
know that you're a better choice for the position than Hazard,
but ..."

"But I'm not a Virginian. I know, Abner. Believe me, I
know. This isn't the first time in my life I've been dealt out of
a hand because of who or what I was."

This comment, delivered so blandly, by a man who showed
no malice in his stance or expression caught Couper off guard.
Seeing his confusion, James gave him a warm, friendly smile.
"I don't remember much of the journey or of my childhood.

What I do remember is my father and the way he was treated because he was a heathen Irish Catholic. Oh, how that man swore that, someday, those who tormented him would pay. That's why he raised me and my brother like he did. We were to be his revenge. We were supposed to become successful, rich, and powerful despite the bigotry that others heaped on him.'' James stopped, looking at Couper for a moment before he continued. ''No offense meant, but I suppose that if I had been allowed to stay in New Jersey I would have eventually become just like you, a member of a society that forgot where it came from.''

Couper recoiled as if he had been slapped. James smiled again. ''I didn't mean it as an insult, though I suppose it was. The reason I'm telling you this is because this entire experience, my going to VMI, serving in the ranks as a private, and watching you, has been an education I wouldn't have missed.''

Slipping from being angry at James back to confusion, Couper shook his head. ''Explain, please.''

James looked up at the dark night sky. ''In my rebellion against my own, I found myself always against something, never for anything. I even used protecting my own brother as an excuse to pick fights with my father when my own behavior wasn't sufficient to anger him. In doing so, I managed not only to make a bad situation worse, I found myself keeping my brother down so I could be the one to decide what to do and how to do it, using him like my father used his business associates. It was becoming a game to me, a game I was enjoying. Then . . .''

The silence that followed was heavy for both men. It was Couper who broke it. ''You never told me why or how it was that you came South. I heard rumors at the Institute, but everyone admitted that no one knew the true story.''

Again, James smiled. ''There is an old saying, Abner, that blood is thicker than water. We Irish believe that. We believe that no matter what our kin do, no matter how evil or mean spirited they are, they are still family. Just as you can't ever forget that you're the member of one of Virginia's leading families, my father could never cast me out and totally abandon what he saw as his paternal obligations to me. So, although my foolishness shattered his cherished dream, he still did his duty as a father.''

"But where," Couper asked innocently, "does that leave you? You know how we feel about ... I mean, surely you understand that you'd have a better chance of making it if you stayed with your own."

James turned away, shaking his head. "Sometimes I feel like the man without a country, doomed to be exiled, forever, for a brief moment of youthful stupidity." Then he added, "I do have one advantage, though."

"Oh? Given everything that's happened to you, what possible advantage could you have?"

"I live," he replied in earnest, "in a forgiving world with people like you."

The rattle of a saber behind him and a hand grasping his shoulder shook James out of his thoughts. Marty, who was already half turned, looked up at the intruder. With a face that showed obvious disgust, he started in. "Ah, geez, Will, what's the matter with you?"

James, rolling over onto his side, looked up at his friend, now kneeling behind him. The face worn by the man returning his stare bore little resemblance to the bright cheery face that had greeted him at VMI in the winter of 1860. Will's skin, weathered by care as much as by the wind and sun, had a sickly pallor to it that made the dark stubble of two days' growth of beard stand out even more. His eyes, sunken deep into his head, were encircled by black rings that melted away into bags under each eye. His hair, dirty and matted, protruded unkempt above and below a filthy rag that served him as a bandage. Most telling, to James, was the expression. Though he was obviously trying hard to hide his pain and suffering, James could see in his friend's eyes a plea for help, for that which he could not give. Not here, not today.

"Will McPherson," Marty continued, "the last thing we need around here is an officer leaking his damned fool brains out all over the ground. You should be back in the field hospital where you belong."

When Will went to speak, no words came out at first. After coughing to clear his throat, he responded as best his voice would let him. "Heard the firing," he said as he nodded his head over toward the cornfield and woods in the east. "Couldn't stay back there."

Disgusted, Marty shook his head. "We shoulda left you back in Virginia. Don't know why I let you talk me and Jimmy out of that. Guess I must be as stupid as you."

Though he felt much the same as Marty, James didn't chide his friend. Taking one hand from the rifle he held balanced on a fence rail, he reached up and grabbed Will's arm. "How you doing?"

Closing his eyes, Will nodded his head slowly. "Head's on fire. Throbs bad, too."

"Well," Marty shouted, "I should say so. That Yankee bullet gave you a crease in the side of the head that beats anything I've ever seen. Another inch to the right and you wouldn't be here 'tall."

Will grunted. "Yes, that's true. But if it were another inch to the left, the damned thing would have missed." Looking beyond James and Marty, out across the pastures that separated them from the Yankees, Will studied the lay of the land for a moment. "Looks like those same black-hatted bastards that we fought back at Groveton."

Marty flashed a sinister grin as he turned his head to look. "Now wouldn't that beat all. I get to give them back what they gave Matty, and more."

James too glanced through the rail fence at the enemy. Rolling smoke from the fight in the cornfield, from both Union and Confederate artillery and the advancing Yankees' brush with skirmishers along the Hagerstown Road, mixed with the lingering morning mist, obscuring whole sections of the Federal battle lines. But James didn't need to see the entire battle line to know that they were coming on fast despite a brutal beating from Confederate guns to the south. He looked back at Will. "You'd best get back to the hospital, Will. This fight's going to be worse than Groveton."

To James' surprise, Will smiled as he looked around, first at the pitiful remains of the 4th Virginia, then at the advancing Yankees. "You know what this reminds me of, Jimmy?"

"No, I have no idea."

"It reminds me of one of Old Jack's experiments. You remember, the one where you divide something in half once, then twice, then three times, and so on and so on until what's left no longer resembles the original object.''

Confused, Marty gave Will a queer look. "So what's that got to do with us and this place?"

Will spread his arms out as if to encompass the remains of the regiment. "Look at us. There's barely enough of the 4th left to make a good-sized company. In a few minutes, even that won't be possible.''

The concern James felt must have shown on his face, for Will dropped his hands and patted James on the shoulder. "Oh, don't you worry about me, Jimmy. The Yankees have gotten the last chunk of me they're going to get."

"Will, I swear, if you don't go back to—"

A command by Colonel Grigsby to the brigade to stand up and prepare to fire cut off all discussion about Will leaving the front. With a speed and agility that surprised James, Will was up and on his feet, shouting to the men of the 4th near him. "Stand up, stand up and come to the ready."

Pushing himself off the ground, James turned to face the enemy, now only scant yards away from them. By the expressions on the faces of those men in the front rank, the Federals had been taken by surprise. Though they continued on, James saw some of the men wavering, frustrated in their efforts to move to the right or left out of harm's way by the presence of a determined comrade on either side. Others, with eyes bigger than saucers and mouths agape, slowed, causing the line to waver here and there. File closers, obscured for the most part by the solid Union ranks, pushed the laggards along, doing their best to keep the ranks closed and up even. All this James took in with a single glance as he mechanically followed Grigsby's orders of ready and aim. As he waited for the order to fire, James fixed his sights on one big fellow who was coming at them with rifle held at the ready and his face set in an impassive stare.

When Grigsby did give the order, the combined fire of the two hundred and fifty men of the Stonewall Brigade swept through the ranks of the 6th Wisconsin with terrible effect. For a moment, the Union ranks staggered, but soon recovered. While sergeants closed up the vacant spaces created by the dead and wounded, officers took their posts and issued commands that resulted in a lively exchange of fire with the Stonewall Brigade. After the first organized volleys, the officers on both sides gave up any attempt to exert control as the men in their commands raced each other in a deadly contest of reloading and firing. Though they were now taking almost as good as they gave, the Stonewall Brigade had checked the Union advance.

That did not last long. From behind the 2nd Wisconsin supporting Union regiments swung out and began to deploy beyond the 4th Virginia's front. Over the din of rifle fire James heard a harried voice to his right shout out, "They're coming round on the left."

As he took the rifle down from his shoulder and slid his hands down the hot barrel to begin reloading, James looked over to the left. Above the wisps of smoke that drifted about between the two antagonists busily hammering away at each other, he could see another Union battle flag, similar to the one carried by the Wisconsin unit to their front, coming around the right flank of the 2nd Wisconsin. Within minutes, after firing and reloading several more times in the interim, James looked back in time to see yet another flag of a different cut come bobbing around the right flank of the new Wisconsin unit. Adding their fire to that already wearing away at the Stonewall Brigade, the new Federal regiments began to have their effect. Aware of the changing situation, officers, starting with Grigsby, began to echo the order to fall back to the woods behind them. James could not tell if they were responding to a retreat that had already been started by men who had decided that they had done as much as they could from where they stood or if Grigsby had ordered it. Not that it mattered. It was time, James knew, to go back.

Moving back slowly so as to keep his front to the enemy and a rough alignment with Marty Hazard to his left and the man to his right, James moved backwards. His foot, extended to the rear in midstride, came in contact with something. Without pausing, James moved his foot over the wounded man lying on the ground and continued back without so much as a glance down or a second thought. Logic, if he had chosen to think about it, would have told him that the wounded man was from the 4th Virginia and, because the regiment was so small, James probably knew him. But this was a battle, one that was shaping up to be a most terrible one. And logic, as any veteran can tell you, is often replaced by cold, thoughtless action when men take to killing each other in earnest.

Upon reaching the wood the 4th Virginia, with her sister regiments, formed on the right of General Jubal Early's brigade of Virginians, already formed and waiting there. When all was set and everyone to the right and left of James had settled in the ranks, the order to advance back into the swirling storm of smoke, noise, and fire that they had just left was given. Even the officers had few words as the regiment surged forward. Will, just to the right of James and Marty, simply kept repeating over and over again in a solemn monotone, "Watch your alignment and keep moving. Keep moving."

The sight of more blue-clad masses moving south through the cornfield toward a small, plain white church where the Confederate artillery was posted, however, checked the advance of the two brigades of Virginians almost as soon as it started. Halting, the men watched in grim silence for a few moments, until a flurry of orders started the soldiers of the Stonewall Brigade around the rear of Early's brigade and over to its left. Forming a line running diagonal to the cornfield and the church that the Union troops were moving on with unswerving determination, Grigsby's brigade began to open a deadly fire from the edge of the woods. Unable to ignore this threat to their flanks, units supporting the Federal advance on the church swung out from behind the lead enemy units and began to push the new Confederate line.

As before, the two enemies, unevenly matched, began trading rifle fire. In the closed confines of the woods, where trees and thick vegetation held both the deafening noise and the choking smoke, the Stonewall Brigade gave ground. Unlike the previous time, the cost to the 4th and the units on either side of it was steep. Alignment of the regiments, difficult to maintain in the woods, was made even more uneven as some men felt obliged to fade back sooner than others and one or two stout-hearted individuals decided to stand their ground. Marty Hazard was one of those latter. The last James saw of him that morning, he was leaning against a tree, biting off the end of a cartridge as he prepared to reload, while half a dozen Yankees swarmed around on all sides of him. Swallowed as if taken by a blue tide, Marty disappeared from sight, leaving James and the pitiful remains of the 4th Virginia to continue the slow, grudging move to the rear.

By the time they reached a field of rock ledges on the far side of the woods, the Stonewall Brigade was bent back double, like a jackknife, on the left flank of Early's Brigade. Though pressed all the way, they had not broken. Quickly, Grigsby's men took up positions among the rocks and prepared for a desperate fight they knew would soon follow. James could hear Union officers, in the patch of woods the 4th had pulled back through, as they drove their men forward in an effort to break the Confederate left that Grigsby's brigade was holding. No one told James, Will, or the other members of the 4th Virginia that it was imperative that they hold where they were; they just did it.

Sharing a rock for cover, James and Will sat back to back. Between shots, as he pulled back behind the rock, James watched as Will fumbled about in his efforts to reload the pistol he had picked up from a Union prisoner at Harpers Ferry. Rather than the nerves that Will had experienced in their first battle at Manassas, James saw that Will's problem was simply a case of trying to work an unfamiliar piece too fast. Though he was managing to get each empty chamber loaded, Will's hasty glances over the top of the rock at the enemy told James he was becoming impatient. It didn't surprise him, therefore, when several minutes later James noticed that Will had discarded the pistol in favor of a rifle that he had taken from a wounded man. Will caught James' smile. With a wink, he brought the rifle up to his shoulder, took a bead on a target, and fired. James, finished with his reloading, went up to fire as Will pulled back to reload.

This contest, along the far edge of the west woods, continued for almost an hour. That it was about to come to an end was signaled by a slight slackening of fire as Union officers made arrangements in their ranks for one more mighty push across from where the 4th Virginia lay waiting. Reinforcements for Grigsby's hard-pressed command were few and far between. In this pause, men reloaded their pieces as quickly as possible, most of them holding their fire for the attack they knew was now just seconds away. Here and there, a man, ready for whatever, took a hasty swig from his canteen. One man, to James' right, having drained his long before, cursed as he shook the upturned canteen. Satisfied that it was indeed empty, the angry man threw the useless container over the rock he was behind, at the enemy.

In this interim neither James nor Will spoke a word. All that had needed to be said between these two men who were more than friends had been said many times before. Neither needed to add anything. In the final seconds before the next attack, the simple knowledge that the man to your back was a friend who would do anything for you was all either man needed.

From across the dead space between the opposing lines came the deep voiced shout of *"Hurrah!"* that accompanied so many Union attacks. Looking up from behind their cover, James and Will could see the Union line jerk to life and move forward. No orders were given as Confederate soldiers brought their pieces to bear and began the deadly drill of firing and reloading as fast as they could. The Union line, after closing the distance some, began to hesitate as individuals, and whole units paused to return the grueling fire that they were receiving with the same desperation with which the Confederates were delivering it. For several minutes, the pitch of battle increased from the steady roar that had characterized it a short time before into a deafening clamor. To James, it seemed that the entire woods was on fire as sheets of flame from Union rifles darted out of the dense grayish-white clouds that lingered in the contested space between them. Though the enemy was close, at times it was hard to take good aim because of the chaos and obscuring smoke. Though he seldom did so, James found himself firing blindly into some of those clouds when a good target wasn't readily available.

In the midst of reloading, James didn't see the sudden and unexpected breaking up of the Union line before them. The first he knew that their fortunes had shifted was when Abner Couper, jumping up from behind the cover he had been fighting from, waved his sword over his head and shouted for the regiment to charge. Without thinking, without hesitation, James was up and on his feet, rushing forward next to Will, who, despite his wound, had managed to propel himself forward like a drunkard lunging after something. The pursuit of the fleeing

Yankees, who had broken after taking more punishment than they could handle, was as uneven as their retreat to the rocks had been. First there were the rocks and their own dead and wounded to contend with. Then, as they moved through the smoke back into the heart of the west woods, there was the vegetation and an occasional body lying about. When they reached the line where the Federals had stood for so long, the number of the dead and wounded scattered about became greater. After that, progress was further slowed as attackers came across the wounded left behind or fleeing Union soldiers too tired to run anymore.

Coming through a patch of smoke, James startled a young, freckle-faced Union soldier who was limping along behind his comrades as fast as his shattered leg would carry him. Glancing over his shoulder, the freckle-faced boy dropped his jaw when his eyes fell upon James, coming up fast behind him with his rifle held at the ready. Picking up his pace as best he could, the Yankee hobbled a few more steps, never taking his eyes off of James, before a tree root tripped him up. Falling forward, the boy sprawled on the ground, rolling over onto his back and looking up just as James came up to him. For a second, James held the muzzle of his rifle not more than an inch from the boy's chest. Seeing that he was done for, the boy closed his eyes tightly and began to weep.

Though James had seen it before, the freckle-faced boy's face masked in sheer terror took the edge off of James' anger. Moving the muzzle of his rifle off to one side, James' right thumb held the hammer back as his finger tripped the trigger, bringing his rifle back to the harmless half-cocked position. The boy, realizing that he wasn't going to die, opened his tear-filled eyes and looked up at James. For a moment, the two strangers looked at each other. Then, without another thought, James moved on, leaving the task of making the dazed freckle-faced youth a prisoner to someone else. Taking his time now, James moved forward to join his regiment. As he did so, the image of the boy he had just spared faded into the memory of a brother he had once had a long time ago.

There would be no more serious fighting for the 4th Virginia that day. When, around noon, the regiment was pulled back with the rest of the brigade to the south edge of the woods to rest and refill their cartridge boxes, less than half a company's worth of men fell in. In their journey through the woods they had fought for, James dropped out of the ranks to search for Marty Hazard. Though he expected the worst, he was not at all surprised to find Marty, his back propped up against a tree, calmly talking to a Yankee as they shared a meal of crackers and dried pork.

"This fella," Marty stated with a cheery voice when he saw James approaching them, "is from Massachusetts. Can't hardly understand him 'cause of his accent but he's a friendly 'nough sort of fellow." James came closer, exchanging a half-guarded nod with Marty's companion. "You got anything to drink, Jimmy? We found plenty to eat in the haversacks scattered about, but no one had a drop of water in the canteens." James looked at the small patch of ground about them, noticing that the contents of most of the haversacks of the dead and badly wounded were strewn on the ground. Though it was a common practice to pick through the belongings of a dead man in search of food, James still found the thought of it uncomfortable.

Without a word, James took his canteen off and handed it to Marty, who immediately uncorked it and handed it over to the Yankee. Given Marty's earlier demeanor and pronouncement of hatred for Yankees, this surprised James. But he said nothing as he watched the wounded Yankee take a drink and then pass the canteen back to Marty, who then took his. Dropping down on his knees before the two men, James pulled his cap off and wiped his brow before asking Marty what had happened.

"Well," he said rather matter-of-factly, "these Yankees suddenly came up all round me. They were as surprised to see me behind the tree I was hidden behind as I was to see them. Well, we fought it out with fists for a couple minutes until one of those bastards drove his bayonet through my thigh here." Leaning over slightly, Marty showed James a dirty handkerchief, with a dark spot where the wound was, tied around his leg. "After them fellows left, another group, Nathan's regiment, the 15th Massachusetts, came along. Nat here was shot in the arm and the foot at the same time."

"And so you two decided to make friends, right here, while everyone else was busy killing each other?" James asked incredulously.

Giving James a look as if James were stupid, Marty countered. "Well, we was hungry. When we both found out that our officers didn't give us a chance to get a decent breakfast, we decided to call a truce and rectify that situation."

James dropped his head, shaking it as he did so. Finally, he took a deep breath and looked up at Marty, smiling. "Well, I hate to break up this budding friendship, but the regiment has pulled back. If you don't want to get lost, you'd best come with me now."

Offering one more drink to Nathan, the Yankee, Marty returned the now empty canteen to James. "Here, boy, give me a hand."

Balancing himself between the tree and James, Marty managed to pull himself up, clenching his teeth as the pain from his wound shot throughout his entire body. When he was well supported by James, Marty turned to face Nathan. "Well, I gotta leave ya. I'm sure your folks will be by here presently. Till then, do take care, hear?" With a forlorn look, Nathan nodded his head in farewell.

Though he didn't bother looking back, James knew Marty was thinking about the Yankee. "I was sort of surprised to see you sitting there, side by side with that Union soldier, Marty."

The older man chuckled despite the pain that shot up from his wounded leg. "Ya know, it's a lot different when ya see 'em like that, face to face and hurt." Then, he stopped as a somber look fell across his face. With his free hand, he motioned to the heaps of dead and wounded men that littered the floor of the woods they had fought in all morning. "We ain't no different, none of us. Yankee, Confederate, Virginian, New Englander. Not really. We just see things differently. That's all. I just wish . . ."

When Marty hesitated, James looked over at him. There were tears in the man's eyes, tears that told James that he was suffering more from the wounds that cut through his memory than the one in his leg. Marty missed his brother with the same passion that James missed Kevin. That Marty had been able to come to terms with his loss and grief so soon was, James knew, a blessing. If only, he thought, he could do the same. "Come on, old boy," James finally coaxed in soft, soothing tones. "Let's go find the regiment."

When the two men reached the southern edge of the woods, they paused. To the east, they could see clouds of smoke ripped by sheets of flame in the distance. "Looks like the fight's shifted over there," Marty stated dryly. "You suppose it'll last much longer?"

James watched for a moment as lines of regimental colors, bobbing above the swells in the earth and the rolling smoke, surged forward. "Yes," he finally answered grimly. "I think this fight will last a long time."

Marty nodded. Both men took one long last look, then turned to continue their journey, neither one realizing that Marty had been asking about that battle when he had asked his question, and James had been thinking of the war when he answered.

When the two men reached the southern edge of the woods, they paused. To the east they could see the reeds of Enmor, ripped by sheets of flame in the distance. "Looks like the fire's shifted over there." Many stated dryly. "You suppose it'll last much longer?"

...me watched for a moment as flack of the mounted riders reaching above the swells in the path and the riding another surged onward. "Yest," he finally answered grimly. "I think this city will last a long time."

Many nodded. Then men took one long last look then turned to continue their journey, neither one realizing that Many had been asking about battle when he had asked his question, and James had been thinking of the war when he answered.

# PART FIVE

# TRIALS & TRIUMPHS

# CHAPTER 20

# September–November, 1862 West of the Antietam Creek in Maryland

THOUGH THE FIRST NEW JERSEY BRIGADE HAD BEEN BROUGHT up to a stand of woods on the eastern rim of what would be called The Cornfield, in support of Hooker's First Corps, they were denied the opportunity to sally from their covered position and assault the weakened enemy holding woods to the west. Like the rest of the Army of the Potomac, Kevin and his men watched in frustration as the Confederates under Jackson defiantly stood their ground through the rest of that day and all of the next. When the following morning revealed that they were gone, Kevin could not hold back his anger. "We had them," he raged as he paced back and forth in front of his assembled command. Stopping in front of First Sergeant Himmel, he looked the old Prussian in the eyes and repeated his lament. "We had them."

Himmel, hardened to disappointment by training, age, and experience, shrugged. "I would not worry so. We will find them again, I'm sure."

While he admired the stoic attitude that Himmel personified, Kevin found it difficult to accept the loss of the opportunity to crush the Confederate Army of Northern Virginia that he and many of the other junior officers of the regiment perceived had been theirs to take. Looking into Kevin's eyes, Himmel saw the anger, the frustration, the helplessness he felt. Quietly, so that the men next to them could barely hear, Himmel spoke. "The

361

company has done well, Lieutenant. *You* have done well. Please, leave it at that.''

Kevin didn't much care for the idea that they weren't going to pursue the beaten Confederates and hound them into the ground. This failure, he knew, would doom him to another year with the colors, another year away from . . . Kevin paused in midthought. He looked at Himmel for a moment, then turned away without saying another word.

Moving off to where he could look out over the shattered landscape that had once been a peaceful farm, Kevin wondered, for the first time, what it was he was in so much a hurry to go back to. His home and father? This thought almost caused him to laugh. The house that he had been raised in was not a home, not by any stretch of the imagination. And his father, the source of so much grief, anguish, and misery in his life, was the last person in the world he wished to see. The fact was, Kevin concluded, the only reason he could muster for going back to New Jersey at all was to confront Miss Harriet Shields herself and find out, once and for all, if she was truly interested in him. The thought of Harriet at that moment brought both a glimmer of hope and a sudden, heartfelt pang of anguish. The idea that Harriet might no longer be his, that she, for whatever reason, had turned her back on him, suddenly seemed more overwhelming, more dreadful than the prospect of another winter in camp and another dreadful summer of campaigning.

Then, like a thief in the night, the memory of his brother crept into his thoughts. He seldom spent time pondering his brother's fate. Perhaps, Kevin thought, he didn't do so because that loss was still too painful for him. Or maybe, he wondered as he peered across the great no-man's-land that separated the two wounded armies, he was afraid that perhaps one day he would come face to face with his brother, clad in gray, in a terrible place like this.

Lost in his dark personal feelings, Kevin paid no heed to the comings and goings of stretcher parties that passed before his eyes, each bearing tattered and blood-soaked wounded soldiers who just now were being retrieved from the battlefield of two days prior. Nor did he hear, at first, the orders issued by the regimental adjutant for the companies of the 4th New Jersey to move out. It was Johnny O'Keeth, sent by Lieutenant Meyers, who finally brought Kevin out of his self-imposed withdrawal. ''The company's moving, sir. We're moving now, away from this terrible place.''

Looking first at O'Keeth, then at the tail end of the regiment, now picking its way through the shattered wood lot, Kevin cleared his throat. ''Fine, fine. You go ahead and tell Lieutenant Meyers I'll be along directly.'' Without another word or a change in his forlorn expression, Kevin turned away from O'Keeth and cast his gaze back across the cornfield whose harvest this year would be measured in graves.

Slowly, the days passed. When no rumors of impending movements or future campaigns filtered down to the men of the 4th New Jersey, the soldiers of Kevin's company settled down into a camp that began to take on a permanent appearance. Tents were brought up, company streets lined out, and amenities of all kinds, sent through the mail from home or bought from the omnipresent sutlers, began to appear. Kevin, as always, threw himself into the tasks of tending to the military and personal needs of the company.

The return of Trevor Ward four days after what was being called the Battle of Antietam did nothing to change Kevin's activities or his manner. On casting eyes on his company commander for the first time since the charge that had gained them Crampton's Gap, Kevin noticed that there was not a trace of dried blood on either the crisp white sling Trevor wore over his shoulder nor on the clean frock coat sleeve on the arm hanging in it. Had this meeting taken place in Washington, Trevor's appearance wouldn't have raised an eyebrow. But this wasn't Washington. This was Antietam, a place where surgeons, lacking bandages of any sort, had used corn husks to bind open wounds. Even now, nearly a week after the last shot had been fired, wounded men were still lined up outside of every barn and structure for miles around. Exposed to the elements, with untended wounds festering, they waited patiently for their turn to be worked on by exhausted surgeons and pitifully small hospital staffs who were overwhelmed by the product of one bloody day's work. Kevin, staring at Trevor's arm, took his time saluting. ''It is good, sir,'' he said while staring at Trevor's sling, ''to see you again. We were, ah, beginning to wonder what had become of you.''

Turning his entire body so that the arm and sling were away from Kevin, Trevor fumbled for several moments. "Well, I was very lucky, you see. The regiment had no sooner started forward when I, ah, went down."

Making it a point to keep his gaze on the "wounded" arm, Kevin made sure he stressed the false sense of concern he felt was obvious in his tone and voice. "Nasty wound, sir?"

Irritated at Kevin's persistent reference to the arm that he so desperately was trying to hide, Trevor was becoming angry. Yet he held that anger in check. "I was," he mumbled, "very lucky. The people in Burkittsville were very kind to me."

Unable to resist the opportunity to take a slap at Trevor, Kevin smiled as he looked up into Trevor's face for the first time. "I should say you were, sir. Why, I'll bet some sweet young thing was even kind enough to stitch up the bullet hole in your coat before she cleaned away every trace of blood from it for you."

The inference that he wasn't wounded at all was almost too much for Trevor to take. For a moment, Kevin feared that he had gone too far. But Trevor choked back his anger, though he did so with difficulty. As he watched Trevor's face, now beet red and puffed out but with lips pursed tightly, Kevin knew that Trevor's wound was a sham, just like Trevor's command over him and the company. After struggling to compose himself, Trevor finally managed to nod. "Yes, exactly so. Now, *Lieutenant*, I must report to the regimental commander." Without another word, Trevor pivoted on his heel and walked away.

With the passing of summer came a period of calm and idleness that was, to Kevin, almost as wearing as the summer's campaigns had been. Slowly, painfully slowly, the wounded that swamped the small farm communities of Sharpsburg, Boonesboro, and all about were moved to more permanent facilities. Many, as was often the case after a major battle, didn't survive long enough to make that trip, succumbing instead to either a lack of medical attention, or just as fatal, to poor medical attention. However, the wounded land began to heal. Fall rains, conspiring with the dropping of autumn leaves, worked to purge the ravaged land of its stains and hide that which could not be cleansed in time for the visitors.

With the Confederate Army now well to the south in Virginia and the worst of the wounded carted away to someplace out of sight, parties of politicians, high-ranking officials, and the idle curious began to frequent General McClellan's stationary army. For those who had the necessary clout, tours of the battlefield were arranged. Though Kevin viewed these tours, at first, as little more than an inconvenience, as the weeks passed and the Army of the Potomac neither went into winter quarters nor showed any sign of initiating an active campaign against a foe now long gone from its reach, the tours became a diversion. Trevor Ward, anxious to find every opportunity to keep Kevin out of camp so that he, Trevor, could exert what little authority he still had with his own company, signed Kevin up as an escort officer on every possible occasion that presented itself.

During one such tour, Kevin had the dubious privilege of being one of several officers charged with showing a party of New Jersey legislators and their ladies the site of the regiment's charge at Crampton's Gap. While the more senior officers of the regiment, men who had a future in New Jersey politics, took the legislators on a walking tour, Kevin was left to supervise the setting up of a pavilion at the base of the mountain his company had attacked. Those ladies who had declined to make the steep climb with their husbands, fathers, and escorts remained at the pavilion, enjoying the crisp, cool autumn day and the beauty of a countryside aflame with the brilliant colors of turning leaves.

One of the ladies, the daughter of a state senator, approached Kevin after he had completed his duties and had drawn away from the crowd of chatting women. Coming up behind him, the lady stood silent for a moment, hoping that he would notice her. When she realized that he was either deep in thought or ignoring her, the lady made several slight movements that caused the crinolines under her skirt to sweep the ground and rustle the fallen leaves. Turning, Kevin acted surprised to see someone behind him. "Oh, I am sorry, miss. I was thinking of something and didn't notice your approach. You have my humblest apologies."

Accepting Kevin's excuse without comment, the young lady

proceeded to her business. "My name is Abigail Milford. My father is Senator Milford, a good friend of Judge Shields of New Brunswick."

The mention of Judge Shields' name erased all traces of the bored, patronizing expression that Kevin had been sporting all day when dealing with the women of the visiting party. When he realized that the senator's daughter standing before him had succeeded in surprising him—by a slight gleam in her eyes and the hint of a smile—Kevin drew back slightly, folding his arms across his chest and, as best he could, masking his emotions behind a scowl. "Yes?" he asked, trying hard to hide his impatience. "How may I help you?"

"It would be, I think," she said coyly as she glanced over her shoulder at the other women gathered about, "much better if we were alone for a moment."

Taking the hint, Kevin offered her his arm and led her away toward the silent stone wall that a scant month before had served as cover for his enemies. When they were well out of earshot, Abigail, her eyes on the ground before her, started. "It would be presumptuous of me to call Harriet Shields a friend, though we have spent much time, of late, together. You see, we both do work for the Soldiers' Christian Relief Agency."

Kevin looked around as they walked, acting as disinterested as he could, though his mind screamed for the young lady on his arm to get to the matter. "Well," she continued, eyes still held firmly on the ground before her. "Harriet—excuse me, Miss Shields—found out that my father was going to come down here to meet with the officers of various units from the state. Though I had not originally planned on making this journey, with the weather being so unpredictable and stories of how dreadful a sight the battlefield was, Miss Shields prevailed upon me to join my father."

For a moment, she let her last comment hang. Whether the pause was out of embarrassment on her part or meant to bait him, Kevin quickly became annoyed. Still, with little choice and not knowing who she was representing, Kevin held his temper in check. "Yes, this can be a difficult time of year to travel," he replied pleasantly.

"Well," Abigail went on, now looking up but away from Kevin, "Harriet asked me if I would be so kind as to deliver a letter for her. She had considered sending it through the post but, since you have failed to respond to all the others, she wanted this one to be hand delivered by a trusted friend, *just* to make sure that it arrived.''

No longer able to restrain himself, Kevin stopped, turning to face Abigail. ''What others?''

Taking her arm from his, Abigail brought her hands together, resting them on the front of her hoop skirt. ''Harriet has been writing you, all summer, at least one letter a day. At first, she was afraid that they were not reaching you because of your, ah, unfortunate imprisonment in June. But when her letters to Captain Ward made it through and received responses, well, she naturally thought the worst.''

''The worst?''

''Well, yes, sir, meaning that you didn't care to associate with her any longer.''

Kevin, with a dumbstruck look of confusion on his face, stood facing Abigail for several seconds. Finally, he spoke, stuttering as he did so. ''Nothing, Miss Milford, could be further from the truth, I assure you. The fact is, I too have been writing, as often as I could. And when she failed to respond, like her, I began to wonder if . . .'' In midsentence, the whole affair became crystal clear to Kevin. Everything, including the reasons why the two young people had been kept from contacting each other, was suddenly as plain to Kevin as the nose on his face. Unconcerned about hiding his feelings now, Kevin took Abigail's hands in his and began to speak rapidly. ''Oh, Miss Milford, you can't appreciate how much I missed hearing from Harriet. Though I don't know how it was done, our letters, hers to me and those of mine that I sent her, have been plucked from the mail. It has to be, for I have been as faithful to her as she, from what you say, has been to me.''

For a moment, Abigail was taken aback by Kevin's sudden change in demeanor. Though she tried to back away and free her hands, Kevin was too excited, too animated. Moving closer to the young woman, he pulled her hands up to his chest as he continued to speak rapidly. ''Dear lady, perhaps, I mean, if you have no objections, maybe you could serve as a bridge between us, Harriet and I. Someone has taken it upon themselves to place a wedge between us and we, *I* need a trusted friend who can work around this obstruction.''

The sincerity, now bordering on desperation, in Kevin's voice eased Abigail's apprehensions. Relaxing, she looked up into his eyes. ''Well, of course,'' she said without thinking. ''That's what I'm here for, to see that the two of you come together.'' Her words, she noted, caused him to smile. Even his eyes seemed to light up, eyes that she noticed were very engaging, very . . .

Anxious to hide the sudden flush of warmth she was sure would show in her cheeks in a moment, Abigail gave a quick tug, pulling her hands free from Kevin's. Turning away from him to hide her embarrassment, she stepped several paces away in an effort to put some distance between them. Kevin, however, caught up in the idea of renewing his romance with Harriet, followed Abigail, unaware that his proximity to her was making her uncomfortable. ''Perhaps,'' he announced, ''I could enclose my letters to Harriet in an envelope addressed to you and you, in turn, could forward them to Harriet, in an envelope addressed in your hand.''

Thinking that she was sufficiently composed now, Abigail turned and looked at Kevin in order to respond. Yet, when she looked at him again, she saw him in a new light. Her eyes darted across his face, a young face that was rugged yet pleasing. His eyes and mouth were gentle without being weak. Adorned in a dark blue kepi that partially covered his brown hair and a frock coat closed with a double row of brass buttons, Kevin's trim yet solid figure was to Abigail everything that a man should be. Unable to take her eyes off of him and unwilling to move back out of his reach, Abigail stood motionless, listening without hearing a single word Kevin said.

It was the return of her father and the party of other civilians and officers that finally broke the trance Abigail had fallen into. Her father's voice, calling her to his side so that he could describe to her what he had just been shown in the mountain pass, caused her to shake. Looking up into Kevin's face, as he still towered over her, Abigail blushed. ''Ah, I am, ah, sorry, sir. But my father, ah . . . my father's calling me. If you would, ah, excuse me for a moment.''

With that, she pulled away. Kevin, however, was not finished. Taking a few quick steps, he moved up behind her. With more force than he meant to, Kevin took Abigail's arm and squeezed it. "Then you will help, Abigail? You will serve as an intermediary between Harriet and me?"

Pausing, she looked down at the hem of her skirt, which touched the ground Kevin and his company had trampled down with their feet a scant month before. The idea of helping him pursue another woman was suddenly too much for Abigail to deal with. "Please, sir," she all but shouted. "I must tend to my father."

With that, Abigail pulled away, leaving Kevin suddenly confused and befuddled. Though he would later regret his conduct, the knowledge that Harriet was still his for the taking was more than enough for him, for now.


## *Near Winchester, Virginia*

Bored with his duties and anxious to get in out of the drizzle and back to the camp where he could write another letter home, the picket watched with casual indifference as a young woman on a horse came up to his post. She was, he decided, not much to look at, though the picket imagined she could be if she bothered to fix herself up. The shawl she wore draped over her shoulders was clean but tattered, like so many of the garments worn by the people of Winchester. Her skirt, the back hem drawn up between her legs and tucked into the front at the waist so that she could ride her horse like a boy, also showed the first signs of becoming threadbare. Even the girl's face, the picket saw as he advanced into the center of the road to block her passage, seemed to be wearing away.

That, of course, was no surprise to him, as one of so many soldiers who had been with Jackson from the beginning. The sight of the lower Shenandoah Valley, spoiled by months of Union occupation, and the condition of the civilian population saddened even the hardest veteran. "Dear Lord," one man promised as he and his comrades marched through the devastated landscape that they were fighting to protect, "if'en we ever go back North, I swear I'll make those damned Yankees howl for what they've done here.''

His companion, after looking at the charred remains of a barn for a moment, shook his head. ''Nah. We'll never get the chance to pay 'em back, not so long as Bobby Lee is in command.''

So little did the picket regard Mary Beth that he didn't even bother to take his rifle out from under the poncho he had picked up off the field at Manassas. While holding the sling of the upturned rifle with his left hand, he raised his right hand. ''Hold it right there, miss. This is as far as you can go.''

Reining in her horse, Mary Beth McPherson stopped just short of the picket. ''Please, let me pass.''

''Where ya headed, young lady?''

''To the camp of the 4th Virginia, Company J.''

Her mentioning of the 4th Virginia caused the picket to screw his face up in an expression of disgust. Though he, like the other soldiers in the brigade, knew that the smallpox epidemic ravaging that unit was probably not their fault, everyone blamed the 4th, and not the smallpox, for the quarantine that canceled all leaves in the brigade. ''Can't let you through, miss. There's smallpox in the camp, and the general don't want it spread around.''

''I've been to the camp before and haven't come down with the pox and don't plan to,'' Mary Beth replied defiantly.

Tiring of this intrusion that was keeping him from the small fire his corporal permitted him while on duty, the picket became determined to be rid of her. ''Look, girl. You either turn that horse around and go home where you belong, or I'll give you what for.''

Jerking the horse's head to one side, Mary Beth turned to face the picket. Her eyes, now alive with rage, glared at the ragged soldier. ''I am not a girl. And I will not go away. Either let me through or bring the officer of the day here to explain to me why you kept me from seeing Lieutenant McPherson.''

The mention of an officer's name and the thought of having to call his own officer out into this miserable drizzle caused the picket to hesitate. As he clutched the sling of his rifle, he looked up into Mary Beth's fiery eyes in an effort to gauge whether this was a bluff. Civilians had, of course, been visiting the camps quite regularly, bringing what meager food and baked goods they could afford to supplement the even more meager rations their sons, fathers, husbands, and brothers were issued. Even now, with a quarantine in effect, pickets were still letting civilians through, but for a price.

Seeing an opportunity to gain something from this encounter, the picket changed his tone. "What's you got in the basket, miss?"

Seeing that he was eyeing the covered basket that hung from the horn of her saddle, Mary Beth jerked her horse's head over so that it blocked the basket from his view. "Trouble for you," she shot back, "if you don't let me through."

Tiring of her, and anxious to get back to his small fire, now threatening to die if it wasn't tended to soon, the picket gave in. "You can go, girl. But woe be it to you if you get caught and my sergeant gives me hell for letting you do so."

Ignoring his threats, Mary Beth spurred her horse and trotted on by, all but knocking the picket over as she did so. Picking her way through the camp, riding just above the smoke layer of haze that rose from hundreds of small cook and warming fires, Mary Beth looked at the faces of the soldiers. Though most were still young men, none that she saw showed the glow of youth that had so impressed many a young lady in Winchester when Jackson's army had first come to that town. Even the beardless faces of the drummer boys, most younger than her second brother, were careworn and haggard despite almost six weeks of rest. Though there wasn't the slightest hint of defeat in the expression of those who bothered to look her way as she passed, the concern for the future they all shared was etched deeply into their faces.

The greeting she received from her brother and James Bannon was less than enthusiastic. Though Will was now an officer and James continued to march along in the ranks as a private, Will McPherson shared his shelter with James. Both men, as dreary in their moods as the weather was, were huddled about a small fire that gave off more smoke than warmth. Will, his head bowed and the blanket draped over his shoulders pulled up around his neck, didn't even look up as his sister dismounted before them. Instead, he continued to stare vacantly at the burning log he hoped would dry his soggy boots and the filthy, threadbare socks he wore draped over his hands, which he held before the feeble fire. Though her own mood was somewhat equally gloomy, Mary Beth sported the best smile she could muster and approached the two men, basket in hand. "I brought you chicken today. Fresh-cooked chicken and biscuits."

Without lifting his eyes from the toes of his boots, Will muttered, "You brought chicken last time."

Looking up, James caught a glimpse of the hurt expression that flashed across Mary Beth's face for a second before she recovered from the effects of her brother's caustic remark. Not knowing whether to apologize to her for Will's rudeness or kick him in the ass, James forced a smile as he looked over to Mary Beth. "Well, I don't know about him, but chicken sounds fine to me."

Still oblivious to the effect that his sour disposition was having on his sister, Will grunted. "Well, then, you can have my share."

Angry now, Mary Beth dropped the basket down at her feet, drew her legs shoulder-width apart, put her hands on her hips, and leaned forward. "William McPherson, just who do you think you are? The chicken in this basket is one of the last ones we have. If Father knew that Mother had killed, plucked, and cooked it for you, you ungrateful wretch, he'd beat her black and blue."

Will, looking up at his sister for the first time, stared at her with sad, drooping eyes. Though he knew that his father wouldn't raise his hand against his mother, for he had never done anything like that in his life, the very thought that his sister would think of such a thing finally shook Will out of his self-imposed isolation. He opened his mouth to apologize, but didn't. Instead, he let his head drop back down between his hunched shoulders and continued to stare at the fire.

For the longest time, the three of them remained where they were, each lost in their own thoughts. Only the appearance of the regimental commander's orderly broke the silence. "Lieutenant McPherson. Major Terry's compliments, sir. He wishes to see you and all company commanders at his tent now."

Mary Beth looked up at the orderly. Both his appearance and demeanor told her that he was one of the new recruits who had been enlisted to fill out the depleted ranks of Will's once proud regiment. Struck by the contrast, she asked the boy his age. "Sixteen, miss. Sixteen last month." Though he smiled bravely, the thought of a boy so young being pulled into the Army sent a shudder down Mary Beth's spine. She, like everyone else who had a relative with the 4th, knew that in a span of six short months the 4th had been reduced from a strength of over eight hundred men to less than fifty footsore survivors at the end of General Lee's invasion of Maryland. And although the ranks were once again filling out, failure in the North had doomed Virginia and the Army defending it to another, perhaps even grimmer, year of war. That it would be waged now by boys barely old enough to shave brought no joy to Mary Beth, or anyone else who cared to see the truth.

Slowly, like a man twice his age, Will stood up, pulling the two socks off of his rough hands as he did so. Sheepishly, he faced Mary Beth. "I've got to go. You're welcome to wait here with James by the fire until I return," he said, motioning to the dry spot on the log that he had been sitting on with James. Turning, he started to walk away, following the orderly, but then paused. Looking back over his shoulder, he nodded at Mary Beth. "Thank you, dear sister, for bringing the chicken. I look forward to enjoying it." With that, he left.

Lifting the basket off the ground, Mary Beth moved over next to James and took the seat vacated by her brother. Like Will before her, she stared into the fire, lost in her own thoughts, while James, conscious of her arm rubbing against his, tried hard to think of something appropriate to say. It was Mary Beth, however, who broke the silence. "He's changed, James."

That solemn pronouncement, issued without a note of emotion, spoke volumes. They had all changed, James thought as he stared at the fire. Even the land that they moved through had been changed by the war. Everything, he knew, had changed. Yet, as bad as things had been to date, more frightening than the past was the future.

"Here, James, go ahead and take your share now," Mary Beth admonished the silent figure seated next to her. "I doubt if any of it is still warm, but I assure you, it's all fresh."

Managing a faint smile, James reached into the basket that Mary Beth had placed between them and had uncovered. While

Mary Beth was somewhat taken aback by the fact that James took the food she offered him in his dirty hands and began to stuff it into his mouth without the slightest hesitation, she said nothing. For a moment, she remembered the October day, two years before, when she had first cast eyes on James. They had all been there, seated around a table brimming with food heaped upon plates set on a nice clean tablecloth in the warmth of a country inn. James had been quite dashing, scrubbed and polished in the tight-fitting uniform of a VMI cadet. She had, Mary Beth realized as she watched him eat, fallen in love with him then. Now, despite having endured many months of worry and privation, with a future that promised nothing but the same, she still loved him.

The love she felt now for this man, however, was a different kind of love. Then, it had been a schoolgirl's love, based more on infatuation than emotions. Now, she told herself, she was a woman who felt a mature and deep-seated love for a man she really didn't know.

When he noticed the steady gaze that Mary Beth was regarding him with, James became uneasy. Choking down the bit of biscuit he had in his mouth, James cleared his throat. "How's Marty doing?"

Though she was annoyed that his question concerning his friend had interrupted her thoughts, Mary Beth smiled. "From the way he carries on these days, you'd never know he was at death's door a few weeks ago. It seems as if his gamble to keep his leg has paid off for him, despite the terrible infection and fever that his decision brought on."

James grunted. "He'd have suffered the infection and fever even if the surgeon had taken the leg. At least this way, he's got everything."

"But it nearly cost him his life, James."

Reaching down into the basket, James fished out another piece of chicken as he casually went on. "As far as Marty is concerned, losing a leg is no different than losing his life. He's a farmer, Mary Beth, a working man. A one-legged farmer who can't tend his fields is no good to anyone." With that, he sank his teeth, yellowed by lack of care, into the chicken leg he held between his black-smudged fingers.

"You really mean that," she protested incredulously, "don't you?"

Looking over the leg bone he held at his mouth, James nodded. "'Course I do," he mumbled as he began to chew his food. "Marty's got no education, no skills other than farming. His brother's dead, his father's an old man, and his mother's a sickly woman. Who'd be left to tend to a cripple?"

James' nonchalant attitude to a matter that Mary Beth took seriously angered her. "And you, Mr. Bannon? Would you rather suffer the loss of your life than give up a limb?"

James stretched his two legs out and looked at them for a moment. "Haven't had to cross that bridge yet, Mary Beth."

Mary Beth pounded her clenched fist down on her thigh in anger. "Why must you and Will always make light of such things?"

Curling his legs back up under him, James shrugged. "Why do you insist on asking questions that aren't relevant? I mean, if and when it comes my time, I'll sort it out then. Till that day comes, and I truly hope it never does, do me a favor and don't worry about me or my limbs."

Exasperated, Mary Beth surprised James by crying out. "I can't not worry about such things, Mr. James Bannon, because I love you." Then, realizing what she had said, she turned her head away from him.

The two were still sitting there, motionless, when Will returned. Mary Beth's head and body were turned away from James while he sat there, staring at her with a half-eaten chicken leg in his hand. Though he quickly surmised that something had transpired between them, Will didn't feel up to pursuing it. Instead, he reached down into the basket that was sitting between James' legs and pulled out a piece of chicken for himself. "Word is," he announced after taking a mouthful of chicken, "the main Yankee Army is finally on the move." When even this piece of information didn't cause James to look away from his sister, Will knew that there was definitely something serious between them.

"The major also told us that Colonel Grigsby is being replaced."

This time, James, with great effort, pulled his eyes away

from Mary Beth and looked over to where Will was standing. "What was that?"

"Grigsby isn't getting the brigade," Will repeated. "Paxton is. Orders just came down."

"But Paxton's a staff officer, a mere major!" James exclaimed. "He never attended VMI or even West Point. Why," James rattled on, excited now, "he was even defeated in elections in the 27th, for major. Why Paxton?"

Will, biting into his chicken, shrugged. "Don't know," he mumbled as he chewed. "Maybe being a Presbyterian like Old Jack helped."

"General Jackson wouldn't appoint a man to command the brigade just because he went to the same church," James insisted.

"We've known that man for over three years now, Jimmy," Will pointed out. "And I'm still amazed by some of the things he does. Not even his own generals know what he's up to."

Conceding to Will's assessment, James settled down as Will reached over into the basket in search of more food. Mary Beth, concerned over her brother's announcement that the Yankees were moving, reached out and touched his sleeve. "Does that mean you're not going to be going into winter quarters here, that you'll be moving soon?"

Dropping the piece of chicken he had grabbed, Will squatted down, taking his sister's hand in his as he did so and looking into her eyes. "Sis, I'm afraid that's what's going to happen, provided the rumors about the replacement of McClellan are true."

James shook his head. "I imagine the new man in charge of the Army of the Potomac is going to have a lot of pressure piled on him to go south for Richmond again. Which means," he added as he looked over at Mary Beth, "that we'll have to leave here in order to stop him."

Mary Beth drew back. "And what about Winchester? What about us? Don't we deserve to be defended? Doesn't your home count as much as the one Jeff Davis lives in? Maybe if Richmond was taken and the people in that town saw what war was really like they'd stop it."

Unable to answer Mary Beth's angry questions, Will and James looked at each other, both knowing that each of them was as disappointed with the prospect of a new campaign so soon as Mary Beth was. Yet both men knew, as did Mary Beth, that it was all out of their hands. What the Yankees would do, what Jackson's corps would do, even control of their own lives, was out of their hands.

Easing back off of the balls of his feet, Will sat on the ground, clutching James' hand while still holding his sister's. Mary Beth, overcoming her own hesitancy, reached over and took James' free hand. For the longest time the three of them sat there, holding on to each other yet lost in their own thoughts as they watched the fire before them consume all that it touched.

# CHAPTER 21

# December, 1862
# New Brunswick,
# New Jersey

FROM HER SEAT ON THE SPEAKERS' PLATFORM, VICTORIA ELIZ-abeth Randolf watched with satisfaction as Harriet Shields made her way into the crowded hall where the monthly meeting of the Soldiers' Christian Relief Agency was already under-way. Victoria Elizabeth Randolf took great pride in the fact that, of all the women of means in New Brunswick, she was the only woman who had been selected to be on the executive committee of an organization made up almost exclusively of women. While a few members did point out that there were many capable women who could administer the agency's ef-forts as well as, if not better than, the three men who served on the executive committee, none was willing to object to the decisions of the head of the organization, the Reverend An-thony J. Binford. To do so, Victoria Randolf pointed out, wasn't proper and, as such, simply wouldn't be tolerated, even though the gentlemen, except for Binford, joined the organization well after it was established and functioning. Since Victoria Randolf was the acknowledged grande dame of New Brunswick soci-ety, nothing more was said.

Harriet made her way through the narrow aisles as quickly and quietly as her hoop skirt, measuring a modest four feet six inches in diameter, would permit. Still, the Reverend Binford, who had been speaking on the agency's special Christmas ef-fort, found it necessary to pause until Harriet was seated. This pleased Victoria Elizabeth Randolf no end, for it just went to show that the Shieldses were the presumptuous upstarts that she had always claimed they were. The Shieldses, after all, had only been part of New Brunswick society for two generations. And despite Elma Shields' best efforts, she and her overeducated daughter would never be able to overcome the advantages that Victoria's lineage, which included a former royal governor dating back to English rule, afforded her.

With a faint smile, Victoria looked down at Elma, who was seated in the front row. Elma, her face red with embarrassment as it often was as a result of her daughter's thoughtless actions, did her best to avert her eyes from Victoria. "If *I* had a daughter like her," Victoria often stated to her cronies when talking about Elma and her only child, "I would keep her under lock and key until I found her a suitable husband, able to teach her to behave as a proper lady born into society does naturally."

Though she was aware of her mother's concern for her future social standing, Harriet found it difficult to adhere to the stringent codes of conduct that her society used to confine her. *"Today I found myself jealous of even the most illiterate Negro slave in Mississippi,"* she noted in her diary on the day Lincoln's Emancipation Proclamation was published. *"While that slave can now dream of throwing off the chains that society has used to keep him in bondage, all my own parents offer me is the threat of marriage to a man I do not love and who will never allow me to be anything more than a wife."*

She was, of course, referring to Trevor Ward, a man both the Judge and Elma promoted almost on a daily basis. Though Harriet didn't have the slightest interest in Trevor and wanted badly to discourage even the hint of such a thing, she found herself unable to resist her parents' persistent threats and pleas. "That poor man," Elma was fond of saying whenever Harriet balked at responding to one of Trevor's letters, "is in the Army, far from his own home, offering up his life to protect you and your rights." Harriet, though often tempted to ask her mother exactly what rights she was talking about, said nothing. Instead, she did as she was told, though often with great reluctance and with an occasional show of defiance. *"What choice do I have?"* she confided to her diary. *"What choice does any woman have? I have an education but no skills, social status but no means. I am as bound to my father, dependent*

*upon him for every morsel of food I eat and the very clothing
I wear, as a black slave is to his master.''*

Lost in a perpetual gloom of self-pity that caused her face to droop in a most mournful way, Harriet made her way to her seat. She didn't pay the slightest bit of attention to the angry stare her mother gave her or the interruption of Reverend Binford's speech that she had caused. Even the fluttering of whispered comments made as many women in the audience commented to their neighbors about how rude and undisciplined such tardiness was didn't faze Harriet. "She'll not be able to find a decent husband who will put up with such behavior as this," an elderly woman seated behind her confided to a friend in a voice loud enough to ensure that Harriet would hear. Glancing over her shoulder, Harriet gave the old woman the sweetest smile that she could manage, then turned back to the front, where the good Reverend was finishing up his protracted and pointless oration.

"While you ladies," he said without even the slightest hint of sincerity in his voice, "can take pride in your efforts to date, you have outdone yourselves during this special Christmas drive." With a sweep of his hand serving as cue, the curtain behind them was opened, revealing stacks of neatly wrapped packages. After letting the patter of self-congratulatory applause subside, Reverend Binford continued. "I have no doubt that all of our brave sons now serving in our state's fine regiments in Virginia will appreciate your efforts and your charity." This comment caught Harriet's attention, causing her to look around the room at the faces of women whose sons were safely tucked away in colleges across the state or holding down "important" government positions in Trenton and Washington. "To present you with some idea of the magnitude of your labors," Binford announced, "I would like to ask our dear, hardworking secretary, the wife of State Senator John Andrew Randolf the Third, to read off the final listing of presents and material we will be sending to our brave boys down South."

While the gathered crowd greeted Victoria Elizabeth Randolf with a muted round of applause, Harriet watched with narrowed eyes as that woman stood up and moved with a slow, regal deliberateness to the lectern, turning every so often to face the crowd and acknowledge their polite adoration with a smile and a bow. As always, Harriet thought, the old biddy was milking the attention her position offered her for all it was worth. That she was there only by the grace of a hefty donation given to Reverend Binford's parish by her husband, the state senator, was well known, just as well known as the fact that since the founding of the agency, Mrs. John Andrew Randolf the Third hadn't lifted a finger to knit a single sock or roll one bandage. Her role, she unabashedly claimed, "was to provide all the fine ladies of our humble community with a role model and icon of feminine virtue during these trying times."

When Victoria Elizabeth Randolf began to enumerate the contents of the packages behind her in great and hideous detail, Harriet returned to her own private thoughts. The failure of her friend, Abigail Milford, as falsely reported by her to Harriet, to find Kevin Bannon and pass on the letter that she had taken such care to write was both frustrating and disappointing. *"After each battle,"* she confessed to her diary, *"I read and reread the casualty lists published in all the local papers. While I half pray that I will not find his name on it, for I do love him so and do not wish to see him hurt, I also find myself hoping that his name is listed with the wounded. After all, a wound would send him to a safe, comfortable hospital which I could go to and find out from him if he still held me in the same regard that he did the last time we saw each other. It is the ignorance, I think, that bothers me the most. Not knowing how he truly feels is, to me, unbearable."*

While these and other thoughts wandered through Harriet's mind, Victoria Randolf continued to go on, and on, and on, doing her best to make the most of this opportunity to stand center stage before all the women of note of New Brunswick. Only when Victoria was nearing the end of her report and preparing to turn the floor back over to Reverend Binford did Harriet pay even the scantest attention to what was being said.

"Thank you," Reverend Binford said with a nod once he had reached the lectern, "Mrs. Randolf, for that magnificent summation. I only pray that all of these gifts of love can make it to our soldiers in time for their enjoyment on the celebration of our Savior's birth. And while I have been assured by the good people who run the shipping depot of our sister agency, the New York City Sanitary Commission, that every effort will be made to ensure the timely arrival of our shipment, we must realize that these are busy times and the needs of the Sanitary Commission must take precedence. Were there something that I could do," Binford stated, raising his eyes and right hand toward the ceiling as if he were evoking the power of God, "to ensure that our boys would be able to enjoy the fruits of your labors, I would move heaven and earth to do it."

Like a flash, Harriet was on her feet. "But there *is* something we can do," she shouted. Stunned by the sudden and unexpected interruption, Binford, his right arm still held high, looked down at her with glaring eyes. After the ripple of shocked murmurs had finished running their course, Harriet looked around the room, sporting the sweetest smile she could manage. "Reverend Binford and dear ladies, why trust others to do our work? Why risk the happiness of our own brave soldiers on the off chance that another agency will give our gifts, gifts that we so painstakingly labored over, the priority and attention that they deserve? Instead, let us resolve ourselves to make one more valiant effort, one more labor, and carry our gifts down to them ourselves."

Pausing to let her suggestion sink in, Harriet looked about the room. With a great deal of satisfaction, she noted that a majority of the heads before her were nodding in approval as the women in the audience discussed it amongst themselves. On the stage, Reverend Binford, annoyed by being interrupted by a woman in such a manner, shot furtive glances at Victoria Randolf. For her part, Victoria was at a loss as to what to do, for while the idea was a good one, one that could bring more acclaim to her organization, the thought that it was being made by Elma Shields' daughter was quite repugnant.

Sensing the confusion those who would oppose her were in, Harriet drove on, determined to seek a quick resolution. "I beseech you, kind ladies, don't fail our dear brave boys now. We have done too much, sacrificed too much time, to abandon our sacred duty. After all, how would it look to our own loved ones in Virginia if we passed obligation and duties on to others to do that which we ourselves should and can do."

With the clamor growing and threatening to erupt into unanimous acclaim before he had an opportunity to squelch an idea that seemed to threathen his authority, Reverend Binford called out above the growing roar of the crowd. "Who, Miss Shields, among us, will do this?"

The Reverend's challenge brought on a hush as faces turned to see how Harriet would respond. With all the poise she could muster, Harriet allowed a measured pause to pass while she looked down for a moment, giving the impression that she was gathering strength. At first, she spoke softly with her eyes still glued to the back of the seat before her. "It would be wrong for me to volunteer such an idea if I, myself, were not ready and willing to see it through." Then, slowly, she lifted her head. With a gentle expression and a steady gaze, Harriet looked about the room, her eyes darting from face to face as she spoke. "We have asked those we hold dearest to go forth and place themselves at risk, as our dear Savior did, in the name of freedom and justice. They have shown, throughout the terrible summer just past, that they are equal to the task that we have set before them. How can we not, then, endeavor to match their sacrifice and their efforts, given freely, by seeing this effort through to the end? I, for one, could not rest peacefully this Christmas Day, wondering if our gifts were delivered into the hands of those they were meant for. Could you?"

While Harriet attempted to gauge the effects of her impromptu appeal, Victoria Randolf gave Reverend Binford a stern, hard look. Reverend Binford, totally at a loss as to what to do, shrugged in return. Determined not to let Elma's little upstart of a daughter spoil her moment of glory, Victoria stood up and moved to the lectern, pushing the befuddled Reverend out of the way. "Ladies," she called in an effort to calm the growing acclaim that Harriet's idea was gathering. "While I applaud the offer of the services Miss Shields has so kindly put before us, we cannot permit a girl of her age or station to undertake such a difficult, not to mention hazardous, task. To do so would be unthinkable."

"But I wouldn't be going to Virginia on my own, Mrs. Randolf," Harriet shouted out quickly before she lost her momentum.

The anger at Harriet's interruption showed in Victoria's face and voice, despite her best efforts to hide it. "Who," she shot back with an unmistakable sharpness, "would dare make this hazardous journey, in the dead of winter, with you, young lady?''

Harriet was ready. With a broad smile, she thrust her right arm out, the palm of her hand upturned, toward the stage. ''Why, Mrs. Randolf,'' she cried with great glee, ''our dear Reverend Binford, of course.'' With great theatricality, Harriet lifted her arms up and out to her sides as she slowly turned to face as many of the women looking at her as she could. ''I ask you, ladies, what better way is there for a man of God to serve the men of this community than to go out into the wilderness amongst them. Think of it. Our very own Reverend Binford would be bringing gifts, gifts that we all toiled so hard to prepare, just as the Three Magi did, but,'' she said, holding her right index finger up to accentuate her point, ''not only that, he would also be there to help our loved ones celebrate the birth of our dear Lord Jesus Christ.''

Stunned, Reverend Binford felt the blood draining from his face as the mass of women before him rose to their feet and, with a resounding round of applause, led by Elma Shields, brought all discussion on the matter to an end.

There was little time to waste and Harriet knew it. Although the idea of taking the gifts to Virginia had come to her on the spur of the moment, her approach to the myriad of obstacles facing her was anything but haphazard. In these efforts, Harriet found many strange allies who helped her overcome the obstructions placed before her by those determined to see her fail.

Reverend Binford, ostensibly in charge of the effort, proved to be the greatest hindrance. The good Reverend, egged on by Victoria Elizabeth Randolf but in a state of panic at the prospect of going so near the fighting, failed to take advantage of every opportunity afforded him to sidetrack or delay Harriet's efforts, including notifying Harriet's father, the Judge. Instead, he relied on what he considered his own mastery of oratory, persuasion, and authority. ''The cost,'' he lamented, ''to move all of this on our own will strip us of every penny we have in our meager treasury. Surely you can see that?''

Harriet, however, always seemed to be one step ahead of

him. Anticipating the Reverend's first ploy, Harriet had risen early the next morning in order to catch the first train to Perth Amboy. Edward Bannon, as surprised to see her on his doorstep as she was to be there, welcomed her into his home with the same graciousness with which the wolf welcomes a sheep into his lair. After they adjourned to his study, he ordered his English maid to prepare tea for Harriet and coffee for himself, while they exchanged pleasantries with all the grace of two people shadowboxing. Realizing quickly that she was out of her depth when it came to dealing with a man like Edward, Harriet abruptly turned to the point of this visit. "I know that there is little affection between you and your son Kevin, Mr. Bannon, and that Kevin would be furious if he knew I had come here to seek your help."

The sudden change in her demeanor, and her bluntness, rocked Edward Bannon back on his heels. Pausing only long enough for the English maid to serve them their tea and coffee, Edward nodded when he was ready for her to go on, watching her, she thought, like a jungle cat watches its prey. Though nervous, and speaking faster than she wished, Harriet explained. "I do love your son, more than you can ever realize, Mr. Bannon. But I am afraid that something has happened, someone has conspired to come between us."

"Well," Edward stated bluntly, "it certainly hasn't been me. Since he left—"

"Oh, no." Harriet hurriedly explained. "I know it's not you. I suspect, I am sorry to say, my own dear father. He and Mother want me to marry Trevor Ward."

Edward Bannon smiled as he nodded his head in approval. "Marriage into that family would be, if I may say so, quite advantageous to your father. And you wouldn't do badly yoúrself, my dear. The Wards have money, old money that is as secure as the Rock of Gibraltar."

Though she didn't quite understand that Edward was taking her parents' side in this issue at the expense of his own son in an effort to test her resolve, Harriet didn't pursue the matter. "Be that as it may, sir, I do not love the man. He is conceited and a bore."

"What, dear girl," Edward shouted out with a chuckle, "has love got to do with marriage?"

That Edward Bannon and her own father viewed love and marriage in the same way stunned Harriet. The essence of Edward's last comment was, in fact, no different from her own father's admonishments to her whenever he was promoting a match between her and Trevor Ward. "My dear child," Judge Shields had told her before leaving for Washington two days before, "the passion that you feel in your heart for that Irish boy will pass, just as the green leaves of summer fade and fall away with the approach of winter. Trevor, and not the Bannon boy, has the means to ensure that the winter years of your life will be safe and secure. Trust me, child, for I know about these things."

Harriet, however, found that she could no more deny her feelings than Judge Shields could turn away from his political ambitions. "Are you telling me, Mr. Bannon," Harriet asked incredulously, "that you would rather see me marry someone other than your son?"

Leaning back, Edward rested his elbows on the arms of his overstuffed leather chair and brought his folded hands up before his chin. For a moment he studied the girl before him. She had spunk, he thought. Determination and spunk, just like Kevin's mother. The memory of what that woman had done for the son of a down-and-out tenant farmer in Ireland who had spent most of his nights dead drunk on the floor of a pub almost brought a tear to Edward's eye. Slowly, ever so slowly, the corners of Edward's mouth turned upward into a faint smile. "Please, Miss Shields, don't mistake my comments. I had to be sure of your reasons, not to mention your mettle. I can see now what my son sees in you." Dropping his hands, Edward leaned forward. "No, I tell you these things because your presence is, to say the least, highly irregular, just as your direct request for my assistance is. I trust," he said hesitantly, "that your father knows nothing about you coming here?"

"No, of course not. In fact, he must not know anything about this until I'm in Virginia."

The mention of Virginia caused Edward's eyebrows to rise. "What, exactly, do you plan to do there? The Army, if you haven't been aware of it, is maneuvering about in an effort to get around Bobby Lee's Army."

"Yes," Harriet acknowledged. "I know all that. But the

special Christmas drive to gather gifts for the soldiers from New Jersey has provided me with an opportunity to go there, in person, to see your son and find out whether or not—''

"He loves you?"

"Yes."

"And," Edward queried, "if he doesn't?"

This caused Harriet to pause. For a moment, she looked down at the hem of her skirt and thought about Edward's question. Then, drawing in a deep breath, she raised her eyes and met his. "Though I do not think that it will come to that, for I am sure that Kevin shares my feelings, I am prepared to face the consequences if he does not."

By God, Edward thought, she does have spirit. "What, dear lady, can I do to help," he asked with the first genuine smile that he had allowed himself all day.

With the dedication of a crusader setting out on an Arthurian quest and a scheming plan that would make Machiavelli proud, Harriet set out to move four wagonloads of goods from New Brunswick to the Jerseymen in the Army of the Potomac, now rumored to be near an old colonial town named Fredericksburg. With speed that both dazzled and befuddled the Reverend Binford and frustrated Victoria Elizabeth Randolf's efforts to interfere, Edward Bannon arranged for the movement of the agency's goods, without cost, by rail to Washington. Though Harriet was never sure if he paid for some of the freight costs from his own pocket or relied solely on favors he called in from railroad men, she was more than satisfied by the speed with which the task was accomplished.

Even more gratifying to her was the manner in which Edward had arranged for the transfer of the goods in Washington. The hired wagons had been engaged and were waiting for the arriving goods without the involvement of any New Jersey politicians in Washington. "If my father gets wind of what I'm up to while he's in Washington, and he will if word gets out, Mr. Bannon, he'll stop me for sure."

With a sly smile that was more unsettling than reassuring, Edward Bannon had replied that the shipment of certain goods about the country, quietly, was, to him, old hat. "I have friends, dear girl, who have made a fortune doing this sort of thing," he'd said with a wink.

While the idea that she was making a pact with the devil crossed her mind when he had said this, Harriet let her fleeting fear pass. *"I have come too far,"* she told her diary that night, *"and the stakes are, for me, too high to stop now."* With that, she packed a small trunk with all that she thought she would need, and, the following morning she left Washington before dawn with four wagons and a reluctant Reverend in tow, on the greatest, and most important, adventure of her young life.

# CHAPTER 22

# December, 1862
# Southwest of
# Fredericksburg,
# Virginia

LISTENING INTENTLY FOR A MOMENT TO THE RENEWAL OF THE cannonading to their north, Will McPherson thought about it for a moment. "They'll be coming today, for sure. I can't imagine them waiting any longer to get on with it."

James, seated on the ground with his back against a tree, also faced the north. After listening for a moment, he disagreed. "If they had been serious about attacking us here, they would have crossed the Rappahannock two weeks ago and taken on Longstreet's corps while we were still spread out to the south. To come at us now, with everyone dug in and ready, would be ..."

"Hell, Jimmy," Marty Hazard chimed in. "Those damned fool Yankees have done dumber things in the past. I mean, remember the railroad cut at Manassas? Remember how they come up on us time and time again, never once suspecting that Longstreet's boys were hoverin' on their flanks like a pack of wolves?"

James Bannon nodded, yet remained unconvinced as he continued to try to gauge the caliber of the guns being fired. "No, Marty, I don't think so. Not even McDowell would be fool enough to try to take on Longstreet's corps on Marye's Heights up there."

"Then," Hazard asked after thinking a moment, "do ya think he'll come after us down here?"

"That," Will said with a grim smile on his face, "would suit

General Paxton just fine. He's spoiling for a fight. So's Old Jack." Then Will looked over to where General Paxton nervously paced back and forth in front of the 2nd Virginia as several brigade and regimental staff officers looked on, waiting like the rest of the brigade. "Our new commander is really itching for a fight."

James, giving in to a yawn, waved his hand. "After the first ten minutes, he'll settle down and do just fine. Though I can't say I agree with the way Old Jack treated Grigsby after Sharpsburg, I'm sure Paxton will be just as good."

Marty grunted as he looked over to General Paxton, now standing still and erect, looking as if he were posing for a photograph. "If you ask me, I'd rather have Grigsby as a colonel in command than this poppycock general. I'll tell you, boys, if he takes us into the fight like he's been drilling us, there'll be a whole bunch of us who'll get to meet our Maker sooner than we want."

From off to one side, a voice called out to Marty. "Sergeant Hazard, you needn't worry about meeting your Maker. The way you carried on in Winchester last month, I'd say you had a one-way ticket headed the other way."

Recognizing the voice, Marty, Will, and James turned to face their regimental commander, Lieutenant Colonel Robert Gardner. "Why hell, Colonel," Marty replied, "you know our dear Lord is the forgivin' kind."

Gardner chuckled. "Well, let's just hope that he's also got a short memory."

Gardner's response caused Will, Marty, and James, as well as the men gathered about them, to laugh. From behind them, one of the new privates, anxious to see his first fight, shouted out, "What do you think, Colonel, sir? Will the Yanks make a frontal attack or go for the right flank?"

With great deliberation, Gardner pondered this question, staring off into the heavy morning fog that stubbornly clung to the woods and trees about them. Finally, after giving the question much thought, he looked over the men who stood or sat about him. "Front, I think. The Northern papers made a big to-do about Burnside's attack over that little bridge at Sharpsburg. The way I figure it, since it worked for him before, he'll try the same thing here. Besides," Colonel Gardner added, "by now he'll know he's facing all three: Bobby Lee, Longstreet, and our own Jackson. They'll not try anything fancy."

"Well, hell," Marty exclaimed. "If I had as many men as they have, I wouldn't mess around with no fancy dance-about either. Straight up the middle I'd go, head down with both arms aflailing."

Colonel Gardner smiled at Marty, then over to Will and James. "And to think they made him a sergeant."

Not knowing how to take the colonel's comment, Marty turned to look at James, who like everyone else, was smiling ear to ear. Marty, knowing they were on the verge of laughing, reached out and pointed at the colonel. "Now there's a fella that knows talent when he sees it."

While everyone around Marty broke out into a chorus of laughter, Gardner shook his head and continued to troop on down the line of troops, pausing here and there to exchange a few words with some of his men. Will, after recovering from his bout of laughter, turned to say something to James but stopped as the sound of a particularly loud and thunderous volley of cannon fire came drifting through the woods. Instead of addressing James, as he had been preparing to, Will faced back to the north to listen to the familiar sounds of battle as they drifted down from the steep hills that frowned down upon the town of Fredericksburg.

"It is time, child," Reverend Binford told Harriet as he kept glancing nervously over her shoulder toward the distant sound of cannon fire, "that we make our way back to Washington as quickly as possible."

The idea that a battle would keep her from completing her self-appointed quest had never occurred to Harriet Shields. It was, as everyone knew, customary for armies to go into winter quarters and wait for the proper campaign season. Harriet looked away from the Reverend Binford at the line of wagons moving up the muddy road to where the Army of the Potomac waited patiently to cross the Rappahannock River. Though she couldn't imagine what was so important about Fredericksburg that compelled the Army's commander to push his men into battle under such foul conditions, his actions and the pending battle didn't, in her mind, change anything.

Looking back at Reverend Binford, Harriet's eyes narrowed. "Meaning no disrespect, sir, but we've come too far to turn back now. If anything, the very fact that our boys are up there, God knows where, preparing to face the enemy under such horrid conditions just makes our mission of mercy more critical." Reverend Binford blinked. His stammering and a nervous twitch in his eyelids that she had never seen before convinced Harriet that he was genuinely frightened. Reaching out, she took his arm in an effort to reassure him.

Reverend Binford, looking down at Harriet, wondered if her concerns for the welfare of the soldiers were sincere, or if she was simply trying to manipulate him, as she had been doing since they had set out on what he considered a foolish and ill advised adventure. Though her words had a ring of truth, and her sweet, innocent smile was beguiling, as always, the thought of continuing forward was simply too much for him. "Harriet, child, this is no place for a young lady such as yourself. It would be unthinkable for me to expose you to such dangers. How could I ever face your father and mother again if something happened to you?"

Seeing that sugar wasn't working, Harriet switched to vinegar. With a jerk, she withdrew her hand from his arm and stepped back, her face darkening as she did so. "And how, dear sir, will you be able to call yourself a servant of God if you turn your back on the sons and fathers of your flock at such a time?"

Harriet's lashing stung him but did nothing to change his mind. "There are those of the cloth with our boys who are better able to tend to the needs of the soldiers. My place, and yours, child, is not here."

"Do not tell me, sir," Harriet thundered, "where my place is or isn't, for I am neither a child nor a slave. I set out to do something and I intend to do it, with or without you."

"Then," Reverend Binford countered firmly in the hope that he could scare Harriet into accepting a decision he had already made, "you shall do so alone."

Looking beyond Reverend Binford, at the four teamsters

who had been watching them, Harriet shouted, "You men, who will go on with me?"

Casting furtive glances at each other, the men began to mutter. Seeing that they were as reluctant as Reverend Binford was, Harriet hastily added, "Any man who goes on will receive double the agreed to price."

Unable to stand there and watch passively while his authority was being challenged in such a manner, Reverend Binford turned to face the men. "I will not be a party to this insanity. Any man who does faces hellfire and damnation."

"And," Harriet shouted, "any man who doesn't forfeits his pay."

Shocked by her performance, Reverend Binford looked over at Harriet, then back at the men, trying his best to stare them down. Finally, one man shrugged. "Well, I sure as hell didn't sign on to join no battle." Turning, he began to make his way over to his wagon. Another man, an old German, shook his head, began to follow him, but stopped. Turning back to face Harriet, he looked her up and down, as if he were gauging her mettle. Finally, he spoke in a broken accent. "If we go, lady, what will you pay?"

Having been forewarned and prepared for just such an emergency by Edward Bannon, Harriet smiled, reaching into her small purse. Pulling out a wad of money, she waved it over her head. "Any man who goes on with me until we find the First New Jersey Brigade will receive triple the agreed upon price."

The other two teamsters who had remained looked over to the old German teamster. "You have dat much there, lady?" he asked.

"I do. If you don't believe me, I will count it out for you now."

The old German smiled, raising his hand. "No, that's okay. I will go."

From where he stood, Reverend Binford shouted, "Fool! You miserable fool."

The old German teamster looked at him. "Ya, ya. Probably so. But I say to myself, Karl, with so many fat businessmen up North becoming rich from this war, you are a fool if you turn your back on a chance to get your share. So I go." Looking over at the other two teamsters, who had not moved, the German advised them, "If you are smart lads, you will come too."

Without further delay, the three teamsters who decided to accept Harriet's offer turned to tend their wagons and teams of mules. Reverend Binford, seething with anger, pointed to the one wagon left unattended. "And who will you find," he shouted to Harriet defiantly, "to take that wagon, young lady?"

With a toss of her head, Harriet shot back without hesitation, "Seeing that there isn't another man worthy of that title in sight, then I shall." With that, she marched over to the first wagon in line and climbed aboard. Gathering the unfamiliar reins in her hands, she settled herself onto the seat, took up the whip, and looked down at Reverend Binford. Seeing that he had been defeated in his last bid to overcome Harriet's stubborn determination, Reverend Binford looked down at the road he stood in and let his shoulders slump. A beaten man, Reverend Binford knew he would no longer be able to hide his cowardliness behind his collar or excuses. Without another word, he turned his back and began to make his way north, on foot, while the sound of cracking whips and cursing teamsters bringing their teams to life taunted him.

After crossing over to the west bank of the Rappahannock River and moving up to the Fredericksburg–Richmond Road, the New Jersey Brigade halted and deployed. They stood in ranks, ready to go into battle but not doing so, for many hours, leaving the soldiers to fidget and speculate. Johnny O'Keeth, always animated when battle drew near, looked over to the man to his right, Henry Wissen. While Henry was a pleasant enough fellow, he tended to be a bore when it came to holding a conversation. Looking to his left, Johnny considered striking up a conversation with the young blond fellow next to him but decided against that too. New to the company, the blond fellow not only didn't know his backside from a hole in the ground, he was too nervous to be of much interest. While some of the others in the company enjoyed taunting new men with tall tales and grim stories of combat in an effort to rattle them, Johnny O'Keeth never found any pleasure in doing so. Besides, the new man's gaze, like everyone else's, was fixed to the front, watching to see what the artillery behind them was firing at.

Tired of standing about in the ranks like a wax dummy between Wissen and the new man and anxious to talk to someone, Johnny looked about to the rear to see if any of the corporals or sergeants were close enough to talk to. He was about to call over to Sergeant Callahan, leaning on his rifle a few feet away, when he saw 2nd Lieutenant Henry Meyers walking about behind the ranks. Though Meyers could be quite snooty at times, he had loosened up some after the fights at Bull Run Bridge and Crampton's Gap. Even Lieutenant Bannon seemed to be more tolerant of a man everyone had once branded as little more than a toady to the company commander. "I suppose," First Sergeant Frederick Himmel had commented one day, "if Lieutenant Bannon thinks well of young Lieutenant Meyers, then he must be a fine fellow after all."

"Lieutenant Meyers," Johnny called out when Meyers was close enough to hear, "do ya think we'll go in today?"

Thrilled that someone was asking him his opinion on a military matter, Meyers stopped when he reached Johnny. Assuming an expression that Meyers considered to be appropriate for such a serious question, he brought his right hand up to his chin. "Well, now," he started after clearing his throat and dropping his tone, "it seems to me that we'd better do something, and soon. I mean, when you consider the fact that the men we're facing belong to Jackson's corps, you really have no choice but to strike fast, 'cause if we don't, he will."

"Then why," Johnny countered, "did we wait so long before crossing? They all but marched our legs off getting us here in a hurry and then let us sit over there, on the other bank, for nearly a week. I don't mind saying, Lieutenant Meyers, that a thing like that doesn't make sense to me."

Meyers shook his head. "Nor does it to me, Private O'Keeth. Though a lot of the other officers who have friends on division and corps staffs claim someone forgot to bring the pontoon bridges up with the main body, I don't place much stock in such gossip. I mean, it seems to me that even the dumbest private in the ranks wouldn't forget something that obvious."

Growing more comfortable as he chatted with Meyers, O'Keeth crossed his arms over the barrel of his rifle and leaned forward upon it, using it as a prop. "I heard the same story about someone forgetting the bridges from an orderly for our general. He says things were really confused after Little Mac was replaced by Burnside. This fellow says that all kinds of things that Little Mac would have thought about were forgotten by the new staff officers. He even said that some of it was on purpose, so as to make Burnside look bad so that Lincoln would have no choice but to bring Little Mac back.''

Meyers looked at Johnny with great skepticism. "I'll admit that there probably were some hard feelings between McClellan's men and the new commander. I surely didn't much like the way they did things. Still, I doubt if those gentlemen would allow such pettiness to interfere with the performance of their duties.''

Now it was Johnny's turn to be skeptical, though he said nothing to the young lieutenant. Like most officers, he defended peers even when they didn't deserve such loyalty. Even Lieutenant Bannon, long considered the real commander of the company by every man in the ranks, never uttered a disparaging word about Captain Ward's cowardly habits. Though some of the noncommissioned officers made it known that they would stand by him if he chose to go before the regimental commander to protest their captain's dereliction of duties, First Lieutenant Kevin Bannon refused to hear them out. "For better or worse," he told them, "Captain Ward is our commander. He holds a commission from the governor and was duly appointed to his post by the regimental commander. Until such time as those gentlemen see fit to replace him, or enemy action removes him from his post, we are bound by law to obey him.'' Knowing full well the captain's habit of making himself scarce when danger threatened, the rebellious sergeants resigned themselves to the fact that Ward would be around for a long time. "At least," Johnny overheard one comment later, "Lieutenant Bannon is here to look out for the company. He'll see us through, by God.''

A sudden explosion down the line, like an unexpected thunderclap on a clear spring day, startled both lieutenant and private. Like most of the men around them, their first reaction was to pull their own heads down, almost between their shoulders, even though, if they had thought about it, the danger was already past. Meyers recovered his composure first. Standing

396

upright, he looked about. "Well, it looks as if the enemy gunners have the range for H Company."

Leaning backwards out of ranks, Johnny looked down to see where Meyers was looking. Above the solid blue ranks, a puff of dirty gray smoke was drifting harmlessly away. The sight of three soldiers on the ground, however, told Johnny that the round of shrapnel that had caused the wispy gray cloud had been anything but harmless. Even from where he stood, Johnny could see blood freely running from fresh wounds. While one man thrashed about violently, lifting a shattered stump that had once been an arm, another man, holding his bleeding head with both hands, stumbled about in a daze. Johnny shook his head. "Lord, I hate standing out here like this, waiting to be struck down by a stray artillery shell like those poor fellows."

"What," Meyers asked, "makes you think that was a stray shell?"

Turning away from the grisly scene down the ranks, Johnny looked at Meyers but said nothing. Though he didn't like the thought of it, every minute they stood there just gave the Confederates more time to find their range.

He was about to say something when the roll of drums and a crash of musketry to their left caught Meyers' attention. Looking around instinctively for Kevin Bannon, Meyers reached down to his side with his right hand and drew his saber. "Well," he announced to Johnny with a hint of nervousness in his voice, "it does seem as if someone is going to go forward after all."

Coming back to a relaxed position of attention, Johnny squeezed back into the ranks between Henry Wissen and the new man. Then, as an afterthought, he looked back at Meyers. "Will Lieutenant Bannon be leading us forward today, sir?"

Understanding the meaning of O'Keeth's question, Meyers blushed in embarrassment. "No, private, not today. Captain Ward, I'm sure, will be back from brigade in plenty of time to lead the company when it comes our turn to go forward."

Looking over to the right down the long ranks, Johnny could see Kevin Bannon already standing in Ward's place at the far right of the front rank in front of First Sergeant Himmel. Johnny straightened up and smiled as he looked back at Meyers. "Well, sir, if he's going to lead us, he'd better hurry."

Torn between his loyalty to a man who held the position as company commander by law and the man who actually did so by deed, Meyers said nothing in response to O'Keeth's snide remark. Instead, he brought the blade of his brightly polished saber up to his shoulder, turned, and marched off to assume the post normally filled by the company's first lieutenant. The fact was, if he had cared to admit it even to himself, he preferred it this way. Ward was, despite his being a gentleman, a coward who no more deserved the rank he held than the team of mules used to pull the regiment's mess wagon.

Just before reaching the Rappahannock River, the cavalry officer of the corps provost guard turned his horse in the center of the road and pointed to a cluster of tents and wagons tucked into a ravine not far from the pontoon bridges. "This is as far as I dare take you, Miss Shields."

Standing up on the buckboard of the wagon she had been driving, Harriet looked about in dismay. Just ahead, past the confused jumble of Army wagons and artillery caissons still waiting to cross over to the south side of the Rappahannock, she could see a cluster of men milling about the tents her escort was pointing at. The encampment was marked only with a dirty yellow flag haphazardly nailed to a post near one of the first tents, and Harriet wondered what this place was and why there were soldiers lying about in the mud doing nothing when there was obviously a battle going on. Though she could clearly see dark stains and tears in their clothing from where she stood, she thought nothing of it.

Looking across the river to the west, she watched the mass of men in blue, deployed in long ranks and columns, standing out on the open plain. Beyond them, across open fields, was a low wooded hill from which clouds of smoke, some seeming like mere wisps from where she stood, rose up. Seeing where she was looking, the cavalry officer spoke. "That's First Corps, commanded by Reynolds. Meade's division has been sent forward to seize that high ground."

"And the Sixth Corps?" Harriet asked anxiously. "Where are they?"

The cavalryman pointed. ''Down there, just across the bridges.''

''Are they to attack too?''

Her escort shrugged as he looked across the river. ''One would think so, since we're facing Jackson's whole corps. But so far, the generals have sent only Meade's division forward.'' He looked over at Harriet. ''They seem to be doing pretty good from here but . . .'' Turning back, the cavalryman never finished his statement.

While he watched the distant battle, Harriet turned her attention to the men coming down the road singly or in pairs. Unlike the wagons and caissons waiting to cross over to the south side of the river, there seemed to be no rhyme or reason to the order of the men coming back. Most walked with an unsteady gait, some even staggering and weaving about from side to side like drunks. Mixed in among them were a few being helped by friends or leaning so heavily on their upturned rifles that the muzzle sank deep into the mud every time they planted it down. Though curious about these men, Harriet had other things to deal with first. Looking back at the cavalry officer, who was preparing to leave, Harriet called out, ''Exactly what is this place, Lieutenant Hansen?''

Surprised by her question, the cavalry officer turned his head back to the farmhouse and considered the scene before them for a moment with a look of confusion. Shaking his head after he was sure that everything about them was as clear and straightforward as he thought it was, he looked back at Harriet. ''Why, Miss Shields, this is the field hospital for the Sixth Corps's First Division. You should be safe here until the battle's over.''

''And then what?'' she asked, still confused.

Realizing that she was truly ignorant of the ways of the Army, the cavalry officer rode up next to Harriet's wagon. He leaned over his horse's neck and looked up into her eyes. ''Well, Miss Shields,'' he said in a tone devoid of all feeling, ''if we win, the surgeon belonging to the 4th New Jersey at this hospital will eventually go forward to rejoin his regiment. When that happens, I'm sure he'll be glad to take you along with him.''

Waiting for a second part that she knew had to come, Harriet stared at the cavalryman. When it became obvious that he didn't intend to volunteer the information, Harriet asked the question. "And if we don't win this battle?"

Sitting upright in his saddle, the cavalryman looked back down the road that they had used to reach the Rappahannock River, then over at the pontoon bridges spanning it. "If it comes to that, miss, and I do pray that it does not, I'd advise you to forget about finding your fiancé. In fact, you'd do him a great service if you got these wagons off the road, abandoned them, and made your way back to Washington as quickly as you could." Jerking his reins, the cavalryman pulled himself away from the wagon and turned his horse about. "Take my word," he shouted over his shoulder at her, "the last thing you want to be part of is the retreat of a beaten army. Now, if you'll excuse me, I've got to get back to my troop." With a wave of his hand that was half salute, half tip of his hat, the cavalry lieutenant dug his spurs into the flanks of his horse and rode off at a fast trot.

For a moment Harriet stood there, watching the cavalryman as he made his way down the road crowded with wagons and soldiers waiting to move on. When she finally realized that he was gone and not coming back, she looked back toward the river, down the road where more and more men meandered their way through the traffic headed across the river and staggered toward her. Above the noise of the slow-moving column and the sharp curses of Army teamsters driving their teams on, she could hear the roar of cannons. Overhead, at regular intervals, a terrible screech reminded her of rockets fired to celebrate Independence Day. To this was added the sound of the cracking and sputtering of distant rifle fire, floating up from across the river.

Absorbed by these sounds and her own thoughts, she didn't hear the old German teamster calling to her from the road next to her wagon. Only after he tugged at the hem of her skirt did she notice him. Taking her eyes off of the distant horizon and looking down, she saw the bearded face of the old German. "Begging your pardon, lady, but me and the other lads don't like being this close to that war over there. Wasn't part of the agreement, you know."

"You can't just go off and leave me and these wagons here."

The old German, his face showing no sign of emotion, shook his head. "We can, miss, and we intend to. We're no soldier boys. We never signed on to fight for darkies and don't plan on starting. Now, if it pleases you, we'll take what's coming to us and be on our way."

"You mean," Harriet said in a voice that she hoped would sway the old German, "you'd abandon me with these wagons?"

"As I said," the old German responded without the slightest hesitation or even a hint of concern in his voice, "we are not soldiers." Looking about him, he pointed over to the soldiers gathering about the hospital tents. "You need help, try asking them. After all, lady, all this stuff is for them, not us. Now, if you don't mind, we'll take our pay and be gone."

Though she did mind, very much, Harriet saw no point in pursuing the matter. Instead, she took the small pouch of money that Edward Bannon had given her, carefully counted out the sum she owed the teamsters, and held it out at arm's length to the old German. "There. It's all there, including the bonus I promised you this morning." Taking the money, the old German tipped his hat, turned, and walked away without another word.

Harriet did not let the fact that she had been abandoned bother her in the least. Instead, she went to dismount from the wagon she had been driving so that she could begin her search for the chief surgeon. A hoopskirt that kept catching on everything, however, made dismounting the wagon, and nearly everything else, hazardous at best. Her efforts to push the hoop and her modest crinolines out of the way came to naught, leaving her no choice but to climb down off the wagon backwards, feeling blindly with her foot for something to step onto. Two soldiers, both with green slashes of cloth sewn to their sleeves, paused in what they were doing to watch Harriet as she fumbled about with her skirts. Though she could hear them, and practically feel their eyes on her, she ignored them until she had both feet on the ground. After smoothing out her crinolines and skirt Harriet spun about quickly and barked at the two leering soldiers. "Who's in charge here?"

Caught off guard, both men jumped back. "Doctor White, ma'am. He's in charge here," one of the men stammered.

Seeing she had a momentary edge, Harriet placed her hands on her hips and leaned forward at the waist. "And where can I find this Doctor White?"

"Over there." The other man pointed. "In the tent on the end."

While Harriet turned her head to look, the two men saw an opportunity to escape this woman and took it. Deciding that she had no further need to bother them, Harriet let them flee as she pulled her wool cape around her tightly to protect her from the cold before heading off in the direction in which the soldier had pointed.

While she was walking down between the rows of tents, ignoring the soldiers she passed and being ignored by them, she heard a voice from one of the tents call out in a weak, pathetic wail, "Help me. Someone. Heeelp meee."

Pausing, Harriet listened until she heard the voice again. This time, though the plea was more desperate, the voice was weaker, barely a whisper. "Please someone help me."

Turning to the tent that she was sure the voice came from, Harriet pushed the flaps of the entrance away and stuck her head through without looking first. Half blinded by the wide brim of the bonnet she wore and concentrating on pulling her voluminous skirts and crinolines through the narrow space between the tent flap and tent pole, Harriet didn't see the soldier who had been calling until she was inside the tent and standing at his feet.

Even before her eyes managed to adjust to the darkness in the tent, her nose gave her a warning. In all her years, Harriet had seldom been exposed to anyone who was sick or injured. Even when she had been allowed to briefly visit her grandfather as he lay on his deathbed, there was, as Harriet remembered, no sign of injury or pain. The room, though kept dark, was clean, as was her grandfather. Even his expression had been one of serene acceptance of what was coming. In contrast, the sight before Harriet now was anything but serene.

Lying upon a dirty gray blanket hastily thrown down on the thin layer of straw that lined the floor of the tent, as were several other wounded soldiers, a youth of no more than nineteen or twenty looked up at her. Shocks of his long black hair, wet from sweat despite the cold, framed a face devoid of color.

The youth's eyes, wild with fear, looked up at Harriet as he pleaded to her. "Please, miss. I'm cold. Please help me?"

Harriet was about to ask what was wrong with him when she saw the empty sleeve of his coat, ripped and still dark with drying blood, lying limply off to the right on the straw. The youth's coat, with only the top two buttons fastened, was open from the chest down. Looking down at his feet, Harriet noticed that his left foot, though dirty and uninjured, was bare. He must have lost his shoe and sock, she surmised, either somewhere in the process of getting him here to the hospital from across the river or after surgery, when he had been unceremoniously dumped into this tent with three other wounded men and left unattended, just as the cavalry officer had left her.

Though the smell of uncleaned bodies, human waste, and fresh wounds was playing havoc with Harriet's stomach, the anger she felt welling up in her over the shabby treatment this wounded man had obviously been subjected to was more powerful. "Dear Lord," she mumbled to herself. "Animals don't deserve to be treated like this." Dropping to her knees, Harriet reached up over the youth with one hand to pull his jacket closed and button it, planting her other hand in the straw beside him for balance. It would have been easier to do this from the side, but the width of her skirt and the stiffness of its crinolines would not have permitted her to fit in the narrow space between the youth and the next man over.

"Still ... cold ... miss," the youth murmured as Harriet fastened the last button on his jacket with one hand. "A blanket ... miss ... if you please."

Looking at the youth's face, she could see his eyes becoming more tranquil now that he knew there was someone at hand who cared. Forcing a smile despite the anger that continued to grow in her, Harriet patted the side of the youth's leg. "I'll go see what I can do. You lie here and be still till I get back."

Her soothing and reassuring words brought the faint traces of a smile to his face, a smile that was quickly wiped away as a spasm of pain racked his body. Unable to maintain her brave front much longer, Harriet pulled back, stood, and quickly left the tent. Once outside, she paused to catch her breath and force back tears that suddenly began to well up in her eyes. While she stood there, soldiers, some supporting or carrying wounded, went by without giving her a second glance. How cold this place was, she thought as she watched men come and go, seemingly detached from the pain and suffering that surrounded them. How terribly heartless and cold.

This thought, like the image of the youth lying on the ground unattended, caused Harriet's anger to rise up again and galvanize her for action. Quickly brushing away all traces of tears from her cheeks, Harriet reached out and grabbed the arm of the first healthy-looking soldier she saw going by. "You, soldier, I need blankets for a wounded man in this tent."

The soldier she had taken hold of spun around and faced her. There was fright in his eyes as he looked up at her. Harriet, who had done nothing more than reach out and grab the first handful of blue sleeve that went past her, was equally surprised, for the person before her looked as if he couldn't have been more than eleven or twelve years old. Letting go, Harriet was about to apologize when she remembered why she had stopped the boy. Clearing her throat, she toned down her demands. "Young man, are you assigned to this hospital?"

Before he responded, the boy looked down, as if he were ashamed. "Yes, ma'am. I'm a medical orderly."

"Well," Harriet continued, "can you tell me where I can find some blankets? There are men in this tent who need them."

The boy looked behind her to see which tent she was talking about before answering her. "They have their blankets already, miss. I know, I checked already."

"But they're lying on them. Besides, in this cold and in the condition they are in, they need more than one."

The boy looked up at her. "They can have only one, miss. Surgeon's orders. If they need more, they're to use their own or their overcoat."

"But the men in that tent," she countered, "have neither."

Shrugging, the boy shook his head. "Sorry, miss. But the surgeon said—"

"Where is this surgeon?" she demanded, her eyes now flashing with the anger she felt.

Backing away a step, the boy pointed to the same tent she had been shown before. Without another word, Harriet pivoted on her heel and marched over to the tent, making her way through a group of men waiting outside.

As she had before, Harriet pushed the tent flaps aside, ducked her head down, and went straight in without hesitation. This time she was greeted with a string of gruff obscenities. "What in the blue blazes do you think you're doing in here, woman?"

Determined to make her point, Harriet stood upright and was about to blast whoever was before her for the abuse they were subjecting the poor wounded to, when her eyes lit upon a scene that beggared description. Standing about a table that stood in the middle of the tent was a cluster of men. One, an older gentleman with the sleeves of his white linen shirt rolled up and a blood-splattered apron hanging about his neck, was glaring at Harriet. Across from him and to one side were two soldiers wearing the green slashes of cloth on their sleeves that Harriet had seen before. Both of them had their gazes fixed on the man on the table, whom they were holding firmly in place. A third soldier, directly across from the surgeon, glanced back and forth from the exposed leg of the man on the table and up at the surgeon, with a worried look on his face.

Looking down despite her better judgment, Harriet saw that the third man's sleeves were rolled up above his elbows, exposing forearms covered with fresh red blood. His bare hands, grasping the patient's leg, were spreading the severed muscles of the patient's thigh apart while the surgeon held a saw on the exposed leg bone. Blood, in tiny rivulets, trickled away from the severed muscles, across the table, and dripped down onto the floor and on the surgeon's boots.

"Damn it to hell!" the surgeon shouted. "Someone get that woman out of my operating room."

Gasping for breath, Harriet reached out and took hold of the tent pole at the entrance to steady herself.

"Good God in heaven! Get her to hell out of here before she passes out."

Shaking her head, Harriet fought back her revulsion. Looking up, careful to keep the sight of the wounded man out of her field of vision, Harriet started to speak but couldn't manage a word with her first attempt.

"Damn it, Brown," the surgeon yelled at one of the men holding the wounded soldier's arms down, "go over there and get her the hell out of here."

Recovered enough to try speaking again, Harriet coughed

once and rattled off her words as fast as she could lest she be thrown out before she had achieved what she had come to accomplish. "Doctor, you have patients lying about in unheated tents, freezing to death. They need more than one blanket if they're to survive."

"Don't you think we'd have issued them more if we had them? There's a battle going on, you little fool. Before this day's done, there will be more men to come across this table than I care to think about. And every one of them, *dear* lady, needs a blanket."

"What about stoves? Haven't you any small stoves for the tents? My boyfriend told me the Army had such things."

The surgeon let out a mean and cynical laugh. "Yes, dear girl, we have them. We have warehouses full of them—in Washington."

"Then why don't you use them?" Harriet shouted, regaining the anger that had driven her into this tent.

"Because some fool quartermaster officer left every one of them in those damned warehouses, just like they forgot to bring the bloody pontoon bridges forward until it was too late." A groan rose up from the man on the table, followed by a shudder that shook his entire body. "Damn it! He's coming out of it," the surgeon shouted to the man holding the leg muscles. Then looking back at Harriet, he growled at her. "I've done everything I can do for those poor devils. I have to get on with taking this man's leg or I'll lose him. Now shut up and get out or I'll have the provost guard shoot you." With that, he looked down at the leg he had been working on, steadied the saw, and gave it a good push.

The sound of the saw's teeth raking across bone sent a wave of nausea up from Harriet's stomach. Clapping her hand to her mouth, she turned and fled the tent, pushing her way through the crowd of laughing men who had gathered about outside to watch and listen.

For several minutes she staggered about on the narrow street between the tents before she ran into the boy soldier she had grabbed before. Reaching out, he took her arm and helped steady her. "Miss, you gonna be all right?"

Resting her hand on his shoulder, Harriet took several deep breaths before responding. "Yes, thank you, I'll be fine."

"Is there something I can do to help you?" the boy offered.

Seeing the concern on his face caused her to smile. Then, remembering the promise she had made to the youth in the tent, she nodded. "As a matter of fact, young man, there is. If that surgeon and the Army can't do anything to help its own soldiers, than I have to. *I* have blankets in one of the wagons. That poor boy may not be from New Jersey, but need knows no boundary. Come, my little friend, and let's see what the two of us can do to make things a little better for the wounded here."

Though the boy had no idea what Harriet was talking about, he gladly followed her. The idea of working with a woman as pretty as she was suddenly had great appeal to him. Together the two spent the next few hours digging through the wagons, ripping apart bundles that had been so carefully wrapped back in New Brunswick, in search of anything that would provide warmth and comfort to the wounded.

"Give way," Will McPherson yelled at his company above the growing din of shouts and musketry. "Open your ranks and make way for Walker's boys." Some of the 4th Virginia grumbled at having to let James A. Walker's brigade of Virginians pass through their ranks enroute to meet the growing Yankee threat at the foot of the hill overlooking the Fredericksburg–Richmond Road rather than going themselves.

"Will," Marty Hazard yelled after a big corporal from one of the passing units bumped him and almost knocked him to the ground, "you just gonna leave us standing here like bumps on a log and let them go up there and do our fightin' for us?"

James, watching the color guard of the 52nd Virginia pass through the ranks of the 4th, shook his head. "Let 'em go, Marty. Let 'em go. We'll be up there in the thick of it soon enough." Then, as an afterthought, James added, "We always are, aren't we?"

True to James' prediction, orders to advance rippled rapidly down the line of regiments. Moving as best they could down the heavily wooded hillside, they came across stragglers headed away from the fight. After catching a glimpse of the palmetto emblem on the buttons and belt buckles of some of the South

Carolinians making their way back to the rear, a few of the veterans around James began to jeer at them while others tried to encourage them to stand and fight with the 4th. "Hey boys," Marty yelled to a group of three South Carolinians as they went by, "you goin' back to Charleston to see ya mama for Christmas?"

A big South Carolinian sergeant, his lips blackened by the black powder of cartridges he had bitten open during the fight he was now leaving, took offense at Marty's comment. Walking up to Marty, he puffed out his chest and sneered at him. "Maxcy Greggs' brigade doesn't run."

Taking up the challenge, Marty straightened himself up and stood as tall as he could, returning the South Carolinian sergeant's stare. "Well," Marty snapped, "looks to me as if you boys are learnin' how to run pretty fast."

Angry, the South Carolinian sergeant shoved his face forward until it was inches away from Marty's. "Those damned Tarheels in front of us gave way and let the Yankees through. We were back in support one minute, then taking fire in the flank the next. Most of my boys didn't even have time to get their rifles from the stacks before they were on us."

Marty looked down at the big sergeant's hands. "Well, I guess it would be a shame to mess up those pretty little hands of yours with a little fistfightin', now wouldn't it?"

The South Carolinian sergeant was about to punch Marty when Will came up and shoved his way between the two sergeants. "Enough!" he yelled as he pushed the two men apart. "We have enough to do beating back the Yanks that have broken through without you two pounding away on each other." Turning to face the South Carolinian sergeant, Will growled at him. "Get back to your company, sergeant."

Still not mollified, the South Carolinian glared at Will. "Half my men are back down there, dead or wounded."

"Then I suggest you find the other half and re-form them," Will shouted back. "Now get out of my company."

Reluctantly, and with several backward glances at Marty, the South Carolinian sergeant walked away. Will, still angry, turned to James, who had been watching this whole affair. "Why in the hell," Will sputtered, "didn't you try to stop them, Jimmy?"

Miffed at Will's unwarranted tirade against him, James shrugged. "I thought Marty was doing just fine on his own. Besides, it's not smart for a private to interfere with a personal fight between two sergeants."

A shell, exploding in the tree branches overhead, caused both Will and James to duck down. After the shower of splinters and branch fragments finished raining down, Will stood up and gave James a dirty look. "Jimmy," he said quietly, "we need to talk later." Then, stepping back on the edge of the military road, Will drew his sword and started to shout out orders. "Company, dress on the center."

Surprised by this command, James looked over to Marty. "What in tarnation," Marty Hazard yelled above the growing noise of shelling and rifle fire, "are we doing?"

"The general is dressing up his lines," Will shot back. "Now hurry up and get your alignment so we can get on with this and off this bloody damned road."

Bringing his rifle up to shoulder arms, Marty looked down the line, mumbling to James above the crash of shot and shell, "Where in the blazes does that man think he is, West Point or something?"

James, concerned about the exposed position they were in and General Paxton's foolish insistence on parade-ground drill in the heat of battle, said nothing as he closed down to the man on his right in an effort to close a gap created by the wounding of two men farther down the line.

They were still in the throes of sorting themselves out on the military road when a spattering of musket fire from the right flank of the brigade brought on a new flurry of orders. Major William Terry, assuming command of the 4th Virginia after Lieutenant Colonel Gardner went down with head and chest wounds, shouted for the regiment to make a right face and move back up hill at the double. "Now where we goin'?" Marty demanded as the regiment faced to the right and every second man in both the front and rear rank stepped forward in between the man to their immediate right. Moving at a pace that was just short of a run, the 4th Virginia headed uphill behind the 2nd Virginia, now deployed in a line straddling both sides of the military road and firing rapidly to their front.

"Looks like we found your fight," James shouted to Marty

as the 4th pulled beyond the right flank of the 2nd and redeployed into line of battle in two ranks. Marty had little chance to respond as Will relayed Major Terry's order to fire by company.

They were still closing and dressing the ranks when Will yelled "Ready!" Forgetting about his alignment, James brought his rifle up waist high, holding it at a forty-five degree angle above his cartridge box and pointed out to his front. He was looking down to make sure that he hadn't lost the percussion cap on the nipple of his rifle when Will yelled out the order to aim. Bringing his rifle up to his shoulder, James sighted down the barrel and, for the first time, began to look for some sign of a target out to his front.

Steadying the long barrel as best he could, he searched in vain for something to fire at out there in the tangled woods, where smoke and noise drifted out. Unable to find anything even remotely resembling a Yankee, James pointed his rifle between two trees in the distance and pulled the trigger when Will finally gave the order to fire. Not surprisingly, as they were in the process of reloading, a ragged volley of bullets came pouring out of the woods that James had just fired blindly into. Though most of the bullets flew harmlessly overhead, one of the newer replacements in the company, just two men down from James, dropped his rifle and grabbed his face before falling to his knees and toppling over facedown onto the ground. Well, James thought as he twirled his ramrod over his head and brought its wide head down smoothly into the muzzle end of his rifle, at least he knew now for sure that there was someone hostile out there. He just hoped that they were, in fact, Yankees.

"Lieutenant Bannon, Lieutenant Meyers, over here."

Captain Trevor Ward's summons caught Kevin Bannon daydreaming. It was his habit, whenever he had little to do, to step back from the terrible realities that surrounded him and mentally compose a letter to Harriet Shields that he would never send. Henry Meyers, anxious to find out what they would be doing, gave Kevin a pat on his arm as he went by on his way to where Trevor stood waiting. "Maybe we're finally moving forward," he shouted back over his shoulder. "Maybe this is the general attack we've been waiting for."

Kevin paused for a moment before following. Off to the west in the direction they had been facing all day he could see the cold winter sun hanging low over the high ground held by the Confederates. While the fighting off to their north, in the vicinity of the town of Fredericksburg itself, seemed to continue in the same sharp spasmodic manner that it had all afternoon, there seemed to be no indication that the fighting to the left by the First Corps was being pursued by either side any longer. Though he had heard nothing of the results of the First Corps's fight, it seemed to Kevin that their best chances for success were fading as quickly as the cold afternoon's light. Still, he could be wrong, he thought. He was, after all, only a lieutenant. With that, he shook his head and trotted on down to join Meyers and Ward.

"The regiment," Trevor announced without ceremony as soon as Kevin joined him and Meyers, "is to go forward. We'll be moving past the left of the 15th New Jersey, over there on the right in that ravine, to secure a stronghold along the railroad at the foot of those hills over there. The rest of the brigade, as well as two more regiments from Russell's brigade, will be in support."

Kevin listened for a moment, waiting for more. When Trevor said nothing else, he wondered if he had missed something. To be sure, he asked what they were expected to do after reaching the railroad. Trevor, looking at Kevin as if he were a fool, responded gruffly, "Why, Lieutenant, we hold. We deploy into a skirmish line and hold."

"That's all we're going forward for?" Kevin stated in astonishment.

"What more do you want? The battle is to be decided over on the right, by Hooker's and Sumner's grand divisions, not us. Though ours is only a supporting attack, it's an important enough task."

Repressing the smirk he felt, Kevin wanted to add, you mean safe enough, but didn't. That Trevor Ward managed to escape censure for his obvious cowardliness in the face of the enemy destroyed all confidence Kevin had in the judgment of the senior officers in this Army. *"It is no wonder,"* he had written in one of the letters he never bothered to send but still faithfully wrote, *"that this fine Army loses as often as it does. We are commanded by idiots who can't tell the difference between skilled leaders and fools."*

With nothing more to say, Kevin returned to his post to await the order to advance. When it came, the regiment, to a man, stepped out in fine order and, despite grueling fire coming from the direction of the railroad that they were advancing on, every man kept his alignment and pace. Even Trevor Ward stayed with the company, although he lagged well behind the line of other company commanders advancing out in front of their companies.

For Kevin, Trevor's tenacity in staying with the company during this advance provided a new and novel experience. In past fights he had always been forward or over to the right of the company, serving as its commander. Today, however, he walked behind it with the file closers. Intrigued, Kevin watched the ranks in front of him as they continued to move forward, taking his eyes away only long enough to determine if a man knocked out of those ranks was indeed wounded or just shirking. Since there were none of the latter, Kevin found little to do but look forward, trying vainly to mark the progress of their advance.

The only warning he had that they were closing on the railroad was an unexpected slackening of enemy rifle fire followed by a sudden shout from the ranks as the pace suddenly quickened. "They're running," an officer in another company to Kevin's right shouted, "After them!" Though Ward gave no such order, the men of Company J also picked up their pace to keep up with their neighboring company. Feeling his blood rising to a fighting pitch for the first time that day, Kevin sheathed the worthless sword that he had been ordered to carry and drew his pistol in preparation for close combat.

There was, however, no need of it when the regiment finally gained the shelter of the railroad. In their enthusiasm the regiment swept over the rail bed itself, revealing to Kevin a scattering of dead and wounded Confederate soldiers lining the opposite side of the tracks. Several of the enemy soldiers, with terror in their eyes, held their rifles up with the butt in the air as a sign of surrender. Colonel Hatch, the regimental commander, was as caught up in the excitement of the moment as anyone else. Climbing up onto the railroad bed, Hatch turned his back to the enemy and faced his regiment. Raising his sword high above his head, he shouted to his excited command. "Boys! Three cheers for our side!" While his men yelled in response to their colonel, Kevin turned to the sergeant next to him and ordered him to take four men from the ranks to disarm and gather up the enemy prisoners. He was holstering his pistol when Henry Meyers came running up to him.

"Good Lord, Kevin." The young officer beamed. "Wasn't that incredible? We swept them from the field like it was nobody's business."

Looking beyond their own lines, Kevin caught sight of several Rebel cannons surrounded by crewmen busily servicing their pieces and pointing them in their direction. "Lieutenant Meyers," he said without taking his eyes off of the enemy artillery, "see to the company's left. Make sure the men take up good positions behind the railroad bed and start taking those people over there under fire."

Not having noticed the enemy batteries before, Meyers looked over to where Kevin was facing. When he saw what Kevin had been looking at, his eyes grew large. "Well, yes," Meyers stuttered after a moment. "Yes, I'll see to the men on the left, right away."

After watching to see that Meyers was doing as he had been directed, Kevin moved over to the right to do likewise without bothering to consult Trevor Ward. He was busy putting the company in order when the first sign of serious trouble came into sight. First Sergeant Himmel called out to Kevin. "Here they come, Lieutenant."

Looking up from what he was doing, Kevin caught sight of a line of battle that must have numbered close to one thousand men moving to the left of the Rebel guns that the men of the 4th New Jersey were starting to take under fire. Seeing only two battle flags, both of which were North Carolinian, Kevin whistled. "Big regiments. They must be new."

Himmel nodded. "Maybe we'll be lucky and they'll stop."

Kevin shook his head in response. "Not likely. If they are new regiments, they'll be filled with all sorts of foolish notions and ideas. It's the veteran regiments that stop and keep a respectful distance when faced with a stubborn foe.'' Looking to his left and right, Kevin decided that all was in order and that the company was ready to receive the new threat as it headed its way.

Coming forward, the two North Carolina regiments moved with a precision and steadiness that rivaled the best parade-ground maneuvers Kevin had ever seen. The steady fire of his own company, now directed solely against the advancing enemy infantry, seemed to have little effect on them, just as the enemy fire had made no impression on the 4th New Jersey as it had advanced on the railroad a few scant minutes ago. At a distance of little more than one hundred yards, Kevin could see the enemy regiment on the right pick up their pace and surge forward. Seconds later, the other regiment did likewise. They were charging.

"All right, boys,'' Kevin yelled as he drew his pistol for a second time that day, ''they're coming. Pick up your fire. Pick up your fire and keep pouring it into them.''

Few of the men who heard Kevin needed to be told this, for the 4th New Jersey was now a veteran unit with three hundred men who had seen enough combat to know what was about to happen. At first the fire of the North Carolinians didn't have much effect, though they blazed away with everything they had. With his men holding their position and returning fire as fast as they could, there was little for Kevin to do. From his post, he watched the enemy as they closed on them, men dropping here and there as a result of the deadly fire from his own men. For a moment, the idea that his men, in response to his orders, were killing other human beings filled his mind. This fleeting thought was followed by the image of Mayor Anderson's daughter, the beautiful young girl he had once loved and had managed to kill.

Shaken, Kevin closed his eyes tight, shook his head, and swallowed deep. When he opened his eyes again the image of Martha Anderson was gone, but not the advancing North Carolinians. The terrible gaps being torn in their ranks by the 4th New Jersey's deadly fire did not seem to be deterring them. If anything, Kevin thought, they were coming on faster. An officer, with the flag of the right-hand regiment, was rushing far to the front, shouting encouragement to his men, who all but stumbled over each other to follow him.

"Keep up your fire," Kevin yelled in an effort to make himself heard over the growing crescendo of battle. "Pour it into them, boys. POUR IT IN!"

Still the enemy came on. Kevin watched with growing apprehension as the officer carrying the regimental colors of his unit reached the railroad bed a few scant yards away and climbed up onto it, just as Colonel Hatch had done when the 4th had reached it. Without pause, without any sign of wavering, the Confederate officer's men came up behind him and surrounded their leader and battle flag, forcing the 4th back and away from the railroad. After dropping back but thirty yards, the men of the 4th New Jersey dug in their heels around their colonel and began to trade round for round with the determined North Carolinians. To their right, several companies of the 15th New Jersey had moved up and were joining the 4th in this desperate struggle. Behind them, only one regiment, the green 23rd New Jersey, could be seen coming up fast to support them. Kevin, moving back and forth behind his line of men, kept one eye on his colonel and one to the rear in a desperate search for more reinforcements.

Seeing no help on its way, Kevin again looked to Colonel Hatch, just in time to see him go down. Torn between going over to see if his commander's wound was mortal and staying with his unit, Kevin was caught by surprise when several men not far from where Hatch had fallen turned and bolted for the rear. Recoiling, Kevin mumbled a silent curse, for he knew what was coming. Turning his full attention back to his own command, he called for Meyers and Himmel.

Only Himmel responded. When a quick glance to the right confirmed that the regiment was falling apart, Kevin shouted back to Himmel. "First Sergeant, keep your post on the right and start bringing the line back. The regiment's starting to give."

Kevin had no sooner said this when some of his men, either seeing others farther down the line break and run or sensing that it was time to leave, backed away from the firing line. With his pistol held high in his right hand, Kevin moved to where he saw these men and pushed them back into line with his free hand. "Back in ranks, men, back into the ranks and keep up the fire!"

Here and there he succeeded in stemming the turning tide, but only for a moment. Sensing that victory was theirs for the taking, the North Carolinians, joined by their sister regiment that the 4th had thrown off of the railroad before, came over the railroad bed and forward with a rush. When he saw that, Kevin abandoned his effort to hold his men any longer. Instead, he stood perfectly still as his command dissolved all about him, lowering his pistol and taking careful aim at the onrushing Confederate line.

"I will tell you, miss, the whole lot of them should be marched to Washington and flogged. Flogged I say."

Harriet, working as quickly as she could in one of the hospital tents she had claimed responsibility for, did her best to make the staff captain comfortable despite his agitated and angry pronouncements. "That fool Burnside spent all afternoon throwing Hooker and Sumner into attack after futile attack against a damned stone wall in front of Fredericksburg while ignoring Meade's breakthrough on the left. Little Mac would never have done that, I tell you. I know, I worked for him before Lincoln put that buffoon Burnside in command. Now . . ."

Hearing other patients that she had just managed to quiet begin stirring, Harriet placed a finger on the captain's lips. "Please, I know you're angry and I appreciate you telling me this," she said quietly and as sincerely as she could, "but you must be quiet. Your thrashing about will only make your wound hurt more."

Being reminded of his injury caused the captain to slump back down into his bed of straw. "Oh, dear lady," he moaned, "would it were a true wound. Instead of being smitten with a noble wound like those other lucky fellows over there, I have suffered a broken leg after being thrown from my own horse, dear girl. My own horse."

As he lamented his fate, Harriet finished tucking the blanket in around the captain. How he, or anyone else, could consider a wound noble was beyond her. Suffering, regardless of the cause, was a terrible thing that should be mourned, not celebrated. Oh well, she thought as she reached into a pan of water for her wash rag. There was much about this Army that she didn't understand, and perhaps telling the difference between an honorable wound and one that wasn't was one of those things.

With the captain quiet now, she busied herself with cleaning his face. Like most everything else she was using, her thin white wash rag had been meant for something else or for other people. The wash rag had been part of her hoopskirt a scant few hours before. That article of clothing, however, had quickly been discarded when it became obvious that maintaining proper attire and working in a busy field hospital were incompatible. Off had come the hoop, as well as her feathered bonnet and heavy wool cape. Albert Merrel, the young boy she had gotten to help her and who stayed next to her all day, had found a private's frock coat for her to wear in place of the cape. Though it bagged on her and she had to roll up the sleeves, it was far more practical than her richly lined cape.

Finished with the captain's face, Harriet was about to clean his hands when Albert stuck his head into the tent. "There you are, miss. I've been looking all about for you."

Harriet turned to face Albert and spoke with a soft, patient tone that sounded like a teacher's. "Yes, Albert, what is it?"

"You told me that your boyfriend was in J Company, 4th New Jersey, didn't you?"

Harriet nodded her head, not knowing why he was asking at a time like this. Still, she responded with the same gentle voice she had been using to calm wounded and frightened young men all day. "Yes, Albert, he is."

"Well, Miss Shields, I just thought you'd like to know, ma'am, there's a lieutenant from that company that's just been brought in."

In a flash, all composure vanished. Jumping to her feet, Harriet dropped the wash rag and rushed for the tent entrance, barely taking the time to watch where she stepped. "Where is he, Albert?"

"They're taking him straight to surgery, Miss Shields. Shot up real bad, they say."

Though she knew that Albert wasn't saying what he was to be mean or cruel, for Albert didn't seem to have a mean bone in his body, his words slashed at Harriet nonetheless.

Pushing her way out of the tent, she didn't even pause long enough to let her eyes grow used to the darkness of the early winter evening. Turning sharply, she made for the surgical tent, a route that she was now quite familiar with. Lying in a rough line were men on stretchers, waiting their turn. "Kevin," she shouted as she looked about desperately in the darkness. "Kevin Bannon, where are you?"

When there was no response, Harriet chided herself for her foolishness. He's wounded, she thought, and can't respond. With that idea, she grabbed the medical orderly posted near the entrance of the surgical tent who was keeping track of patients waiting to go in. "They just brought in a lieutenant from Company J, 4th New Jersey. Where did they put him?"

The sergeant, having seen Harriet all day but in no mood for pleasantries, simply pointed over at a nearby stretcher. "Over there," he grunted and then went back to the task at hand.

Without bothering to thank the sergeant, Harriet turned and rushed over to the stretcher he had pointed at, dropping to her knees beside it. In the darkness, she couldn't quite make out the features, at first. Scooping up the wounded man's hand she placed it next to her cheek. "Kevin, can you hear me?"

A spasm, a cough, then a gurgling sound rose up from the stretcher. Then, to Harriet's relief, a voice she didn't recognize. "Meyers. Hen . . . ry Meyers."

Harriet pulled back but held the man's hand. "Are you . . . do you belong to Company J, 4th New Jersey?"

With a slight movement that was barely evident in the darkness, Meyers nodded his head. "Comp . . . any second lieu . . . ten . . . ant, ma'am."

"Kevin Bannon? Is he all right? Have you seen him?"

Meyers shook his head. "Last time . . . he was with the comp . . . any, fight . . . ing."

"Then he's all right?" Harriet asked, great apprehension in her voice.

"Don't . . . know. Reg . . . iment routed, again. Every . . . one scat . . . tered. Can't say what hap . . . pened." Then, sensing her disappointment, he added, "Sorry."

Realizing how selfish she had been while this man had been lying here in pain, Harriet forced herself to forget about Kevin for the moment. "Where are you hit, Lieutenant Meyers?"

"Hen . . . ry, please. Leg. Right leg."

Though she could do nothing, Harriet glanced down at the leg, then back at Meyers' face. "I'm sure it will be all right. The surgeon here is good, they say."

In the faint light, she saw Meyers smile. Squeezing her hand he nodded. "With you here, I know it will be all . . . right."

From behind them, the sergeant who had been at the surgical tent entrance barked. "He's next. Step aside, miss, this man is going in now."

When she went to stand, Meyers refused to let her hand go. "Please, stay with me?"

Remembering the sight of the amputation she had barged in on, Harriet swallowed deeply to fight back the surge of nausea she felt rising. "I can't, Henry."

Squeezing her hand tighter, Meyers pleaded. "I'm no coward, miss. But . . ."

"We have to get him in there now, lady," the sergeant insisted.

Again Harriet tried to back away and again Meyers tightened his grip. "Please."

The sergeant, frustrated, faced Harriet. "Either let go or go in with him."

Despite her better judgment, Harriet didn't let go. Following the stretcher bearers, she entered the surgical tent.

"Dear God in heaven," the surgeon barked. "You back again, woman?"

Avoiding as best she could the bloody mess that lay about the floor and table, Harriet looked into the surgeon's eyes. "I know this man. He wants me . . . has asked if I would stay with him."

"Girl," the surgeon snorted, "this isn't your mother's front parlor. You want to hold hands, do it elsewhere."

Angry at the surgeon's harsh remarks, Harriet straightened her back. "I have no intention of leaving until you have finished working on this young man. I gave him my word."

In no mood to argue and seeing a way of ridding himself of this bothersome woman once and for all, the surgeon smiled.

"Fine, have it your way." Then, with a gruff bark, he shouted to the sergeant. "Get on with it, man. Get him on the table."

With much bumping and clumsiness, the stretcher with Henry Meyers was placed on the table. Harriet, turning her back to the surgeon, forced the best smile she could manage and looked down into Henry's eyes. "This won't take long."

After arranging themselves about the table, the surgeon and his assistants went about examining Meyers' wound, ignoring Harriet. "It'll have to come off," the surgeon announced without any hint of emotion. Henry, hearing this, squeezed Harriet's hand.

Taking her free hand, Harriet ran her fingers over his forehead and through his hair, trying hard to suppress her own tears while comforting Henry. "It will be all right," she whispered. "Please, relax and don't worry. I'll be here."

There was a smile on Henry's face when the medical assistant placed the dirty white cloth over Henry's nose and mouth and began to pour the chloroform onto it. Harriet, holding her hand still on his head, looked into his eyes, still sporting her forced smile until she was sure he had passed into unconsciousness. When Henry's breathing became noisy, the surgeon announced it was time to get on with the amputation and started in.

Making his way among the tents, Kevin felt more exhausted than he had ever imagined was possible. Though their advance to the railroad and the fight there hadn't taken much time, and their losses hadn't been as bad as he had first feared, the humiliation of being routed as they had again was too overpowering to bear. The wounding of Henry Meyers, a fellow he was just starting to like, only added to his misery and exhaustion.

Catching sight of a small boy coming out of a tent, Kevin took him by the arm. "Lad, I'm looking for a wounded lieutenant, his name's Meyers."

To Kevin's surprise, the boy smiled. "Oh, why he's over here, in this tent." Taking the lead, he showed Kevin into the tent and pointed out where Meyers was lying, bundled up in a gray Army blanket. Pushing past the boy, Kevin made his way into the tent, easing his way past a woman who was kneeling over a man across from Meyers. Coming down on one knee, Kevin looked down at the stricken officer. In the dim light provided by the lone lantern hanging in the center of the tent, Kevin studied Meyers' face. Though it was drained of any trace of color, it was clean and he looked to be resting comfortably. Looking down at the blanket, Kevin was tempted to pull it away to see where Meyers had been injured, but didn't. Besides, the shape of the tightly wrapped blanket did away with the need to do so. The absence of most of Meyers' right leg was painfully obvious after Kevin took the time to look.

Standing up, Kevin looked down at Meyers one more time before backing away toward the entrance. In his grief, he had forgotten about the woman behind him, as she had forgotten about him. Standing up just as Kevin stepped back, she bumped into him, causing her to fall forward. Only quick thinking kept the woman from falling on the wounded man she had just been tending to.

Realizing what he had done, Kevin spun around in the narrow space that separated the two rows of patients and reached down to help the woman up. Stuttering, he began to apologize. "I'm sorry, miss. I . . ."

When Harriet turned around and faced the man who spoke with a voice that was so familiar to her ears, she all but broke into tears. Without a word, with no need to explain, Harriet bounded up and wrapped her arms about Kevin's waist, while he gathered her up in his. For the longest time they stood there holding on to each other. And it was there, surrounded by the grief and the wreckage of war, that each of them pledged silently to themselves that they would never, ever, again let go of the other.

"Jimmy boy, wake up."

Marty Hazard's hushed voice and shaking surprised James Bannon. Curled up in his blanket and huddled behind a log, not far from where they had fought to hold the hill overlooking the Fredericksburg–Richmond Road, James had fallen asleep.

"Come on, Jimmy, wake up."

Opening his eyes, James was blinded for a moment by the light of a lantern Marty held close to his face. "What's up? We got picket duty, or what?" James protested.

"Just hush up and come along."

Reluctantly, James pushed his thin blanket away, losing what little heat he had managed to trap in it. A spasm of shivers racked his body as he gathered up his blanket and rifle. "I shouldn't be due for guard, Marty. Not yet."

"You ain't goin' on guard. Now hush and come on with me and Adam."

At the mention of Adam Page's name, James looked about and saw the short, dark-haired private standing behind Marty in the shadows. James gave Adam a slight nod before following Marty into the woods, back along the route they had taken after their fight with a Pennsylvania unit. "We going back to look for wounded?" James queried. "I thought they'd all been gathered up."

Now that they were away from the rest of the company, Marty spoke louder, but only slightly. "Ain't lookin' for no wounded. We're after overcoats and blankets."

James recoiled slightly and stopped. "From the Yankee dead? We're going to go and strip the dead?"

Marty stopped and turned to face James. "Can't say that I like it any better than you, but Lordy, it's cold and those overcoats and blankets ain't doin' those dead Yanks any good. And besides," he added before turning back to face the front, "if we don't get them tonight, someone less deserving will get 'em tomorrow."

Though the idea of rummaging about amongst the dead didn't appeal to James, he knew Marty was right. Besides, they had all done it before, though mostly in search of food, which the Federal troops always seemed to have plenty of.

Reaching the site of their fight, Marty stood back and held the lantern high while Adam and James rummaged through the woods. When one of them came across the body of a Yankee, he would make a quick inspection of the upper torso to see if the overcoat had been ripped or was too stained by the wearer's blood to be of use. When they found a coat that was in good shape, James and Adam would work together to strip the accoutrements off the stiff body, then remove the coat, being as careful as they could not to let it touch any open wounds. Not that this was much of a problem, for the blood and bodily fluids of the dead were as frozen as their corpses. As Marty pointed out as they went about this grisly work, "fightin' in the winter sure does have its advantages. No flies and a lot less stink." James, unhappy that circumstances required him to handle dead men like this, took small comfort in Marty's observations.

The three had been working for some time when James, finding a man lying facedown, turned him over. When the man groaned unexpectedly, James jumped back.

"What's the matter?" Marty shouted as he caught sight of James' sudden movement and started to shed the piles of coats slung over both shoulders to get at his rifle. "Trouble?"

"No," James replied. "This one's still alive."

"Well," Marty responded with a sigh of relief, "leave him. We got all the coats we can carry."

James started to back away when the Yankee's eyes opened and he muttered, "Mama?"

Pausing, James looked down into the Yankee's face. In the faint light of Marty's lantern, the boy bore a striking resemblance to his brother Kevin, a resemblance that caused James to shiver. Everything about him reminded James of his younger brother. Even the Yankee's eyes, frozen wide open and betraying a lost, forlorn look, reminded James of the expression Kevin often wore whenever he needed James' help and comfort.

"Mama," the boy pleaded again, "is that you?"

Without thinking, James bent over, and whispered back. "No, boy, I'm not your mama."

The boy, however, didn't hear James. "Oh, Mama, I'm hurt. Hurt bad."

James looked down at the boy's torso and saw the coat covered with dark stains. Though he could not see the holes, James had seen enough of war to know that the boy had been gut shot. Dropping down on the ground next to the boy, James reached up and pulled the Yankee's hat back. "Yes," James whispered. "You've been shot, boy. But it'll be all right."

"No, Mama," he protested, shaking his head slowly. "I'm done for, Mama. I know I'm done for. I can feel it."

Though the boy was his enemy, and James knew he could

very well have been the one who shot him, James was suddenly swept by an overwhelming sense of grief and loss. Whether it was the mournful thoughts of his brother that the Yankee's likeness had evoked or a sudden release of emotions and tensions that he had managed to hold back until then, James began to break down. As tears started to well up in his eyes, he reached out and softly brushed the boy's cheek with the back of his rough hand. "Don't you worry, boy," James said in a voice choked with emotion. "Everything will be over soon."

A slight upturning of the corners of his mouth and a momentary passing of his pained expression was as close to a smile as the boy could manage. "I know that, Mama. But now that you're here with me, I'm ready to meet the Lord. I wrote you a letter here, tellin' you how much I love you and Pa and asking that you'll pray for me."

The growing brightness of the light from behind told James that Marty was approaching. "What in tarnation are you doing over here, Jimmy?"

"This Yank's dying." James responded without looking behind him. "He thinks I'm his mother."

"Well, tell 'em he's sadly mistaken and let's go. It's too blasted cold to be foolin' round out here with wounded Yanks."

"You and Adam go back if you must. If you don't mind, I'm going to sit here with the boy for a while."

A year ago Marty Hazard would have berated James for such foolishness. But he, and everyone else who had been with the 4th Virginia throughout the brutal course of 1862, had seen much suffering. He himself had spent an entire night holding and rocking the body of his own dead brother before he finally was able to accept the terrible truth. Though Marty had no idea why this particular Yank had affected James as he had, he said nothing about it.

After a moment or two, James looked back at Marty and Adam. "You two go back. I'll be all right here."

Handing the lantern to Adam, Marty took a Union overcoat from his shoulder and carefully draped it over James' shoulders. Then, without another word, he turned to Adam. "Let's be gettin' back."

Alone and in the dark, James sat with the wounded Yankee, responding to his pleas and cries with soothing words and an occasional gentle touch on the boy's cold cheek. In the darkness, images of a home that was no longer his merged with those of a brother whom he still loved dearly. Slowly, as he sat with the boy who looked so much like that brother, James began to realize how alone he was. Like the boy at his side, circumstances had cast him adrift from those who knew and cared for him. Even his father, James finally realized, must have loved him, once, in his own, twisted way. That it took a war and such terrible suffering for him to see that bothered James, just as it bothered him that he, like this Yankee boy, could do nothing now but ignore the pain and cling to life, no matter how tenuous or cruel it was.

When dawn finally ended that terrible night, and the thick fog that encased the forest like a shroud began to lighten, James saw that the boy was gone. Sometime during the long night, while James had been wrestling with his own troubled thoughts, the boy had slipped away quietly and found a peace that had been denied him during his last hours on earth. Though cold and spent himself, James gathered the boy's body in his arms and carried him to an unspoiled patch of woods. There, after removing the unmailed letter the boy had spoken of, James dug out a shallow grave in the frozen ground with his bayonet, laid the boy in it, and covered him over.

# CHAPTER 23

# April, 1863
# Winchester, Virginia

PUSHING HER WAY PAST THE GUARDS AT THE DOOR, MARY Beth McPherson made her way into the home that served as headquarters for the Union military commander of Winchester. Bursting into the large downstairs hall, she was greeted by the sergeant of the guard. "Hold it right there, girlie," he warned Mary Beth, his hands held up to block her advance. "Just you hold it right there."

Determined to force her way past the sergeant as she had past the two guards, now stumbling through the door to catch up with her, Mary Beth lowered her head and rushed forward in an effort to duck under one of the sergeant's outstretched arms. And while Mary Beth was quick, her actions literally played into the sergeant's hands. When she was nearly past him, the sergeant dropped the arm Mary Beth was passing under and wrapped it about her waist, sweeping her off her feet. Caught off balance, the sergeant went tumbling down onto the well-polished floor with a thud, while Mary Beth screeched, "Let go of me, you brute," for all she was worth.

The commotion brought everyone in the building scurrying out of the rooms they used as offices. Even the hated commander of Winchester, Major General Robert Milroy, was preparing to leave his desk to see who was disrupting the early-morning tranquillity of his headquarters when his adjutant, recognizing the female voice wailing in the hall, jumped to his feet and rushed for the door. "You don't need to concern yourself with this matter, sir. I'll deal with it."

Milroy snorted. "See to it, Major Sutton, immediately."

That proved to be easier said than done. Sutton left his desk and walked out into the hall. The crisis that had disrupted Milroy's headquarters was now little more than a comic wrestling match as the burly sergeant of the guard fought to gain control of the squirming mass of skirts and woman he held onto, and Mary Beth struggled to free herself. "Don't just stand there, you two jackasses," the sergeant yelled to the soldiers Mary Beth had so easily pushed aside. "Get hold of this . . . this . . ."

Both soldiers, however, were laughing too hard at their sergeant to be of any use. "We'd like to, Sergeant Kennedy, but there's not enough girl there for all of us to grab hold of," the shorter of the two soldiers replied to the amusement of all the Union soldiers now gathered about and watching. Even James Sutton, standing on the third step from the bottom of the stairs, found it hard to suppress a smile. Holding back for a moment, Sutton straightened his coat, forced a frown, and cleared his throat loudly. "Sergeant Kennedy, let that woman go."

Sutton's sudden sharp order brought the wrestling match between the sergeant of the guard and Mary Beth to an end and scattered the ring of spectators that had gathered in the hall. Scrambling to his feet, the sergeant of the guard took a step back away from Mary Beth, leaving her sitting on the floor to straighten out the tangle of skirts and crinolines that exposed practically everything that shouldn't have been. Decorum, however, was the furthest thing from Mary Beth's mind at the moment. As soon as she managed to cover most of her legs, she was up on her feet and flying at Major Sutton. Only a quick bob to the left saved him from being struck by a wild swing of Mary Beth's right hand. "You bastards," she screeched as she turned to have another go at Major Sutton. "What have you done with my father?"

Reaching up with his own right hand as she again raised hers to strike at him, Sutton grabbed her by the wrist and squeezed for all he was worth. With his brows furrowed in anger, and in a voice that was more of a hiss, Sutton warned her. "Miss, you either control yourself or you'll join your father."

It was more the shock of being treated like this by James Sutton than the pain he was causing her right wrist that caused Mary Beth to back off. She had never seen him angry, never heard him raise his voice. Whenever he rode by to visit the McPhersons, usually at night, he had always been charming and sweet, especially to Mary Beth. That he was interested in Mary Beth could not be denied. That she also appeared to be interested in him was evidenced by the fact that since the reoccupation of Winchester by Union forces shortly after the Battle of Fredericksburg, in December, Mary Beth had not asked him to pass a single letter through the lines to James Bannon.

Seeing that Mary Beth had been mollified by his action and threat, Sutton let her hand go. "Now, miss," he said in a loud and impersonal tone, in an effort to keep up the fiction that they weren't even acquainted, "if you would be so kind as to follow me, I will be *glad* to hear you out, in private." Though none of the members of Milroy's staff or his headquarters guards understood why the major hadn't just slapped the secessionist woman in irons, no one was interested in finding out. It simply wasn't worth their time or the trouble to deal with a troublesome woman like her. "That's," one of the two soldiers who had been on guard dryly remarked to his companion on the way out the door, "what we've got officers for. It's best we let them get their eyes scratched out by the likes of her."

Even after they were in Sutton's office and the door was closed and locked, neither Mary Beth nor Sutton could bring themselves to break the icy silence of the room. Instead, she stood before his desk with her arms held across her chest, her chin stuck out, and her eyes glaring at him while he moved from the door to his chair. Seeing that she was going to be obstinate, which under the circumstances was understandable, Sutton dropped down into his seat and leaned back to study Mary Beth for a moment. During the Union's first occupation of Winchester, when they had first met, Sutton had harbored no doubt that Mary Beth strung him along simply to use him and his position to pass letters through the lines to her boyfriend serving with the Army of Northern Virginia. Now, he wasn't sure how Mary Beth felt about him. After his return, and despite his association with Milroy, a man whose administration engendered hatred in the people of Winchester, the McPhersons had encouraged Sutton to visit them often, and Mary Beth no longer asked him to serve as an intermediary for her letters. Though he kept telling himself that there simply was no way that there could ever be anything serious between them, the idea that someday Mary Beth could see past his uniform and learn to love him as a man kept forcing its way into his consciousness.

Seeing that he had no intention of initiating the conversation, Mary Beth finally spoke. "You have no right to hold my father."

Sutton grunted. "Mary Beth—"

"Miss McPherson to you, *sir*."

"Mary Beth, not only did the captain of cavalry have every right to arrest your father, he had no choice. Your father struck one of his troopers and threatened another with an ax."

"Well, they threatened to take my horse," she shot back.

Without the slightest hint of remorse, Sutton countered. "Under orders of the Federal government, those soldiers have the authority to confiscate all materials, animals, and foodstuffs required by our armies for the suppression of states in rebellion from citizens living in those states who fail to take the required loyalty oath."

Mary Beth dropped her hands to her hips and leaned forward. "James Sutton, do you really think that my father would take that accursed oath while his older son was off serving with Bobby Lee?"

Sutton narrowed his eyes. "If he had wanted the Federal authorities to safeguard his property, then he should have, regardless of what his son was doing."

Straightening up, Mary Beth threw her head back and laughed. "My brother Will was right about you Yankees. You don't know the first thing about family loyalty, do you?"

Sutton smiled. "I suppose you and your boyfriend would know more about that than I."

The mention of James Bannon's failure to return to his native state and fight for it hurt her as much as if Sutton had slapped her across the face. Recoiling, Mary Beth glared at him for a moment, then dropped her eyes to the floor. When she spoke again, she did so with a soft, almost sorrowful tone. "What will happen to my father?"

Speaking with a cold monotone, Sutton rattled off the elder McPherson's fate as a judge passing sentence would. "He is to be escorted to Confederate lines tomorrow morning and passed through them, with orders never to return, under pain of death.''

Mary Beth looked up. "Just like that? No trial, no chance to defend himself in a court of law?"

With a slight nod, Sutton responded. "Just like that." Then he added in an effort to comfort her, "Mary Beth, it's best he wasn't put up before a military court. For striking a Union soldier and threatening death to another, your father would have been hanged, no questions asked."

"And I suppose," she challenged him defiantly, "my family has you to thank for that?"

"As a matter of fact," he replied, "you do."

"Well, if you think I'm going to thank you for what you and that mongrel you call a general have done to us, you're mistaken." With that, Mary Beth turned and stormed out of Sutton's office.

As she left the building, no one paid her any more attention, other than the two guards she had shoved aside before, who gave her wide berth. She was halfway down the street when she stopped in midstride. Though she had said that she had no intention of thanking James Sutton for his role in keeping her father from the hangman's noose, she knew she owed him at least that. Turning, Mary Beth was about to head back when the door of the home housing Milroy's headquarters flew open and Sutton, bareheaded, came rushing out. When he saw Mary Beth standing in the street, looking back at him, Sutton took the steps two at a time and began to rush toward her. Then, spying two local women standing across the street watching both him and Mary Beth, Sutton slowed his pace and changed his expression. "Young lady," he growled as he neared Mary Beth, cocking his head toward the two women watching, "I want you to know that if you ever come into my headquarters again, I'll have your entire family thrown out of our lines."

By the time he had finished, he was face to face with Mary Beth. Knowing that the words were simply show to keep the two nosy women from detecting any feeling between them other than one of animosity, Mary Beth stood still and said nothing in return. Reaching out, Sutton held a folded piece of paper out at her. "This is your final, written order, miss. If you fail to comply with it, I cannot be held responsible for what happens to you and your family." Without waiting for a response, Sutton turned and walked back to the headquarters, nodding his head at the two women across the street, who responded by turning up their noses and walking away.

When everyone had gone their own way and was no longer paying any attention to her, Mary Beth turned her back and headed toward home. After going around the corner, she unfolded the paper and read Sutton's hastily scrawled note.

> I'll be by your house this evening at seven to pick up whatever clothing and personal items you can pack for your father in a small valise.
>
> J. E. Sutton.

Mary Beth smiled. Sutton knew that the McPhersons ate their evening meal at seven like clockwork. Well, she thought to herself as her smile grew, you'll not be disappointed, Major James E. Sutton. Not tonight.


In the past, the McPhersons had always endeavored to be cordial whenever Major James Sutton paid them a visit. For the father, Major Sutton provided a receptive male ear of one who was willing to debate the merits of the Southern cause as well as listen politely to his ramblings on the issues and news of the day. Daniel found it intriguing to have "an enemy soldier" in the house who was not the least bit hostile and who was willing to pay attention to him despite an occasional comment by Daniel concerning Southern military prowess and victories. At first Mary Beth saw him as nothing more than a useful means of keeping in touch with James Bannon. Only Elizabeth McPherson held back. Memories of the pillaging of her home by Union soldiers and the thought that James Sutton was part of an army that endangered her older son's life were never far from her mind, though she never spoke of it. Rather, she chose to keep her feelings to herself and perform her duties as a mother and a wife as was expected of her, even in the presence of her enemies.

Nothing would have come of Sutton's befriending of the McPherson family had he not returned as part of Milroy's staff in late December, 1862. Mary Beth was confused and disheartened by James Bannon's failure to respond to her affections, and the uncertainty of his future and his long absences did much to cool the passions that her earlier notions of romance and love had enflamed. Had she been left to herself, as so many of the other girls her age in the valley had been, Mary Beth would have clung stubbornly to her efforts to win him over. James Sutton's return, so soon after James Bannon's less than enthusiastic behavior while the 4th Virginia was camped nearby, created a dilemma that was too much for Mary Beth to deal with, for there was no doubt that Sutton's interest in her was undiminished, just as it soon became apparent that she too felt more for the blond-haired and blue-eyed New Yorker than was appropriate under the circumstances. How much she had become infatuated with Sutton became very clear when she received word that her father had been arrested and was scheduled to be passed through Confederate lines. For despite the pending loss of her father and the terrible straits that loss would place the rest of the family in, Mary Beth couldn't find it in herself to blame James Sutton.

Her mother, on the other hand, found no difficulty in doing so. "How could you have accepted his offer?" Elizabeth McPherson screeched when Mary Beth told her of Sutton's note. "I'd rather see your father ride through the lines naked than open my house again to the very man who signed the orders exiling him from his family and home."

All efforts by Mary Beth to explain that Sutton had no choice did little to mollify her mother. "It was expulsion or hanging, Mother. James saved Father's life."

"And what of us?" Elizabeth McPherson wailed. "How are we to get along without your father? What am I ever going to do? In twenty-five years of marriage, I've never spent a night alone without him, Mary Beth. He's always been here, right here, with me, tending the farm and helping me raise you children. What are we to do now that he's gone?"

Though it worried Mary Beth that her mother was speaking of her father as if he were dead and buried, Mary Beth pushed that problem aside as she tried to focus on Sutton's pending visit. "If you don't want to see or talk to James, I mean Major Sutton, Mother, then don't."

Partly out of concern for her daughter's safety and well-being, and partly out of the need to strike out at someone, Elizabeth McPherson stared Mary Beth in the eyes. "And what about James Bannon? What are you going to tell him when he finds out that you're being courted by a damned Yankee?"

Her mother's question rocked Mary Beth like a slap in the face. Though everyone in the McPherson household save Will knew of Sutton's interest, no one had said a word out loud about it. That her mother would choose to bring that issue up at this time and in the manner she did doubled the severity of the blow. Turning to walk away before she said something she would regret, Mary Beth paused only long enough to call back to her mother over her shoulder. "You needn't trouble yourself with anything tonight. I will tend to the major. All I ask is that you have Father's bag ready before seven tonight." With that, she left the room.

The meal that night was eaten in silence. Daniel, taking his father's place at the head of the table, glared at James Sutton throughout the entire meal. Mary Beth, seated across from Sutton, was as on edge as Sutton himself was. The two ate their meal with their heads bowed down and without a word passing between them. Though Elizabeth McPherson stayed in her room and made a point of not making a sound, her absence from the table weighed heavily on both Sutton and Mary Beth. Whether her mother was doing this out of spite or was truly mourning the pending exile of her husband was beyond Mary Beth. All she knew was that, for the first time, she felt very much alone and unwelcome in a place that had been, up until that day, a refuge from the troubles of the world outside.

When they were finished, Mary Beth began to tell Daniel to clear the table but wasn't allowed to finish. Looking straight at Sutton, Daniel stood up. "With Father imprisoned by the *enemy*, I'm the man of the house. I'll have no time to tend to woman's chores around here anymore."

Mary Beth, her face flushed with anger, jumped up out of her seat and leaned over the table as if she was going to slap her brother. Daniel met her advance with a hard, defiant gaze. Sutton, seeing no point in making things any worse than they already were, stood up and cleared his throat loudly. "Mary Beth," he announced loudly, "I've got to be getting back." Turning to face Daniel, he asked in a firm and forceful voice, "Daniel, would it be possible to have your father's things, now?"

Torn between continuing his demonstration of hatred for Sutton and the need to give this man the things that his father would need during his upcoming journey, Daniel hesitated. For a moment, the three of them stood there, waiting for the boy to decide. When he did, both Mary Beth and Sutton breathed a silent sigh of relief that no one would come to blows. Still, Daniel refused to be completely cowed. "I'll go and see if Mother has them ready," he announced with a sharp, unrepentant arrogance in his voice.

This angered Mary Beth, causing her to lose all restraint. Raising her hand, she leaned over to slap the back of her brother's head as he moved away. James Sutton, however, reached up and caught her hand. Looking over to him, Mary Beth gave him a questioning look. Sutton only shook his head as he released her arm. "Outside, please," he whispered.

Stepping back from the table, Mary Beth stormed out of the room and out into the cold night air without pausing to take a wrap. Sutton followed slowly, grabbing his overcoat and pistol belt off the peg rake at the door as he passed it. He was about to step out into the darkness to join Mary Beth when he paused at the threshold. Folding his overcoat over one arm, Sutton unsnapped the cover to his holster and withdrew his Army Colt .44. Setting his pistol belt down for a moment, he pulled the trigger back to the half-cocked position and gave the pistol's cylinder a quick twirl, checking to make sure all the caps were still snugly in place. Satisfied that his pistol hadn't been tampered with, he picked up his holster, slid the Colt back into it, and strapped his pistol belt about his waist. It was sad, he thought as he did so, that every passing day took the war, and everyone touched by it, further and further away from the idyllic, almost innocent bliss that had once covered the entire nation like a warm comforter. It was, he thought, as if the leaders of the Southern rebellion had eaten a forbidden fruit, and now all America was being punished. That they would never be able to turn back and live again together in blissful happiness was becoming more and more evident with each passing day. For every day Sutton saw new wrinkles of hatred creasing the faces of the people about him, both Northerners and Southerners, just as age withers the complexion of a fading beauty. With a heavy heart, James Sutton passed from the warmth of the well-lit room behind him and plunged into the cold darkness that surrounded the McPherson home.

Outside, Mary Beth stood alone in the chilly darkness. Holding her arms tightly across her chest, she stood looking vacantly out over the darkened landscape of her beloved farm while random thoughts and feelings tumbled through her head. It had been a mistake to allow James Sutton to stay for dinner. She realized that now. It had only served to encourage him when she knew, in her heart, that she had no intention of giving in to his advances. Though she was flattered by his persistence, everything, including her own foolish infatuation with a boy who had shown little interest in her, made any kind of romance between her and Sutton impossible. She hated herself for stringing him along as she had, just as she hated herself for having allowed a stranger to come between her and the members of her family. Though he had saved her father, Mary Beth began to wonder if she could pay the price that James Sutton might demand for that salvation.

She was still standing there, slowly swaying back and forth with her arms crossed, when she felt a pair of hands encircle her waist. Though Sutton's unexpected touch sent a shiver up Mary Beth's back, she did not resist. "Mary Beth," Sutton whispered in her ear, "I've been wanting to tell you, for a long time, how much I—"

Sutton's words were cut short by the sound of a packed valise being thrown down into the dirt beside them and the slamming of the front door. Lunging forward, Mary Beth broke Sutton's hold on her and spun around. Taking several paces backwards, she raised her hands when Sutton began to advance on her with his arms outstretched. "James Sutton, I'm sorry, but this just can't be."

Stopping, Sutton dropped his hands at his sides, then threw them up. "What can't be? I don't understand."

"You understand perfectly, sir. You and I. We can't . . . I can't ever love you."

Dropping his hands, Sutton went to advance again. "Mary Beth, please. You're all upset and excited by what happened today, I know. And the reactions of your mother and brother were, well, to be expected. But that doesn't change anything between you and me. The two of us can—"

"There is no two of us, James Sutton. Don't you understand? It just can't be. There's just too much between us."

"You mean that Irish boy with Jackson?"

"Yes," Mary Beth said angrily. "*That* Irish boy. For better or worse, I love that boy. I guess I always have and I hope I always will. And nothing you say or do will ever change that."

Sutton was about to ask even if it meant the life of her father but stopped short when he realized how cynical and evil such a threat was. Seeing that there was no point in pursuing the matter any longer, Sutton turned away from Mary Beth without another word. Mary Beth, he was sure, would see that he was right someday. Still, that thought did nothing to soothe the disappointment he felt as he walked over to his horse, picking the valise up from the dirt as he passed it.

Unsure how he would react to her outburst, Mary Beth stood still while Sutton mounted his horse and rode off toward town. Only after the sounds of the horse's hooves had faded into the night did she finally return to her house, where she hoped that she could undo all the pain that her actions had brought down on the family that meant everything to her.

## North of the Rappahannock, near Fredericksburg

As had become her habit, Harriet Shields walked through the camp of the First New Jersey Brigade after spending most of the morning with Dr. White at the field hospital that tended those soldiers who were not ill enough to be evacuated to a general hospital in Washington. Though he still made a show of informing Harriet that he preferred to keep women out of his hospital, Dr. Emmit C. White realized that she was a valuable addition to his staff. "The men absolutely adore her," his chief hospital steward reported to Dr. White every time he began to complain about her presence. "She's worth three men and a boy to me when it comes to cleaning and caring for the sick and injured," the burly steward told White with pride. "Though she's still a bit queasy when it comes to dealing with an open wound, there isn't a thing she can't handle."

"Though it's against my better judgment," White would counter with a growl, "she can stay, so long as she keeps out of the surgical suite. Can't afford to worry about a woman while I'm up to my elbows in a man's leg."

Even before she reached the company streets of the 4th New Jersey, Harriet was surrounded by soldiers from other regiments of the brigade, anxious to greet her and share a moment with her. Running up behind her, a corporal from the 3rd New Jersey waved a letter. "It's a boy, Miss Shields. My Dorothy gave birth to a healthy boy."

Pausing, Harriet turned to face the beaming soldier who had run up to her. Flashing a smile that was every bit as broad as his, and sincere, Harriet reached out and gave the corporal's arm a squeeze. "Franklin, that's wonderful. And how's Dorothy?"

The corporal lifted the letter and pointed to a line scrawled across the page. "She says right here that they're both doing just fine."

"Have you named the baby yet, Franklin?"

Doing all he could to keep from bouncing, the corporal shook his head. "No, that's what I wanted to ask you. My Dorothy here is asking me what we should name him, and I thought maybe you could help. Would you?"

Remembering how the corporal had once mentioned to her that he had lost his father at an early age, Harriet smiled. "I think it would be just grand if you named your first son after your father. Maybe then some of the loss you still feel over his death will be eased every time you're with your new son."

The corporal blinked as he thought about it, then smiled.

"Miss Shields, that's a wonderful idea. I . . ." Choked up by a sudden surge of emotion, the corporal lowered his head as he wiped his teary eyes.

Harriet gave the man's arm another squeeze. "I'm glad you like it, Franklin. Now how about writing your Dorothy a quick letter before the mail orderly leaves for division?"

With a smile and a nod, the corporal thanked Harriet and turned to run off and do as she had suggested. With his problem solved, Harriet went about her business, pausing to greet and talk with another dozen or so soldiers who came up to her for advice for their own problems or to relay news to her from their families. When she reached the company street for J Company, 4th New Jersey, she felt as if she was amongst family. The men, just back from morning drill, made way for her as she greeted each and every man by name with a smile and a slight nod of her head. Almost without exception, the soldiers returned her greeting and smile. The one exception was a private by the name of Miller, Kenneth Miller. Every time Harriet approached, Miller's face would droop into a frown just before he turned and all but fled in the opposite direction. Today was no exception.

Coming onto J Company's street, Harriet exchanged greetings with two men as they removed their accoutrements. Turning to continue on, she suddenly found herself face to face with Miller. Miller, also surprised, blinked twice before turning and walking away without a word. For a moment, Harriet stood there and watched Miller, trying to decide if he was being rude or just inhospitable. Everyone was comfortable with having her in camp, and even the most outspoken critic was civil to her face-to-face.

From behind her, Harriet heard a chuckle. "He's a strange one, he is."

Looking about to see who had said that, Harriet saw Johnny O'Keeth sitting on a rickety stool in his shirt sleeves, trying to sew his brand-new corporal's stripes onto the sleeve of his sack coat. "Oh," Harriet commented as she caught a last glimpse of Miller as he ducked around the corner, "he's entitled to be a little shy, I suppose."

Harriet's comment caused O'Keeth to chuckle. "Shy isn't

the word for it. Sometimes you get the idea he's afraid of his own shadow.''

Interested in finding out more about Miller, Harriet took a seat on a cracker box that was sitting next to Johnny. Watching him for a moment as he tugged at a long thread that had become hopelessly knotted behind the sleeve, Harriet reached out to take the coat. "You're making an utter mess out of that, you know."

Defensively, O'Keeth pulled the sack coat away from her. "I can manage. See." With this, he tried to pick up the sleeve that he had a stripe half sewn on, but he found that he couldn't since his stitches had not only penetrated the entire sleeve but also snagged some of the pant leg the sleeve had been sitting on. In bewilderment, O'Keeth pulled at the sleeve. When two men across the way who had been watching him in amusement broke out in laughter, Johnny got angry. "Shut up, you two miscreants. They promoted me 'cause I could fight, not for my sewing."

While Johnny glared at his detractors, Harriet reached over and took the stripe and sack coat away from him, giving the whole mess a good tug in order to break the threads attaching the coat to the trousers. "I'll do this for you, Johnny, if you don't mind."

Though he had wanted to finish the job on his own, if for no other reason than to satisfy his pride, Johnny was proud of his new rank and wanted his stripes to be sewn on right. Realizing that he couldn't have both, he handed his needle and thread over to Harriet without a fight. "Well," he said sheepishly when he was sure the other two weren't paying him any more attention, "I'd truly be obliged if you did, Miss Shields."

After cleaning up all remains of O'Keeth's feeble attempt, Harriet set about sewing the stripes with a deftness that amazed O'Keeth and drew a small crowd of admiring soldiers. Though a few were, in fact, interested in watching how she sewed, most of the dozen or so men who gathered about were only interested in being near a woman. All of the men knew that Harriet was more or less engaged to their own Lieutenant Bannon, and none harbored even the slightest thought of wooing her away from him. Yet just having someone like her to look at, to listen to, and have her smile at them while they told their stories was enough. To many of the men who had been away from their own wives, mothers, sisters, and girlfriends for better than a year and a half, Harriet was a link to a life that sometimes seemed to be as foreign and distant to them as the far side of the moon. One day, after she'd helped one of the men with a little bit of mending, the soldier took the repaired sock from her hands and held it in his own for a moment as if she had given him a piece of gold. After studying the neat job she had done, the soldier looked up at Harriet with teary eyes. "Miss Shields," he said haltingly, "just having you here and being able to talk to you every now and then makes being a soldier bearable."

It was such feelings, more often left unsaid, that led Harriet to decide that she would ignore her father's pleas and demands and stay with the regiment, despite its hardships and the constant threats of being disowned by her own family. *"If these men are so willing to risk everything for a cause,"* she wrote in the privacy of the tent the regimental commander had provided her, *"the least I can do is make their lives more bearable, and perhaps a little brighter, while I can."* So, like hundreds of other women, Harriet Shields turned her back on the conventional and easy path and allowed her heart to lead her down a path few women of her day were willing to take. *"I do not feel myself a crusader,"* she confided to her diary one night, *"for I do not have the courage that many of the other women, such as Clara Barton, Kady Brownell, or Anna Etheridge, seem to possess plenty of. Yet I know I can make a difference, in my own way, here and now. To turn my back on these men, and this cause, would be, for me, unthinkable. Whatever the consequences, I am committed."*

With her eyes glued to the sleeve and stripes before her, Harriet began to gently probe for information concerning Private Miller. "You know," she said in a most casual manner, "I've been with this regiment now since December, and I don't think I've heard Private Miller speak two words."

A tall soldier sitting crosslegged on the ground in front of Harriet chuckled. "I've been with this regiment for a year and a half and he hasn't said two words at the same time to me, so don't feel too badly, Miss Shields."

Another soldier, standing behind him with his hands in his

pockets, shrugged his shoulders. "Some people aren't made to be gabbers. I guess Kenny's just one of them."

"Well," a third soldier added, "if you ask me, I wouldn't give a hoot if Miller never said anything. He stands shoulder to shoulder with the best of them in a fight."

The tall man on the ground laughed at this remark as he turned to look at the last speaker. "You mean, he tries to stand shoulder to shoulder."

The third soldier wouldn't be denied. "For a man barely taller than his own rifle, he gives a good account of himself. If more men in this regiment were half as reliable as he is in a fight, we wouldn't have the reputation we do."

The mention of the regiment's reputation, which to date had been spotty at best, cast a pall over the gathering. Johnny O'Keeth looked around after a moment of silence. "Let's face it, lads, we're not well liked in the brigade. Except for our charge up the mountainside at Crampton's Gap, we haven't done very well."

Johnny's comment angered the soldier with his hands in his pockets. "We did good in just about every fight we've been in. Was it our fault some fool forgot to tell us the whole blamed Army had retreated during the Gaines's Mill fight?"

This was greeted with a rough chorus of murmurs and nodding heads.

"And at Second Manassas, how could anyone expect us to stand in the face of all those Rebels when the rest of the brigade was skedaddling."

"No one," the tall man on the ground responded, " 'cept those Ohio fellas."

"And I dare any man to say we didn't do as good as any last December, given the odds that were against us."

"That's right, you know," another man chimed in. "If'en they hadn't pulled back all our support, I'll bet we could have held them Rebs."

"Oh," Johnny exclaimed, throwing up his hands, "there's no doubt of that. No, boys, we've had some tough luck. It's just too bad we won't have a chance to redeem ourselves in the next fight."

Johnny's reminder that the regiment had been assigned to train guard for the Army, with three companies, including J

Company, serving as provost guard for the Sixth Corps, caused the soldier with his hands in his pockets to fume. Turning away from the crowd, he saw a clump of dirt in the middle of the company street that he kicked in anger. It wasn't until Kevin Bannon's voice boomed above the sour grumblings of the men gathered about Harriet that the man with his hands in his pockets realized he had accidentally sent the clump of dirt flying toward Kevin, who had been coming up the street while the group discussed their new orders. "Private!" Kevin shouted. "What's the meaning of that?"

Shocked, the private jumped back, pulling his hands out of his pockets and coming to attention as he did so. "I . . . we, well . . ."

Everyone about Harriet who had been sitting jumped to his feet and turned to face Kevin. Johnny, realizing what had happened, stepped forth just as Kevin came up to the man who had kicked the clump of dirt. "He wasn't meaning no disrespect to ya, sir. I guarantee it. It's just that we boys were sitting talking about how unfair it was that we've been assigned to provost guard, what with a big battle coming up and all."

Kevin, despite his earlier feelings about the war and his service in the Army, felt very much the same way about their relegation to duty in the Army's rear. Taking deep breaths, he looked about the group and was about to say something when he spied Harriet in the background, still sitting on her cracker box. Immediately the hard lines on his face softened. Looking over at the soldier who had kicked the clump of dirt, Kevin nodded. "I'll accept the explanation that it was an accident." Then he looked back at the other soldiers. "Some of you men have been neglecting your rifles since we got the word about our new duty. That I won't accept. Jeb Stuart and his cavalry are always looking for a chance to add to their collection of government-issue wagons, something that I'll not allow to happen while we're watching them. Now, unless you have business here, I'd advise you get to work on those rifles before this afternoon's inspection."

"What inspection?" Johnny asked.

"The one Captain Ward will be holding."

Though the mention of another inspection and Ward's name in the same breath was unwelcome, none of the men uttered a sound as they scattered to the four winds, leaving Kevin, Harriet, and Johnny. Without moving, Kevin called out to Harriet. "Could I have a word with you?"

The tone of his voice told her that Kevin's request was actually an order. Harriet lifted up a half-finished stripe. "I'm almost finished with Corporal O'Keeth's coat. Would it be all right if I finished?"

Except for shaking his head, Kevin didn't move. "Please, Harriet, I'd like to speak with you, now."

Harriet sighed as she let the sleeve she had held up to Kevin drop down to her lap. She knew what Kevin was going to tell her and she didn't relish the thought. Passing the coat back over to O'Keeth with the promise that she'd be back in plenty of time to finish the job before the afternoon inspection, Harriet rose up, gathered her long, sweeping skirts about her, and walked over to Kevin. When she came up next to him, Kevin turned and walked toward the open end of the company street. Together they walked, side by side in silence, until they had left the close confines of the camp and were wandering along the edge of the woods the camp was near. Still neither one spoke, the quiet broken only by the sounds of an army in camp and the occasional buzz of a fly.

Finally, Harriet broke the silence. "Kevin Bannon, I know what you're going to say, and the answer is still no."

Kevin stopped and looked at the woman he loved. "Harriet, when I mentioned Stuart's cavalry, I meant it. Given the chance, he and his boys will be all over us. If and when the bullets start flying, I'll have to do my duty and I may not have the time to protect you."

Harriet looked up into his eyes. "I'm not asking you to neglect your duties or to protect me."

"Harriet," Kevin pleaded, "this isn't a game."

Narrowing her eyes, Harriet took a step closer to Kevin. "How could you say such a thing? How could you? I sat there and watched Colonel Hatch die despite Dr. White's best efforts. I held Henry Meyers' hand while they hacked off his leg. I've cleaned blood and pus from dozens of wounds and stood by your side every time you buried a soldier who died from one godforsaken disease or another this past winter. To think that I

443

would hike up my skirts and run home now, when the regiment needs me the most, is—"

"Harriet, you're not a soldier."

"And neither are most of those men back there in camp. They're boys! Many of them are just boys, away from home, fighting for something that is becoming harder and harder to believe in."

Though he shouldn't have been, Kevin was taken aback by Harriet's show of defiance. He took her hands in his. "I understand what you're saying. I really do. Like them, I sometimes wonder if we're really the soldiers we think we are."

His admission took the harshness out of Harriet's eyes. Lifting his hands up, she gave the back of one of them a gentle kiss before looking back into his eyes. "Kevin, I know how hard all of this is on you. I now realize how wrong it was of me to push you into the Army like I did. Though it was the right thing to do, it was wrong for me to insist. I know that now and I'm sorry."

Kevin made no attempt to contradict her statement. Rather, he let his eyes drop down to look at their joined hands. After a pause, Harriet continued. "As hard as it may seem, it would be more painful for me to go back home and be away from you again. There, I am nothing, a nobody waiting for something to happen. Here, I make a difference. Though I'll never shoot a Rebel and truthfully have no desire to do so, I do have real value here. I am important, perhaps not to your colonel or the Army, but to the men. In my own little way, I make their burden easier to bear."

Kevin nodded as he looked up into her eyes. "I know, darling Harriet, I know. Everyone from the colonel on down admires you and appreciates your contribution to keeping the morale of the regiment up during this miserable winter. Even Doc White praises all the work you've done with the sick, though he still does so grudgingly." Mention of White's attitude caused them both to chuckle. Then Kevin went on. "And while I know it means so much to you to be here, with me and the regiment, I don't think you understand how much you mean to me." Grasping her hands tighter, he stepped closer. "Dear Harriet, you're everything to me now. I lost my mother at birth, my only brother was taken away from me four years ago, and my father can't stand the sight of me. Except for you, I have no one. The thought of losing you is . . .''

A smile lit Harriet's face. Using their clasped hands for support, Harriet stood on her tiptoes. Leaning forward, she planted a light kiss on Kevin's forehead. After easing herself back down, she smiled again. ''You're not going to lose me, First Lieutenant Kevin Bannon.'' She gave their joined hands the tightest squeeze she could manage. ''I simply will not allow that.''

Knowing defeat when he saw it, Kevin could do little more than look into Harriet's big green eyes. There was strength, he knew, in those eyes. Strength that he would need, today and tomorrow, if he was going to survive this war. With a smile, he took her arm in his and began to walk along the edge of the woods until the roll of a drum called them both back to the war that could only promise more suffering and pain for them and all that it touched.

# CHAPTER 24

# May, 1863
# South of
# Chancellorsville,
# Virginia

THE DAMP GROUND MADE THE MARCH SURPRISINGLY EASY.
Rain the night before gave the soil a sort of springy, moist
texture that gave off no dust as rank after rank of the Army
of Northern Virginia's Second Corps moved to the west in
virtual silence. Though there was the usual chatter between
soldiers, and an occasional good-natured comment shouted
out at a young staff officer as he passed the lines of scrawny
infantrymen, there was no cheering. Instead, when the hardened veterans saw their commander, riding bent over on his
small sorrel, arms loosely hanging at his sides, the men
in the ranks would give him a wide toothy grin, a deep, respectful nod, or a wave. When he wasn't engaged in conversation with one of his commanders or an aide, Lieutenant
General Thomas J. Jackson returned their nods and smiles
with a fierce glance from his brilliant blue eyes that always
seemed to be partially obscured by the brim of his dingy cadet
cap. The men recognized that look. They called it his war
look. Their steady pace, the hustling of staff officers to and fro,
and that peculiar look told them that there was going to be a
fight that day, a big one. The long winter of waiting while they
froze, starved, and buried comrades who had succumbed to
sickness and diseases was over. The war had come back to
Virginia.

On and off during the long day's march, various commanders came up and rode with Jackson. For a while, Brigadier General Robert E. Rhodes, the commander of his lead division, and Colonel Thomas T. Munford, the commander of the 2nd Virginia Cavalry and the vanguard of the Second Corps that day, were riding with him. Jackson's talkative manner that day told his companions that he was in a good mood and satisfied with the progress that his command was making, for Old Jack seldom engaged in small talk or idle chatter.

When Brigadier General Raleigh E. Colston, acting commander of the division following Rhodes', joined them, Jackson hit upon the common bond that all four of them, together with many of those in the ranks they were passing, shared: VMI. Jackson, though a West Pointer, had served the Institute for ten years as an instructor of artillery and natural and experimental philosophy. Colston had graduated from VMI in 1846 only to return three years later to teach French. Rhodes, class of '48, taught tactics and physical science, while Munford had graduated in 1852 after serving as the cadet adjutant during his first-class year. As the four men rode together they freely reminisced about their days in Lexington and all those friends and associates that they had served or gone to school with there who were now somewhere along that very same route of march, headed into battle with them.

Every now and then, as if it were staged, a familiar face from those days marched by, adding his name to the list of those being discussed by the four mounted officers. Though the topic had drifted back to the pending battle by the time the four old associates had scattered and the 4th Virginia Volunteer Infantry came by where Jackson stood watching his command, the thought of his old students was still fresh in his mind. With a nod, he acknowledged the greetings given by Abner Couper, Will McPherson, James Bannon, and Charles Clifton Burkes, also of the 4th Virginia, as they went by. Later that day, after ordering Colonel Munford's 2nd Virginia Cavalry and the Stonewall Brigade under Paxton to drop out of the line of march to cover the corps's flank, Jackson would comment to Munford as they parted,

"The Virginia Military Institute will be heard from today."

Other than to nod, James Bannon paid little attention to his former instructor. Nor did he listen to the flurry of rumors that flew back and forth from one side of the column to the other. For despite the almost cheerful, sangfroid spirit that possessed the soldiers of Company J that day, James was lost in a sea of troubled thoughts. This was, he calculated, the beginning of the third year of the war, a war that everyone had once thought would be decided by one swift battle. With great anger he recalled the claim by one U.S. Congressman that he would be able to wipe up all of the blood that would be spilled in the upcoming war with his handkerchief. Too few people, James reasoned, had seen the congressman's boast as a foolish one. But then, that was to be expected. Even after two years of war, generals on both sides continued their pursuit of that mythical great, decisive battle that would end the war with a single stroke. "This war is going to go on and on, Will," he lamented one night after returning from picket duty. "We're going to be fighting it till the South's bled white or the people back home get tired of the killing."

James' reference to the North as "back home" was not lost on Will. After Fredericksburg, he had been using those words more and more. Though he said nothing, Will realized that his close friend was, for whatever reason, drifting further and further from whatever convictions had once compelled him to throw his lot in with Virginia.

"Hey, Jimmy boy," Marty shouted as he shook James' arm and broke his concentration. "You with us or what?"

Not understanding, James looked at Marty with a questioning look on his face. Then, after trying hard to figure out what he meant, James just shook his head. "Sorry, I was just thinking."

Marty grunted. "If ya ask me, you've been doin' too much of that lately. You're startin' to worry Will and me."

James tried to put Marty off with a laugh. "Is that all my company commander and first sergeant have to worry about?"

A serious look crept across Marty's face. "We're more than that, James. We're your friends."

He wanted to correct Marty by adding that they were his only friends that mattered, but didn't. He knew Will already knew that and suspected that Marty did too. Instead, James tried to change the subject. "Okay, Marty, what was so hellfire important that you had to wake me up?"

A smile lit Marty's face. "I was tellin' Sidney here that we're sneakin' around the enemy's flank, like Old Jack likes to do. He keeps insistin', though, that we're retreatin'."

Sidney Thompson, marching in the rank in front of James, turned his head. "Course we're retreatin'. We just turned south again. If we were gonna fight, we'd of stopped before, when those Yankee cannons took potshots at us. We're marching away from them."

"No we're not," insisted Marty. "We're just gonna go around their flank. You can ask Jimmy here. Old Jack was his instructor when Jimmy was a keydet."

Though he wasn't sure which way they were marching, since he had paid scant attention to where they were going and the forest they were in made picking out one's orientation almost impossible, James nodded in agreement. "Marty's right. We're going to fight them, today."

"Well, how do you know that?" insisted Thompson.

"His eyes," James answered. "Did you see his eyes when he went past? His fighting blood is up."

"That's what I said," Marty added. "Those blue eyes of his were burnin' like two blue flames. If I know our boy, he's got the Yankees right where he wants them."

From behind Marty, Will's voice called out. "First Sergeant."

Marty looked about. "What's up, Will?"

"We're starting to straggle. Get back there and keep the boys up close. Give 'em the boot if you have to."

Hopping on one foot, Marty held the other bare foot in the air. "Now, Will, you know I haven't even got a pair of boots for myself. How can I give 'em anything?"

Some of the men laughed. Even Will shook his head as he tried to hold back his smile. "Just get back there and keep them up, will you?"

With a wave of a hand, Marty saluted his company commander. "Okay, Will, I'm goin'." Then he nodded to James and Thompson. "See you boys later."

With Marty gone, Will moved up next to James. "Hey, Jimmy," Will asked in a hushed voice. "You all right?"

James let his head drop down for a moment before turning to face his friend. He smiled. "Yeah, Will, I'll be okay. I've just been thinking a lot about this war and home lately."

For a moment, Will looked away from his friend. "Who hasn't," Will answered with a distant, almost painful sigh. Then, after pushing aside whatever image he had held before his own eyes, of a home that was never far from his thoughts, he turned back to James. "Marty and I were talking about you the other night."

"So I hear."

"Please, don't get us wrong, Jimmy. We care about you and, well, we're worried."

"Will, it's been two years since we walked out of the sally port at VMI. This will make the third year of war. And what have we got to show for it other than a long list of names of men who have been killed or maimed during those two years?"

Will was surprised by James' outburst. "Jimmy," he said wide-eyed, "we've still got our freedom."

James looked into Will's eyes with a hard, fixed stare. "Yes, the South has its freedom. But at what price? Will, how much longer can this nation of yours go on sacrificing its sons in bloody battles against a foe that just keeps coming back, year after year, with bigger and bigger armies? We can't take much more of this, you know, we just can't."

Now it was Will's turn to gaze back at James with a determined gaze. "James, we, those of us who call this state home, have no choice. We didn't ask for this war. It came to us. To just up and give up, now . . ." Will looked down at the ground he was moving across, shaking his head several times before looking back up at James. "James, I have no choice. It's that simple."

Drawing in a deep breath, James looked ahead, focusing on the back of the man just a few feet in front of him. "Will, I'm lost." He looked over to his friend to see how he had reacted to that comment. Will's expression had softened. He was watching him, waiting for him to continue. "When I joined with you, I did so because you were my friend and your friendship was all I had." He paused, thought about what he had said, then hastened to explain. "Don't get me wrong, you're still my friend, and I love you as dearly as I do my own brother. But . . ."

450

Will nodded. "It's your home you've been thinking about, isn't it."

With tears welling up in his eyes, James nodded. "Will, as much as I hated that place, it's still my home, a place where *my* only kin still lives, God willing."

"You're afraid that you might run into your brother, aren't you?"

James could only nod as he turned his head away to hide tears that were now streaming down his cheeks.

Will, feeling James' embarrassment, also looked to one side for a moment. Then, when he was sure that James had managed to collect himself, Will put his hand on James' shoulder. "We'll get through this, you know. Somehow, we'll see it to the end, whatever that end may be. And when we get there, I'm sure your home will be there, just as I'm sure mine will be. Do you believe that, Jimmy?" he asked as he shook his friend's shoulder. "Do you?"

Though he tried hard to imagine it, the only image that came back to James was one of a cold, corpse-strewn forest, permeated by a freezing mist and fog. At that moment, in the middle of a mass of men stepping out smartly through a thick forest alive with freshly budding spring leaves and wild growth, all James could see was darkness.

## At the Chancellorsville Inn

Though he was used to being sent on fool's errands, Kevin Bannon hated them with a passion. This particular errand had been doubly painful, given that he had had to ride a horse, a particularly obnoxious horse that spent half their journey to the Chancellorsville Inn trying to turn its head around and nip at his feet. Only after exhausting all other measures without results did Kevin finally hit upon a reaction that the horse understood. In frustration and anger, Kevin had drawn his pistol and cocked it while the horse was trying to nip at his foot for the umpteenth time, almost throwing him in the process. By the time Kevin had regained his balance, sanity had prevailed. Kevin carefully released the hammer back to the safe position.

He was about to reholster the pistol when he saw the horse's head begin to turn. Without any hesitation, Kevin brought the barrel of his pistol down in a wide sweeping arch and smacked the side of the horse's head with it. This surprise blow caused the horse to shake its body and snort. But it also caused it to turn its head back to the front and keep heading down the road crowded with wagons and ambulances. Kevin smiled. ''That'll teach you, you black-hearted beast.'' Not trusting the animal, Kevin kept his pistol out, held high and ready as he continued on his way with one eye on his mount and the other on the road ahead.

After arriving at the Chancellorsville Inn, where the commander of the Army of the Potomac had his field headquarters, Kevin regretted not having shot his horse when he had had the chance. Sent by a corps staff officer to pick up orders from the Army commander, Kevin found out that whatever problem the Sixth Corps had been having with its telegraph lines had been repaired and the orders he was after had already been transmitted. Unable to face the prospect of making the return trip at that moment, Kevin took his reluctant mount and led it away from the calm and serene atmosphere that had settled down over the Army's command group as the sun sank slowly in the west. Other than the sound of rifle fire from skirmishers and an occasional exchange of cannon fire in the distance to the south, little seemed to be going on. Every now and then a messenger rode up and handed a dispatch to a staff officer who carried it over to the white-pillared verandah of the Chancellorsville Inn where the Army commander, Major General ''Fightin' Joe'' Hooker, sat chatting with his aides. There was, Kevin noted, none of the concern or apprehension here that he had seen at the Sixth Corps headquarters. Perhaps, he thought, things weren't really as badly managed at Army level as he and his fellow officers had always assumed.

Tying the horse to a branch, Kevin eased himself onto the ground, cursing loudly as he did so because of the tenderness of his bottom. Ignoring his mount's impatient snorts, Kevin pulled his cap over his eyes, folded his hands over his chest, and dozed off. Even the rumble of cannon fire, now drifting down from the west as well as the south, did little to disturb him. It wasn't until he felt the earth under him begin to tremble that Kevin pulled his cap back up for a look around. When he did, he was shocked to see dozens of men in blue streaming past him.

Jumping to his feet, Kevin looked first to the old inn. The staff officers who had been idling away the hours were now mounted and galloping toward him and the Turnpike. Even Hooker was up and mounted, brandishing his sword as he ran head-on into the crowd of frightened men that had engulfed Kevin. "What in the blazes," Kevin yelled as he grabbed a fleeing soldier by the sleeve, "is going on?"

Hatless, without a rifle, and thoroughly panic-stricken, the man looked at Kevin with large brown eyes. "Wo ist der pontoon?" the man shouted in German.

Innocently, Kevin lifted his arm and pointed in the direction of the road that led to the river-crossing site. "Over there."

Satisfied, the frightened soldier broke free of Kevin's grasp and took off at a dead run just as a staff officer rode up next to Kevin. "Damn you, sir," the major yelled at Kevin. "Get on your mount and rally the bastards."

Still confused, Kevin stood where he was for another moment before it finally sank in what was going on. From the west, a jumbled mass of men, most without weapons, came flooding down the Turnpike. Though he could clearly see officers mixed in amongst them, none, other than those of Hooker's staff and Hooker himself, seemed to be trying to stop them. It was a rout, Kevin decided. Some unit had broken and it was fleeing the field. Having been involved in more routs than he cared to remember, Kevin realized as he watched that there was little that he could do. These men were not from his unit. Fact was, he didn't even know whose command they belonged to. And if their own officers couldn't stop them, then what chance, he thought, had he?

Stepping back to seek some protection from the tree he had been sleeping under, Kevin, however, began to feel the same old anger begin to well up in him that he did every time he saw a badly botched battle. The circumstances surrounding this disaster didn't matter to Kevin. Even the fact that the soldiers running past him were not his responsibility didn't matter. In his growing rage, Kevin turned to his mount and swung himself up into the saddle. He could not and would not sit by, impassively, and watch good soldiers run away because some fool officer had blundered. Though he doubted that he would have any better luck at rallying troops than Hooker and his staff did, Kevin was determined to give it a try. Besides, Kevin thought to himself as he drew his pistol, if there is one thing I know about, it's retreats and routs.

*Near the Wilderness Church*

All about James Bannon the confusion and chaos was complete and overwhelming. After having stood along a road Will said was named the Plank Road while the rest of Jackson's corps slammed into the Union flank, the 4th Virginia and the rest of the brigade finally were ordered forward. Slowed in part by the growing darkness, the 4th Virginia was nonetheless in time to add its number to the pursuit of the broken Union forces. "Come on, boys," Will yelled at those who stopped along the way to pick through the deserted camps and the haversacks of the dead and wounded. "There'll be plenty of time for that later. We've got the damned Dutchmen on the run." Though most of the men of the Union Eleventh Corps, the corps that the full weight of Jackson's attack had fallen upon, weren't of German extraction, everyone came to think of it as being made up almost exclusively of Germans, or Dutchmen as they were popularly called.

Though most men responded to Will's plea, the pace of advance, the intermingling of units, and stiffening enemy resistance, not to mention the almost junglelike nature of the woods they were passing through, finally stopped their advance. When they finally did stop, James discovered that he was alone with only two other men from the company. One minute James and his two companions were following Marty Hazard through thick underbrush, and the next, they found themselves falling in with a group of Georgians. Whether they had lost the company or the company had lost them didn't matter. Though both of the other men felt that it would be better to stay with the Georgians and wait until dawn, James decided to find their own unit. "They couldn't have gone far, boys," he told his two companions. "Best we find them now before the brigade gets up and moves to the far side of the field."

In their travels, the full magnitude of the Union defeat and the confusion that had resulted from Jackson's attack became apparent. There were Union dead and wounded everywhere, mixed in with Confederate casualties to mark where someone had tried to make a stand and had failed. While James tried to avoid tripping over or stepping on these poor souls, the darkness and tangled forest floor made that impossible. In one instance, he went to step over a large log that was lying on the ground. But instead of finding firm ground on the other side, James' foot came to rest on a soft, moving mass. Pulling his foot back, he fought to regain his balance while bringing his rifle up to the ready.

From behind the log, a dark form jumped up. "Don't shoot me, dear God. Please don't shoot me."

Excited and angered at the same time, James yelled out at the form. "Well, tell me who in the blazes you are first."

"Todd Patterson."

James shoved his rifle forward, closer to the man's chest. "What regiment?"

"107th Ohio, McLean's brigade."

Leaning forward, James could make out the scabbard of a sword hanging on the side of the Yankee before him. "You an officer?"

"Captain. I'm a captain, commander of Company E."

One of the men with James chuckled. "Well, you ain't commandin' no Company E anymore."

When the other man broke out in nervous laughter, James yelled for them both to shut up before turning his attention back to the Union captain. "How about handing over your sword belt, if you don't mind."

Quickly Patterson reached down and unsnapped his belt buckle, all but throwing belt and sword over the log at James. James picked it up and saw that there was no pistol in the holster. "Where's your pistol, Captain?"

"Lost it."

Not knowing if he was telling the truth or hiding the pistol under his coat, James ordered one of the men with him to go over and check out the Yankee. The levity of a few seconds ago was now replaced with a sense of foreboding as the closer of the two went past James, over the log, and searched the man. "There's nothing on him, James. He's unarmed."

The other member of the lost trio came up next to James. "What are we going to do with him, Jimmy?"

Letting his rifle come down to a more relaxed position, James considered their predicament. "Well, boys, we're as lost as this here Yankee is. The only difference is that we're behind our own lines, I think."

This last comment made the man next to him jump. "You mean we could be behind Yankee lines?"

"I mean," James explained, "I don't think there's anything even resembling a line out here tonight. Chances are, there's groups of Yanks scattered all about, lost just like us."

"Then why in the devil did you insist on leaving those Georgians, James?" the man who was with the Yankee demanded.

"Because I thought it was the right thing to do," James insisted.

"And what in the blazes do you think is the right thing to do now?"

James sighed. This night, he thought, was like the whole war wound up into one tight little nightmare. All about him was darkness, death, and confusion, with no clear or simple path to follow. "Right and wrong doesn't matter anymore, does it. All that matters is making our way through this tangled mess as best we can," he mumbled more to himself than in response to the question that had been posed to him.

Confused by James' sudden philosophical lapse, the man next to the Yankee demanded impatiently, "Well?"

Looking about, James shook his head. "Let him go. If we run into more Yankees, I don't want to be burdened with a prisoner."

"Jimmy," the man next to him pleaded, "let's stay here, at least till all the shooting stops and everyone settles down for the night."

Again James shook his head. "I don't think anyone's going to settle down tonight. And staying here could be just as bad as going on. So we might as well go on."

Reluctantly, James' two companions agreed. With a wave of his arm, James signaled the Yankee to leave. Then, lifting his rifle up and resting it across his shoulder, James grunted to his companions. "Let's go."

The three of them hadn't gone more than fifteen or twenty yards when a volley of rifle fire broke out behind them. Pausing, James thought he heard the cry of a wounded man as the echo of the volley faded away. "You think someone shot that Yankee we let go?" one of the men with him asked.

James didn't respond. Instead, he just turned his back on the other two and plunged forward into the woods.

## Near the Chancellorsville Inn

When the first faint rays of dawn finally made their way through the dense overgrown trees where Kevin Bannon and his small force of stragglers were deployed in line, Kevin was surprised to find that the number of men with him had grown rather than diminished. Though he knew that this had occurred more because the new men had simply grown tired of running and had joined up with the first unit that they found rather than because of his inspired leadership, Kevin didn't mind. He had a good thirty or forty men, fully armed, under his control, and ready for battle. Standing up next to the tree he had been leaning against, Kevin stretched his legs and called for the sergeant who had helped him form the line the night before. "Sergeant."

A squat, barrel-chested man came up to Kevin and came to attention and shoulder arms. "Vhat is it you would like, sir?"

A smile lit Kevin's face. Even in his own company, where he was well respected, his NCOs didn't respond with such precision or smartness. "First, Sergeant, I would like your name."

"Heizelmann, sir. Karl Heizelmann from New York."

"Good, Sergeant Heizelmann. And my name is Kevin Bannon."

Kevin didn't know whether it was the friendly manner with which he addressed Heizelmann or the mention of an Irish name that caused the squat sergeant to smile. The idea of being under an officer who was from another minority group was quite popular among men who had recently immigrated to the United States, for many felt that their shared background of racial hatred and disenfranchisement from the mainstream of American society made for a stronger bond between officer and enlisted man. After watching Trevor Ward for almost two years, Kevin shared that belief.

"Our first order of business, Sergeant Heizelmann, is to sort out our charges. Let's go find out if there are any other NCOs mixed in here and start making this company look like a company again."

Heizelmann smiled. "Ja, das is goot. Ve vill straighten zem out und den, coffee und crackers."

In the process of sorting out the men who had assembled under Kevin, Heizelmann found that many of them were from his old unit. When he saw a familiar face, he would greet the man with a smile. "Dat man, Herr Lieutenant," he would comment to Kevin, "ist a good fighter. Very good." Or, he would shake his head and frown. "Ve must vatch him. Troublemaker."

They were finishing this chore when the major from Hooker's staff who had ridden up to Kevin the evening before and had admonished him to do something came up to Kevin again. "You've done a right smart job, Lieutenant, rallying these men. The general himself noted your coolness during our little crisis and would like your name."

Though Kevin didn't consider the previous night's fiasco a little crisis, he didn't comment on that. "I am First Lieutenant Kevin Bannon of the 4th New Jersey, First Brigade, First Division, Sedgwick's corps."

For a moment, mention of the Sixth Corps caused the staff major to stare at Kevin in confusion. Then he remembered.

"Oh! You're the man they sent over yesterday when the telegraph was out."

"Yes," Kevin grumbled, "I'm the one."

"Well," the major said with a smile as he slapped Kevin's arm, "lucky for us."

Remembering the ride over, Kevin rubbed his sore bottom. "Yeah, lucky."

In the midst of this rather one-sided conversation, a captain with a double-breasted frock coat and a well cared for mustache came trooping up toward them, behind the line of troops. Kevin, out of the corner of his eye, noticed that Sergeant Heizelmann's expression soured when he too saw the approaching captain. "You, sir," the dapper captain shouted out to Kevin, "what is your name?"

Angered at the rude interruption, the staff major turned to the approaching captain. "What business, sir, do you have here?"

"One of my corporals informed me that someone's taken over my company and I demand that man's name," the captain insisted.

"And where have you been, Captain, while your company was holding the line here?"

The staff major's question caused the captain to wince. "That's none of your business."

"Oh?" responded the major, his own anger rising. "I don't think so."

"Listen, you," the dapper captain shouted as he turned on the major with the index finger of his right hand held up in front of the major's face, "this doesn't concern you. This man has usurped my command and I intend to break him for his insubordination."

Kevin saw, even if the captain didn't, that this last comment made the major angry. Puffing out his chest, the staff major took a step closer to the captain, pointing to Kevin as he did so. "This man, *sir*, rallied your company last night when no one else could and you were cowering under a rock somewhere. General Hooker himself seems to think this man's efforts played a big part in stemming a rout that could have carried away the entire Army. I was coming over here to inform the young lieutenant of his promotion and temporary assignment to the general's staff. But now that I've met you, I'd be a damned fool if I took him away from this company and turned these men back to a cur like you. Instead, I'm afraid I'm going to have to convince the general that we need to postpone that assignment in favor of leaving the lieutenant here, for now, to command this company.''

"You can't do that," the dapper captain hissed.

The staff major smiled as he leaned forward and jammed his finger into the captain's chest. "Sir," he said as he pulled his finger back and then jammed it home again, "consider it done. Now, get out of my sight and go back to whatever hole you hid in last night and don't ever come back. We have a battle to fight."

Throughout this whole affair, Kevin kept a straight face, looking from one man then to the other. Only after the dapper captain had flinched, backed down, and turned to walk away, did Kevin speak. "Begging your pardon, Major, but can you do that?"

The major didn't say anything for a moment as he watched the captain walk away. Then he turned to Kevin and shrugged. "I sure hope so."

Kevin blinked, looked at Sergeant Heizelmann, then back at the major before he burst out laughing. The major, now over his fit of anger, also began to laugh. "You mean," Kevin asked between laughs, "that was all show? Hooker never sent you over here to reassign me?"

After a moment or two the major finally regained control. "Well, he did mention that he wanted to thank you for your efforts. The rest, well, I wasn't about to let that pompous ass come in here and push you around. Not after what you did last night. I'd best go back to headquarters and see to it that the necessary orders are written to confirm everything I've just said here. It would be a terrible waste to see a good fighter like you get in trouble because of a buffoon like that and my temper. What did you say your name was?"

"Bannon, sir. First Lieutenant Bannon."

"Captain, you mean," the major stated as he clapped his left hand on Kevin's shoulder and shook his right hand. "You can put money on that. Now, I think we're in for another hard pounding today. See to your new command."

Kevin let the major's hand go and saluted. Though he didn't quite know whether to be happy about his new circumstances or not, the irony of being recognized for his trivial efforts here, after having done the same for so long in the 4th New Jersey, didn't escape him. Unfortunately, he had no time to dwell on those thoughts. Cannon fire and the sputtering of ragged volleys to the west and southwest told him that the battle was close and would, no doubt, be a lot closer before long. Turning to Heizelmann, he smiled. "All right, Sergeant. While I go find out who's in charge of this regiment, have the men cook up some coffee and breakfast."

"Ja," Heizelmann responded with a lusty smile. "And I vill save some for du."

Kevin smiled. "That, Sergeant, would be just fine, just fine."

## West of the Chancellorsville Inn, near the Turnpike

With the early morning light came the sound of battle. From the sound of the fire and its nearness, James realized that, unlike yesterday, there would be no waiting, no long delays before they would be thrown into the fight. As if to underscore this, an aide from J. E. B. Stuart, now commanding Jackson's corps after Jackson had been shot the previous night, rode up to General Paxton and repeated Stuart's urgent orders to take his command forward at once.

As the brigade was forming up, Will walked the line as was his custom. Stopping before James, kneeling on one knee and leaning heavily on his rifle for support, Will put his hand on his friend's shoulder. "You going to be all right?"

James looked up at Will, revealing a face that was more careworn and haggard than the previous night, bad as it was, could justify. Even James' response betrayed a deep, mournful melancholy that bothered Will. "Yes, Will," James answered in a heavy, monotone voice. "I'll be fine."

Will was about to recommend to James that he step out of ranks and follow behind the regiment but didn't have the chance. Major William Terry, commanding the 4th Virginia that day, relayed Paxton's order to advance. Turning his back on his friend, Will hustled off to his post at the far right of the line, drew his sword, and ordered Company J forward.

James, with a push that seemed to take all his strength, managed to rise up in time to step off with the rest of the front rank. His mind, still troubled by thoughts of home and fatigued by a frightful night without sleep, was unable to focus on the battle they were rushing off to. Though he tried hard to concentrate on what he was doing, all that his brain kept repeating over and over again was a line he had once read from a Shakespearean play. "Once more unto the breach, dear friends, once more," he recalled with terrible clarity, "or close the wall up with our English dead!" Though he wasn't afraid, or thought he wasn't, James moved forward with a dread that was almost as crippling.

Hearing the man next to him speak, James looked over. His companion, Ben Douglas, was laughing at a man crouched on the ground behind a series of breastworks they had come across. "Get up and watch how Virginians clear a Yankee line."

The man, wearing the palmetto emblem of South Carolina, said nothing. Instead, he continued to crouch behind the earthworks and glared at Douglas as the 4th pressed on. Looking back to the front, James could hear Will out front, shouting for the men to keep up and dress to their right. The boggy ground, tangled vines, and sheer denseness of the forest they were moving through, however, made that nearly impossible. James, looking over to his left, past Douglas, to see if they were still on line with the 5th Virginia, was startled when a sudden mass volley was fired at them.

Haltingly, the entire line staggered to a stop, some men doing so before others. While Will and the other officers of the regiment ran back and forth in an effort to push back those who had gone too far forward, sergeants in the rear of the company pushed forward those men who were hanging too far behind. Douglas, excited by all of this and too impatient to wait for the order to fire, brought his rifle up to his shoulder, aimed in the general direction from which the Federal volley had originated, and fired. Though Marty Hazard shouted for the men to hold their fire, most of the company, including James, ignored him. With Yankees behind breastworks less than one hundred yards to their front, delivering devastating fire on them, James figured it was a good time to say the hell with parade-ground tactics.

Will McPherson, seeing that the men in his charge were pretty much re-formed into a line of battle, elbowed his way into the ranks next to James. Though it wasn't where the company commander should have been, Will figured that in this fight, where he stood and fought really didn't matter. Marty Hazard too gave up his efforts to restore order and edged his way into the front rank between James and Douglas. "Hot fight today," Marty yelled into James' ear while they were both reloading. James, his eyes glued to the front while his hands went through the mechanical process of ramming his next round home, only nodded.

## West of the Chancellorsville Inn, near the Turnpike

Slowly, Kevin Bannon moved along the rear of his newly adopted company, watching his men as much as he did the line of Rebel infantry deployed a little less than one hundred yards to their front. Knowing that he'd be wasting his time, since he wasn't that good a shot at long range, he didn't even lean forward to fire his pistol. Instead, he had to suppress his urge to strike out and content himself with shouting an occasional order or words of encouragement. He also needed to make sure that his ad hoc collection of stragglers stayed in place and kept to the task at hand.

Everything, that morning, was jumbled up and confused. From the fact that his men belonged to a regiment that had been moved to another part of the field to the discovery that the regimental and brigade commanders that he was currently serving under hadn't even realized that Kevin's little company had fallen in with them until Kevin had introduced himself a scant two hours before. "While I am sure," the brigade commander told Kevin, "the general whom these good men belong to is worried about them, I'd be much obliged if you stayed where you are. I fear we'll need all the help we can get right here in this spot before the day's out." Kevin, not having any particular loyalty to the regiment or brigade that the company he commanded belonged to, agreed and spent what little time he had left preparing for the day's fight.

When he reached the end of the line where the squat form of his newly appointed first sergeant, Karl Heizelmann, stood, Kevin paused. "The boys seem to be holding to it this morning."

Heizelmann stepped back and turned to Kevin. "Zay are good boyz, zay are. Ve are ashamed, heartzick, about vhat happened last night. Today, ve make it richtig, right."

Knowing the feeling, Kevin smiled. "Yes, Sergeant Heizelmann, today we will all make it right." Then, noticing the movement of Union troops coming up on the right flank of the Confederate battle line to their front, Kevin pointed at them. "Keep an eye on those men, Sergeant. As that unit rolls up the Rebel flank, make sure the men at this end of the line shift their fire to the right."

Seeing what Kevin was pointing to, Heizelmann smiled. "Ya, I vill do dat."

For the better part of an hour, the 4th Virginia, wedged between the 5th on the left and the 2nd on the right, stood there and blazed away at Union forces, who returned their fire, round for round. In a firefight like this, one not only loses track of time, most soldiers become almost hypnotized by repeated firing and reloading. After a while, even the roar of the battle itself is blocked out, leaving soldiers numb to all but the most violent pain or action. It therefore came as a surprise to James, who was about to take a shot, when Will grabbed his arm and shouted at him. "COME ON, DAMN IT! BACK, we've got to go back."

As if wakened out of a trance, James shook his head and looked blankly over at Will. Will repeated his order. "Pull back, Jimmy. The 2nd Virginia's been flanked and has given way. Now we're flanked.''

Looking over his friend's shoulder, James could see that there no longer was a battle line off to their right. Instead, he saw angry red flashes that marked a partially hidden line of men in blue where the 2nd should have been. Glancing to the rear, he could see it and the rest of the 4th staggering backwards, with great reluctance, toward the earthworks where they had passed the South Carolinians. With a nod, James acknowledged the order but didn't start back until he finished taking the shot he had been preparing to make. When he was ready, he started back.

At first he tried to step backwards, so as to keep his front to the enemy. It was a great embarrassment to be shot in the back. Conventional wisdom had it that a man who was shot in the back was shot while running away, no matter what the actual circumstances had been. Though most of the men in both armies that spring were seasoned enough to know that there were times when a unit had to retreat, the fear of being shot in the back was still as powerful as it had been in 1861.

The boggy and tangled floor of the forest they were in, however, made walking backwards impossible. As hard as it had been advancing, retreating while walking backwards was even harder. After a few steps, during which he stumbled all the way, James hit upon a compromise. He turned and walked with his feet and hips headed toward the rear, but kept his face and rifle pointed toward the enemy by twisting his trunk at the waist, as far around as he could. Taking quick glances, he watched where he was going while keeping an eye on the Union lines.

Only when they reached the position where the South Carolinians still held did he finally turn completely around. When James stepped over the log barricades, the same South Carolinian whom Ben Douglas had chided looked up at James with a broad smile. "So," he said with great pleasure, "this is how you Virginians sweep the Yanks from a position."

Though infuriated by the remark, James didn't take the time to respond. Instead, he headed to where he heard Major Terry, the commander of the 4th, and Will rallying the regiment. As he was passing Will, who stood in front of the diminished line of soldiers, Will grabbed his arm. James looked into his friend's eyes. They were bright and alive. His entire expression, despite his having lost a number of his men, seemed to be cheerful. "James," he said, "good to have you back."

While he fell in and dressed on the man next to him, James thought about Will's comment. For the first time, he realized, since Fredericksburg, he had been animated, fully alive and functioning. Whatever doubts had clouded his troubled brain were gone. Whether it was the smell of gunpowder or the sheer excitement of battle, James felt strangely at ease with himself and his surroundings. Why he did, he hadn't the foggiest idea. All that mattered, he decided, was that he did.

While his small band of New Yorkers cheered the retreat of the Confederates, Kevin looked nervously to his left and right, watching to see if someone from regiment or brigade was going to give the order to advance. When he was sure that they weren't going to leave the safety of their earthworks, Kevin ran down the line to where Heizelmann was opening a new package of cartridges and reloading his cartridge box.

"First Sergeant," he shouted as he grabbed Heizelmann's arm. "Have the men remove the dead and wounded from the firing line. Then get them back to work improving our position. The Rebs'll be back, and soon."

Heizelmann looked down the line, noticing for the first time that several of his men were lying on the ground or staggering to the rear holding a wound. "Ya, ya," he responded looking back at Kevin, "I vill get to dat, right away."

With a smile and a pat on the back, Kevin nodded. "Good, good. I'm going to find the regimental commander and find out if he knows what's going to happen."

To this, Heizelmann nodded his agreement. "Goot, you do dat. I vill tend the company." Then, as an afterthought, as Kevin was getting ready to leave, Heizelmann added, "It ist a goot company, Herr Captain. Zay fight vell."

Kevin nodded. The same, he knew, could be said for his own company back with the 4th New Jersey. He just hoped that someday he would be able to prove it to his own company. "Yes, they fight well. Now, get to it, First Sergeant."

Their respite from the fight was short. Colonel John Funk, who had commanded the 5th Virginia, now commanded the brigade, since General Paxton had gone down with a mortal wound. Abner Couper, acting as the 4th's second in command, was busy dressing the line at one end while Major Terry did the same at the other end. In the midst of this, J. E. B. Stuart, seemingly unaffected by the carnage about him and joyful as ever, rode up to Colonel Funk. "Order your men to fix bayonets and go forward again, Colonel," Stuart commanded with a wide, sweeping gesture of his arm. "And," he added as he turned his horse away, "remember Jackson."

Whether it was the chant to remember Jackson that all of the officers quickly took up as they ordered their regiments forward, or it was the order to fix bayonets—an order that always meant their commanders wanted them to close without fail on the enemy—or it was because of the humiliating retreat they had just made, the Stonewall Brigade stepped off with determination and fire in their hearts. Back over the earthworks where the South Carolinians still cowered the 4th Virginia went. Back over the same ground they had advanced and retreated across, which was now covered with their own dead and wounded, the 4th swept. And back into the teeth of Yankee rifle and artillery fire the men of the 4th advanced. This time, however, there was no pause, no hesitation. Though their losses were staggering, and their ranks were being torn apart by enemy fire that became increasingly desperate, the brigade went on.

Caught up in the excitement of the moment and unable to hold himself in check any longer, Will McPherson, after waving his sword over his head twice and letting go a shriek, began to run at the Union earthworks. James, infected by the same drive, let loose a high-pitched yell, leveled his rifle, and took off after Will. Together with several other men, they rushed forward as fast as their feet and the miserable ground permitted. They would not be denied this time, and they would end it, now, whatever the price.

The reappearance of the enemy was expected, almost anticipated. The viciousness of their attack, however, was quite unwelcome. From behind their positions, the men under Kevin's command loaded and fired as quickly as possible. It was, Kevin thought, as if the anger and desperation of the Rebels was leaping across the open space between them and infecting his own men, for Kevin could see a noticeable increase in the speed and animation of his men.

"STEADY!" he yelled as he paced back and forth behind the line. "STEADY." Unsnapping his holster, Kevin prepared for the desperate fight the Confederates seemed so eager to push.

From the flank, a voice yelled. "They're breaking in!"

Pushing his way forward, Kevin could see a group of Confederates, moving forward at a dead run, coming up to the earthworks just off to their right. A quick glance to his left and right, then to the front, told him that the entire Union line was about to buckle. Rather than wait until the enemy was amongst them and face losing control of his unit as the company commander to his right already was, Kevin shouted out to Heizelmann over the growing din of battle and screams of the advancing Confederates. "We're going back by rank. You stay with the second and keep them together."

Nodding that he understood, Heizelmann stepped back and waited for Kevin to give the order. "FIRE BY RANK," he shouted. "SECOND RANK, OBLIQUE FIRE TO THE RIGHT."

Kevin paused to take a deep breath. "READY," he screamed, his voice cracking from the effort. "AIM!" he shouted in an extremely high-pitched screech. "FIRE!"

The second rank, leaning well over the first rank, let loose with their volley. "Second rank, fall back twenty paces. First rank, READY," Kevin started again, shouting as he moved to one side to avoid being knocked over by the jostle of men from the second rank, now moving back. "AIM!" he repeated with a yell that was even shriller than his previous commands. "FIRE."

Even before the men could bring their rifles down, Kevin ordered the first rank back, turning his own back to the enemy, this time, to join them. Though he shared the same fear that many men did about being shot in the back, his greatest fear, at that moment, was whether he could re-form his unit and keep it together under such heavy and determined enemy pressure. To his surprise, and great relief, when the gray smoke of battle parted, he saw Heizelmann and the second rank holding fast and busily reloading their rifles. Making his way through their rank, Kevin patted Heizelmann on the shoulder. "Good job." Then he looked around. "Everyone else is giving way, First Sergeant. We will continue to fire and fall back by rank."

Heizelmann looked around too, then nodded. "Ve are ready, Herr Captain."

Without hesitation, Kevin turned to issue his next orders. "Second rank, ready." As he waited for the men of the second rank to bring their rifles up to the ready, he could see Confederate soldiers climbing up over the earthworks they had just pulled back from. Drawing his pistol he moved up, stuck his arm through the ranks to his front and took aim. "AIM ... FIRE!"

With a great leap that seemed almost effortless, Will McPherson jumped up on the freshly abandoned Federal earthworks. He paused for a moment, catching his balance as he looked to the rear. James came up next to him, with Marty Hazard close behind. "COME ON, 4TH VIRGINIA!" Will yelled. "COME ON!"

Unable to keep his balance and wanting to get a good shot at a group of Yankees re-forming some twenty yards away, James stepped down on the Union side of the earthworks and dropped to a kneeling position just before they fired. The crash of their volley was followed by a sharp scream to his rear, then a heavy thud on the ground next to him. Pausing only long enough to take aim and fire, James turned to see who had been hit.

"Oh, Lordy," Marty Hazard cried out in pain as he doubled up and grabbed his bloody leg. "They've shot me in the same blamed leg."

Bringing his rifle down to rest, James leaned over to look at the wound Marty was clutching between his hands. "Doesn't look too bad, old boy."

"Hurts like the blazes, Jimmy," Marty hissed out between clenched teeth. "Can't keep goin'."

James nodded. "Don't worry. I'll be back for you later."

Marty opened his eyes as James got up to continue the advance. "Don't forget me, hear?"

James smiled. "I won't forget you."

On his feet, James all but bumped into Abner Couper. Despite the carnage that was all about them and the mortal danger they themselves were in, the two men looked at each other for a moment. Then, James smiled. "Come on, Abner, what are you waiting for?" With that James went forward.

Abner, looking at James going on, smiled. Then he raised his sword and yelled at the ranks of the regiment now re-forming behind the Union earthworks. "Come on, 4th Virginia. Forward!"

## At the Chancellorsville Inn, on the Turnpike

For three-quarters of a mile Kevin kept his dwindling little band of New Yorkers falling back by rank. First one rank, then the other would pause, turn, and fire before moving farther to the rear. Their efforts, however, didn't seem to deter the Confederates. As maddening as it was to Kevin, they just kept coming. "Damn," he shouted at one point, "why won't they stop?"

Heizelmann, coming up next to him, looked back at the oncoming Confederates with a cool eye, then turned to Kevin. "Because, Herr Captain, zay are goot soldiers too."

Angry, Kevin cocked his pistol and took aim. "We're just as good, damn it. Just as good."

"Ah," Heizelmann added. "But zay have better generals. Dat, I think, makes all the difference."

Unable to contradict his first sergeant on that, and needing to continue their fighting withdrawal, Kevin took a shot, looked behind him, and shouted. "All right, second rank, get ready." As before, he issued the series of orders that took his small company back, firing as they went. When they reached the area where the Chancellorsville Inn was, Kevin was surprised to see the old inn engulfed in flames. The scene in the front yard and all about bore no resemblance to the idle headquarters it had been just twelve short hours before. In quick order, it had been a rallying point for broken units, then a field hospital. Now, it was a battlefield, one that Kevin could not hold.

Seeing a line of Federal troops to his rear, across the road on the far side of the inn, Kevin pointed Heizelmann toward it. "There, First Sergeant. Make your next move over there and pass through those people."

With his usual nod, Heizelmann acknowledged Kevin's order and continued to go about his business.

With a suddenness that was startling, James Bannon and the men with him broke out of the woods into a clearing. In the center, a large brick inn with white columns burned furiously. In front of it, bloody rags and discarded blankets were spread out on the ground and in heaps. They were in the Yankees' rear, James realized. They had routed the enemy again. He turned back to shout to his comrades. "Come on, boys, we've got them on the run."

But a sudden clap of rifle fire from positions in a tree line just beyond the burning building told him that their foes weren't completely vanquished. Facing back to the rear, James reached back into his cartridge box for another round but found none. Leaning his rifle up against him, he pulled out the tin dividers that separated the ammo in the cartridge box but still found none. A quick pat of his left and then right pants pockets told him that he had used those rounds too. Turning to the man next to him, he yelled over, "You have any ammo left?"

The soldier, grim faced and tired, shook his head as he brought his rifle up to fire. "This here is my last."

As soon as it became apparent to the regimental commanders and Colonel Funk that the Union troops to their front weren't going to yield and that their own men didn't have enough ammunition left to make a fight of it, the Stonewall Brigade began to go back, again. Though angry that they had to, everyone, including James, knew that they had done all they could and, for now, they had no more to give. Whatever final, decisive, masterful stroke waited to be launched to end this contest, it would have to be carried out by another unit. All the Stonewall Brigade could do now was fall back, lick its wounds, and prepare for the next fight, a fight that always seemed to come.

## In Fredericksburg, East of Chancellorsville

Like the tides ebbing and flowing, the stream of wounded coming back to the Sixth Corps hospitals told Harriet how the battle was progressing. Left to face Fredericksburg along with one division from the Second Corps, General Sedgwick's Sixth Corps didn't take part in the early fighting to the west, of which rumors abounded. While one man told Harriet that Hooker was in the process of winning a great victory, the next would lament about the great rout that endangered the entire Army of the Potomac. Though she listened politely, winning or losing the battle didn't matter for Harriet at that moment. Instead, she spent the early part of the day worrying about Kevin, who had been sent over to the Union right and, as far as she knew, had not returned.

Only the arrival of casualties from the Sixth Corps's attack through Fredericksburg against the Confederate forces on the hills west of that town took Harriet's mind off of Kevin. Though still appalled by the sight of blood and torn flesh, Harriet managed to control her revulsion as she became more and more involved in handling and tending to the wounded. She even found that she was able to force a small smile when caring for a badly wounded man. Since Harriet did seem to have a decided calming effect on the wounded, and she did well enough with the cleaning and bandaging of minor wounds, none of the doctors or hospital stewards objected to her presence now as they had back in December when she had first appeared. Some even began to call her over when they needed help in settling a man who was fighting them. "Miss Shields," Doctor White would say to her in a hushed voice, "we've got to settle that lad over there so that we can work on him. Please, explain to him it's either his arm or his life." Though she soon began to hate being handed what she considered the surgeon's real dirty work, she did so, for there was, she knew, no one else there who would or could do it as tenderly and well.

In the process of working with the wounded, Harriet found that she could keep track of how the battle was going. In the late morning, a man wounded during the assault on Marye's Heights told her in great detail about their attack while she was binding his wound. "When we was told we were going out there across the same fields where so many good boys got slaughtered last year, we was scared, I'll tell you. Then," he said, leaning forward closer to her with his eyes wide open, "our captain told us we was gonna do it with rifles unloaded and bayonets only. 'Just keep on goin', boys' he told us. Well, we thought the old general had gone plum crazy. But ya know what? It worked! We stormed over that stone wall like a freight train and didn't stop till we reached the top of the hill. I'd still be goin' west if'en a Reb cannon hadn't fired a round of canister in our faces."

Listening to these stories made Harriet wonder what drove Kevin and these men to go out and so casually risk their lives in the manner in which they did. Raised by a father who prided himself on his logical and scientific view of life and the world, Harriet found the idea of willingly placing oneself in mortal danger, in a word, insane. *"How foolish I have been,"* she often chided herself in her diary. *"Had I known how terrible war was, I'd have never pushed Kevin to stay in the Army like I did. Should anything happen to him, I fear that I will always blame myself."*

"*Yet,*" Harriet recorded one night, after lamenting and reflecting upon her past decisions, *"I don't see that either Kevin or I had any other choice. It is as if we were both caught up in*

*a great, cruel drama in which we had no control over the roles
we were chosen to play. Only now can I begin to appreciate
why my mother and many of her friends are like they are.
Perhaps they realized, a long time ago, that our world isn't a
logical place and that to believe otherwise is foolish and waste-
ful. Still, I cannot sit back, like her, accepting a woman's lot in
life without protest. Even if, in the end, my efforts make little or
no difference, I must do something. I must try."*

In the evening, when a new wave of wounded began to
arrive, the demeanor of the men told her that the tide of battle
was starting to go against them. Here and there she began to see
soldiers from the First New Jersey Brigade. "They've stopped
us cold," one man who recognized her told her as she was
helping him onto a table to be worked on. "We were driving
them pretty good till we reached a ridge with a stone church on
top." After wincing from a spasm of pain, the soldier looked
into Harriet's eyes and began again in a very apologetic manner. "We gave 'em everything we had, Miss Shields. You've
got to believe me. It was just too hard," he concluded as a tear
appeared, "too hard."

Easing his head down onto his folded sack coat, Harriet
swept back his hair and smiled at him. "You did good, Jack.
You all did good."

As the surgeon began to look over the soldier's wound, the
man looked up at her, as a child does to his mother. "Do you
think so, Miss Shields? Did we do good?"

Harriet nodded as she continued to smile despite the nausea
she felt rising in her throat and the tears she was struggling to
hold back. "Of course you did. Now, you just lie back and rest.
This doctor is a good one and he'll take care of you." Then,
unable to hold back either the tears or her sickness, Harriet fled
out of the room into the darkness.

She was out there, alone, when young Albert Merrel found
her. "Miss Shields," he whispered even though they were
alone. "You've got to come with me."

Standing upright, Harriet sniffed a few times and wiped her
eyes. "What is it, Albert?"

Albert raised his lantern above his head in an effort to see
what was wrong with Harriet. After she turned away from the
light in an effort to hide her teary eyes, he lowered the lantern

and stated his business. "Private Miller's been wounded and wants to see you."

Running her hands over her hair, Harriet took a deep breath and then turned to Albert. "All right. Lead on."

To Harriet's surprise, Albert didn't take her back to the hospital. Instead, he led her to a small tumbled-down shed. "Albert, what are we doing here?"

"Well," he protested, "this is where Private Miller asked me to bring you."

From the darkness of the shed, a low, frightened voice called out. "Who's out there?"

Not ever having heard Miller speak, Harriet didn't realize it was he until Albert pushed the door of slat boards open and shoved his light into the small confines of the shed. Shutting his eyes, Miller raised one hand up over his eyes to shield them from the lantern's light. "It's me, Miller, Albert Merrel. I've gone and got Miss Shields like you asked."

Slowly, Miller lowered his hand and squinted at Harriet. "I'm sorry if I've inconvenienced you but . . . well, I . . ."

Looking down, Harriet saw Miller's right trouser leg was ripped near the crotch and drenched in blood. "Good Lord, sir," she said, "why didn't you come right to the hospital? You need a doctor."

Mention of a doctor caused Miller to scream. "No, please, no doctors." Then lowering his voice, he asked, "Would you look at my wound?"

Harriet shook her head. "Private Miller, I am not a doctor. I cannot . . ."

"PLEASE?" Miller screamed out with a pained desperation. Then lowering his voice again, he repeated his request. "Miss Shields. Look at my leg, here and now."

Unsure of what she was getting into, Harriet slowly knelt down next to Miller. "Albert, bring that lantern around."

Miller looked at Albert, then Harriet. "He's got to leave," he commanded.

Tired of Miller's attitude and somewhat frightened by the situation she found herself in, Harriet refused to give in. "Listen, you're in no condition to say who goes and who stays," Harriet snapped. "I need someone to hold the light while I, ah, look at your wound."

Bending over, Harriet could see the tear in the trouser leg was nearly a foot long. "How did this happen? I thought J Company was at corps headquarters on provost guard?"

"Shrapnel," was all she got back as a response.

"I need a knife to cut the trouser leg open so that I can, ah, examine the wound."

Moving the lantern from one hand to the other, Albert stuck his newly freed hand into his pocket. "I've got one right here." Pulling it out, he handed it to Harriet, who opened it and carefully began to make the slit in the trouser leg wider. As she did so, it occurred to her that she had never in her life seen a man's genitals. Finished cutting, she took the pant leg, held her breath, and pulled it aside.

She gasped as she saw the gash that the jagged shrapnel had cut into Miller's leg. With blood all over, it was difficult to distinguish between flaps of skin and the shredded material of Miller's long johns. "Albert," she commanded, "bring that light down closer. I've got to see what I'm doing here."

Obediently, the young hospital steward leaned over, watching as Harriet began to slowly pull material away from the wound starting just above the knee. Then, as curiosity got the better of him, Albert began to look along the length of the wound. When his eyes finally reached the crotch, the boy jumped back. "Oh, my God! Miss Shields!"

Angry at him for jerking the light away like he had, Harriet looked up at Albert. "What on earth is the matter with you?"

Unable to speak, Albert merely pointed at Miller's crotch.

Still angry at Albert, Harriet glanced over to see what he was pointing at. Then, without letting go of the blood-soaked material she was holding, Harriet looked up at Miller's face, wide-eyed and speechless.

Propped up on one elbow, Miller nodded her head. "I'm sorry, Miss Shields," Miller responded to Harriet's stare. "I . . ."

"My God, girl. Why?" Harriet asked in amazement.

With tears streaming from her eyes, Miller tried to say something, but couldn't. Instead, she just lowered herself to the ground and covered her eyes with both hands. "I didn't want to hurt anyone. Honest," she lamented between sobs. "I just wanted to be a soldier. I wanted to do something important, not stay at home like all the other girls. For once in my life, I wanted to stand on my own two feet and make a difference.''

Miller's words, sounding so much like those Harriet herself had committed to her silent diary, struck home. Letting go of the bloody scrap of long johns she held, Harriet wiped the blood from her hands as best she could and reached over to grab Miller's hands. Pulling them from her face, Harriet looked down into Miller's eyes and smiled. "Don't worry, dear. It will be all right. Believe me, I understand."

Only after Miller finally managed a smile did Harriet look back to Albert, who was still standing in one corner of the shed, watching with wide eyes. "Albert," she commanded in a stern voice. "You go back to the hospital and fetch me a pan, fresh water, towels, needle, thread, and bandages, lots of them."

"What are we going to do?" the boy asked in a quivering voice.

"We work in a hospital tending the wounded. Private Miller is wounded and needs our help, so we're going to do our job."

Albert was still unsure. "But he's a girl."

Harriet snapped at him. "Private Miller is a soldier, a brave soldier who's been wounded and needs our help. Now, leave the lantern and be off with you, boy, quickly."

As he was turning to leave, Harriet called out. "And, Albert," she added, "not a word to anyone, do you understand?"

Though still shaken, the boy nodded and disappeared.

## *East of the Chancellorsville Inn*

Two days after Kevin's assuming command of his collection of stragglers, a courier from Army headquarters handed Kevin a set of orders. "Signed by the Chief of Staff himself," the courier announced as Kevin read the order. When he was done, he looked up at the courier, who offered him his hand. "Congratulations on your brevet to captain and assignment to Army headquarters."

Still amazed that the staff major he had met two days before had actually managed to follow through with what he had pledged, Kevin offered his own hand up and gave the courier a weak handshake before the courier mounted up. "You're to report by tonight," he added before digging his spurs into the flanks of his horse and riding off to his next destination.

Sergeant Heizelmann, who had been listening to the conversation, came up to Kevin, who stood in the roadway, orders in hand, while he watched the courier disappear. "It ist too bad, Herr Captain, that you must go."

At first, Kevin didn't respond. Rather, he just continued to look down the road. How ironic, he thought, this war was. A year ago, he would have given anything for these orders. Now, even though he knew that this war would continue forever, he wanted to go back to his unit. He wanted to be with men whom he had had nothing in common with until fate had thrown them together. With a shake of his head, he looked down at the paper in his hand. How ironic, indeed.

With a snap of his head, he looked over to Heizelmann. "Yes, First Sergeant, I must go." After slowly folding the orders and tucking them into his breast pocket, Kevin took a step over to Heizelmann. "I must go now and find the regimental adjutant. I'm sure he'll want to appoint someone to take over from me before I leave."

"Ve do not vant someone else, Herr Captain. Ve," he said, motioning to a group of men from the company who were now gathered about them, "vant you. Der Rebels, they beat us again, true, but you, you gave us back our pride. You treat us like men and lead like a lion."

Kevin smiled as he looked down at his boots before looking around the circle of dirty and ragged soldiers. "I thank each and every one of you for your vote of confidence. And I share your sentiment. Leading you has not only been easy, for you are good soldiers, it has been a privilege." As he spoke, Kevin could see the twinkle in the men's eyes as they straightened up their backs and puffed out their chests. "Unfortunately, even if I didn't have these new orders," he said, patting his breast pocket where they were, "I'd have to leave you. You see, I have my own company that I must look out for. I am their lieutenant and it would be wrong for me to turn my back on them, even though you men are such fine fighters."

Heizelmann came forward and took Kevin's hand. "Zay are lucky men to have a leader like you." Then, with his free hand, Heizelmann reached into the pocket of his trousers and fished out two epaulettes. As he offered them up to Kevin, he looked about his gathered company. "Ve vere going to gib these to you later, but . . ."

Taking the epaulettes, Kevin saw that they were those of an infantry captain. Though he had no idea where Heizelmann had gotten them, that did not matter. It was the thought that moved Kevin to tears. "I . . . I thank you, each and every one of you." Then looking back at Heizelmann, he shook the squat German immigrant's hand one more time before turning to leave. Though he had no idea what he would find at Army headquarters in the wake of such a disastrous battle, he had something now that he had never had before: confidence. Though it had taken him two years, he had finally realized that he had come into his own. From now on, he told himself as he walked down the road, glancing back every now and then to look at the New Yorkers that fate had thrown him in with, he was his own man. And nothing and no one, not his father, not Trevor Ward, not even death, would ever be able to take that away from him.

## West of Chancellorsville

Moving slowly along the long rows of wounded, James Bannon alternated between watching where he put his feet and looking into the faces of the men lined up waiting to be tended to or evacuated to a more permanent facility. James hated going back to the field hospitals, hated it with a passion. For as bad as the carnage of the battlefield was, nothing could compare to the sights, sounds, and smells of a field hospital after a major battle. Besides the usual odors of dirty men who hadn't bathed in weeks, those peculiar to festering wounds were added. The stench of blood, both fresh and old, human waste, rotting flesh, and body fluids that seeped from open wounds permeated the air, causing even battle-hardened veterans to cover their mouths. How anyone, James wondered, could survive such treatment was beyond him.

It took him two hours before he found Marty Hazard, lying on the bare ground. Marty didn't recognize James at first. Lifting his friend's head up, James poured a little water into Marty's mouth. Weak from the loss of blood and the growing infection that was now spreading from his leg wound, Marty coughed and spit up most of the water. A second try was more successful. After easing Marty's head back to the ground, James sat next to him. "I see you still have your leg, Marty," James offered when he could think of nothing else to say to the ashen-faced figure.

"Won't let the bastards have it," Marty whispered. "I'll die before I let them take it."

Looking at his friend's thin, frail body, shivering despite the heat of day, James realized that the odds were he'd lose both his leg and his life before too long. Marty was, James thought, like the Army of Northern Virginia. Though he was as determined and stubborn as ever, physically he was a mere shadow of himself. How much longer this man, and the Army he represented, could hold on was beyond James.

"How's the company, Jimmy?" Marty asked when he had gathered up enough strength to speak again.

James shook his head. "The regiment lost over half the boys we started out with four days ago. Can't say how many for sure since there're still some fellas straggling in yet. Still, we were pretty well used up again."

"Jimmy," Marty asked in a weak voice. "You find Will yet?"

"No, Marty, I didn't. I was told he was here with you. Do you know where he is?"

For a moment, Marty stared into James' eyes. Then, slowly, he closed his eyes and nodded his head.

James Bannon found his friend and former roommate right where Marty told him he would. Making his way along the line of breastworks they had taken from the Yankees on the 3rd of May, James found the spot where the 4th Virginia had broken the line. Here and there he saw a familiar face, many now blackened and bloated in death. One of them belonged to William McPherson, the son of a Winchester farmer, a member of the VMI class of '63, and a man who had come forth and filled the void left in James' life when he had thought he was alone in the world.

Dropping onto the dead leaves that lay next to his dead friend and comrade, James felt a pain go through him unlike anything he had ever imagined possible. Will was gone. There was nothing that he could do to change that. Nor was there anything that he could do to understand it. Like the war, Will's death was a hard, cruel fact, laid bare before his eyes, that now had to be lived with. All that James could do now was to fulfill the promise he had made his friend so long ago and take him home.

But before he could do that, before he could do anything, James Bannon had to grieve. And although he thought he was mourning the passing of a man who had been more than a friend, James Bannon was, in truth, mourning for himself.

# PART SIX

# A TERRIBLE SWIFT SWORD

# CHAPTER 25

# May–June, 1863
# Winchester, Virginia

BUSY SCRATCHING OUT THE ORDER BEFORE HIM, JAMES SUT-
ton ignored the sentry standing in his open door, in a very
baggy blue sack coat, as long as he could. Finally, when he
couldn't do so any longer, Sutton looked up and snapped,
"What is it?"

"Sir," the young private responded after taking half a step
back, "the sergeant of the guard has a man out here that the
cavalry patrols picked up coming through our lines early this
morning."

After waiting a moment for more, Sutton shook his head.
"So?"

"Well, sir, the provost marshal wanted to know what to do
with the man."

Annoyed at being disturbed over such a trivial matter James
Sutton threw down his pen. "Damn it! Can't anyone in this
headquarters think for themselves?"

The soldier inched back out of the doorway, glancing to his
rear as if he were weighing his chances of escaping. Calming
himself, Sutton brought his arm up, rested his elbow on the
desk, and planted his head down into the open hand. He was
tired of garrison duty, sick and tired of it. He longed to be back
with the 39th New York again, in the field. Though many of the
problems the adjutant of a regiment faced were not much different from those he faced in Winchester, at least a regiment in
the field was doing something that was tangible and honorable.
Tending to the needs of a community that was hostile and
remote was anything but glorious. Besides, he told himself as
he rubbed his forehead against the palm of his hand, he would
be away from Mary Beth McPherson. The nearness to a woman

485

he loved, despite her lack of interest in him, was just as unbearable as his mundane duties were.

"Sir, are you all right?"

Sutton opened his eyes and looked up at the soldier still standing at his door. He forced a smile. "Yes, I'm fine." Then, rather sheepishly, he added, "Thank you."

Bringing his other hand up to the desktop, he rested his arms from the elbow forward on the desk and clasped his hands together. "Now, what is this about a man coming through our lines?"

"Well, sir," the sentry started again, "a cavalry patrol picked up this Irish teamster, driving a one-mule wagon, coming up through our lines this morning."

"What did this teamster have in his wagon, son?" Sutton asked when it became obvious that the soldier wasn't going to volunteer this information.

"A body, sir. Says it's the body of a Reb lieutenant."

"And what, may I ask, is this Irish teamster hauling around dead Confederate officers for?"

"Well, sir," the soldier stated, now becoming more relaxed, "seems the Reb officer lives, or I mean lived, here in Winchester before the war. The Irishman, it seems, was hired by the family to haul the dead Reb all the way from Chancellorsville to here for burial."

Leaning back, Sutton pulled his arms back onto the arms of his chair and looked at the soldier as he thought. It was not unusual for families, both Union and Confederate, to hire someone to bring a loved one who died with the Army back home for burial. Undertakers, following the armies like buzzards, had a lucrative trade in catering to this desire. They provided everything from coffin to shipment. Sutton had vivid memories of solemn-looking gentlemen, dressed in black frock coats and tall black beaver hats, hawking their wares to soldiers when rumors spread that a battle was pending. He hated the practice, just as he hated those who profited from a family's grief. But, he knew that the traveling undertakers provided a service that neither army did. So, like garrison duty, he tolerated the undertakers. "Is this teamster here?" Sutton asked.

"Yes, sir. We got him waiting outside, around back."

"Why outside?" Sutton asked as he stood up and lifted his hat up to his head.

The sentry made a face. "The teamster had no ice to pack the body in. All he did was wrap it up in a rubber ground cloth and plop it into a cheap box."

Pausing with his hand still on the brim of his hat, Sutton reconsidered whether or not he really needed to go down and check this out. If the Confederate had, indeed, died at Chancellorsville, that would mean that the body was now almost two weeks old. Sensing Sutton's thoughts, the soldier shook his head. "I sure hope the folks who hired the Irishman are paying him well. Lordy, that Reb is ripe."

Sutton grunted. God he thought, how he hated this job.

While he waited, James Bannon dismounted from the rickety wagon he had been driving and pretended to be tending to his scrawny and footsore mule. He had become used to the stench of Will McPherson's body by now and depended upon it to keep the curious away. For James, that was paying off now, for the armed soldiers in blue were making him nervous. The idea of being in the presence of these men, soldiers who were from states that surrounded the one he was born and raised in and serving the flag he should have been serving, made James far more uncomfortable than he, at first, had imagined.

"I'm taking Will home to be buried," James had told Marty Hazard during his last visit to his wounded friend.

"Jimmy," Hazard had protested, "they won't let you go home for that. And you can't desert. They'll hunt you down like a coon and shoot you dead when they find you."

James, however, wouldn't be convinced. "I promised him, Marty. I promised that I'd take him home. The way I figure, at least one of us should be laid to rest with his loved ones."

Knowing that James Bannon was a determined young man, Marty gave up trying to talk him out of going. "You're gonna come back, ain't you?"

James, standing next to his friend, didn't answer. Instead, he looked down at Marty, stuck out his hand. "So long, Martin

Hazard. It has been an honor and a privilege to serve with you. I wish you the best of luck."

Propping himself up on one elbow, Hazard took James' hand. "I hope you find someplace you can finally call home, Jimmy. You're a damned fine man and a hell of a fighter. I'm gonna miss ya."

The tramping of feet and the shout for the men guarding him to come to attention told James Bannon that an officer had arrived. Giving his mule one more pat, he turned to meet the officer, flashing the widest, most innocent smile on his face that he could as he quickly removed his hat in the same manner that workers in his father's brick works used to do whenever his father approached them. "Good day to you, me lordship," James shouted out to the blond-haired, green-eyed Union major of infantry who approached him. "Sorry to trouble you, me lordship, on such a hot day over so trivial a matter."

As the major stopped well short of the wagon, James Bannon could see the stench of the decaying corpse had hit him. After a slight gag, which he tried to hide, the major wiped away the sickly look that had flashed across his face when he had taken his first whiff and replaced it with a stern expression. "We do not consider travelers passing through our lines from enemy territory without proper authority a trivial matter in this command," the major barked.

"Oh," James Bannon exclaimed, lifting his right hand with the index finger pointed toward the major. "That's right, me lordship. I don't have me papers. Well, you see . . ." James started to explain as he began to move toward the major.

When he realized that James Bannon smelled as bad as the corpse in the wagon, the major put his hand up and took a step back. "That won't be necessary, sir. I can see, ah, that you are, in fact, what you claim to be."

James Bannon's smile broadened. "Well, now, that's very Christian of you and all," he exclaimed in the heaviest Irish brogue he could manage. "The poor folks will be much obliged that you, the good Christian gentleman that you are, did all you could to speed the body of their poor dear departed son to its final resting place."

"It, ah," the officer said, turning his head away from the smell, "is the least we can do."

"Well then, me lordship, I'll be going."

Turning, James Bannon replaced his hat and began to move back to his wagon when James Sutton called out. "By the way, sir, what is the name of the family that hired you?"

A chill ran down James Bannon's spine as he stopped. Pivoting about, he wondered if he should lie or tell the truth. The McPhersons hadn't hired him. They didn't even know he was coming. In fact, James had no way of knowing if they even knew that Will was dead. Deciding that it was better to err on the side of the truth, James answered. "The McPhersons, me lordship. George and Elizabeth McPherson."

The reaction of the Union major after hearing the mention of the McPherson name told James that he had made a mistake. The Yankee officer stiffened noticeably as he cocked his head back to reveal two large round eyes peering straight into James' own. For a moment, the two men stood there, as James Sutton glared at James Bannon. "And your name?" Sutton demanded.

Having already given one name to the cavalrymen who had picked him up, James had no choice but to follow through. "O'Bannon, me lordship," James whispered. "James O'Bannon."

Despite the stench, Sutton took a deep breath. "Sergeant," he ordered without taking his eyes off of James, "open the coffin."

Though he had no idea what the Union major knew or what would happen, James understood that something serious was wrong. Standing perfectly still and trying hard not to take too rigid a military stance while he waited, James Bannon watched as the sergeant and another man, both obviously displeased with the major's order, moved past him and went to the rear of the wagon. With the aid of their bayonets, the two men pried the top of the box open. When they managed to lift one side of the lid, the private stepped back, gagging uncontrollably. Though the sergeant wanted to yell at him to get back to work, he was more anxious to finish the job and get as far away from the wagon and its cargo as possible. This he did as the box lid finally came off and fell over into the wagon bed next to the box.

While the sergeant beat a hasty retreat, the major walked up to the wagon and peered over the edge into the box. He had seen dead men before, perhaps too many. In many ways, this was just another one. Still, the flurry of flies disturbed from their meal, the stench of rotted flesh, and other pungent odors that permeate the unwashed dead caused Sutton to gag. After hesitating for a second, Sutton stepped back from the wagon and looked back at James Bannon, while his stomach struggled to settle itself. He was about to order James to undo the ropes that held the blanket tightly in place around the corpse but didn't.

Instead, he walked over to James, looked at the wagon for a moment, then at James. "What, sir," Sutton asked James, "are your intentions after you deliver the McPhersons' son?"

James was nervous, but didn't show it. "Oh, Lordy, I don't know. I suppose I'll look for work around here. Maybe the McPhersons, may the Lord keep them safe, could use a hand now that . . ."

The smile that crept across the Union major's face troubled James. But he didn't dwell on it. Instead, as soon as the major told him he could proceed, James hopped up on his wagon, hurriedly replaced the lid to the coffin, and took off out of Winchester as fast as he could. Whatever trouble he was in, he decided, he'd keep from Mary Beth and her family for now. The loss of a son, James reasoned, would weigh heavily enough on them without him adding his own burden.

Though the McPhersons knew of Will's death, the presence of his body and the humble burial service they held that night hit them harder than the first word of his death had. After a cheerless meal that only James, Daniel, and Mary Beth partook of, Mary Beth explained. "With no reliable way of getting news through the lines from our own people, folks around here are always being told that a loved one was shot or was sick in the hospital or . . ."

Even now, with Will finally resting in the cemetery that held the remains of every McPherson who had passed away since the family had come to Virginia in the late 1700s, Mary Beth found it difficult to use the word "dead." James, knowing what she was going through, for he had experienced the same pain, the same stunned disbelief on more than one occasion, said nothing. Instead, he left her alone. Rising from his chair, James lifted his hands to his nose. After taking a sniff, he went over to a counter where a pan of soapy water sat. Immersing his hands into it, he fished for the bar of lye soap that he had left in it before dinner and began to scrub the front and back of his hands for all he was worth, wondering if he would ever be able to clean the stench of death off of them.

Though she had noticed James' compulsion with scrubbing his hands, Mary Beth said nothing. Instead, she busied herself with the clearing of the table. Though just about everything she had put out had been eaten, she pondered what little remained with great deliberation. Nothing could be wasted, for she knew that with James, there wouldn't be enough to sustain them until the new crop came in. Somehow, she would have to stretch what little they had.

"Except for when we were outside, Mary Beth, I haven't seen your mother. Is she not feeling well?"

Mary Beth sighed as she let a plate drop to the table. Though James' question was meant to be nothing more than a sincere inquiry, the thought of her mother's frail state of mind, coupled with the funeral of her beloved brother Will, was too much.

James, hearing the plate hit the table and a soft sob, stopped what he was doing and turned to see that she was on the verge of tears. Pulling his hands from the soapy water, James stepped over to where Mary Beth stood, wiping his hands on his trouser legs as he went. "Dear Mary Beth," he whispered as he placed his wet hands on her shoulders. "I didn't mean . . ."

Spinning about, Mary Beth buried her head in James' chest. "It's all coming apart, James. Everything Pa ever worked for. Everything that we ever dreamed of. It's all coming apart."

Though he wanted so badly to tell her that everything would be all right, he couldn't lie to her. He had seen all of this before: smashed dreams, shattered futures, and human suffering. It was, James thought as he held Mary Beth close to him, as if he were cursed. The things that seemed so plentiful to other folks, including simple happiness, it seemed, would never be his to enjoy. He had lost his mother before he had ever known her. He had been raised by a father who had never seemed to have any use for him other than to further his own ambitions. The first girl he had loved had been taken from him by his own brother, and he had been exiled from the only family and home he had ever known. Now, even here in his adopted state, grief followed as war tore him from VMI, killed his friends one by one, and tore apart the family he had hoped one day he would be part of. At times he wondered if he carried a plague or the mark of Cain. Such heartbreak, he thought, was just too much for one person to bear. Dear Lord, he prayed silently as he looked up while stroking Mary Beth's hair, give me the strength. Please, give me the strength.

The clatter of hooves coming up the road from town sent a chill down Mary Beth's back. Pushing away from James, she wiped her cheeks and eyes on the sleeve of her blouse as she headed for the window. James, not sure what he should do, started to come over to where she was, but was stopped by her before he reached the window. "James," she told him in a hushed, desperate tone. "You have to stay in here and out of sight."

"Why, what's up? Trouble?"

Mary Beth lied. "No. Just a Union officer out riding about. They do that sort of thing, to check on the farms, their patrols, and such."

Not believing her because she was acting so fearful and as best he could determine there was only one rider, James pressed her. "Is there something going on that I need to be aware of, Mary Beth?"

Looking up into his eyes, she shook her head. "No, James. Nothing. Now you stay in here and I'll go out there and handle it. Okay?"

Though he didn't believe her, he had no choice. The brush with the Yankees in town that afternoon had been enough for one day. He had no intention of pushing his luck, especially since he had now, by his simple presence, placed the rest of the McPhersons in danger.

Rushing out of the front door and down the path, Mary Beth reached the gate before James Sutton had a chance to tie his horse off. "Major Sutton," she announced as she resisted making a quick rearward glance at the house, "I thought I made it perfectly clear that you were no longer welcome on this property."

Unsure of his own feelings, just as he was unsure of what he should do, Sutton didn't speak at first. Instead, he took off his hat, held it in front of him, and fumbled with it for a moment. Finally, he looked up at the girl he loved with all his heart. "Mary Beth, I came by to pay my respects. Though we don't see eye to eye on many things, especially our feelings toward each other, I cannot but help feel for the loss of your brother. If there is anything I can do to ease this burden of pain, please—"

"How did you know about my brother's death?"

Noting the rearward glances that she was struggling to conceal, Sutton straightened himself up. "Well, the teamster you engaged to bring your brother Will home didn't have the right papers when he reached our lines this morning. He was brought to me for verification and disposition."

The idea that James Sutton and James Bannon had met was almost too much for Mary Beth to handle. Still, she managed to keep herself composed. "Well, I trust that you found all in order?"

"Why didn't you apply for permission to do this?" Sutton demanded. "You know this sort of thing goes on, officially and unofficially."

Thinking fast, Mary Beth fought off the urge to look at the house behind her. "Major Sutton, you know that we are already beholden to you for what you did for our father."

"Not to mention," he added with a wicked smile that almost totally unnerved her, "the letters I passed through the lines to your beau with the Army of Northern Virginia."

His reference to James pushed her to the brink. "James Sutton," she shrieked, "how dare you come here at a time like this? How dare you play with my emotions as if I were a . . . a trollop. Don't you have any decency? Don't any of you *men* from the North have even the slightest bit of compassion? I mean, good Lord, man, my father's gone, my mother mourns him like he's dead already, my older brother is fresh in his grave, and I haven't even had time to mourn him."

Stung by Mary Beth's anger, Sutton backed up. He was about to respond, but didn't. Instead, he let his head drop. Unsure of what to do, he pulled his hat onto his head, walked over to his horse, and mounted it. Looking down at Mary Beth, he started to say something, but stopped before he had uttered a sound. Instead, he jerked the reins of his horse sharply to one side, dug his spurs deeply into the horse's flanks, and galloped off down the road, as confused as to what to do about the woman he loved as ever.

Mary Beth, standing at the gate, waited until he was gone from sight before she turned to head back into the house. Though she didn't know what had passed between James Bannon and Sutton, she decided to say nothing to James about this—and anything else that had ever transpired between her and Sutton. There was, she reasoned, no need to upset James with something that didn't concern him.

## North of the Rappahannock River in Virginia

After the Army's retreat from their latest defeat, at Chancellorsville, Harriet found she had precious little time to sit and talk to Karen Miller. And even when she did, she had to be very, very careful despite the fact that she had managed to settle Miller in a tent Dr. White had had set up at the end of the line of hospital tents belonging to the First Division's field hospital for her use during her daily visits and during battles. When she did manage to find time to speak in private with Miller, Harriet posted Albert Merrel outside as a lookout while Harriet and Miller spoke in hushed voices that never went above a whisper. "I am much obliged," Miller told her every chance she could, "for what you've done for me. I just hope that I don't get you in trouble with the doctors or Captain Bannon."

Harriet always passed off Miller's concern with a smile. "Dear, you're not going to get anyone in trouble. I just keep telling everyone that you're too shy to stay in a crowded hospital tent."

"And they accept that?" Miller asked incredulously.

"Dear girl, they accept anything I say as gospel, whether they believe it or not." Then, with a serious note, Harriet added, "Besides, there isn't an officer or a man in the brigade who doesn't admire your courage and skill in battle. If there's one thing that I've found out in my short time with this Army, it's that if you pull your weight when the fighting starts, you can do just about anything without anyone saying boo."

Whenever she heard that, Miller would look down with a forlorn look on her face. "That is, except be a woman."

To that, Harriet had no response, for she knew that there were certain limits of "social decency" that even the most compelling crisis would never remove. Harriet had no doubt that, if discovered for what she was, Karen Miller, serving in the 4th New Jersey since August of 1861 as Private Kenneth Miller, would be unceremoniously drummed out and shipped home without a second thought.

To prevent that, Harriet protected Miller like a mother hen. After the Army of the Potomac had withdrawn north of the Rappahannock, she had managed to move Miller with the regimental baggage trains and had installed Miller in her own tent. While the regimental command thought this was highly irregular, and even Dr. White frowned upon it, Harriet insisted. "With all these other men to tend to, Dr. White," she had countered, "I would think you would be glad to be free of one. Besides," she added with all the charm she could muster, "after working with you, I am sure that I can handle Private Miller's wound and recovery."

Though still skeptical, Dr. White relented, bringing the regimental commander over with him. "Just remember," he admonished her every day before she left the field hospital after finishing her regular rounds, "if you get into trouble, don't wait till it's too late, girl. This is a man's life you are playing with, a good man's life." With a smile and a twinkle in her eye, Harriet would thank Dr. White for his concern and head on over to her tent to tend to Miller.

At first, Harriet hadn't been sure that she could handle the responsibility of nursing Miller back to good health on her own. Besides her own revulsion at the sight of blood and wounds, Harriet was fighting ignorance. The skills she had learned working in the field hospital helped, but they weren't enough. While there were moments when Harriet thought that she couldn't go on, she reminded herself that failure meant the end of Miller's dream. *"Though she has chosen a different path, how can I betray a sister,"* she wrote in her diary, *"who seeks to make something of herself, as I am trying to do? To do so, especially given all that she has already endured, would be unthinkable."*

So Harriet did what she could to improve her own skills as a nurse. She even managed to pry Dr. White's manual on military surgery from him. "Good Lord," he bellowed when she asked him for it. "Now that you've managed to destroy the proper decorum of my field hospital for all time and bend any regulation and rule as you see fit, do you plan to become a surgeon and do away with me as well?"

Having learned that Dr. White's anger was a great sham, Harriet smiled as he handed her the volume. "Well, I hadn't thought about that, but now that you've mentioned it . . ."

While Harriet was removing the dressing from Miller's leg and carefully cleaning the wound and skin all around the wound, Miller watched. "You know," she whispered to Harriet, "it's been so long since anyone's called me Karen or dear, it sort of, well, sounds strange."

"Do you want me to stop, then?" Harriet asked without looking up from what she was doing.

Miller thought for a moment. "Well, no. I kind of like having another woman I can talk to about everything. You don't know how hard it is, sometimes, to keep all your thoughts, all your dreams, all your feelings penned up inside. Sometimes, before you came, I felt like I was simply going to burst."

Harriet smiled. "Well, though I haven't quite undergone the same experiences that you have, I know the feeling." Stopping for a moment, Harriet looked up at Miller's face. "That's why Kevin is so important to me. He's the first person in my life who I ever felt comfortable sharing my deepest thoughts with. I don't know what I'd do without him."

Miller smiled. "You really love Captain Bannon, don't you?"

Harriet went back to work on Miller's leg. "Yes," she said with a smile. "Very much."

"How is he doing on General Hooker's staff?"

Harriet let out a laugh. "Oh, he hates it. Hates everything about it. There isn't a day that passes that he doesn't ride by to beg Colonel Birney to be reassigned to the regiment. 'I'll gladly guard mules and wagons,' he bellows when he manages to come by and see me, 'before I ever accept an order to serve on a general officer's staff again.' "

Miller and Harriet were both laughing when Albert Merrel, posted as a trusted lookout, came up to the flap of the tent. "Miss Shields," he called out without entering. "The adjutant and some politician from New Jersey are at the colonel's tent looking for you."

The two women looked at each other. Then Harriet called out to Albert, "Come in here and finish dressing Private Miller's wound."

There was a moment of hesitation. "He won't bite you," Harriet called out, remembering to refer to Miller to everyone, including Albert, as a he. "Now get in here while I make myself presentable."

Shyly, Albert entered the tent and came over to where Harriet sat. After handing the boy the clean bandage and watching him to make sure he was starting it right, she turned to a small mirror she had hung on the tent's front pole. As Albert slowly wound the bandage around Miller's wound, Harriet fussed with her hair, pausing only when she noticed Miller's reflection in the background. Miller's expression reminded Harriet of her own when she had been an admiring little girl watching her mother dress and tend her hair before going out to meet someone. How hard and lonely, Harriet thought, life had to be for this woman. To endure what she did for a cause was, to Harriet, laudable.

With the same skill and grace that she used to tend the wounded, Harriet set her broad-brimmed straw hat on her head, gave the front brim a slight downward bend, and stood up straight. "Well," she announced as she turned to face Miller and Albert, "I'm about as ready as I can get. Albert, you stay with Private Miller till I return." With that, she left the tent and headed for the regimental commander's tent.

Her approach brought the heated discussion that had been in progress between a civilian, whose back was to her, and the adjutant, who saw her coming, to an end. Standing up, the adjutant picked his cap up off the table that separated the two men sitting under the canvas fly. "I am sure, Judge Shields," Harriet heard the adjutant announce, "that while you *gentlemen* back in New Jersey see things more clearly, those of us with the Army have no illusion as to what your proposal would mean to this country. The resolution you and the state legislature propose is an insult, sir, to the memory of the fine men of this regiment and every regiment from the state of New Jersey."

Harriet stopped for a moment, held back as much by the anger of the adjutant as by the thought of facing her father. The resolution of which the adjutant was speaking called for New Jersey to leave the war. Though many of the men in the First New Jersey Brigade didn't agree with everything that the Lincoln administration was doing, few supported the idea of going home before the South was thoroughly crushed. "We've shed too much blood," Kevin had stated solemnly, "to settle for anything less."

Without waiting to say farewell, the adjutant left the area of the tent and headed toward Harriet. With a slight bow and tip of his hat, he stormed by her. He was angry, she thought as she watched him go by, which meant that her father would be too. Taking in a deep breath, Harriet pulled her hands together at her waist and went forward to greet the Judge.

Sporting a cheery voice and a casualness that would have been more appropriate in the parlor of the Shieldses' New Brunswick home, Harriet came up and greeted her father. "Well, it certainly is a surprise to see you here, Father."

Judge Shields, making no effort to hide his displeasure, snapped. "I'm here to take you back home, Harriet. Now go gather up your things and be quick about it. I have no intention of staying one more minute in this camp than is absolutely necessary."

Though she was angered by her father's effort to bully her, Harriet kept her poise. Moving around the table to the seat where the adjutant had been sitting, she gathered up her hoopless skirts in front of her and sat down. After becoming quite comfortable, she placed her two hands together in her lap, looked up into her father's eyes, and smiled.

Her obvious act of defiance caused Judge Shields' face to

redden. "I have no intention of playing silly little games with you, young lady. You will do as I say or—"

"Or what, Father? You'll have me shot? Oh, no, I'm sorry, I forgot. You're a civil judge. They hang people in New Jersey."

When Judge Shields slammed his hand, open palm down, on the table as he always used to do to intimidate Harriet when she was a small girl or to silence her mother, Harriet didn't bat an eye. Instead, she smiled. "Now, Father, calm down. It will do you no good—"

"I will not calm down," he bellowed. And, wiggling his index finger at her, he added, "And don't speak to me as if I were a child."

"Then do me the honor, Father, of not speaking to me as if I were one."

"When one acts like a child, one deserves to be treated like one," he countered.

When she spoke, Harriet did so slowly, looking right into her father's eyes. "I am sure that you and Mother see things differently back home. That, I have found, is to be expected. Since I've been with the regiment, I have learned so much about people, about life, and what this war is all about."

Judge Shields laughed. "Ha! What do you, a young girl, know about war?"

Harriet narrowed her eyes. "Obviously far more than you and your cronies back in the statehouse do. To imagine drafting legislation to make peace with the Rebels while this Army is down here, fighting and bleeding to defend the very Union that has made you what you are, is, is—"

"Is none of your concern, young lady. You are a woman. What the state legislature does is not your concern. Obeying your mother and father and starting a family of your own, is." Standing up in a gesture that he often used to signal that all discussion was at an end, Judge Shields lifted his top hat and put it on. Looking down at his daughter, he grumbled, "I will be leaving here within the half hour. I expect you to have your things in my carriage over there by then."

Looking up, Harriet shook her head slowly. "I am not going with you, Father. Don't you understand? I can't." Taking her eyes off her father, she looked about at the soldiers coming back from morning drill. "Though I know that what I am doing is frowned upon by proper society, I belong here. These soldiers, all of them, are doing something important, something vital. I don't understand it, not all of it. But I don't think that really matters."

When she looked back up at her father, there was a serene smile on her face. "I do miss home, Father. I miss being there with you and Mother. Yet, I cannot go back. Not until this is finished, one way or the other, can I rest. I have found something here that I don't think I ever would have found in New Jersey, no matter how long I lived. I have found out who I really am. And do you know what, Father? Not only do I like me, but others do too." Looking back toward the soldiers, some of whom waved at her when they saw her looking in their direction, Harriet continued. "They need me, Father. Many of those boys will never see their homes or their loved ones again. How can you ask me to turn my back on them? How?" she asked as she turned her head to face her father again.

When she looked, however, he was gone. Looking about, she finally caught sight of his figure rapidly disappearing down the long row of white tents of the regimental officers' row. Harriet sighed. Though she was sorry that he had left angry, she didn't grieve. There came a time, she knew, in every girl's life when she had to leave the security and safety of her parents' world. That, after all, was the order of things. Casting her gaze across the camp of the 4th New Jersey, now alive with soldiers digging into haversacks for their lunch, Harriet smiled. That this moment would come at a place like this, in the midst of a terrible war, was more than her father could handle. In time, she hoped, she could make him understand. But for now, she was where she belonged, doing what was right for her.

## Winchester, Virginia

Making his way through the chaos that had overcome General Milroy's Winchester headquarters, the provost sergeant called to James Sutton when he caught sight of him. "Major, sir. We have that woman."

Sutton, standing at the head of the stairs leading up to his office, looked down at the provost sergeant for a moment. Even from where he stood, the sergeant could see Sutton's expression darken. "I'll be right down," he finally responded as he turned his attention back to the two junior staff officers he had been talking to. Only when he was finished did he take off down the stairs, taking them two at a time. Walking up, he placed his hand on the provost sergeant's shoulder and leaned over close so that no one else could hear what he was saying. "You do have the right woman, don't you?"

The provost sergeant nodded. "Yes sir, the young McPherson girl. She was in town, getting something or other for her crazy mother, when—"

Sutton clapped his hand on the provost sergeant's shoulder. "Good, good," he said as he looked up and around at officers and soldiers moving boxes and files out into the street to be loaded onto waiting wagons. "Now, I want you to hold her for an hour, just one hour."

When the major didn't say anything else, the provost sergeant looked up. "And then?"

"Let her go," Sutton responded.

"Just let her go? What do we say? What reason do we give for holding her?"

Becoming annoyed, Sutton leaned forward. "We are the military government here. We do not need a reason. Now, go on and do as you have been ordered."

When the provost sergeant left, Sutton ran back up to his office to fetch his cap and pistol belt. As he pulled his .44 Army Colt out of the holster and checked to make sure that it was loaded and that all the caps were in place, he informed his clerk that he'd be back in less than an hour. "Sir," the clerk protested, "we're supposed to be leaving in an hour."

This did nothing to dissuade Sutton. "If I'm not here when it's time to leave, inform the general that I'll catch up with the wagons outside of town."

"And where, sir, should I say you are if he asks?"

Lifting the pistol up before his face, Sutton looked at it as he carefully brought the hammer back to the full cock, then eased it down. "That, Corporal, is not your concern."

James Bannon was in the barn, tending to a split wagon

wheel spoke, when James Sutton rode up. James neither heard Sutton nor sensed there was anything wrong until Sutton's shadow fell across the entrance of the barn. Jumping up, James Bannon spun around and started to reach for a pitchfork leaning against the side of a stall. "Don't do it, Private James Bannon, 4th Virginia Volunteers. Don't give me another reason for shooting you."

The voice, James realized, belonged to the same major who had examined the wagon with Will's body when he had come into Winchester. That he knew who and what James was un-nerved James. Slowly, he lifted his hands above his head and backed away from the pitchfork, turning to face the intruder as he did so. "What do you intend to do with me?"

Sutton, standing in the open doorway with his pistol trained on James, didn't answer at first. Instead, he just stood there, motionless and sweating. Carefully, James looked beyond the Union major to see how many men he had brought. From where he stood, he couldn't see any. But that didn't mean that the Yankee didn't have a detail waiting outside or at the house. Becoming impatient, James lowered his arms. "Well, Major, what are you going to do?"

Still, the figure standing in the doorway, with the sun to his back, said nothing. Instead, he stood there, motionless, as if he were thinking. After what seemed like an eternity, the Yankee finally spoke. "Private, do you love her?"

Caught off guard by this question almost as completely as he had been by Sutton's appearance, James blinked. "Do I love her?"

Sutton took a step forward and barked, "Yes, damn you. Do you love her?"

Ignoring the threatening gesture or the reason why this Yankee officer was so concerned over Mary Beth's personal affairs, James looked down at the ground before him. He had known Mary Beth McPherson now going on three years. That she had been interested in him, from the beginning, was obvious to all who had eyes. But his own feelings, his own thoughts about her were, at best, confused, just like his life. Looking up, James shook his head. "I don't know. Honest to God, I don't know."

Prepared for anything but this, Sutton hesitated. Then, slowly, he lowered his pistol to his side, dropping his head as he did so. When he looked up again, James thought that he could see tears in his eyes. "I love her, Private. I don't know why, I don't know how, but I do love her."

Finally, it dawned upon James that there was something more going on than he had ever imagined. The incident in Winchester when he had come into town with Will's body and Mary Beth's reaction after the major's appearance that night finally made sense. Though he didn't know how Mary Beth felt about the Yankee, there was little doubt that he was deeply in love with her. "Major," James said in a soft, caring tone, "would it help any if I told you I know what you're going through?"

"How could you ever know what I'm feeling, Private? How?"

The memory of Martha Anderson, his first love, and that terrible cold night so long ago when his own brother had stood, just as the Union major now stood, holding a gun on him, came flooding back to James. "I loved a girl once," James finally responded, "but she was taken from me. And you know, I don't think I'll ever get over that."

The sincerity of James' admission and the foolishness of his own predicament finally calmed Sutton down. Lifting his pistol up before his face, Sutton examined it closely. "You know, Johnny Reb, I had every intention of shooting you. All I kept thinking about as I rode over here was how good it would feel to do so. But . . ." Lowering his pistol, Sutton slid it into the holster.

"So if you're not going to shoot me, what are you going to do?" James asked.

Sutton looked up. "Me? Well I'm going to mount up on my horse, ride back into town, and find the column. You know your people are coming this way."

Though they had heard rumors, many in Winchester refused to believe them. James nodded. "Ewell's corps, I hear."

Sutton shrugged. "We're leaving. I have orders, finally, to rejoin my regiment, the 39th New York. I expect to be with them in a few days, thank God."

"And me? What are you going to do about me?"

Sutton sighed. He was about to tell him that he knew how much Mary Beth loved him and that he could never do anything that would bring further harm or grief to her, but he couldn't bring himself to do so. Instead, he looked James in the eyes. "If my guess is right, you're a deserter. I don't have to do anything to punish you, Private. All I have to do is leave. If your own people catch you, they'll deal with you, I'm sure, appropriately."

"I can always run away," James countered.

"Then," Sutton responded, "you'll do so alone. Mary Beth will never leave this farm or her beloved Virginia. If you go, you'll go alone and never be able to return. That," Sutton concluded, "will be punishment enough."

Without another word, James Sutton turned and walked over to where he had left his horse, leaving James alone in the barn to ponder his fate.

Though there were signs of grief and melancholy here and there as the Stonewall Brigade marched into town and loved ones failed to see their sons, brothers, or fathers in the ranks, the return of Winchester to Confederate control was overall a time for celebration. The reign of Milroy, whose heavy-handed occupation had made him the most hated man in town, was brought to an end after a sharp battle that had cost Milroy much of the loot he had sacked from private homes as well as a good portion of his force. At a cost of forty-seven dead and two hundred and nineteen wounded, General Richard S. Ewell had inflicted four hundred and thirteen Union dead and wounded, taken an additional forty-four hundred Yankees prisoner, and captured twenty-three pieces of artillery. Though such one-sided victories were always a reason for a celebration, Abner Couper of the 4th Virginia had one nasty chore to tend to before he could join it.

Sitting in his tent, he looked down vacantly at his desk, pondering the fate of Private James Bannon. Appearing out of nowhere during the battle and joining a Louisiana regiment at the height of the fight, James Bannon, Couper was told by the sergeant who brought him back to the 4th Virginia, "fought in the grandest tradition of the Louisiana Tigers." With Colonel Terry, the commander of the 4th Virginia, away for the moment, Couper was the senior officer in the regiment and, as the adjutant, responsible for tending to these matters.

As he sat there, Couper was struck by the irony of the situation he was now placed in. His duty was clear. Army regulations left him little choice but to prepare charges against Bannon. Still, Couper found that he couldn't do what he had always wanted to do. His desire to ruin the Irish upstart from the North whom he had hated for so long simply wasn't there any longer. Too much had transpired since those foolish days at VMI, he realized. Too many good men, Couper remembered, whom he had once marched with, gone to class with, and shared a meal with at the institution, were now dead. Those who were still alive were, with few exceptions, still with the colors, serving the Confederacy. One of them was James Bannon, a man who, against all logic, had stood by the South for two hard years and now had come back to do so again.

Leaning back in his chair, Couper let his arms drop limply to his sides as he stared up at the ceiling of his tent. How easy, he thought, it would be for him to write out the charges against Bannon. Once done, Bannon would be brought up on trial and found guilty of desertion. Of that, Couper was sure. Then, all he would have to do was watch as someone else administered the punishment he had once thought Bannon deserved simply because of who he was and where he had been born. But Bannon's loyalty to the regiment and to the South, as well as Couper's loyalty to a fellow cadet, obscured the issue. To turn on Bannon, Couper rationalized, at a time when the South needed every able-bodied fighting man it had, would be foolish.

Still, he thought, as he looked down at the blank piece of paper sitting on his desk, waiting for him to initiate action against Bannon, something had to be done. To let him slip back into the ranks without a word would encourage others to desert. Something had to be done with Bannon.

Like a thunderbolt, it came to Couper. Sitting upright, he brought his hands up to the desktop, looked down at the blank sheet of paper, and thought for a moment. When all of his thoughts were sufficiently organized, he reached over, grabbed the pen out of the inkwell, and began to write a personal note to Colonel John Mercer Brockenbrough, commanding officer of the 40th Virginia Infantry and a graduate of VMI.

# *CHAPTER 26*

# July, 1863
# West of Gettysburg,
# Pennsylvania

THE RUMBLE OF CANNONS TO THE EAST HERALDED ANOTHER day's fighting. Those men of the 40th Virginia who had managed to sleep were stirred from their rest by the cannonading. Throwing off their thin blankets, they rose off the ground and looked to where the rising sun was beginning to make its appearance. A sergeant, walking along the straggly rows of sleepy soldiers who were still lounging about, called his men by name. "All right, boys, day's a-wasting. Get up and get yourselves something to eat."

One soldier stopped rolling his blanket as he looked first to the east, where the clap of rifle volleys now mixed in with the sound of cannonading, then up at the sergeant. "Think we're gonna go join that ruckus over there?"

The sergeant as well as several other men looked over to the east. "Lord," the sergeant finally said in a low voice. "I hope not." Then, with his eyes still fixed over to the east, he continued down the line while men gathered around watch fires to cook up their day's rations. There was none of the heady gaiety that had characterized their march north through the rich farmlands of south-central Pennsylvania. "We've found the land of milk and honey, boys," one of the men had shouted as they rifled the foodstuffs from an Amish farm. And for an Army used to campaigning in a country where all that was eatable had long been picked over by their comrades and the enemy, Pennsylvania had been a rare treat. Were it not for the heavy hand of their officers, all agreed that they would have made the rich

Yankee farmer howl in payment for the devastation that the Union Army had visited upon northern Virginia. "The Yankees 'round here," one man complained bitterly, "should fall down on their knees and thank God for Bobby Lee. For if it weren't for him, I swear to God these people would pay, I tell you. They would pay dearly for what they did to Virginia."

Still, there was enough "authorized" foraging to more than meet the needs of an army long used to doing without. Even when they moved into an area already picked over by another unit farther up the road, the soldiers of the 40th Virginia found plenty left over. Even firewood was abundant along the line of march as soldiers used fence rails and stocks already cut by the farmers for their own use. Though Army regulations forbade soldiers from taking any more than the top rail of a fence, one member of the 40th Virginia sarcastically noted as he took a rail that had once been the third down but was now the top one, "Seems like we can never quite figure out which rail really is the top, can we?"

All this easy living came to an abrupt halt on the first day of July, when the brigade, commanded by Colonel John M. Brockenbrough, found itself swept into a bitter fight just west of a small Pennsylvania town named Gettysburg. Rather than facing militia, which had been the only opposition the Army of Northern Virginia had met since moving north, they found themselves face-to-face with the troops of the famed Iron Brigade, distinguished from all others by their tall black felt hats, which they held on to as stubbornly as they held their ground. It had been a bitter fight, one that had cost the regiments that made up Brockenbrough's small brigade over a third of their number. The brigade, as well as the rest of Heth's division, had been so badly mauled that it sat out the second day of the battle as new fights flared up south and east of where they had been left to lick their wounds in peace.

Even now, two days after that terrible fight, no one seemed much interested in going back into the fray. As a group of half a dozen soldiers sat around a fire, cooking their bacon and chunks of ham in small frying pans or on sticks, few found anything to talk about. Even those few who did, however, quickly lapsed into silence as James Bannon ambled up to the fire. One man who had seen him coming nodded to his comrades, two of whom gave way without a word so that James had a clear space near the fire.

James, his head perpetually bowed down, dropped to his knees and set his small dirty black frying pan on the ground. Reaching into his haversack, he pulled out a shapeless clump of meat wrapped in a greasy bit of cloth. Carefully unfolding the corners of the cloth, he exposed the bacon, which he took in one hand while he stuffed the dirty rag back into his haversack. Pulling out a knife, James cut irregular strips of meat and fat off of the chunk of bacon into his frying pan. Finished, he lifted the frying pan and set it carefully on a bed of hot coals near the edge of the fire.

After watching the bacon for a few minutes, never once looking about the gathering of men who stood around him, James went back to fishing in his haversack. This time, he pulled out two hard crackers, which some called hardtack. He didn't even try to break them in half, for to have done so would have been a waste of time. Instead, he gently set the two crackers into the frying pan, which was now filling with bacon grease. Satisfied with his work, he eased back on his haunches, placing his hands on his legs as he watched his breakfast cook.

Ignoring the spitting grease that dotted the back of his hands in the same cold silence as he ignored his messmates, James didn't move or utter a sound until his food was ready. Even then, all he did was fish out the dirty old cloth that had once covered the bacon from his haversack and a silver spoon that he had picked up somewhere along the way. Wrapping the rag about the handle of the frying pan, James gave the pan a slight jiggle as he poked at the crackers to make sure that they were soft enough to eat and flipped the bacon over and about. When he was satisfied that his meal was done, James stood up, balancing the frying pan so as not to spill the grease his food was floating in. Turning slowly, he walked away from the circle of silent men, who watched him leave. Only after they were sure that he was out of earshot did someone finally break the silence. "Well," a tall scrawny soldier announced, "if you ask me, he scares me."

The sergeant who had gone about waking the men of his company grunted. "Well, no one asked you."

"Yeah," a short, dark-haired youth next to the sergeant added. "He ain't hurtin' no one."

With a look of surprise on his face, the tall scrawny soldier looked about the circle of men, who were now nodding in agreement. "Well," the tall scrawny soldier stated with indignation, "that's a fine how do you do, now isn't it? I mean, three days ago there wasn't a one of you who would have given two hoots for that glum has-been from VMI."

"That," the sergeant announced solemnly, "was three days ago. A lot has changed."

Unwilling to be bullied, the tall scrawny soldier persisted. "No it hasn't. He still keeps to himself as if we weren't good enough to associate with. He still refuses to do anything unless you or an officer orders him to. He even marches along the side of the road, away from the rest of us. Besides," he added with a note of concern, "he scares me."

The black-haired youth looked up. "Scares you?"

"Yes," the tall scrawny soldier insisted. "He scares me. I ain't never seen a man fight with such, such . . ."

"Abandon?" another man volunteered.

"That's right," the tall scrawny soldier agreed. "Abandon. It's almost like he wanted to kill every Yankee himself. Either that or . . ."

When the tall scrawny soldier didn't finish his sentence, the black-haired youth looked up. "Or what?"

The tall scrawny soldier stared into the burning embers of the fire at his feet. The hot coals shone brightly in his sad, tired eyes as he spoke barely above a whisper. "Or he's trying to get himself killed." Looking up, the tall scrawny soldier glanced about the men gathered about the fire. As he had just a minute before, most of them were now looking into the fire with thoughtful, reflective expressions on their faces. It was as if they were all sharing a common vision that no one outside of the small circle could see. And perhaps they did, for each of them, after almost two years of war, had seen men so tired of living that they did whatever they could to bring an end to the misery that had come to dominate both their lives and the land that they had once loved so dearly.

It was the sergeant who finally broke the spell. Looking about, he once again cast his eyes over to the east. "Well," he admitted. "If that's what he's after, then I'm sure he'll find it, and soon."

## Cemetery Ridge, South of Gettysburg, Pennsylvania

With nothing to do and little desire to stand around while general officers came and went, Kevin Bannon asked for and received permission to go over to where the Third Division of the Second Corps was posted. "I have a friend," he told General Butterfield, General Meade's chief of staff, "serving with the 12th New Jersey, whom I haven't seen since I left Rutgers to enlist. Since I'm not of much use right now . . ."

Butterfield, his attention distracted by an approaching courier, waved Kevin off. "Go, Captain, go. Just let me know when you're back."

Intending to take full advantage of Butterfield's carte blanche, Kevin saluted, turned, and made his way up the slope from where Meade's headquarters sat to where he thought the 12th New Jersey might be. The first unit he came across was a New York regiment, the 39th New York, which Kevin knew to be in the Third Division. Seeing their major standing off to one side, alone, Kevin walked up to him. "Excuse me, sir, but I'm looking for the 12th New Jersey. I was told they were in this division."

The blond major began to speak as he turned to face Kevin, but stopped in midsentence when his green eyes reached Kevin's face. After standing there for a moment while the major stared at him, Kevin finally asked if there was something wrong.

With a wave of his hand, as if he were clearing away an unseen cobweb, Major James Sutton blinked, shook his head, and laughed. "No, nothing at all. I just thought . . ." Then he stopped midsentence again as he pondered the resemblance between this captain and the Rebel who owned the heart of the girl he loved. "Yes, well, the 12th New Jersey, you say?"

"Yes, sir. I have a friend who's a captain in that regiment."

"Well, now, the 12th is in the Second Brigade, about a hundred yards over there," Sutton announced as he lifted his left arm and pointed, "along that stone wall, just short of the white barn."

Looking over at the barn, Kevin could see regimental colors he took to be the 12th's. Then, he looked back at Sutton with a smile. "Well, Major . . . ?"

"Sutton, James Sutton of New York."

Kevin was about to mention that he had a brother named James, but didn't. It was of no importance and besides, whenever he thought of his brother, he was always taken with a bout of melancholy that followed him for days. After saluting Sutton, Kevin headed over to where the 12th New Jersey was supposed to be.

He found his friend right off, crouching behind the stone wall with several other officers, looking out over the open field to their front. When a zing ripped through the air not far from Kevin's head, he too crouched down as he made his way forward. "Spencer," Kevin called out when his friend caught a glimpse of him and smiled. "Spencer Rains, how are you doing?"

Making room for Kevin up against the wall, Rains took Kevin's outstretched hand and shook it firmly. "We'll all be doing a whole sight better after we rid our front of those pesky sharpshooters in that barn out there."

Carefully lifting his head above the level of the wall, Kevin looked out in the direction that Rains was pointing in. At a distance just slightly more than a quarter of a mile, Kevin saw a substantial two-story stone-and-wood barn standing just in front of an orchard. To the right of the barn was a two-story wooden house. Here and there, a telltale puff of smoke from the barn or the house or the orchard rose. Lowering his head, he looked at Rains, who was smiling. "Some of the boys went out there last night and chased the Rebs away, but they've come back in force. They've been making life miserable for us here all morning. Dick Thompson here," Rains stated as he pointed to a captain, who nodded politely at Kevin, "is going to take a battalion of us out there and see if we can get rid of those fellows for good." Then, with a glint in his eyes, Rains added,

"Would you care to join us, Kevin? You can march with my company."

Without even a sideways glance back to where Meade's headquarters was, Kevin smiled. "It would be a pleasure, Spencer."

"Well then." Rains beamed. "Follow me." Keeping low, he led Kevin over to where his first sergeant was forming up his company. After a quick introduction to him and several other members of Rains' small command, Kevin looked over to where Thompson was preparing for their sortie.

"All right, boys," Rains ordered his company. "Check your pieces and get ready."

When Kevin saw that they were armed with the ancient caliber .69 smoothbore muskets, like the ones that the 4th New Jersey had been issued after being exchanged in 1862, he almost balked about going. Since the muskets were all but useless at anything but the shortest range, few units in the Army of the Potomac still carried them. That a line unit like the 12th New Jersey should be armed with them bothered Kevin. Still, he said nothing. Instead, he pulled out his own pistol, gave the cylinder a quick spin to make sure all the caps were in place and ready, then reholstered it. Though he didn't know a single man in this unit other than Rains, the idea of going forward into an attack excited him to the point where he started to chafe at the delays that kept them back. It would soon be two years ago, he realized as he fought back his growing excitement, that I set out, reluctantly, on my first campaign. "Two years," he repeated, out loud now. God, he thought, how this world has changed; how I've changed.

With a crisp shout, Captain Richard S. Thompson started to give commands to his small command, consisting of Companies A, C, D, F, and K of the 12th New Jersey. Rains' company was the second in line. After a quick right face, the column was marched behind the regiment, given a file by the left, and led around the white barn building the regiment's right was anchored on and down a farm lane that led out toward the enemy-held barn and orchard. As soon as the head of the column came around the north end of the stone wall and past the white barn there, the 12th New Jersey began to take fire.

The first shots missed their mark, for the most part due to

partial cover provided by a broad, flat knoll and the haste with which the Confederates fired. The cover of the knoll, while not much, allowed the assaulting column enough time to cross the road that led north into Gettysburg and south to Emmitsburg. Once across this road, Thompson ordered his command to swing out into columns of company. Company F, the lead company, deployed in line of battle, with the other companies following doing likewise. When each of the five companies was in double line of battle and covered down on the company line in front of them, Kevin heard the order to charge. Drawing his pistol, he followed his old friend and took up the double-quick pace.

Once they were up and over the knoll, Kevin was surprised to see movement off to his right. Without pausing, he kept up with Rains but turned his head in the direction of the movement in an effort to get a better view of what was going on over there. A sudden spattering of rifle fire quickly told him all he needed to know. The same knoll that had served to cover their deployment into columns of company had hidden from their view another group of Confederate skirmishers, who were now taking the 12th's right flank under fire.

Picking up his pace and looking back to the front, Kevin was about to shout a warning to his friend when he suddenly tripped over something. Staggering forward several feet with arms flailing, Kevin managed to keep his balance. Out of curiosity, he craned his neck about to see what he had stumbled on. What he saw sickened him. His friend, his right arm still outstretched and grasping his saber, was lying facedown on the ground. Spencer Rains' hat was gone, exposing his light brown hair, stained bright red on the side where he had taken a bullet.

Looking back to his front, then to his left, Kevin instinctively moved forward to fill the void left by Rains and waved his pistol high over his head. "Keep up with Company F," he shouted down the swaying line of panting men who once belonged to Rains. "Dress on me and keep up."

By the time Kevin's newly adopted company reached the barn, the soldiers of the lead company had swept into it. With a wave of his arm and a shout, Kevin ordered his men to swing to the right and establish a firing line to the right of the barn, facing to the northwest at an angle. The house, less than two hundred feet from where they formed, seemed to be vacant. Beyond the house, the enemy who had taken the 12th under fire as they had advanced were continuing to snipe at them. But because of their smoothbore muskets the men under Kevin's command could do nothing to discourage this. Besides, there was plenty to their front that was a lot closer to worry about.

In the orchard to the west, Kevin could clearly see Confederate officers moving about, pointing and shouting as they tried to rally their men and direct their fire against the 12th New Jersey. Off to their right, the Confederates who had taken them under fire as they had advanced were still active, though their attention was now being directed against another unit Kevin could not see. Even though Kevin's men and the other companies with them were returning their fire as rapidly as possible, he quickly realized that not only were they outgunned by Confederates armed with better rifles, they would soon be engulfed by superior numbers. And as if this wasn't bad enough, a Confederate artillery battery, sited across the field in front of a tree line to the west, was beginning to take the barn under fire. Though their fire was directed squarely at the barn with telling effect, near misses as well as splinters and chunks of brick and stone from hits on the barn were peppering those men of Kevin's command who were next to it.

Kevin was about to go off and see if he could find Captain Thompson when Thompson came up to him. "Where is Spencer?" Thompson shouted above the roar.

Kevin pointed back across their line of advance. "He was struck down before we got here." Then, without thinking, he added, "I've taken command."

At first, Thompson made a face at Kevin's announcement. After glancing up at the red Greek cross that served as the symbol for the First Division of the Sixth Corps sewn to the top of his cap along with the number 4, however, he changed his mind. Though the 4th New Jersey didn't have the greatest reputation as a fighting unit, Thompson realized that the man he was looking at probably had seen more action than any officer in the 12th. "All right then," he finally announced. "We're going to move along this stream to our rear, take those Rebs up there in those bushes in the flank, and then fall back to the wall. Your company will form the right. When you are ready, sir, move your men out and form up facing to the north. I'll bring the rest of the battalion along and form on you.''

Kevin nodded, then turned to find his first sergeant. Pointing to a spot across the small stream with his pistol, Kevin shouted, ''Over there. We're going to re-form the company in line facing that way, to the north.''

Looking to where Kevin pointed, then farther on, to where the enemy in the bushes were now being engaged by another Union unit to the east, the first sergeant didn't say a word. Like Kevin, he could see that by forming there, they would be able to take the Confederates in the flank, just as the Confederates had done to the 12th during their advance. Instead, he turned, and headed out to comply with his orders.

After giving the first sergeant a few seconds' head start, Kevin went down his line of men, starting on the right. Coming up behind them, he repeated his order as often as necessary to get his company moving and redeployed. ''Re-form on the first sergeant, over there,'' he said, motioning over to where the first sergeant was headed. Though most of the men didn't recognize Kevin's face, they saw that he was an officer and that he was in control of both the situation and himself. While some acknowledged Kevin's order with a nod and others with a grunt, all followed his directions. By the time he was finished and had himself turned to follow, other companies were streaming down to form up on the left of Kevin's company.

It took only a few minutes. For Kevin, whose company was in place first and therefore had to wait the longest, they were long minutes. If the Confederates who had run from the barn to the orchard were quick, they would be able to rush forward and take the detachment of the 12th New Jersey in the flank before the 12th had a chance to do that to the enemy they now faced. Thompson's command to move forward, therefore, came as a great relief.

As they moved astride the stream, with half the detachment on one side and half on the other, Kevin could see that the Rebel riflemen who had fired on their flank during the advance to the farm were now occupied with an Ohio regiment that had advanced on them. If any of the Confederates did see the 12th New Jersey coming, they did nothing about it. It was only after Thompson, judging that they were near enough, stopped the

line and ordered his command to fire by battalion that the
Confederate officers took note. By then, it was too late, for
their men, startled by the sudden volley in their flank, took to
their heels and fled. Thompson, seeing that his men had
achieved the effect he desired, then began to order his companies to fall back, picking up their wounded as they went.

## Seminary Ridge, Southwest of Gettysburg, Pennsylvania

By early afternoon, all hope that they would be left out of that
day's fight had pretty much vanished for the men of the 40th
Virginia. No one had to tell them that they were going to attack.
They were all veterans. They knew the signs. First came the
mounted couriers, shouting for the brigade commander. Then a
brigade staff officer came by each of the regiments, requesting,
in the politest of terms, the regimental commander's presence.
Upon his return from his meeting with the brigade commander,
the regimental commander would call his own officers together
and pass on to them whatever orders and information he felt
they needed. By the time those orders, much abbreviated to
nothing more than "All right, 40th Virginia, fall in," reached
James Bannon, he was already on his feet and ready to march.

Though their move was a short one, it took time, for there
were many units converging, as one officer pointed out to
James' sergeant as they waited for a battalion of artillery to
move by, in the center. "Seems Longstreet's effort to get
around the Yankee left didn't work yesterday," the smooth-
cheeked lieutenant stated with an air of authority. "Neither did
Ewell's attack on their right, the one we heard last night and
this morning."

The sergeant, after thinking about it for a moment, looked
back at the lieutenant with a worried look on his face. "So
Bobby Lee thinks we can break them in the center?"

"No." The lieutenant beamed. "He *knows* we can."

The sergeant looked down at the ground and shook his head. "Well, sir, I'm only a sergeant, but it seems to me if the Yankees couldn't break Old Pete's line at Fredericksburg, what makes General Lee think we can do it here?"

The lieutenant took a step back as if he had been slapped. "Sir, we are Virginians. This Army has never been beaten, and I highly doubt that General Lee would gamble so much and so many on something that he wasn't sure would succeed."

James, like the sergeant, shook his head. Though he wanted to remind the lieutenant that, at best, Sharpsburg was a draw, he kept his peace. After two years of war, the only things that never seemed to change were the idle chatter soldiers engaged in before a fight and the desire of the men in the ranks to second-guess their commanders, neither of which James had any interest in pursuing.

The sergeant, sensing that his lieutenant was no longer in the mood to discuss the matter in a reasonable manner, decided to back off. "Well, sir," he said rather diplomatically, "I suppose you're right. It surely wouldn't make sense to throw us all away on a gamble that didn't have a chance in hell of succeeding."

Believing that he had won over the sergeant, the lieutenant cocked his head back and pulled at one side of the scrawny mustache he had grown in an effort to hide his youth. "Of course not, Sergeant, of course not." With that, he strolled over in search of an officer with whom he could discuss the pending fight.

When the sergeant, seeing that there was a break in the artillery column, looked back to order his men to shoulder arms, his eyes met James'. For a moment, they looked at each other. Then the sergeant shook his head, signifying that he, like James, wasn't convinced. James, in return, nodded as he brought his rifle up to shoulder arms. Whether they believed in their odds of succeeding really didn't matter. For while they, as battle hardened infantrymen, knew what would happen once they stepped out into the attack, they also knew that many a battle was decided not by superior numbers or tactics, but by sheer determination and courage. Perhaps, James thought, as the 40th Virginia's short column lurched forward, the lieutenant was right. Perhaps.

## Cemetery Ridge, South of Gettysburg, Pennsylvania

Sitting with his back against the two-foot-high stone wall in an effort to stay out of the hot afternoon sun, Kevin Bannon chatted idly with a corporal and a private who flanked him on either side. The private, sitting with his legs spread apart and the contents of his cartridge box poured out on the ground before him, was busy repacking the cartridges for his caliber .69 musket. Each of the issued cartridges, big hefty things, contained one round ball, slightly smaller than the bore of the musket. On top of these balls, in each cartridge, were three buckshot pellets. This type of cartridge, known as buck and ball, was meant to compensate for the incredibly short range of the percussion-cap muskets. Some of the men were convinced that the Confederates would try the center after failing on both flanks. Since they, the 12th New Jersey, sat almost smack in the middle of the Union line, they suspected that before the day was out, there would be heavy fighting.

So rather than sit by idly in the hot sun, they began to reload their cartridges. No one ordered them to do so. And no one told the men how many buckshot to repack in each round. The corporal, to Kevin's right, had reloaded nine buckshot per cartridge. The private, to the left, seemed to prefer anywhere between twelve and fifteen, with the count varying from round to round. Kevin toyed with the idea of taking some of the buckshot himself and reloading his pistol, as a few of the officers were doing, but didn't. It was too hot and the Confederates were, for him, being too quiet.

Finished with his reloading, the corporal gnawed at a cracker he held in one hand. "You gonna stay with us for a while, Captain?" the corporal asked nonchalantly.

Kevin took off his cap and wiped his forehead with his sleeve. "Well, I suppose I should head back to headquarters and ask, but, if I do, someone might say no."

The private, carefully dropping buckshot into an open cartridge he held in front of his face, paused and looked over at Kevin. "Won't you get in trouble if you don't go back?" he asked innocently.

"Well," Kevin pondered, "I suppose I could, if anyone missed me. But in all the time I've been on that staff, the only thing I ever got to do that was even remotely important was hold the general's horse while he sat under a tree and talked to another general."

The private's eyes betrayed his wonder. "My Lord! To be there like that, when the generals are planning their battles. It must be exciting."

Both Kevin and the corporal looked over at the private with amazed expressions on their faces. Kevin didn't have the heart to tell the young man that all the two generals talked about while he held the horse in the baking sun was how beastly hot it was. Instead, Kevin finally smiled. "Yeah, sometimes it is, I suppose."

Satisfied, the private went back to reloading his cartridges while the corporal continued to gnaw angrily at the stubborn piece of cracker. Kevin, pulling his cap back on so that its brim was low over his eyes, looked around. All around him soldiers lay about and loitered, some talking, others eating, a few even sleeping, all doing their best to escape the heat, sun, and boredom that seemed to consume the entire Army. Behind the 12th New Jersey, the men of the 111th New York sat out in the open, doing much the same as the Jerseymen did. The officers of the New York regiment, as well as those of the brigade and division staff, were gathered here and there in little knots, chatting and debating. Seeing the regimental and national colors hanging limply on their staffs, Kevin noted that the air was as still and calm as death itself. Then, with a slight shake of his head, he started to correct his own thoughts. For despite his long association with war, he didn't like comparing anything to death.

He was in the midst of thinking so when the report of a lone cannon, firing from somewhere across the valley behind him, shattered the early afternoon calm.

## Seminary Ridge, Southwest of Gettysburg, Pennsylvania

Deployed in line of battle and with their rifles laid out neatly on the ground before them, the soldiers of the 40th Virginia watched as the gun crews in front of them went to work pounding the Union line that sat little more than one mile across the shallow valley.

"Lordy," one man next to James exclaimed as he watched the avalanche of shot and shell crash down on the Union-held ridgeline. "Them boys is catching hell for sure, I tell you."

The sergeant grunted. "I just hope the lieutenant is right about them Yankees being on the brink of breaking."

James, sitting against a tree, looked up and over at the sergeant. "You really don't believe that, do you?"

Surprised by the fact that he had spoken as much as by the comment, the sergeant and several men about James just looked down at him for several seconds with their mouths agape before someone finally responded. "Well, hell, of course we do. We've beat them to a standstill every time we've come against them, haven't we?"

"But they keep coming back, don't they?" James responded calmly. "Did you ever think of that?"

"I guess they're just a little thickheaded, that's all," a private countered. "Maybe today will be the day they up and decide that they've had enough."

"And maybe," James shot back, "those boys feel the same way about defending their homes here and about as you do about yours back in Virginia."

"What," a burly corporal challenged, "makes you such an expert on Yankees?"

With only the fury of the cannon fire itself to move it about, the smoke from each discharge clung stubbornly to each cannon, obscuring James' view of the far ridgeline. "I was born and raised in the North. I know those people. Except for their accents and beliefs, they're no different than you. And like you, many of them are willing to fight for those beliefs, no matter how terrible the cost.''

His announcement that he was, by birth, a Yankee stunned some of the men about him. Two of them, whispering so that he could hear them, commented that they now understood why the 4th Virginia had been so anxious to get rid of him. Finally, one of that pair smiled and looked James in the eyes. "If'en all those folks up north are so blamed dedicated to what they're fightin' for, then how come you're here fightin' with us? What's so impo'tent to ya that makes ya want to fight ya own kin?"

James stared at the grinning scarecrow of a man but didn't answer him. He couldn't, for he really didn't know any longer what he was fighting for. Once, he had convinced himself that he was fighting for his friend Will, but Will was gone now. Then, he fancied that he could make a new start in Winchester with Mary Beth, until the Yankee major had come out of nowhere to threaten that dream. Now, he was just fighting, as he always had, not for something that he loved, but against everything before him.

Tiring of a discussion that most saw would be fruitless, and anxious to watch the effects of the artillery barrage, one by one the men turned away from James, leaving him in peace to ponder what, exactly, it was that he believed in.

Across the valley, separated by little more than a mile of rolling farmland and a small insignificant stream, the tranquil afternoon that the 12th New Jersey had found so boring was over. Those who could dove for the cover of the knee-high wall. Even the soldiers of the 111th New York, with no natural cover of their own, ran forward in leaps and bounds, and plopped down in amongst the Jerseymen of the 12th. Officers, for the most part, threw away any false pride that they might have carried into this battle with them and cowered behind whatever cover they could find alongside their men. Those who didn't, for the most part, paid a terrible price for that pride.

From his spot against the wall, Kevin propped himself up on an elbow and looked about at the scene behind him. Off to his right, a caisson caught a Confederate shell, sending it and two of the six horses still harnessed to it flying through the air. "Oh, Lordy," a man near Kevin shouted as he watched the fragments of caisson and horse come raining back down. "I don't want to see no more."

With great relief, Kevin saw that most of the Confederate shelling was going overhead, either directed at the artillery batteries interspersed along the front line or going harmlessly over the ridge. Remembering the congestion in and around General Meade's headquarters, which was directly behind the ridge, Kevin imagined that they were catching hell there. Since he had no close personal friends there, he experienced no great anxiety at that thought. Rather, he chuckled when the thought came to him that perhaps the Confederates would do what he had been wanting to do since Chancellorsville, which was to kill the damned horse he had been issued.

The private, who had still been busy repacking his cartridges when the shelling began, at first tried to gather up all his scattered rounds and stuff them away before taking cover. But after several seconds of futile effort, during which he saw that he might lose his spot right up against the wall, the private gave up, satisfying himself with the few handfuls he had managed to scoop up, and nuzzled up next to Kevin at the wall. "Dear God in heaven!" he exclaimed as he brought his hands up to cover his ears. "How long they gonna do this?" he shouted to Kevin.

Feeling the effects of the strange calmness that seemed to possess him now whenever he was going into a fight, Kevin looked into the frightened eyes of the young private. "Till they attack, boy."

"Then what?"

"Then," Kevin responded with a smile that befuddled the private, "it's our turn."

Even as the last few rounds were being fired, the brigade and regimental officers began falling their men into ranks in preparation for their advance. The Union guns that had been responding to the massive Confederate barrage had, for the most part, ceased. Though ineffective, that return fire had inflicted some casualties, not only on the Confederate gunners whom it had been aimed at but also on the infantry, waiting patiently to their rear in the woods. Carefully, the soldiers of the 40th Virginia stepped over their fallen comrades, shouting out words of encouragement to those who were wounded. Few realized, at that moment, that those already wounded were the lucky ones.

As he had many times before, James Bannon lifted his rifle and took his place in ranks. Like the men to his left and right, he was jostled about while arranging his cartridge box, cap box, and haversack before looking to his right to check his alignment. This was a veteran unit, a long-service regiment that had seen many battles and much hard campaigning. Like every other man in those ranks, James knew what was about to happen and what he needed to do to prepare for it. Every man about him knew what was expected of him. And every man, whether he wanted to admit it or not, knew, even before they stepped out of the shade of the woods, how much more they had to give.

After counting off their men by twos, the officers took their posts and drew their swords. Officers, including their division commander, rode by and shouted a few words of encouragement that James didn't pay much attention to. His head, cluttered with memories and images of his own troubled past, spun off from one thought to another without rhyme or reason despite his best effort to grab onto one, any one, in an effort to justify his life. He was still struggling with this invisible fight when he felt a nudge from behind, indicating it was time to advance. Mechanically, he lifted his left foot and stepped out with his eyes fixed straight ahead.

Emerging from the dense cloud of smoke that still lingered from the artillery barrage, the 40th Virginia moved through the guns that had been pounding the Union-held ridgeline little more than a mile off to the east. The gunners, grim and sweaty from their labors, stepped aside and shouted encouragement to the infantry as they went by. For the most part, none of the infantrymen responded, concentrating instead on the long line of blue that seemed to stretch across the entire horizon before their eyes. Even James was struck by the terrible beauty of the spectacle before him. The contrasts were, he thought, most startling. Set against the pale blue sky, the dark blue uniforms of the Union soldiers seemed to merge into a single long ribbon. Only the flash of their rifle barrels, a stand of colors, or a break here and there where a battery of artillery stuck their muzzles over the short gray wall gave contrast to that terrible sight. With a gray wall no taller than knee height obscuring their legs, the enemy looked to James as if they were an army of scarecrows set up to intimidate them.

Yet, as James now thought as he emerged from his own confused reflections, if anyone in the Confederate ranks was intimidated, they weren't showing it. To the immediate right of the 40th Virginia, a brigade of North Carolinians was advancing, well to the front of the 40th. To the left, James couldn't see the rest of the brigade but knew that it would be over there, perhaps moving forward in echelon. In front, a thin line of skirmishers, six feet apart, moved across the lush green fields that separated him from the formidable host they were attacking.

If Kevin was nervous, no one about him noticed, for they were all so engrossed with their own thoughts or the spectacle of the advancing gray host coming at them that few men made the effort to consider what was happening to their immediate left or right. Even when Kevin, tired of pacing back and forth behind his adopted company, pushed his way back to the wall, no one said anything, no one even bothered to glance his way. Some of the men occupied these last few idle moments by slowly stacking up small piles of cartridges before them on the wall while keeping their eyes on the soldiers of Pettigrew's division as it continued to close the distance between them at a steady, irresistible pace. Here and there, behind him, Kevin could hear the occasional click of a musket hammer as soldiers nervously flipped their thumbs across the hammer and let it go without cocking it.

Behind them soldiers of the New York regiments were closing up on them, giving the line the effect of having four, instead of two, ranks' depth. General Hays, the commander of the division to which the 12th New Jersey belonged, rode behind the lines, repeating as he went along, "They're coming, boys.

We must whip them." When he noticed the men about Kevin were armed with the big-bore muskets, he paused. "You men with buck and ball, don't fire until they get to that fence," he shouted as he jabbed his gloved fist toward the Emmitsburg road. Kevin looked over to where the general was pointing and noted that even that road was too far for the short range of the muskets. Still, Kevin understood what the general wanted and nodded in acknowledgment before Hays rode on. Not long after that, Major John T. Hill, commanding the regiment that day, ordered the 12th to hold its fire until the enemy soldiers were within twenty yards.

When the Confederate line, staggered off to the right, reached the slight rise of ground behind and to the right of the Bliss farm, where the 12th New Jersey had advanced to earlier, Union artillery began to take them under fire. Though slow to start, it soon began to spread, though with little response other than a continuation of their steady, determined advance, from the enemy.

It was impossible to ignore the enemy artillery fire. Nor was there any more doubt that it was increasing with every passing moment. As the men to the left pushed down to close ranks and men behind them staggered forward in an effort to step over the dead and dying, James remembered the statement Major Thomas Jackson had made a long time ago, in the quietness of his section room, before he had become Stonewall Jackson. "If the time comes," he had admonished James and his fellow cadets that April day, when talk of the impending war inflamed every young heart, "then draw your sword and throw away the scabbard." Someone, James realized as he bent over as if he were walking into a heavy wind, had done just that. They were going to go forward now, regardless of the wisdom, regardless of the cost. There was no longer any need for him to think, James told himself. No longer any chance to appeal to logic. He would go forward, he decided, with them, consequences and reasons be damned.

Like James, the men around him held their own thoughts. Some of those thoughts would never find expression, for even as James and the tortured mass of men who made up the 40th moved onward, men continued to go down all about him, taking their unspoken thoughts and questions to their graves. Down they went, in increasing numbers. Sometimes a single man would fall, unnoticed by his comrades to his left and right, proving to be nothing more than an inconvenience to those who followed him as they were forced to step over his body. Sometimes they fell in groups as a round of solid shot bowled its way through the ranks or a shell exploded in the midst of a knot of men, throwing whole men and many small parts of men's bodies this way and that.

And yet the lines moved on, those who still stood moved forward. Steadily, unhastened footfall after footfall brought them nearer to the gray stone wall. With the rising tempo of Federal fire raining down upon them came a steady increase of activities, within the ranks of Pettigrew's division. Officers and noncommissioned officers up and down the lines of battle were shouting louder and louder as they competed with explosions, screams of the dying, and moans of the wounded. All around him, James began to hear the cries of officers, "Close it up," or "Dress on the colors. Push on and dress on the colors." Sergeants and corporals, with few words, closed gaps torn in the ranks. James suddenly began to feel worse than useless; he felt alone. As he had some four years before, he faced a dark and fearful crisis surrounded by strangers.

"By God," the corporal next to Kevin shouted, "they're stopping!"

Kevin, who had been looking down, jerked his head up and scanned the long gray lines, now less than half a mile away. After watching for a moment, he shook his head. "No, they're not stopping for good. They're just adjusting their alignment, dressing up their ranks before they make the final charge."

"Well, now," the private on the other side said, "isn't that cheeky? Who do they think they are, anyhow?"

Kevin looked over at the private and smiled. He too had been thinking the same thoughts, becoming angered by the display of utter contempt that the advancing Confederate soldiers were hurling at them. "Well," Kevin responded slowly as he looked to his left and right at the line of troops waiting at the wall, "I doubt if those ranks will be as pretty as they are now after we empty a few volleys into them."

The private laughed nervously. "Oh, no, sir. They surely won't. They surely won't."

Though it only took a minute, maybe two at the most, to finish realigning the 40th Virginia in the shallow streambed that provided little cover from the brutal Union artillery fire that seemed to be concentrated on them, something happened to the resolve of Brockenbrough's brigade in those two minutes. Such things were not uncommon, as James knew. Most attacks that James had seen fail did so because the men making the attacks decided, collectively or individually, that they had done enough and stopped moving forward or following orders. And while, on occasion, an officer's inspired leadership or example could manage to get the stalled attack back on track, more often than not, even the most vehement haranguing or the most vicious threats of their officers could not push a man beyond his limit. The officers of the 40th, as well as the rest of the brigade, rediscovered this terrible truth about human nature when they gave the order to go forward again.

James, along with several other men, stepped out without hesitation. A few, those who were wavering, lifted one foot, then the other, but did not move forward when they saw that there were too many holding back. The rest, the bulk of the regiment, simply stood fast, in ranks with their rifles at shoulder arms. The officers who had survived up to this point at first didn't believe what was happening. Thinking that their orders had been drowned out by the grueling pounding the enemy artillery continued to rain down on them, the officers stopped, turned, and repeated their orders. This time, however, not even those who had wavered before budged. "Forward, *damn you*. Forward," the smooth-cheeked lieutenant with the scrawny mustache screamed as he jabbed his sword toward the stone wall, "forward or I'll shoot you all right here myself." Still, no one moved. When the regimental commander, seeing that his command was no longer responding, turned and began to curse and admonish his men to advance, even the color guard failed to respond.

Sensing the Confederates' difficulty, Union infantrymen who had been deployed as skirmishers to the front of the brigade surged forward in what many thought would be a suicidal attack against the left flank of Colonel Brockenbrough's brigade. To their surprise, the opposite was true. Even before they had covered half the distance to the wavering mass of men their desperate charge was directed against, their enemy broke. James, looking first at their assailants, then to his own companions, who were either slowly stepping backwards or turning and fleeing in abject terror, couldn't believe what was happening. Even from where he stood, he could see that the brigade, with one good volley, could check the mad Union charge. But the men of the Brockenbrough brigade simply didn't have even one good volley left in them. Even the smooth-cheeked lieutenant forgot all his idle boasting of that morning and turned to join his men as they rapidly retraced their steps, bothering neither to look back nor to pick up their own wounded as they did so.

Suddenly, for the first time in a long time, James felt angry, truly and uncontrollably angry. He was not going to run. He was not going to turn his back on those who attacked him, not again. Deciding that he had done all the running in his life that he could, James screamed at the advancing enemy, brought his rifle up, and fired at the nearest Yankee, knocking him over backwards. Without taking his eyes off of his assailants, James dropped the butt of his rifle to the ground, grabbing the barrel with his left hand while he reached around behind his back with his right to fish out another cartridge. When he brought the cartridge up and clamped it between his teeth, grains of black powder showered out of the end as he jerked it away and poured it into the upturned muzzle. With quick easy steps, he drew his ramrod, rammed home his charge, replaced his ramrod, brought his rifle up, cocked the hammer back, flicked off the old cap, put on a new cap, and prepared to fire again.

Having achieved all that they could, the Union commander leading the attack by the 8th Ohio halted his men and led them back. James, after taking one more shot, looked about. In a moment, he realized he was alone. To his right, a freshly burned barn still smoldered. Behind him, the scattered remains of his brigade staggered back as individuals or in small groups of not more than half a dozen. To his left, there was nothing other than the retreating Ohio Yankees. Only to the front, just off to the right where the North Carolinians were still advancing, did James see any prospects of useful employment. Quickly reloading as he started forward again at the double, James headed for the wavering lines of North Carolinians, now nearing a rail fence along a road just short of the Union-held ridge.

On all sides of the 12th New Jersey, regiments opened fire on the mass of Confederate infantry as it climbed over or pushed down the fence that lined the Emmitsburg Road. Together with the artillery, which had switched from shell and solid shot to canister, the effect that the rifle fire was having on the Confederates was both spectacular and appalling. The nice neat lines that regimental and company officers had taken the time to dress not minutes before were no longer in evidence. Now, when the real killing was beginning, those who still had the resolve to go forward merely followed the nearest flag, officer, or their own path. Yet, Kevin thought in amazement, they were *still* coming forward.

Sensing that his own men were becoming anxious to fire, Kevin leaned over and shouted above the din. "Hold your fire. Fire only on command." Though half of the men in his small command didn't hear him, no one fired. All stood there, grim faced and transfixed by what they saw before them, waiting. Kevin, knowing that the time was near, drew his pistol and brought it up, muzzle aimed at the sky. Turning his head, he looked until he saw his regimental commander. Then, without even a glance to the front, he watched and waited until Major Hall raised his sword and began to issue his orders to fire.

All around James there was now nothing but chaos. The neat regimental and brigade lines of battle were gone. Instead, the

North Carolinians were simply surging ahead through the drifting clouds of dirty gray smoke in small groups centered around their regimental colors or a trusted officer. Deafened by the roar of battle, James heard only bits and pieces of desperate orders or shouted encouragement. "Forward, North Carolina!" one colonel yelled. Another officer, a captain, was waving his hat over his head, screaming at the men behind him, "Stay with the colors!" Mixed in with these stirring orders were the cries of the wounded. "Help me," one man on his knees kept repeating over and over to each passing figure as he tried to maintain his balance. "Help me." Another man, whom James had to step over, lay on his back, his hands resting upon a mass of intestines that spread to either side of his ripped abdomen. With a wide-eyed look of shock on his face, the boy stared at the sky, softly whispering, "Mama, oh, mama."

James reached the rail fence along the road, where a number of dead and dying men lay in a tangled heap. He was just about to pull himself up and over it when the ragged line of men he was running to join on the other side was knocked over by a single volley of rifle fire, delivered at appallingly close range. Those who survived staggered backwards a moment, looked about in a daze, then went back to loading their rifles in the same mechanical way all veterans did. An officer without a hat, seeing his regimental colors go down, stepped over and on the writhing bodies that surrounded the flag and bent down to scoop it up. Throwing his sword to the ground, he waved the flag over his head. "Rally, boys! Rally!"

Once over the fence and across the road, James did just that. Though winded, soaked with sweat, and with no clear idea of what was happening any longer, James could think of nothing better to do than head for the flag that now drew him like a magnet.

"Hurry, men! *Hurry!*" Kevin harangued his men as he looked between his line of men along the wall and the shattered groups of enemy soldiers who still staggered forward under the colors of a regimental flag now being waved by a bare-headed Confederate officer only yards in front of him. "Come to the ready when you are loaded and *hurry!*"

Having just managed to make it to the rear of the mass of men now following the hatless officer, James was startled when another loud clap of a massed volley erupted from the wall, now less than ten yards to their front. The man in front of James flew backwards, knocking him down onto the body of another man who had gone down in the first volley. Pinned by the dead weight of the man who had knocked him down, James let go of his rifle and gave a mighty shove, pushing his fellow soldier off of him. Scrambling to his feet, he looked about.

The wall was there. It was right there, almost close enough to touch. Behind it, rows of blue-clad soldiers were busily reloading their muskets, and some of them were looking right at him. There was fear in a few of their eyes, fear that seemed to make them move faster. Others, however, wore a hard look of hatred. Those men eyed James as if they were personally marking him.

There was no real thought behind his actions, no real purpose either, for just about everyone who had been with him a moment ago was now down or already streaming back to the rear. Still, James would not give in. Seeing the regimental colors lying on the ground next to the hatless officer, now writhing in agony, James coolly stepped over, bent down, and grabbed them up. Then, with a scream that pierced even the deafening sound of battle, he ran straight for the first Union officer he saw standing at the wall.

When he looked back to his front, Kevin Bannon was shocked to see a Confederate soldier, regimental colors in hand, charging straight for him and screaming for all he was worth. Though his first instinct was to step backwards, he didn't. Instead, he lowered his gun, laid the muzzle of his pistol against the man's chest as he came up to the wall, and reached out to grab the staff of the colors with his left hand.

It wasn't the feeling of a muzzle against his chest that stopped James Bannon. Nor was it the realization that he was about to die. Instead, it was the sudden appearance of his brother's face, right there in front of him, that brought him to a sudden halt.

In an instant, everything was silent, everything all about him disappeared. Kevin blinked once, then opened his eyes, still not believing that the man in front of him was his brother. Even when the wide-eyed Confederate before him mouthed his name, Kevin couldn't believe it.

As the pistol was lowered, James could see tears welling up in his brother's eyes. Finally, Kevin stuttered, "James! Dear God, James, come over to this side."

James looked down and saw that his brother had dropped the pistol from his right hand and was now offering his hand to him. Then he looked back up into his brother's eyes. How long, James thought, had he dreamed of this moment. How long had he prayed for it. Yet now, when it was here . . .

James, his hands still grasping the regimental colors, looked behind him. Through smoke clouds that were now starting to part, he could see the lush green fields he had crossed littered with mounds of gray and butternut for as far as the eye could see. Other figures, some staggering, some crawling and all with their backs to him, were retracing their steps. They weren't his people. They weren't his countrymen. Yet when James looked back, he saw that the men who were glaring at him weren't his countrymen either, not anymore. Whatever Kevin had meant to him belonged, he realized, to the past. To meekly give up again, as he had when his father had thrown him out in 1859, and again when he had blindly followed Will McPherson off to war two years later, would wipe away everything that he had been fighting for, whether he knew he had been fighting for it or not.

Letting go of the colors, James stepped back, shaking his head as he did so. "No, Kevin, I ..." Then without another word, he looked away from his brother and started back across the field to rejoin a cause that had suddenly become his.

All around Kevin Bannon the men of the 12th New Jersey looked back and forth between the two brothers, not realizing what had transpired. Why the captain from Meade's staff, still holding the Confederate battle flag in one hand, had let this Confederate go was beyond them. But that they knew each other, and that some kind of strong bond existed between them that transcended the hatred that war generates, was obvious. So none of them fired. Instead, they watched in silence as the shattered remains of a once mighty host limped away in defeat.

# EPILOGUE

# July, 1863

*Southwest of Gettysburg, Pennsylvania*

As IT DID EVERY DAY, THE SUN SLOWLY ROSE IN THE EAST, bringing a new day to the small Pennsylvania town of Gettysburg. And though all eyes, in both North and South, were still turned to that obscure little farm community, the fate of the enterprise that had seemed so promising just days before for the South was being sealed by the conclusion of another campaign, one in which the Confederate forces were being led by a Pennsylvanian.

In the fields, woods, and along the ridgelines all about Gettysburg itself, the contestants didn't yet know that their trails were at an end. Many expected the Union commander to throw his two unused corps, the Fifth and the Sixth, against a still-defiant but much diminished foe who stood his ground throughout that day. General George Meade, however, felt that his Army had done all that it could for the moment and chose not to press the advantage he had gained in three days of hard fighting. Thus, the costliest battle in American history came to a close without a cheer, without a flourish. Rather, the still-proud Army of Northern Virginia simply slipped quietly away at night, as it had done at Sharpsburg, to begin its long, tortuous march back home, leaving the Army of the Potomac to follow the next day at a respectful distance.

Marching through the rain behind a wagon filled with wounded, with his head bowed and his rifle slung over his shoulder, James Bannon thought about his life. He didn't dwell much on the past, for he had already done a great deal of that. In fact, he had written to Mary Beth on that 4th of July a letter in which he expressed feelings he had, for so long, held hostage in his own mind.

*I have spent all too much time pondering what should have been and why it wasn't. In doing so, I fear that I have missed the opportunity to make myself a new life, one in which I was the master of my fate and not simply a poor lost soul being tossed about by others.*

*My dearest Mary Beth, I have been a fool. When Will offered me his friendship, I held back because I thought he could never take the place of a brother I thought I had lost. When you offered me your heart, I ignored that too, for I had convinced myself that I could never love another as I had the girl I had helped destroy. And when the men of the 4th Virginia offered me a purpose in life and a home to fight for, I turned my back on them. Had fate struck me down yesterday, I would have died in peace, knowing that my death was atonement for the self-pity and sadness I carried in my heart like a rock. But I didn't die, though I still wonder why I didn't and so many good men who went forward with me did. While I sometimes question whether or not there truly is a God in heaven, I must trust that there is some power greater than all of us, controlling and guiding us.*

*Yesterday, I saw my brother. He stood in front of me, less than a foot away. When he looked into my eyes and saw who I was, a smile lit his face. Mary Beth, he still loves me. Despite years and many miles that have lain between us, despite the fact that I was on the other side of the wall, trying to kill him as he had been threatening to do to me, he is still my brother and he loves me and I him. Yet, when he offered me his hand, I could not take it. I could not go back to a life that was no longer part of me. In that terrible moment I suddenly realized that my fate is tied to you, Virginia, and the South. For better or worse, my fate, like Will's, is tied to a state I have grown to love. I cannot explain any of this, for such things, I have learned, often defy logic. But I feel it to be true, truer and more sure than anything I have ever felt before.*

*I apologize if this all seems like so many nonsensical ramblings, but the feelings that I hold for you, and Virginia, are genuine and pure. Now, as we prepare to come back to Virginia, I only pray that the same fate that has allowed me to see all of this so clearly will give us, both you and me, enough time on earth to enjoy whatever happiness this war allows us in the coming months and years.*

Though he had yet to mail that letter, for there were many pressing things that took precedence over mail for an army in retreat, James was at peace. And while he heard every scream of pain and the steady moans of the wounded who were being jostled in the springless supply wagons on the rutted road before him, he was at peace because for the first time he was going toward something, and not away.

### First Division, Sixth Corps Field Hospital, South of Gettysburg, Pennsylvania

News that the Confederates were gone brought Harriet Shields little cheer. Instead, she rose from the blanket spread over straw she had been resting on in the barn that the doctors and medical orderlies were using for sleeping quarters. Already everyone else was awake and busy tending wounded who were still being brought in from the field. Walking over to the well, past rows of wounded and dying men, Harriet rolled the blood-soaked sleeves of the white soldier's shirt she wore over her own torn and blood-soaked dress without looking to one side or the other.

Picking up the bucket that sat under the pump, she looked in to make sure that there were no used bandages or dirty water left in it by a lazy orderly. And even though she didn't see any, she filled it part way, swished the water about, and threw it off to one side just to make sure that the bucket was clean. Satisfied, she began to fill the bucket. Her mind, numbed by four days of unending labor and the suffering that surrounded her, sought escape but found none. Instead, as she pumped the handle and watched the water laboriously dribble out of the spout, Harriet wondered if she would ever be this tired or dirty or hungry again. How easy, she thought, it would be to turn her back on all of this. How easy it would be to go back home where she could live in a nice, safe house that was cleaned by maids and where meals were always warm and plentiful. At that moment, there seemed to be nothing more inviting than to find some place, any place, where she could bathe herself and change into a clean, crisp dress with ruffles.

She was thinking about this, ignoring the water that now overflowed the bucket and was running on the ground about her feet, when Dr. White called to her from across the barnyard. "Miss Shields." Startled, Harriet looked up. "Please hurry, madam," he snapped. Then, after looking about the rows and rows of wounded, he added, with a sad tone in his voice, "The butchers have finished their work and have left us to clean up after them. Please come to surgery as soon as you can."

Without another thought, Harriet reached down to grab the handle of the bucket. Then she saw him standing next to her. She hadn't heard Kevin approach, and he hadn't done anything to let her know he was there. Instead, he just stood there, looking at her with a blank expression on his face. At first she thought he was wounded, but a quick check didn't show any sign of blood or a tear in his uniform. Letting go of the bucket, she took a step toward him and began to ask what was the matter, but wasn't given the chance.

"I saw him, Harriet," he said as if in a trance. "He was as close to me as you are."

Confused by Kevin's expression and statement, Harriet stepped back. "Who?"

"James. My brother, James."

Though he had never spoken much of his brother, and she suspected that there was much that he was hiding, Harriet always knew that there was an affinity between Kevin and his brother that was strong. Coming up next to Kevin, she took his arm. "Was he . . ."

Kevin shook his head. "No, he's not dead. At least not when I saw him last." Kevin looked down into her eyes. "I asked him to come over to our side of the wall, Harriet. I offered him my hand," he said as he stretched his hand out as he had to James. "But he said he couldn't. There were tears in his eyes, Harriet. I know he still loves me. But he said he couldn't. Instead, he turned away from me and went back."

"Went where?"

Kevin looked off in the distance, then down at the ground. "Back with the rest of the Confederate Army, I guess."

Though she wanted to know what Kevin's brother was doing with the Rebel Army, she didn't ask. Instead, Harriet took Kevin's hands in hers. "If he's still alive, then there's hope, isn't there?"

Kevin looked up at her with a forlorn expression. "But this war, dearest Harriet, is going to go on. And as long as he stays over there and I'm with the Union, there's the chance that we might meet again. There's the chance . . ."

"And," Harriet said as she pulled his hands up to her bosom, "there's the chance you won't, isn't there?"

Slowly, he nodded. "You're right, you know." Then he looked into her eyes and smiled. "Somehow, my dearest, you always seem to have the right answer."

"No," Harriet responded with a sudden melancholy. "I wish that were true. But," she said as she tried to cheer herself and Kevin up, "all we can do is hope that we are right and keep on living. We'll find your brother, Kevin, together."

Taking Harriet's right hand, streaked with the dried blood of a dozen wounded men, he lifted it up to his lips and planted a light kiss on the back of it. Then he smiled at her. "You are, and always will be, my love. You know that. Just as I suspect that you somehow know that we will find James."

Harriet, blushing with joy and rising passion, was about to embrace Kevin when Albert Merrel cried out, "Miss Shields, come quick. Dr. White needs you, right away."

In an instant, Harriet's expression turned to one of exasperation. Kevin, seeing her look and the look on the young boy's anxious face, smiled. With a nod and a wink, he gave her hands one final squeeze and then let go, leaving her to tend to her duties.

As he watched her go, he wondered if any of them would survive this all-consuming war. He wondered what kind of a world those who survived it would find. They were hard questions, he knew, questions that neither he, nor anyone, could answer. All he could do, he realized, was to do what he could to bring the war to an end and wait, like everyone else, to see what happened then. And though this sounded simple and logical, he also knew, as he looked about the barnyard crowded with wounded men, that doing so would not be easy. The war would go on. All he could do, as Harriet suggested, was to do likewise. With that, he turned and began to make his way back to his duties and responsibilities, just as his brother James had done.

**HISTORICAL
NOTES**

# October, 1994
# Leavenworth, Kansas

Let there be no doubt about it, this book is a work of fiction.
The Bannon family, the Shieldses, the McPhersons, Johnny
O'Keeth, Frederick Himmel, the Hazard brothers, Abner
Couper, Trevor Ward, and many of those who come into frequent contact with them, have never, as people, existed. The
events that these fictional characters are cast in, as well as the
societies depicted, are, however, quite real.

In the telling of my story of men and women caught up in
the crisis known generally as the Civil War but also as the
War Between the States, I have endeavored to keep faith with
historical events as they occurred, not as I or someone else
would have liked them to. To this end, I have placed my
fictional characters in military units that existed, mixing on
occasion with historical figures and taking part in events that
really occurred. Even when creating my characters and telling
their stories, I used first-person accounts of actual participants
in the events to model the actions and reactions of my characters.

In doing this, I have mixed fact with fiction, which, at times,
may become disconcerting to some of my readers. To assist in
untangling some of this, I am including this section in which I
will point out what is historical and what is fictional.

## Prologue

On the afternoon of May 23, 1856, John Brown, four of his sons, and two other men belonging to Brown's Liberty Guards left their homes near Osawatomie, Kansas, to avenge pro-slavers' attacks on Lawrence, Kansas. On the night of the 24th, Brown's party, dedicated to the abolition of slavery, dragged five men identified as pro-slavers from their cabins in Pottawatomie County and murdered them. The young farmer with second thoughts is fictional. John Brown, his son, and the sentiments expressed here are not.

## Chapter 1

In 1859, the city of Perth Amboy, New Jersey, like the rest of the state as well as many other locations in the Northeast, was in transition, moving away from an agricultural economy to one based on industry and commerce. Though the Bannons and all the characters depicted in this chapter are fictional, the setting, conflicts, and sentiments, as well as the political, economic, social, and ethnic forces at work, are real.

The near riot referred to in this chapter took place. It was caused by the rumor that the bodies of two of John Brown's Harpers Ferry raiding party were to be buried near Perth Amboy in a Utopian community known as the Raritan Bay Union. The bodies of these men were eventually buried there but were exhumed in 1899 and moved to Elmira, New York, where they were buried next to their leader, John Brown.

## Chapter 2

In the 1800s, nearly every state in what was to become the Confederacy had a state-owned and -supported military college, of which the Virginia Military Institute is one of only two survivors. Unlike the United States Military Academy at West Point, New York, these state-run military colleges were not created to educate professional soldiers but, in the words of VMI's founder, "to produce citizen soldiers ready, in the time of need, to come to the defense in their native state." By the close of the 1850s, the superintendent of VMI, Francis Smith, and his faculty were instructed to prepare their students to do just that. Assisting him in these efforts was Major Thomas J. Jackson, a graduate of West Point, class of 1846, a veteran of the Mexican War, and, from 1851 to 1861, the professor of natural philosophy and experimental philosophy and instructor of artillery at VMI. Jackson would gain fame in the Civil War as Stonewall Jackson. After his death, in 1863, he was buried in Lexington, Virginia.

## Chapter 3

Much of western Virginia, including Rockbridge County, where VMI is located, and Winchester, Virginia, was pro-Union in 1861. Even Thomas J. Jackson spoke out for the pro-Union movement. This sentiment was not shared by many of the cadets at VMI, some of whom were from states in the Deep South. This gave rise to conflicts both within the corps of cadets and between the corps and the citizens of Lexington, Virginia.

## Chapter 4

Conditions in Ireland resulted in the migration of millions of men, women, and children from that land to the United States throughout the 1800s. This massive influx was viewed by many in the United States as a threat to their institutions and their society. Efforts by what we today would call the Establishment to suppress the Irish and defend Establishment institutions are well documented and quite familiar. I have, throughout this book, attempted to depict as accurately as possible the sentiments and attitudes on both sides of this issue.

## Chapter 5

The firing on Fort Sumter on April 12th, 1861, brought pro-Union and pro-secession sentiment to a head in Lexington, Virginia, and resulted in the flagpole incident, which has been depicted in this chapter as accurately as possible. All subsequent actions and events, including the mass meeting in the section room in which Jackson was called upon to address the corps of cadets, occurred as depicted.

## Chapter 6

The coming of war found the United States with an army of approximately 16,000 men in its ranks, garrisoned in many company-sized posts throughout the United States and on the Plains. Of the one thousand officers, three hundred and thirteen went south to stand with their native states. The dearth of professional soldiers left both sides heavily dependent on established militia companies and newly raised companies. Under the militia laws then in place, state governors were responsible for the raising and manning of militia regiments requested by the central government. This gave them the power to appoint officers, which was all too often used to gain or pay back political favors. Though some officers appointed in this manner eventually rose to prominence and learned their new trade well, in 1861 all but a handful were amateurs.

As part of the Virginia militia system, the VMI corps of cadets was included in Virginia's war efforts. While the bulk of the corps was ordered to Richmond, where they were to serve as drill instructors for the newly raised companies, a small contingent was left to guard the arsenal at VMI. Eventually, the arms and equipment stored there were moved and issued out, and the forty-seven cadets who were left behind left their posts and joined companies being raised to defend Virginia or their own home state. Both the Rockbridge Rifles and the Rockbridge Grays were real units. The Lexington Defenders, and all characters associated with it, are fictional.

### Chapter 7

The 2nd Regiment, New Jersey Militia, was a real unit and was part of the New Jersey Brigade, consisting of the 1st through 4th Regiments, New Jersey Militia. This brigade was the first fully formed brigade to reach Washington, D.C., in early May. At the end of May, the brigade moved across the Potomac and took up positions on Arlington Heights. There it served as part of the Washington defensive force, along with other units assembling around the city, as part of what was then known as the Army of Northeastern Virginia.

### Chapter 8

The Battle of Falling Waters, which took place on July 2nd, 1861, between Harpers Ferry and Winchester, Virginia, was, by later standards, a small affair, little more than a skirmish. Only the 27th Virginia Infantry, one gun of Captain Sandy Pendleton's battery, and some cavalry of the 1st Virginia under Colonel J. E. B. Stuart were actively engaged. Colonel T. J. Jackson had brought his entire brigade up and was ready to stand and fight had the Union forces under Major General Robert Patterson continued to push south, but Patterson did not, leaving Jackson free to return to Winchester and join General Joseph E. Johnston, his division commander.

### Chapter 9

Called Bull Run in the North and Manassas in the South, the first major battle in the East was, by later standards, a small affair. It was, however, what we would call today a media event. For the first time, the premier army of the Union was marching from its capital with the goal of seizing the capital of the Confederacy, newly moved from Montgomery, Alabama, to Richmond, Virginia. The armies that met at Manassas Junction, just south of the Bull Run Creek, were amateur armies, led by a handful of professional soldiers, few of whom had ever seen an entire regiment formed at once in a single place, let alone led one.

The 2nd Regiment, New Jersey Militia, did not take part in the actual fighting. The New Jersey Militia Brigade and the First New Jersey Brigade, consisting of the 1st, 2nd, and 3rd New Jersey Volunteers, were posted as reserves in a small town named Vienna, under the command of Brigadier General Theodore Runyon. Only parts of Runyon's division were ever committed that day in the effort to halt the rout of the rest of the Union Army. This effort failed miserably, with many of the Jerseymen joining the dispirited mob as it fled back to Washington.

The actions of the 4th Virginia, brigaded together with the 2nd Virginia, the 5th Virginia, the 27th Virginia, and the 33rd Virginia under the command of Brigadier General Thomas J. Jackson, occurred as depicted. Individual accounts by participants and Jackson's official report were used when writing this section.

## Chapter 10

Between August and October, 1861, New Jersey raised seven additional volunteer infantry regiments, enlisted for three years of service, in response to Lincoln's second call for troops. The 4th New Jersey was one of those units. Kevin Bannon's company, Company J, and all the people associated with it are fictitious. The rest of the 4th New Jersey, and its actions, are real.

## Chapter 11

On January 1st, 1862, Thomas J. Jackson, now a major general commanding the Valley District of Virginia from the town of Winchester, commenced an expedition to seize the town of Romney, Virginia (now West Virginia), some thirty miles away. Weather turned out to be the major enemy in this operation. Although he did manage to reach his objective and seize it, the harsh conditions claimed up to one-third of his command in sick and injured, which overwhelmed Winchester and gave that town its first taste of war. Eventually, Romney was abandoned and all forces returned to Winchester to recoup.

## Chapter 12

The appointment of Major General George McClellan gave the Army of the Potomac, newly renamed, two things that it didn't have before: sound military and administrative organization and pride. Part of McClellan's efforts to build unit pride and cohesion was the staging of grand reviews, gladly attended by politicians, news reporters, and civilians from all over the North. Yet, while constant drill and better administration reduced many of the problems the earlier amateur army had been troubled with, its commanders and the men in the ranks were still untried in battle.

The 4th New Jersey was brigaded together with the 1st, 2nd, and 3rd New Jersey in what was known as the First New Jersey Brigade. For a while, the brigade was commanded by the colorful one-armed hero, Brigadier General Philip Kearny of New Jersey.

## Chapter 13

On Sunday, March 23rd, 1862, believing that the Union forces before him were in full retreat and wanting to press them, Jackson ordered his command to attack at once, just south of a place named Kernstown. In the course of that fight, there was confusion between Confederate commanders as to what Jackson wanted. This was not helped by Jackson's direct intervention in the ordering about of regiments, especially those of his old brigade, now commanded by Brigadier General Dick Garnett. The exhaustion of the troops, the muddled orders, and the strong reaction of Union forces resulted in Jackson's first and only defeat. It also resulted in the relief of Garnett and the presentation of court-martial charges against him. Garnett never had an opportunity to defend his actions in a military court of law.

## Chapter 14

On the second day of what was to be known as the Seven Days Battle, Confederate forces managed to trap Major General John Porter's Fifth Corps north of the Chickahominy River, on a hill where Dr. William Gaines had a grist mill. The First Division of the Sixth Corps, of which the 4th New Jersey and the First New Jersey Brigade were part, were sent across the Chickahominy to assist the Fifth Corps. The incidents involving the 4th New Jersey and other units around it occurred as depicted.

Jackson's command, coming down from the north, had difficulty making it to the battlefield and did not join the action until Union forces were in the process of collapsing and night was falling. Again, the actions of the 4th Virginia are depicted here as accurately as I can determine.

## Chapter 15

The practice of exchanging prisoners was carried out well into the war. Exchange commissions met to determine which prisoners would be exchanged and when. Until exchanged, soldiers were forbidden to participate in active campaigning even if they had already been sent back across the lines to their own side. The 4th New Jersey, captured on June 27th, was returned to Union lines at Harrison's Landing in Virginia and exchanged officially on or about August 12th. When the exchange was completed, the regiment was reequipped with smoothbore caliber .69 muskets that had been refitted with percussion-cap trigger mechanisms.

## Chapter 16

To counter the threat posed by Major General John Pope's newly created Army of Virginia, Robert E. Lee dispatched Jackson, now commanding better than half Lee's army, renamed the Army of Northern Virginia, north to counter Pope. In a series of maneuvers, Jackson managed to make his way into Pope's rear and seize Pope's main base of supply, located at Manassas Junction. Knowing that he couldn't hold the massive stores of supplies or move them away, Jackson allowed his troops to loot the supply base, then burn what was left before withdrawing to the west.

Colonel Herman Haupt, chief of the Union military railroad system, thought that the Confederate forces at Manassas Junction consisted only of cavalry making a quick raid. He seized the first major unit disembarking in Alexandria, Virginia, after returning from Harrison's Landing and sent it to Manassas Junction to recapture Pope's supply base. This unit was the First New Jersey Brigade with the rearmed 4th New Jersey. Except for the fact that I moved Company J to the right of the Bull Run Bridge (this position was held by another company), all actions in this account are as accurate as I can determine.

## Chapter 17

One of the great ironies of the August 27th Battle of Groveton was that two of the most famous brigades in both armies, the Stonewall Brigade and the Iron Brigade, faced each other. In a stand-up fight fought at a distance of eighty yards and less, those two units pounded away at each other for nearly two hours with neither side giving ground. Though this minor fight was to be overshadowed by the Second Battle of Bull Run, or Second Manassas, fought over the same ground during the next two days, it stands as testament to the determination, courage, and savagery both sides brought to the growing war.

It also highlighted some of the deficiencies both sides had in dealing with the masses of wounded that these battles were now generating. Many men wounded at Groveton on the 27th were still there, unattended or untreated, three days later when the battle concluded. When you consider that this action took place in August, in Virginia, you can begin to appreciate some of the horrors of this war.

Actions and events, including the prayer meeting on the night of August 29th depicted in this chapter, occurred during the course of that battle.

## Chapter 18

The fight at Crampton's Gap on September 14th was part of what is collectively called the Battle of South Mountain. As a result of this action, the 4th New Jersey regained favor and was awarded a new set of regimental colors, depicting the fight at Crampton's Gap. Unfortunately, the purpose of this fight, the relief of the besieged Union garrison at Harpers Ferry, was not realized. Through bluff and boldness, Major General LaFayette McLaws of Jackson's corps was able to keep the victorious Union forces at Crampton's Gap from pushing on to Harpers Ferry, only six miles distant.

## Chapter 19

Antietam, or the Battle of Sharpsburg, fought on September 17th, was the single bloodiest day of the war, resulting in the death or wounding of some 23,400 Americans. The 4th Virginia, as part of the depleted Stonewall Brigade, faced the Union Iron Brigade again, in what was to be known as the West Woods. By the end of that day, the 4th Virginia had less than fifty men left with the colors. I have tried to re-create, from a number of sources and without embellishments, the desperateness of that fight as viewed by the 4th Virginia.

## Chapter 20

Few units of the Sixth Corps participated in the fighting at Antietam, coming up late in the day and being held back in reserve in the East Woods. Like the rest of the Army of the Potomac, the Sixth Corps stayed in the vicinity of Sharpsburg after Lee retreated under the cover of darkness on the night of September 18th–19th. While enjoying this respite, the Army was visited by civilians and politicians, including President Lincoln, who came to see the battlefield, visit loved ones, and discuss strategy for the next campaign.

## Chapter 21

Throughout the North, many local church groups banded together to form relief agencies whose aim it was to provide items for the health, welfare, and comfort of the troops in the field. The most famous of these was the Sanitary Commission, which had chapters throughout the Union, held fairs to raise funds, established depots in major transportation centers to handle the movement of the material they gathered, and sent agents to accompany the armies in the field to oversee the administration and distribution of material. In this way, many Northern women were able to contribute to the war effort in a manner that was, in their time, socially acceptable.

## Chapter 22

The appointment of Major General Ambrose Burnside to replace McClellan as the commander of the Army of the Potomac came with instructions to resume active and vigorous campaigning at once. The result was the Battle of Fredericksburg, fought on December 13th, 1862. While much has been written about the brutal and costly frontal attacks made against Marye's Heights just west of town, a division under Major General George Meade managed to break Jackson's line southwest of town and could have caused Lee serious problems had the senior Union commander on that part of the field reinforced Meade's success. This, however, did not occur, and Meade's penetration was beaten back. Both the actions of the 4th Virginia and the 4th New Jersey that day are depicted as they occurred.

The presence of women in field hospitals, though frowned

upon, was becoming more and more common. Clara Barton, a volunteer with no official status, made her way onto the field at both Antietam and Fredericksburg, providing both badly needed medical supplies and assistance. The actions of Harriet Shields are modeled after those of Ms. Barton, the woman who eventually would be credited with the founding of the American Red Cross.

## Chapter 23

As the war progressed and became more vicious, Union forces occupying areas of the South with sympathies toward the rebellion became harsher in their dealings with the local populace. More and more repressive measures, aimed at breaking not only Southern sympathizers' ability to resist, but also their wills, were applied. While some of these actions were intentional, many were brought on by war weariness and frustration. It wasn't until 1864 that war against the citizens of the South became a recognized and systematic part of the Northern war-winning strategy.

The presence of women in camp, especially during long periods of inactivity, was not unusual. Besides the officers' wives and laundresses, some Union units had what they called "The Daughter of the Regiment," a woman who stayed with the unit and served as a sort of housemother for all its soldiers. The great majority of the troops enjoyed having this female presence amongst them. While many debate the value of such women, no one can deny their existence or the fact that, for many soldiers, the women were an important part of their camp life.

The debate about the resolution by the legislature of New Jersey to seek an accord with the South is real. New Jersey, a predominantly Democratic state, had close ties with the South before the war and had actually sought, in December of 1860, to secede from the Union along with South Carolina.

## Chapter 24

Chancellorsville saw the Army of the Potomac under another new commander, Major General Joseph Hooker, and another effort to march on Richmond defeated. Lee's victory, however, cost him Thomas J. Jackson, wounded accidentally by his own men on the night of May 2nd, just after he completed what was probably his most daring and brilliant maneuver. (Jackson died of pneumonia eight days later.)

The conversation between Jackson and various VMI alumni, as well as Jackson's quote, took place as depicted.

Seven companies of the 4th New Jersey were assigned duty as train guard for the Army's trains, with three companies being retained to serve as provost guard for the Sixth Corps. The actions of Kevin Bannon at and around the Chancellorsville Inn are fictional but based on accounts of other officers who found themselves in similar circumstances when the Eleventh Corps broke under Jackson's flank attack.

The 4th Virginia, as part of the Stonewall Brigade, did not finish Jackson's march around the Union right flank. It was, instead, left to guard a road junction on the Brock Road. It did, however, participate in the vicious fighting on May 3rd in the dense forest known locally as the Wilderness and did advance as far as the Chancellorsville Inn before being forced back by a lack of ammunition and Union fire.

A number of women, wanting to serve the Union or the Confederacy in a more active role, disguised themselves as men and enlisted. Little or no medical screening at the time of enlistment and the practice of sleeping fully clothed aided these women in keeping their identity hidden. Though some were discovered, many managed to hide their gender until wounded or killed. How many made it through the war undetected will never be known. Though Private Miller is a fictional character, her story is based on the documented accounts of some of the more than two hundred women who fought in the ranks of the two armies.

## Chapter 25

The Second Battle of Winchester, mentioned here, fought from June 12th through the 15th, was part of Lee's opening moves that led up to the invasion of Pennsylvania. The story concerning James Bannon, Mary Beth McPherson, and Major James Sutton is fictional. The practice of families retrieving their beloved dead from far-off battlefields was real. Undertakers made a good living transporting the dead back to their home-towns. They even sold soldiers going into battle package deals that included recovery, embalming, a coffin, and transportation. I have no reliable data on how efficient such services were.

## Chapter 26

From the 1st to the 3rd of July, 1863, Lee faced the Army of the Potomac, now under the command of General George Meade, at Gettysburg, Pennsylvania. The 40th Virginia Volunteer Infantry, which James Bannon had become part of, fought on the 1st and was badly battered. It took no part in the second day's fight but participated in what history calls Pickett's Charge on July 3rd.

The 12th New Jersey, part of the 2nd Brigade, 3rd Division of Major General Hancock's Second Corps, was posted along a stone wall south of Brian's farm, a structure that still exists and is immediately west of where the Visitors Center stands today. Four hundred strong, the 12th New Jersey was armed with the old smoothbore caliber .69 musket. On the evening of the 2nd, and twice on the morning of the 3rd, parts of the 12th sallied from their positions near the Brian farm to chase away Rebel skirmishers who were using the barn and house of the Bliss farm for cover. The action in which Kevin Bannon took part occurred, as did all other actions concerning Pickett's Charge.

The incident at the wall between James and Kevin Bannon, while fiction, is based upon a true incident that occurred at the same spot. After making their way through the grueling fire thrown at them by Union artillery and riflemen, a lone Confederate standard bearer and his companion found themselves at the stone wall in front of the Union troops. Rather than shoot these men down, the Yankees nearest them ceased fire. One man called out, "Come over to this side of the Lord." The Confederates, seeing their predicament, did so, crossing the wall with the aid of the Union soldiers. Today, the colors of the 26th North Carolina Volunteers, taken by the 12th New Jersey on the 3rd of July, 1863, hangs in the Lee Chapel on the campus of Washington and Lee University in Lexington, Virginia.

## *Epilogue*

As he had at Sharpsburg, Lee stood his ground on the 4th of July, 1863, and tempted Meade to come out and attack him. Meade, however, like McClellan, thought his command too badly battered and refused to attack, leaving Lee free to slip away with his wounded, unmolested, on the night of the 4th. The cleanup of wounded from the battlefield in and around Gettysburg took almost a week and taxed the medical resources of the Army of the Potomac. Altogether, almost 40,000 Americans were killed or wounded in three days of fighting.

Simon & Schuster
Proudly Presents

# *UNTIL THE END*

## HAROLD COYLE

Coming in Hardcover
from
Simon & Schuster

The following is a preview of
*Until the End . . .*